A.E. RAYNE'S SUGGESTED READING ORDER

This is the order in which I wrote the books and for me, the optimal way to enjoy them (although *Kings of Fate* works well as an introduction to *Winter's Fury*), but honestly... you can choose your own adventure!

THE FURYCK SAGA

1. WINTER'S FURY

2. THE BURNING SEA

3. NIGHT OF THE SHADOW MOON

4. HALLOW WOOD

5. THE RAVEN'S WARNING

6. VALE OF THE GODS

7. KING OF FATE
[prequel novella which links to *The Lords of Alekka*]

SUGGESTED READING ORDER

THE LORDS OF ALEKKA

8. EYE OF THE WOLF

9. MARK OF THE HUNTER

10. BLOOD OF THE RAVEN

11. HEART OF THE KING

12. FURY OF THE QUEEN
[features *The Furyck Saga* characters]

13. WRATH OF THE SUN

FATE OF THE FURYCKS
[begins after *Fury of the Queen*]

14. THE SHADOW ISLE

15. TOWER OF BLOOD AND FLAME

16. HOME OF THE HUNTED

17. GODDESS OF SECRETS AND WAR
- releases December 2024 -

TOWER OF BLOOD AND FLAME

FATE OF THE FURYCKS : BOOK TWO

A.E. RAYNE

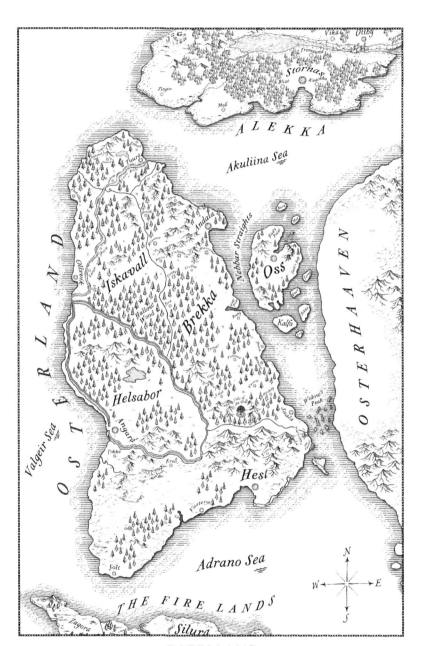

- OSTERLAND -

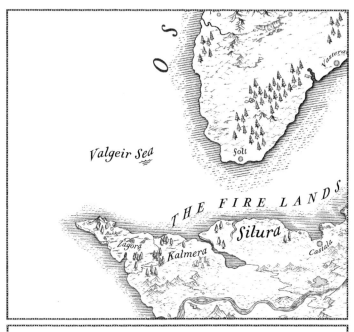

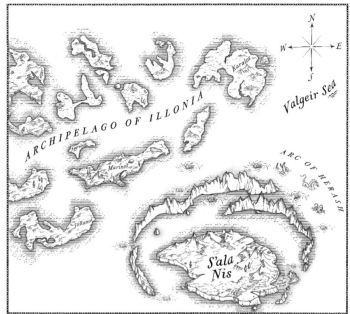

- S'ALA NIS & ARCHIPELAGO OF ILLONIA -

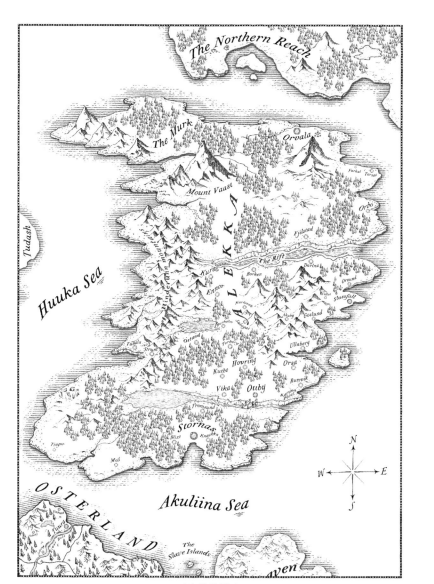

- ALEKKA -

CHARACTERS

In Andala

Axl Furyck, King of Brekka
Amma Furyck, Queen of Brekka
Getta Vandaal, former Queen of Iskavall
Gisila Olborn, Axl and Jael's mother
Hal Harbak, Axl's best friend/councillor
Erling Venberg, Axl's best friend/councillor
Eren Venberg, Erling's sister
Gerald Hogen, Axl's steward
Ragnar Olveggen, garrison commander
Helga Brugen, dreamer
Linas Brugen, her grandson
Gully, the dog

At Sea

Eadmund Skalleson, King of the Slave Islands
Thorgils Svanter, his best friend
Fyn Gallas, warrior
Mattie Bilso, dreamer
Bolder Oysten, *Bone Hammer's* helmsman
Kolarov Radic, explorer
Arras Sikari, Commander of the Waves
Nico Sikari, his son
Anika Edlem, former slave
Otter, the cat

CHARACTERS

On the Road
  Rexon Boas, Lord of Saala
  Gant Olborn, Axl's stepfather

Travellers
  Edela Saeveld, dreamer
  Bertel Knutson, elder
  Sigfrida 'Siggy' Larsen, novice dreamer
  Katalyne, the bone sister
  Korri Torluffson, Alekkan trader
  Zen O'yun, taverner's grandson
  Raymon Vandaal, former King of Iskavall

On S'ala Nis
  Jael Furyck, Queen of the Slave Islands
  Kalina Sardis, Queen of S'ala Nis
  King Ronin Sardis, her father
  Dessalene Sardis, his wife
  Pye, her man servant
  Alek Orlan, slave foreman
  Quint Gillum, overseer
  Krissia, his wife
  Argo Kosta, Commander of the Rocks
  Rigg Alred, slave
  Noor of the Dragon Blood Tree, seer
  Inesh Seppo, seer
  Ratish Feros, physician
  Gardi, stone mason

CHARACTERS

In Hest
    Karsten Dragos, King of Hest
    Bayla Dragos, his mother
    Berard Dragos, his brother
    Meena Dragos, Berard's wife/dreamer
    Ulf Rutgar, Master of the Fleet

Also mentioned
    Iker Rayas, Siluran warrior
    Oren Storgard, King of Iskavall
    Lina Storgard, Queen of Iskavall/dreamer
    Herold Valens, King of Helsabor
    Freya Valens, his daughter/betrothed to Karsten
    Isaura Svanter, Thorgils' wife
    Milla Ulfsson, Alekkan girl
    Mutt Storman, outlaw
    Edd Arnsten, Lord of Borsund
    Henk Layborg, Lord of Rosby
    Ayla Adea, dreamer

PROLOGUE

'You were gone when I woke,' the man frowned, touching his wife's face. 'Is something wrong?' Leaning forward, he brushed his lips over her cheek, kissing her soft skin until he found her mouth. Now, he took her in his arms, pulling her close. 'Some reason you left our bed?'

The woman laughed, playfully pushing him away. 'How desperate you are for me, dearest one. So needy. But no, I merely had matters to attend to.'

'Problems?'

The woman turned towards the balcony, where the sun was rising, curtains fluttering like golden wings across the open doors. 'But you can never rise as high as you desire without encountering the odd problem.' She spun back to her husband with a gleaming smile. 'Though nothing that can't be fixed. I will just... leave ahead of you.'

'Leave? Why?'

Now the woman slipped back into his embrace, nuzzling him. 'You haven't set foot on the isle in twelve years, my love. I think your daughter deserves a little notice. Besides, I wish to spend some time with her before you arrive and send her into a spin. Let me go, and we will be reunited in no time at all.' She kissed him, wanting him distracted and pliant.

She couldn't let him know there were problems on the isle. Problems of his foolish daughter's making.

She simply had to placate her curious husband and leave in haste, hoping to arrive at S'ala Nis in time...

PART ONE

Wolves

CHAPTER ONE

The noise on board *Bone Hammer* consumed Eadmund's every thought.

Bolder had turned them around, away from The Maiden's Reach, though everyone was still arguing, no one truly able to comprehend why they were leaving without Jael.

Without Jael?

Looking up, Eadmund saw the dripping figures of the two men and the woman he had helped escape.

Leaving his wife behind.

She had wanted him to rescue them but not herself?

Bile flooded his mouth, and turning away, he stumbled towards the stern, the chill wind freezing his wet body. Drops of water fell from his hair, into his eyes, blurring his vision.

And in that great blur, he saw Jael.

Frowning, he spat, numb hands gripping the stern, fingers tightening, wanting to tear the wooden strakes in two. He spat again, hearing Kolarov sneezing, Thorgils barking, and Bolder yelling orders. The wind groaned, and his wife's pleading voice rang in his ears.

'Leave!' she urged. 'You have to leave now!'

Looking up, Eadmund Skalleson, King of Oss, stared at the island of S'ala Nis – its sheer cliffs like walls, keeping his wife imprisoned. The great statue of the maiden had her arm raised, pointing them home. Though he wouldn't leave Jael here. He more words out of the dreamer. 'Where are these ships? *Mattie*?'

Fyn glowered at him, Eadmund ignored him, Kolarov nibbled a nail.

And eventually, Mattie's eyes sprang open. 'They have prows... like nothing I've seen. The ships are nothing I've seen before. Dark wood. Painted heads in gold. Heads of... wolves. They're wolves!' She blinked at Arras, who appeared ashen-faced before her.

'The king's ships,' he breathed. 'It's the king. The king is coming.'

***

Kalina Sardis, Queen of S'ala Nis, paced her golden throne room, seething with anger.

Her body was rigid, a great throbbing knot of tension.

Guards stood silently by the golden doors, slaves flanking the throne. Her ladies hovered pensively near the open balcony doors, sheer curtains threaded with silver billowing around them like clouds. And standing like a plinth in the middle of the gilded chamber, eyes closed, was the old seer, Noor of the Dragon Blood Tree. There was a calmness in his still body, a peace in his expressionless face, as though he was immune from all that roiled the chamber.

Hearing footsteps approaching, Kalina swung around, clenching her fists so tightly that her nails dug into her palms. She felt the pain of it and dug them in deeper, wanting to pierce her flesh, to feel the warm ooze of her blood.

Anger and pain blended in a seething miasma, pain pulsing at her temples. 'Open the doors!' she screamed, sensing Noor stiffen as she strode past him, eyes trained on those opening doors.

Four guards marched inside, dragging Jael Furyck between

them, depositing her on the shining marble floor. She was dressed in a soldier's uniform, the sight of which was so unexpected, so at odds with everything Kalina had been anticipating, that she pulled up in confusion.

Heart galloping like an escaping horse, she turned her attention away from the dark-haired slave towards one of her guards. 'Give me a knife.' His hesitation angered her. 'Give me a *knife*!' she roared so loudly that her voice crackled in her ears, throat aching.

Jael looked up, watching the guard unsheathing his knife, offering its leather haft to his queen. Her focus, blurred since her capture in the tunnel, suddenly sharpened.

Four men had brought her in.

She had passed two more manning the doors.

An old man in a white robe was peering at her.

Two finely dressed slaves were staring at her from the doors.

Two slaves stood by the queen's throne.

She kept seeing Sunni lying dead on the tunnel floor, the girl's blood staining her hands. Guilt had claimed her. Guilt and grief. They had claimed her as their prisoner, and she felt almost compelled to submit to the queen and her knife.

Worthy of her retribution. Almost seeking it.

Hopelessness swept over her, joining in the great churn of despair, and once again, her thoughts fractured.

'*Whose* ships?' she heard someone splutter. 'Who's after us?'

It was Thorgils, she realised, suddenly no longer in the queen's throne room. She stood on a ship amongst a circle of panicking men, towering over a woman.

The dreamer. Mattie?

Eadmund was there, those familiar hazel eyes stricken with pain, wet curls buffeted by the wind, blowing back from a tense face. Arras was trying to get his attention, she saw, wet through and frowning as ferociously as ever.

Turning to look between them, Jael saw a line of ships pointing directly at them, and she shivered.

The queen screamed at her, and the vision was gone.

'Where is he? What did you do to Arras? What did you *do*?' Kalina snarled, teeth bared, eyes ablaze. 'Where is he?' Jabbing with the knife, she threatened Jael with its sharpened tip, aiming at her eye.

Jael didn't flinch.

Everything slowed around her.

She saw the old man approaching, her eyes drifting to him as he held out a hand.

'My queen,' he murmured. 'Your father –'

'My father!' Kalina spat. 'My *father*? But this has nothing to do with my father!' Ignoring the old seer, she kept her eyes on Jael. 'Get her up!' The guards' hesitation irritated her further. 'You will get her up! She will stand before me! She will confess everything!' She glowered at the guards, who hurried to drag Jael up to her feet, holding her there as the queen stepped forward with her knife. 'Tell me what you did with Arras! *To* him! Where is he?'

Jael saw that ship in her mind again.

She saw Milla Ulfsson on Oss with Bo in her arms, Axl in Andala, and her grandmother walking into a great fog. Images charged at her, worrying her, taunting her.

Seeking to reach her.

To wake her out of this stupor.

To pull her back from the pit she was slowly sinking into.

'He...'

Kalina lunged at her.

'He... took... me,' Jael said in a halting, quiet voice, so unlike her own. 'He... kidnapped me.' Lifting her head, she stared into the queen's eyes, seeing her rage but also her pain.

'*Kidnapped* you?' Kalina's shock made her still. Knife trembling in her hand, she simply stared. 'But... why would he do such a thing? What are you talking about?'

Jael sensed the old man watching her with narrowing eyes.

He was Noor, she realised. The seer. Arras had told her about him.

'After the tournament, I was... in the physician's room, on a stretcher. The commander burst in. He... hit the physician, made me put on this uniform,' Jael explained, standing straighter, strengthening her voice now, finding her path. She had as good as killed Sunni, but she couldn't abandon her family. They needed her. 'His son was there, and they threatened me. He said he would ransom me to my husband. That I would earn them a great prize.'

Kalina shook her head, incredulous. 'You are lying!' she spat, spinning to Noor. 'She is lying! Tell me you see that! You must!' Now the knife was pointed at the old seer's face, though he remained as serene as ever.

And taking his time, aware of the queen's shuddering arm and that jerking hand wielding its blade, he closed his eyes, making gentle humming sounds.

Inciting the queen to even more fury.

Opening his eyes, Noor stared into Jael's, and stepping forward, he placed his right hand on her shoulder, reaching down to touch her hand with his left.

A surprised Jael heard his voice in her ears. He spoke rapidly and certainly, words that confused and shocked her. Her eyes remained open, her expression neutral.

His lips never moved.

'Aleksander is waiting for you. He will show you what to do. Trust him.'

Releasing his hold, Noor turned to Kalina with a long sigh. 'She speaks the truth, my queen. The commander took her. He had been making plans to escape for some time, believing the slave queen would bring him the gold he needed to start a new life with his son.'

Kalina stumbled backwards, the shock of Noor's words striking her like a bolt of lightning. Her heart, once so full of hope for the future, shattered. 'No, no,' she mumbled, eyes sweeping the marble floor. 'No, it is impossible.' And now she looked around, first at Jael and then at Noor. 'I do not believe you.' Shaking her head, she repeated herself. 'I do not *believe* you!'

Jael's eyes widened, watching the queen bring up her knife. 'No!' she shouted, lunging at the seer. '*No!*'

The guards dragged Jael back, holding her tight.

Though her eyes remained on Noor, who held his ground, maintaining his stoic expression as the queen plunged her knife into his heart.

***

Nico Sikari sensed that no one on the ship trusted anything his father was saying. He hovered near Arras' right elbow, wanting to show his support, though he doubted he'd be able to get a word in.

A bustling Kolarov Radic had pushed into the centre of the panicked huddle, equipped with decades of knowledge that he was attempting to share with Arras, who kept shaking his head.

'The king left S'ala Nis twelve years ago,' Arras explained, holding up a hand to try and stem Kolarov's babble. 'Though those ships you described?' he said, eyeing Mattie. 'Those are certainly his. Golden wolves? It's what he called himself. The Golden Wolf of S'ala Nis.'

Kolarov had heard that, and he became quiet.

'What are we doing?' Bolder shouted from the steering oar, needing direction from someone. 'What are we doing?'

'The king had a dreamer when he left the isle,' Arras warned. 'A powerful woman by his side.'

The information floated around Eadmund like specks of dust that soon merged into a dense cloud, revealing no clear answers. He needed more information, though, and blinking, he stared at Arras. 'But how do we know those ships are after us? Perhaps the king is simply going to visit his daughter?'

It was a possibility they clung to for a few moments until Mattie dropped a hammer and shattered all hope.

'I have seen it. They will chase us!'

Kolarov fell against Arras, who grabbed his arm, pushing him upright. 'We cannot go to Castala now!' the explorer fretted. 'We cannot!'

'Why?' Thorgils wanted to know.

'The King of S'ala Nis has powerful friends among the merchant class. He was no ally to Silura's king, though he always held great sway with the wealthy lords,' Arras explained. 'We'll be walking into a trap if we go there. We must turn north. We have to turn!' Panic vibrated at the edge of reason, for he didn't want to imagine what danger he'd brought upon his son by escaping and upon Jael's husband and friends, whose lives were now at risk too.

Finally, Eadmund's vision cleared, a path emerging. 'We'll go to Hest. It's closest. Karsten will help us.'

Thorgils thought so, too, though glancing over his shoulder, he saw that the line of wolf ships was edging closer.

Fearing that soon, they would hunt them down.

***

Kalina didn't look at the dead seer, whose blood spread over the marble floor, pooling around him. His eyes stared up at her, wide open in death, yet somehow still serene.

Still brandishing her knife, now wet with Noor's blood, she jerked it at Jael's face. 'You are lying,' she hissed. 'As he was lying.' She stepped closer, one deliberate, slow step. 'I am no seer, but I can smell it! Arras would never betray me. You did something to him. You bewitched him!' Glancing down, she saw that her prisoner no longer wore the iron fetters. 'Yes, of course, when your bonds were removed, your powers returned. Your powers returned, and you entrapped him. Made him a tool to help you escape. Him and his son! And now you will tell me where they are! What have you done with them?'

Jael didn't move her gaze from the queen's frantic face, though her attention remained on that shuddering knife, on the guards behind her and the slaves hovering nearby. Every threat now came into view.

Clarity returned.

In that moment, she knew she had to survive.

'I did not trick or trap them. I swear to you,' she said calmly.

Kalina twitched the blade near Jael's right eye.

Though Jael didn't blink. 'I could help you. I can search for them. They were taking a ship, though I don't know to where. But I can look for them.'

Kalina laughed. 'You want to help me? *You*? You who took everything from me? You want to *help*?' She released her grip on the knife, letting it fall into the bloody puddle, splattering the hem of her gown. Oblivious, she spun away, shoulders knotted, heart throbbing. 'Take her to the pits!' she ordered. 'Bury her alive!'

Jael's eyes bulged. 'But I can help you! You can't kill me. You said it yourself. You can't kill me!'

Though her words had no impact on the queen, who swept

out of the chamber, leaving the dead seer and the bellowing slave in her wake.

***

Since her escape from Tuura, Edela had been having visions of the two sisters and their mysterious bone tree, bursting with questions. Though now that she was here, sitting before one of the women, those questions were nowhere to be found.

She remembered Elmer and his crew down on Aggralaia's beach. The old helmsman had been so fearful of these women that he had called them outside the gods.

She still didn't understand what that meant.

What were you if you existed *outside* the gods?

Edela watched as the pretty young woman calmly moved around her cauldron, occasionally dropping in pinches of herbs before stirring with a long wooden spoon.

Lifting her eyes from the cauldron to the woman, Edela wondered how old she was. No more than thirty, she decided, seeing few lines on her pleasant face and no grey in her chestnut hair. It surprised her, for after her conversation with Elmer and her own dreams, she had been expecting a much older woman.

'The thought of a hot drink may not seem appealing at first, not in the heat,' the woman smiled, turning her heart-shaped face towards Edela. 'Though this is my favourite tonic for a warm day. It is especially reviving for one who has experienced a journey as trying as yours.'

A nodding Edela brightened her smile. 'Well, I can't deny that I'm in need of some reviving. It has been quite an ordeal.'

'And yet, here you are,' the woman said, silent again as she finally unhooked the small cauldron, and using a striped cloth, carried it to a table where two pottery cups waited. Edela saw the intricate blue patterns encircling the cups, inhaling a delightful aroma that had her salivating.

'I call it pira,' the woman told her, and after pouring equal amounts of the boiling liquid into each cup, she left the cauldron on the table and topped up the cups with water from a jug. 'My sister's creation, I confess, though I have made it my own over the years.' She brought the cups towards where Edela sat perched on the edge of a simple wooden chair, nervously fiddling with her fingers. 'I do apologise for taking so long. After your journey, you must be eager to begin.'

Edela nodded, feeling parched, though she took the cup with trepidation. She wasn't sure she could trust the woman, who hadn't even provided her name. She had been welcomed into the tiny cottage, shown to the uncomfortable chair, which could certainly use a fur, and left in silence while her hostess prepared the sweet-smelling tonic.

And now, she wasn't even sure she should drink it.

'My name is Katalyne,' the woman said, taking the chair opposite Edela and cradling her own cup in two elegant hands. 'I should have introduced myself earlier. Do forgive my rudeness.'

A slightly more reassured Edela bobbed her head. 'You know me, knew I would come here, so does that make you a dreamer?'

Katalyne stared at her, eyes sharpening. 'Dreamer? No, I am something else entirely.'

A shiver shot up Edela's spine, her smile faltering. '*Something else?*'

'Do drink up,' Katalyne urged. 'I assure you it is quite delicious.'

***

Siggy was bored.

She decided to move out of the sun, heading to join Bertel, who had long since decamped for the shade. There were no boulders in the leafy spot he had chosen after careful consideration and much grumbling, though he had finally made himself comfortable on a log, where he'd set about sharpening his knives. He had collected three on his travels, wanting to feel useful, more like the man he had once been. That man had made a terrible mistake with life-changing consequences, but he was still in there somewhere, so surely he could be of some use?

'I can help,' Siggy offered, sitting down beside him. 'Do you have another whetstone?'

Bertel shook his head. 'But why not rest? Or see if you can find something to eat? I fear Edela will be all day in there.' He frowned now, eyeing the tiny stone cottage in the distance. He couldn't smell any smoke or see any rising from its thatched roof. He had hoped Edela's hosts might bring out refreshments, though the door hadn't opened.

Siggy shrugged, heading away from him. 'What could they be talking about?'

'Who knows? Some illuminating wonder! Some explanation for why we've ended up here, so far from Tuura.'

Siggy turned back. 'Do you think you'll ever go back? To Tuura?'

Laying his sharpened knife on the log beside him, Bertel felt weary. 'I'm not sure there's anything to go back to. Not now.'

'Though the dreamers will still need help,' Siggy reminded him, tipping back her head to take in the vast landscape of clouds. White and grey and fluffy, they surged across the sky like horses. She watched them bleed into each other, changing shapes, remembering how the elders had instructed her in the ways to bring dreams to her.

The clouds, they would say. It was all about the clouds.

Clouds hid the truth, they revealed the truth, and it was up to a dreamer to choose which path to follow. Which secret to uncover.

Closing her eyes, feeling the sun on her face, Siggy slowly turned around, twigs snapping beneath her boots. Bertel was quiet now, though she heard birds in the distance squawking loudly, as though they were screaming at each other. Wrinkling her nose, she took a deep breath and opened her eyes.

The trees appeared to part like curtains, and keeping perfectly still, Siggy watched as they revealed the most horrifying scene.

***

Edela finished the delicious tonic, leaving her empty cup on the low table between the two chairs where Katalyne's cup was already waiting. 'That was lovely,' she smiled, feeling energised. 'Most refreshing.' The young woman looked pleased to hear it. She had busy eyes, though Edela couldn't tell what colour they were. Dark blue, she thought, though sometimes they appeared almost black.

'It is the lemon myrtle,' Katalyne revealed. 'There is something so deeply restorative about it. It calms the chaos and relaxes the mind. It grows like weeds in my garden.'

Edela clasped her hands in her lap, eyeing her. 'I imagine my companions would like to try some themselves. Perhaps when I go, I may take them a cup?'

'Of course! Yes. There will certainly be enough, though I fear they may be waiting some time yet, for we have much to discuss. Why you are here, why you have come, and how we can help one another. We must discuss it all before you go.'

Edela felt a sharp pain in her chest, another in her belly, and she blinked, eyes on her empty cup, belatedly remembering the seeress Govana. On Karalos, she had been a fool, walking into a trap so deadly it had nearly killed her.

And now?

Katalyne smiled at her, those busy eyes suddenly still, and Edela couldn't stop shivering.

couldn't.

Bolder would take them back to Castala. They would get more ships and –

A shout from Mattie rose above the rumbling din, and Eadmund turned to see her swaying towards him before she tripped, lost from view.

'Ships!' she kept calling, drawing everyone's attention out to sea. 'I see ships!'

Bolder had threaded *Bone Hammer* through the stone spires surrounding The Maiden's Reach into the Valgeir Sea, which would take them back to the Fire Lands and Castala. That had been the helmsman's hastily formed plan.

But ships?

He looked around, as confused as everyone else.

Mattie was soon on her feet, refusing Kolarov's offer of assistance as she bustled towards the king, wheat-coloured hair whirling around a worried face. 'I counted at least nine! Nine ships!'

The dripping man arrived in haste; Eadmund couldn't remember his name. He felt no warmth towards him, only resentment that he was here and Jael was not. Frowning at Mattie, he took her arm, steadying her swaying body, which threatened to fall again.

'What ships?' Bolder called, wanting to know more, though he couldn't give up his steering oar now; the swirling currents heading away from the isle demanded his full attention. 'Where?'

Mattie kept her eyes on Eadmund. 'From the south. They'll soon be behind us!'

An alert Arras Sikari tried to claim the dreamer's attention. 'What did they look like? Sails? Flags? Anything?'

Mattie's lips parted, staring blankly at him before closing her eyes. She seized Arras' sodden arm as *Bone Hammer* was hit by an enormous wave. Sea spray showered over them, but no one moved.

'What's happening?' Thorgils demanded, desperate to shake

***

'Why are you standing there? What are you doing?' Bertel called, seeing a rigid Siggy staring into the trees. She hadn't spoken in some time, and unused to such a prolonged silence from the girl, Bertel drew his full attention towards her.

She didn't respond – not even a twitch to indicate that she'd heard him.

And feeling concerned, he placed his whetstone on the log and stood, heading towards her. 'Siggy?' he asked, touching her arm.

She jerked around, big eyes wide open, mouth ajar.

She looked terrified.

Grabbing her arms, Bertel tried to focus her. 'What is it? What's happened? Siggy? Siggy, look at me,' he demanded. Then, getting no response, he shook her. 'Can you hear me?'

She swallowed suddenly, the visions retreating, seeing Bertel's worried face come into focus before her. 'I... I... I had a dream, Bertel. I... I had a real dream! But it, it wasn't a dream at all. It was a nightmare!'

CHAPTER TWO

A bruised and battered Jael had been hauled into a wagon, where she sat, restrained by two guards, while two more stood behind the driver, issuing orders.

The clattering noise as the wagon rumbled over cobblestones was so invasive that she was struggling to think.

What had Sunni said about the pits?

Sunni...

Dropping her head, Jael felt ripples of grief rising into great waves again. Why had she forced Sunni to leave the isle? She rubbed her eyes before remembering the blood. And turning over her hands, she saw her palms – dirty and blood-stained. Those hands had killed Otho Dimas and the queen's spy, though they couldn't save Sunni.

She had cradled the dead girl with her hands.

Dead because of her.

The wagon struck a rut, and Jael fell against one of the guards, who shoved her upright. Reminded of Arras, her mind drifted away from S'ala Nis, seeking the ship she had seen him on, though now she saw only water: a great empty sea, dark and cold. Fears rising for her husband and her friends, her attention drifted far away from her own precarious situation.

Her fetters were still off, though perhaps when they were returned someone would discover that she'd scratched through the symbols? Perhaps there wasn't much time left to communicate with Eadmund? To warn him?

Waking herself up, she remembered what the queen had said. *Bury her alive.*

And if that was the case, there wasn't much time at all.

***

'We have to go faster!' a tense Eadmund growled, shoulders hunched, prowling behind Bolder Oysten, who ignored the king, shifting his eyes right, seeing the clouds rolling in.

The sky was rapidly darkening, just to add to the mountain of things that had gone wrong since Eadmund had swum into the tunnel to rescue his wife. Then, remembering that Eadmund had returned without his wife, Bolder blew out a frustrated breath. 'I'm pushing her, the wind's pushing her! She won't let us down!' he promised. *Bone Hammer* was like a loyal, big-hearted horse, though oftentimes, he knew you were simply no match for a faster horse.

He blinked stinging eyes, trying to shut away his fear that Eadmund was right.

That they were gradually being hauled in by the wolf ships.

Further down the deck, Kolarov and Thorgils had cornered Arras, desperate for more insight.

'What will the queen do to Jael?' Thorgils wanted to know.

'And if that is the king, what will he do to us?' Kolarov added, wiping a trembling hand over his wet scalp. He wasn't sure if it was sea spray or light rain falling, but without any hair to mop it up, every drop of liquid landing on his head tended to trail into his worried eyes.

Arras feared for Jael, though he also feared what would happen when Jael's husband found out that he was the one who had taken her from Tuura in the first place. He didn't answer the two men, his eyes drifting towards the dreamer, who stood with a tall young man, watching him.

'What is it?' Fyn wondered, nudging Mattie. 'Don't you trust them? That man and his son?' There was a woman too. Anika, he remembered. She had barely left the bow, where she'd remained alone, occasionally on her feet, vomiting into the ocean.

Mattie shrugged, hair in her eyes, blue dress and blue cloak tangling around her legs, though she didn't have enough hands to counter the determined wind. 'I can't say! I've barely spoken to them!'

Fyn frowned at her, frustrated that she couldn't tell him more. 'Jael helped them. We need to remember that. She wouldn't have saved them unless she'd wanted to.'

Mattie thought so, too, though that didn't necessarily make sense of everything she'd seen and what she'd seen Arras do.

Arras turned away from the dreamer's intense stare, trying to put Thorgils' mind at ease. 'The queen cannot kill Jael. I've never known why, but she told me so herself. That she had sworn an oath never to kill her. Hurt her, yes, but never kill her. The intention was that Jael would remain on the isle as a slave, die a slave. A very old slave. She will be safe.' Though despite his assurances, doubt blossomed, for Kalina was not her father. Ronin Sardis was a man of singular vision and uncompromising discipline. He had never let emotion cloud his judgement as his daughter was certainly wont to do.

Arras' words took the edge off Thorgils' rising fears, though there was still their own safety to worry about. 'And this king? What will he do to us?'

Arras stared at the big man with the wild red curls, choosing his words with care. 'The king created S'ala Nis as a paradise for his friends and allies, for the wealthy. He intended to keep it private, secret, a hidden oasis. He forbade anyone from escaping. Anyone. What he will do...' Guilt flashed in Arras' eyes, and perhaps if he'd been alone, he would have jumped overboard and sacrificed himself, leaving Jael's husband and friends to escape.

But he couldn't let anything happen to Nico and Anika.

He wouldn't.

An unhappy Thorgils muttered under his breath, and with a final look at Kolarov, he turned away. 'Well, we'd better hope that Bolder can get us out of here fast.'

***

'We, I... we can't stay, we, we... I saw!'

Siggy blurted out a flurry of words that made no sense to Bertel. Feeling panic rising and glancing over his shoulder at the little cottage in the distance, fearing that Edela had once again made a grave error of judgement, Bertel tried to coax some sense out of the girl. 'You had a dream,' he soothed, distractedly patting her shoulder, wishing he had more than a few old knives to hand. 'And it showed you something. Something we must... escape from? We must escape here?'

Siggy started nodding, brown curls trembling around a noticeably paler face. Shaking off Bertel's hand, she stumbled back, spinning around. And without a word, she hurried towards the edge of the cliff they had recently climbed.

'Careful!' Bertel warned, following close behind. 'Siggy! You must be careful.' Stopping beside her, he kept back from the cliff edge, and craning his neck, he tried to see what she might be looking at, though they were so far up that nothing registered. 'What is it? What did you see?'

Siggy jerked around, body ablaze with a fiery terror that surged up her legs and arms, burning painfully in her chest. 'I saw Elmer!'

'Elmer?' Bertel swallowed. 'What about him?'

'Down on the beach! They're dead, Bertel! Elmer and his men... they're all dead!'

***

'It was our tree that drew you here, wasn't it?' Katalyne smiled warmly, though seeing the distress in Edela's eyes, she frowned. 'Is something wrong?'

Edela gulped down strange feelings. The pain in her chest felt as though it was coming from her heart. There was an increased rhythm, a discomfort that, once it had made itself known, had been swiftly aided by a sense of panic that told Edela something was wrong.

She tried to ignore it, for what could she do here? Now?

'Oh, it's nothing but a sudden weariness. I think I am simply old and tired,' she admitted with a chuckle. 'The climb to your cottage was certainly a challenge for someone of my advanced years.'

Katalyne laughed. 'We ask a lot of our visitors, that is true. Though they always find the effort worthwhile. Especially when they see the tree.'

Edela's eyes brightened. 'Yes, I do long to see it myself. The glimpses I had in my dreams were enticing. A tree of... bones?'

'It is a tree of history,' Katalyne said as she stood. 'The story of Varmyr from its very inception. Each bone records an important event in our history, and we are the keepers of them. From the very beginning, we have kept them safe here.'

Edela shuddered, Elmer's words echoing back to her. 'The *very* beginning?'

Katalyne headed through the modest kitchen area, aiming for another door. This was even smaller than the front door, painted a cheerful yellow. 'You have waited a long time to see the tree, Edela, so please, come.'

That sharp pain in her heart returned and Edela gasped, turning away from Katalyne, remembering Bertel and Siggy. 'I...'

'Edela?'

And feeling herself turning towards the woman, almost

against her will, all thoughts of her companions drifted away as Edela stood and followed Katalyne towards that yellow door.

***

'Elmer? Is dead?' Bertel's eyes returned to the cottage. 'Dead how?' he asked, turning back to the terrified girl. 'What exactly did you see? Raiders? A battle?'

Siggy shook her head, anxiously nibbling her lips before clamping them together.

Bertel frowned at her. 'We have to stay safe and warn Edela, so you must tell me what you saw.'

'Creatures!' Siggy eventually blurted out. 'There were these... creatures! They... tore the men with claws. They pulled them apart. They were just... pieces!'

A shocked Bertel hadn't been expecting that, and clutching his throat, he swung around, squinting eyes taking in their rocky surrounds. Atop Aggralaia's great cliff, there was no easy escape and no other visible path down to the beach except the one they had only recently climbed.

Trying to ignore the images Siggy's words brought to mind, Bertel posed a more practical question. 'And the ship?'

'It was still there.'

'Then we have to get Edela. We have to leave this place at once!'

Siggy trembled before him. 'We can't fly, Bertel! And we can't go down to the beach. What if they're still there?'

What if they're coming up here, Bertel wondered, but didn't say. 'Go grab my knives! I'll get Edela. She'll know what to do!'

***

Jael didn't know what she was going to do or what was even possible now.

Standing beside the wagon, restrained and waiting while the guards talked to a man, she surveyed the great rows of pits before her, unable to shoo a swarm of flies away from her face.

The graveyard of offerings to Venusta, Goddess of Souls, was a wasteland – dirt and gravel and dust. She saw freshly dug troughs and sweat-soaked slaves digging more. Enormous stone plinths were positioned to mark each row. There were mounds in the distance, beneath which lingered skeletons, stripped of every vestige of life.

The smell of death and decay hung over the pits like a foul blanket – a promise of what was to come.

Fear swelled in Jael's chest, mingling with grief and guilt now.

Fear for herself.

She saw her father staring at the row of pyres – the loss of hope in his eyes.

The devastation.

Was this it?

The guard who'd been talking to the man in charge signalled for Jael to be brought forward.

She pulled back, eyes flaring. 'No! You... I'm not supposed to be killed! The queen isn't in her right mind! I am not supposed to be killed!'

No one appeared to understand her.

They started dragging her now.

Fighting back, Jael tried yanking her wrists out of their grip. One man hit her on the back of the head and she staggered, unbalanced, making it easier for them to pull her along. At least for a while.

Arching her back, she screamed, writhing and kicking, but

with little purpose. She had no weapons; there were too many men.

More soldiers came; she counted at least twelve now.

Her head pounded, thoughts blaring like warning bells, seeking her attention.

The curly-haired man in charge was pointing to a tower in the distance, laughing, and suddenly, she could understand what he was saying. His lips moved with different words, though she heard his meaning. The tower under construction by the temple was proving so challenging that his men were having to dig faster. Soon he feared they would need to find a new island to bury all the dead slaves. He thought they should just toss them into the sea for Herash's serpents to chew on.

He kept laughing, some of the guards with him.

She realised she could understand them too.

'This is the bitch who killed Otho.'

'Otho? Why? How?'

'She was a queen. A warrior. She fought in the Arena, though the commander defeated her. Defeated her, then tried to escape with her. And after he could've been a consort? Husband to the queen?'

The foreman laughed. 'You know how many of her husbands I've thrown in here? Arras Sikari wasn't wrong to see where that path would lead.'

And though it was unwise to joke about the queen, a few of the guards smirked, one chuckling.

Fear started freezing Jael's thoughts.

There was a path out of here. She just had to find it.

The heat of the afternoon sun was oppressive. Squinting, she couldn't see, couldn't think.

'Buried alive, you say?' the foreman grinned, turning to look at Jael. 'She looks half-dead already, but if the queen commands it...' He motioned towards a series of wooden hatches sitting atop the ground.

The smell intensified, dark clouds of flies hovering above them.

'No!' Jael dug her boots in the dirt, seeking purchase, though she was soon overpowered, pinched and squeezed, and eventually, kicked forward. One of the guards pulled her hair, wrapping it around his hand, bringing her close as he hissed in her ear. She headbutted him, kicking him in the balls, though she was quickly dragged away.

Laughing now, the ever-jovial foreman chose a hatch, and holding a hand over his mouth and nose, he slid an iron bar out of the locking mechanism. Slotting it into a hook, he pulled it open. Looking down, he scanned the small barrel-like hole and nodded. 'This will do. Just cleared it out. He must've died overnight.' Winking at Jael, he motioned with a dirty hand. 'Drop her in then!'

Jael's eyes widened; she was surrounded.

The man she'd spat at stepped forward, grabbing her by the tunic. 'You will suffocate. You will end your life in this small hole. A dead queen tossed away like rubbish.' He spoke the common tongue to her, knowing she was Brekkan. 'Not even your gods can save you now, bitch.'

Jael feared he was right, though as she was hauled towards the open hole, she remembered the old seer and what he'd told her. He had died with acceptance, with dignity. He had saved his last words for her.

But now?

Was it too late?

Jael tried to turn, to hold her ground.

But it was hopeless.

And soon, she was falling.

***

In his panic, Bertel didn't see the hole in the ground, and falling into it, he sprawled in front of the cottage door. Scrambling back to his feet, he hammered away at the little door, glancing over his shoulder at Siggy, who had scooped up his knives and whetstone and was running towards him.

Turning back to the door, Bertel remembered the giant seeress on Karalos, and his heart raced. 'Edela!' he called, banging again, then too impatient to wait another moment, he grabbed the old iron handle in the centre of the door. It squeaked and groaned but eventually turned. Pushing open the door, confronted with an eerie silence, he immediately felt on edge. 'Edela?'

The cottage was almost bare.

There was scant furniture to be seen: a small table with two chairs, a wooden bench pushed against a row of shelves, two beds, and two more chairs.

Two fire pits scraped clean.

And no Edela.

Siggy pushed past a stunned Bertel, and eyes bulging, she turned around in horror. 'But... but... where are they? Where's Edela? They didn't come out, did they? We were watching.'

Bertel nodded. 'We were, and no, they didn't.' His thoughts slowed, sinking into thick, unctuous mud. He could find no clarity of thought. No sense at all. 'There's only one door.'

Siggy spun around again, surveying the cottage. 'Look!' And moving to the table, she ran a finger over it, scooping up a thick line of dust. 'No one's been here in a long time.'

Bertel's shiver was explosive. 'Edela's gone! She's... gone. But where?'

***

'Where have they gone? Can you see them?' Bolder called, wanting to know where the wolf ships were. He was thirsty, throat strained from constant yelling. He was starting to lose his voice too. 'Thorgils! Where the fuck are they?'

Clouds had dropped from the sky like leaden curtains, masking their pursuers, though everyone crowded the stern, trying to catch a glimpse of them.

'Still there!' Thorgils told him. 'Getting closer!'

Bolder cursed, eyes snapping to Eadmund, who had taken to striding up and down the ship, as though by moving himself, he could push *Bone Hammer* on. He shook his head, needing to see, shoulders burning, hands locked around the steering oar. 'Talk to the dreamer!' he urged. 'What can she see? What will happen?'

Eadmund nodded, cloak snapping as he turned, heading for where Mattie sat, backed into the starboard gunwale, clutching Otter. Fyn and Kolarov stood over her, the explorer clinging to the younger man as the wind intensified, though they were both swaying.

Otter miaowed and Mattie opened her eyes, immediately plonking the cat on the deck and hurrying to her feet. *Bone Hammer* tilted, and she fell against Fyn. 'My lord?' she said, sensing Eadmund's need of her.

'Bolder wants to know what you've seen. Anything?'

Mattie had been sitting with her eyes closed for some time, trying to find a path to safety, though nothing had emerged from the darkness of her mind. She hadn't been able to shut out the keening wind, the muttering crew and the bellowing helmsman, or her fear that she was destined to die at sea. Glancing at Otter, she shook her head. 'Nothing at all. Which isn't as bad as it sounds,' she added with a measure of reassurance. 'I see no threat.'

A frantic Kolarov snorted. 'You hardly need to see what is already apparent to those of us riding this doomed coffin! Oh no, for despite those murderous-looking clouds, the threat is painted all too vividly!'

Eadmund grabbed his arm. 'Get hold of yourself, man! We don't survive this unless we're united and calm, so keep your fears to yourself, Kolarov. If you want to see your home again, then help. Do what you can to help!'

'There!' someone shouted over the roaring wind, and every head turned, seeing a row of ships surging through the clouds.

'They're closer!' Thorgils warned, heading for Bolder with a shaking head.

'Arrows! Bows!' Eadmund ordered. 'Let's prepare!' He hadn't thought it would come to this, or at least, he'd certainly hoped it wouldn't. Though it was obvious now that the wolf ships would catch them before long. They were faster, sleeker. They cut through the waves like blades – a different class of ship altogether – and Eadmund feared there was nothing Bolder could do to make *Bone Hammer* outrun them.

'How many days away is Hest?' Fyn wondered.

'Too many,' Kolarov muttered. 'Far too many to help us. We could try for Zagora, though I fear that fickle queen's loyalties. Her family has never been a friend to Osterland.' He turned to the dreamer. 'But you, my dear. *You* have the power to save us!'

No one spoke as Bolder's crew ran to uncover their store of bows and arrows, bringing them back to the mast.

'Me?' A confused Mattie shook her head, ears throbbing with cold, buzzing with fear. 'I can't make us go faster! I'm not the wind!' Hazel eyes bulging indignantly, she glared at Kolarov.

'But dreamers are chosen by the gods!' Kolarov declared. 'They have gifted you powers almost as great as their own. Not merely to see and hear the unspoken, the unlived, but to *do*. You can do a great many things, Mattie. It is in you, waiting for moments such as this, where all your hopes and dreams, your very life is on the line!'

Mattie squirmed, not wanting this put on her. Not the survival of an entire crew. Not the life of Jael Furyck, who needed them to mount another rescue attempt. Quickly nauseous, she shook her head. 'I'm not that sort of dreamer!' she insisted angrily. 'I haven't, I didn't... I didn't train to be that sort of dreamer! You can't simply do what you don't know! It's impossible!'

Eadmund stared at the dreamer, seeing fear and doubt

shining in her big eyes. 'You're wrong, Mattie. Those gifts you have are like weapons. You were born with a belt full of them and the talent to wield them too. You just need to believe in yourself. Trust that you will know what to do at the right time.' And then he was gone, turning to organise Bolder's men – his men now. They were all his men to care for. He saw the two men they'd rescued coming to join him. 'Soon they'll be in range.'

Arras picked up two bows, handing one to Nico. 'You're risking your lives for us. Least we can do is risk ours for you.'

Eadmund nodded, resisting the urge to pick up a bow himself; it was better if he took charge of the archers. He inclined his head for Fyn to grab one himself.

Thorgils joined them. 'I'll test the range,' he decided, selecting one of the remaining two bows.

'Just the one,' Eadmund warned, seeing the meagre pile of arrows the crew had collected. 'We can't afford to waste any.'

Thorgils turned for the stern.

'Eyes open!' Eadmund called after him. 'Go with him,' he told Fyn. 'Keep a watch. If we're trying for the range, you can be sure they'll be trying too.'

A sneezing Mattie bent down to pick up Otter, seeing Kolarov holding out his arms.

'Let me take him, my dear. I will look after him for you.' She backed away, holding Otter tightly. 'I've seen what dreamers can do, how powerful they can be. Their minds! *Your* mind, Mattie. You just have to open it up and the impossible will quickly become possible!' He stared imploringly at the dreamer clutching her cat until, eventually, she loosened her hold on Otter, and he scooped him into his arms. 'We'll head to the bow, out of the way, for I fear things are about to get rather messy!'

Mattie's lips parted, moving, though she couldn't find any words. She stared at Otter, remembering the last morning she'd seen her husband. She could still feel his cold lips on hers; the soft bristles of his beard brushing her cheek; the look in his eyes that silently conveyed how much he regretted leaving their warm cottage for the bitter sea.

He would return, he'd promised.

To her.

He would return, and they would be together again.

They would have a child, a house of children and animals and laughter. She would not be alone for long.

Tears stung her eyes, the wind tormenting her, and she blinked, turning away from Kolarov towards Eadmund Skalleson, who was trying to save them all.

Taking a deep breath, she realised that it was time to stop thinking, to stop fretting and worrying and doubting.

There was no time for any of it.

If they were going to escape the wolf ships and return to save Jael Furyck, she was going to have to become the dreamer the gods had chosen her to be.

CHAPTER THREE

Katalyne led Edela into the most wondrous garden.

Fenced by pale stone walls taller than either woman, it was dominated by the magnificent bone tree, whose ivory boughs reached from one side of the garden to the other, shimmering in the sun.

She heard bees buzzing and birds singing in smaller trees dotted around the garden, though she saw none in the bone tree itself. Sweet scents of rose and jasmine wafted towards her, the verdant greenery soothing her as she stepped on spongy grass with bright eyes, taking everything in.

Though despite the wonders of Katalyne's garden and the many questions flooding Edela's mind, she continued to look over her shoulder, worrying about Bertel and Siggy.

'Is something wrong?' Katalyne wondered as she watched the old woman's eyes dart towards the cottage again.

'It is my... companions,' Edela explained, not wanting to draw attention to her discomfort, though she still felt physically strange. 'They'll be so hot and tired out there. I don't wish to keep them long.'

'Though there is a shaded copse and a well nearby. I'm sure they'll enjoy the rest and peace after such an arduous time.'

Edela's shoulders dropped as she released her hold on that worry. 'Of course. I'm being silly. Bertel's certainly old enough to look after them both.'

'As long as you are sure? We can go back at any time.'

'No, no, I came to see the tree. And to meet you, of course. It would be rather foolish to give up now.'

'Good, then come, and we will continue,' Katalyne purred, holding out a hand.

Touching it, Edela felt an odd chill in that flesh, though she smiled as she followed the woman towards the tree.

Upon reaching it, she tipped back her head to take in the breathtaking sight. Its trunk was as tall as a mast, its leaves made of glistening bone. It was exactly as she had seen it in her dreams.

'The tree led us here,' Katalyne explained, stroking its smooth alabaster trunk. 'To Aggralaia. My sister and I. We shared a dream of what it was, of what it could one day be and what we were born to do. We are twins, you see. Two bodies but one mind.'

An intrigued Edela wondered where Katalyne's sister was, though she didn't want to interrupt.

'Please, don't be shy. You may touch her.'

'Her?'

'Lystora. She is a tree of bones to some but a living creature to those of us who can see beyond the shells we hide in.'

Edela didn't hesitate. She had been drawn to the tree like a bee to pollen, and now that she was here, before it, eyes on its towering majesty, she felt a powerful compulsion to touch its trunk. Reaching for it with both hands, she soon lifted one higher, aiming for a leaf.

'No!' Katalyne snapped, moving towards her. 'Not the bones! Forgive me, I should have explained. Some are thousands of years old. Please, there is time for that.' Turning, she inclined her head to a circle of stools carved from the familiar white stone Edela had seen on her travels around the archipelago. 'Let us sit, and when you have answered my questions, I shall allow you to retrieve a bone.'

***

Standing in the empty cottage, a panicked Bertel Knutson was dripping with sweat. He felt it trickling down his back, beading across his forehead, and mopping it out of his rapidly blinking eyes, he tried to compose himself for Siggy, who trembled before him.

Taking hold of her shoulders, he sought to focus them both. 'We can't help Edela. Not yet.'

It was true but shocking to hear, and Siggy gulped.

'She would tell us the same. We have to save ourselves first. We cannot think to rescue her while we are in danger, so tell me about these creatures. I... you've never had a dream before. Is that right? And now, you think this vision was real? I'm not sure we should tie ourselves in knots without some proof.'

Siggy took no offence, for she was beginning to fear she'd imagined everything she'd seen. That it had simply been boredom leading her mind on an adventure, the way it had as a child, conjuring up all sorts of fantasies that would eventually lead to terrifying nightmares. She glanced around the cottage, eyes on that tiny front door. 'We have to go back to the beach.'

A nodding Bertel scoured the cottage, peeking under a bed. He pulled out a small wooden box, hoping to find something useful, though it was empty. It was as though the occupants had packed up and moved away.

'We'll go to the beach,' he echoed, standing up with a grimace, tension tightening every muscle. 'See for ourselves.'

Siggy waited for him to lead the way out of the cottage, and glancing over her shoulder, wondering what had happened to Edela, she headed through the door, quietly closing it behind her.

***

Rain came down in big icy drops; it felt like being struck by stones.

The noise was thunderous, though sheltering under a fur, a grimacing Kolarov did wonder if he heard thunder too. It was hard to make out much. Eadmund was shouting at Bolder, who was rasping back, both men starting to lose their voices. Clutching Otter and sitting next to the terrified woman they'd rescued from S'ala Nis, Kolarov tried offering some reassurance. 'We have a king protecting us. A king! And he won't let us falter now. His wife is back on the isle. He must survive to return to her!'

A tearful Anika nibbled wet lips, hunched under her own fur, trying to keep out the worst of the pounding rain. She kept searching for a glimpse of Nico, though in the darkening gloom, it was hard to make him out. Those with bows had made a wall across the stern in preparation for what might come, and from the raised voices of the crew and helmsman, Anika feared that what might come was nearly here.

'And you are from Brekka?' Kolarov asked as though they had encountered one another in a market, chatting over twists of spice and pots of honey. 'Where in Brekka?'

'North. Past Andala. A village called Folen.'

Kolarov nodded blankly, not knowing it. 'And you were taken from there? By slavers?'

Anika shook her head. 'I left with my father. He carved ivory figurines and combs. Drinking cups too. He thought to trade in the Fire Lands. He'd tried it once and brought back many wonderful things, so I begged him to take me with him. I wanted an... adventure.'

Her body was soon heaving with sobs, leaving Kolarov regretting that he'd asked. 'Well, I –'

The first arrow struck one of the archers, flinging him backwards, head slamming on the deck with a sickening crack.

Arras jerked around, seeing Nico staring at the man in horror. The man who, only moments ago, had been standing next to him.

'Fire!' Eadmund shouted, unable to offer any guidance, for their enemy was once again masked by the rumbling storm clouds. 'Someone else grab that bow!'

The fallen man had been hit in the chest.

He wasn't moving.

Bone Hammer's archers silently released a volley of arrows, listening, hoping they might land true. Though over the rush of waves and the drumming rain, it was impossible to tell whether the arrows had landed in the sea or hit a target.

Then a shout.

Eadmund turned, catching Thorgils' eye. 'Shields!' he called, turning further to find Bolder. 'We need to move! Push into the clouds!'

Bolder leaned on the steering oar, hoping the wind would drive *Bone Hammer* out of the range of those archers.

The enormous raindrops soon turned into hail, pummelling the sodden crew and hitting the deck with real force.

More arrows scythed through the sinking clouds, one striking the mast, another hitting one of Bolder's men. He cried out in surprise, dropping his bow and grabbing his shoulder. Staggering, he backed out of the wall.

Eadmund thought about the little wooden houses Jael had built on their ships in Oss. She'd been so bullish about her plan, ignoring the derisive looks and muttered doubts, especially from the resistant old helmsmen. But those wooden houses had saved their lives and those of countless men.

Here on *Bone Hammer*, they only had shields.

'Mattie! Grab a shield!' he snapped, seeing the dreamer rising unsteadily to her feet. 'Take a shield and head to the bow!' Spinning back to the archers, he sent another man to pick up the dropped bow.

Bending down in search of a shield, the crew's fears flooded Mattie's mind. She heard them praying to their gods. They wanted to live. To see their homes and families and live.

'Arrows!' she called, an intense whistle drilling into her ears. It didn't seem as though anyone on board had heard the warning. And reaching for the shield rack, she tugged out a round wooden shield made of faded blue boards, and crouching down, she swung it over her head.

One of the arrows struck it. The rest hit the deck, a few splashing into the sea.

Taking down the shield, Mattie stared at the arrow in horror.

Dropping his own shield, Eadmund looked back at her in surprise. 'You can hear the arrows?'

She nodded, feeling equally shocked. 'Yes, I can hear them coming.'

***

The more time she spent in the walled garden, the more Edela's thoughts raced around her mind like panicking children.

She didn't trust Katalyne, she didn't know what to make of her, so what could she offer that wouldn't reveal something she needed to keep to herself?

'Perhaps begin by telling me why you left Tuura behind? To have come so far without your family? You must have been driven by a purpose? A reason?'

Edela nodded. 'I was... sent away.' Katalyne twitched, and though it was barely perceptible, Edela became even more reticent, seeking to clarify her words. 'I... had a vision. I saw trouble coming to Tuura, I saw the danger, so I took the girls and Bertel, and I... escaped.'

Katalyne leaned forward. 'You had a vision?'

'I did. The urgency of our departure made sense, but then? Well, I soon discovered that I couldn't simply return to Tuura, to Osterland at all, for I was being hunted. Perhaps I still am?'

'And you seek to uncover your enemy? Is that why you came here? Someone told you to come?'

Edela glanced over her shoulder at the little stone cottage, neck tingling. She looked back at Katalyne, who remained a statue before her.

'I can help you, Edela. Lystora can help you. We will, but only if you open yourself to us. A closed door reveals no secrets, and perhaps that is your intention, though it also prevents insight. Lystora's leaves are yours for the taking, but first, you must tell me the truth.'

Edela sensed that Katalyne was fishing for one answer in particular. She readjusted herself on the stool, slipping her right hand under her leg.

Sitting on it.

'I do want to help you,' Katalyne promised, reaching out to touch Edela's left hand. 'I have helped many...' Her words trailed off as she stared intently into the dreamer's blue eyes.

So sharp and wary.

She squeezed that old hand, seeing inky veins bulge beneath thin, pale skin.

Edela remained perfectly still, holding her breath. 'For a price?'

'Well, yes, dear Edela. Here? On this little island with just my sister for company? There are things we need for our very survival. Important things. Knowledge...'

The pressure on her hand became so intensely painful it brought tears to Edela's eyes.

The grip wasn't human.

Icy and stone-like, it wasn't human at all.

Panic rising, she eyed the tree.

'Though the price is merely a simple answer to a simple question. Tell me what I need to know, and you may avail yourself of Lystora's wisdom and then return to your friends.'

'And what do you wish to know?'

'Oh, it is nothing to fear!' Katalyne tittered, though her strange eyes were unblinking, her pressure on Edela's hand unflinching. 'Nothing that would grieve you to reveal, I'm sure. I only want to know who sent you away from Tuura. Who that vision was from?'

Edela sought to look bemused rather than concerned.

Though she was desperately concerned.

She kept her eyes on Katalyne, resisting the urge to peer over her shoulder at the door.

Where was Katalyne's sister?

The tree seemed to shudder, or perhaps it was a shimmer of light escaping a bank of clouds, now tinged with red.

Edela swallowed a great lump of tension, sweat beading along her upper lip. 'Who sent me? But I told you, *I* had a vision, *I* saw the danger in the fort. It was me.'

Flinging away the old woman's hand, Katalyne stood with a snarl, towering over her.

Edela saw strange things as she stared up at the woman now: hints of age on that previously flawless young face, as though her skin was rippling like waves in the sand.

And rage.

The woman's eyes had darkened further, now seething like a stormy sea.

'That is untrue!' Katalyne growled, teeth bared. 'You *lie*!'

'If you are so certain I'm lying, please, read my thoughts,' Edela dared, rising to her own feet, holding her ground against this woman or creature, who appeared to have grown in size. The pain in her heart returned in force, accompanied now by a tightness in her throat that threatened to steal her breath. Though pushing back her shoulders, she revealed no outward sign of discomfort.

'You were sent from Tuura, from Osterland, by someone who knew what was planned! Someone who knew what would unfold! Someone who sought to save the Furycks!'

Edela couldn't hide her surprise, though she quickly recovered, strengthening the protections around her mind, sensing Katalyne trying to pry open those defenses now. Pain throbbed at her temples, sweat trailing down her forehead, settling in her eyebrows.

'You will tell me who it was! Who warned you of what would

come!'

The woman's voice roared around the garden like a storm, the reddish clouds hovering above it sweeping low, whirling around the tree, which shuddered again, its ivory trunk turning a dull ashy colour.

'I have told you!' Edela roared back. '*I* had a vision! In the forest, I had a vision. I saw the danger coming. I did! It was *me*!' She sensed Katalyne's magic coming like a vibration in the air, like a flap of wings, and swaying back, she flung out both hands as sparks from the woman's palms struck her own.

And crying out in agony, Edela dropped to her knees.

***

Bertel was breathless, his tunic stuck to his back as he finally reached the bottom of the long trail of steps carved into the cliff.

A hesitant Siggy waited for him, holding her breath.

She wasn't sure how she felt.

If she'd had a real vision, a dream, then she truly was a dreamer.

But if what she'd seen was real, then Elmer Falson and his crew were dead.

Bertel peered at her, seeing the terror in her blinking eyes. Unsheathing one of his knives, he offered her the plain wooden haft. 'It's not much, it won't do much, but it's always better to have an option. You get behind me, though. And stay close. I'll lead the way.'

Siggy stumbled into a shallow hole as she stepped down onto the sand.

'Ship's still there!' Bertel called, moving ahead. Then, lowering his voice, he turned back to her. 'That's something.'

'I saw it was still there. I told you,' she reminded him.

'I can't hear anyone,' Bertel murmured. Eyeing the trees where they'd collected wood for the fire, he motioned for Siggy to head that way. 'Let's get under cover. Out of the sun would be good too.' He attempted to sound calm, though he feared the girl's gift had finally announced itself and that an arrogant Edela had led them into certain danger once more. The foolish woman, he scolded, muttering to himself.

What had she done?

***

Edela's teeth were gritted as she struggled back to her feet, knowing she was better suited to making teas than battling malevolent creatures.

Surely such things were Jael's job?

Her tingling hands reminded her of Furia and the symbols she had discreetly marked on her palms before she'd ventured up that long chain of steps. And now she pushed her hands forward again, straightening her spine.

Katalyne blinked in horror at those symbols. 'What are you?' she hissed, her face distorting more obviously now.

Edela saw gums where once there had been teeth. Small ears became great drooping lobes, a delicate snub nose thickened into a hooked beak and hair that had been lush and chestnut turned wiry and grey.

There was no time to wonder what was going on. With the sky darkening and lightning tearing through those odd red clouds, Edela knew she had to act.

Katalyne tried again to break through.

Edela felt a burst of heat strike her ankles, her elbows burned, though she focused on her own symbols, weaving them together like threads on a tapestry. And hastily making a new symbol, she strengthened it with a powerful chant. It was like flint to tinder, and soon, she felt the symbol ignite inside her.

Katalyne lashed out with an arm and a curse, sending the old woman flying, crashing into the tree. It shook, bony leaves knocking together. It reminded a dazed Edela of wind chimes, and she felt wistful for her home and family.

They were in danger.

She had been sent away to help them because they were in danger.

And somewhere on the island, she feared that Bertel and Siggy were in danger too.

Edela felt the icy tree trunk behind her as she struggled back to her feet, watching Katalyne striding towards her, long arms sweeping from side to side. Edela's heart stuttered, strained breaths burning her lungs. She tasted blood and spitting on a hand, she pressed her palms together before lifting them to her mouth and blowing out a powerful breath. Flinging out her arms, she sent a shower of blood spraying over Katalyne.

The woman screamed, raising her hands in vain, unable to prevent the great wave of it striking her. Edela had infused her blood with a dark curse, and now it struck Katalyne, binding to her.

She could not escape it.

Moving forward, hands extended once again, ignoring every ache and pain, the red storm howling above her head, Edela now chanted her curse upon the creature. For now, she truly was a creature, she saw, as Katalyne's human form degraded further until she was little more than a fleshy, bent skeleton. Like a dragur. As though she had been raised from the dead.

'No!' Katalyne pleaded, falling onto her side and curling into a ball. 'No! You... you cannot kill me –'

'Kill you? I have trapped you, and you will give me answers! Why did you bring me here? What are you?' Edela could barely see the creature now. The red sky was darkening to night, her dress snapping around her ankles, wisps of hair in her eyes, her mouth. 'Who are you?' she repeated as the angry wind swirled, nearly knocking her over.

Though Katalyne didn't answer.

She lay in that ball, trapped by Edela's binding spell, eyes closed tight.

And despite the noise and the effort it took to remain on her feet, Edela soon realised that Katalyne was chanting, gripping an amulet around her neck. She closed her own eyes, doubling down on the binding spell. Then, hearing a shriek and seeing a flash of white light, she was blown off her feet, tumbling back across the garden all the way to the cottage.

CHAPTER FOUR

Crashing over swelling waves, *Bone Hammer's* crew became nauseous, quickly running low on arrows.

'Hold fire!' Eadmund ordered, gripping the shield rack.

Bolder was working the steering oar, trying to keep their enemies guessing, though it mostly kept his own crew guessing. More than one man had lost his balance, ending up red-faced on his knees in the bilge water.

Another two men had been injured by arrows, helped to the bow, where Anika worked to stitch them up with Kolarov's clumsy assistance.

Mattie had been shouting warnings, which had saved many more injuries. As soon as she heard the whistle in her ears, she would call out, and the men would raise their shields, holding a defensive position. And when the danger had passed, they would resume their own attack.

Though they were one ship against nine.

Or seven.

They hadn't counted nine wolf ships in some time.

Eadmund was growing tired. It had been only hours, yet it felt like days since the terrifying swim into the tunnel and the heartbreaking departure without Jael. He saw glimpses of her in their bed, cuddling their children and dogs. She was laughing, smiling.

She was his.

He had to keep alert, he had to keep everyone alive.

He had to get back to her.

'Arrows!' Mattie called, raising her shield. A stream of arrows burst through the storm clouds, two piercing *Bone Hammer's* sail, another striking the bow near Kolarov, who had been bending over an injured man.

He yelped in surprise, throwing himself on top of the man.

'They're close!' Arras warned, eyes sweeping past a worried-looking Nico to where Eadmund Skalleson emerged from behind his shield. 'We need a plan!'

Eadmund was all ears. He moved towards the man. 'You have one?'

Arras nodded. 'No more arrows. We just defend.'

'Against nine ships?'

'Seven. I only see seven now.'

Fyn left them arguing, returning to Mattie, who looked unsteady on her feet. 'Are you alright?'

She was working hard not to vomit. The deck kept tilting; every lurch as the waves rolled beneath *Bone Hammer's* hull felt like a mirror of what was happening in her stomach. Wrinkling her nose, she shifted her eyes, willing Fyn Gallas on his way. Though he remained, watching as those eyes now widened in horror.

'What?'

'*Move!*' Mattie stumbled away from him, pushing past those men, all taller and bigger than she was, though just as wet and scared. She slipped, heart thumping an urgent rhythm in her ears.

Thump, thump, thump.

Otter miaowed.

Whistle.

Thump, thump, thump.

Pulling herself to her feet, Mattie slid past Eadmund, who turned to her, expecting her to speak. Though lips clamped shut, she hurried on, running past Arras and Nico to where Thorgils stood in the first row of archers, and now she ducked under his arm, eyes on the stern. Head up, neck extended, she flung her arms towards the sky.

There were no voices, no noises, no words.

She saw a symbol. Unblinking eyes blurring with rain, wind searing her face, Mattie Bilso took in every aspect of that symbol. And now, arms pushing so high that she thought they would separate from her shoulders, face tilted back, washed in rain, she saw a dark wave of arrows coming.

And then nothing.

Mattie held those arrows in the sky. Hands splayed and trembling, she stopped them midair.

They didn't move.

Fingers stiff as iron nails, hands burning, bile swilling in her mouth, Mattie felt her legs shaking as though the weight of the arrows was bearing down upon her, pushing her back.

Heart skipping wildly now, her vision darkened.

Otter miaowed. She focused again.

Tightening her grip.

Her fingers became claws, folding in towards her palms.

Every arrow. She wanted every single arrow. She would draw them all to her. Not just those hovering in the air, threatening *Bone Hammer* and her crew. She wanted every arrow on every one of those wolf ships.

Closing her eyes, she sought them out, lifting them into the air, joining that great storm cloud of arrows.

And now, limbs strengthening, balance steady, eyes clearing again, she threw down her arms, sending every single arrow into the sea.

***

Bertel and Siggy crept into the trees, forcing their way through until they were stopped by a dense tangle of branches. The trees were similar to the pines of Osterland, with a fresh scent and bristly leaves, poking them as they tried to move further.

'There!' Siggy hissed in horror. '*See!*'

Bertel squinted through the branches, unsure of what he was seeing. The sand rose ahead of them, tiny grains swept around by a light breeze. He saw no men standing as he had hoped, though there certainly appeared to be something scattered across the sand.

'People,' Siggy told him, clasping his arm. 'Bits of people!'

Bertel didn't want to believe her. 'Keep a firm hold of that knife,' he whispered. 'And quiet. You're too loud.' He crept closer, pushing branches out of his path, wanting confirmation of Siggy's fears. And his own.

Seeing a head, he jerked to a stop, recognising the face of Elmer Falson lying in the sand: mouth wrenched open, a bloody hole where his ear should have been. There was no sign of the rest of his body. Not anywhere Bertel could see.

Hand over his mouth, he turned to Siggy, urging her back into the trees.

'What? What did you see?'

Bertel didn't answer. He kept pushing Siggy, head swivelling, searching for threats. They needed to be somewhere less exposed. The trees were hardly that, but he wanted a solid surface at his back. Somewhere to defend from.

Spotting a pair of enormous boulders, Bertel hurried Siggy towards them. And when they arrived, he pushed her down behind them. 'It was Elmer,' he panted. 'I saw Elmer. Or, at least, his head.'

Siggy covered her mouth, eyes bulging over her hand.

'You had a dream,' he whispered breathlessly. 'Which means that you're a real dreamer, Siggy, so I need your help. We all do. You have to tell me everything you saw. What it was that did this. And Edela. What can you see of Edela?'

Siggy was too stunned to speak. A real dreamer?

Tears flooded her eyes as she shuddered before him.

Lifting her chin, Bertel peered at her, trying to focus the girl. 'We've all done brave things on this journey, haven't we? To keep alive, to stay together? But we can't stop now. We must get back up that cliff and find a way to Edela. So tell me, what were these creatures, and where did they go?'

***

Fyn had hold of Mattie's arm, though he didn't know what to do with her.

She wasn't moving, wasn't speaking.

After she'd drawn those arrows from the sky and the wolf ships, sending them into the sea, she'd collapsed to the deck in a heap. He'd pulled her to her feet, and now she leaned against him, limp and quiet, eyes fluttering.

'Bring her here, Fyn! Bring her here!' Kolarov was bellowing, heading for his cabinet for more of his precious jara, hoping to revive the dreamer once again.

Thorgils took Mattie's other side, leaving Eadmund to try and wrap his head around what had just happened.

A stunned-looking Arras arrived with Nico. He was as confused as everyone else, though his mind soon surged ahead. 'I'll talk to your helmsman. We must try to lose them.' Hearing thunder surging closer, seeing the clouds turning black, he knew it wouldn't be long before the storm was upon them.

Eadmund nodded, turning away from the two men as they moved down the watery deck towards Bolder. He saw a ship in the distance, just making out its wolf head prow, fearing they had gained on them.

'Here, here,' Kolarov fussed, urging Fyn and Thorgils to ease the dreamer down onto a chest he had just covered in a damp fur.

'Sit down, Mattie, and I'll give you a little of this.'

Having finished stitching the two wounded men, Anika helpfully brought over Otter, who seemed to awaken a flicker of interest in Mattie. Sitting on the chest, she wrapped a trembling arm around her cat. Her eyes had no focus, though, until Kolarov tipped a few drops of jara into her mouth. And suddenly, everything sharpened, and she cried out, rising off the chest with a gasp.

'What *is* that stuff?' Thorgils wondered with a scowl. 'Sounds like you're poisoning the woman!'

Ignoring him, Kolarov tucked the bottle of jara into his pouch and patted Mattie's hand. 'You are here again, my dear. And we are all so glad of it! Aren't we?' he asked of his audience: Fyn, Thorgils, Otter and Anika.

Fyn stared at the dreamer. '*You*... stopped those arrows?'

Mattie's head was clearer, though what had happened was hard to describe. She hadn't been herself at all. She wasn't sure if she'd even been the one to do it.

That she could suddenly make magic?

How was it even possible?

'I saw...' She struggled to speak, but coughing, she tried again. 'I saw what would happen,' she remembered. 'The arrows, the wolf ships... there were so many arrows. I knew we'd be finished. The sail, the archers, and Otter. I saw that they would kill Otter and...' She glanced at Fyn, then quickly looked away, back to Kolarov.

Thunder clapped overhead.

Anika shuddered, eyes on Nico, who motioned for her to join him, though she remained where she was, wanting to hear the rest of the dreamer's story.

'I can't remember much of what happened after that,' Mattie admitted, avoiding Fyn's searching gaze. 'I just tried to stop it. I just... tried.' Tears stung her eyes now, shoulders sinking as lightning flashed over *Bone Hammer's* bow.

'You did more than just try,' Kolarov assured her. 'You did

save us, Mattie. You did!'

Mattie didn't look pleased or relieved. She simply felt exhausted.

'We're not out of danger,' she added with a frown. 'Not yet. But they are out of arrows.'

***

Jael wanted a knife.

She had nothing. No weapon. Not even those dratted fetters.

She laughed hysterically before coughing, gasping for air.

The dark hole she'd been dropped into was oppressively hot, barely a breath of air creeping in.

She needed a knife to scrape at the walls, to dig a hole she could crawl through. To escape.

The hole.

How long had she been in this hole?

Fine shafts of light filtered through the trapdoor, shining on her hands.

It was still daylight. Only hours then.

It was still daylight!

The hole was barely tall enough for her to stand, not wide enough to lie down in; she could easily touch the sides. It was small, airless. Dark.

Sweat poured down her back, soaking the soldier's uniform, reminding her of her failed escape. What a mess she'd made of things. And Sunni?

Not just a mess, a tragedy.

Leaning back, Jael heard shouting coming from above.

She was underground. Panic sparked again, her chest rising and falling at speed. She didn't like tight spaces. It felt as though the dirt walls were coming closer; that they would collapse upon her, burying her alive.

'Panic won't help you survive. And you must survive!' her father bellowed in her ears. Turning her head, she imagined him sitting in the cramped space beside her.

'Do you think you are meant to die here, Daughter? And not just my daughter, but Furia's daughter too. And you think this is your end? That such a nothing fate has been woven for you?'

Jael snorted, mind unspooling now. 'I think you died in your bed, Father, soiled by sickness and decay. The great Furyck king! You died on your back like a wasted wreck. We are Furycks, not gods, not heroes. We are just people.' Ranuf laughed bitterly, then her vision of him was gone, and she saw Sunni smiling at her, running and skipping away. Tears came like a deluge, and lifting her hand to her head, Jael sobbed. 'Oh, Sunni, I'm sorry. I'm so sorry.'

***

Siggy's description of the creatures she'd seen tearing apart Elmer and his crew left Bertel more confused than ever. 'But how many were there? How many did you see?' He swallowed, inhaling foul odours for the first time, noticing that the breeze had strengthened.

The afternoon sky was darkening.

'I...' As much as she tried, Siggy could only recall fleeting glimpses of what she'd seen: fur and teeth and claws; blood and bone and terror. They were glaring, colourful images that heightened her fears but gave her little ability to describe the threat they were facing. 'I'm not sure. I'm sorry, Bertel.'

'That's alright. It's alright,' he assured her, feeling grit in his eyes. He scrubbed them, quickly making everything worse. 'I think we'd better stay here for now and see what happens. Keep alert, though, and if you see anything, if you have another vision, tell me straight away.'

Siggy nodded, and immediately feeling the hairs on her arms rising, she dragged up her knife. 'Now! I think something's coming now!'

***

Pulling herself back to her feet in the garden, a panting Edela saw that Katalyne had disappeared.

Glancing at the cottage door, she knew she had to leave, fearing for Bertel and Siggy, though she couldn't go without seeing what the tree might reveal. All their efforts to get here surely couldn't be for nothing? So, taking a breath, she headed for the tree, which now appeared dimmed, as though it was no longer illuminated from within. Perhaps it was just that strange sky, Edela thought, eyes on the red clouds sinking overhead.

Turning back to the tree, she placed her hands on Lystora's trunk and closing her eyes, she sought an answer to her most burning questions: to where did her path lead, and for what purpose had she been sent away?

Opening her eyes, she reached up a still-trembling hand, aiming for one bone in particular. Plucking it from the tree, she turned it over, expecting to see something carved there – symbols, words, a message.

Though it was entirely blank.

Confused by that, Edela tried again, numerous times, though every bone was the same. There was no message to be found on any of them.

Placing her hands on the tree, she tried drawing its power to her, but opening her eyes, Edela soon discovered that the tree was just like Katalyne.

An illusion.

Just a way to lure her here.

And realising it, she hurried away from the whole mess, heading for the cottage door, eager to find Bertel and Siggy.

***

What Siggy had seen coming turned out to be a ship.

And having discovered that, Bertel debated what to do for some time.

Though ultimately, they had to get off the island. And if Elmer Falson and his crew were now pieces of meat roasting in the sun, there was little choice but to try and attract the ship's attention. He certainly couldn't attempt to sail a ship with a crew of Siggy and, hopefully, Edela.

'We must go,' he decided with a sigh. 'There's no sign of whatever was here, whatever did... that. But perhaps that ship won't linger? We need it to moor here. To wait for us so we can find Edela.'

Siggy nodded, agreeing in theory, and though the prospect of heading across the sand terrified her, she straightened up, following Bertel down a stony path, through the trees, and up onto the sand.

Bertel carried two knives, one in each hand, though he felt unprepared and vulnerable, certain he stood no chance of defending them against whatever had killed Elmer and his crew. 'Don't look,' he urged, fixing his eyes on the ship, avoiding the horrors scattered across their path.

Siggy shrieked, seeing a foot, an arm, a head. 'But that's –'

'No time!' Bertel snapped, turning back to glower at the girl. 'And move!' He started waving at the ship as he waded through the warm sand. 'Hello!'

Seeing Bertel brandishing his knives and the body parts scattered in the sand, Siggy hurried forward. 'They might think you did it!' she warned. 'That you killed them all!'

Stumbling to a stop, Bertel lowered his arms and sheathed his knives. 'You go ahead, Siggy. You're faster! Try to attract their attention. I'll be right behind you.' He pushed her ahead, glancing over his shoulder, quickly becoming aware of an unsettling noise.

***

Edela couldn't find a way out of Katalyne's garden.

The reddish clouds hovered above her, the tree still and pale behind her, though try as she might, Edela couldn't pry open the cottage door. Tension tightening her aching limbs, exhausted beyond measure, she turned to stare up at the clouds again, starting to wonder where she actually was. So, abandoning the door, she began exploring the little garden.

Her eyes went to the walls, almost touching those strange clouds.

She couldn't smell the sea or feel a breeze.

And becoming more disturbed by the moment, Edela knocked over one of the stone stools, rolling it across the grass until she reached the wall. And carefully clambering onto it, she grabbed hold of the top of the wall.

She almost fell off the stool.

There was nothing.

Nothing.

Nothing on the other side of the wall but a dark void.

She was nowhere at all.

***

Armed men had jumped down from the ship, landing in the shallows. The sky was now seething with clouds, though it remained just as hot.

A running Siggy felt twinges of fear as she moved across the sand, gagging at the sight of a headless torso and quickly lifting her eyes once more. She waved at the new arrivals, trying to attract their attention, though they were far away and didn't appear to see her or Bertel.

Turning around, she realised that Bertel had stopped. 'What's wrong?'

The sky darkened, her twinges of fear becoming great shudders.

'It's... a... bear!' Bertel shouted. 'Run for the ship, Siggy! *Run!*'

Siggy turned back, immediately falling into a dip in the sand, landing on her knees, hands resting on the arm of one of Elmer's men. Screaming, she was hauled to her feet by Bertel, whose panic she could hear loud in her ears.

Glancing over her shoulder, she saw the enormous creature: a great brown bear charging towards them.

The sand vibrated beneath their feet as they ran, trying not to fall or trip over the remains of Elmer's men. Gulls and ravens squawked in annoyance, not wanting company. Then, seeing the bear, they took off, black and white wings flapping in a flurry of panicked noise.

'*Run!*' Siggy screamed, digging her boots into the warm sand, her speed soon taking her away from Bertel.

He let her go, unsheathing one of his knives, flinging it at the rapidly gaining bear, who pounded across the sand towards him. He'd had little time to steady himself, no time to consider his aim, but Bertel's knife struck the bear in the shoulder. It growled in surprise, breaking its momentum.

The men wading through the shallows had seen the bear

and its running prey and were calling out now, hands in the air, urging them to hurry.

The bear roared in anger, a strange, almost human sound. Stopping, it stood on its hind legs, and then dropping down to all fours again, it dug its lethal claws into the sand and charged.

'Get down!' one of the ship's crew ordered, running towards them, spear in hand. More men trailed behind him, carrying weapons. 'Get down!'

Siggy glanced at Bertel, who had caught her up. She couldn't breathe, a stinging pain in her side making her eyes water.

Spinning around, Bertel released his last knife, striking the charging bear again before throwing himself forward. Siggy landed beside him with a grunt, swallowing a mouthful of sand. They kept moving, wriggling forward like snakes, feeling the thumping vibrations beneath them.

The spear flew past the bear, missing.

The bear kept coming, wounded by Bertel's two knives, though otherwise unimpeded.

Siggy heard the ship's crew calling for more spears; she didn't think they would be in time. And head swivelling, she saw that Bertel had wriggled away from her. '*Bertel*!'

The bear was nearly on them.

Injured, angry, and growling, it swung for Bertel's trailing leg, but smelling the creature almost on top of him, Bertel dragged it away. And grabbing the sword he'd seen glinting in the sand, he swung it up into the air, rising onto his knees with a pained cry, spreading them apart for balance. '*Aarrghh*!' he roared, thrusting the sword into the bear's chest as it rose over him. Pushing harder, he drove that blade into its heart.

The bear bellowed, jaws prised open, saliva dripping from vicious-looking teeth. It tried to swipe at Bertel, who released his hold on the sword and fell back to the sand, quickly rolling away.

'Run!' he rasped at Siggy, who was on her feet again, staring at the bear. 'Get to the... ship!' He couldn't breathe. He doubted he could even lift a leg.

The sand made everything impossible.

The crew was coming again, armed with bows. Bertel didn't think the bear had much left in it. And then, as he started moving, breathless with terror, he felt an enormous thud ripple beneath his feet as the bear dropped to the sand.

Dead.

CHAPTER FIVE

The only enemy coming for *Bone Hammer* now was the storm, though there was little to do but hunker down and try to plan for what would come next.

Eadmund decided that if he was going to die in a storm, he wanted his last thoughts to be of Jael. He kept hearing her voice in his ears, seeing that brief glimpse of her before the door had closed. Before she had locked it.

What was happening to her?

It was all he could think about as he sank further under his cloak, knees pulled to his chest.

What was happening to his wife now?

***

Breathing was becoming more challenging.

There wasn't enough air.

The heat drained Jael – the late afternoon sun at its most intense. She was thirsty, breathless, throat like sand.

Her head pounded, arms too heavy to wipe away the sweat dripping into her eyes. Her wet hair clung to her, her sweat-soaked clothes too.

Dropping her head, she tried to think, though no thoughts would form.

She had no power, no strength.

The prison hole was winning the battle.

Without any weapons to fight it, it squeezed the life from her body, the breath from her lungs, the hope from her heart.

There was no escape, no air, and soon, she guessed, no light.

And no way out.

'It is what you deserve,' snarled a woman. 'For who you are, for what you have done. You will die, your family will die, and the Furycks will cease to exist. The end of Furia's corrupt, evil line finally at an end. Ha! What? You thought because you sprang from the womb of a goddess, that you were immortal? All of you? Is that really what you think, Jael Furyck, soon to be the last of her name...'

***

Aggralaia's sky was heavy, dark and foreboding, though Bertel and Siggy felt lighter beneath it, gifted a reprieve from certain death.

'One bear did all this?' a man asked, staring at the carnage spread across the sand like a battlefield. He stroked his coppery beard, tied into two long braided ropes.

Staring at him as though he was an apparition, Bertel was still breathless, shaking his head.

'There must be more,' Siggy panted, realising that the creatures she'd seen in her vision were bears. 'I thought I saw more.'

The man glanced around, seeing the dark mass of trees. 'Then I don't think we should linger. It's the first time we've stopped here, but it'll certainly be the last.' He looked from Siggy to Bertel.

'We're on our way to the Fire Lands. We can take you with us, if you like?'

Bertel glanced over his shoulder up to the cliff. 'Yes, yes, please, but our friend is up there. Perhaps in trouble? She's old. If you can get the girl on board, I'll go and try to find her.'

The man nodded. 'I'm Korri Torluffson. I've come down from Tingor, in Alekka.'

'Bertel Knutson, and this is Siggy,' Bertel said, pushing the girl towards the friendly-looking man. 'From Tuura.'

'And you're on your way to?'

Bertel shrugged. 'Well, that remains a mystery, to be honest. It's our companion who is leading us.'

'The old lady?' Korri laughed. 'What? Is she a dreamer?' The looks on Bertel's and Siggy's faces mostly answered his question.

'Well, no, I...' Bertel spluttered, not wanting to be abandoned now.

'I've no problem with dreamers,' Korri assured him with an easy smile. 'The ship's mine. The crew's mine too. Friends and kin. You've nothing to fear from us. Dagmar! Get the girl on board, find her something to eat and drink. I'll come and help you find your friend.'

***

After checking on Nico and Anika, Arras searched for somewhere to sit. His previous place had been taken, and in the darkness of the howling storm, it was almost impossible to see. He nearly fell on the dreamer, who looked up at him with a frown. Then, staring at him with searching eyes, she quickly frowned some more.

Arras stepped past her, one hand out, water sloshing over his boots, waves crashing over the shield rack. Shaking wet hair out of his eyes, he finally spied a space to sit and moving quickly, he dropped down, seeing the bowed head of the King of Oss beside him, immediately regretting his choice.

Eadmund moved over, making room. 'Everything alright?'

Arras nodded. 'My son's woman... she's ill.'

'She's not the only one.'

The towering waves had *Bone Hammer* bucking and diving, under attack from the crashing thunder and howling wind. Arras could hear the retching sounds of those vomiting up their stomach contents. He felt sick himself, though more with worry than anything else. The storm was one thing, but if it didn't blow away their chasers, he was certain they'd be hunted down again soon enough.

Was it really the king on board one of those ships? Ronin Sardis?

Eadmund leaned towards him. 'Tell me about my wife.'

Arras flinched, searching for something to say. 'Jael? Well, I... she did this,' he said, motioning to the cut across his forehead. Anika had stitched it, though the rain often sent rivulets of bloody water trickling into his eyes.

Eadmund stared at him, smiling for the first time since he'd left Jael behind. 'Does that mean you're her enemy or her friend?'

Arras looked down at his hands, squeezing them into fists. 'You'd have to ask her. I'm the one who captured her in the first place. I took her to S'ala Nis. She's there because of me, though I also helped her try to escape. We worked together to leave.'

'You took her? *You?*' Eadmund sat perfectly still, though every muscle in his body burned with the need to lunge at this man, to grab him by the throat and shake him until his heart stopped beating. Anger throbbed at his temples. He slid his hands under his legs, sitting down hard.

'I had no choice. I'm not a king or a queen. I follow orders or I die. My son dies too. That's how it is on the isle. I followed my queen's orders, and she sent me to Osterland to find Jael. To bring her back.'

'Why? For what purpose?'

Arras shrugged, sliding into one of Bolder's men, who pushed him back. Righting himself, he swept wet hair out of his eyes, ran a hand over his dripping beard and frowned. 'As I said, I'm no king or queen. Not privy to their thinking either. She's just there, on the isle. For life.'

'What?' Eadmund hadn't heard him. 'For what?'

'Life! She's there for life! I told you. They won't kill her!'

'But they will hurt her.'

'I imagine so, though she seems like a woman who can handle the pain,' Arras decided. 'She's not afraid of it, at least. She won't shy away from it. I saw that first hand.'

Eadmund swallowed, not wanting to even imagine what Jael was going through. 'Why did she cut you?'

'We were forced to fight! In a tournament. I was supposed to defeat her, and she let me.'

'Defeat her?' Eadmund grinned. 'That was generous of my wife.' Despite his smile, he felt tears coming now, blinking the unwelcome sting of them away.

'She wanted to escape. Badly.' Arras couldn't help but smile, thinking of the dogged woman who had obviously sensed his own long-held desire to leave the isle. 'She hounded me from the moment she arrived, wanting my help.'

'And why did you help her? Why did you want to leave?'

Arras looked down the deck to where he'd left Nico and Anika, though he couldn't make them out now. 'I was to marry the queen, a petulant child of a woman. A dangerous woman! She killed six husbands because they couldn't give her an heir, and I knew that if I became her seventh, I wouldn't live long. Nor would Nico.'

'So Jael helped you escape?'

It was true, Arras realised. He was only here because the Queen of Oss had helped him – not the other way around. He had wanted to leave for years but had never actually tried to take the next step. Never been brave enough to attempt an escape on his own.

'She sacrificed herself for you and your son?'

'She did.'

Eadmund leaned his head back against the gunwale. 'Sounds like my wife.'

He shivered, closing his eyes, not wanting to talk anymore.

***

'Sky's strange,' the coppery-headed Korri noted, tipping back his head. 'Still hot, though.'

There had been many strange occurrences since he'd met Edela, and Bertel didn't want to think about what terrible portent that moody sky signalled. He simply had to focus on trying not to faint from exhaustion. Climbing the cliff once had been bad enough, but on his second journey up to Aggralaia's peak, his legs trembled so violently he feared they would snap at the knees before long.

Eventually, they reached the top of the cliff, and after a short break, which helped Bertel catch his breath, they were soon approaching the little cottage.

Korri looked to be no more than thirty, lean and energetic, and he turned around to Bertel with a sweaty grin, revealing teeth marked with tiny symbols. That surprised Bertel, who staggered to a stop, bending over to suck in another breath.

'How about you find a perch, and I'll go get your friend?'

Bertel quickly straightened up, shaking his head. 'No, no. I... no. There's a problem, see. We can't... we can't –'

The cottage door opened, and a blinking Edela tottered out. 'Ahhh, there you are, Bertel. I wasn't too long, was I? I do hope you and Siggy weren't bored without me? Oh, it's rather dark now, isn't it? You must be ready for supper!' Her eyes shifted to the man with the extravagantly long beard. 'I'm not sure I know you. Are you one of Elmer's men?' She frowned, gripping her throat in horror. 'Oh.' Her eyes shifted to Bertel, and now they shone with tears. 'Oh, dear.'

'Yes, I'm afraid there's been an... accident, Edela. Down on the beach.' A breathless Bertel glanced at the cottage in confusion, remembering how he had searched it with Siggy, finding no sign it had been recently occupied. 'This is Korri Torluffson. He's got a ship to take us to the Fire Lands. And there's Elmer's ship too,' he added, realising that there was no point leaving the unmanned vessel behind.

Korri smiled, offering an arm to Edela. 'If that's where you're heading?'

'And Siggy?' Edela turned from Korri to Bertel, who nodded reassuringly at her.

'She's safe, down on the beach, and...' Bertel sucked in some air. 'She'll have a story to tell you. As you, I hope, have a story to tell us?'

A disturbed Edela stared at him, too upset to speak, though she managed to choke out a handful of words. 'Yes, I do. I most certainly do.'

**

Between listening to *Bone Hammer's* unsettling creaking sounds and the howl of the wind drilling into his ears, Fyn couldn't sleep. He yawned, stroking Otter, who had crawled onto his knee when Mattie had fallen asleep beside him.

She appeared to be having a bad dream, for she was making whimpering sounds, occasionally shifting around as though trying to escape it.

Kolarov sneezed on his other side, and Fyn turned to him.

'If the storm doesn't drown us, I'm sure to die of an illness!'

the explorer fretted, huddled beneath a dripping fur. He shook with cold, feeling unsettled.

'Do you want to hold the cat?' Fyn offered. 'He's warm.'

Kolarov's eyes bulged, and he nodded greedily, opening up his fur as Fyn handed Otter over. 'That's very kind of you.'

A sleepy Otter seemed eager for the protection of the fur and soon curled up beneath it, making himself comfortable next to Kolarov's big belly. Adjusting himself, Kolarov wrapped the fur tightly back around his chest, feeling slightly more content.

Fyn turned back to a whimpering Mattie, but Kolarov tapped his arm.

'Let her sleep. Her dreams are her work and perhaps our salvation. We need her seeing what will come, what dangers lurk in the distance, and those still behind us. We need her looking for answers.'

Turning back to him, Fyn saw the sense in that.

'You saw what she did today, didn't you?' A blinking Kolarov was still dazed by it himself. He had witnessed magic before and was no stranger to it, though such other-worldly experiences always took his breath away. That something so implausible could be conjured by the hands and minds of dreamers? It was exhilarating. 'She doesn't know what she's capable of, though I have tried to encourage her, of course. But I didn't anticipate that. Those arrows? I didn't expect her to rise to the occasion so majestically!'

A shivering Fyn remembered the sight of Mattie holding her hands up to the clouds as though seeking to bend them to her will. She had certainly bent those arrows to her will, saving them all. And now, because of her, they still had a chance.

A chance to get help and return to TOWER OF BLOOD AND FLAME.

For Jael was still there, and she needed their help.

***

In the darkness, Jael's fears hopped about like hungry fleas.

Being stuck in the hole was like being stuffed into a barrel. The struggle to breathe and the awareness of the tight space overwhelmed her thoughts.

She had gone into battles facing enemies threatening her with arrows and knives, spears and fire. She had walked forward with a confident swagger, partly, she realised, because she hadn't cared if she lived.

Once.

The flashing images of her children, her husband, and her home tormented her.

Without her, what would they do? Who would keep them safe?

Who would...

The darkness was swallowing her whole!

She was light-headed now, and curling forward, she slumped towards the wall. It was exhausting to sit up, to hold up her head, which felt like a lump of stone upon her weak body.

She needed air, though the urge to reach her face up to the trapdoor to try and steal some breaths of warm night air was not as demanding as the desire to close her eyes. To simply rest her head on the dirt wall.

Her body hurt. Her lungs ached.

She would just close her eyes and think of something.

There had to be something she could do...

***

Siggy had burst into tears upon seeing Edela, hugging her as though she would never let go, though no one had wanted to linger on the beach, so Korri had divided his men, sending half to crew Elmer's ship, urging his helmsmen to get them going.

Once night had fallen, and Siggy had been fed a welcome meal of smoked sausages, nuts and cheese, she curled against Edela, wanting to hear what had happened in the cottage, though it wasn't long before she was sound asleep, causing Edela to pause her tale.

'Start again,' Bertel grumbled when Edela had finished covering the girl with a fur provided by their agreeable host. 'I didn't understand a word of your mumbles.'

Edela sighed. 'I'm not surprised. I feel turned inside out. I can barely keep my own eyes open.'

Bertel edged closer, clasping her arm. 'I killed a bear!'

'Yes, yes, so you said.'

'I killed a bear, Edela. I climbed up and down those maddening steps, fearing for our lives. And you were simply gone. Not to mention poor Elmer and his crew. I could sleep till winter, but not until I hear where you were, for you weren't in that cottage! I know because we looked. Nothing was there at all!'

Korri Torluffson seemed perfectly comfortable having a dreamer on board his ship, *Sea Queen*. In fact, he'd almost welcomed it, so Bertel didn't feel the need to lower his voice, though he saw Edela flinching.

'As always, you are far too loud, Bertel Knutson,' she scolded with a hiss.

He frowned at her. 'You weren't in that cottage, Edela. No one was. There wasn't even another door! No other way out. So where did you go? And what happened with the sisters and their tree? Did you see them?'

Edela shuddered, wanting to tell him everything but not wishing to relive it. She ached where she'd hit the ground, her head still pounding. Despite facing death more than once recently, she certainly wasn't getting used to it. 'It was all a trick.'

'Again?' Bertel was aghast, though he had suspected it. 'What sort of trick?'

'I'm not entirely sure, but there were no sisters, just a woman... thing.'

'*Thing*?'

'Well, when she welcomed me into her cottage, she was a pleasant young woman, attractive and hospitable. Though by the end of our... encounter, she was a haggard old crone. Perhaps not even human?'

Bertel's eyes bulged.

'At first, she tried kindness to get what she wanted, seeking to make me reveal something I had no intention of revealing. Then she tried to kill me.'

Bertel was shocked. 'Reveal what?'

Edela clamped her lips together. 'Nothing for you to worry about.'

'Is that so? After all of this? This... *this*!' Bertel's hands were busy, pointing at Siggy, at the ship, and at Edela herself. 'And you won't tell me, even after all we've been through together?'

Edela took his hand, surprising him into silence. 'That creature wanted to know something only I know. Only me. The world, Varmyr, it's full of dreamers, Bertel. Dreamers and gods. They're not all friends and allies, and not all possess good intentions. In fact, I fear that many don't. I can't share it with you because someone may be listening, waiting to hear my answer, to use it as a weapon they can wield.' Voice lowered to a whisper, she stared into Bertel's eyes. 'Do you understand? It isn't that I don't trust you. It is because I fear the damage it might do if I speak it.'

A quiet Bertel nodded, noticing that Edela still had hold of his hand.

She smiled at him, finally releasing it. And sitting back now, she sighed. 'The woman's name was Katalyne. If it really was her name. She took me through a door into her garden to show me her tree. Though none of it even existed. It was all magic, created to lure me there, assuming my curiosity would render me a willing participant. And when I refused and she... left, I was marooned in this strange void. The door to the cottage wouldn't open. It took some time to figure out how to escape.'

'But you did?'

Edela chuckled, blue eyes twinkling. 'Oh, yes. Eventually. I might not remember what I did two minutes ago, but I can almost see every page of my book back in Andala. I found a way through that door and into the cottage. And there you were, my rescuer once more!'

Bertel stared at her, thinking of Siggy's vision and the horrors they'd left behind on that beach. 'I am sorry about Elmer,' he said quietly. 'You seemed fond of him.'

Edela looked surprised, then sad. 'He stayed on that beach for me. I may as well have killed him with my own two hands, the poor, poor man.'

'But you're not to blame for a bear attack, Edela. It wasn't your fault.'

'Do you think so? Truly?' Edela shook her head, not wanting to reveal anything further or to lead Bertel down the dark path she herself had embarked upon. Now was the time for sleep. She turned away from him towards Siggy. 'I must close my eyes before my eyeballs drop out from exhaustion. Sleep if you can, Bertel Knutson, and I will see you in the morning.'

**

In the early hours before dawn, no one was asleep on *Bone Hammer*, whose creaking noises had become steadily louder and more foreboding.

Bolder had been forced to take a break from the steering oar, seeking to keep them on course through the crashing storm, for now there was no course and nothing to see but a dark, watery wasteland. He could only imagine that they were still heading north, though they could just as easily be heading for the Fire Lands or further south.

Squeezing some life back into his stiff hands, he strode up and down the deck, urging everyone to hold on. Everything had been secured, tied down, though he feared tying down his crew. If they were going to lose their battle with the ocean and the gods of the deep, he wanted his men free to swim.

Buffeted by a gust of wind, Bolder tumbled down the deck past Thorgils, who flung out a hand, grabbing his arm.

'Abandoning ship?' he joked, gulping down big drops of rain.

Bolder pulled himself up on Thorgils, deciding it was time to sit down. He squeezed in beside the big man, wedging himself between Thorgils and Eadmund.

'Not quite the journey you promised,' Thorgils winked at him, sweeping wet curls out of his eyes.

'Oh, really? *I* promised, did I? I could say the same! We'll just go rescue the queen and be back before you know it, you said!'

Thorgils' smile faltered, though he knew that Jael had an unfailing ability to make a joke in the direst of situations. So, keeping thoughts of his queen firmly in the front of his mind, he nodded. 'And we will! We're just taking a longer route. Makes it more interesting, don't you think?'

Bolder peered at him. 'And you think the King of Hest will help us? Give us some ships and men?'

'I like your optimism, thinking we'll make it that far!' Thorgils laughed, sliding against Fyn. He felt like vomiting, though he kept smiling, not wanting the gods to hear his fears, certain it would only make them determined to torture them some more. 'If we're still afloat by morning, talk to me of Karsten Dragos. For now, how about some dice?'

Bolder eyed him with a scowl, though realising there was nothing to do but twiddle his thumbs, he dug an aching hand into his pouch and pulled out his dice.

Beside him, Eadmund closed his eyes, wanting to keep to

himself. He wondered if they were doing the right thing by aiming at Hest. He felt mostly confident that Karsten would help them, but how long would it take? He could only imagine the back and forth, the interference of Karsten's mother, perhaps his brother, Berard. And what about the wedding? Maybe the King of Hest was in Helsabor already, preparing to marry Freya Valens?

Thoughts tangling in knots that quickly made him nauseous, Eadmund leaned his head back against the gunwale, seeking Jael's face in the darkness, imagining he was holding her hand.

CHAPTER SIX

The elegant woman walked with purpose, in through the open doors of the queen's throne room.

Though there was no queen sitting upon S'ala Nis' throne now.

The woman was extravagantly dressed in a green silk gown embroidered with swirls of fine golden thread, a mane of flaming auburn hair cascading in waves down her straight back. She turned to snap at a slave hovering by a table of refreshments. 'Where is your mistress? It is long since dawn, and she is?'

'Asleep,' the surprised slave said. 'My lady.' She bobbed her head, fixing nervous eyes on the marble flagstones.

'Asleep?' The woman's anger was palpable, her sharp cheekbones seeming to lift higher as she sucked in her cheeks, narrowing unimpressed blue eyes. 'She. Is. *Asleep*?'

Lifting her eyes, the timid slave now shrugged. 'She took to her bed yesterday, my lady. She has... not emerged.'

'Hmmph.' And spinning on her heels, the woman swept her dress behind her, leaving the throne room and aiming for the stairs. Various slaves approached, though not acknowledging them, she walked with purpose and pace, her green gown slithering along the flagstones behind her. She was nearing fifty, a handsome woman with a steely gaze and a frightening reputation, long since seen on S'ala Nis.

Dessalene Sardis.

The queen's stepmother.

Reaching Kalina's bedchamber, Dessalene paused, resettling her garments and sweeping away a stray hair. And with a determined breath, she pushed open the door, striding into the dark fug of the room. Wrinkling her thin nose, she turned to see the sleeping queen sprawled in her giant bed like a drunken lord. Further irritated, she aimed for the curtains, dragging them open and quickly pushing open the balcony doors, she welcomed in both air and light.

Turning back to the bed, Dessalene stared, tapping a soft-soled shoe.

Kalina croaked, struggling up into a sitting position with her eyes closed. She had drunk so much wine that her throat was stripped of all moisture, tongue stuck to the roof of her mouth, head pounding like a drum being struck over and over again. Swaying, she immediately became aware of the need to vomit. Her body flamed with heat, and lurching over the edge of the lavish bed, she threw up on the floor.

'Well, aren't you the picture of a perfect queen!'

Kalina blinked, retching, and quickly wiping her mouth, she turned to peer at the woman. '*Dessalene?*'

'Your father would be so proud. And pleased. To have gifted his precious isle to you, his only child, and to see how well you are carrying on in his absence. I'm sure none of the slaves are gossiping about this unfortunate situation. I'm sure they're not at all!'

Kalina vomited again.

'Girl!' Dessalene called, spying Mali lurking outside the bedchamber.

And soon, the young slave woman hurried in.

'Your queen appears in need of a bowl. And I would suggest you find something to clean up the floor. Something to freshen the air too. That smell...'

The slave nodded, nostrils flaring, quickly disappearing.

Revolted by the smell and by the sight of the dishevelled

queen, Dessalene headed for the welcome respite of the balcony. It was an oddly dull day, the sky heavy with clouds, still lingering from the previous day's storm. She had sailed through that storm herself and still felt nauseous. Though perhaps that had less to do with the weather and more to do with why she had come to S'ala Nis.

Eventually, wrapped in a robe, a squinting Kalina joined her on the balcony. 'Why are you here? Why have you come? Is it my father?' she croaked, running fingers through her messy hair.

'Your father?' Dessalene's laugh was more of a snarl as she swung around to her stepdaughter. 'You *care* about your father? Care for him and his wishes?'

'I –'

A seething Dessalene clamped a beringed hand over the queen's mouth. 'Do not speak to me of excuses, Kalina. *Excuses?*' Removing her hand, she spun away, eyes on the sun, now pushing out of those clouds, reminded of how unforgiving it could be. 'After what you have done? What poor judgement you have exercised? You can only pray now that Jael Furyck lives. For if she doesn't...'

***

In her dream, Jael was dead, sitting next to Aleksander.

They had known each other since they could talk. They had been best friends and lovers and in love... once.

The loss of him had cast a spell over her for years, and she still grieved for him. It never felt real. Even now.

She loved Eadmund, she wanted to be with Eadmund, but she felt certain that only Aleksander truly understood her. They had gone through so much together – failed, succeeded, and learned together – and then been torn apart.

'What happened in Tuura –' Aleksander said.

They had shared in that trauma; that one night had shaped both their lives.

'I don't want to talk about Tuura.'

Ignoring her, Aleksander nudged her arm. 'And nor do I because what happened in Tuura is done, Jael. Over. It doesn't define you. It isn't you, and you aren't it.'

'Though it made me.'

'No, it broke you. You made yourself, you fixed yourself. Tuura is nothing, nothing you can't defeat, so let it go. Free yourself from its yoke. It cannot control you anymore. You are free if you believe you are.'

'Why? Because I'm dead?'

'Do you want to be dead?'

'I want my husband.'

Aleksander didn't blink. 'And he wants you. He needs you. So do your children. And Axl. He's in grave danger, Jael. Your family needs you, they need you, but how can you help them if you're dead? If you give up and simply die here?'

Jael drew in an unsteady breath. 'I am... not...giving up, but I...'

'Killed that girl? Sunni?' Taking Jael's hand, Aleksander dragged her attention towards him. 'And what would your father say about that?'

Jael's shoulders sank. She felt dizzy.

She couldn't feel Aleksander's hand anymore.

He squeezed harder, and her eyes sprang open. '*Jael*? What would Ranuf say about that? To you? If we were in Andala, what would he say?'

'That I should... that I...' Jael dropped her head, seeing tiny pinpricks of light on the dirt.

Daylight.

She slumped against the wall, drifting in and out of consciousness, clutching her knees to her chest. And then, not clutching them at all, her body going limp.

Seeing Sunni's face.

The trapdoor opened with a creak that drilled deep into Jael's unconscious mind, though she didn't stir, and even when the ladder came down and a slave was sent to prod her, she didn't move.

'Is she dead?' the foreman called. 'She'd better not be dead!'

The slave dropped to his knees, squeezing in between the woman and the wall. The airless hole was suffocating, and he was struggling to draw in a breath himself, even with the trapdoor wide open. Leaning over, resting his head on the woman's chest, he listened closely, unable to hear a heartbeat.

***

A swollen-eyed, soaked to the skin Bolder Oysten swigged from his cup of ale like a man who had claimed a great victory.

And it was.

For though the sea was still a choppy, angry swell around them, the storm had blown away overnight, and *Bone Hammer* had survived.

'We made it!' Thorgils declared happily, banging his cup against the helmsman's. 'Told you we would!'

'And when did you become such an optimist?' a yawning Eadmund wondered, wanting a cup of ale himself. He thought he may have snatched an hour's sleep overall, but no more than that. His eyes hurt, his back ached, but he was soon up and moving.

'Well, I figure the gods need us to save Jael, so they'd hardly drown us now!'

Eadmund shoved him. 'Ever heard of the God of Tricks?'

A bashful-looking Thorgils took another drink, keeping his eyes down.

'No sign of the wolf ships,' Arras announced as he joined them.

Eadmund eyed him sourly, though as much as he wanted to hate the man for causing all this trouble in the first place, the less tired, less worried version of himself knew it wasn't Arras' fault. 'What do you think happened to them? Will we see them again?'

Arras could only shrug, though Bolder offered his thoughts. 'I'm guessing we've been blown off course, but we'll need to stay alert. They may have lost a ship or two, but likely they'll still be after us. We just have to put our heads down and get going.'

'To Hest,' Eadmund told him.

Kolarov stumbled into him, a yawning, sneezing mess. 'Or Castala!' he suggested, thinking of his house and his bed, desperate for a pillow and thick walls to block out the bitter wind.

'Though Hest is safer,' Eadmund said firmly, turning to place his hands on the explorer's arms. 'You don't have to return to S'ala Nis with us. Once we reach Hest, you can take a ship back to Castala, but I must go there. I need a fleet, and Karsten Dragos owes Jael one.'

'Owes?' Arras was confused, taking a cup of ale from Thorgils.

Eadmund nodded. 'Jael saved Karsten's life. His brother would have killed him, likely would've kept Hest's throne, too, if not for her. Karsten knows it, so he'll give us a fleet to save her. He will.'

A newly arrived Fyn blinked at Thorgils, who lifted his coppery eyebrows in surprise.

'Karsten Dragos?' Thorgils spluttered. 'But that family has always talked out both sides of their mouths. And their arses. I'd hardly wager all your silver on that man.' For though Thorgils now called Karsten a friend, he knew the Dragos' ambition knew no bounds.

'Yes,' Kolarov agreed, nodding vigorously. 'The son of Haaron Dragos must have learned something at his father's knee. That man was wily. Dangerous too. I agree with Thorgils. There's no guarantee of what help we'll find in Hest. No guarantee at all!'

***

Dessalene Sardis ordered Kalina to dress in haste and meet her in the throne room, where they would discover Jael Furyck's fate.

She strode up and down the long, gilded chamber, pursing her lips and sneering at the garish additions her stepdaughter had made to the once tastefully decorated room. Knowing Kalina as she did, she wasn't surprised that everything screamed loudly of need, of wanting to be seen.

Ronin Sardis had ruled here with silent power.

A confident, secure man, he had never needed to raise his voice to achieve his ambitions. Though Kalina was like her highly-strung, childish mother, and despite his wisdom and insight, Ronin remained blind to her weaknesses.

The queen arrived looking unusually unkempt and dull-eyed, her skin oddly grey, Dessalene noticed, nostrils flaring. For despite lathering herself in perfumed oils, she stunk like a drunk.

'What news?'

Dessalene cocked her head as her stepdaughter approached. 'Oh, you are interested? *Now* you are interested?' Once again, she tapped her shoe, eyeing the marble flagstones. 'And here is where you killed your seer. Why, haven't you been busy, dearest queen! The stain of Noor's blood will never be removed. You have cursed it. This room, this palace, your line. You have cursed S'ala Nis itself with your desperate recklessness!'

'I am still the queen here,' Kalina hissed, head thumping; Dessalene's voice attacked her like a hammer, and she sought a reprieve. 'Get me some wine,' she snapped at Mali, who had followed her down from her bedchamber.

'Well, that will surely help! More wine! Yes, why not? More wine for the queen!'

Kalina's face flamed. She could not abide being mocked, and in her own palace? In front of her slaves? Though there was nothing she could do or say.

Nothing.

Arms hugging the sides of her golden gown, she sighed.

Dessalene approached, holding her tongue until she was within whispering distance. 'To kill a seer? One chosen by Eyshar? The god responsible for your father's rise? For bringing him to this isle? And what will you do now, Kalina? To have insulted that noble god so grievously, a great payment must be made, or he will surely have his brother Herash send his serpents to drag S'ala Nis to the bottom of the ocean!'

Kalina held Dessalene's wild-eyed gaze, though it took some effort. At times, she feared the dreamer was reading her thoughts, aware of every feeling.

They heard footsteps, and turning, the two women saw guards entering the throne room, carrying what appeared to be a dust-covered body.

Kalina's horrified eyes widened, though Dessalene was quickly striding away from her, shaking her head.

'Leave her on the floor,' the older woman ordered. 'And go, back to the doors. Remain there until you are called for.'

The four guards deposited Jael on the flagstones, backing up to the golden doors which had closed behind them.

'Is she dead?' Kalina wanted to know, hand clasping her throat. She thought of Arras and half hoped she was. Though her father...

Kneeling beside the still body, Dessalene placed her hands on Jael's head, closing her eyes. Breathing out, she bent lower, chanting in Jael's ear. Rocking back on her heels, she saw that there were no fetters clamped around the woman's ankles and wrists, and she frowned.

'If you had let this Furyck woman die, I wouldn't have been able to stop your father from throwing you into the pits, Kalina. In fact, I would have helped him! After all he's done for you? All he's sought these years? And you would take that from him now?' She stood, kicking Jael, who groaned. 'No, she is not dead. Of course not. Though a few hours longer, a day more, and she would have been a corpse, Kalina. And then, so would you!'

Kalina sought to regain her footing, indicating for one of her slaves to bring water to revive the prisoner. More slaves came, propping Jael up into a sitting position. Her eyes rolled around the room, focusing nowhere, mostly closed. Soon water was forced into her mouth, and though it dribbled down her tunic, some made it in, and she gulped, quickly retching.

'There,' Dessalene smiled, turning to Kalina with cold blue eyes. 'All better! And lucky for you, my dear. Lucky for you that I came when I did.' Heading to the table, she felt ravenous. She saw pretty little sweetmeats – a treat she hadn't seen in years – pomegranates and pastries. Though perhaps a slice of the honey cheesecake was what she felt like most of all?

Ignoring her stepmother, Kalina's eyes remained on Jael Furyck, gagging in a dusty, dripping heap before her. Dessalene's voice was just a whisper in the distance now; she heard no words. Her anger bloomed again when she thought of Arras, surging through her body like hot liquid, pulsing at her already throbbing temples. Hands in fists, she thought about kicking the woman herself. Though thinking better of it, she pointed to the guards flanking the golden doors. 'Take her away,' she ordered. 'To Ratish. He will revive her and send me word. And you will retrieve her fetters! I want this woman unable to help herself!'

The four guards hurried forward, each man taking an arm or a leg, and moving with ease and silence, they removed the slave from the queen's throne room.

Kalina watched them go before spinning around to Dessalene, now licking her lips, cheesecake in hand.

'You have far more pressing matters to attend to than which task to assign Jael Furyck, dear queen. For what are we going to do about the seer you murdered?'

***

Korri Torluffson had a menagerie on board his ship, *Sea Queen*. The animals kept Siggy occupied, and she happily milked his black goat, Nellie, before searching for eggs from his caged chickens. There were six, and they'd produced five eggs between them for breakfast.

Korri had a brazier, and a griddle and a cook, who took the eggs and milk and proceeded to whip up a batch of hot cakes that soon had everyone salivating. Apart from Edela and Bertel, who sat elbow to elbow in the stern, furs draped over their knees and around their shoulders. After the whirlwind of the previous day, they were too nauseous to be tempted by food.

'In my dreams, I saw more about what happened on Aggralaia. In that garden,' Edela murmured. 'At the time, it was so terrifying. I was focused on trying to survive, to escape and find my way back to you. But now I think I understand more. When I peered over the garden wall, the void there felt reminiscent of something I'd seen before. I'm sure I was in the Dolma.'

An exhausted Bertel was gobsmacked. 'The Dolma? Prison of the gods? But what *was* that creature?'

'I'm not sure. Perhaps some sort of shape-shifter?' A confused Edela had slept fitfully, reliving every moment of what had happened, slowly forming a clearer picture. 'It took the form of a young woman seeking to put me at ease, though it ended up looking much like a dragur. It lured me there with the promise of the bone tree and the sisters, though everything felt wrong from the moment she opened the door. If I'd been thinking clearly, I wouldn't have stepped inside.'

'Well, you were desperate for answers. For an understanding.'

Edela smiled at Siggy, who motioned to a trencher of hot cakes. Shaking her head at the girl, she returned her attention to Bertel. 'Mmmm, though it was the creature who wanted answers from me. She wanted me to help her!' Edela snorted, feeling oddly irritable. Regretful too. Her folly had nearly gotten them all killed.

It had certainly gotten poor Elmer and his crew killed.

She dropped her head, sniffing.

'Did she say anything to you? Anything about why she'd lured you there? About what she wanted to know?'

'I've already told you. She wanted me to reveal something that only I know. Well, it appears that only I know it, or why else would she have gone to so much trouble to draw it out of me? And –' Edela blinked, sitting up.

'Yes?' Bertel's empty belly growled, overriding his intention not to eat. 'What is it?'

Realising that she couldn't say anything to him, Edela shook her head, worry like a wet cloak draped across her shoulders. 'It's nothing. I... I'm just very tired now. I don't want to talk anymore.' And with that, she turned away.

An open-mouthed Bertel peered at her, certain, once again, that Edela was keeping things from him. Though if she never let him in, never shared her secrets, how was he ever going to truly help her?

***

The physician had a black eye, his cheek was swollen and bruised, but he was smiling as he raised Jael's head, plying her with a tonic. 'This will help,' he promised kindly.

Jael stared at him in confusion. 'You... speak the common tongue?'

'A little. Yes. Well, more than a little,' Ratish admitted eventually. 'I am a private man. I do not wish all of S'ala Nis to know my secrets.'

Jael closed her eyes, feeling the sweet, warm liquid flowing down her throat, seeking to revive her. Though it would take more than a cup of Ratish's sweet tonic to make her feel human again. She felt boneless, without a spine, as though her limbs were just dangling parts. Her mind cantered down paths like a wild horse she had no control over. Her lips were dry, too cracked to mould into shapes.

And finally, she sank into the bed, drifting away, thinking of home.

CHAPTER SEVEN

The dishevelled messenger apologised profusely to the King of Brekka. He had been set upon by outlaws, robbed of every coin and weapon, his horse stolen.

And then he'd been flung into a ditch.

'You're lucky they didn't kill you!' Gisila exclaimed beside her son, worried eyes surveying the filthy young man. 'Where have we come to that Brekka is beset by thieves and outlaws?'

Ignoring her, Axl took the dirty but still sealed scroll from the man's hand. 'You did well to find your way home. Gerald!' he called, eyes snapping to his steward, who had entered the hall from the kitchen with crumbs in his beard. 'Find Torun some food and dry clothes. We'll need to replenish his coins too. And his weapons.'

'Thank you, my lord,' the messenger sighed, bowing before his king before turning after the old steward.

'It's Gant's hand!' Gisila exclaimed, drawing closer to her son, attempting to read the note.

'Ssshhh,' Axl told her, trying to concentrate. Gant had a creeping scrawl, hard to decipher at the best of times, but Torun's ordeal had caused the vellum to become damp, the ink blurring in places, making it even harder to read. 'It's about the trouble in Valso. Gant says it's someone called Mutt... Storman?' The name sounded familiar, though he couldn't quite place the man.

Gisila looked surprised. 'That's a name from the past.'

She shuddered. 'A horrible man. He murdered Hans Steffen's daughter, Klara. Do you remember her?'

Axl shook his head.

'She was just fifteen, I think. Mutt Storman was as old as your father, as old as Hans himself, and he wanted her for his wife, but she didn't want him. Eventually, when Hans forbade him from marrying her, he killed her. Horrible business.'

Axl looked back down at the scroll. 'We need a meeting. Can you find Getta and Amma?' He thought of Hal and Erling, frustrated that they were both still away. Gant too. 'We need to discuss what we're going to do.'

***

'You killed Noor as though he was some pointless slave!' a furious Dessalene hissed at the queen when they were alone in the throne room. Kalina had sent everyone away, and now the two women sat on opposite sides of a round table, glowering at each other. 'To spit in the eye of a god? To betray the trust your father placed in you?'

Kalina heard her, though her mind was elsewhere.

And sensing it, Dessalene leaned forward, slapping the table. 'You must forget Arras Sikari! Your obsession is a weakness, and that weakness will continue to undermine you until you are in real danger, Kalina. Are you so blind that you cannot see your reflection? That you cannot look yourself in the eye and confront the truth?'

Kalina started. 'But Arras –'

'Arras Sikari will be found and brought to justice!' Seeing the queen's shock, Dessalene smiled smugly. 'I did not sail here all alone, dearest. Of course not, for I saw how things would go. Your father's wolf ships are hunting down the traitor as we speak. And when they find him, they will kill him. Unless I do so first.'

Lurching forward, Kalina's heart thumped wildly, nails clawing the table. 'But I ~'

'What? You think I would trust you to deal with him if he were brought back here?' Dessalene laughed. 'But you have a weakness, child. Your desperate heart! Your father has always been blind to it, but when it comes to love, you simply cannot be trusted. The number of husbands you have discarded? The poor choices and reckless decisions you have made? Your heart leads you astray, Kalina, so the wolves will see to Arras. They will kill him for the good of all.'

Kalina's eyes bulged. She was broken-hearted, embarrassed, ill with what had happened, and desperate to see Arras again. Though she couldn't deny that Dessalene was right.

After what he had done, Arras Sikari deserved to die.

***

Thorgils nudged a thoughtful Eadmund, who, much like the rest of *Bone Hammer's* crew, had his eyes peeled open, searching for signs that their pursuers were still in the hunt. 'So what do we think of our guests then?' he wondered quietly, inclining his head to where Arras, Nico, and Anika were talking to Kolarov, who wobbled before them as though he would soon topple over.

Eadmund's eyes drifted to them as his cloak billowed around his face. Grabbing handfuls of the woollen cloth in frustration, he tucked it behind himself, leaning back to trap it against the stern. 'Well, Arras kidnapped Jael, so I'm not overly fond of him.'

A shocked Thorgils spun around to his friend. 'He what? Kidnapped Jael?'

Eadmund nodded. 'Though according to him, he had no choice. Besides, no one was more aware of that than Jael, and she helped him escape. She sacrificed herself so he could leave the isle. I doubt she'd have done that if she hadn't thought him worthy of his freedom.'

Thorgils didn't know what he thought about that.

'Jael's no fool,' Eadmund reminded him. 'Not one to choose worthless allies either. And she left him with a few scars to remind him never to cross her again.' Smiling now, he tried imagining how that fight had gone. He would've loved to have seen it. To have seen her...

Thorgils sighed. 'Well, whatever the case and whatever Jael may have thought of him, likely we're being hunted because he's on board. If those ships survived the storm, they'll find us again. And when they do?'

Eadmund was worried about that too. 'Go talk to Mattie. She might have seen something.' A muttering Thorgils headed off, leaving his frowning king behind. And watching him go, Eadmund became increasingly tense. Everyone kept turning his way, trying to catch his eye, and on a ship, there was no escape from it.

He closed his eyes, seeing that tunnel, hearing the slamming door and the sound of his wife calling his name.

***

Jael felt almost alert when she woke for the second time.

Ratish was washing her face with a wet cloth, and pulling away from him, she sneezed.

'Black pepper,' he told her with a smile. 'It does not agree with everyone.'

Nose running, Jael sat up, eyes sweeping the room, seeing the busy shelves Sunni had been so drawn to.

She dropped her head, wiping her nose on the back of her

filthy sleeve, feeling nauseous. She saw that the fetters were back. The weight of her arms was suddenly heavy, and so was the weight of despair.

'There are soldiers outside, waiting for you. I would have liked to keep you here longer, though the queen sought word when you were revived. I am not sure where they will take you now or what may happen.'

'Who was the woman?' Jael wondered, returning to her encounter in the throne room. 'There was a woman with the queen. A dreamer?'

Ratish was confused, and frowning at Jael, he dropped the dirty cloth into a bowl of water. 'A dreamer? Why, what did she look like?'

'Tall, with reddish hair. Very thin. Middle-aged.' Jael closed her eyes, trying to retrieve something more descriptive from her memory. 'She wore an amulet of a bird. A golden bird.'

Ratish's swollen face noticeably paled. 'That sounds like Dessalene, but she –'

'She saved me. I'm certain she saved me. But why?'

'Dessalene is the queen's stepmother. Some call her dreamer, others offer less complimentary names. She is married to the king. There are many rumours about the woman and what she might have done to the king's first wife. Though it is better not to speak of her. Safer.'

A knock on the door was immediately followed by it opening, and a glowering soldier came in, talking in an impatient voice. Ratish headed him off with flapping hands, shooing the man back outside and shutting the door.

'They want to take you now,' he told Jael. 'I'm sorry, but you must go.'

Jael swung her legs over the side of the bed, staring down at her fetters. She stood, feeling oddly unsteady. Her wobbling legs appeared to be trying to decide if they possessed the strength to hold her up. And not certain herself, she leaned on the bed. 'Thank you. I hope not to return.' And now she smiled. 'Though

I have a tendency to get in trouble, so you never know.' Once again, she caught a glimpse of the surgeon's jars filled with his collection of disturbing oddities, and her heart sank.

Ratish patted her arm, guiding her to the door. 'We do our best,' he whispered. 'To survive. Man or god, we do our best. And sometimes, we fail. But you will carry on, Jael Furyck. I am sure Sunni would want that. She would want you to be happy.'

***

Axl found himself thinking about his sister as he listened to Getta, Amma, and Gisila debating the many challenges Brekka was now facing, certain she would have strong opinions about everything.

He had sent Gerald to find Ragnar Olveggen, commander of Andala's garrison, though having been retrieved, Ragnar sat beside his king in silence, a man of few words who didn't know his place in such a situation.

Axl turned to him, hoping to draw him out. 'How is the count coming along?'

A surprised Ragnar cleared his throat. 'The tallies are trickling in from the settlements and forts. Down south will take longer, but we're getting a picture.'

'And how's it looking then, this picture?'

'Fair, I'd said, lord.' Ragnar wriggled a leg, which had gone to sleep. He squirmed on his bench and generally couldn't sit still at all. His eyes drifted to the women, who had fallen into silence, all three staring at him. 'There's been a drop off of men after all the sickness, but it's not marked. Not in the numbers I've seen. Though we may have to assist the settlements in terms of providing weapons. It would make sense,' he added, mumbling now.

Ragnar was in his late forties, rising through the ranks

during Ranuf Furyck's reign and then Lothar's. And though Axl had been in charge for four years now, the garrison commander was still struggling to find a firm footing with him. The king was usually flanked by his unserious friends, who had a habit of confusing everything. And now, without them, he wasn't sure how to behave.

'Andala is the prize our enemies will need to claim if they wish to unseat me, so I will have to think carefully before parting with a single arrow. Once all the numbers are in, we can discuss further.' Axl turned to his mother. 'I'm not sure I can go to Karsten's wedding now. In fact, I'm sure I can't.'

Gisila looked surprised, Amma was disappointed, but Getta nodded. 'Your departure would signal an opening to your enemies, and you wouldn't be able to go south alone. The amount of men needed for such a journey?' She shook her head. 'Word of your preparations would quickly filter back to Oren Storgard. Perhaps he is choosing to remain behind himself?'

Axl scratched his beard, fearing he would. 'I will send you by ship,' he decided, smiling at his wife. 'It will be an easier journey, I imagine. And faster. It will be nice to get away from here, to see new sights and make new allies.' He kept smiling, seeing fear in Amma's eyes. The journey would be challenging for her either way, though he needed her to go, to represent Brekka to the rest of Osterland while he remained behind, keeping everyone safe.

He could almost see his sister nodding, and he felt strange, realising how far apart they would soon all be. Edela and Jael were lost, and there was still no word about either of them. Gant was in the south, and soon Amma would sail away with Gisila. It was unsettling, especially when he considered that Iskavall was in the hands of an enemy, his brother dead.

Though now Axl imagined his father and straightening his back, he took a sip of ale, ready to press on with the next matter at hand.

His steward popped his head around the door. 'There is someone to see you, my lord. A woman.'

Axl looked up with a frown. 'That's not especially informative, Gerald. Who is she?'

But the portly man could only shrug. 'I don't know, my lord. She says she must speak with you urgently. She would not give her name.'

Everyone turned from Gerald to Axl, who stood. 'Well, you carry on, and I'll see what this mysterious woman wants. I won't be long.'

***

After Kalina had eaten and sipped a little wine, Dessalene took her for a walk in the palace gardens, where they discussed what would happen to the body of Noor of the Dragon Blood Tree.

And their plans for Jael Furyck.

'Will you stay?' Kalina wondered, unsure how she felt about it either way. She started, seeing a little man appear from the bushes. 'Who are you?'

Dessalene laughed. 'Ignore my little toad. He does tend to creep about.'

'What is he?' Kalina stared in horror at the strange creature, who was the size of a boy with the face of a man. He had bulbous, greedy eyes, leering at her in a way she wasn't used to.

'He is Pye, my crooked little helper.'

'A slave?'

'No, a willing attendant! Isn't that right, Pye dearest? He serves me out of a desperate need to be useful. To me. I assure you I barely endure it, though he has his uses, as we will both find out.' Dessalene eyed the hunched little man. 'You must stop creeping about here, though. Go out into the city and bring me back what I need to know!' And with a flapping hand, she shooed Pye away.

Kalina watched as he hobbled off, almost hopping. 'What was his name?'

'Pye. It's what I call him. He has a ridiculous name, so I much prefer that.' And without further explanation, Dessalene hurried through a flowering arch into the next garden.

Named the Garden of the Goddess, in honour of the Goddess of Fertility, Olera, it had been designed by Kalina's mother, who, like herself, had also struggled to fall pregnant. And despite her best efforts, she had died, leaving behind just the one child. And a daughter at that. 'What will we do about Noor?'

'Everything!' Dessalene announced, swinging around with bright eyes. 'We must hold the greatest funeral ever seen on S'ala Nis! A vast procession with weeping slaves and singing children. There will be flowers and wine and sacrifices. We will soak the temple in blood to remind Eyshar of our unfailing loyalty and gratitude. Anything else will be less than the god deserves. Remember, our words of contrition will have no meaning without offerings. Bounteous ones!'

Kalina nodded. 'And Jael Furyck?'

'Well, I'm sure we can find something suitably unpleasant for her next challenge. The woman likes to go about as a man, so perhaps it's time to treat her like one?'

***

Axl's visitor was a sour-faced old woman who didn't offer a smile or a bob of deference as he approached.

She waited for him in the middle of the hall, eyes on the burning fire pit. It was a warm day, and she was dressed in mostly rags. Wide and short, she had messy shoulder-length greying hair and a ruddy face. Dirty, Axl thought. Her eyes were dark, pinched with suspicion as she waited for him, thin lips pursed in a scowl.

'And you are?' Axl wondered, sensing that Gerald had followed him out of the meeting room, though he didn't feel inclined to offer this rude creature refreshments.

'Helga,' the woman almost spat. 'I have come to help you.'

'Help me?' Axl cocked his head to one side. 'Are you a dreamer?'

The woman's nod was imperceptible. She was perhaps sixty, Axl thought, as still as a boulder as she glared at him. A strange, strange creature.

But a dreamer?

'And where are you from, Helga?'

'Where all the other dreamers are from, I suspect. Tuura. North of the River. I live in the forest there. My grandson and me.'

Axl looked around, not seeing a boy.

'He is out in the sunshine. I set him exploring.'

Axl found it disconcerting that she never smiled, for though this woman was offering her services, she didn't appear happy about it. 'And you came here, why?'

'Because I saw what was happening and what would come. Dreamers are being killed. Strung up and cut up. Shut up. I have never been especially fond of my own kind or insidious Tuura and all its ambitious power brokers. It was once my home, though I left it behind years since, never seeking to be drawn into that sticky web. And where I live, I'm happy enough. We are. But now? Darkness is coming to this land.'

Axl felt compelled to lighten the mood. 'Though the Darkness was defeated. It will not come again.'

Helga's glowering face became stormy. 'You think the only darkness was contained in a book of spells? That when Raemus was defeated, all evil was banished with him? That no one with evil intentions exists?'

'Well, I –'

'Do your enemies wish you well, King of Brekka? Do they want you and yours to live?' Helga grunted, shaking her head.

'No, they seek to grind you into dust, you and those of your name. Do you not feel it? In the air? The earth? The rain that pours down and ruins the crops? Do you not feel a great stirring of evil?'

Axl shivered. The woman eyed him as though she was seeing into his soul.

'I have come to help you,' the dreamer repeated. 'Your grandmother is gone. I have seen that.'

'Did you know her?'

'In Tuura. Many years ago now. We were not friends. Not enemies either,' she added, seeing Axl's concern. 'I will need a place to sleep big enough for me and the boy. He's eight, so he doesn't take up much space, though he does tend to run around.'

Axl didn't appear to have much say in the matter, though he had been searching for a dreamer, desperate for insight. 'Yes, of course. And you... will you be able to find my grandmother? My sister? They are missing, and I –'

'What I will be able to do is up to the gods. I am guided by their hands and their hands alone. I will do what I can to aid you, though I can never go against the gods. And nor can you.'

'Of course.' Axl spun around to Gerald, who hovered a few paces away with a look of displeasure on his round face. 'Please inform everyone that the meeting is finished, Gerald. You may tell them that I appear to have found a new dreamer. I will take her to Edela's cottage.' He turned back to Helga, who appeared ready to snarl at him. 'You and your grandson may stay in my grandmother's cottage. It is small but warm and comfortable.'

Helga nodded curtly. 'That sounds acceptable.'

Axl thought about demanding the respect he was owed as king, though seeing her scowl intensify, he thought better of it, instead ushering her out of the hall to where her short-haired grandson had commandeered a dog. He smiled at the skinny boy, dressed in rags like his grandmother. 'That's Gully. He'll be your friend if you give him something to eat.'

The boy grinned toothlessly at him. 'Can he be mine?' he said to his grandmother.

She shook her head. 'No, he cannot. Though you may be his friend, and play with him when he allows it. But not now, boy. We must go and see our new home.'

The boy looked excited to hear that, so hugging the dog, he hurried to his grandmother's side. And with the slightest bob of her head, Helga indicated for Axl to lead the way.

***

Her ordeal in the prison hole had Jael ready for a long sleep. Though after being returned to the slaves' quarters and made to change into a clean grey tunic, trousers, and sandals, she'd been taken across the city towards the south of the isle, where she'd been reassigned to the expansive temple compound.

She stood on a gravel road, eyes roaming the grounds, seeing a circular platform, ringed by what looked like a moat, a temple with an enormous tree sprouting from it, and a stadium, looking down on it all.

'Queen's orders,' a tall, lean man told her in a hesitant voice. He'd seen this woman fight in the Arena, defeated by Arras Sikari, though she had put up a mighty fight for a time, and with those fetters around her wrists?

He held his ground, remaining watchful.

'You'll be working on the tower behind you. See? The Tower of Eyshar. I've just had word we need it completed in time for the funeral, so you'll be putting in long hours with the rest of the men.'

The sun blazed into Jael's eyes, and she squinted up at him. 'Funeral?' Her eyes drifted to the tower. It was taller than any structure she'd seen on the isle, reaching into the hazy blue sky, now free of clouds. The tower was made of the same pale stone used elsewhere – almost white. She saw an arch at its base, where men in yellow robes came and went, stepping in and out of the shade.

Much of the tower was wrapped in wooden scaffolding, though Jael could see that its top remained unfinished.

'For Noor of the Dragon Blood Tree. He died suddenly. Yesterday. Just dropped dead, apparently, which isn't a good omen. No one's happy about it. The funeral, that is. We're going to have to move all these stones out of the road too,' he muttered, motioning to where great lumps of dressed stone and piles of rubble blocked the route to the temple.

'What's your name?' Jael asked the chatty man.

'Quint,' he told her, reminding himself that the woman was a slave. Though she was also the Queen of Oss, daughter of the famous Ranuf Furyck.

He didn't know how to act.

'I'll take you to Alek. You can be on his crew. He'll show you what to do.' And with that, Quint fixed a frown on his naturally genial face and strode away. He had a compact torso but long legs and was soon well ahead of a weak Jael, who made little effort to catch up.

They headed for a courtyard, where squinting slaves hefted stone slabs into carts, some lifting them onto their shoulders, acting as carts themselves, aiming for the tower.

The men stared as she passed, whispering to each other.

Jael assumed that many recognised her from the Arena, though it soon became apparent that they were also staring because she was a woman.

Every slave she could see working on the tower appeared to be a man.

Quint eventually stopped before a slave with the bluest eyes Jael had ever seen. They burst brightly from a bronzed face, liberally dappled with freckles. He wiped a hand over a high forehead, staring at her with interest.

'I've brought you another worker,' Quint said, and seeing the man's mouth drop open, he held out a hand, pre-empting his complaints. 'Queen's orders. Find something that won't kill her. She's tough enough, but we've carted enough warriors away from here to know that being good with a sword doesn't help you down here.' He motioned to the dark shadows in front of the tower. 'Good luck,' he said to Jael, smiling crookedly. 'Alek will take care of you.'

A blinking Jael didn't reply, remembering Noor's words in the queen's throne room. She turned to the blue-eyed man with a frown. 'Aleksander?'

The man nodded, interest sparking in those intense blue eyes. 'Though I prefer Alek. And you're Jael Furyck.' He lowered his voice now, stepping closer. 'I've been hoping to meet you.'

CHAPTER EIGHT

'Tell me about my father,' Kalina said as she returned to the palace with Dessalene, a silent Mali trailing behind them.

'Tell you what?' Dessalene wondered, happy to escape the sun and the flies. 'He is as busy as ever. No man has ever worked harder, which is why he's been successful beyond his wildest dreams.' Upon re-entering the throne room, she indicated for Mali to pour her something to drink. 'Yet Ronin will not rest until he has accomplished his vision. Our job is to help him. It has always been to help him, dearest.'

Kalina was thoughtful, fiddling with her rings, seeing the bare finger she had been saving for her wedding band. Her stomach clenched as she trapped a furious scream in her mouth.

Dessalene placed a hand on her arm. 'You were reckless in your choice of Arras Sikari. You can't have imagined your father would have approved of such a union? He liked him well enough, but as your consort? A son-in-law? But you didn't even seek his opinion! Your quest for this child has gone on long enough. It has been indulged for far too long, and it is now over. It is, Kalina. You are barren, and it is simply time to face the truth of it!'

Kalina's eyes flared, glancing over her shoulder at Mali, who dropped her head, coming forward to offer both women little beakers of wine. 'To speak to me as though I am nothing? With such cruelty?'

Dessalene placed a bony hand on her stepdaughter's arm.

'The cruelty comes from those who say nothing! Who won't tell you the truth. You will have an heir, though the child will not be born from your body, Kalina. It is time to stop pretending that the fault is anyone but yours. You need a husband and an heir, and that is all. You needn't worry, there will be a solution.'

Kalina curled towards her. 'And is there nothing you can... do?'

'Magic, you mean? You wish to have an unnatural child?'

Kalina thought to say yes, that she would have any sort of child. Any child of her own. She was desperate. Desperate to hold a baby in her arms.

Dessalene squeezed the queen's arm, demanding her attention. 'What matters is your legacy, not your feelings, not your needs, for they cannot rule after you are gone! If you truly wish to help your father establish a great dynasty, then you must accept that your feelings do not matter at all. No. I shall think on it and dream on it and find a way forward, and that is all.'

***

After leaving the dreamer and her grandson to get comfortable in Edela's cottage, Axl returned to the hall, eager to discuss things with Gisila, who had sensed it and found him on the way.

'You finally have a dreamer?' his mother asked with gleaming eyes. 'A real dreamer?'

Thinking of surly Helga, Axl felt less enthusiastic. 'A reluctant sort of one.'

Gisila turned around, following her son to the hall. 'What does that mean?'

'Well, she's not an overly friendly woman.'

'No?'

'But she saw what was happening to the dreamers and wanted to help. She has a grandson. A young boy. I've set them up in Edela's cottage.'

Gisila was surprised by that but soon nodded. 'It will surely help her find Edela. And Jael.'

'Well, I hope so, though I fear she won't bend to my will, Mother. To ours. She seemed quite obstinate.'

But Gisila only laughed. 'Though dreamers come in all shapes and sizes, don't they? I'm certain she will help us.' Approaching the square, she frowned. 'As long as we can trust her. As long as she's not a Follower.'

'She doesn't seem overly fond of Tuura and its kind, so I don't think she's a Follower. Or if they even exist now. Not since the Vale.'

'Mmmm, though we must try and make sure,' Gisila warned, clutching Axl's arm as they entered the busy marketplace. 'We cannot be fooled again. We have to ensure this woman is an ally who can help us.'

***

Alek Orlan led Jael towards the shade, which made her like him immediately.

'I come from Brekka, my lady,' he told her as they walked. 'A small village on the coast. Stora. Lived there my whole life. Well, until I went and got myself captured at sea. My brother and I did. My twin. He was a man of the sea, got into trading. I was happy working as a silversmith, though he convinced me to join him. In hindsight, it wasn't my finest decision.'

He seemed excited to meet her, and though he was friendly and had an open, easy manner, Jael was soon on edge.

'I'm surprised you've been assigned here,' Alek said, once again wiping sweat from his forehead. His short hair was sandy-blonde, similar to Eadmund's, mostly darkened with sweat.

It was scorching.

'Summer's only just arrived,' Alek went on. 'But the heat's taking more men by the day. The heat and the strain of the work. It's not for women, even one as useful as you. This job will maim or kill you before long.' He scratched his head, looking her over. 'I'll try and find you something lighter.'

Jael scowled at him.

'You might think it doesn't look hard, and maybe you'll be able to lug a few of the smaller slabs,' Alek grinned. 'But try doing it hundreds of times from sunrise till sunset. And these days, the sun's setting later and later. You try that for just one day, and you'll never want to move your arms again. But then you'll get up and do it again and again. It's brutal, unforgiving work that changes you forever, one way or another. I'll find you something lighter. Trust me, it's for the best.'

A doubtful Jael peered at him, thinking fondly of her little buckets of urine, which led her mind immediately back to Otho Dimas and Sunni.

She saw the girl's body lying in the tunnel, and her husband, who had been so close.

It had all been so close...

Shaking her head, Jael remained dazed, attempting to focus on her new surroundings, on the new tasks and the new men. And this man in particular, whose name was Aleksander. She eyed him with interest, remembering Noor's words. 'Well, I may as well get started. There's plenty of hours left in the day.' And pushing back her shoulders, she followed a smiling Alek out of the shade and into the blazing sun once more.

***

There was an almost relaxed feel on board *Bone Hammer* for the first time since they'd left S'ala Nis.

An exhausted Bolder had taken a real break, sitting down to supper with Eadmund, Thorgils, Kolarov and Fyn, leaving the ship in the hands of his second-in-command: a steady older man named Raal. And feeling the relief of stepping away from the steering oar, Bolder finally felt free to let his shoulders drop.

'What do the clouds say?' Thorgils wondered, for though it had been a relief not to see any sign of the wolf ships for the past few days, he wasn't foolish enough to imagine that such luck would hold until they reached Hest.

He'd never wanted to see Karsten Dragos so much in his life.

It was light enough to still see the outline of the clouds that had followed them all day, of which there were many, though Bolder only shrugged, tipping back another cup of ale. 'They say enjoy the respite! Rest while you can!' He shook his head at Fyn, who held the ale jug, not wanting any more. Well, wanting it but deciding that the pleasant, light-headed feeling would end up becoming a detached inability to function if he drank another cup.

Raal was useful, Bolder knew, trustworthy, but *Bone Hammer* was his responsibility, and so were the men. Though looking at the King of Oss, he smiled, realising that they were all Eadmund's men now. 'If we reach Hest and you can convince the king to bring his fleet back to S'ala Nis, what's the plan? We won't be able to hide this time. They'll have men up on The Maiden's Reach. Men everywhere, looking for trouble.'

Kolarov belched loudly, gripping his chest. 'How right you are! And their ballistas, primed for action! We must ask the commander about that. He will know what their plans will be. And the dreamer. She's sure to see things.'

Eadmund held up his free hand. 'Let's not get ahead of ourselves. After what's happened, we can't tempt fate. I think we just focus on getting to Hest. That's all. That's all I want to think about for now.'

Sitting next to Thorgils, a quiet Fyn was of the same mind.

He couldn't believe they were sailing away from S'ala Nis

without Jael.

It was impossible to stop thinking about what had happened to her or what her captors were doing to her. He filled his own wooden cup, placing the jug on the deck beside Thorgils.

Who knocked it over in a hurry to scramble to his feet when the shout went up.

And then everyone was on their feet, cups abandoned, ale spilling down the deck.

For the wolf ships had returned.

***

Having escaped her needy stepdaughter, whose side she'd been at since she had arrived, Dessalene was thrilled to finally be alone, and she shut her chamber door that evening with an audible sigh.

Hearing a knock.

Swinging back around with clenched fists and aching shoulders, the dreamer snarled at the door. 'Go away!'

Silence.

She frowned, certain she could hear something.

A grunting sort of noise.

'Go away, Pye!' she snapped. 'You lost your chance to speak to me. I will hear whatever you have found in the morning!'

'But, but, where will I sleep, Mistress?' came the plaintive voice. 'I do not have a chamber!'

'*Chamber*?' a horrified Dessalene laughed. 'But the animals sleep in the stables, Pye. Don't you remember? Run along, my pet, and find yourself a bale of hay!' She turned away with a smile, not needing to open the door to see his miserable face.

She heard an indignant spluttering, which soon faded, and then silence.

She had given one of Kalina's slaves instructions to deliver nine braziers to her chamber. To prepare them with kindling and tinder, ready to light.

And now she arranged them in a circle.

Taking a flaming candle, she carefully lit each one, shutting herself off from all that lurked beyond her door. She repeated a chant, murmuring it until her lips became numb.

It was the beginning.

She would go into a trance. She would seek out her enemies.

She would offer them up to the God of Death and his serpents of the deep.

***

Bolder couldn't stop cursing as he returned to the steering oar, sending Raal to organise the crew.

He had steadily pulled them back on course, past Zagora, and with no sign of their pursuers, they'd pushed on into the Adrano Sea, aiming for Hest's golden city, where they'd hoped to find a safe harbour amongst powerful allies.

But now?

They had quickly counted five wolf ships hunting them again.

'Head to shore!' Eadmund called to Bolder. 'Head to shore, and we take our chances!'

'With what? One crew against five?'

A frowning Eadmund swayed towards him. 'You think another storm's coming to save us?'

Bolder didn't. 'I'll aim north, though southern Hest won't make it easy. There are more cliffs than coves. We could try for Castala instead? Disappear into Silura?'

'Which is closer?'

Bolder stared at him, deciding. 'I'd say both.' It was a well-informed hunch, supported by years at sea, though still just a hunch.

Arras Sikari made his way up to the steering oar. 'What's the plan?'

Bolder glanced his way. 'We're aiming for shore.'

'What? Castala?'

Eadmund thought for a moment, then shook his head. 'No, we still go for Hest, but try for Vastera. There's a cove there.' He turned from Bolder to Arras, whose face betrayed nothing. 'We're safer in Hest than Silura. I'm sure of it.'

Arras just stared at the king, hoping he was right.

***

In the slaves' dining hall, it was finally supper, and though the meal promised to be a watery, tasteless slop, Jael sat down with real enthusiasm. Though after three days of hard labour, she half doubted she had the strength to lift her spoon.

Her friendly foreman, Alek Orlan, had been right – the work was brutal.

She had strong arms, she was used to working and fighting hard, but spending hours lifting and carrying bricks and stones had her body aching in places she hadn't even known existed.

Alek tapped her arm and she winced. 'Sit with me,' he said, indicating for her to take her bowl and join him outside. 'It's slightly cooler out there. Private too.'

Jael had seen a lot of the Brekkan since being assigned to his crew. She sensed there were things on his mind, though initially, they'd only spoken of the work.

But now?

A curious Jael picked up her bowl and headed outside. She saw they weren't alone in wanting some privacy, for despite a few flaming torches and braziers lighting up the courtyard, it was welcomingly dark outside, a light breeze teasing them with the promise of cooler air.

Alek led her to a stone bench big enough for two, and motioning for her to sit, he joined her. 'You're likely missing the cesspits and shit holes,' he joked. 'I've done that work, done nearly every task you could imagine in this place. I often think of lugging those little buckets with fondness. As light as a cat.'

'Perhaps,' Jael said, sensing him dancing around the subject he actually wanted to discuss, and fearing what that might be, she sought to cut him off. 'Do you have a knife?'

Alek was taken aback. 'Knife?' He shook his head, lowering his voice. 'Most slaves aren't allowed to have knives. Not to keep.'

'Get me a knife and two small, flat stones, and we can talk,' Jael told him. 'Until then, it's best not to.'

'Quint has a knife. He often lends it to me to trim my beard.'

'Good, get it then, and the stones. In the meantime, you can tell me how long you've been here. How you've survived.'

Alek smiled. 'Too stubborn to die, I suppose. My brother died within a year of arriving here. Our crew didn't last much longer than that. I've been here six years come summer.'

'Six years?' Jael shook her head. 'And what did you leave behind? Who?'

Scooping up a spoonful of the watery stew, Alek looked sad. 'Two sons. Twins.' Losing his appetite, he poured the stew back into the bowl. 'The Goddesses of Fate work in mysterious ways. When my sons were born, I felt like the luckiest man alive, then a few months later, I was dragged to this place. I thought there'd be some way out, some hope, but there was nothing until I heard that you were –'

Once again, Jael hurried to cut him off. 'How long have you been working on the tower?'

Alek's mouth dropped open, though he soon followed Jael on her sharp turn. 'A year now. It's been beset by problems, though. Taken twice as long as it should have. It's made for the god, Eyshar. Apparently, he's the one who led the king here, to the isle. He gifted it to him. Gifted him a seer too. Though now he's dead, so we're under orders to finish it for his funeral. Though unless we work every hour of the day and night, I don't see how that's possible.' He frowned then, fearing that under pressure from the queen, that might just end up happening.

'And what's Eyshar the god of?' Jael wondered absentmindedly.

'Providence,' Alek smiled. 'But also the God of Fire.'

***

Darkness could be both a friend and an enemy.

Though Eadmund was yet to determine whether it would work in their favour as he called for every shield to once again be drawn from the racks and every bow and spear retrieved from their storage places. There were few arrows left, though he hoped Mattie had deprived their enemies of their own supply.

Thorgils came up to his shoulder, and losing his balance, he bumped into him. 'They're fast.'

Eadmund could see that. Gripping the stern before him, wet knuckles turning white, he peered at his friend. 'They won't let us escape.'

'No.' Thorgils' muscles felt tight, legs vibrating. Trapped on a ship in the middle of the ocean at night... he felt tied in knots. They were at the mercy of the sea, the gods, and soon, he feared, their enemies. 'I'll try Mattie again. She has to see something that could help!'

Eadmund nodded, watching him go.

A frantic Kolarov took Thorgils' place. 'Catasla might have been the better choice, my dear king.' Feeling himself slipping, he snatched Eadmund's arm. 'If these are indeed Ronin Sardis' ships, we should be cautious. That king is favoured by the gods! Oh, the fortune bestowed upon him!'

Eadmund didn't need to hear it. 'Is that so? Well, to my knowledge, I'm not favoured by a single god, but my wife is. And if her gods want her to live, they're going to have to help us escape. Wouldn't you say?' He almost bellowed in Kolarov's face, for he was burning with rage as the sea splashed over him. 'Let those wolves try and stop us here, and they will die regretting it!'

***

Dessalene used her right index finger to stir the dark liquid. The reek of the balm she'd rubbed on her skin made her eyes water, tears trickling down flushed cheeks. Hot fires blazed in the braziers she had arranged in a circle in the centre of her spacious bedchamber.

She was alone, and apart from the burnished glow of those braziers, sending light shimmering across the marble flagstones, it was entirely dark.

She heard nothing but the sound of waves.

Her body swayed as though she stood on the deck of a ship, a hint of nausea stirring in her belly.

Picking up a small bowl, she whispered a chant – a growling sound so unlike her own voice. And now, she submerged her entire right hand into the bowl before bringing it up to her face, eyes bursting open, her chanting sounds rising as though cresting a wave. She flicked her dripping hand at the brazier before her, watching the flames hiss before turning to the next, and then the next, repeating the process until her bowl was empty and the flames blazed like a circular wall of fire.

Casting aside the bowl, hearing it clattering across the marble floor, Dessalene lifted her arms into the air, encouraging the flames to rise higher, until she stood, caged in fire.

CHAPTER NINE

Fyn had abruptly sent an enquiring Thorgils on his way, and Thorgils was muttering in annoyance as he turned, smacking into Arras, who staggered backwards, knocking into Nico behind him.

'What is it?' Arras asked, checking on his son.

'Just my cousin,' Thorgils grumbled. 'Acting as the dreamer's minder. Apparently, she won't speak to anyone.'

'It's a good thing!' Arras assured him loudly, buffeted by the wind and by his fears of what was about to happen. The wolf ships had hung with them, slowly gaining. He felt certain that before long, they would strike. 'She gave all their arrows to the sea! Let her show them what else she can do!'

Mattie heard the wind, the voices, the waves and the creaking as Bolder pushed his beloved ship further into the dark night. She felt the warmth of Otter nestled in her arms, the rhythmic vibrations of his purring against her chest. A wave of intense heat washed over her, the bright light of flames blaring into her eyes. She suppressed a scream, struggling to see, and rising to her feet, she dropped Otter to the deck. He scampered away as she reached Fyn, pushing past him, unable to catch her breath, to find her voice.

Eventually, she stopped by Bolder, who glanced her way.

'Fire!' she croaked, touching his arm. 'We have to turn! South! Go south! *Now!*'

But it was too late, and as Mattie and Bolder looked towards

Bone Hammer's prow, they saw flames rising out of the sea like a wall of fire, blocking the ship's path.

***

After supper, the slaves were allowed some time to themselves. They could gather in the high-walled courtyard, sit at the tables, finish their meagre ration of food and water and talk with their friends. But the hot days were so draining and absent any respite that most took straight to their beds.

The thought of being the only woman sleeping amongst hundreds of men had given Jael some pause, unarmed as she was. Though, much like her fellow tower workers, she'd been too tired to think once her head hit the floor.

There were no pillows, just the same thin mattresses that had been provided in the women's quarters. Sitting down, nauseous from her meal, confused by her conversation with Alek, Jael didn't immediately lie down. Her attention drifted back to the tunnel again, to Eadmund and then Sunni. Looking down at her hands, throbbing before her, she couldn't see any blood. It had been washed away, replaced with dirt, dust, and blisters, but in her mind, it was still there. The blood of Sunni's death would always stain her.

It was her fault – all of it.

And now, what would Eadmund do? Ships had been hunting him – she'd seen that – so what would he do?

She dropped her head, feeling a sharp pain run from her neck all the way to her lower back, where it spread into a throbbing ache. Shifting her body, she rolled her shoulders, feeling but avoiding the attention of the men lying around her.

Those who hadn't seen her fight in the Arena had heard about it from their friends. Most were suitably wary, but perhaps not all?

Refocusing, she posed the question again: what would Eadmund do now?

'Find ships.'

His voice was loud in her ears, as though he stood speaking directly into them. He would return to Oss, get the fleet, arm the Islanders and return. Perhaps seek support from Axl? Even Karsten?

He would get a fleet and return for her. Risking how many lives?

'If he makes it that far.'

Shuddering, Jael jerked around, wondering who had spoken. Someone had. A woman?

Looking down at the fetters locked around her wrists, she saw hints of the symbols she knew were there, though she had scratched through some of them.

So who was in her head, and how did they get there?

And more importantly, what did they mean...

***

'Sail down!' Bolder shouted at his experienced crew, who had anticipated his order, moving with speed as they hurried to drop the sail.

They needed to slow *Bone Hammer* down fast.

Mattie had asked Kolarov to keep Otter safe before rushing to the bow.

Eadmund thought about following her, eyes drawn to that strange wall of fire, though he needed to see what the wolf ships would do. Turning back to the stern, he thought of Jael and her sea-fire.

Only heavy rain or snow had put that deadly weapon out.

But this? This wasn't sea-fire at all.

'They're gaining!' Thorgils warned.

'Bring every weapon we have!' Eadmund barked at him. 'All of it, into the stern! Arras! Nico!' And as the crew hurried to stow the sail and yard, gathering the oars, Bolder watched with sinking hopes as the fire spread, quickly blocking any chance of escaping.

And realising it, Eadmund yelled at Thorgils. 'Wait on me!' He almost fell as the ship tilted, but rebalancing quickly, he reached Bolder. 'Turn all the way if you can! We'll aim for the flames!'

The wind was whipping the flames around, and though Bolder saw it was possible, he thought it insane. 'And then what?'

'Do you trust her? What she can do? And you?'

Bolder nodded, not needing to think about that.

'Good! Then run her close as you turn her! We need to get near those flames!'

***

An entranced Dessalene was surprised, wondering what that ship was about.

She saw the familiar face of Arras Sikari glowing in the flames.

The traitor.

And though she had no love for her foolish stepdaughter, her shame would be avenged. The king, she knew, would insist upon it, and she would not let her husband down.

***

Bolder's teeth were jammed together, eyes stinging from the fire's heat as he took *Bone Hammer* close to those flaming walls, the steering oar groaning beneath his vibrating grip, his crew now at the oars.

Thorgils was the tallest on board, with the biggest reach, though Eadmund wasn't far behind. Both men hung out over the port gunwale, spears in hand. Fyn, Arras, and Nico joined them, hurrying to knot the scraps of cloth they'd hastily wound around the necks of their spears before dipping them into a barrel of pitch.

Suspended out over the water, fearing he would set himself alight, Thorgils' hand shook as he reached farther than he thought possible. The tip of his spear caught fire, and convinced that his arm would go up in flames, he jerked back into the ship, quickly moving to the bow beside Eadmund, whose spear was also alight.

Fyn, Arras, and Nico surrounded them, carefully lighting their spears, and soon all five men held flaming weapons, though in the swirling breeze, they feared they wouldn't be alight for long.

'Go! Go! Go!' Eadmund bellowed at Bolder, who tugged *Bone Hammer* away from the fire wall, now turning her into the path of the oncoming wolf ships.

There were five of them.

Five flaming spears.

'Row!' Bolder ordered, struggling to see but well aware that they now needed speed. 'Row hard!' His men steadily increased their rhythm, oars scything through the sea, as Eadmund and his spear-wielders reached the bow. He glanced at the dreamer, sitting behind him, seeing her eyes closed, hoping she was helping as he aimed *Bone Hammer* between two of the wolf ships.

In the darkness, it was impossible to gauge if there was enough space, though Eadmund and his men had their heads fixed forward.

Bolder could only hope they would alert him to danger.

'Can't miss!' Thorgils called, though as the spear burned in his hand, it was a message mostly to himself. They had tried to use the cloth sparingly and the pitch lightly, but now, holding that flaming shaft in his hand, Thorgils feared it wouldn't fly. Though there was no time for fretting, so with a grunt and a prayer, he launched his spear into the air, aiming for the nearest ship's sail. Fyn remained with him while Eadmund, Arras, and Nico hurried to the starboard gunwale as *Bone Hammer* drew closer to the wolves.

Thorgils' spear tore through the enemy's great square sail, hitting it high, near the mast, flames quickly spreading. And turning back to Fyn, he remembered Jael on board *Sea Bear*, wishing they had a catapult. They'd be able to fling that pitch at their enemies and set them all ablaze.

Eadmund launched his own flaming spear, and soon two sails were on fire.

Bolder felt the wind strengthening, knowing that if he got too close to either burning ship, *Bone Hammer* risked catching a spark and going up in flames herself. Their enemies appeared too preoccupied trying to put out their sails to launch a counterattack, and seeing the great wall of fire moving further around to block their escape, Bolder realised he had no choice but to turn again.

Three more ships. Three more spears.

His jaw ached, and realising it, he opened his mouth, inhaling a smoky breath.

Hearing Bolder shouting for everyone to hold their places, Fyn used his free hand to brace himself against the gunwale as *Bone Hammer* started turning. Now they would come from behind and cut through the middle of the remaining three ships.

He stood with Arras and Nico, each man fearing his flame would extinguish before they got close enough to launch their spear.

Eadmund feared that too. Heart in mouth, he watched as *Bone Hammer* made her move. Seeing that their enemy had outflanked them, the wolf ships started veering away, and with their sails still up, he knew they would soon be out of range. 'Fyn! *Now!*' he urged, eyes darting back and forth, seeing Fyn almost tipping overboard as he released his spear, hearing the roar of his effort.

His spear lit up the darkness, flame flickering, struggling. Rising.

And then it went out.

'No!' Fyn was furious, devastated, but there was no time for it. And not giving up, he swung around, looking for something else to set alight.

Trying not to let his disappointment unsettle the crew, Eadmund shouted at Bolder to push on, and soon they were coming up behind two wolf ships. There was no space between them. Arras and Nico would have to fire on their sails from behind.

Eadmund was tempted to take the spears from their hands, though Arras had risen to the rank of commander, so likely he knew how to handle every kind of weapon with skill. And as he thought it, the two men released their spears, one aiming left, one right.

Both of them striking their targets.

And soon, four wolf ships were on fire.

***

Standing in the centre of her circle of crackling braziers, Dessalene was outraged.

Feeling an oddly cool breeze, she shivered, becoming distracted, wondering if one of the slaves had left a door open. Then, realising she couldn't be in two places at once, she pulled down the curtains of her mind, enclosing herself in her vision.

At once, seeing the dreamer.

Swooping over the ships like a bird hunting for prey, Dessalene saw the woman hunched up on that enemy ship, eyes closed.

What game was she playing? What could she do?

But not waiting to find out, the dreamer curled her fingers as though plucking a harp.

Drawing closer.

***

Shutting out the ships and their crews, Mattie remained in the silence of her mind. Her need to protect *Bone Hammer* grew in strength, power, and size until she felt like a giant standing astride the ship, feet touching the ocean floor. As though, with one enormous hand, she could bend down and sweep their enemies away. She thought of Otter and Fyn; Eadmund, Kolarov, Thorgils and Bolder.

In Sonderberg, apart from Otter, her only real companion had been loneliness, but on *Bone Hammer*, on this adventure, she had found friends, and she wanted to keep them safe.

Four ships were on fire, some of those crews now looking for weapons they could use against their enemy. Bolder was veering away, heading after the one ship whose sail remained intact.

Yet, they were now encircled in flames, and realising it, Mattie the giant bent down and started blowing.

***

The flames rising from Dessalene's circle of braziers now swept around as though they stood outside in a storm. Soon one was extinguished, and then another. The dreamer's eyes sprang open in horror, seeing no curtains blowing in her chamber. The balcony doors were closed, and she felt a heavy warmth in the air. A perfect stillness.

It wasn't that.

It was the dreamer.

And closing her eyes again, a furious Dessalene started chanting, squeezing her right hand into a fist.

***

Two of the wolf ships collided, and the explosion of bright flames shooting into the darkness revealed an arrow abandoned on *Bone Hammer's* deck. Quickly scooping it up, Fyn tore a strip from the bottom of his tunic, hastily making a fire arrow. Dipping the cloth in pitch, he hurried across the ship and leaning over the port gunwale, he hoped to catch a flame.

Thorgils grabbed hold of him, allowing his cousin to extend his right arm even further.

He sensed that the fire walls were lower, though how they were going to pass through them unscathed, he didn't know.

The wind was strengthening, *Bone Hammer* shuddering as she ploughed through the waves, Bolder aiming her at their last target.

Seeing that his cousin had managed to set his sleeve alight in the swirling wind, Thorgils yanked him back into the ship. 'Give me that!' he yelled, taking the arrow so Fyn could drop to his knees, soaking his sleeve in the bilge water sloshing over his boots.

Quickly back on his feet, Fyn drew the bow from his back, reaching for his arrow. Though catching a glimpse of Mattie clasping her throat, eyes bulging, he hesitated, handing Thorgils the bow instead. 'You do it!' And running past his nodding cousin, he headed for the choking dreamer.

'Fire!' someone shouted, and Thorgils turned to see a flaming spear land in the back of one of Bolder's men, who spun around, howling in agony.

'Get him down!' Eadmund bellowed. 'Get him down!'

Nico Sikari was closest to the man, and he tackled him, knocking him down to the deck, quickly smothering the flaming spear, though not before it had burned him.

Fyn reached Mattie, trying to pull her hands away from her throat. 'Mattie!' he called, unable to free them. 'What's wrong?' Those fire walls, which had seemed to be shrinking, suddenly shot up higher, and the intense glare of flames revealed terror in Mattie's blinking eyes. 'Mattie!'

Thorgils heard his cousin yelling the dreamer's name as he reached *Bone Hammer's* starboard gunwale, nocking the flaming arrow with wet fingers, breathing too heavily to feel confident about anything. The wolf ship was drawing away from them as he pulled back the arrow string, fingers parted, bringing it past his ear, knowing this was their last chance.

Releasing the arrow, he prayed to Borli, watching its tiny flame leap into the darkness.

Fearing for it.

And then nothing.

It was as though his heart had stopped.

Then suddenly, the wolf ship's sail burst into flame.

***

Dessalene hissed with fury.

She would kill the dreamer. She would burn that ship to ash.

There was a knock.

Blinking in confusion, she didn't understand.

Ignoring the odd distraction, she clenched her fists until she feared her bones would snap, squeezing the air from that little dreamer's throat. She was young and surprisingly useful, though she had made a mistake thinking she could –

'My lady?'

Another knock.

'My lady!'

Eyes springing open, a furious Dessalene rose to her feet, wheeling around like a fire-breathing dragon, eyes on the slave cowering at her now open chamber door. 'You think to enter unbidden? That I want you here, in my private chamber? *Now*?' She screamed so loudly that her ears rang. 'Get out! Get out before I have you thrown from my balcony! Before I do it myself!'

The slave was Mali, Kalina's most loyal servant, and though she felt frightened of the screaming dreamer, she didn't leave. 'My lady, please. It is the queen. She has tried to... kill herself. She is dying!'

Dessalene stared at her, lips parting, jaw clenching.

Not moving.

Turning to glance back at her circle of braziers, she bared her teeth.

Growling.

CHAPTER TEN

Every wolf ship was now on fire.

Sails burning to ash, flames spreading, their helmsmen had no choice but to order the crews to the oars. And despite the chaos and burning carnage, Eadmund feared their enemy still stood a chance. He pushed up the sloping deck towards Bolder. 'We have to run through the fire wall! We have to escape it now!'

Bolder thought he was mad.

But right.

Blinded by the glare of flaming ships and fiery walls, he tried to find the best place to aim his precious ship.

Behind him, Mattie fell forward, releasing her neck. Rasping and gasping, she pushed Fyn away. 'Go!' she hissed. 'Get away!'

Fyn stumbled backwards, hearing a crack and a crash as one of the wolf ships' masts came down. And looking at Mattie, he saw that her eyes were once again closed. He rose to his feet as his triumphant cousin returned.

'What's the plan?' Thorgils panted.

'We're escaping!' Eadmund told him, glancing around as Arras Sikari arrived. 'Arras, take the bow. Thorgils, go to the stern. Fyn, you've got starboard. I'll take port. We're going through the fire! Everyone's eyes open. Fill every bucket with water and watch for sparks!'

'Take down the prow!' Bolder ordered. 'We're rowing through it!'

It made sense, Eadmund knew, though they wouldn't be fast. And seeing the speared man lying on the deck, tended to by a useful Anika, and knowing they'd already lost a few to injuries, he called to Nico Sikari. 'Nico! Take an oar!' Eyes shifting to Kolarov, clinging to Otter, he pointed. 'Grab that bucket of water! Eyes open for sparks!' And thinking of water, he stalked the deck as those men not rowing scurried about like rats, responding to their helmsman's orders.

Doing his part, Eadmund collected buckets of bilge water, leaving them with those he'd charged with watching for sparks; the rest of the crew was stowing the prow, and finally ready, *Bone Hammer* started moving again.

***

'We pulled her out of the baths, my lady, but she is weak,' Mali explained, voice trembling, eyes on the bed where a bedraggled Kalina lay, ashen-faced and covered in blood.

'Find a physician!' Dessalene ordered with an unimpressed snarl. The smoke from the braziers was trapped in her throat, as was her anger, and she coughed and spat, too wild to think what to do with the foolish woman.

The king loved his daughter more than he'd ever loved his wives, Dessalene knew. Perhaps she was even jealous of her pretty stepdaughter?

Perhaps...

Hearing Mali leave, and shooing the rest of the ogling slaves away, Dessalene sat on Kalina's bed. She swept away the covers, grabbing one of the queen's bloody wrists, hastily wrapped in cloth, now entirely soaked in blood. 'What were you thinking, you fool! And if those slaves talk?' Spinning to the door, she called the slaves back into the chamber, and after giving them a warning about spreading gossip, aided by a little spell sure to tie their tongues, she once again sent them on their way, turning back to the queen. 'Your father always told you how beautiful you were, how special, and in that, he failed you terribly, Kalina. For you still see yourself as a child, cherished by all, seeking to be pleasing and to please those you wish to admire you. What a meaningless queen you truly are. Yet...' And now Dessalene stood, feeling the pull of her chamber, the threads she had been ready to tie in knots, all flapping loose, now out of reach.

And unwrapping the bandages around her stepdaughter's wrists, she sighed.

***

The oars turned with purpose and precision as *Bone Hammer* surged forward, leaving the burning wreckage of the wolf ships in her wake.

As they approached the flaming wall blocking their exit, Eadmund took up his position in the bow, bucket of water in hand. The crackling flames dared them to approach, warning what would befall them for even attempting such folly, but Eadmund chose to think of Jael walking straight through them.

She would, he thought, turning to urge the crew on. She would.

'Row! *Row!*'

Mattie heard him, working to push herself back into her trance, though it was harder this time. Now there was the lingering fear that someone was watching her, seeking to hurt her. Attempting to ignore that and her aching throat, she focused on reclaiming the vision of herself as a towering giant, blowing out the flaming walls.

Bolder's eyes were on those walls, too, every instinct urging him to turn *Bone Hammer* away from the danger. He glanced over his shoulder, seeing the five burning ships. They had no sails between them, though if they could put out those flames, they would row soon enough.

They had to escape now.

So, echoing Eadmund, he ordered his men to pick up their pace. 'Row! Faster! Go faster!'

The heat from the flames soon warmed a shivering Eadmund, who wasn't breathing as he braced himself, clutching the bucket. Bolder's men had taken down the dragon head prow, limiting the damage the flames would inflict, though he still wouldn't take a breath.

Not until they were safely through.

'*Row!*' he heard Bolder scream, then a strange silence amidst the creaking oars and splashing waves; amidst the roar of the fire and the exploding ships behind them.

Mattie blew out an enormous breath. She made it cold, like frost, as though by blowing on those flames, she was powerful enough to freeze them all.

Eadmund felt a cold breeze on his face as the heat from the fire walls diminished. They came close to licking *Bone Hammer's* strakes, and he quickly dashed a bucket of water over them, though it was as if the flames were being sucked away from the ship now. And as *Bone Hammer* edged forward, they appeared to part, inviting the ship to escape.

Turning around, Eadmund strode down the deck, past the men straining at the oars, backs to him. He saw Arras, Thorgils, and Fyn, unblinking on the gunwales; Kolarov standing in the stern, clutching his own bucket, Otter sitting at his feet.

But most of all, he saw that the flames weren't touching them.

Bolder didn't look his way, eyes peeled open, jaw pulsing, waiting for word that they were all the way through.

And as Eadmund moved past the helmsman, down to Kolarov, he saw them leave the last of the flames behind, watching as the walls closed after them.

Finally, setting *Bone Hammer* free.

***

Finding Jael's bed, Alek crouched down beside her.

Waking in fright, she shoved him in the chest, knocking him over, disturbing those men sleeping around her.

A shocked Alek pulled himself back onto his knees, touching her arm. 'Jael, it's me. Alek. I don't wish to hurt you.'

She panted, heart racing, and sitting up, she stared at him through a curtain of dark hair. Parting it and sweeping some behind her ears, she frowned. Moonlight leaked through holes in the ceiling, and she saw his blue eyes before her like tiny pools.

Tugging him forward, she shivered. 'What are you doing?'

He leaned even further forward. 'I have a knife.'

'And stones?'

'Yes, two.'

'Then go back to bed. Quick. Don't draw any attention to yourself. Leave them here with me, and I'll see you in the morning.'

Alek hesitated; he had wanted to wait, to talk to her. Though nodding, he turned the knife, laying it in the queen's hand before placing the two stones on her mattress. They were smooth, flat, and not too big. He left them there, watching as she rolled onto her side, concealing the knife and the stones.

And soon a confused Alek rose to his feet with a creak and crept back to his bed.

Hearing him go, Jael lay perfectly still, wondering what the dreamer would see? Or the men sleeping around her?

What would they hear?

She waited, struggling to keep her eyes open for what felt like an hour. The sounds of the men's sleeping quarters would take time to get used to. There were rustles, murmurs and the odd familiar rhythmic sound, though no one was moving about. Everyone appeared settled. Tired.

And finally, inhaling a deep breath, Jael picked up one of the stones, angling it towards the rays of moonlight, and with the knife in her hand, she started scratching.

***

Kalina hadn't opened her eyes, which kept Dessalene by her bed.

The physician had been roused, brought sleepy-eyed to stitch her wounds.

Dessalene Sardis was a dreamer, not a healer; blood mostly disgusted her unless used for her own purposes. She felt reluctant to even attempt to save her stepdaughter, who had caused such a mess. And not for the first time.

Now, having tended to the queen's self-inflicted wounds, the physician was looking to be dismissed, suppressing a yawn. Dessalene eyed him, feeling jealous. He would escape back to his house, and she would –

'The queen must be watched, my lady,' Ratish told her as he edged backwards. 'When she wakes, there may be regret, though perhaps, I fear, a desire to try again...' His voice trailed away as he dropped his eyes.

'Yes, yes, you may go. Return in the morning, though. I will not have the queen's wounds festering.' Straightening up her aching body, in need of sleep herself, Dessalene eyed the physician, who had almost reached the chamber door. 'I am sure I don't have to tell you that no word of this is to escape your lips. If it does, I will have them cut off. I've seen it done, you know. Nasty business. I can't imagine it makes eating a very pleasant task, or speaking, come to think of it. And you'd never kiss again, though at your age, would you even want to?' Smiling, she shooed the old man away before turning back to the bed.

And now she sighed.

The queen was propped up on perfectly plump pillows, sheathed in a clean silk nightgown, her glistening black hair smoothed under her head. Kalina's slaves certainly knew how to care for their mistress, how to pamper and indulge her, though they did not know how to modify her ridiculous behaviour. That much was obvious.

Yawning now, Dessalene aimed for a lounge chair. She couldn't trust the slaves to ensure that her stepdaughter lived, and imagining her husband's worried face, she knew he would want her sitting there. So, running her tongue over thin, sullen lips, Dessalene Sardis took a seat, eyes on the bed.

***

In the hours before dawn, Korri Torluffson, owner of the *Sea Queen*, lord of his men, took a seat beside the dreamer.

Neither of them appeared able to sleep, so he thought they may as well keep each other company. His tawny cat, Alvi, an expert ratter, was laid out across the dreamer's lap, pink tongue poking out.

'You cannot conjure up a sleeping spell?' he wondered with a wink, thinking he should have found a fur to cover himself with; the wind was rising off the sea like a vengeful whip.

Edela chuckled. 'I've never tried to, truth be told. I'm not usually awake at this hour, even at my age. Dreamers tend to sleep a lot, but not tonight.'

Korri frowned. 'Do you have a bad feeling?'

'Plenty! Yes, plenty of bad feelings, especially in the dark. It's where they all like to gather, isn't it? In the darkness, waiting to frighten us, when in the sunlight, perhaps they wouldn't be so scary at all?'

Korri was thoughtful, enjoying the silence. 'We'll stop in Zagora, the city of Bakkar, in a few days.'

'I've never been there,' Edela admitted. 'Which is something I've been saying a lot lately.' She smiled again, seeing the man relax. He had an open manner, a friendliness she warmed to; she knew few people who were so forthcoming. 'I do not have a bad feeling about you, however,' she added. 'In case you were wondering?'

'I'm glad to hear it. So just for yourself then?'

'For me and my companions, yes. For my family too. I fear the future and why I am here. Of what I will do and who I might hurt. Like poor Elmer and his crew.' Which, Edela realised, was at the heart of her sleeplessness. Guilt had given her a bad case of indigestion. She felt a sharp pain in her chest, a flood of bile in her mouth, sickening her.

'Though you didn't cause the death of those men, Edela. The bear did that.'

Edela stared at him, saying nothing further. It would do no good to draw another innocent victim into the web of danger she was weaving.

Korri turned to her. 'I met a dreamer as a boy. She told my father to stop farming. That he should sell his farm and take to sea. That if he didn't, it would be the death of him. And though he'd paid her for her insight, he didn't listen to the woman, too stuck in his ways to change. He was dead within a year. Fire destroyed the place, killed my parents and my sister, so I didn't go into farming...' Korri grinned. 'And since then, I've always been open to the words of a dreamer, both good and bad. It's like day and night, storms and clear skies. We can't choose one or the other, can we? We have to live in the world as Daala made it. A world carefully balanced between good and evil. Between darkness and light.'

Edela looked surprised. 'You're rather wise.'

'What? For a man of the sea?'

'Perhaps.' Edela saw glimpses of a pregnant woman and Korri's hands wrapped around her belly, his long beard draped over the smiling woman's shoulder as he nuzzled her neck. 'And your children? Your wife?'

'I've none of those,' Korri laughed. 'Not yet. This sweet ship is my only mistress. Perhaps there's nothing else in my future? No one else?'

Edela shook her head. 'I don't think you have to worry. I see a very happy family in your future. A very happy family indeed.' The old cat began to stir, and beside her, Bertel flopped over, interrupting his steady stream of snores.

Korri's mouth gaped open. 'You've seen it? My future?'

'A happy glimpse of it, yes, which is rather reassuring, I must say. For both of us!' Now she yawned, finally feeling a break in the darkness, as though its hold on her had lessened. Elmer and his crew were gone, and though it grieved her, she could not dig back into the past and save them.

The only way now was forward. The only path lay before, not behind her.

Flicking out a hand, Bertel touched Edela, and finding her hand, he held it.

***

When morning dawned, Jael had only just fallen back to sleep. She'd hidden the knife inside her thin mattress, knowing it remained on the floor each day, mostly undisturbed, reserving the place of its owner.

She slid the two symbol stones into her new shoes, feeling grateful that now she was working on the tower, she had been provided with more purposeful footwear. The covered shoes were too big for her, mostly given to men, and the stones helped keep them on her feet.

As the leader of his crew of thirty-four men and one woman, Alek Orlan was up earlier than the rest, responsible for getting them hydrated with cups of warm, cloudy water and handing out small shoulders of stale bread. And though his men gratefully took whatever he handed them, it wasn't the breakfast they needed to prepare them for the day ahead.

Sunshine streamed into the dining area, already strong and bright, though it hadn't been long since dawn.

Jael peered at Alek with one eye, struggling to peel open the other. She thought wistfully of her perfect bed and her husband lying beside her, his legs entwined with hers.

'Where's the knife?' he wondered with a whisper.

Jael was trying to swallow down the tough bread and couldn't answer. Tipping some warm water into her mouth, she attempted to soften it, eventually gulping it down, feeling grit in her teeth.

Scratching her nose, she scowled at Alek, knocking his cup of water to the floor.

He blinked in surprise before bending down to pick up the now-empty cup. Jael dropped down with him, and slipping one of the stones out of her shoe, she wedged it into Alek's.

They both straightened up.

'I'll need some more water,' he said. 'You too. I thought you could come with me today. I'll be at the top of the tower for much of it. As you can see, that's where our attention is focused now.'

He was an awkward-looking man, Jael noticed. Though he was of average height, his hunched, crooked posture made him appear much smaller. Still, there was a manic sort of energy about him as he hovered around her.

She kept scowling, not wanting to draw attention to either of them.

He couldn't favour her.

'I'll be fine carrying on,' she muttered as they headed outside to the well. 'No special treatment. If the dreamer gets wind that

I'm being given an easier time, she'll think of something worse.'

'I'm not sure there is worse,' Alek told her with a grin. 'I've done most tasks since I arrived, and I can't think of anything I'd want to do less. Working at the top of the tower is still hard, the hours are still long, but you're not doing all that lifting. That's what broke me. My body will never be the same after my time in the quarry.'

Perhaps that explained it, Jael realised, seeing his unnatural way of walking.

And he wasn't the only one.

The men around them moved as though sleepwalking, bent over with shuffling gaits, as though their arms and heads were too heavy to lift.

'What are the stones for?' Alek asked, smiling at a slave boy filling buckets from the well. And scooping his cup into one, he gulped down a mouthful, grimacing before encouraging Jael to do the same.

She glanced over her shoulder. 'Hopefully, to protect us. To hide us from that dreamer and anyone else who might be looking at what we're doing.'

Alek watched in silence as Jael filled her cup. Men filtered out of the dining hall, stretching and sniffing, squinting at the sun – their arch-nemesis.

That and the massive lumps of stone.

One or the other was sure to kill them in the end.

'I'll get everyone underway, then we can talk,' he whispered. 'I'll see to it. There's so much to talk about, but we don't have much time.'

And wheeling away from her, Alek Orlan soon left Jael behind.

CHAPTER ELEVEN

The bright glow of the morning sun revealed that there were no flaming walls and no sea wolves hunting them.

Eadmund dropped his head, nauseous with exhaustion.

Beside him, Thorgils chomped into a hunk of salted pork, eating with his mouth open. 'We still aiming for Vastera?'

Jolted out of his stupor, Eadmund shook his head. 'No need.'

'Though this is the last of the pork,' Thorgils frowned. 'There's no cheese, little ale, and we're low on water.'

That was true, and Eadmund pulled himself to his feet. 'I'll speak to Bolder.' And leaving Thorgils chewing as though his life depended on it, he headed for the stern, tipping back his head, seeing *Bone Hammer's* faded red sail as full as a pregnant belly above his head. It reminded him of his daughter, who had writhed like a sea creature in Jael's belly. He'd been fascinated by it, lying in bed beside his wife, irritating her with his exploring hands, eager to feel his child, to imagine her.

Bo.

She had certainly arrived like a bellowing beast, he thought, a smile now brightening his face.

His father would have spoiled her rotten. His sister too.

If they had lived.

Mattie stood and stretched before him, mirrored by Otter, who yawned.

'You're awake,' Eadmund noted. 'Thought you might have

been trapped in a dream again.'

Mattie was in a surprisingly good mood. She was used to waking up feeling the need to scratch her claws on something, but this morning, she felt light and at ease. 'No, just resting, I suppose. It was a long night.'

'And you worked hard,' Eadmund reminded her. 'We all saw that. You helped us, Mattie. You've helped a lot.' As a leader, it was important to give everyone confidence in their abilities, and it had taken a distracted Eadmund some time to realise how little belief the dreamer had in herself. She covered it up with a brash manner and a loud voice. She bustled and scowled and generally looked in charge of whichever situation she encountered, though over the past few weeks, Eadmund had seen how afraid she was.

Afraid that she wasn't good enough.

He patted her shoulder. 'Jael has a chance because of you.' And feeling tears coming, he bobbed his head, abruptly turning away, nearly tripping over Otter.

Fyn approached, clutching a cup of ale. He looked wary, knowing the dreamer well enough now to anticipate an abrupt dismissal, though she beamed at him as a purring Otter weaved through his legs. Surprised on both counts, Fyn couldn't find anything to say.

'It's a beautiful day,' Mattie smiled, staring up at him. 'A better day.'

Peering into her eyes, Fyn thought they looked emerald green in the sunshine – green with a shimmer of gold. 'It is. I didn't think it was possible. But who did that? The fire walls?'

Now Mattie frowned, curious about that herself. Bending down, she scooped up the cat, rubbing his head. 'Someone who wants to stop us. Someone watching, so likely a dreamer. Hopefully, not a god.'

'A god?' Fyn didn't like the sound of that.

Mattie chuckled. 'Likely a dreamer,' she repeated. 'A powerful one too. I felt a hand around my throat, like a vice tightening. Not flesh and bone but metal.'

'And you stopped it?'

'No, I think it stopped on its own. I wasn't doing anything. It just stopped, and I felt released.' She shook her head. 'It wasn't me.'

'Then we had some luck,' Fyn decided, hearing Kolarov calling for him, and seeing the explorer, red-faced and pointing at Thorgils, he rolled his eyes, guessing he was being called upon to settle another dispute between the two stubborn men, who had been facing off against each other since Castala. Though seeing the bright sun and the full sail and the relaxed dreamer, he smiled.

They weren't out of danger, they didn't have Jael, but for the first time in days, Fyn Gallas felt hope stirring.

***

Kalina saw nothing but darkness.

She sat on her bedchamber balcony, propped up against a wall of cushions beside a table laden with refreshments. Ignored by the queen, they were now attracting flies.

She stared as if at nothing. Her swollen eyes were without focus, her body no longer her own.

She felt suspended in pure darkness.

Sitting beside her, Dessalene rolled her eyes, looking away for a moment to silently scream at the wall before turning back to her stepdaughter. 'The physician will be here soon. I shall order another tonic. Something uplifting! You will see the sun again, Kalina.'

Kalina remained mute and lifeless beside the dreamer, and resisting the urge to prod her with a sharp fingernail, Dessalene brightened her forced smile. 'There is much to plan. You enjoy that, don't you? Festivities and the like? Though,' she added, 'I hardly think the funeral should be too festive. And we must use the time before it to draw your lords around you, Kalina. After what happened with Arras Sikari, you need to refocus everyone on what comes next, not on what has been. On what has gone wrong.'

Kalina still didn't reply, and too irritated to fake it any longer, Dessalene snapped. 'And what will your father think when he hears of this?' She saw a flicker of something in the queen's eyes. 'To hear that your response to your mistakes was to run away from them? Not to fix them or make things right, but to end your own life? After the trust he put in you? I cannot think that would please him, dearest.'

Kalina had grown up fearful of her father.

He was a smiling, gregarious man until some slight irritation set him off and then, like a spark on dry moss, he would ignite and turn into a bellowing ogre. Sitting in the heat of the balcony, she shuddered at the memories of his rage, stomach clenching.

Dessalene smiled. 'We are never parted, though when I saw what you were about, I... I wanted to help you, for if Jael Furyck had died in that hole?'

Kalina slumped forward with a heavy sigh. 'And though I am grateful you came, you need not stay, Dessalene. You can return to my father.'

Staring at the oddly pale queen, Dessalene shook her head. 'No, I will stay. I must. Eyshar must be more than simply appeased for your error. His trust in you, in the isle and its people must be fully restored. That will require more work than you are capable of managing, especially in your... present state.' Touching Kalina's hand, she closed her eyes. 'You will have a child,' she breathed. 'I see a boy, dark-haired and handsome. Strong and healthy.' Opening her eyes, she tried to infuse her stepdaughter with hope, wanting to snap her out of her catatonic state.

Though Kalina's eyes remained lifeless. 'Yet you said I am barren.' She didn't care who heard. She didn't care about anything. Her heart ached for Arras, for the mess she had made of everything, for the child she would never carry.

'You will never give birth, for not even a dreamer of my ability can change what Olera herself has ordained. But a child, a baby given into your arms after his first cry? That will be your child in every way. You will raise him. You will be his mother in all the ways that matter.'

'What child?'

'Argo Kosta's. It became clear to me last evening while I sat by your bed. I have chosen Argo Kosta's unborn son to be your heir. And when the boy is born, he will be yours to raise, beside your new husband.'

Kalina scrunched up her face. 'Argo Kosta? But he is –'

'An experienced man of high rank. A friend of your father's. And it just so happens that he's impregnated a slave. When she delivers her boy, we will take him and kill her, and you will have your child!'

Kalina stared at her. 'But he is –'

'A man worthy of being your consort. He was never a slave, so he does not pine for his freedom as Arras Sikari so obviously did. No, Kosta will remain by your side, enjoying the power and prestige you gift him. And happily content to play amongst his whore slaves, he will provide you with many heirs, my dear. You see!' Dessalene threw up her hands, ready to leave the sweltering balcony for somewhere cooler. She eyed Pye, who, sensing his mistress' need of him, had popped his head around the door. 'It will all work out perfectly. It will! But first, there is the matter of the funeral and the new Noor. Your people are unsettled, and unease does tend to fester amongst the masses. As pervasive as disease! Do not let your feelings undermine all your father has built. He trusted you, Kalina. For you to let him down now?'

Dessalene's words seared through Kalina's cloudy consciousness, and soon she was blinking. Her wrists ached, the bandages hidden beneath long, draping sleeves. She suddenly felt embarrassed, enraged that Arras had left her, foolish for falling in love.

Her heart ached.

A pain she had never experienced before.

Dessalene stood. 'You rest, and tomorrow, we will make our preparations together. By then, I am sure you will be yourself again, Kalina. Do not forget now, you are a queen first, a woman last and your father's daughter above all. You must not let him down.'

***

Hidden away on the scaffolding at the top of the Tower of Eyshar, Alek spoke to Jael in hurried whispers, hoping not to attract attention.

In charge of his own crew, Alek Orlan had more freedom than that offered to most slaves, so when he'd chosen to keep Jael with him, no one had raised an eyebrow. Alek had taken her up the tower, intending to have her help the stone masons, though he wanted to speak to her first.

To share all he knew, hoped, and desired.

Now that she had arrived.

'It is possible,' he began. 'To free ourselves. I've thought about it since I arrived. I've counted, studied, watched, listened, planned it out myself. I've made allies and talked to others of the same mind, though I've never been a warrior, never fought in a battle. I'm good with numbers, I can organise, but I can't lead the slaves into battle. And that's always been my problem, what I've waited all these years for. A true leader, someone to organise us. And now you're here. You can lead us, Jael.'

'Into battle?' Jael's voice was so low she could barely hear herself. They had squatted down while Alek acted as though he was outlining the tasks he needed her to do. She squinted at him, seeing those intense blue eyes.

Aleksander is waiting for you. He will show you what to do. Trust him.

Inhaling sharply, Jael pushed herself up, realising how the deep throbbing pain in her back already had her stooping. She squeezed her hands into fists, trying to feel her fingers.

Looking at Jael's face, Alek could see he had some work to do. 'Those in positions of power in the army are generally weak and ineffective. Sons of the queen's lords. Most haven't earned their places with any particular skill they've honed over the years. They're not experienced leading men like Arras Sikari. He was different, but now he's gone and –'

'What about the other commander? Commander of the Rocks?'

Alek nodded. 'Argo Kosta. He'll be here soon enough. It's his job to see that the tower is finished. He's a beast.'

'A smart beast?'

'A ruthless killer. The king was friends with him, from what I've heard, so Kosta rose quickly until he became head of the army. Though it appeared that the king had a change of heart, for before he left the isle, he divided the position into two roles. Commander of the Waves and Commander of the Rocks. I think he wanted a more powerful fleet, and he saw Kosta as less suited to that.'

'A ruthless killer?'

'His daughter's married to Quint. Krissia. I suspect Quint tells her everything that happens here, and she reports it all to her father. He turns up sometimes with his whip. Takes it to anyone she tells him is disloyal or not pulling their weight.'

Stepping back, Jael was troubled. 'We can't just hide here and talk all morning. Quint's already staring up at us.'

Alek agreed. 'Come, I'll take you to Gardi. You can stay up here and help him for a while. You're like a gift from the gods, Jael. You'll help me free the slaves. I know it.'

She eyed him with doubt.

'They keep us imprisoned by threatening us with weapons, with torture and pain. They make us fearful and afraid, fill us with doubt that nothing else is possible but this. They keep bringing in more slaves to build their homes and towers, their sanctuaries and gardens, never thinking of how outnumbered they are. But those they've captured are farmers and seamen, traders and merchants. Warriors too. Many know how to fight. More than our oppressors might imagine. We just need weapons and you. You to lead us out of here, Jael. You to show us the way home.'

PART TWO

Reunions

CHAPTER TWELVE

They would reach Bakkar today, Edela knew, savouring a cup of goat's milk with Siggy, who appeared to be enjoying her time on *Sea Queen*.

'Do you think we'll be safe there?' the girl asked, big curls bouncing in the wind. She kept shaking them away, trying to see, though they blew straight back into her eyes. 'Wherever we've gone, someone's tried to kill us. Except Marinos,' she said with a cheeky grin. 'We were safe there.'

Edela laughed. 'Is that what you think? Though there I was lured to that horrible Aggralaia, wasn't I? Someone was obviously watching, laying a honey trap that I certainly fell for.' She saw Siggy shudder. 'Though let's not talk about that! We've barely had a chance to discuss what happened to you on the island.'

'To me?' Siggy wiped her milky lips on the back of her hand, leaving a faint moustache behind. 'What about me?'

'Your dream! You saw that bear.' Though any joy about Siggy's progress was dampened by the memory of Elmer and his crew's terrible fate, and soon they were both frowning.

'I didn't think it was a bear,' Siggy admitted. 'In my vision, I saw dark creatures. They were big, with sharp teeth, but they weren't bears.'

Edela felt tremors of worry about that, though putting down her empty cup, she patted Siggy's hand. The goat bleated, ready for her breakfast, which Edela knew was Siggy's chore, though she kept holding her hand. 'You are a dreamer, Siggy, you've always been a dreamer, though something was stopping your dreams coming. Maybe fear? Or sadness? Though now that first dream has come, many more visions will flood your mind, awake or asleep. They'll be confusing, unsettling, and sometimes nothing at all, but I want you to tell me about them so I can help you. Everything you see. There's no Tuura, no temple anymore, though you're fortunate enough to have your own dreamer and elder on hand.'

Siggy looked nervous.

The goat bleated again.

Nellie, Edela remembered with a smile. 'You'd best go give that beast something to eat. After all, she's given us a lovely drink this morning. We must return the favour.'

Siggy hopped to her feet and turning to look down at Edela, she shrugged awkwardly. 'I do want to help. I'll tell you everything I see so I can be useful. I promise.'

Edela nodded. 'I know, now hurry along. I might close my eyes and see if I can find anything about our destination. Bakkar. I wonder what it will hold for us?' She smiled at Siggy, who spun away before muttering to herself. Bertel waved to her from near the mast, where he was deep in conversation with one of Korri's men, and she bobbed her head, still smiling. Though inside, everything was a great swirling mess.

For she had woken from a dream that had left her fearing she was going in the wrong direction entirely.

***

It had quickly become apparent to Axl that nothing he said or did would tease a smile out of his new dreamer. She stomped around with a face like thunder, though her grandson, Linas, appeared oblivious to it, and the boy continued to smile and chatter as though she was enjoying his company.

Perhaps she was, Axl thought as they walked away from the harbour towards the cove.

He had been showing the dreamer around Andala, wanting to learn more about her. Hoping to trust her.

'My mother wishes to meet you. She's been busy, though, preparing for the wedding in Angard.'

Helga called out for Linas not to throw stones before turning back to grunt at Axl. 'I know nothing about it.'

'Mmmm, though it does affect Brekka. With my Southern neighbours uniting in marriage, it very much affects us.'

'Though your neighbour in the west is more of a problem. That man is a messenger of darkness.'

'Oren Storgard?'

'Yes. Some are like that, born to evil. He seeks vast power. He seeks to rule Osterland itself.'

Axl stumbled to a stop just before the little rise in the path. 'Osterland?'

Helga grunted. 'Securing your borders will not save you from a man who intends to fly over them.' She kept walking, once again calling out to a dark-haired Linas, who swung around, flashing a toothless smile before running off again.

Having experienced flying creatures, Axl was shivering when he caught up to the dreamer. 'Though what power does he have? Surely he's just a man?'

Helga shrugged. 'Desperate men, hungry, obsessive men, can seek out many remedies for their weaknesses. With gold, great power can be bought, so you underestimate the man if you are only thinking of iron and steel as a defense. Of mortal warriors to aid you.' The dreamer shook her head, finally stopping to turn to the king. 'I do not wish the boy to grow up in a land of darkness. And the Brekkan throne will soon be the only one standing against that darkness. With your grandmother gone, you need my help.'

'But what can we do?'

'Plenty,' Helga promised. 'There are no warriors breaking down your gates, no enemy ships in the harbour, so you have a chance. We do. Brekka will be isolated, but she cannot fall, my lord. And if we work together, I am certain she won't.'

It was the first acknowledgement of his standing, though Axl barely heard her. Heart pounding, he peered at the woman, whose scowl hadn't shifted. 'And my child?' he wondered. 'My heir? Will he live?'

But Helga had turned away from him, heading after Linas, not stopping to answer.

***

Bolder had kept them in Vastera for two days.

Bone Hammer's sail had needed repairing, her hull caulking, and with Eadmund's help, he'd replenished their supplies too.

Now they were sailing to Hest's capital, which the Hestians simply referred to as The City, though despite Eadmund's reassurances that they would be welcomed by their allies, he wasn't going there defenseless.

They had stocked up on arrows, pitch, tinder and spears.

And now, with *Bone Hammer* caulked, cleaned, and restocked, they set sail again.

Kolarov bubbled with energy. He had purchased a new hat in Vastera's bustling market. It was blue, made of wool, and a little floppy, though he felt more like himself with something covering his scalp. More respectable.

'There was talk about a wedding in Angard,' Eadmund remembered, scratching his head. He'd slept in a bed in Vastera's tiny tavern, which had been almost comfortable, though he'd been scratching ever since.

'You did mention something about it,' Kolarov said, gripping the lid of the chest he had commandeered for the journey. 'Do you fear the king may have already decamped for Angard?'

A frowning Eadmund nodded. 'I'm losing track of time. I should have asked in Vastera. Why didn't I think to ask?' He scratched his beard with two hands, drawing Kolarov's attention.

'You have certainly caught lice,' the rotund explorer told him, inching backwards. 'You'll need to shave, dear king! All over, I'd advise.'

Eadmund sat on a chest opposite the explorer, slipping his hands beneath his thighs, though the itching sensation became even more maddening.

'I never travel anywhere without my pillowcase.'

'Your pillowcase?'

'Oh yes, made of the finest silk! I purchased it in Tudash many years ago. A luxury of the finest order, not cheap, though one I heartily recommend. It's cool and soft, and most importantly of all, no lice!'

'Though you have little to attract lice anyway,' Eadmund reminded him with a grin. 'I doubt they'd be drawn to your eyebrows.'

'Don't be so sure about that!' Kolarov laughed. 'They're insidious creatures, creeping into those places you often forget about. Like enemies! They like to find those weak spots, to slip through shadows, embedding themselves in the darkness and then...!' He lunged towards Eadmund with mad eyes before dissolving into a fit of giggles, belly jiggling. 'I don't like lice.'

Eadmund absentmindedly scratched his head. 'Well, let's forget about invisible enemies for now.' He saw Arras coming towards them and frowned. 'We need to talk about those enemies we can see and what we're going to do about them.'

Feeling conspiratorial, Kolarov lowered his voice. 'You don't like the man? Arras?'

Eadmund didn't move his head. 'After what he did to Jael, I've no reason to trust him, though she did. She gave up her place on this ship for Arras and his son, and I can only hope she didn't sacrifice herself for an enemy.'

***

Jael caught her first glimpse of Argo Kosta that morning.

Alek had told her that the imposing Commander of the Rocks liked to make unannounced visits, hoping to catch the slaves off guard and punish those failing to carry out his orders.

As it was that morning when he arrived in the company of the seer, Inesh Seppo. After the funeral and sacrifices had taken place, the seer would be anointed the new Noor of the Dragon Blood Tree. In his early forties, handsome and tall, he looked nothing like his predecessor, apart from the air of calm that radiated from his long face and his slow, graceful movements.

Alek was one of four foremen working to complete the tower under the supervision of the commander's son-in-law, Quint, though there had been no sign of Quint that morning, and his absence had led to a loosening of discipline, which was quickly pounced on by a barking Kosta.

Jael had returned to the bottom of the tower, sent for supplies by Gardi, the stone mason, and she remained in the shade of an arch, watching as Alek hurried forward, called to account for the mess in the tower courtyard. The commander was twice the width of a lopsided Alek, at least a head taller and physically imposing. And though he'd appeared ready to throttle the smaller man, he merely pushed him away, snarling for another of the foremen to come forward – this man, the one ultimately responsible for the courtyard side of the tower.

Alek edged back towards his men and Jael, not looking at any of them. There was a palpable tension in his body that had her concerned, and looking at the brutish commander, now rendering the foreman a stuttering mess, she soon joined him in his worries.

It wasn't long before Kosta drew out a knife, stabbing the apologetic foreman in the cheek.

Jael swallowed, hearing the man's cry of anguish, seeing a flash of horror on the seer's face, which he was quick to mask.

'This tower is months overdue! *Months*!' Kosta bellowed. 'The funeral is to take place in twelve days, and a great sacrifice will be carried out here. Before the tower! So you will have this fucking tower finished, or you will *all* suffer like your worthless foreman here!' And now, grabbing the sobbing man by his tunic, he slashed open his throat, throwing him to the ground. 'Take him to the pits!'

Swinging around, he took in the rows of slaves now cowering before him, eyes lowered, hoping not to draw the commander's attention.

Inesh Seppo sought to intervene. 'Commander, we must not keep the queen's stepmother waiting. She is to meet us inside the temple.'

Kosta was still bristling with anger, incensed by the unfinished work and the poor standards of Quint's foremen and their crews. Though reminded of the seer beside him, he allowed his attention to be reassigned. Turning with the blue-robed man, he caught sight of Jael and stopped as though struck.

Curling a thick, calloused finger in her direction, Kosta's eyes narrowed as he waited.

Jael heard a hush weave through the slaves as she walked towards him, wishing she had a weapon to hand.

The commander, she could see, had plenty.

She kept her eyes up, back straight, as she stopped before him, barely blinking.

He still held the bloody knife he'd killed the foreman with, and though Jael could smell the blood and the trail of shit the foreman's body had left behind, she didn't look. She didn't flinch beneath that intense gaze.

Kosta took a thumping step forward, aware of the seer's discomfort and the slaves' interest. 'You are the woman Arras

Sikari sought to kidnap. A wealthy woman. A famous woman. A warrior.' He had seen the match in the Arena; he knew what this woman was capable of. 'And a precious, precious prize.'

His breath was smoke and wine and meat. Skin that had spent decades baking in the sun was a rippled, leathery mass. He peered at her with yellow-tinged blue eyes narrowed to slits, as though surveying a great feast.

Jael didn't answer him; she hadn't heard a question.

Roughly taking her chin in his hand, Kosta squeezed it, jerking it upwards. 'But not to me,' he rasped in warning. 'You are not a prize to me.' And now he shoved her backwards, watching her stumble, disappointed that she didn't fall. 'I will have my eyes on you. On all of you!' he shouted. 'This tower will be finished before the funeral, or you'll all be sent to the pits. Every last one of you useless fucks!' And with a nod of apology to the clearly disturbed seer, he led the man away.

Jael watched him go, still inhaling the stink of that smoky hand on her face as Alek came up behind her.

'Are you alright?'

Annoyed by his fussing, she brushed him aside, simmering with anger. 'I'll have to kill him,' she decided, far more interested in Alek's plan now. 'Before we leave this place, I'm going to have to kill that bastard.'

***

'What is troubling you, Edela?' Bertel muttered in a distracted voice. Bakkar, Zagora's noisy capital city, was a whirlwind of delights, and his attention was everywhere but on his companions. Siggy roamed ahead of them, turning around to announce where she was leading them next. Beside him, Edela was silent, as though not entirely present. The streets were swarming with people in a way they hadn't experienced on any of the islands. Instead of bright blue skies and little white cottages fronting cobblestoned alleys, Bakkar was like a dark, steaming maze of narrow paths, old roads and impossibly tall buildings. They rose like towers, crammed together, blocking out the sun, allowing little air through, making everything even more claustrophobic.

Bertel stood on a woman's foot. 'Oh, I'm sorry!' he declared in horror. The young woman's husband swung around, shoving him with a look of disgust, and though incensed by that, Bertel allowed himself to be tugged away by an insistent Edela.

'Are *you* alright?' she asked, showing signs of life now as Bertel peered at her with furrowed brows. 'I hardly think getting into a fight serves us.'

'Well, I...' A flustered Bertel didn't go on, realising that they'd lost Siggy. 'Hurry up, Edela!' And taking her hand, he shouldered his way through the crowd, finally spying that familiar curly head.

Siggy turned back to them. 'I don't know where I'm going!' she admitted with a laugh.

Edela laughed with her, though she felt uncomfortable in her own skin. Bakkar was an unsettling, overcrowded place, and though the sun was out, it felt strangely dark. She was becoming less convinced that she was going in the right direction, more fearful that her every move was being watched – even her thoughts studied by some invisible enemy. But smiling at Siggy, she tried to move them forward.

Though they didn't get far, for soon, they came across the friendly Korri Torluffson and a handful of his men, who had left the ships early, hoping to offload their stock of honey and furs, and by the look of their empty hands, they'd succeeded.

'Glad I've found you,' Korri smiled at Edela, nodding at Bertel. 'If you're still keen to earn some coins, I've heard of an opening that might interest you.'

Bertel frowned at him, one hand on Edela, who he sensed was ready to leap forward at any moment. 'What sort of opening?

What would I have to do?'

Korri laughed. 'Not you. Edela. It's a fortune teller they're looking for. An old man and his grandson, they own a tavern called The Crescent Moon. A small place, but very busy. You wouldn't be short of customers!'

Edela turned to Bertel, shaking off his hand. 'Well...'

Bertel wasn't sure what he thought. 'I suppose you wouldn't have to do it for long,' he suggested. 'And you could use a different name.'

'It pays well,' Korri added. 'According to the grandson, at least.'

'You should only do it if you want to, Edela,' Siggy told the dreamer.

'Though will it be safe?' Edela wondered.

'I'm not sure anywhere's safe,' Bertel said, leaning close. 'I can try down at the harbour, see if anyone needs help –'

'No, no. No, this makes perfect sense,' Edela decided. 'I'll tell some fortunes, make a few coins, and then we'll be on our way.'

Happy to hear it, Korri and his men soon took their leave, eager to return to their ships.

'Well, that was a stroke of luck,' Edela chuckled as they turned back into the crowd, though she shivered, wondering if she was doing the right thing.

Revealing herself as a dreamer?

Not a dreamer, a fortune teller, she reminded herself. And anyone could set themselves up to tell fortunes. No one had to know she was a dreamer.

'The sign of the crescent moon?' Bertel muttered, seeing how many stalls, shops, and signs populated their path. 'Perhaps we should have asked Korri to guide us?' Narrowing tired eyes, he tried to sharpen his vision, though he wasn't looking where he was going, soon standing on another foot.

Now Edela laughed, almost relaxing for the first time in days. 'Perhaps we need to find a cart so Siggy and I can push you? It might be safer. At this rate, you'll end up with a knife in your chest!' Though a scowling Bertel took her hand, squeezing into a gap in the crowd, pulling her after him.

***

Mattie's hands were so cold they were turning blue. Her red nose was dripping.

'Oh, I long for hot water,' she sighed, smiling at Anika, who had proven a friendly, if shy, companion. And though it was agreeable to have another woman on board, Mattie was so unused to female company that she could never think of anything to say to her.

They sat side by side in the bow, keeping to themselves while the men sharpened weapons, played dice and chatted amongst themselves. The weather was fair, the wind bitterly cold, and they were well on their way to Hest.

Anika, who had arrived on board in a thin grey dress with sandals on her feet, nodded. 'Hest will be warm. I lived there as a child.'

That was more information than she'd revealed about herself so far, and Mattie peered at her with interest. 'You're Hestian?'

Anika shook her head. 'No, I was born in Brekka, but my grandparents were Hestian. I lived with them for a time.'

'Near The City?'

'No, further north. Near the border with Helsabor. It was a hot place compared to Brekka. Very dry.'

The women looked wistfully at each other before a jet of sea spray fired over the bow, showering them both. They burst out laughing, frightening a sleeping Otter, who bounded off Anika's knee, scuttling towards Bolder.

'So will you stay in Hest then or go back to Brekka?' Mattie asked, dragging a clump of wet hair out of her eyes.

Anika immediately sought out Nico, feeling a fluttering in her stomach, still amazed to think there was a future to talk about. 'I'm not sure. We haven't discussed it. I know Nico and his father will want to go back for the queen. For Jael Furyck. After what she did to help us escape, they won't leave her behind.'

***

Gisila recognised Helga Brugen at once.

Beside her, Axl was surprised when his mother didn't speak. He knew Gisila was desperate for answers about Jael and Edela, worried about him and Amma, yet she had no questions and certainly no welcome for his new dreamer.

'I didn't expect you would ever leave the forest, Helga,' Gisila frowned.

Helga had no smile either, though that was less of a surprise, Axl realised.

'The forest sustained me, fed and nourished me for years and will again, though for now, my place is here, helping your son.'

Gisila's frown didn't budge. She stood in the centre of the hall, too close to a fire pit, feeling a warmth on her back that was almost burning. 'You were sent out from memory. Banished from the temple.'

Helga's beady eyes sparked. 'Not quite. Though I imagine the elders sought to turn everyone against me after I left. My daughter said as much. It was a corrupt place, and I would not remain silent, so I spoke up and left.'

'Which seems like a wise choice in hindsight, don't you think, Mother?' Axl said with a raised eyebrow, hoping to set his mother right again.

Gisila offered a grudging nod, hearing the truth in Axl's words. 'Tuura has certainly fallen far these past few years. You were well out of it.'

'These past few years?' Helga sneered. 'Oh no, but Tuura has always been rotten to its core.' Straightening up, she looked past the former queen to where servants were laying the high table, realising that before long, Linas would come searching for food. 'I would like to help myself to your kitchen stores.'

Ignoring his mother's blinking eyes, Axl nodded. 'Of course. You will need to feed your grandson and yourself. I can show –'

'I can take myself,' Helga assured him, stepping away from the fire pit. 'You must have better things to do. More important things, perhaps?'

'I... yes. Well, do help yourself. I shall be paying you for your services, Helga, but in the meantime, take what you need.'

The dreamer bobbed her head at the king, eyed Gisila coldly, and strode towards the kitchen with purpose.

When she had disappeared from view, Gisila swung around to her son, grabbing his arm. 'Helga? You didn't say her name was Helga!'

'Why, what does it matter what her name is?'

'Helga Brugen was no friend to dreamers in Tuura. I'm not sure we can trust her. That you can, Axl.'

Axl had been fearing that himself, though he was determined to push back, not wanting to think he was making a mistake. 'There is no one else, Mother. Besides, Helga sees danger on the horizon, and she wants to help me.'

'*We* see danger on the horizon, so that's hardly illuminating!'

'But she sees danger for all of Osterland. For every kingdom, not just us. Oren Storgard's ambitions are more than we could ever have imagined.'

That was news to Gisila, who finally moved away from the fire.

'We need help. I do. And for now, that help is Helga. You were desperate for a dreamer, and she has come, so let her help us, Mother. Let her help us save the kingdom.'

CHAPTER THIRTEEN

Having been brought down from the top of the tower by Quint, who wanted another pair of hands to help unload the wagons, a struggling Jael tried to order the horrors of her current experience, seeking to determine which was the most unbearable.

There was the heat.

It was so hot she felt burned from the inside out. Her skin sizzled in the sun. It gave her a pounding headache, dried her throat and soaked her clothes with sweat.

Which led to the smell.

The reeking stink of sweating bodies and the rank odours from the pits and latrines drifted towards her in hot waves.

And the pain.

That was constant. Slabs of stone were hefted onto wagons, brought up from the quarry, some as large as a man, many smaller but still incredibly heavy. Jael's arms felt as though they were coming apart.

One man's had. A young slave called Wibo.

Something had popped that morning, his right arm suddenly changing shape, withered and dangling from the shoulder joint like a piece of overcooked meat. The pain must have been unbearable, though the man had looked almost removed from his own body – a level of exhaustion Jael was certain she would soon approach herself.

Then there was the enslavement.

That was discomfort in a way she couldn't put into words. To be enslaved, where no decision was your own. Where your time belonged to someone else, your energy, joy and pleasure.

Your body.

Someone owned all of it.

And though Jael had been made Queen of the Slave Islands, sympathetic to the plight of all slaves, as the daughter of a king, she had always been removed from the experience of actually being a slave.

Until now.

Now she felt like a horse shut in a stall, a dog tied to a post.

She wanted to scream.

Nudged in the back, she turned with a snarl, surprised to see Alek, who had been gone for most of the day. 'Where'd you disappear to?'

His blue eyes glowed with pleasure. 'A meeting with the foremen and Inesh Seppo about the tower and the funeral. He spoke to the queen's stepmother about Noor's wish to give the slaves a day of rest in honour of the occasion.'

'So they'll be invited to watch? The slaves?'

Alek nodded. 'They want a crowd, so yes, we'll get to watch. Which will suit our plans.'

Jael peered at him. 'Did you know the old seer?'

'Yes. The queen has many plans for the temple grounds and Noor helped her refine her vision. He worked closely with Quint and the foremen.'

'He knew your name?'

Alek stepped closer, glancing around. The slaves were being given a water break, many dipping scraps of cloth into their cups and wetting their faces, wiping the backs of their burning necks. The water wasn't cool, but some liked to tie the cloths around their necks, though they didn't remain wet for long. 'Why do you ask?'

'I watched him die,' Jael whispered. 'The queen stabbed him, and before he died, he spoke to me about you.'

Alek was gobsmacked. '*Me?*'

'Unless there's another Aleksander you know of?'

'No. Not around here.'

The slaves were already being ordered back to work, so Jael quickly gulped down the remainder of her water.

'I'm sending you back up the scaffolding,' Alek told her. 'Gardi could use the help. If you don't mind heights?'

Jael frowned. 'Do you ask every slave's preference for where they want to work?'

'No, just those who are queens,' Alek grinned. 'Those who need to conserve their strength for what lies ahead.' He whispered the last part as he turned away, heading for the rickety tower of scaffolding.

Watching him go, Jael wondered if it was truly possible.

To free the slaves and leave this place?

And tipping back her head, eyes on the intense blue sky, she thought of home.

***

After finally finding the sign of the crescent moon, Edela had left Siggy and Bertel outside the narrow little tavern while she went inside to enquire about the position.

The taverner was a wily old Tudashi man, intent on haggling with her, though she eventually struck what she hoped was a fair bargain, and finally emerging into the sunshine, she flashed her companions a triumphant smile.

'At last! We thought you might have disappeared again,' a red-faced Bertel declared. 'What have you been doing?'

'Negotiating,' Edela said with a wink.

'Successfully?' Siggy wondered.

'Very successfully! I start work this evening.'

Bertel wasn't sure what he thought about that.

'And what's more, the man has a room to rent above the tavern. We can stay there as part of my agreement. Free of charge!'

'Well, I hope you haven't talked yourself into some form of bondage, Edela,' Bertel fretted. 'I didn't think we'd chosen to stay in Bakkar. In Zagora at all. It's not where we want to be.'

'Isn't it?' Edela shielded her eyes from the sun, which suddenly seemed so bright after the dingy tavern. 'I'm not sure we know that. Every destination has provided one more clue, so why not this?'

'So you have to tell people's fortunes?' Siggy asked, squinting at the boy who'd emerged from the tavern. He eyed her briefly before starting to wipe down the tables. 'And can you do that?'

Edela laughed. 'Well, I'm sure I'll see some things. I just need to stop myself becoming too dark and gruesome. I want to leave my customers feeling optimistic about their futures.'

'*Your* customers?' Bertel snorted. 'Sounds as though you've lost hold of your purpose, Edela, which certainly isn't to become a fortune teller!'

'Is that so? But wasn't it you suggesting I offer myself up as one to poor Elmer and his men?'

Nostrils flaring as though he'd inhaled some horrible odour, Bertel turned away. 'Well, as you say, we do need to earn our way, and I don't expect we'd make very good thieves.'

Siggy laughed. 'I don't think so. Edela's far too slow to run away.'

A chortling Edela agreed. 'Yes, we'd be caught for sure!' Everything suddenly darkened, and she heard a voice in her ears urging her to run.

To run far away.

'What is it?' Bertel asked. 'Edela?'

Edela stumbled, swinging around, and finding Bertel, she took his arm, steadying herself. 'Nothing. It's... nothing.' Which neither Bertel nor Siggy appeared to think was entirely true, though avoiding their eyes, Edela was soon on her way. 'Let's go back to the harbour and see if we can find Korri,' she suggested. 'He might allow us to help ourselves to some of Nellie's milk. This sun is unbearably hot!'

Siggy turned after Edela, though Bertel didn't move. Jostled and growled at, he ignored the crowd seething around him. Instead, he saw images of Tuura and his simple chamber in the temple, the quiet company of the elders, the plentiful food and comfort his former life had afforded him. And though he was a tense, starving, aching mess, far removed from that world, he knew it had been slowly killing him with boredom.

Edela Saeveld was a secretive witch, a mysterious healer and visionary dreamer leading them to who knew where, though Bertel felt certain he was meant to be by her side.

He was meant to help her find the answers she was so desperately looking for.

***

The sun was sinking in the sky, blinding Jael as she tottered near the edge of the scaffolding, only half-listening to Gardi lecture her about the importance of keeping her trowels clean. She was transfixed by the incredible view and occasionally by the wobbling scaffolding as the pulley was drawn up and the next bucket of bricks was delivered.

From here, she could see the palace. She could see into the temple, where the majestic Dragon Blood Tree commanded a mosaic-floored courtyard. She could see the sea to the west and the great pits where she'd been dropped into a hole and left to die. The memory of that had her shivering as she turned around to Gardi, who was now shielding his eyes, hoping to see her own.

'You're looking in the wrong direction,' the white-haired old man grumbled. 'Unless you're thinking of flying? Won't have been the first. They sometimes send soldiers up here to stop men throwing themselves off. At such a height? You're guaranteed a fast death. Not painless, though. Wouldn't try it myself. Now come on.' He turned back to the wall, where a stack of bricks waited. 'Alek says you're my new assistant.' He muttered noisily, not sounding thrilled about that as he motioned to the bricks. 'For now, you'll hand them to me. I need to stay down on my knees. See?' And easing himself down onto his aching knees, Gardi held out a hand. 'Once we've laid out the row, I'll apply the mortar. Watch me carefully, and perhaps you'll have a turn. Perhaps...'

Picking up a brick, Jael attempted to focus on Gardi's process, though her mind remained busy, exploring every area of the city. She saw a side road heading out of the grounds, around the back of the temple. And that road appeared to lead towards the harbour.

***

The smell of supper, still hours away, wafted into the dining hall, and Kalina felt a stirring of hunger. It was a new and surprising sensation, for she'd had no appetite for days. It had felt as though she no longer possessed a body, just a mind and a heart, both distracted and in pain. She had no body, no need to care for it, no need to worry if she lived.

In those first few days, she hadn't wanted to.

Dessalene swept into the room in a rush of silk and gold, her auburn hair unbound, whipping around like a horse's tail. 'We shall announce the engagement after the funeral!' she decided gleefully. 'That will put us all back on an even keel, won't it, dearest?' Seeing Kalina's emotionless eyes, she brightened her own. 'You will make such an attractive couple, such a talked-about pair, that all the mess with Arras will be gone as though it never existed. Brushed away like yesterday's crumbs. Soon no one will even remember his name!' Though thinking of Arras Sikari, Dessalene was aware that the traitor had slipped away from her wolf ships, and when he heard about that, her husband would be furious.

'I thought you might mention it this evening. My betrothal.'

'No, dearest. This evening is all about the Noor-Elect and introducing him to your lords and ladies.' Dessalene frowned. 'What a strange custom that is, not allowing the man to keep his own name. Pretending they are all one and the same. Whoever thought of that, I wonder?'

'My father,' Kalina said dully, aiming for the door. She wanted to bathe. Her stitches were itching, and she wanted to soak them. Whatever Mali added to her baths was soothing and reduced the irritation. The heat, her clothes, everything else simply irritated them. 'And have you heard anything of Jael Furyck?' she wondered, heading out of the throne room into the entranceway leading to the grand staircase. 'Whether she lives?'

Following her, Dessalene blinked. 'She does, of course! Nothing will happen to her now. I've arranged it all, so you needn't worry. I have my eyes on her, and my little toad is checking on her, so if she gets up to any mischief, I'll soon see it. We must keep her safe, mustn't we, for your father will want to see her when he arrives.'

Kalina jerked to a stop. 'My... father is coming? Here?'

'Of course! He was always coming to inspect his prize. I merely hurried on ahead to fix your... mistakes before he arrived. You know how he can be. And we want things to be pleasant, don't we? This way, he will arrive with everything smoothed over!' Dessalene spun around, running a critical eye over the dining table, pleased with the work of those dedicated slaves, before turning back to Kalina. 'Besides, he is only in Zagora. I don't expect he'll be long at all.'

***

That evening, Korri met up with Edela, Bertel, and Siggy at The Crescent Moon, where they shared a meal at an outside table.

It wasn't what any of them had been hoping for.

The ale was too strong, with a bitter aftertaste, and the stew was unappetising: little chunks of meat sunk into a thick brown gravy with nuts sprinkled on top.

Thankfully, Edela realised in time that the meat was, in fact, rat and the bowls went untouched by her hungry companions.

Feeling bad about that, the taverner's grandson, Zen, suggested they try some bread, which a starving Korri promptly ordered four servings of.

And while they waited for that to arrive, they sat outside the busy little tavern, in the busy little road, far too close to the crowds for comfort, occasionally jostled by people hurrying by.

Bertel was annoyed on every count, though he tried to smile for Korri, who had been generous with his hospitality from the moment he'd rescued them from Aggralaia. 'And how long do you plan to stay in Bakkar?' he wondered, glancing at the open tavern door, yet to see any sign of that bread. He did see the taverner's grandson, though, and raising a hand, sought to claim his attention. Though the boy – a tall, slumping sort of youth – turned away without noticing.

'A few more days, I reckon,' Korri said. 'I need more men to crew the new ship.' He didn't feel comfortable about acquiring Elmer's ship in such tragic circumstances, though she deserved a careful owner and a useful crew, and he was determined to succeed on both counts. 'And I'll have to think about how I'm going to pay them. I've still got the ivory, which I was planning to sell in Castala, but I may need to part with my pelts here.' His freckled face momentarily lost some of its cheerful enthusiasm, but he was soon smiling again. 'And you? What are your plans?'

Zen brought out the plates of bread, and all conversation

ceased, for it was warm, soft, and white. And soon gone.

'If only we had something better to wash it down with,' Korri grinned. 'I'm not sure you can call this ale. Tastes like spicy bilge water.'

Edela couldn't help but agree. 'Well, there's always Nellie. She can be relied upon for a nice cup of milk.'

'True, and maybe it's worth finding another goat for the new ship?' Korri mused. 'We'd never go thirsty then.'

They chatted for a while, discussing the animals, the ships, and what they'd discovered in Bakkar until Edela stood, adjusting her cloak and belt. 'I must excuse myself, for it is time to get to work. I did tell my employer I would start after supper.'

Korri hopped to his feet, along with Bertel, who blinked at Edela with worry in his eyes. 'You've secured a place here?'

'Well, a temporary position. A way to pass the time!'

Siggy rose to her feet with a yawn. The air felt warmer than ever, a kind of sleepy haze falling over the sky now, turning everything a deep shade of copper.

'We won't be far away,' Bertel promised, glancing at the patrons, who seemed loud and drunk.

'I'd say that's a good idea,' Korri said, then seeing that Bertel had only a few knives in his belt, he smiled. 'Come down to the harbour with me, and I'll give you a sword. After Aggralaia, we've plenty to spare.'

Bertel looked pleased about that, turning after the helmsman before swinging back to Siggy. 'Are you coming?'

Siggy shook her head. 'I think I should help Edela. You might need some help,' she insisted, sensing the dreamer's resistance before she even opened her mouth.

Edela was certainly ready to protest, though seeing how eager the girl was to be useful, she nodded, squeezing Siggy's arm. 'Yes, I think that sounds like a sensible idea.' Shivering, she glanced over her shoulder, feeling the same ripple of fear from earlier.

It was odd – a new sort of sensation.

As though a snake had slithered over her bare feet.
A long black snake with glowing eyes.

***

Bone Hammer slid into Hest's harbour, searching for somewhere to moor. It was bustling and busy, every spot on every pier seemingly occupied, though eventually, Bolder's man Raal found them a berth.

It brought back memories for Eadmund and Fyn, who stood by the prow with Thorgils, eyes on the enormous castle in the distance, seeing the improvements Karsten Dragos had made to the harbour since their last visit. It felt similar to Castala in many ways now, blessed with the same sort of golden hue, though not quite as chaotic.

'He's been busy,' Thorgils noted, enjoying the welcome onslaught of warm, still air. Overhead, the blue sky was tinged with gold and he saw a hint of the moon. 'Looks like he's built five more piers since we were last here. How's he managed that so quickly?'

Eadmund tidied up his beard, running stiff fingers through his hair, itching his scalp again. He wanted nothing more than to fall asleep, though he needed to be alert and move with speed. And he needed to find Karsten.

'With all the trade coming from the Fire Lands, I imagine he had to get the harbour back up and running,' Fyn said, raising his voice as Bolder shouted at his crew. 'It's certainly busy!'

Kolarov stumbled into him. 'What a sight!' he declared cheerfully. 'Oh, what a magnificent sight! I do hope your friendship with the king wasn't overstated,' he murmured to Thorgils, who turned to peer down at him. 'I do so wish to sleep in a real bed! A real bed in that majestic castle. I had occasion to meet the old king a few times, though I never found him an especially hospitable man. Nor that wife of his. A quite vicious woman from memory.'

Thorgils slapped him on the back, recalling his own memories of Bayla Dragos. 'Oh, you think so? A room in the castle?'

'Well, I'm not one of the crew,' Kolarov muttered. 'They'll have to make do with whatever they find, but a chamber in the castle would be more suited to me, an advisor to the king!' And licking a finger, he smoothed down his eyebrows, ignoring a laughing Thorgils.

Eadmund's eyes were on the docks, where their arrival had attracted the attention of three men dressed in green tunics trimmed in gold, who quickly headed towards them, muttering to each other. He turned to see Mattie with her cat, Arras and his son, and Anika. They had remained in the stern while Bolder and the crew secured their possessions, tidying up the ship. 'What matters is what I can procure in terms of heading back to the isle. Not beds, not food, but ships and men and weapons. We have to rescue Jael. Don't forget that now.'

That silenced everyone, though Kolarov had to pinch his lips together to stop any contrary thoughts from escaping his mouth.

'You needn't worry,' Thorgils assured the man. 'The Dragos' will have fond memories of us Islanders. I'm sure they'll lay on a warm welcome.' Hearing a snort from Fyn, he smiled, thinking of the night Jael had set fire to Hest's harbour.

Jael Furyck, he thought, still smiling.

Wherever she was and whatever she was doing, he hoped she was causing some trouble.

***

'I've just been to see Quint. The commander wants us working through the night until the funeral,' Alek told Jael as he joined her at the top of the tower. 'So I'm going to make a new roster.'

'Through the night? But how will anyone see?' Jael wondered, and though the thought of what such a schedule would do to the already under pressure slaves, the darkness would provide opportunities for her and Alek not afforded by revealing daylight.

'Lamps are on the way. Quint's having more braziers brought in from the city too. We'll do our best. And you? How are you finding it up here?'

'Informative. It's been very informative,' Jael murmured, and inclining her head, she moved further along the scaffolding, feeling the wooden planks bouncing beneath her feet. She'd never had a problem with heights before, though that lack of concern was being sorely tested by her precarious new occupation. 'On your roster, find time for us to be together. Surely there's a task we could do side by side? Anything?'

Alek stared at Jael, seeing the last of the sun reflected in her green eyes. 'You'll help us then? You'll lead us?'

She didn't blink. 'Roster us together, and we can talk about what's on my mind.' And now she smiled, feeling a familiar tremor of urgency emerge from her grief-stricken stupor.

Ideas had been percolating for days, and finally, she was ready to make a plan.

CHAPTER FOURTEEN

As he reached the wide swathe of steps leading up to Hest's stone castle, Eadmund stopped, turning back to his friends, running his eyes over those who had trekked from the harbour. Two servants scurried out to greet them, but ignoring them, Eadmund pointed to Thorgils, Fyn, Mattie and Kolarov. 'You four come with me. Bolder, see that everyone else is watered and fed. I'll see what I can do about somewhere to stay.' Then, thinking again, eyes on Arras, he pointed at the man. 'You'd better come too. Your insight will be important.'

Turning back to the castle, Eadmund felt his shoulders tightening as he mounted the steps, trying to think of what he would say to Karsten. Of how to say it.

'Eadmund? My lord?'

An older man emerged through the castle doors, stopping abruptly. He was finely dressed, though his grey hair was shaggy, and he carried himself without the poise of one raised in a castle.

Eadmund started. 'Ulf? Is that you?'

Ulf Rutgar, formerly of Brekka, emerged from the shadows of the castle into the golden evening, seeing more familiar faces lined up behind the King of Oss. 'Yes, still here! Not sure how Bayla has kept me prisoner for so long, but I seem too content to leave. I've been put in charge of the fleet, you know. About time, I must say. That shit Ludwig Berner died in a knife fight, though he was never the right man for the post.' Realising he was rambling, Ulf blinked. 'You're here for the wedding? You did know it's taking place in Angard?' Now he looked around. 'And where's Jael?'

Hearing his wife's name, Eadmund swallowed, though there was some hope in that familiar old face, some hope in being in the presence of allies once again, and he smiled. 'Well, that's why we're here, Ulf. Jael's in trouble, and we... need some help.'

***

Axl walked up the path to his grandmother's cottage, feeling strange.

He remembered coming here as a child with Jael and Aleksander. They'd usually been forced to take him with them, and they'd always let him know how much of an inconvenience that was.

He remembered how Edela would fling open her door with a big smile and then open her arms for a bigger hug. This place had always felt safe and nurturing. In the hall, his mother had often been miserable or sharp-tongued, and his father had been in a hurry, barely glancing his way. But in Edela's cottage, he'd always felt seen and heard.

The boy, Linas, opened the door, cocking his head to one side. He had an uneven haircut, much like his grandmother. As though she had taken a blade to it in the dark. There were patches where she'd gone too close to his scalp, Axl could see, and he smiled sympathetically at the cheerful boy.

'Are you the king?' Linas wondered.

'Yes, I am.'

'But where's your crown?'

'Back in my chamber, as it happens. Sometimes I forget to wear it.'

Linas didn't welcome him inside, for he had many more

questions, though his grandmother soon yanked him away from the door. 'Move yourself, boy, and let the king in. His questions are more important than yours.' Now Helga opened the door wide, ushering Axl inside.

He almost gasped. Though the cottage appeared just as Edela had left it, it no longer smelled like his grandmother. He saw the fur-lined chair by the fire, the stool waiting before it and felt an overwhelming longing to see her again.

'You want to know about your family, I expect,' Helga said in that blunt way of hers. 'Well, I've seen one or two things, so you'd better sit down.'

***

Edela's strange feeling continued as she made herself at home in the smelly back room of The Crescent Moon. The taverner's grandson, Zen, had been quiet but helpful, bringing in a small round table, which wobbled, and giving it a wipe. Siggy tried to balance the table while Zen disappeared, returning with four stools of varying heights.

'Do you have any cloth?' Edela wondered. 'Something to make it look...nicer?' Despite Zen's attempts to clean it, she saw stains and holes in the table. 'Anything?'

'I'll see what my grandfather has upstairs,' Zen said, smiling at Edela before disappearing again. Though he was soon back with an armload of fabric, which Siggy helped Edela sift through. They chose an ivory-coloured muslin for the table and scraps of thicker, woollen cloth for the four stools.

Siggy asked Zen if he had a cushion or sheepskin, for she wanted Edela to sit in comfort, and Edela requested more lamps and candles, seeking to brighten the dingy chamber.

And eventually, they were ready.

Bertel returned with his new sword, promptly sent on his way by the two dreamers, who didn't want him frightening Edela's customers. Though he was soon put to work by the taverner, who offered him ale in return for keeping a watch outside the back room door.

Edela settled down on her cushioned stool, smiling at Siggy, who sat in the corner braiding her hair. 'This is hardly what I should be teaching you,' she admitted ruefully. 'And not what dreamers were born to do, though we must eat! We'll certainly be no use without food.'

Siggy agreed, remembering that delicious bread. It had been dusted with spices she could still taste when she licked her lips. It almost made up for the horrible rat stew. She shuddered. 'And then we can leave.'

'Leave? You have plans, do you? Something you've seen? Somewhere we must be?' Edela's eyes snapped to the door, which opened, revealing a man and woman. The woman was barely more than a girl, the man a brutish sort of lump. And quickly assessing the situation, Edela offered her customers some wine. Though not understanding the common tongue, they stared blankly at her.

Zen appeared from behind the man.

'I'm to translate for you, madam!' he announced loudly, repeating this in the Zagoran tongue before boldly winking at Siggy and taking his place behind Edela.

She turned to peer at him, flapping a hand to move him away. 'Over there, I think, by Siggy.' And ignoring the girl's horrified look, she turned back to the couple with a beaming smile. 'Please, do sit and tell me how I can help you.'

***

The Dragos family had just finished supper, retiring to a chamber off the hall, when Ulf brought the news of their unexpected visitors.

Bayla Dragos, the king's mother and a former Queen of Hest herself, scrunched up her face in confusion. 'Did they not read their invitation?' she sneered. 'It certainly does not say come to The City. What are they here for? What do they want?' Eyeing her heavily pregnant daughter-in-law, Meena, she hoped for some insight, though despite being a dreamer, the silly girl remained a mostly mute irritant who trembled and shook around her.

Tidying up her shoulder-length silvery-blonde hair and dabbing a napkin at the corners of her mouth, Bayla eyed her eldest son.

King Karsten Dragos was just as surprised, though ignoring his mother's enquiring look, he urged Ulf to take his guests into the hall. His younger, one-armed brother, Berard, joined him, followed by an uptight Bayla, leaving Ulf to help Meena to her feet.

They trekked from the chamber into the hall, where their bedraggled guests huddled near the massive stone hearth, warming their hands before a blazing fire almost taller than they were.

'Islanders!' Karsten called cheerfully, adjusting his eye patch. 'You have come!'

Eadmund and Thorgils turned with smiles, and soon the men embraced.

Karsten glanced past them in surprise. 'But no Jael? Don't tell me you've managed to get another child on her?' He laughed, eyeing Eadmund. 'Perhaps you're skilled in magic yourself?'

More greetings followed between Eadmund and Bayla, Berard, and Meena, and when that was done, Eadmund completed his own introductions, and soon Bayla's steward was organising wine.

'My mother is concerned that you Islanders can't read,' Karsten said with a straight face. 'That you misunderstood the wedding invitation.'

Hearing a snorting Thorgils behind him, Eadmund turned to the former queen, who was attempting to conceal her annoyance at her son. A chuckling Ulf took her arm, pulling her close. 'I'm afraid we haven't come for the wedding but for something less celebratory.'

Meena gasped, holding her belly. 'Jael!'

Her husband, Berard, frowned at her before turning to Eadmund. 'What's happened to Jael?'

All eyes were soon on Eadmund, who saw flickers of past visits here with his wife – not all of them pleasant. 'She was kidnapped.' He felt rather than saw Arras Sikari's eyes on him. 'In Tuura. Edela disappeared, and Jael went after her, and then... she was taken.'

Meena gasped again.

Ulf looked worried. 'What sort of disappeared?' Having lived in Andala for many years, he was particularly fond of the old dreamer.

'I don't know. Tuura was attacked by Silurans, and during the attack Edela seems to have vanished.' Again Eadmund felt Arras' eyes on him, knowing he hadn't spent nearly enough time asking the man what he knew about the events in Tuura. 'In her search for Edela, Jael was kidnapped, transported to an island in the Valgeir Sea. She's being held there.'

'For ransom?' Berard asked.

Only Karsten was still smiling, his smirking face more deeply lined than when Eadmund had last seen him. The worries of being a king, he imagined, feeling them himself. He sighed. 'No.' He motioned for Arras to come forward. 'This is the man who took her.' That evinced a murmur of horrified surprise from the Hestians.

Arras looked embarrassed and uncomfortable in the presence of two kings, both glowering at him.

'And he's not in chains? Or in the sea?' Karsten wondered with a growl. 'He took your wife, and he still breathes?'

'He did, though she ended up saving him,' Eadmund explained. 'They were escaping the isle together, but Jael remained behind, saving Arras and his family. She sacrificed herself for him, but she's still there.'

The fire spat a spark at Mattie, who flicked it away, blushing as everyone turned to her with questions in their eyes. She edged closer to Kolarov, whose head was up, eyes bright, hoping to be invited into the conversation.

'What island?' Ulf asked. 'Where?'

Eadmund indicated for Arras to speak.

'It's called S'ala Nis. Ruled by Queen Kalina Sardis and before her by her father, Ronin.'

'I've heard of it,' Ulf said.

Karsten nodded. 'And him. Though the King of Silura had nothing nice to say about him.'

'They were rivals,' Arras added.

'And you kidnapped Jael for your king?' Karsten wanted to know.

'For my queen,' Arras admitted, strengthening his voice. 'They took me from my home in Silura before I was even a man, made me a slave, though I fought for my freedom and became a commander. But I was never truly free on the isle. I sought to escape so I could give my son a better life. And yes, I am only here because of Jael, so I will do anything to help her.'

'So you want ships?' Karsten concluded, his one eye snapping to Eadmund. 'My ships? And my men to sail them?'

'But we are leaving for Angard in seven days!' Bayla blurted out, sensing where this was going. Her son had been champing at the bit for months, seeking anything to delay his impending nuptials, and now perhaps he saw a way to do just that. 'The wedding!'

Both Karsten and Berard cringed, and dropping her eyes, Meena shuffled awkwardly, cradling her pregnant belly.

Only Ulf looked unconcerned by Bayla's screeching. 'Though Karsten can spare a few ships,' he told her with an encouraging smile. 'We were never taking the fleet to Angard.'

Arras glanced at Eadmund, who spoke. 'We have one ship. We left Osterland in one ship, though we need more than a few. I thought...'

Karsten looked torn, shifting his weight from one leg to the other.

'You owe Jael,' Thorgils reminded him sharply. 'You're here, a walking, talking, breathing king solely because of her. You owe her more than a few ships, Karsten Dragos.'

'I'm well aware of my debt!' Karsten snapped, glowering up at the big red-headed man. 'You think I've forgotten what she did? I promise you, I remember that moment every day of my life. Every night I close my eye.' It was an admission he'd barely made to himself, and admitting it in public made him furious. 'But I have a commitment to this wedding. I have no choice but to go. Two kingdoms are holding their breath for this fucking marriage. When it's done, though...'

'How many ships will you need?' Berard wondered, eyeing his wife. Meena was a dreamer, though still not an experienced or confident one, and she rarely volunteered any visions. Despite her love for him and her happiness in the castle, the trauma of her life before Berard still kept her prisoner.

'There is a dreamer,' Meena whispered, staring at the flagstones.

Bayla rolled her eyes. 'Isn't there always!' She spied a familiar figure amongst those visitors huddled around the fire. 'I know you. Come, come, let me see you!'

Kolarov barrelled forward with gleaming eyes. 'My lady, yes.' He bowed deeply, one hand on his blue hat, which, straightening up, he swept from his bald head. 'Kolarov Radic, explorer extraordinaire –'

Karsten cut the man off, looking at Eadmund. 'You wish to topple this queen? Is that your intention, or do you want to slip in and out? To take Jael and escape?'

'We've tried that,' Eadmund told him, exhaustion flooding

his body. The warmth of the chamber had surprised him, the taste of the wine, the meaty smell of the Dragos' evening meal still lingering in the hall. He had spent days frozen by tension and an always bitter wind, and now, in the castle, surrounded by allies, maybe even friends, he felt his body almost collapsing around him.

He eyed Arras, then Thorgils. 'No, this time, we'll be going in the front door.'

***

Helga spoke of Jael as though she knew her.

It was unsettling, Axl thought, watching the dreamer propped up like a boulder before him in his grandmother's favourite chair.

'I sense that she was lured away by magic.'

'Magic?' Leaning forward, Axl was surprised. 'Why do you say that?'

'Because she is a smart woman, an experienced warrior. To have walked into a trap with all her senses working? I can't imagine you think that possible?'

Axl supposed not.

'And after she was taken, there has been no sign of her. You say this dreamer, Ayla, that she found a wall when she searched for her? Such walls are only erected by dreamers. Those who understand how to shield and hide what they wish to remain secret.'

'Ayla suspected as much.'

Helga grunted, jerking her head towards Linas, who hurried to add another log to the fire.

Axl was hoping it would slowly die. He was melting.

Helga narrowed her eyes. 'Your sister and grandmother will free themselves. They are dreamers, and in your sister's case, a warrior. They are the only ones equipped to undertake such a rescue. I am not here for them. I am here for you. Linas, boy, bring me my box.'

Linas scurried away, as obedient as a well-trained dog, promptly returning with a scuffed wooden box. Taking it onto her lap, Helga opened the lid, lifting up a bronze amulet hanging from a plain leather cord. 'You must wear this.'

Now Axl narrowed his eyes.

'Doubt me all you like, but know that my life was in the forest. My freedom too. I do not like people, do not wish to live around them. I like the quiet and my own company. I mostly like the boy's company, but I did not come here for me. The Furycks are no friends to Tuurans, though without them? I see no one else capable of standing up to our enemies.' Helga jerked the amulet at Axl, who finally took it, studying it carefully.

On one side, he saw an image of a man holding what appeared to be a spear.

On the other, an intricate knot of symbols – nothing he had seen before.

'What does it do?'

'It keeps you safe from danger, of course. Not the danger you will see coming but that which you won't. Keep it on you at all times. Wear it around your neck, next to your heart. This I offer you as a form of protection.'

Looking up, Axl wanted to see a comforting smile giving him confidence, though instead, he saw grubby Helga glowering at him with beady eyes.

It was hard to trust the woman, though what choice did he have?

So, with a nod and a sigh, Axl slipped the amulet over his head.

***

After sitting at her table for many hours, seeing a steady stream of customers, Edela was desperate to stand and stretch out her back. It was cramping in a most uncomfortable way. Her right leg too. She wiggled her toes, shifting around on the cushion as Zen ushered her next customer into the tiny room. The candles were either burning low, or she was growing blind, for the man appeared shrouded in darkness. She blinked, hoping to sharpen her vision, though everything only became blurrier as Zen led the hooded man to a stool.

More men attempted to enter the room, past an indignant Bertel, though the man urged them to remain outside, nodding at Siggy, who poured him a cup of wine. She felt a great responsibility for Edela, who looked like a tiny grandmother hunched over the table. Though, she reminded herself, that grandmother had ably defended them on their dangerous adventure. They were all still standing because of Edela, so whoever sought to trouble her was likely to bring trouble on themselves.

'Please, do make yourself comfortable,' Edela smiled at the man, hoping to encourage him to remove his hood. She wanted to look in his eyes, to see his face, for there was already something about him that troubled her.

Zen translated her words into Zagoran, though the man held up a hand. 'No need. I understand perfectly.'

His voice sent a chill up Edela's spine, and she watched as he drew back his hood, revealing a thick head of dark hair, liberally oiled. He wore a short beard, covering much of the lower half of his face, which remained in shadow. He was incredibly still with his body. Commanding.

It was as though he was in control, Edela realised, becoming unsettled now.

'I am Inga,' she said. 'A wise woman from the North.'

'Inga? Is that so?' the man smiled. 'And where in the North are you from, Inga? Hest? No, you don't look Hestian to me. Perhaps further north than that? As far as Tuura?'

Edela held his eyes, feeling her insides clench into a fist. 'You are a well-travelled man.'

'Did you see that about me? Have we begun?' The man placed his hands on the table, turning them over. 'Do you need to look?'

'At your hands?' Edela became acutely aware of Siggy hovering nearby. The girl's heartbeat had quickened, matching her own. 'Yes. May I see?' The man nodded, and she took his right hand, holding it gently.

A burst of light blinded her, and she heard a great buzzing in her ears.

'But why kill the dreamers?' someone asked.

'Not for us to question,' came another voice. 'They're the queen's orders. She wants them all dead, so we kill them. All of them.' He sounded almost gleeful at the prospect.

'And you?' the first man asked. 'What did the queen task you to do, Iker Rayas?'

Now Edela saw the man with branded cheeks, eyes glowing like lumps of coal. 'I am to kill the one they call Edela Saeveld.'

Eyes springing open, Edela dropped the man's hand.

'Is something wrong?' he purred, a hint of a smile playing around his hairy lips.

Hearing Edela's voice in her ears, a surprised Siggy quickly aimed for the door.

The man turned to her. 'Where are you going, girl?'

Siggy froze. 'To get... more wine. I won't be long, sir.'

Slipping around the table, she grabbed the door handle, pulling it open to two burly men who blocked her path. They looked familiar, she realised suddenly, swinging back to Edela.

'Though I've had enough wine,' the man said, returning his eyes to the dreamer. 'Finally, I have everything I want right here before me. There's no need to go anywhere. Not now we're all together.'

There was a commotion as the two men at the door moved aside to make room for a now weaponless Bertel Knutson, who was shoved inside, falling onto Siggy. She cried out in surprise as the men moved back into position, closing the door and blocking it.

'As I was saying,' the man at the table purred darkly. 'Now that we're all together, let us begin...'

CHAPTER FIFTEEN

Karsten took Eadmund and Thorgils into his private chamber, leaving his family to entertain the rest of their guests. His mother tended to override every conversation with her demands, and Berard had gained his own voice since the death of their father. Sometimes their interference was too much, especially with the wedding around the corner.

'You need to take a moment,' he insisted as Eadmund swung around to him with blazing eyes. He held up a hand. 'And what, you think I'm wrong here? Being patient?' Laughing bitterly, he eyed Thorgils. 'I remember being stuck in Andala, going out of my mind, watching people I loved die. I remember what it felt like to scratch the walls with the need to do something. You're the one who held me back, Thorgils. You told me to wait it out, to be patient. And you were right, weren't you, in the end?' He turned to Eadmund, who paced the chamber like a wolf. 'To do it properly is what your wife would advise. You remember her, the one with all the plans? How carefully did she plot out attacking Skorro? You can't think she was wrong to take that time?'

'Says the most impatient man in the world!' Thorgils scoffed, seeing threads of silver glinting in Karsten's long blonde hair. He had grown it out over the years, and it gave him a more regal appearance; older, too, he thought distractedly.

'And what if it was your wife?' Eadmund added. 'You'd hardly sit on your hands if it was this Freya Valens.'

Karsten laughed, topping up his goblet. He studied the burgundy liquid with disinterest, swilling it around before turning back to his guests. 'I'd let them keep the bitch,' he grinned. 'They could have her with my permission and a chest of gold!'

'So it's no love match then?' Thorgils suggested.

Karsten threw back the wine and immediately refilled his goblet. 'A king needs heirs, and for that, a king needs a queen. I've no choice in the matter.' His easy demeanour vanished, replaced by a look of sadness. 'When my son died, I...' Gulping down more wine, he took a moment to compose himself. 'I have one son left, one heir, and he was desperately ill last winter. Whatever that plague was, it took my nephew, Valder, too. I realised I couldn't keep going, hoping...' His words became stilted, his thoughts elsewhere. 'A king must have sons,' he ended abruptly. 'So prim and proper Freya Valens it is!' He eyed Eadmund with more sympathy then. 'I want to help you, but we must do it properly. You can't afford to fail again.'

Eadmund's chest rose and fell, the stem of the goblet cold in his hand. Thinking about what Arras had done, he wanted to snap that stem in two.

Though it wouldn't help. Arras had followed orders.

Then tried to help Jael escape.

He scratched his head. 'I need to organise beds. I've a crew of tired men out there. I need to see to them.'

'Of course. I'll find my steward and he can organise a meal too. I'm sure there's something Berard hasn't stuffed into his little mouth. Or Meena. She eats like a wild boar when she's pregnant.' Karsten became thoughtful again, eye shifting to the door. 'We'll talk more about what to do and what's possible. I can't get out of this wedding, but I'll do what I can, I promise.'

Eadmund wanted to scream, but instead, he nodded.

Karsten placed a hand on his arm. 'It's Jael,' he reminded the king. 'No matter what you think or fear, never forget who your wife is.'

***

It wasn't any cooler as Jael and Alek met that evening on the mostly finished southern side of the tower. Alek's crew had been assigned their tasks, and in the darkness, there was a silent rhythm about the work. Few spoke, as those who had been rostered to work through the night were long past exhausted, struggling to coordinate their bodies and minds.

'This slave revolt of yours...' she began with a grin.

'Will work,' he cut in, seeing only shadows on her face.

'A battle where the attacking side has no weapons requires coordination,' Jael said in a hushed voice. 'And that's a challenge while there's a dreamer in the palace. And the new seer,' she added. 'What is he? I'd heard that Noor wasn't a dreamer, but he spoke into my mind.'

A surprised Alek blinked at her. 'But the stones we have stop anyone spying on us, don't they? Including the dreamer?'

'In theory. I think so.' Still, Jael glanced around. 'I'll make more, and you can distribute them to those you trust. You have to keep talking and planning with your allies.'

'Of course. I've told them all about you. They're ready.'

Jael sighed. 'To attempt this, you need to be fully aware of what failure would mean, Alek. I don't appear to be someone they want to kill, so my life likely won't be in danger if we attempt this, but yours will. Yours and whichever men are caught, especially any leaders.' Hearing a noise, she popped up her head, but seeing only cats chasing each other across the courtyard, she bent back down. 'You need to be sure this is something you want to do. To risk dying?'

'I'll die here if I don't try,' Alek told her in desperation. 'I've watched my brother die and my friends. If I'm to die, too, then so be it, but I'll have no chance of ever seeing my sons again, of ever tasting freedom if I don't try.'

'And what about your wife?' Jael wondered, realising that

he'd never spoken of her.

Alek looked away. 'I imagine my wife has a new life now and certainly a new husband. She never wanted to marry me. Not me. She wanted a family, to be prosperous and respected, though I see now that she simply grew impatient with being married to a craftsman. I thought I could earn the fortune she so desperately desired, trying my hand at trading, that I could convince her to be happy somehow. I loved her once, though the truth is, she never loved me.'

'I'm sorry.'

Alek shook his head. 'I only hope my boys are alive. I don't want to leave them in that woman's hands.'

'Well, if you're determined to do this, then the funeral is the best opportunity we could hope for. To gather so many slaves in one place? It's not a smart move... for them.'

'There's no Arras Sikari anymore. Likely he'd see things that way and consider a different approach, though Kosta's a man who barely sees out of one eye, and that one's always fixed on petty squabbles. He lost overall command of the isle because of his inability to manage his men. He's a bully, not a leader.'

'Well, I hope that remains the case. That no one points out the risk he's taking, packing so many slaves in here.'

'Mmmm, hopefully not.'

'The soldiers will be distracted, watching the sacrifice. It's not something you can look away from. There'll be drumming and chanting and blood... enough to take their minds off what's happening behind them,' Jael mused. 'So we just need a signal, and the slaves will overpower the soldiers here. If we can get enough weapons quickly, we'll drive the momentum in our favour, push them onto the back foot. Though they won't stay there long if we don't work quickly. And effectively.'

'So you agree then, we attack at the funeral?'

'Yes,' Jael whispered, feeling the certainty of that settling within her now. 'At the funeral, we take back our freedom.'

***

Edela tried to delay whatever the branded man, Iker Rayas, was planning, hoping to get some answers.

Chest tightening, legs trembling, she sought to press him. 'You were sent here by who?' The man's surprise froze his momentum, and Edela quickly ploughed on. 'There is little chance of me escaping,' she smiled sadly. 'In fact...' And now her eyes met Bertel's. 'I see no chance.' He visibly shuddered. 'But I've been running from you for some time now, and I would like to know why.'

The man rested his elbows on the table, grinning at her. 'You think I'm privy to that information? Ha! If you're such a famous dreamer, why not see for yourself? Here,' he offered, holding out his right hand. 'Try again. You might be able to see what I don't know.'

Edela nodded, clasping that big hand.

Bertel's tension overflowed like a bucket of water, though seeing the taverner's grandson and poor Siggy, he sought to calm himself, to remember the warrior he'd once been. Thirty years ago, he would have felt confident taking all three men on, weaponless as he was. Now, he feared he would only end up getting them all killed.

He remembered the attic room in Esby, the symbol on the floor and the bloody-eyed bodies lying in a heap.

And the little dreamer presiding over them all.

And clenching his fist, he willed Edela on.

***

In the castle hall, Berard Dragos had helped his wife into a chair, bringing pillows to make her more comfortable. And helping himself to another goblet of wine, he'd sat down beside her while she chatted to the dreamer.

Mattie Bilso.

'Did you know Edela?' Berard interrupted, then sensing that neither dreamer wanted his company, he stood, eyeing the men. 'Meena has visited Tuura and Andala many times. She's met Edela. A very giving woman.'

Mattie shook her head. 'No, though I knew her name.'

Now Berard took his leave. 'I do hope they find her,' he said. 'Jael is especially fond of her grandmother.'

'Have you seen anything yourself?' Mattie wondered when Berard had gone. He seemed like a kind man, though his constant fussing hadn't offered his shy wife a chance to speak. She was an odd creature, timid yet determined, Mattie thought, sensing strength in the woman, though it appeared trapped behind a great barrier of fear.

Smiling wryly, she imagined the same could be said about her.

Meena looked uncertain. 'My dreams have been different lately,' she confessed. 'I used to see glimpses of this or that, but recently, I've been having the same dream. Different versions of the same dream. Don't tell Berard, he does tend to worry, but I've, I've been dreaming of volcanoes.'

Mattie was taken aback. 'Volcanoes? Are there volcanoes here? In Hest?'

Meena shrugged. 'Possibly, though I don't believe it's something that *will* happen. I don't get that sense at all.'

She didn't say any more, fussing with the sleeve of her voluminous gown. She was exquisitely dressed, though despite her jewels and her gown, made of fine silk and embellished with delicate patternwork, there was a wildness about her, crowned by a mop of frizzy red hair.

Having heard Mattie's appraisal of her, a frowning Meena sat up straighter. 'I was at the Vale of the Gods and not by choice.

What happened that day makes me fear the power of dreamers and gods. I watched my own family consumed by dreams of power. Berard's brother too. Karsten and Bayla are always asking what I see, what I think, though I don't want to open the door to those answers. For what lies beyond?' Shuddering, she clutched her belly, blinking rapidly. 'You wouldn't understand, you can't, unless you've seen how dark this world can be. How truly cruel and evil.'

Mattie, who had only just started embracing her own powers, felt disturbed. She had been excited to meet a fellow dreamer, wanting to talk about what had happened on the ship, but now she felt reluctant to speak of it.

'I have children,' Meena went on to explain. 'This will be our third. A girl. We will have three daughters, and I must shield them from this world. I was, I, I...'

Leaning forward, Mattie patted her hand. 'You have been through a lot. I sense that, at least. I only want to know more so I can help, not hurt anyone. Not claim anything for myself.'

Meena narrowed her bulbous eyes. 'But you know that isn't true, and being a dreamer, so do I. The path you're walking down will trip you up, but maybe by then, it will be too late? I have known dark dreamers, old crones, menacing witches, and those raised from the dead to become something even worse. And in the beginning, I'm certain they were just like you and me, searching for something they truly thought mattered. But darkness is an enemy cloaked as a friend, and once you welcome it in, it infests you, breeds within you, and then it is you. Please, I beg you, turn away from this path now, Mattie, before it is too late. Before you become one of them...'

***

Edela held Iker Rayas' hand, eyes closed, seeking to trap him, hoping to mine whatever information she could before she killed him. Just the thought of it was horrifying, but she had to keep Bertel and Siggy safe. She had to –

Eyes springing open, she turned as Zen whipped a knife from his belt and flung it at the branded man's face, striking him in the eye. 'No!' she shouted, seeing the two men guarding Bertel draw their swords, charging at the boy. Though one quickly saw that as a mistake and turned back to keep an eye on the old man.

A panicking Siggy unsheathed her own knife and flung it at the man, missing him entirely and hitting the door, just above Bertel's head. Yanking the knife out of the door, Bertel drove it up into the man's throat. He jerked back, gurgling, trying to lift his sword, but kicking it out of his hand, Bertel sent it flying. Squinting in the dark room, he saw the bulky shadow of the branded man rising to his feet with a bellowing howl, lunging for Edela, and a screaming Siggy trying to pull Zen out of the path of a scything sword.

Everything slowed to a blur, Bertel's thoughts extending from him like long threads as he sought to pick his next step.

'Save the boy!' Edela yelled, falling off her stool with a thump.

'Edela!' Bertel moved with speed now, ducking under the arm of the gurgling man, scooping up his sword, and in two steps, he'd driven it into Iker's man's back. The man gasped, swinging around in surprise, sword vibrating in a shuddering hand.

Siggy dragged Zen away, urging him towards Edela, who was crawling away from Iker Rayas. Knife jammed in his eye, blood coursing down his cheek, he chopped wildly with his sword.

Edela couldn't think. She'd fallen onto her side, hitting her head so hard that her ears rang like bells. No thought would come to her, and certainly no symbols.

The door was flung open, banging against the wall, Iker Rayas was looming above her, and more men were fighting in the tavern.

She could hear screams now, clashing blades and furniture smashing.

So could Zen, who fell to his knees beside Edela, dodging Iker's blade. Though Iker wanted the old woman more than the boy, and sensing that, Edela urged Zen to leave. 'Run!' she croaked, unsure if anyone could hear her. She could barely hear herself, though she could see images of what was unfolding in the tavern, and rising to her knees, she tried to urge everyone to follow her.

'Aarrghh!' Siggy cried, kicked by Iker Rayas, who turned to slash his blade at the irritating boy blocking his path to Edela.

Edela felt a hand on her back, and swinging around, arms extended, she was surprised to see a bloody-faced Korri Torluffson bending down, pulling her to her feet.

'We've got to get you out of here!' he urged, eyes sweeping the back room. One man was down, bleeding from the throat. Another, bigger man had a sword in his back, but he was still going, using his own sword to try and kill Bertel. He saw the tavern boy, Zen, and Siggy, and a gruesome-looking man with a knife in his eye who looked ready to kill them all. 'Bertel!' Korri bellowed. 'Forget him! We have to go!'

Bertel swung around in surprise, and feeling a cool breeze of relief wash over him at the sight of the Alekkan, he kicked his attacker in the balls and hurried towards Zen and Siggy.

Korri helped a stumbling Edela through the door.

Her ears were buzzing so loudly that she knew she would soon faint. She tried to turn her head, wanting to see Siggy and Bertel. And Zen. That boy didn't deserve to get trapped in the middle of their mess.

She caught a glimpse of Bertel's tall shadow, watching as he swung a punch at the back of Iker Rayas' head.

And then, feeling Korri's strength like a wall beside her, she sagged against him.

The tavern was a battleground and seemingly on fire, and though Korri's men were under attack from the Silurans, there was little he could do but try to get the dreamer and her friends to safety. He was useful with a sword but no great warrior. His men didn't need him as much as the dreamer did.

Edela had gone limp, her eyes closed, and sheathing his sword, Korri bent down, throwing her over his shoulder. 'Bertel! *Hurry*!' he yelled, seeing Bertel shoving the two teenagers ahead of him, out of the back room.

Zen staggered to a stop, seeing the chaos in the tavern, the great battle unfolding, flames licking a corner wall where someone had tipped over a lamp. 'Grandfather!' he panicked, ducking a flying knife and heading for the counter.

'Zen!' Siggy called, ready to go after him, but Bertel held her back.

'We have to get out of here! Now!'

'But he tried to save us!' Siggy implored, and seeing Bertel rolling his eyes, she held her ground.

They were jostled by fighting men, and pulling Siggy close, Bertel hissed in her ear. 'Well, hurry up then!' And bending down, he yanked an axe out of a dead man's back. One of Korri's, he saw, recognising the tattooed scalp. 'Hurry!' Eyes on the back room door, he saw no one coming after them, though he didn't imagine that would remain the case for long.

Zen cried out, holding his face in horror, and then he was gone from view, lost behind the counter.

Jugs were being brandished as weapons, ale and wine splashing everywhere.

Siggy slid over, falling onto her knees just in time to avoid a man who'd been launched into the air. Bertel jerked to a stop, waiting until the way was clear before dragging Siggy back to her feet. Though shaking him off, she hurried behind the tavern counter, where she saw a sobbing Zen lying over his grandfather's body. It was dark, though the flames revealed that the old man was dead. His eyes were wide open, staring lifelessly at him.

Bertel felt sympathy for the boy, but swinging around, he could no longer see Korri and Edela, and he tugged Siggy's arm.

'We have to go!'

Siggy reached for Zen, watching the flames surging across the ceiling. 'You can't help your grandfather now! He'd want you to live! Come with us! *Please*! You'll die here!'

Zen was ready to; his grandfather was everything to him. Everything.

Though the girl was right. So, leaning down to kiss his grandfather's head, Zen unbuckled the old man's belt, replete with knives and pouches. And crawling now, tears streaming down his face, he felt around until he found a loose floorboard. Lifting it, he retrieved a satchel, and with one look at his grandfather, he turned to Siggy and Bertel. 'Let's go.'

CHAPTER SIXTEEN

Eadmund had been shown to a chamber by Bayla Dragos, who was as uptight as ever. She reserved her smiles for Ulf alone, it seemed, for she was dull-eyed and frowning as she motioned to the bed.

'I'm sure you'll find everything you need. Though if not, just ask. We are so busy preparing for the wedding, but someone will be able to assist you, I'm sure.'

She turned to go, but holding out a hand, Eadmund stopped her. 'I am grateful,' he said haltingly. He thought to say more but felt overwhelmed by sadness.

He had stayed in this chamber with Jael.

He remembered it well.

Bayla's face appeared to soften before him, though she remained as stiff as before. 'Your wife has a quality about her that few possess. A pig-headedness perhaps?' And now she offered half a smile. 'I doubt she is sitting on that island waiting for you to come. I imagine she's busy making her own plans.'

Eadmund returned the half smile, nodding as he followed Bayla to the door, and when she was gone, he closed it. Boots stuck to the flagstones, he stood there for some time, resting his head against the door.

The fire behind him wasn't needed, for it was a warm evening, but its gentle crackle reminded him of home. Of his bedchamber and his family, his chair and his horse. His children and his wife most of all.

Life was so fragile, so easily shattered. And once broken, could the pieces ever be put back together as they once were, or did the scars left by what had broken make it impossible? Tears came, and finally, truly alone, Eadmund didn't stop them. They fell from his eyes onto the pale stone beneath his feet, splashing his dirty boots.

He smiled. Bayla Dragos was right.

His wife was pig-headed – more stubborn than anyone he'd ever met.

Now he laughed, and straightening up, he wiped his eyes and turned to look at the bed, seeing himself lying there and Jael moving on top of him, her black hair sweeping over her breasts, eyes glowing like emeralds.

She was wild and unpredictable.

His.

He shook his head, knowing that tears wouldn't bring his wife home. And nor, by the sound of things, would Karsten Dragos and his fleet.

So it was time to make another plan.

***

Korri quickly hashed out a plan, and when Bertel, Siggy, and the boy came charging after him and Edela, he led them down the nearest alley to where he'd earlier purchased a pair of boots. He had taken a liking to the shoemaker – a confident woman who had recently taken over the business from her deceased father. She had fitted him out with the most comfortable pair of boots he'd ever owned, and now he hoped she would provide them with a place to hide.

Banging on the door, he jiggled a still-unconscious Edela

over his left shoulder.

'Put her down,' Bertel urged, squinting at the dreamer. The alley was narrow and dark, few lamps lighting up windows or hanging from doorways, and he couldn't see anything more than shadows on her face. 'Let me see.'

A nodding Korri lay Edela on the ground, turning back as a tiny shutter opened in the door. And soon, the door itself was opened.

'Is something wrong with your boots?' the shoemaker asked in surprise, a leather apron tied around her waist, curly brown hair hanging loose around a tired face. Then glancing past Korri, she saw the old woman lying in the alley, an old man, and two teenagers, and stepping back, she grabbed the door.

'We need somewhere to wait for a few hours,' Korri told her, eyes darting to the end of the alley, certain someone was yelling about a fire. 'Please. Just a few hours.'

The shoemaker's hesitation was only momentary, for the man with the long beard had a trustworthy face, and soon she was ushering them all inside.

***

Berard Dragos couldn't help his fussing.

Meena was quiet, rarely speaking for herself or voicing her own needs, so he felt an obligation to try and anticipate them. Though on nights like this, he had no idea how she might feel or what she might need.

Wriggling in the bed beside him, she was unable to get comfortable. Her pregnant belly had made sleeping a challenge lately, and as she flopped back and forth, it tended to disturb a light-sleeping Berard. He generally gave up trying to sleep until Meena herself was snuffling away beside him.

He often wondered if she was avoiding the dreams that waited for her.

Reaching out his hand, he took hers. 'You haven't said much.'

Her eyes were closed. 'I'm trying to sleep, Berard. Talking doesn't help with that.'

Peering down at her, he saw that she was smiling. 'But did you know they were coming? Eadmund and his friends? Or what happened to Jael? Did you see?'

Meena shook her head, feeling her belly. 'No. I told you I didn't. I didn't.'

'I hope she's alright. I can't believe she let herself get kidnapped. Jael Furyck?' Berard chuckled quietly. 'I imagine she's giving her kidnappers a hard time.'

'That man took her,' Meena reminded him. 'The one downstairs.'

'Mmmm.'

'But he had help.'

Berard propped himself up on his elbow. 'Help? Whose help?'

'A girl with freckles and long blonde hair. She led him to Jael. She showed him the way.'

Berard realised that Meena was almost asleep. Her voice had become strangely liquid. She spoke in stuttering mumbles most of the time, lacking confidence. But here, she sounded dreamlike. He yawned. 'What girl?'

'She's not a girl!' Meena spat suddenly, eyes springing open. 'She's not a girl at all!'

***

Thorgils and Fyn were sharing a chamber with Kolarov, all three men grateful for the comfort of Hestian mattresses, generously stuffed with wool, and plump feathery pillows to rest their weary heads upon.

It made Thorgils wistful for home.

'If Karsten's not going to part with his fleet, we may as well head for Oss tomorrow,' he yawned. 'Unless Eadmund wants to make another midnight escape from Hest?'

Rolling onto his back, Fyn smiled. 'I don't think we'd get very far. We don't have the men to steal more than one ship.'

'Mmmm, so Jael will have to hold on.' Thorgils felt tense at the thought of it. He heard the squeaking noises as a muttering Kolarov adjusted himself in his bed – something that had been going on for some time. 'And you?' he asked, eyes shifting from his cousin to the explorer, whose bed lay along from Fyn's. 'What do you think about our next steps then? What are your plans?'

Kolarov, who needed total silence to fall asleep, sighed loudly. 'I would like sleep! Yes, that's my next step. And yours? To talk all night and keep us awake with your pointless mutterings?'

A surprised Thorgils burst out laughing. 'Well, true. Maybe it's a conversation better saved till morning?'

'I would say so,' Kolarov carried on, though his frown had lessened, for he had found a comfortable spot where his hips didn't ache and his back was supported, and even his legs appeared to have stopped twitching. Closing his eyes, he remained perfectly still, trying to ignore a sudden urgency in his bladder. 'Karsten Dragos is no coward,' he added. 'And as much as the king wants to hurry us all back to S'ala Nis, it won't be easy breaking in. No, I remember thinking how secure its harbour was, how tricky to navigate. And those ballistas!' Eyes springing open, Kolarov wondered if he should simply return home to Castala? Back to his quiet old life, which suddenly didn't seem as dreary as it once had.

'Mattie will help us,' Fyn insisted, eyes closed now, imagining the dreamer peering at him in the darkness as though she could see through every veil he attempted to drape over his weaknesses. She wasn't fooled by his words or bravado. Her inquisitive eyes were sharp and judgemental, though he found himself thinking of them often. They were hazel, bigger than the average eye – like windows into her soul. And once you saw past that sharpness, sadness lingered. A desperate sadness, he thought, becoming sleepy now.

'Well, you might be right about that,' Kolarov conceded. 'A powerful dreamer can be a more useful weapon than an entire army. Or a fleet. With Mattie on our side, those ballistas won't stand a chance.' And smiling now, Kolarov Radic closed his eyes, remembering that great hail of arrows frozen mid-air by the dreamer, who had then thrown them into the sea.

Magic.

It was simply breathtaking.

***

Edela couldn't catch her breath.

When she'd fallen off the stool, she'd landed on her ear, though she also felt a pain in her chest and a shortness of breath as though she'd been running.

Everyone was fussing over her, though she didn't have the strength to tell them to go away. Blinking at Siggy, she sought to reach her.

'We need to give her some space!' Siggy soon called over the chorus. She stood next to Zen in the shoemaker's narrow main room. He slumped on a stool, head in hands. 'She can't breathe!'

Bertel, Korri, and Anna, the shoemaker, turned her way before dropping their eyes to the dreamer.

'Edela?' Bertel touched her shoulder. 'Is she right? Do you want us to step away?'

A silent Edela nodded, grateful when they did. She dropped her head, hands on her knees as Siggy left Zen behind and joined the worried huddle.

'I'm sorry to have burst in on you,' Korri said to Anna, whose plump face was pinched with worry. 'There was an attack at The Crescent Moon.'

Anna's eyes widened, realising where she knew the boy from.

'The taverner was killed,' Korri added softly. 'His customers were attacked, and my friends... they had to fight for their lives.'

Anna looked concerned. 'The city can be a dangerous place, especially at night. You are welcome to stay, and I will organise a drink for your friend. I have something that should revive her.'

Edela watched the woman turn away. She saw Bertel and Korri exchanging worried glances, and beside her, she felt Zen's grief.

Siggy looked frozen in place, those big doe-like eyes full of fear as she turned from one to the other. And though Edela was staring at what lay before her, and who, her mind was back in The Crescent Moon, in that little room, where she had touched Iker Rayas' hand. Shivering, she brought the vision back to her, closing her eyes, wanting to go deeper. To understand what it meant.

A queen wanted to kill all the dreamers.

She had sent men to Osterland to carry out her plan.

Determined men. Warriors.

But why?

And what did it mean for those she loved, like Jael and Ayla? Or her friends in Tuura?

Edela gave only a fleeting thought for herself, though those men who survived the battle at The Crescent Moon would keep hunting her. Of that, she was certain.

Opening her eyes, she saw Bertel watching her, though she looked away, desperate for a moment alone.

***

Jael wanted to go back to sleep.

Her eyes ached, her weary body vibrating with exhaustion. Though try as she might, she couldn't send herself back to sleep.

She knew that soon the roosters would start crowing, the cooks would put on the onions for whichever tasteless broth was on offer today, and the hammering, grunting, groaning noises from the tower would filter in through the sleeping hall's open windows.

She curled her fingers and squeezed as though holding a hand. In her mind, it was Sigmund's, and they were walking to the stables. He loved horses. Bo was scared of them, but Sigmund would have ridden all day if she'd let him. He had a little black pony called Shadow, which Jael was teaching him to ride. She imagined Sigmund's beaming face as he tugged her along, turning back to look up at her with urgent eyes.

So much like Eadmund.

And then Eadmund was before her, and her hands were in his hair, and she was bringing his face towards hers. She closed her eyes, body heavy now, releasing a sigh, muscles softening, feet flopping to the side. Then a smell and a grunt, and a man was over her, reaching a hand under her tunic. She saw the shadow of him in the inky pre-dawn light and immediately flung up her right leg, smashing her ankle fetter into the back of the faceless man's head.

And now she was moving.

Her attacker staggered sideways, and rising to her knees, Jael smashed her wrist fetter into the side of his head, helping him on his way. She hit him hard, grunting, nearly losing her balance with the effort. And now, up on her feet, she stood over the man, snarling.

He didn't move.

Body heaving, Jael wondered if he was even breathing, though eventually, she caught a glimpse of his chest moving up and down. And not sure how she felt about that, she left her bed behind, heading to an open window, needing some air.

A sleepy Alek soon joined her. 'What happened?'

'Some idiot forgot I was armed,' Jael said, brandishing her wrists.

'He tried to touch you?'

'He tried, though he won't try again.'

'He's alive?'

Jael nodded. 'Seems so.'

Alek stroked his stubbly beard, seeing that few had been woken by the disturbance. He hadn't been asleep, his mind whirring with ideas. For though he was always exhausted, he didn't sleep much these days. 'You need to meet someone.'

Turning towards a whispering Alek, Jael frowned. 'Who?'

'Rigg. My friend. My number two for what I've been planning. He took ill, so Quint sent him to the physician's but he'll be back today. He'll help us.'

'And you trust him?'

Alek nodded. 'With my life. He's a little rough around the edges but a good man, I promise.'

Jael heard groaning sounds coming from the direction of her bed. 'And you're sure you want to do this? That you're able to?'

Alek grabbed her arm, feeling her flinch. 'I'll use whatever I have to get out of here. A needle, an elbow, my teeth. I will do anything to crawl out of here, swim out of here, be carried out of here. I just want to go home, Jael. I need to. I won't die here. My boys need me. I'll do what I have to to escape, for them.' He'd hissed with such force that he started coughing, bending over, trapping his face in an arm, not wanting to wake anyone up.

'Though I can't protect you,' she warned. 'If you want me to lead this, then I can't focus on you, Alek. When it begins, whatever it turns out to be, it'll be chaos. Bloodshed, death, panic, fear. A living, breathing nightmare. One you'll have to survive on your own.'

Alek straightened up, pushing back aching shoulders. 'And I will. I promise you, Jael. I will.'

***

Edela woke with a thumping headache and ringing ears, seeing the shoemaker sitting beside her bed, a cup nestled in her hands, eyes closed.

She stifled a yawn, not wanting to wake the poor woman they'd imposed themselves on, but as her mind wandered back to what had happened in the tavern, she was unable to prevent an explosive sneeze.

Anna jerked in fright, spilling hot tea on her knee.

Shaking her head, Edela propped herself up. 'I am sorry,' she said, promptly sneezing again. 'You've got ragweed in that cup, haven't you?'

A nodding Anna smiled, though she remained wary. 'I still don't understand why those men were trying to hurt you. Or if they still want to?' She glanced at her front door, half-expecting blood-drenched warriors to burst in, brandishing axes.

'I imagine they still want to, yes. Though we will not stay. We cannot.' Edela felt chilled to the bone – not by the morning air, which was anything but cool – but by her own fear of what lay waiting outside the door.

Or who.

A thoughtful Anna got up, and heading to her kitchen, she brought back a cup for Edela. 'It's just hot water, though I often find that soothing in itself.'

Smiling at her, Edela saw a faint rim of light around the front door now. 'Thank you. And yes, I agree. I would bathe in the cup if I could. Disappear into all that lovely hot water!' She turned as Bertel roused himself, soon followed by Korri, knowing that the two teenagers would be the last to wake. She thought of Zen and his grandfather, wondering what they were going to do with the boy. Then looking back at Anna, she sighed. 'We will leave promptly. It's for the best. I don't want to bring further trouble to your door.' Edela had carved a handful of symbols on the back of

Anna's door, though she was losing confidence in her ability to see danger coming.

'I'll prepare some food to take with you.'

Edela was ready to protest, though it would certainly help. 'Thank you. You're very kind.'

Korri approached, adjusting his swordbelt with a mighty yawn. 'I'll go out first, get the lay of the land. See what happened at the tavern and how my men fared.' He felt guilty for leaving them to it, though he'd wanted to ensure that Edela and her friends were safe. They had no one to protect them, and those men appeared quite determined to kill them all.

Seeing the pretty shoemaker, he smiled. And noticing Edela staring at him, he wondered if there was perhaps another reason he'd felt the need to stay the night? Feeling his cheeks heating up, Korri smoothed his wrinkled mud-brown tunic, untangled his beard ropes and headed for the door. 'I'll return soon, so get yourselves ready to leave. Soon as we can, we'll make our way down to the docks. I don't think Bakkar has anything more to offer. We may as well head to Castala.'

Bertel nodded, feeling much the same. Glancing over his shoulder, he saw the sleeping boy, Zen. 'And what are we going to do with him, Edela? I'm not sure we need another mouth to feed.'

Edela frowned. 'I think we're the reason that boy's grandfather is dead, so if he wants to come along, then he shall, Bertel Knutson. We owe him that. It's the least we can do.'

***

Karsten Dragos had woken up feeling strange.

He was due to leave for Angard in six days. After months of planning, negotiating, arguing and compromising, the wedding was coming far too quickly for his liking. When his marriage had been a distant proposition, he'd merely felt a niggle of discomfort, but now with it all but staring him in the face, he wanted to scream.

Marriage itself wasn't a problem – he'd missed having a wife. He hadn't often been happy with his first wife, Nicolene, but he'd enjoyed the certainty of her presence in his bed and having a mother to his children. And shuddering with the memories of the loss of both his wife and son, he turned to the balcony, walking out to view the harbour. He soon found the ship Eadmund and his friends had arrived in.

And his strange feelings intensified.

Every instinct made him want to set sail today. Now. And not to Angard but to this mysterious isle, S'ala Nis.

It had been years since he'd felt free. He had been focused on remaking Hest into his own kingdom, and without his father barking at him or his brothers bossing him about, he'd been free to. His mother had always been a clanging voice in his ears, but with Ulf to fuss over these past few years and her motherless grandchildren to care for, she had mostly left the kingdom's business in his hands. Despite having only one arm, Berard had proven to be surprisingly useful and eager to handle the more mundane tasks, so Karsten had happily delegated most of those to him. Meena had even been helpful at times, offering some insight and ideas when she wasn't breeding.

Things had been going well.

And yet?

The restless energy flooding his veins, waking him in the night, driving him to the training ring twice a day wasn't going to be sated by marriage to the prickly daughter of the King of Helsabor.

Karsten didn't burn for Freya Valens.

He burned for adventure, danger, action.

And...

Turning away from the balcony, heading back to his chamber, he thought of breakfast and his guests, certain that his mother would already be down in the hall, seeking to make an impression on her royal visitor.

And Hanna, Karsten eventually admitted with a sigh.

He burned for Hanna Boelens.

CHAPTER SEVENTEEN

Korri Torluffson returned to the shoemaker's house with good and bad news. A number of their enemies lay dead in the tavern, a handful of his own men, too, and the tavern itself had burned down, everything in it now just smoking ash and charred wood.

A swollen-eyed Zen looked in disbelief from Siggy to Edela and back to Korri, though he didn't speak. Korri had offered him passage on one of his ships, though Zen had been in Bakkar since he was nine-years-old – seven years now. He didn't know if he was ready to leave the only home he could remember.

Anna patted his arm. 'You can stay here until you decide what to do, if you like? I've been looking for someone to help me in my workshop.'

Korri smiled at her, feeling an odd sensation stirring. And then Anna turned to him and that sensation rippled through his body. He couldn't look away.

'No,' Zen decided. 'No, I shouldn't stay. My grandfather would tell me to go. I should go with you.'

Korri nodded, patting him on the back. 'Good. And go we must before those men are out scouring the city.'

'Do you think they will be?' Bertel asked, taking a wrapped bundle of food from Anna with a grateful nod.

Korri headed to the door. 'According to Edela, their mission is to kill her, so yes, they'll have to keep trying if they wish to please their queen.'

Bertel muttered something under his breath, which Edela heard perfectly, and she shook her head, turning back to Siggy. 'Put your hood up, dear. You've got rather recognisable hair. The less we stand out, the better.'

Korri thought so, too, tucking his beard ropes down his tunic.

Siggy did as she was told, stomach growling loudly, though there was no time for breakfast. They simply had to get away from Bakkar in haste. She glanced at Zen, feeling his pain. Not just imagining it but actually feeling it, for his loss had awakened her grief over her mother's death, and she felt even more upset.

'Thank you for your help,' Korri told the shoemaker. 'And once again, apologies for the inconvenience.'

'I was happy to help,' Anna promised. 'And if there's anything else I can do, you know where I am.' Her brown eyes shone as Bertel opened the door, ushering in the sun, trying to shepherd everyone out into the alley.

Korri remained, staring at her. 'I won't forget your kindness. And perhaps we'll meet again? I've a feeling I'll return to Bakkar before long.'

***

Eadmund had piled his plate with the breakfast bounty on offer in Hest's hall, seeing that both Fyn and Thorgils had done the same. It had been some time since they'd eaten so well. In fact, scratching his head as he made his way to the high table, he couldn't remember the last time he'd even had an appetite. Though he'd begun to feel a weakness that had come from a prolonged lack of food, and knowing he needed to be strong in both mind and body when he returned to S'ala Nis, Eadmund had decided to fill himself to bursting.

Bayla Dragos was watching, and with a smile, she indicated

that he should sit beside her. He tried to mask his reluctance, for the former queen was always happy to offend, eager to dig for gossip, and he didn't want her company. Thankfully, Karsten headed towards him, inclining his head to where he'd chosen to sit, at the far end of the high table, next to Thorgils.

Eadmund shrugged apologetically at Bayla and aimed for Karsten instead.

Sitting beside Bayla, Ulf laughed.

'You men are all the same,' she snapped, lips thinning into a scowl. 'You think we women have nothing to offer, no useful information to impart. Why Eadmund thinks Karsten has anything other than smutty jokes to share, I don't know.'

Ulf eyed her, licking hairy lips. 'Is that so? More likely you fear Eadmund will sway Karsten about the wedding. Convince him to take the fleet to sea and him too?' Seeing a flare of anger in Bayla's clear blue eyes, Ulf thought he'd hit the nail on the head. Nudging her arm, he placed a hand on her thigh. 'Karsten's promised to go through with it, so he won't back out. Not now, Bayla. You can trust him.'

Bayla let out a strained breath. 'I worked very hard on this marriage. He has no idea. The visits, the endless feasts and meetings with that vile Herold Valens and...' She leaned towards Ulf. 'Though for what? Karsten's heart isn't in it.'

'It's not his heart that will get him an heir, though, is it?' Ulf joked. 'He doesn't need to love or even want the woman, just to do his duty and strengthen his hold on the throne. And he will. Karsten's not the same man who went to the Vale. You know that.'

Bayla mostly did, though seeing her son sniggering with Eadmund Skalleson, she was suddenly reminded of how reckless he could be. That impatient, boyish man who thought little of the consequences of his actions.

Yes, she remembered that man well.

Leaning out, she poked Berard, who sat next to Ulf, talking to the explorer. 'Go and sit with your brother,' she hissed. 'I don't want him changing his mind!'

Karsten could hear the chairs being moved, scraped across the flagstones, and soon he saw a lop-sided Berard approaching with a nervous look. 'Here comes Mother,' he joked to Thorgils.

'Well, my mother always told me what a bad influence I was,' Thorgils laughed. 'So if that's still the case, perhaps I can convince you to postpone this inconvenient wedding of yours and come to S'ala Nis with us instead?'

Ducking his head and ignoring Berard, Karsten lowered his voice. 'Can't say I haven't thought about it. It's certainly a more attractive proposition than bedding Freya Valens.'

'Ugly, is she?' Thorgils asked, seeing Berard quickly look away as he took a seat beside him.

'All women look the same in the dark,' Karsten supposed with a shrug.

'She's not ugly,' Berard assured them. 'Perhaps a little... plain featured?'

'A little?' Karsten shuddered. 'The woman could sour milk, though it's not her features that bother me as much as her sneering, whining voice. In all of Osterland, in all of the Fire Lands, that's the woman Bayla thought would make the best Queen of Hest?'

Thorgils was confused. 'But what happened to Hanna?' He glanced at Karsten and Berard before turning to Eadmund, who looked on with interest.

Berard immediately sat back, eyes on his breakfast plate.

Karsten didn't speak.

'Thorgils has a mouth big enough to stick two boots inside,' Eadmund said, breaking the suddenly awkward silence. He turned to glare at his friend. 'I imagine if Karsten and Hanna had wanted to marry, he would be marrying her instead.'

More silence ensued as Karsten squirmed and Berard knitted his lips together, neither Dragos speaking.

'I asked her to marry me,' Karsten admitted softly. 'Hanna. But she...'

Thorgils patted him on the back. He couldn't think of anything to say. Whatever words he offered would be mere platitudes.

When he'd lost Isaura, such words had been spoken to him, though nothing had truly felt right until they'd been reunited. Looking at Eadmund, he imagined he felt the same.

'And you have to go through with the marriage?' Eadmund wondered with a darting glance at Bayla, now talking to Arras Sikari, who appeared to be charming her.

'I do... and though I'd rather come with you to this hidden isle, as king, I simply can't. Though you should still have my fleet. I may not be able to come, but you must rescue Jael. I'll talk to Ulf. The fleet's his, so he can go along and take charge. Either way, Bayla won't be happy, but at least this way, I won't make an enemy of Herold Valens.'

It was spoken like a king, and a surprised Eadmund nodded, understanding all too well how it felt to put your own needs and desires to one side and do what was right for your kingdom. 'I'm grateful, Karsten. Very grateful.'

Karsten didn't even nod. It was the right thing to do, though he didn't feel happy staying behind. Still, seeing Bayla now eyeing him suspiciously, he smiled, taking pleasure in knowing that he'd be irritating the woman who had organised the wedding in the first place.

Eadmund didn't know what else to say, so deciding to change the subject, he turned to Berard. 'Can I speak to Meena? To see if she's seen anything? Anything that might help us?'

Meena hadn't come down to breakfast. She had tossed and turned all night, and Berard had left her sleeping, though with two little girls in the chamber next door, he doubted she'd have slept for long.

He looked uncertain.

'You'll need help from the gods to drag a vision out of Meena,' Karsten laughed. 'She tends to keep them all to herself. Though we've had no great need of her dreams, thankfully enough.'

Berard started spluttering, ready to defend his wife, when Meena herself waddled into the hall, quickly overtaken by her two toddlers, who hurried towards their father. Meena's eyes, however, went to Eadmund, and seeing her staring at him, he lost his appetite entirely.

***

Breakfast for those slaves who had worked long into the night was spoiled and warm. S'ala Nis' heat was draining, the arduous work under an always-bright sun exhausting, and sitting at the table, faced with watery gruel, Jael couldn't bring herself to lift the spoon to her lips.

Sitting opposite her, Alek ate like a hungry dog, slopping the gruel into his small mouth with real enthusiasm. He was as thin as a stick, with protruding cheekbones and shoulder blades that jutted out from his back. His vivid blue eyes were bright with energy, though she continued to worry about the man's chances of escaping the isle in one piece.

A shadow fell over the table, and looking up, Jael squinted at a new arrival. He loomed over her like a standing stone, with small beady eyes and a thin slash of a mouth. His short dark hair was thinning, some missing where a scar angled across his scalp, down to his right ear, which, Jael could see, was missing its tip. He looked about Eadmund's age, perhaps older, though perhaps not, for she sensed that work in the quarry and on the tower was ageing them all.

Alek lifted his face with a beaming smile. 'Rigg!' Turning to Jael, his smile widened. 'I told you about Rigg. And you're finally back!'

'They wanted to keep me longer, but that weak cunt Quint sent one of his minions to bring me back.'

Rigg's voice was stone-like, too, Jael heard as he plonked his massive weight down on the bench beside Alek, who was forced to move along.

'So you're still not well then?'

'Well enough, though I'd rather be lying in the physician's room with one of those pretty slaves spooning soup into my mouth.' And that mouth now curled into something resembling a smile. His small eyes disappeared as he chuckled, his flat cheeks swallowing them up entirely.

'But now you're back, and just in time.'

'For what?' Rigg wondered, opening his eyes and shifting them to Jael. 'And why's she here?'

Alek ducked his head, dropping his voice to a whisper. 'This is Jael Furyck, Queen of the Slave Islands. She's here to help us. Help with the...' And now he mouthed the word. 'Plan.'

Rigg burst out laughing. 'What? This loser? I saw her in the Arena, beaten up like a nobody. And what, you think because she's a queen, we want her helping us?'

Despite having known Rigg for three years now, Alek was still mortified. He looked towards a surprised Jael with supplicating hands. 'You'll have to forgive my friend for his... manner.'

Rigg glared at Alek. 'What's wrong with my manner?'

There was a sudden flurry of noise as Quint entered the dining hall, blowing his conch shell for the change of shift.

Rigg stood. 'No,' he spat at Jael. 'I saw you fight, I know who you are, and the answer's no. I'll lead our men, as I've already said, Alek.'

Jael stared up at him, slowly getting to her feet. 'I'm not sure it's up to you.'

Quickly scooping the last of his gruel into his mouth, Alek joined them. 'I've got Jael working up the scaffolding, but let's talk on the way. Hang back with me,' he hissed. Though seeing Quint waving for him to join the other three foremen, he frowned. 'I'll catch you up. Listen to Jael, Rigg. Give her a chance.' And with that, he ran a hand over his mouth and strode away.

Rigg was the same height as Jael; a solid man with impressive balance. She imagined that not even a strong wind would have him swaying. There was no movement, not even on his face, as

Alek left them behind.

'We should talk,' Jael began. 'About Alek's –' But before she could finish, Rigg had stomped away.

***

The walk from the shoemaker's to Bakkar's harbour was led by a grief-stricken Zen, who knew the crowded city better than anyone.

Though he didn't speak.

Siggy took the lead beside him, leaving Edela and Bertel behind them and Korri bringing up the rear.

'Are you sure you want to leave?' Siggy asked, eyes sweeping the alley, stacked with carts, buckets, and piles of rubbish, where dogs were sniffing around. Zen appeared to be avoiding every public square and market, though she feared, as the alleys became steadily narrower and shrouded in shadows, that they would soon come to a dead end. 'Bakkar? It's your home. Those men aren't after you.'

Zen didn't answer her. Instead, he strode out ahead, taking a left turn. And head up now, he appeared to be thinking.

'I'd hold your nose, Edela,' Bertel warned, inhaling what smelled like a latrine or perhaps dead bodies. Whatever it was soon had him covering both his nose and mouth.

Edela was looking over her shoulder at Korri and didn't answer.

'I may as well talk to myself for all the company you are this morning,' Bertel huffed, and lengthening his stride, he left Edela in his wake.

She barely noticed. Her attention kept being drawn back to Korri.

Though she didn't know why.

Then, feeling that same strange sensation, as though a snake was crawling over her boots, she pulled up, dragging Korri onto the dark porch propped up beneath an overhanging house.

He grunted in surprise, but as they crouched there silently, masked by shadows, he soon saw two men heading past them. 'Silurans,' Korri mouthed at Edela, who nodded with worried eyes, recognising the leathery tunics worn by Iker Rayas' men.

The two men hung back slightly, not wanting to be seen, and as Korri made to step off the porch, Edela snatched his sleeve, holding him back. She pointed at the sword he was about to unsheathe, shaking her head.

Pulling out her knife, she quickly cut a symbol into her palm, wincing as the blade bit into her thin flesh. 'Hello!' she called. 'I was wondering if you could help me. Hello?' The two men, who'd been about to turn the corner after Bertel, jerked to a stop, swinging back to find where that voice was coming from, but in the darkness of the alley and shade of the porch, there was little clue.

Edela and Korri remained perfectly still.

Clasping her hands together, feeling the pain of the symbol and her coursing blood, Edela tried to release a breath, knowing that a calm dreamer was a powerful dreamer.

Breath ignited the magical symbols.

So did chants, and whispering words under her breath, she now brought the symbol to life. It glowed on her palm, urging her to act. Edela didn't recognise either man, almost relieved that it wasn't that terrifying brute with the brands, Iker Rayas.

She stepped off the porch.

The men looked slightly confused and wary but pleased to see the dreamer alone. Though, as they approached, they saw Korri with his sword.

'Don't hurt us!' Edela pleaded as Korri stepped past her into the alley.

Having discovered that Edela and Korri were no longer behind him, Bertel had headed back around the corner, and seeing the two armed Silurans, he'd hurried to alert Siggy and Zen. Now all three stood blocking one end of the alley while Edela and Korri commanded the other.

Edela saw Bertel unsheathe his knife and quickly sought to reach him, telling him to wait. Korri too.

Holding her burning hand up to the Silurans, the symbol on her palm glowed red. 'Do you feel your legs? How heavy they are? How you can barely lift them? How hard it is getting to move?'

Both men scoffed at her words, though it was soon apparent that their boots were stuck to the ground, holding them in place. Panic flared, the Silurans exchanging a frantic look before returning their attention to the old dreamer and her glowing symbol.

'Put down your swords!' Edela ordered, voice sharpening now. 'On the ground. Throw them away, far out of reach!'

They heard a loud slap and someone crying out, a door slammed, though the alley remained theirs alone.

The men threw their swords away; metal clattering on stone.

It grew darker in the alley as the symbol on Edela's hand became brighter.

Siggy watched it, feeling strange. Beside her, Zen didn't know what was happening.

'Close your eyes!' Edela warned the men. 'And down on your knees!' She started walking towards them as the men followed her orders, calling out in pleading voices, begging for mercy.

It was hard to hear, but these men sought to kill them. They would not stop.

So she would have to stop them.

Now the men became perfectly still, faces wrenched in fear, lips and eyes frozen. Edela had claimed their bodies, though she would not claim their lives.

Not her.

'Korri! Bertel!' she called. 'They are all yours!'

Neither man hesitated – Korri taking the first man in the

chest, Bertel slitting the second man's throat. Their deaths were silent for those in the alley, though not for Edela, who could hear the men's pained cries as the blades bit, and soon their mournful howls were choked off.

And Edela no longer heard the sound of their hearts beating with life.

CHAPTER EIGHTEEN

Upon returning from his meeting with Quint and his fellow foremen, Alek gathered his crew together, revealing that the date for Noor's funeral had been confirmed by the palace.

It would be held in eleven days' time.

That news was greeted with gaping mouths and audible groans. Alek didn't blame his men, for they could all see what it meant for them. The foremen had agreed with Quint that the timetable for completion of the great tower was weeks.

Not days.

So much of it had been finished, though the work to complete the top, which would be crowned with an elaborate arch, was laborious and, in many instances, fiddly.

It wasn't something they could rush.

Though he couldn't change any of it. Eleven days gave him a chance to work with Jael, Rigg, and their allies to ensure that everything was in place for the slave revolt.

Though if Argo Kosta was going to drive them all into the ground, would any of them have the energy for it?

'It's doable!' Rigg bellowed in support of his friend. 'Why not? That fuck Kosta's looking for reasons to throw us into the pits. Let's not give him any!'

Jael watched the men, seeing little belief in Rigg's words.

Or Alek's.

She didn't blame them. Sweat had soaked through their

clothes already, and it had only just gone breakfast. One man started sobbing, banging his hands against his head.

After offering more words of encouragement, Alek dismissed his crew, his smile soon becoming a grimace. 'The queen's expectations must be met, though they're not based in reality.'

'Course not,' Rigg grumbled. 'Queens think only of themselves, don't they? Of their own wants and needs as they sit upon their thrones and look down on their people. We're like ants to them up on their mighty perches. Mere ants!' He eyed Jael with scorn.

She eyed him right back. 'And how many queens have you known? You're thinking they're all like this one? Believe it or not, some of us actually care for our people. Some of us put our lives on the line for them.'

Rigg laughed in her face. 'Well, you don't need a great storyteller in your hall. You can tell your own tall tales, it seems! But I see you here, before me. You're a slave. I saw you in the Arena when the commander defeated you. You're a loser! A slave and a loser just like the rest of us!'

Stepping forward, Jael jutted out her chin, but Alek quickly pushed in between them. 'We need to get up the tower, Jael. And you need to see Goran at the quarry, Rigg. And both of you are far too important to kill each other!'

'You don't need her,' Rigg insisted. 'To do what?'

Alek rolled his eyes. 'She's Ranuf Furyck's daughter. She was by his side for those famous battles with Hest. And Brekka was never defeated. She helped her father see to that. Haven't you heard the stories? She's Furia's daughter!' Usually calm and even-tempered, Rigg had finally pushed a genial Alek too far. 'I brought her in because she knows battle. She's the leader we've been waiting for.'

'But I was to lead us. That was the plan,' Rigg hissed, bending down to drive his point home. 'And then, I get sent to the physician's and –'

'Why?' Jael interrupted. 'Why were you there?'

'I was poisoned!' Rigg growled in a loud voice. 'Poisoned, I tell you!'

Alek threw his hands in the air, leaving them both behind. 'I have work to do, and so do you. We'll get nothing done while you're blathering about that again.'

A curious Jael followed after Rigg, who had turned after Alek. 'Poisoned by who? And why?'

'Attilo Balda. Over there. Big bruise on the side of his face.'

Jael saw the man, wondering if he was the one who had touched her in the night. He certainly looked in pain, holding his swollen, bruised face. 'What does he have against you?'

'Nothing that's any business of yours, loser.' And with that, Rigg walked off.

Jael stared after him in surprise, and shaking her head, she tilted it back, looking at the great web of scaffolding leading up the side of the tower, fixing her mind on Eadmund.

***

Meena took Eadmund to the winding gardens.

They were her gardens now, and though the bad memories of her grandmother and her aunt and even Draguta lingered, she had worked hard to make a fresh start.

There were more healing plants now, less tools of darkness.

She had encouraged birds to visit by planting honeysuckle and milkweed. There were bees and butterflies and all manner of insects. And her children.

Willa and Lila.

When they were with her, the garden felt the happiest of all.

Sitting on the stone bench beside Eadmund Skalleson, she regretted not bringing the girls, though Willa had a tooth coming through and wasn't good company. It was better that they stayed with their nursemaids.

'I expect you want to know about Jael,' she said, becoming nervous. A dreamer was expected to provide answers to kings, and though Karsten had mostly given up on her, she could feel the weight of Eadmund's concerns and his need for her insight.

He nodded, turning to her. She was still a squirming, awkward creature, he saw, watching her curl over beside him. But happy. Meena looked happy. 'Anything. Just anything. I don't understand why this is happening. Why Jael was taken.'

Meena felt troubled, twisting swollen fingers on her lap before lifting her blinking eyes to Eadmund. 'I've been sensing ripples lately. Sometimes in the earth, like the where-worms from the Vale.' She shuddered, immediately shutting those dark memories away. 'Sometimes they're in the clouds or in the air. As though... it is hard to explain.' And now she twitched, becoming entangled in nerves.

An impatient Eadmund saw that rushing the dreamer wouldn't help matters, so he sat perfectly still, drawing his attention to a hovering hummingbird dipping its long beak into a pink foxglove.

'The ripples are a sign that something is happening,' Meena said at last. 'I feel it myself, here. This alliance with Helsabor? Bayla wants Karsten to have a wife. She never thought Hanna would make a suitable queen, and she made that known to Hanna herself. There was talk of a Siluran princess, though she died, so when Herold Valens reached out with an offer, Bayla worked quickly. Karsten was too drunk at the time to argue, which he likely now regrets.' Eadmund looked confused. 'Raymon Vandaal is dead!' Meena blurted out as though it should all be obvious to a king. 'Hest and Helsabor will make an alliance, someone has kidnapped the Queen of Oss, and Tuura has been attacked.'

'So something bigger is happening? The ripples?'

Meena's eyes widened, and she started tapping her leg. 'I th-th-think so. I fear it, for no ripples happen in isolation. They are always connected. So to find answers for one, you must find an answer for all.'

Her words were confusing and not especially encouraging, though they certainly focused Eadmund.

'Volcanoes.'

'Sorry?'

'Somewhere, somehow, this has to do with volcanoes. I feel that.' Grimacing now, Meena rubbed her belly.

Seeing her discomfort and doubting he would get much more out of the dreamer, Eadmund stood, and taking her hand, he pulled her to her feet. 'Thank you, Meena. I will... think on what you've said.'

She became flustered, drawing in a shaky breath. 'It wasn't much. Mostly nonsense.'

Slipping her arm through his, Eadmund helped her back down the steep path with a smile. 'No, not nonsense. I'm grateful for any insight you can give me. Any at all.'

Feeling his arm, Meena shivered, seeing glimpses of an unexpected sight. And blinking up at Eadmund, she immediately looked away, not wanting to reveal the horror she was sure had blanched her face.

'Is something wrong? Meena?'

'No,' she mumbled, eyes on her boots. 'No, it's nothing.'

***

They encountered no further trouble on their way to Bakkar's harbour and quickly finding *Sea Queen* and Elmer's ship, and pleased to see that every man still standing was on board, Korri Torluffson bid his helmsmen to get them underway.

'Are you alright?' Siggy asked Zen, who looked ready to jump overboard. He kept eyeing the pier as though he regretted stepping down into the ship.

Korri eyed the lanky boy. 'Can you row? We've lost a few hands, and now with two ships... it would help.'

Zen shrugged. 'I don't know.'

Placing an arm around his shoulder, Korri guided him towards a chest. And feeling a twinge of grief at those friends he'd lost, he pushed Zen onto it. 'Just match the rhythm as best you can. You've certainly got the arms for it.' Clapping the boy on the back, he turned to Siggy. 'Make yourself scarce in the stern. And Nellie could use a milking.'

Nodding and feeling slightly dazed, Siggy turned towards the little black goat, pleased to see her. Nellie bleated urgently, so shaking off the strange morning and the terrifying night, Siggy took a deep breath and headed for the milking stool.

Watching her, Edela was consumed with guilt.

She was forcing the girl down a dark path. And to where would it lead?

Beside her, a frantic Bertel wanted Korri to hurry everyone along. *Sea Queen's* helmsman was a genial, relaxed sort of man, but it was Korri's voice everyone listened out for. Though now, when there was such an urgency about the situation, he strolled around with the air of someone arriving for a feast. Bertel feared that at any moment, a half-dead Iker Rayas and the dregs of his warband would appear and launch a last stand.

Placing a hand on his arm, Edela squeezed gently. 'Stop your fretting and sit down beside me, Bertel Knutson. We don't need to get in their way.'

Swinging around as though stung, Bertel was ready to snap, though seeing exhaustion in Edela's blue eyes, he sighed instead. 'I should have killed that man in the tavern. I shouldn't have left until I knew he was dead.'

'Well, if you'd done that, perhaps his men would have trapped us there? No, we had to escape. But if he finds us again, I will kill him. I promise you that. We cannot go on like this, hunted like animals. And all because of me?'

Bertel stared at Edela, then past her to the pier, where his view was obscured by men hefting barrels into a wagon. 'But can you tell me why? Why these men are after you? What they actually want?'

'It's a very good question,' Edela sighed, feeling her palm stinging. She heard a muffled voice like a distant rumble of thunder, though no actual words. Shaking her head, she smiled again. 'Castala!' she announced confidently. 'I'm sure we'll find answers in Castala.'

***

Jael peered over the edge of the scaffolding, seeing Argo Kosta motioning up to her. She recognised Quint next to him, and Alek, and soon all three men were urging her to come down.

It took some time. The scaffolding planks were narrow, restricting who could pass – the ladders too – though, eventually, Jael reached the ground, where the three men waited.

'You're to be reassigned,' Alek told her with blinking eyes. 'The commander wants to move you to the quarry. You'll be loading wagons.'

An expressionless Jael clenched her jaw. She had no issue with hard work, but that was a task her body was ill-suited to.

'Quint will show you,' Kosta said with a wrinkly grin.

There was a malicious delight in his eyes, which Jael wouldn't indulge. She simply nodded her head and followed after Quint.

Alek made to follow, but the commander thumped a big hand on his drooping shoulder, holding him back. 'You thought to make things easier for her? Why? Do I need to think about sending you with her? I'm sure you'd last a few hours at best.'

His growl sent shivers up Alek's spine, tingling the back of his neck. 'I was trying to work with speed. She doesn't have the strength others do. She would be slow. I thought her better suited to the top of the tower. She worked with precision up there. The work is laborious, lord, but also intricate. I chose her for that role.'

Kosta squeezed Alek's shoulder, watching those bright blue eyes intensify until he saw tears of pain. '*You* thought? *You* chose? But your place is under Quint, who is under me. I decide all, and I'll tell you if there has been a change in my decision. Understood?'

Alek nodded, shoulder burning. He wanted to twist out of that grip, to free himself from the pain, though legs trembling, he focused on merely keeping to his feet.

'I want that tower completed as much as anyone, and we'll all work to please the queen. Give the bitch a day at the quarry. Have Rigg keep an eye on her. He can report back to you at supper.'

A trembling Alek gasped as the commander finally released his shoulder.

He couldn't help but stumble down onto his hands and knees.

Kosta laughed. 'Are you made of sticks, man? I wonder how much more you have in you? Just enough to get my tower done, I hope. Though you'll die either way soon enough.'

Alek bowed his head, then looking up, he saw the commander spin on his heels and stride away, laughing as he scuffed up a cloud of dust.

***

Fyn Gallas had been oddly distant since they'd arrived in Hest, which had Mattie frowning. She was used to him hovering around, checking on her. He didn't appear to like her or enjoy her company, but he did like it when she gave him answers.

Though here, in the golden city, he'd become quiet, keeping to himself.

She found Thorgils on a bench outside the castle, and sitting down beside him, she decided to find out why.

'Wrong?' A cheerful-looking Thorgils peered at her. 'With Fyn?' He turned to the castle, where he'd expected his cousin to emerge with some food, though there was still no sign of him. For a moment he frowned, then his face cleared. 'That would be Milla.'

'The Alekkan girl?'

Thorgils nodded, sweeping unruly curls away from squinting eyes. 'It's about time, you know. No one's needed to find someone more than my cousin, though he does tend to scare easily.' He chuckled, seeing Mattie's deepening frown. 'Why? Have you seen something? About Fyn?'

'No, no, just curious. He's been so quiet since we got here. I just wondered if something was amiss.'

'And you can't see for yourself? You have no clues?'

Mattie smiled. 'My head is full of clues, though they're no more use than a cloud of flies buzzing around me. It takes time to wade through them all and find out what's important.'

Thorgils bent down to her. 'Though you need to, Mattie. What matters is attacking that island and reclaiming our queen. Nothing will feel right until we have her home with us. Though,' he added with a wink, 'don't tell her I said so. No one's got an ego as big as that woman.'

It was hard not to like Thorgils Svanter, Mattie thought with a smile, watching as he excused himself and headed to where Eadmund and Arras had emerged from the castle, aiming for the harbour. She thought to close her eyes and enjoy the hot sun for a while, letting her mind wander, though it wasn't long before Kolarov was upon her with a flurry of questions.

Seeing Mattie waving her hands at the explorer, Arras was momentarily distracted, though sensing Eadmund's impatience, he cleared his throat, drawing his eyes back to him. 'Jael had iron fetters around her wrists and ankles. They had symbols inside to stop her dreaming, though she had no problem using them as weapons. She smashed more than one man in the face.'

Eadmund didn't smile; the thought of his wife as a prisoner

made him wild with anger. He glanced at Thorgils as he fell in beside them. 'Though she found a way out? She's the one who showed you the tunnel?'

Arras nodded. 'She never said, but I imagine she found a way around those symbols, for she certainly appeared to read my mind.'

'In the tunnel, she wasn't wearing them,' Eadmund remembered. 'At least I didn't see them.'

'No. Before our fight in the Arena, they were removed.'

'So we might be able to reach her? Mattie might?'

Arras sighed, knowing Kalina Sardis as he did. 'The queen is a petty woman, vengeful and short-tempered. I doubt she'd allow Jael the freedom she had before.' He didn't want to add how much he feared for Eadmund's wife. Kalina couldn't kill Jael – according to the queen, she'd been forbidden – but she would blame Jael for his escape.

She would take her anger out on her.

'Noor of the Dragon Blood Tree is bound to the queen. To the isle. He may be forced to reveal our plans.'

'He sees the future?' Eadmund asked.

Arras shrugged. 'He speaks to the gods, advises the queen and her lords. It's likely he'll tell the queen what is coming, whether he wants to or not.'

'Us, you mean?' Thorgils muttered, looking concerned.

Arras nodded. 'Yes, us.'

Eadmund smiled. 'I don't mind that. Let them be waiting. We have our own dreamer, and she's proven herself quite useful so far, so let them be waiting.'

And Jael, he thought.

Let Jael be waiting too.

CHAPTER NINETEEN

With Jael and Rigg at the quarry and two men throwing themselves off the scaffolding, progress at the top of the tower slowed.

The relentless pace was too much for some to bear. The heat turned them mad with exhaustion. It sapped energy and stole hope from bodies and souls. It burned skin and broke minds, and for some, there was no longer any point in living.

For this was no life.

'Do you think they'll want us back?' a panting Jael asked Rigg when he'd shared the gossip. 'Alek's crew needs more men if we're to finish on time.'

Rigg laughed. 'And you think they'll need you? What? Are you a stone mason? Do you have the skills they need?'

Jael swung around. 'What's your problem with me, Rigg? I'm a prisoner here, same as you. I'm as miserable as you, as desperate to get home as you.' She lowered her voice, suppressing a cough. It felt as though she'd sunk into a great pit of dust, feeling tiny particles in her eyes and up her nose. When she wasn't hefting the slabs and bricks into wagons, she was wiping her eyes and sneezing. 'I want to help Alek as much as you.'

Rigg lurched forward, grabbing one of her wrists. 'You think I have a home to go back to, do you?' Seeing Quint heading towards them, he dropped Jael's arm, lifting a slab of newly dressed stone onto his shoulder. 'Thanks to you Furycks, my home, my family, everything I know, everyone I loved... they're all gone.' And spitting on the ground, just missing her shoe, a red-faced Rigg lumbered away.

Quint stopped behind Jael. 'Do we have another problem, your highness?'

Hearing the sarcasm in his voice, she didn't turn around, merely shaking her head. Her arms were mostly dangling by her sides, entirely numb, though bending down, she slid her hands beneath a stone similar in size to Rigg's, and with a grunt, hefted it up, bracing it against her shoulder as she staggered towards the wagon.

Quint watched her go with a frown, knowing she was better used elsewhere. For though his father-in-law wasn't a man to cross, he wondered if Kosta had thought through the ramifications of Jael's reassignment. He watched as she struggled under the immense weight of the stone, pleased to see a scowling Rigg turn and take it from her, easing it down into the wagon, which soon buckled under its weight.

'You two!' he called. 'Drive the wagon up to the tower! Stay there for the rest of the afternoon and help Alek. His men are dropping like flies. I'll have you back tomorrow if he doesn't need you!'

Jael's eyes brightened at the unexpected gift, though as she turned to Rigg, she saw that his were still dull and unblinking. Though dropping her head and choosing to forget about her miserable companion, she aimed for the wagon bench, eager to sit down.

***

Amma was tired of lying down, and knowing she would soon be heading to Helsabor, she decided to leave the hall behind and see the sun, hoping to infuse herself with energy. Getta was busy with Gisila, organising their departure, and Axl had left early, though she wasn't especially eager for company. Sometimes, it was simply nice to be alone with her thoughts.

She saw a boy playing with Gully, who had never had an owner. A friendly, happy dog, he was well looked after by everyone. Perhaps a little too well looked after, she thought, seeing how plump he was getting. The scrawny boy looked up as Gully took off, scampering towards her.

'Well, hello,' Amma smiled, bending down to pat the black dog, who quickly flopped onto his back, offering up his big belly for a scratch. She laughed, seeing the boy coming, watching her with curious eyes. 'Perhaps you could give him a scratch for me?'

'Is he your dog?' Linas wondered.

'No, Gully has always been his own master. He goes where he wants, when he wants.'

'Are you the queen?'

Amma nodded. 'And you are?'

'I'm Linas. I'm new!'

'New? To Andala?' Amma stood up now as the boy crouched down, vigorously scratching Gully, who flicked out a hind leg in ecstasy.

'I came with my grandmother. From the forest. We always lived in the forest.'

'In the trees?' Amma wondered with a smile. 'Did you live in a tree house?'

Linas shook his head. 'But I can climb trees!' He looked around, seeing that the queen was alone. 'Do you have children? They could come with me, and I could teach them!'

Amma's smile faltered. 'No, not yet, but soon. Soon, I hope.'

Gully wriggled up to his feet, bounding towards a waddling Helga, who immediately shooed him away.

'That's my grandmother!' Linas called, waving to her. 'She can make magic!'

Helga glowered at the boy, who paid her no mind and was soon scampering after Gully. She turned her attention to Amma.

'The boy talks too much. Linas. He's never had a friend.'

Amma was surprised. She had met the dreamer once and wasn't sure what she thought of the intimidating woman. She was coarse in both appearance and manners, so she hadn't expected her grandson to be such a joyous and happy boy. She smiled nervously. 'I had thought to come and speak to you about –'

Helga held up a grubby hand. 'I have seen nothing of your child. Nothing of you at all. My lady,' she added somewhat begrudgingly, still scowling. 'I must see to the boy. He needs to eat.' And with that, she wheeled around and headed after Linas and Gully.

Gisila arrived, scowling herself. 'That woman has the manners of an ogre. The face of one too.'

A horrified Amma turned to her. 'She will hear you, Gisila.'

'I've no doubt she will, though I'd happily say it to her miserable face. Speaking to a queen as though she's a servant? No, I shall ask Axl to have a word with the woman. She may have come to help, but she must be taught her place.'

'I imagine she lived in the forest because she didn't want to have a place,' Amma murmured. 'She didn't want to live under anyone's rules.'

Gisila peered at her. 'Helga lived in the forest because no one wanted her in Tuura. She has a habit of saying things people don't want to hear. I'm not sure having her here makes sense. Not for Axl.'

'Can we trust her?'

Gisila shrugged. 'I've no idea why Helga's truly come. Axl hasn't really explained it. He says she wants to help, which doesn't sound like the Helga I remember. If only Edela were here or Gant...' Gisila tensed, realising that perhaps her ornery mood wasn't about the dreamer at all.

Since her husband had left, she'd felt rudderless. She had flitted about Andala, looking after her family and fulfilling her duties. She and Gant had often passed like ships during the day, though there was always a smile and a few words, a touch and a kiss. And then, after supper, they would retire to their chamber to be alone.

Together.

Her favourite time of the day.

It had been weeks without that ritual taking place. Weeks since she had felt his touch, heard his voice or seen that rugged old face – her handsome husband – and she didn't feel like herself at all.

'I'm not sure when I'll see Gant again. Perhaps he's just enjoying escaping from under my thumb!' Though both women knew that Gant wasn't the sort of man to let anyone tell him what to do. Gisila felt worried. 'I only hope he's safe, wherever he might be.'

***

Gant and Rexon were nearly at Saala.

They had spent weeks roaming Brekka's southern borders, gathering information, speaking to farmers, warriors, and villagers. They had hidden out, following tracks, leading them to an abandoned camp once occupied by Mutt Storman, the disgruntled Andalan outlaw stirring up trouble. Gant hadn't wanted to return to Axl with only half a story and one idea. He'd wanted to be fully armed with information before returning to Andala, seeking to survey the true extent of Mutt's corruption of Southern Brekka.

In Saala things had remained stable under Rexon, but their journey had been eye-opening and both men rode with increasing urgency, sensing that Mutt Storman had stacked a great pyre of kindling in the South and was merely waiting to set it alight.

They'd ridden out with Gant's thirty men, imagining they'd feel safe, though it had quickly become apparent that things had shifted. A few villagers had spat when Gant had mentioned Axl's name. Others had threatened them. And, unable to guarantee the safety of his men, Gant had made the decision to return to Saala, where he would decide his next move.

'Where is Mutt Storman getting all his silver from?' Rexon wondered, eager to see his wife and children. Eager to free his numb arse from the saddle too. 'Someone with deep pockets.'

Gant nodded, wiping a cloth over his neck. Sweat dripped from his long hair, trickling down his back. He sought to stop it at its source and soon lifted the cloth to his head, trying to soak up moisture there.

It was a warm day, and though he didn't generally mind the heat, they'd long since seen a stream and were all getting thirsty. Gus shook his dirty white head, growing impatient with the slow pace, refocusing Gant's wandering attention. He patted his horse, shifting his eyes to Rexon, who looked a few shades darker than when they'd left Saala.

Summer certainly had arrived in a burst of sunshine.

'Well, that's the one thing we need to know,' Gant muttered. 'An outlaw doesn't mount such a bold challenge with empty pockets. Ranuf tossed him out of Andala without even a cloak on his back, so how did he end up leading an army? How did he take Valso?'

'Take it and claim it,' Rexon said bitterly, for not even he had realised how successful Mutt Storman had become.

'Perhaps only a dreamer could tell us?'

Rexon didn't like the sound of that. 'Please tell me there are no more dark dreamers stirring up trouble in Osterland. I –' Lifting his head, he sniffed. 'Smoke.'

Gant tightened his grip on Gus' reins, scanning the trees. 'Where are we near?'

'Only Saala. Though perhaps someone's camping nearby?' The smoke was oddly strong, and fearing what it might mean, Rexon's stomach started cramping.

***

The journey back to the tower gave Jael a chance to ask Rigg about his earlier statement. 'What do you mean the Furycks took everything from you?' she wondered with a frown. 'Took what?'

Bouncing along on the wagon bench beside her, Rigg was initially reluctant to say any more; the memories were too painful, even now. 'My family,' he admitted eventually. 'My father, my three brothers. They all died in your war with Hest.'

'You're Hestian?' Jael asked, though Rigg grumbled something she couldn't understand. 'I thought I recognised your accent.' He didn't reply, so she carried on. 'But we had no war with Hest.'

Rigg spun around, snarling at her. 'You wanted our riches, our city, our gold! You never stopped trying to claim what belonged to us. To take and take until you controlled all of Osterland. You Furycks swallowed up Tuura, destroyed their people, and now, now you seek to claim it again.' Tugging the reins, Rigg steered the oxen out of the path of an oncoming wagon. He paused there, simmering with rage. 'Haaron Dragos didn't have to convince my family to fight for him. We were never going to surrender to the likes of you.'

Jael was speechless. 'But who told you that? It's not true. It's not what happened at all.'

'You think I'm lying?' Rigg growled, wrapping the reins around his hands until his knuckles turned white.

'What were you and your family? Lords or warriors?'

'Ha! You think I'm lying because I wasn't a lord? Just a grunt with a sword? You think you know more than I do about what happened? That you know why my family died?' Rigg's voice had risen until it strained with pain.

'I do,' Jael insisted. 'I was beside my father when he read the scrolls from Haaron Dragos announcing his intention to defeat us, to take *our* kingdom. He wanted Brekka. The fact that he told you the opposite was just a ploy to convince you to fight. It wasn't what happened, Rigg. My father fought to keep Brekka safe. He had no intention of expanding our borders. In his entire reign, he didn't.'

'Not for want of trying!' Rigg spat, and flicking the reins, he urged the pair of oxen up the hill.

'Did you ever meet Haaron Dragos? Ever talk to him or his sons?' Jael asked, temper sparking. 'Did you ever ask him what he was doing, driving up out of Valder's Pass every spring? You left your kingdom to attack ours. I was there.'

'So was I!'

There was no getting through to him, Jael realised, sinking back onto the bench, deciding to save her breath. Though still feeling incensed and unable to hold her tongue, she tried one more time. 'I'm sorry for your losses, sorry for your family, though I fear we've no choice but to disagree and move on.'

'Move on?'

'What? You wish to die here? We can argue about who had the right of it when we're standing in Hest or Brekka. I don't care. But for now, we have to work together to escape.'

'With you as our leader?' Rigg scoffed. 'A woman who got herself captured? Who couldn't defeat a rusty old man? *You're* the chosen one? But what do you know about this place? How have you suffered?'

'So *you* want to do it then? That's what's at the heart of this? You thought you'd lead the revolt?' They were approaching the entrance to the temple grounds now, and Jael leaned closer to Rigg, lowering her voice. 'Alek is your friend. He trusts you and I trust him, but for this to work, you and I need to trust each other.' Seeing that his scowl hadn't budged, she held out a hand. 'Just until we leave, until we're away from this place. Then you can try to kill me.'

He peered at her now, squinting eyes once again disappearing into his big, flat face. 'Oh, I will, Brekkan,' he promised with a snarl. 'You can be sure of it.'

***

A panicking Rexon was now sure where the danger lay, and he pushed his mare on, ignoring Gant's warnings.

The smoke intensified, a grubby pall smeared across the summer sky.

His wife loved summer, Rexon remembered, his horse's hooves digging up clumps of dirt, flinging them at Gus, who pounded the road behind him.

Demaeya loved summer, and summer loved her. It turned her hair brilliant shades of gold. It sprinkled her perfect nose with freckles, it deepened the colour of her cheeks, and the fine, dry days lifted her mood. With her children playing outside, the hall airing, and their winter stores replenished, she was always at her happiest and most fertile.

Summer was the perfect time to plant seeds of every kind, she would say with a wink, drawing him into her arms.

Rexon's heart was a throbbing lump in his chest as he urged his horse on, barely needing to guide her as she took each turn with ease, for this was the way home.

They both knew that.

The way home, now veiled in smoke.

He coughed, hearing Gant coming up behind him, coughing too.

'Wait!' Gant spluttered. 'Rexon, wait!'

Though a desperate Rexon ignored him, and dropping his head, he kicked his horse towards the fort.

***

Karsten held up a hand to shade his eye.

He'd headed down to the harbour to join Eadmund, Thorgils, and Arras – who had now been joined by Bolder – eager to show them his fleet.

'We managed to put it back together after your wife destroyed it,' he laughed. 'That was a memorable night. For all the wrong reasons!' He still had a bit of a limp from where Jael had stabbed him.

Arras looked confused, though no one bothered to explain it to him.

Seeing the array of ships moored in the harbour, Eadmund knew it was only a portion of Karsten's fleet. 'Are they all seaworthy?' he wondered, pointing to the enormous ship sheds facing the docks, where he assumed the remainder of the fleet was stored.

Karsten nodded, feeling pleased about that. 'Every last one of them. I keep them ready in case you Islanders attempt to threaten us again.' He laughed, seeing Arras' puzzled face. 'They sought to take one of my islands a few years ago, though that didn't work out.'

'Well, it worked out fine for us,' Thorgils grinned. 'Your father paid us all that gold to go away. We've never been disappointed about that, have we?'

Eadmund frowned at him, only wanting to talk about the near future, not the distant past. He felt an impatience to get on with planning, unlike Karsten and Thorgils, who were too busy reminiscing.

Sensing his tension, Karsten had one of the harbour workers open a ship shed. 'I keep these locked as they contain something I'm not interested in sharing. Not with whatever spies lurk in my city.' And thinking about that, he glanced over his shoulder.

Eadmund leaned forward, craning his neck as the shed doors were pulled open.

He saw a fine-looking ship with an unusually short prow, revealing a catapult mounted in the bow. Turning, he saw Arras' wide eyes and Thorgils' blinking surprise. Bolder's mouth had dropped open.

'And here,' Karsten said, enjoying himself, 'is another. I've five in all, though I'm planning for more.'

Arras smiled for the first time since he'd left S'ala Nis. 'Yes,' he breathed, turning to Eadmund. 'With these, we can rescue your wife.'

***

'My wife!' Rexon cried, pulling up some distance from Saala's fort. Something was burning – likely the hall. Dense clouds of smoke billowed across the path leading to the gates, hiding the ramparts, and seeing that his friend had stopped, Gant slid off Gus and ran to him, trying to pull him off his panicking horse. 'I need to save my wife! My children!'

Gant imagined how he would feel if Gisila was trapped inside a burning hall, captured by enemies, though he couldn't let Rexon throw his life away. He glanced over his shoulder as his men rode to join them before turning back around. He needed the Lord of Saala to hear him, to follow his commands. 'We don't know how many there are! You'll be killed if you get any closer!'

'I *want* to die!' Rexon screamed at him. 'If my family is in there, then I want to die! Let go! Let me go!'

'Archers on the walls!' one of Gant's men called in warning.

Rexon spun his horse in a circle. 'You stay!' he bellowed at Gant. 'Stay safe! But I need to do this!' And unsheathing his sword, a coughing Rexon Boas drove his horse towards Saala's gates.

Gant ran to mount Gus, calling his men to him. 'We back him up! Ears open! If we have to get out of here, we need to move with speed!' And swinging Gus' head around, Gant spurred him after Rexon, praying they weren't too late.

CHAPTER TWENTY

'You're back!' Alek exclaimed, pleased to see Jael and Rigg return to the tower. 'For good?' He eyed one then the other, sensing with some disappointment that they hadn't resolved their differences.

Rigg shrugged, jumping down from the wagon. 'Quint sent us back. Once Kosta gets a whiff of it, he might have something to say, but in the meantime, we're all yours.'

Alek looked relieved. 'You heard about Kol and Akon then?'

Rigg nodded. 'Not a surprise. If you take a man from his family, if you take his freedom, his dignity, his choices, you take away his hope. Eventually, he must question what there is to live for.' Eyeing Jael, he called two of Alek's men over to help him unload the wagon.

'He's still not convinced by you as our leader then?' Alek asked discreetly as Jael hopped down from the wagon. She looked stiff, he thought, sore, and knowing the damage such work had done to his body, he wasn't surprised.

'I'd say he intends to kill me.'

'What? He said that?'

'Well, he implied it, at least. And he's welcome to try. As long as we get out of here, he can try what he likes. Arsehole.' She muttered the last word under her breath, though Rigg swung around, glaring at her.

'I'm saddened to hear it, Jael,' Alek sighed. 'He's always been a loyal friend to me. He's saved my life more times than I can count.'

'Though where family's concerned, his resentment runs deep,' Jael warned. 'And he blames my family for the death of his, so likely he won't rest until he makes me pay.'

'Well, I know what passion the thought of my sons stirs within me. The thought of anyone hurting them, let alone killing them? I understand his anger, his sadness, though he must see that we're on the same side here? That you'll help us?'

Jael stared at the frail man, trying not to dash his hopes. 'I'm sure deep down he does. And to get you out of here, I sense we're going to need him.'

***

'Pull up!' Gant bellowed. 'Rexon! Pull up!'

Saala's gates were slammed shut; he heard the locking bar dropping into place.

And screams.

Over the shouted orders and crackling fire, Gant could hear people screaming in terror.

Behind him, those armed with bows shot at the men on the ramparts, striking one. Gant swung around to them. 'Cover me!' And spurring Gus down the path, he aimed him at Rexon's galloping chestnut mare. '*Rexon*!' Arrows flew in both directions – he felt one skim his arm – and dropping his head further, he was soon alongside the Lord of Saala.

Rexon turned to him, eyes bursting with the need to do something.

But the gates were shut.

What could he do on his own? What could they do with so few men?

'We have to leave!' Gant pleaded. '*Rexon*! Do not die here!'

Rexon turned his mare in circles, eyes darting to the ramparts, back to Gant, then further back to those archers trying to keep them safe. Smoke burned his throat, his racing heart a pain deep in his chest now.

He couldn't breathe.

'Let's go!' Gant urged, nudging Gus forward.

Rexon's hands trembled as he tightened his grip on the reins. An arrow speared his horse in the rump, and she reared up in shock. He clung to her, urging her down to the ground, and with a look back at his fort, now in enemy hands, he flicked the reins, reluctantly aiming her at the trees.

***

When Erling finally returned from Hest, Axl called a council meeting.

'I've decided on horses,' Gisila told her son as they waited to begin. Amma and Getta hadn't arrived, nor had Erling. 'I spoke to Nils, and he has two possible contenders. A brother and sister from Saldis. It feels a worthy gift, suitable for a Brekkan king to give.' She lifted an eyebrow at her son, who seemed distracted. And noticing that he was crushing a scroll in his right hand, she frowned. 'Have you had news?'

Axl nodded. 'Another note from Gant. He suspects Mutt Storman has powerful allies, for how else is he managing to acquire so many weapons? So many men?'

Gisila sighed, forgetting all about horses now. 'I do fear his ambition.'

Axl was starting to as well. He ran a hand through his beard, becoming tense. 'But who could they be? These allies?'

Gisila didn't know. 'Your father had little trouble amongst his own people over the years. Nothing that flared up threatening to become something more. He battled the Islanders and the Hestians. Iskavall was like an annoying sibling but generally manageable, and Helsabor just hid away behind its walls, seeking to disappear.' Gisila clasped her hands in front of her dark blue dress, feeling a chill. 'What else does he say?' They stood in the meeting chamber where a brazier was burning – almost suffocating in the small space – though she felt as though someone had dropped a block of ice down her back.

'Just that he'll remain with Rexon until he has a clearer picture of what's happening.'

Erling Venberg entered the chamber looking markedly different from when he'd departed Andala some weeks ago.

'You've had a haircut,' Axl noted in surprise, seeing his friend's closely cropped black hair, which had always touched his shoulders.

A frowning Erling ran a hand over his fuzzy scalp. 'There was an... incident with a barrel of mead, an arm-wrestling competition and a candelabra,' he joked. 'Hopefully, it'll grow back by winter.'

Gisila didn't smile as she took her seat. 'And where is everyone else?' she muttered as Gerald led two servants into the chamber, carrying trays of nuts and ale. 'I had hoped to start by now.'

Axl glanced at the open door, though he couldn't even hear a sign of Amma or Getta. 'Perhaps they've gone to visit my new dreamer? Amma did mention wanting to take Helga and the boy a basket of food. To help them settle in,' he added, seeing what his mother thought about that.

'New dreamer?' Erling almost dropped the cup Gerald had handed him, turning to Axl in surprise. 'What dreamer?'

'Helga,' Axl said. 'She's not to everyone's taste,' he added, hearing Gisila snort. 'Though she's come to help.'

Erling shook his head as though dazed. 'I don't understand. Where did she come from? She just... turned up?'

'From Tuura. She heard about what's been happening and wanted to do her part.'

'Well, that's her story, at least,' Gisila muttered, turning from Axl to Erling. 'Though I have my doubts. She certainly wasn't wanted in Tuura.'

'No? Why is that?' Erling wondered, though his question went unanswered as an apologetic Amma swept into the room, followed by her sister.

'Your hair!' Amma exclaimed in surprise. 'I... you look quite different.'

Erling smiled ruefully, once again running a hand over his scalp. 'Yes, it's quite a change. My mother isn't especially taken with it.'

Gisila laughed. 'No, I imagine not. And how is your sister? I heard she was ill.'

'She's a little better today, though still in bed. Mother is hovering over her, attending to her every need. Hopefully, she'll be well enough to travel to Angard. It's all they can talk about.'

Gisila's tension rose, and she remembered the horses and how much else there was to do and only three days left to do it in. 'Well,' she smiled at Axl as he took his seat, 'shall we hurry on? I can't be sitting around all day!'

***

'Perhaps you could teach Meena something about dreaming?' Bayla said with a beaming smile, eyes shifting from the comely Mattie Bilso to her red-faced lump of a daughter-in-law, who sat opposite her, fussing over her crying daughter.

Mattie looked surprised, caught between two opposing forces. She saw Meena blush and Bayla sit up straighter, that confident smile never faltering.

'She was not trained as a dreamer, you see,' Bayla went on, ignoring her granddaughter's tantrum and Meena's struggle to deal with it, encumbered as she was by her enormous belly.

'Willa, please, that is Lila's, not yours. You must let her have it, sweetheart,' Meena tried, looking around for the girl's nursemaid, who had disappeared to find Willa's favourite toy.

'You can play with my cat if you stop crying!' Mattie called over the noise, eyes on the girl, who soon swung around, peering at the strange woman stroking the cat on her lap. 'His name is Otter, and he's a very special cat. A magical cat.'

Even Bayla looked interested in that, and soon all eyes were on the fluffy brown cat with the white-tipped ears who, sensing the attention, lifted his head, lengthening his neck.

Willa reached out to touch him, but Mattie shook her head. 'Are you sure you've stopped your tears? That they're all gone now?'

Willa Dragos nodded with enormous moist eyes, bottom lip protruding.

'Alright then,' Mattie smiled, and plonking Otter down on the balcony floor, she left her cat in the care of the toddler.

'Perhaps we need a cat?' Bayla mused as peace returned. 'Is it really magical?'

Mattie grinned, though she didn't answer.

Which led Bayla back to her previous thought. 'And you were trained at Tuura?'

Leaning forward, Mattie helped herself to another sweetmeat. She couldn't get enough of the miniature delicacies, though she was becoming aware that she was the only one eating and that the plate was nearly empty. 'For a time, though I left when I was fifteen. The elders and I came to realise that we wanted... different things. So I taught myself after that.'

'And you are Eadmund's dreamer? He has so many now, I think. If he still has that woman on Oss?'

Mattie shook her head. 'No, I don't believe I am. When the queen was kidnapped in Tuura, I offered to help find her.'

'So you'll return to Tuura when Jael's safe?' Meena asked, finally getting a word in.

'I expect so. My home is there. Though not until I help the king. He needs me.'

'Yes, I agree,' Bayla hummed, eyes returning to Meena. 'The advice of a dreamer is invaluable to a king, wouldn't you say, Daughter?'

Meena gulped down a mouthful of bile, feeling strange. 'I, yes, of course...' She winced, a burning pain shooting up the back of her leg. This pregnancy, quick on the heels of the last, had been a more uncomfortable ordeal than her previous two, and she was looking forward to feeling like herself again. She blinked, gripping the armrests of her chair.

Sighing, Bayla turned back to her granddaughter, who was becoming more confident with Otter. 'Gently now,' she urged the little girl. 'You don't want a scratch.'

'Are you alright?' Mattie asked Meena. 'Have you seen something?'

Meena shook her head, trying to push herself out of the chair, though she appeared quite firmly wedged in place. 'No, no, I... I... the baby is coming!'

***

'My children!' Rexon raged. 'My *wife*!' He wasn't sure if he was crying or whether the swirling smoke was merely stinging his eyes, but he couldn't see. His heart throbbed, every muscle knotted, every breath like heavy fog. 'I need to...' And coughing violently, he bent over, retching.

Gant patted his back, eyes darting around the gathered men, who huddled in the trees near their horses. His men. Rexon's Saalans were all back in the fort with their families. With Rexon's. 'We have to go,' is all he could say; the only option to advise. 'Saala has fallen. We won't know about your family for some time. As the wife of the lord, Demaeya has a good chance.'

Flinging up his head, Rexon bared his teeth. 'A good chance? And what if I said that about Gisila? Would you just leave? Do nothing?' Ignoring the curious stares of the Andalan warriors, he strode away.

Gant let him go, calling over his second-in-command – a useful man named Saki. 'How are we with supplies?'

Saki rubbed his own stinging eyes. The smoke from the fort was being driven west on a stiff breeze now, and their horses were shifting around, growing disturbed. 'We're low. We had enough for today but after that? We'll have to hunt. Eat on the road.'

Gant scratched his beard.

They needed more men, though his time in the South had shown him that former allies could no longer be counted upon. The growing resentment bred by poor harvests and devastating plagues was festering and spreading. He didn't know where he could be guaranteed to find a lord still loyal to Axl. And realising that, he shook his head.

They could aim east, head to Borsund, whose lord had ships. Take one, head home. But could he still rely on the man?

He could lead them west instead, but that way was paved with treachery, he was sure.

Then there was south. Hest.

Was Karsten Dragos still an ally?

Saki took a waterskin from one of his men, offering it to Gant, who shook his head, indicating that he give it to Rexon.

Gus nudged him, nudging harder until Gant turned towards him.

And there he saw the path.

East.

***

A waddling Meena Dragos was hurried upstairs in a fluster of noisy panic.

She remained mostly calm, though Bayla became frantic, calling for help, then quickly sending her servants on their way, demanding someone find Berard.

Mattie tried to calm her, though that didn't improve things, and eventually, she left the Dragos women to it and the nursemaid to deal with the children, hoping to find Berard Dragos herself. She imagined he would want to be as close to his wife as possible.

Heading downstairs, she became distracted, remembering her own doomed pregnancy, and then just as quickly, trying to think of something else.

A wide-eyed Berard was charging up the steps as Mattie walked outside.

'Meena?' he panted.

'She's upstairs. Your mother's with her.'

Berard didn't wait to hear any more, and soon Mattie was alone again. She inhaled a breath, feeling tension building in the pit of her stomach, eyes on the busy square, and past that to the bustling harbour.

Soon they would head back to S'ala Nis.

She remembered her conversation with Jael Furyck in the tunnel and Eadmund's grief when he'd returned to *Bone Hammer* without his wife.

She thought of Berard and Meena; Fyn, who couldn't wait to see that girl on Oss; Thorgils, so worried about his own wife and children.

And sighing, tears flooded her eyes as Mattie realised how desperately lonely she felt.

How unbearably sad.

***

As the afternoon progressed, the heat intensified around the Tower of Eyshar.

It was getting hard to breathe.

A breeze had picked up, though it wasn't cooling, just troublesome. Sifting dust, it whirled it around, into eyes, up noses and down throats. So now those slaves with parched mouths and grainy eyes were further hampered, made even more miserable.

They needed water – anything to drink.

As Jael exited the tower, she felt as though she'd entered a fire pit. The swirling heat from the blazing sun threatened to knock her over. Seeing no sign of Alek, she aimed for Quint, who stood like a signpost in the middle of a cluster of wagons and slaves, arms pointing in every direction. He'd tied a wet cloth around his head, holding another to his mouth to keep out the dust, though he was still croaking and coughing.

Jael headed for him, then hearing a crunching noise, she turned around to see a man collapse. He'd been carrying a heavy stone slab, and unable to hold his balance or the slab in his weary arms, he'd dropped it on his foot. 'Gaspar!' she called, and hurrying forward with another slave, they lifted the slab off the young man. Seeing the crushed mess of his foot, she stood, signalling for the overseer. 'Quint!'

He came quickly, grimacing at the sight of that mashed foot. 'Get that stone up the tower!' he ordered the other man. 'And you,' he said to Jael. 'We need a stretcher. Bring it back with two men. Have them take him to the physician's.'

'I can take him,' Jael quickly offered. 'I know where it is. And the physician needs to look at my wrists. Under the fetters, it smells rotten.'

Quint frowned at her. 'Rotten?'

Jael nodded with big eyes, showing him a glimpse of the wounds beneath one of her wrist fetters. 'If they get any worse, I may die.'

'*Die?*' Quint scoffed. 'What are you talking about?'

Jael's nodding was enthusiastic. 'That's what the physician

said. It's like any wound that turns bad. Once it fouls the blood, it can kill you.'

Quint had seen many amputations in his time, so with a shudder, he nodded, not wanting to be responsible for his most famous slave's sudden demise. He saw Rigg coming with a stretcher. 'Take Rigg. But quickly! We can't lose more time!' And erupting in a coughing fit, his attention was soon claimed by another slave with another problem.

Alek wasn't far behind Rigg, and quickly assessing the situation, he sought a word with Jael. 'You're to take him to the physician's? You and Rigg?'

Jael nodded.

'They won't spare a wagon, so you'll have to walk. Perhaps it will give you an opportunity to... smooth things over?'

Jael looked doubtful. 'I have to go.'

Alek touched her arm. 'Someone said you wanted me?'

'Gardi does,' Jael told him, turning away. 'He needs more bricks, but there's something wrong with the pulley.' She hurried to Gaspar, who writhed in agony, stirring up dust. Rigg stood by his legs, ready to lift the man. 'We need to drag him onto the stretcher,' Jael told him. 'But first, we have to deal with that leg.'

'That's what the physician's for,' Rigg snapped, bending down to grab Gaspar's good leg.

'No! Leave him!' And rushing to the nearest wagon, Jael helped herself to a thin strip of wood, which she snapped in half. And tearing off the bottom of her tunic, she braced a now-sobbing Gaspar's foot, doubting Ratish would be able to save it – the bones were crushed.

Hearing Rigg muttering under his breath, she made knots in the cloth and stood. 'We'll go as quickly as we can,' she promised. And coming around to Gaspar's left side, she indicated for Rigg to help her. 'We'll drag him onto here, then we'll go.'

Rigg scowled but offered his help, and with a yelp and a sob, their patient was soon on the stretcher.

Inesh Seppo hurried towards them, brandishing a cup. He

said something that neither Jael nor Rigg understood, though bending down, he offered what smelled like wine to the injured man.

Straightening up, the concerned-looking seer fixed his brown eyes on Jael, now speaking the common tongue. 'I am Inesh Seppo, the Noor-Elect.' He glanced down at Jael's fetters before raising his eyes again.

'We must go!' Rigg barked, tugging the stretcher.

And with a hasty smile at the seer, Jael stumbled after him.

Watching her go, Inesh Seppo bowed his head, closing his eyes.

***

Berard Dragos' eyes were moist with tears when he entered the hall later that afternoon. The joy of his wife safely delivering a healthy child had him feeling emotional and slightly giddy.

'Another daughter!' his brother called, holding up his goblet. 'Another princess of the realm!'

Berard was thrilled to have three daughters. Three vibrant little lives. It was a gift greater than any he'd thought would be bestowed upon him. And his wife.

She was a joy like no other.

'And how's Meena?' Eadmund asked. They had been discussing plans around Karsten's map table when Berard had burst in with the good news.

'Relieved. I think we're both just so relieved. So much can go wrong. And yet?' He shook his head. 'I will sacrifice to Thita in thanks!' he decided loudly. He saw Karsten's eye narrow and tempered his enthusiasm, knowing his brother was still grieving his lost son.

Tipping back his wine, Karsten looked away. He didn't

begrudge Berard his happiness, for sometimes it felt as though his family was cursed by the gods. So much had gone wrong, so much had been taken from them. He was smiling, full of good humour when in company, but in private?

He felt deeply alone.

Brightening his face, he smiled at Berard. 'Well, you go and take Meena our best wishes. And little...'

'Sasha.'

'Sasha. Take her our best wishes too.' Karsten turned back to the map table, all thoughts of babies and dreamers quickly gone from his mind. 'We must get on with the planning,' he told his friends. 'For if we don't leave on this rescue mission soon, Bayla will never forgive me.'

Eadmund turned to him. 'We? But I thought –'

'What? Me?' Karsten laughed. 'No, Ulf. He's promised he'll join Bayla in Angard, so we need to get him there and back as soon as possible. Though ask Ulf and I think he'd happily stay at sea for weeks.' He laughed, imagining what his mother would think about that. She'd never said, thought it was obvious to everyone how much Bayla had come to rely upon Ulf over the years.

And love.

Karsten knew she had come to love him too.

'Well, you'll get no argument from me,' Eadmund promised. 'The sooner we leave, the sooner I get my wife back. We just need to ready the ships. Ready the ships and make our plans.' He was raring to go, impatient to leave, though he knew it was important to do this right, certain that if they failed, none of them would see Oss again.

CHAPTER TWENTY-ONE

Ratish was occupied when they arrived at the physician's rooms, so Jael and Rigg deposited the injured slave with another physician, who seemed ill-tempered and unprepared. Though there was little to be done, and they were promptly sent on their way, back to the tower.

Leaving the building, they bumped into Ratish, who looked surprised but pleased to see Jael.

'You are well?' he whispered. 'And those wrists and ankles?'

Jael shrugged. 'I've more important things to worry about.'

'That sounds... concerning.'

She smiled, feeling a rush of energy. Just being out of the sun for a moment was a relief. She saw glimpses of Sunni dashing down the hall, though, and her good mood vanished. 'Tell me about the seer, Inesh Seppo? Is he like the old seer?'

Ratish peered at her. 'The old seer?' Then, only guessing at her meaning, and sneaking a glance at a glowering Rigg, he shrugged. 'He came here as a young man many years ago now. He learned everything from Noor. They were especially close. Why do you ask?'

'No reason. I met him at the tower.' And brushing off Ratish's attempts to inspect her wrists, she spun around. 'We have to get back. Hopefully, we can find our way!'

Rigg grunted at the physician and turned to follow, soon catching her up.

'What are you doing? Making your own plans?' he snarled. 'Doing whatever suits you?' They headed across the cobbled street, immediately seeking the shade offered by a wall of fresh-smelling pines. Jael slowed down, trying to get her bearings. She had been led here more than once by Sunni, though she was still not certain where to go. 'Where's the harbour from here? How do we get there?'

'You want to go to the harbour? Now?'

'Why not now? I doubt we'll be free to go anywhere until the funeral. This is our only chance.'

'To do what?'

A pair of finely dressed ladies headed towards them, eyes on Jael, whispering to each other. They looked disgusted but also intrigued. Stepping out of their path, Jael dragged Rigg after her. 'Someone will find us soon enough, so we don't have much time. When the attack starts, we have to push up from the temple towards the harbour. No matter what's happening at the tower, they'll keep men stationed there. And if I'm leading, I need to understand the path to get there. When I arrived, I was brought in through tunnels.'

'It's one of the ways in,' Rigg said, beady eyes darting up and down the street, fearing they'd be stopped. He led Jael down the alley that would take them back to the main road. 'But not the way I came. They take the female slaves that way. They get sorted into those worthy of pleasure and those only good for work.'

'Pleasure? Whose pleasure?' Jael snorted, keeping her head low, not wishing to draw any unwanted attention. She followed after Rigg, who stomped with uncertainty ahead of her. 'What is it?'

He grunted, sniffed loudly but remained silent, focusing on heading towards another row of trees. 'We should go around the back. Less chance of being spotted.'

'Though more chance of looking suspicious,' Jael decided. 'Let's stay on the main road.'

Rigg pulled up now. 'Are you in charge of me? The boss

here? *My* boss?'

'For now. Seems that I am.'

'I don't think so, loser.' And jerking around, Rigg strode off, not wanting the queen's company.

Though Jael soon caught him, eager for that shade. 'I can get us out of here.'

'*I* can get us out of here.'

'And you've been here how many years? Do you stay because you enjoy it?'

A simmering Rigg clenched his fists, seeing a troop of soldiers heading their way. Jael was drawing everyone's eyes, and he was becoming increasingly tense, not understanding the point of what they were doing. 'I... the timing needs to be right. It's taken Alek a long time to build connections across the isle. We've worked solidly over the years. Together. Now there are allies in the palace, the stables, the Arena. Even at the harbour. You may have just swanned in, but we've been making plans for years now.'

'You!' a soldier shouted, and nudging one of his friends, they headed across the road towards Jael and Rigg. 'Stop right there!'

***

Korri Torluffson's two ships arrived in Castala after an unremarkable journey from Zagora.

Edela wondered if Iker Rayas would follow them. One-eyed Iker Rayas, she remembered, watching Zen offering to help Siggy over the side of *Sea Queen*, down onto the pier.

Siggy appeared insulted by his offer, though perhaps remembering that he was grieving, she shook her head and took his hand.

Bertel held Edela back. 'We tell no one you're a dreamer,' he whispered hoarsely. 'Never again. Not till we're safe in our own beds.'

'Our own beds?' she frowned, spinning around to him. 'And where exactly might that be? I can't remember what it feels like to have a home anymore. Or a family.'

'Well, be grateful you still have one, Edela, for both Siggy and I have lost ours. And poor Zen. The only one of us who isn't a homeless orphan is you.'

Edela felt terrible. She'd barely slept on the journey from Bakkar to Castala and had been in a fractious mood. 'I'm sorry,' she sighed, turning back as one of Korri's men offered her a hand. 'Oh, thank you,' she smiled. The young man had been experiencing terrible spasms in his right shoulder, and she had used the last of her lavender and yarrow salve to release it.

Bertel nodded as he reached up to take her in his arms, lifting her over the shield rack.

Edela's first glimpses of Castala had her heart sinking. It was a sprawling city, much bigger than Bakkar, from what she could make out. Though just as busy. If she was meant to find something here, it was going to be a hard task. She thought wistfully of the pretty little islands of Illonia. Though despite their beauty, they had also lured her into traps of her own making.

Here, in Castala, she had to be careful. And clever.

Bertel was right. No one could know she was a dreamer.

***

Jael wished she could simply make herself invisible.

She had hoped to get to the harbour, wanting to assess the route for herself.

But now?

'What are you doing here?' one of the soldiers demanded, right hand hovering near his sword.

Rigg twitched beside the slave queen, hoping she didn't drag him into her mess.

'We've been sent with a message for the commander,' Jael told him. 'Argo Kosta. Our overseer said to find him at the harbour. Apparently, he's there.'

'The harbour? And then?'

'Then we're to report back to the temple grounds. We're working on the Tower of Eyshar.'

The soldier eyed her with suspicion, though his friend sought to draw him away. Jael recognised him as one of Nico Sikari's friends.

'Come on. We have to report to the palace. Do you want to be late? They'll be whipped soon enough if they've left the tower without permission.'

How right he was, Jael thought, not liking the sound of that. She bobbed her head, keeping it down until Nico's friend managed to drag the other soldier away. And when they were gone, she hurried up the road.

She could smell the sea.

The breeze that had stirred up so much dust was blowing in from the harbour.

'How many ships?' she wondered, glancing at Rigg, who exhaled loudly. 'In the harbour? I never asked Arras. Not sure why.'

'Oh, Arras, is it? Your friend, the commander?'

Ignoring him, Jael carried on. 'If we're escaping an island, how many can fit on the ships? We don't want to leave any behind.'

'That's not the plan. The plan is to stay, not to sail away.'

Jael peered at him. 'Though one plan is never enough. You and Alek have your numbers and your allies, but I've led men into battle. Vast armies. I know how useless plans become when one thing or another goes wrong. So, if we have to leave, I need to know how many ships can take us.' Rigg grunted, which was his most common method of communication, Jael realised, and ignoring him, she lengthened her stride, eager to reach the harbour before they were stopped again.

***

'Seven days,' Arras decided, leaning over Karsten's map. It stopped before ever reaching S'ala Nis, though seeing the distance from Hest's capital to Bakkar, he could guess how long it would take. 'Eight at most, but we should aim for seven.'

Beside him, Kolarov tottered about, ready to burst.

'Yes?' Eadmund wondered. 'Is something wrong?'

'The... *trouble* we encountered on our way here, my lord,' Kolarov said with great deliberation, eyes darting from one king to the other. 'That unexpected trouble... what if something similar were to... occur again once we get within distance of the... isle?'

Karsten scanned the gathered party, seeing something resembling horror blooming on every face present: Fyn, Mattie, Thorgils, Arras and Bolder. Ulf was there, too, though he simply looked confused. 'Trouble?'

'Well, there was a little fire,' Eadmund mumbled. 'Though we survived it well enough.'

'What sort of fire? Sea-fire?' Karsten asked.

Thorgils laughed. 'We would've liked some sea-fire!'

Karsten didn't understand. 'What fire then?'

'Walls of fire,' Mattie explained, sensing Eadmund's hesitation but knowing that they couldn't hide the danger from the King of Hest, for what if they did encounter such trouble again?

'In the sea?' Ulf didn't understand, glancing at Karsten.

Who scratched his beard. 'Not sea-fire?'

'It was a dreamer,' Mattie said. 'A dreamer did it.'

'So the island Jael's imprisoned on has a dreamer?' Karsten's bravado retreated. It had been years since they'd had to face a dreamer, and he wasn't sure it made sense to do so again.

Arras spoke up. 'No, though the king is married to a dreamer.'

'A dark one?' Karsten snapped, turning to look at Eadmund and Thorgils, who certainly looked disturbed. 'A dark fucking dreamer? And you thought to keep that to yourselves? You were just going to borrow my ships and lead them into a sea of fire conjured up by a dark fucking dreamer?'

'Mattie stopped her!' Fyn blurted out, directing everyone's attention towards the dreamer, who looked unhappy to receive it.

'Well, I...'

'Mattie helped us escape,' Eadmund explained. 'We were set upon by a handful of ships likely belonging to the king. And yes, there were walls of fire, but we got through those too. I wasn't keeping it from you, Karsten. We're discussing it now, aren't we?'

'Only because your explorer brought it up!' Karsten huffed, feeling Ulf's hand on his back.

He remembered the night he'd met Ulf.

He remembered what had happened to his brother.

A dark, powerful dreamer...

Shuddering, he looked towards the hallway entrance, as if seeking an escape. 'Who is she? What does she want?'

No one knew, so there was no answer.

'To keep Jael on the isle?' Kolarov eventually suggested with a shrug. 'Though for what purpose or reason, we still have no idea.' And now every head turned towards Arras.

Eadmund stared at the man, convinced that he hadn't revealed everything he knew. Though perhaps not intentionally, he conceded, for Arras likely didn't appreciate the significance of every morsel of information he possessed. 'The queen never spoke of Jael before? Of what she might want with her?'

'In my presence, no,' Arras said, becoming uncomfortable. His rescuers had been understanding about his role in Jael's kidnapping, though he remained on edge, fearing that one wrong word would set them against him. 'I knew nothing about Jael until the night the queen brought me in to discuss her plan.'

Thorgils leaned across the table. 'Tell us everything she said. Were you alone? You and the queen?'

Arras shook his head. 'There were two other men with me. I'd been asked to bring them along.'

'And what did she say?' Eadmund wondered.

Arras was immediately back in that enormous chamber, reeking with fragrant smoke, the queen staring at him with intense eyes.

'I have a very special mission for you,' Kalina purred, eyeing each man in turn, though her attention lingered longer on Arras. 'A mission that will take you all the way to Osterland.'

Karam looked excited, Iker intrigued, but Arras frowned. 'Osterland, my queen? For more slaves?'

Kalina shook her head, indicating for her own slave to pour wine for her guests. 'Well, one slave,' she conceded. 'You, Arras, will bring me a very special slave. A slave queen.'

Arras blinked. 'A queen?'

'Her name is Jael Furyck, a Brekkan warrior of some renown. Now Queen of the Slave Islands.'

'And she will be in Osterland?'

'Yes. That is what I've been told.'

Arras had thought about it then as he thought about it now.

By who? Who had told her that?

'And you, Karam. I have set you the most distasteful task. You are to kill Osterland's dreamers. Every old crone you can find. I want them strung up and torn apart. Make it gruesome. I seek to encourage their silence, so you must frighten those who remain into hiding. Do you understand?'

Karam nodded, a hungry look in his eyes.

'And that leaves you, dear Iker,' Kalina smiled, patting his arm. 'You must hunt down one dreamer in particular. The most troublesome one of all, I imagine. Edela Saeveld. She is Jael Furyck's grandmother. If anyone is going to cause us problems, it will be her. You will find her at the Temple of Tuura, I understand. At the very tip of Osterland.'

None of the men understood what their mission was about, though they hadn't felt entitled to press for clarification.

Kalina had encouraged Karam and Iker to drink, taking a moment to approach Arras alone. 'Your mission matters most of all, commander. And when you return, we shall have other, more personal matters to discuss.'

When Arras had finished speaking, Eadmund blinked. 'So the queen wanted the dreamers silenced and Edela unable to help Jael? To warn her?'

'It seems that way.'

'Though the question remains why?' Karsten put in, still frowning. 'For if your queen went to so much trouble to find Jael, there must be a reason. A reason important enough not to want to lose her.'

Thorgils frowned. 'The king's wife. The dreamer. She must have told your queen that Jael would be in Osterland, for we didn't know we'd be there ourselves, did we? And certainly not in Tuura.'

Eadmund nodded.

Karsten brandished his empty goblet at the nearest servant. 'Well, they sound like people who need to be stopped!' he decided loudly. 'First Jael and Edela, then who? They want to kill all the dreamers? I have a mostly useless one, though I don't intend to lose her. Likely Meena's daughters are dreamers, too, so we have to do something. Whatever they want, whatever their plan, you need to stop them.'

Eadmund raised his lips into a smile, though he didn't feel happy.

Just desperate to begin.

'We'll float the fleet tomorrow, get all the ships into the harbour,' Karsten decided, eyeing a nodding Ulf. 'So we'd better finalise your plans.'

***

They had been riding in silence for hours, and a bereft Rexon could no longer take it. Thoughts burned like hot flames in his mind. Fears and hopes wrestled in a desperate battle to see which would come out on top.

He jerked his injured mare to a stop, and jumping down, he ran towards a row of brambles, vomiting violently.

Gant jumped down after him, ordering Saki to keep watch and the rest of the men to take a break. 'You alright?' he asked Rexon when he turned around. It was a stupid question that had rushed out of an exhausted mind. 'Sorry, I mean –'

'I am no more,' Rexon said starkly, unable to focus. He wiped his beard, spitting. 'If my family is dead, which likely they are, I am no more.' Tears came, and bending forward, he covered his face with his hands, sobbing.

Gant took him in his arms, tears in his own eyes. Just the thought of those poor little children. And Demaeya? It didn't seem real. 'We'll head back as soon as we can. As soon as we have the men.'

Rexon's arms fell to his sides. He felt encased in a tomb of pain, so oppressive that he struggled to even breathe. The grief was too much to wrap his mind around. It was as though the gods had torn out his heart and flung it far from his body. As though he was no longer alive.

'As soon as we have the men,' Gant repeated. 'We'll return as soon as we have the men.'

'They must be stopped,' Rexon panted. 'And we must stop them, Gant. Whatever we have to do, we must tear the flesh from their bones!'

***

Dessalene Sardis tore the flesh off a pork bone like a starving beggar.

Sitting opposite her, Kalina cringed, still nauseous and miserable.

'I do like a well-cooked pig!' Dessalene announced as she tossed the bone onto her plate and picked up a napkin, dabbing her glistening lips. 'You have such talented cooks here, Kalina. I had almost forgotten!' Her eyes snapped to the archway leading into the hall, where her little spy had appeared. 'Pye! Are you lost, precious thing? Or have you come upon a juicy tidbit?'

Turning her head, Kalina soon saw the odd-looking creature creeping into the dining hall. The oily little man made her shudder. His protruding eyes were evasive and smug. He would never meet her eye, which she found highly disconcerting, though she was certain he was always watching her.

'My queens,' Pye smiled, bowing deeply. 'I had no idea it was supper time.'

'Shut up with your charm!' Dessalene snapped, good humour vanishing as though it had never truly been there, just a veneer masking a seething anger that blazed like fire. 'We have no need for it, just your information. What do you know, Pye? What have you seen?'

Brushing off the insults, which he took as a form of endearment, Pye bowed some more. 'Your favourite slave has been wandering about the city, my queen.'

Kalina jolted forward. 'What do you mean, wandering about?'

Pye shrugged, wide-eyed with innocence. 'I couldn't say, though the matter was brought to my attention, so I felt it necessary to bring it to yours.'

'*You* felt it necessary?' Dessalene flapped a hand. 'You impertinent toad! Have Argo Kosta sent to the palace. The queen must have a word about how he is managing his slaves.'

Kalina stared at her stepmother as Pye turned away.

'The commander has his talents, though he has never been

particularly attentive to his responsibilities,' Dessalene told her. 'It is quite apparent why your father sought to put Arras Sikari in charge. According to him, Kosta had a habit of *disappearing*. I imagine that's still the case? Disappearing into the arms of those wanton concubines in the harem!' She sneered now, not understanding the weakness of men. To undermine their futures with such self-defeating behaviour?

'I must find someone to replace Arras,' Kalina said blankly.

'I would leave your father to do that. It's better if it's him, Kalina. He won't be happy with the mess you've made. I imagine he'll seek to make changes in that way of his.'

And reminded that her father was returning to the isle, Kalina shuddered, thoughts of Arras Sikari and Jael Furyck fleeing her mind. 'My father, he... hasn't even returned for my weddings.' She ignored the plates of steaming ox hearts the slaves delivered to the table. The dish itself smelled enticing, though her attention remained on her grinning stepmother, who was always one step ahead of everyone.

'Though what choice have you given him, dearest? He has thought about returning many times over the years, but this? You have outdone yourself, Kalina. Throwing his prize into the pits? Murdering his beloved seer, displeasing the god your father owes his success to? And then, seeking to escape your great litany of misjudgments, you took a knife to your wrists and opened them into a warm bath, trying to end your life, thereby depriving your father of his only heir!' She smiled at the queen, fluttering thick eyelashes. 'There is simply so much to choose from! So much your father will wish to discuss!'

Kalina was growing more uncomfortable by the moment, and she certainly didn't want more food. Reaching for her goblet, she gulped down a mouthful of wine that quickly burned her throat. 'What will he do with her? Or me?' she asked in a small voice.

'Ronin? I imagine he will inspect Jael Furyck like a treasure stolen from his enemies. Then he will return her to the heat and the sun and the back-breaking misery. And you? We shall have to wait and see!' And rubbing her hands together, Dessalene picked up her knife and stabbed it into a steaming heart.

***

Jael and Rigg didn't return from their adventure until supper, much to Quint's annoyance and Alek's horror.

After a barracking from Quint, they joined Alek at his table, where Rigg quickly shooed away his companions so they could speak in private.

'But where were you?' Alek hissed. 'Did something happen? I thought Quint would send for Kosta. He should have done so immediately, though I imagine he didn't want to get in trouble himself.' Alek saw Quint cuff one of the slaves around the ear – he was obviously in a foul mood. Though he wasn't a cruel man, just married to the daughter of one.

'Your queen decided to take a tour,' Rigg grunted, pulling his bowl towards him, too hungry to be disappointed by the small helping of stew. An oily film clung to the top of whatever lurked beneath, and grabbing his spoon, Rigg broke through that film with gusto.

'A tour?' Alek blinked at Jael.

'To see the harbour,' Jael explained, the smell of the stew turning her stomach. She looked away, seeing a commotion at the door and Quint disappearing through it. Lowering her head, she eyed Alek. 'We need more than one plan. You may think you've calculated every number and all the possibilities of what might happen, but battle changes plans. It changes minds. Those who insist they'll be with you? When you blow that shell and they're faced with a wall of soldiers, armed with swords and capable of killing with them, there's no guarantee every slave will be able to find the courage to keep going, especially when the soldiers rally.'

Alek looked thoughtful, but Rigg scoffed loudly.

Unsurprisingly.

Jael rolled her eyes. 'You think differently? Every battle you've been in has gone to plan, has it? Or perhaps you never knew the plan to begin with, only having second or third-hand knowledge of your king's intentions.'

Rigg dropped his spoon and lunged across the table. 'Don't you speak about my king. What do you know of him?'

'That he's dead.'

Rigg sat back in horror. '*Dead*? Haaron Dragos? What? Killed by your father, was he?'

'My father's dead too. A lot's changed since you were last in Osterland.'

Rigg saw sadness in Jael's eyes, and picking up his spoon, he stirred his stew, hoping to awaken some flavour.

Jael took a breath. 'All I know is that if this revolt fails, it's the slaves who will suffer. They can't kill everyone, but they'll certainly kill the leaders, and you can be sure that those trying to save their own lives will point a finger at you.' She looked from Alek to Rigg, then past them to where Kosta had entered the dining hall, rendering it silent.

He strode around the tables until he reached theirs.

And there he stood, watching Jael.

CHAPTER TWENTY-TWO

'What do you see?' Linas asked his grandmother, who sat before the small fire with her eyes wide open, as though watching something in its flames. He was hungry, wanting her to turn her attention to the meal fire instead.

Surely it was time for supper?

Gully lay curled up at the dreamer's feet, tongue lolling from an open mouth. He'd followed Linas and Helga home and didn't appear inclined to leave.

Linas thought that Gully would need supper too. He didn't want him running away.

'I see a boy who won't have any supper if he keeps interrupting his grandmother. Now hush and let me finish. Pat that dog and keep him quiet. Do that, and you will eat soon enough and well. I have smoked trout, cabbage, and beans. Some bread, too, so be patient, child, and you will feast when I'm done.'

Nodding vigorously, Linas crouched down to the dog, stroking his thick black coat.

Helga returned her gaze to the flames, brow furrowing into deep troughs. She saw things that made no sense. It felt as though the ground was quaking beneath her feet; all that was certain, all that had stood for centuries, crumbling like great towers around her.

She heard her grandson's heartbeat and that of the dog's.

When her daughter had died in childbirth, she had sworn to

care for the boy. Her blood. The only family she had now.

'Kings will fall, the Furycks will die, and Brekka will stand alone.'

That same voice spoke to her from the flames – a warning that sent shivers through her body.

'A time of darkness will return. You cannot escape what is coming, Helga. Not by hiding. You won't. It is time to choose your side and enter the fray.'

***

Grabbing a handful of Jael's filthy hair, Kosta yanked her to her feet.

'My lord!' Alek was immediately on his own feet. 'But what has she done?' He glanced at Quint, who looked away, heading out of the dining hall.

Rigg's head remained down as he continued to eat.

'You were seen strolling around the harbour today. Looking to escape?' Kosta spat at Jael, and releasing his hand from her hair, he tightened it around her tunic, twisting the rough homespun until it started choking her.

Preventing her from speaking at all.

'She, she went to the physician's, my lord,' Alek explained, holding out an unsteady hand. 'You... she took an injured man to the physician's at Quint's direction. His foot was broken, and... and Rigg went with her. Though they got lost. They simply lost their way, lord.'

Kosta kept twisting Jael's tunic, further cutting off her oxygen.

And now, veins bulging in his thick neck, he started pulling her off her feet.

'Well?' he demanded. 'What do you have to say?'

'My lord, she can't speak!' Alek insisted.

And completely aware of that, the commander now turned his ire on Alek. 'Seize him!' he ordered, eyeing two of his men. 'You will come too!'

'Come where?' Alek panicked. 'But, my lord, I –'

He was knocked to the ground, kicked by one of Kosta's men.

Jael had thought that Kosta only meant to scare her, knowing that she'd already been pulled out of the pits, though now she feared what he intended to do.

Calmly placing his spoon on the table, Rigg stood. 'Alek's telling the truth, lord. Gaspar dropped a slab on his foot. Quint sent the woman with me to take him to the physician's. We left him there and –'

'And?' Kosta demanded, releasing Jael, who gasped in a breath, staggering. Her eyes flicked from Rigg to Alek, who had been hoisted into the air. 'And?'

'And she wanted her freedom,' Rigg snarled, eyeing Jael. 'It was nothing to do with Alek. He didn't send her anywhere. Quint did. And when we left the physician's, she wanted to see the city. I followed her, eventually convincing her to return.'

Kosta narrowed his eyes. 'You went along? Why? Because you feared her? What? You couldn't knock her out and throw her over your shoulder? Or seek help from someone braver? Stronger?'

Rigg's expression remained neutral, unchanging, as though carved into his stony face. 'I heard she was special, to be protected. I thought I could get her back in one piece.'

'Heard from who?'

'Gossip, lord. Whispers. Everyone talks about the woman.'

Jael wished Rigg would shut his mouth. She had no idea what he was doing except trying to get her thrown back into those pits.

'Well, then, let's give them something more to talk about!' Kosta grinned, wrinkles folding up like curtains, and dismissing Rigg with a grunt, he motioned for his men to release Alek. Then, grabbing another handful of Jael's hair, he tugged her through the hall and out into the night.

***

It was decided that they would sleep on *Sea Queen*, though Bertel wasn't pleased, having thought Edela's full pouch of coins meant that they could afford a room.

But Edela was not to be swayed. 'I would much rather know we can leave if we need to.'

'Though to do that, we need a helmsman and a crew,' a tired Bertel grumbled. 'And none of them are currently on board. Likely they've found actual beds, surrounded by walls and doors.' He flung out an arm, seeing that they were alone, bar Siggy, Zen, and the two men Korri had left to watch over them. Though Bertel didn't think they'd be much use against Iker Rayas and whatever men had escaped death in Bakkar.

'It's quieter here,' Edela added, remembering another of her arguments for why the ship made sense. 'Private too.'

A confused Bertel glanced around. '*Private*? With all these ships? All their crews? Not to mention whoever's making that noise! Sounds like cats being strangled!'

'Bertel, do sit down,' Edela sighed. 'I've no energy for a fight.'

'Fight?' Bertel slumped down onto a chest opposite her. Siggy and Zen were playing with the goat and cat. The girl was trying to cheer him up, though in the occasional flash of a swinging lantern, Bertel could see the abject misery in Zen's eyes, doubting she stood a chance. 'But we're not fighting, Edela. I'm merely pointing out that a more comfortable arrangement could have been organised. By me. I would have been happy to seek out accommodation for us.'

'Though here is where I want to be.'

And with a defeated sigh, Bertel left the subject alone.

'Tomorrow, we will take leave of our hospitable host and continue on this journey alone. To draw attention to ourselves will only hamper our progress. We must be like specks of dust, imperceptible to the naked eye.'

Bertel's frown dug a deep canyon between his grey eyebrows. 'Do you have any clues?'

'How ridiculous you are, Bertel Knutson, asking such questions. You know I never have a clue about what I'm supposed to do next!' She winked at him, smiling for the first time in a while.

He smiled back, shoulders dropping slightly. 'We are certainly living boldly,' he decided. 'Not dribbling and quivering in a corner like some our age.'

Now Edela laughed. 'Though I'd happily curl up and dribble on myself for a while. After what we've been through, it would be quite appropriate.'

'And what is to come? Do you think we'll ever see Osterland again?'

Edela saw Axl's face and Jael's, overcome by a desperate fear for her grandchildren. 'I... I really must make a decision about that. When we left Tuura, I was given the impression that I was not to return.'

Bertel saw how troubled she was. 'You should dream on it, Edela. Whoever gave you the warning about Tuura, the warning to leave, perhaps they had ulterior motives? Perhaps they didn't want to help you at all?'

Edela didn't want to admit that he might be right, though the thought nagged at her. She had left behind everyone she cared about, and it was long past time to decide if that was the right thing to do.

***

Jael was dragged into the courtyard, scalp burning, fearing that Kosta would tear out clumps of her hair. She tried to push herself towards him to lessen the pain, though he kicked her leg, and she lost her balance, crying out.

'Kilo! Hector!' Kosta called, motioning two of his men forward. 'Chain her up!'

The slaves had followed the commander towards the dining hall doors, wanting to see what would happen in the courtyard, though Quint had ordered them closed, and now the only witnesses for what was about to happen were Kosta, Quint, and four of the commander's men.

She would have fancied her chances...

Though then what?

There was simply no way off the isle on her own.

Dragged towards a stone arch she hadn't given much thought to before, Jael now saw that it had a particular purpose, as Kosta's men brought down chains with fetters, which they clamped around her wrists. And once her arms were secure, they dropped to the ground and drew out another pair of chained fetters, securing them around her ankles.

Panic started fraying Jael's thoughts. She felt flashes of dread, bracing for what would come next.

'Get back!' Kosta snapped at his men. 'Unless you want to lose some skin yourself? Kilo! Tear her tunic!'

Now Jael did brace herself. Closing her eyes, seeing she had no choice but to let everything unfold as Kosta intended, she sought to disappear inside herself.

She heard the commander scuffing his boots, grunting as he unfurled his whip.

'Are you afraid?' her father growled in her ears. 'Afraid of pain? After all that you begged me to make you a warrior, Jael, and now you're too afraid to get in that ring and fight?'

He was angry, but his voice was a comfort.

She heard Kosta barking orders, wanting to hear her father instead.

'But you still have a choice, Jael. I give you a choice, here and now,' Ranuf Furyck said to her. 'To choose the path of your mother, the pain of the childbed, the pain that comes from losing babies and children. Or you could choose my path, where I promise you will be bruised and broken and cut open. You will bleed and cry, and it will hurt. But it's your choice, Jael, for life is pain either way. You just need to choose your path...'

Jael heard the flick of the whip, and legs trembling, she tensed her body.

'I choose your path,' she whispered, gritting her teeth. 'I choose your path, Father.'

The whip cut her skin like a blade, searing across her back, tearing open her flesh. She reared up silently, mouth wrenched open, body singing with pain. Her eyes flooded with tears, and shaking now, Jael slumped forward, hearing Kosta's joyful laugh.

'You want to beg, bitch? Plead? Make me stop? Then tell me what you were really doing at the harbour! Tell me what plans you're making!'

Jael shut out his voice, taking herself back to Andala.

Closing her eyes, she saw Aleksander in the training ring. Gant was talking to him, giving him advice.

Her mother was holding Axl and shaking her head, and her father's arm was around her shoulder as he whispered in her ear. 'Whoever tries to stop you, Jael, they are your enemy. Never let them see weakness or fear. Never let them win.'

And now that vicious whip came for her again.

***

Standing on benches, watching through the high windows in the dining hall, Alek cringed, turning to Rigg in horror. 'Why did you do that?'

Rigg looked incensed. 'What would you've had me do?' he hissed. '*She* took the risk, *she* chose that path. I didn't! Let her suffer for it. Let her think next time she chooses to be reckless.'

Alek shook his head. 'I thought I knew you, that I understood you. I thought we were doing this together.'

'She's a Furyck!' Rigg snarled. 'A Brekkan! You have no idea what her family has done!'

'*I'm* a Brekkan!' Alek cried. 'My father put his sword behind Ranuf Furyck, as did my uncle, my grandfather, my brother. They were proud to serve the Furycks. Proud of our people. I don't know what you think you know, but you're wrong! Jael could have blamed you, brought you into it, but she didn't. She's out there suffering, no thanks to you!' Now he lowered his voice, which trembled, as his entire body trembled. 'And what do we do now? Without her to lead us?'

'We have me!' Rigg insisted. 'As we always have done. You never needed her, Alek. You have me!'

***

Jael thought she was swinging in the air. She felt like she was moving. There was no ground, no bones in her legs. She was just swinging.

Just flesh and pain and –

'What are you doing?' came a screeching voice.

She blinked. The rhythm was broken.

The whip didn't come again.

And now she opened her eyes.

It was nearly dark. Or perhaps that was the great cloud of pain descending upon her, blocking out anything real.

'What are *you* doing?' Kosta growled at the strange-looking man. He hopped about like a frog, flapping small arms, his bulging eyes almost popping out of his head. 'Interrupting me? Get away from here, you fucking turd!'

'I am sent by the dreamer, Dessalene, who bids me to inform you that you are abusing the king's prized slave! The king who will soon arrive to view said prized slave. And you? You brute! What have you done to her? You were to discipline her, not deface her!'

Jael hung suspended from the arch, blood oozing down her naked back, dripping on the ground. Despite the warm air, she shivered uncontrollably, thoughts mashed together. She could hear someone trying to stop that whip. She hoped he would succeed. Eyes closing, she knew it wasn't up to her.

What happened next wasn't up to her at all.

She saw Eadmund smiling at her.

Steam rose up to cloud his face, and she imagined they were in the hot pool outside Oss' hall. She saw his chest, shoulders, wet beard. He was smiling, eyes narrowed to slits.

One of those smiles.

Edging closer, his lips parted, and she felt herself moving, wanting to touch him, wanting to –

She dropped to the ground, unable to break her fall.

The fetters and chains binding her to the archway had been released, and now those holding her to the ground were unclamped as well.

'You will see that she is carried to the physician's at once!' Pye ordered imperiously, though he barely came up to Kosta's elbow. And suddenly conscious that the hulking brute might simply swat him away, he grew quieter. 'She needs a stretcher. Look at her! Look at what you've done!'

Rolling up his bloodied whip and hooking it onto his belt, Kosta spat on the ground. 'I never want to look at that bitch again. The king is welcome to her.'

The commander's men opened the dining hall doors, searching for a stretcher. They tended to be stashed everywhere, for slaves were constantly dropping dead or injuring themselves.

The slaves who'd been locked into the dining hall poured outside, eager to know what was happening. Alek and Rigg were first in line, their eyes drawn to the prone figure of Jael Furyck, slumped on the ground. And though it was growing dark as they approached, both men could see the bloody lines crisscrossing her back.

Watching from inside the dining hall, Alek had counted thirteen lashes. He imagined that Argo Kosta had intended to deliver many more, feeling grateful for the little man who had given Jael a reprieve.

'You will ensure she is delivered to the physician's!' Pye repeated, uncomfortable with the arrival of so many filthy, smelly slaves. He shuddered, seeking to leave. 'And I shall tell the Queen Kalina exactly what I have witnessed. This is not what she intended at all!'

'Is that right?' Forgetting all about Jael, Kosta stepped towards Pye, wanting to flick the little snot away. 'And how will you do that with no tongue?'

'I... the dreamer can see! The dreamer can see!' Pye reminded the man before spinning around and scampering away.

Kosta laughed, burning with unsated rage. 'Get the bitch on a stretcher!' he commanded. Though aware that every slave was simply staring, he turned with a snarl, seeing that Jael was moving, attempting to stand on her own.

No one spoke.

The silence descending on the square was only broken by the loud buzzing of cicadas.

'Do not let him defeat you,' Ranuf Furyck rasped in Jael's ear. 'Do not let him win. He may hurt you, yes, cut you, make you bleed, but defeat is something that happens in the mind, not the body. Remember that. Whatever happens, you get up and you walk out of that ring with your head held high. Because you're a Furyck, my daughter, and you will never be defeated.'

Jael's back had frozen, numb, her arms and legs were wobbling, but she wasn't about to be carried out on a stretcher, spat on by a sneering Kosta.

Soon she would lead the slaves in a revolt against the army, the lords and the queen. And why would they ever want to follow someone who couldn't stand up and fight for herself?

So, pushing her hands against the dirt, she gritted her teeth, feeling the weight of her fetters like enormous slags of iron pinning her to the ground. But sucking in a breath, she lifted herself onto her knees. And now, squatting there, sensing all eyes on her, she filled her lungs with air, ears ringing. Pain screamed loudly, like a bell someone was hammering, an axe thumping against a shield. She saw glimpses of her horse, Tig, and vibrating all over, she pushed off her knees and finally stood.

Turning around to face Argo Kosta.

Dropping aching shoulders, eyes wide and blinking, she held her head high. And with a look at Alek and Rigg, she turned and started walking to the physician's.

***

Korri and his crew had returned to *Sea Queen* with a bounty of food and drink, which cheered Bertel up no end. Siggy was hungry and eagerly took the trencher of fried fish and flatbreads she was offered, though a grief-stricken Zen refused to eat anything. And seeing that, Bertel offered a sympathetic smile as he helped himself to the boy's food too.

He had taken a plate to Edela, who had asked to be left alone in the stern, where she was keeping Korri's old cat company. Though knowing she needed to eat, Bertel soon joined her. 'You need your strength,' he said sternly, peering down at the dreamer. 'It was a tasty meal, I must say. Korri did well.'

'He did,' Edela agreed blankly, staring at her full trencher. 'Perhaps Siggy might like it? She certainly has a healthy appetite.'

Bertel nodded, though instead of delivering the trencher to Siggy, he sat down beside Edela, groaning quietly. 'What is it then? You can tell me. No one can hear us down here.'

Edela shook her head.

'You don't even want to try?'

Thinking about it, she peered at him, cocking her head to one side. 'Well, there is something we could try. I'm sure it's safe.'

'Safe?'

Edela took his hand. 'Just stay still now and close your eyes.'

Though Bertel stared at her, eyes wide open.

'Please. It won't work if you don't trust me.'

Eventually, Bertel closed his eyes, hearing Edela release a long breath. He stayed still, listening to Siggy's laughter and Nellie's bleating, the gentle splash of water against the ship. Men were talking as they ate, their voices bleeding into a comforting hum of noise.

And then Edela.

'I am in your mind, Bertel. Can you hear me?'

Feeling surprised by that, he nodded.

'I can hear your thoughts, so relax and set them free.'

'What are you doing? That is the only thought I have, Edela. What are you doing inside my mind?'

She smiled. 'I am going to tell you my secret. I need to, for I want your help deciding whether I've been an old fool. Whether I've made the right decision or merely led us all on a wild hunt far away from where I'm supposed to be.' Bertel's hand twitched, but she held on.

'Tell me.'

***

Walking to the physician's felt like plunging into a blazing fire.

Jael's back burned, the pain flooding every part of her until she wanted to wail like a dog. Though lips pressed together, jaw clenched, she remained silent. The four men walking with her left her alone, for the most part, merely attempting to lead her.

Though by now, she knew the way.

Had it been worth it, she wondered? That trip to the harbour?

Flashes of pain blinded her, and she stumbled.

She thought of Alek and that misguided prick, Rigg.

Perhaps it had? Though perhaps not...

Halfway through his supper, Ratish was surprised to receive news of a patient. Though quickly seeing what had happened to Jael, he bid her to come into his chamber, shooing the guards away. They promised to wait outside the door, for they were under orders not to let the slave wander off again.

'Wander off?' Ratish snapped irritably. 'I'm surprised she can even stand!'

And when he'd shut the door on the men, he saw Jael's legs bow, almost giving way as she turned to him with an ashen face.

'Oh, dear,' he tutted, switching to the common tongue as he gently helped her sit on his linen-covered bed. 'But what am I going to do with you, Jael Furyck?'

CHAPTER TWENTY-THREE

'I was visited by someone in Tuura's forest, just after I saw you,' Edela explained, sending her words directly into Bertel's mind. Her lips remained pressed together, her eyes closed as they sat facing one another in *Sea Queen's* stern.

'*Someone?*' Bertel's thoughts were loud and impatient.

Ignoring him, Edela carried on. 'It was what that shapeshifting creature Katalyne wanted to know. Who had told me to leave Tuura? Well, it wasn't who, it was what. A goddess. I was visited by Furia.'

Bertel's eyes flew open, and he stared at the dreamer, who remained before him with her eyes closed. So, closing his own again, he urged her on.

'She bid me to leave Osterland immediately, to save the Furycks from their doom. Those were her words, and I took them to heart. I did not question them. I did not look back. That a goddess would visit me and request my help? Well...' Edela tightened her grip on Bertel's hand. 'At the time, I believed everything was as I had seen. But what if I was wrong?'

'Wrong?'

'I have a pain in my chest, in my heart. It is growing in intensity, leading me to fear that I should be there, helping them, not here, running and hiding, killing and maiming, turning into who knows what. Perhaps it wasn't Furia at all but another shapeshifter? Or something else? Perhaps even some delusional thought! Some ridiculous daydream!'

Edela sounded oddly overwrought, and Bertel had to resist the natural urge to open his mouth and speak. He thought hard instead. 'Tell me exactly what she said. Furia. Can you remember?'

'Yes, as though she is speaking to me now,' Edela insisted, proceeding to relay every word as though Furia herself was saying them. She saw the goddess' face and those bold green eyes. Like Jael's, she realised sadly.

Listening to the dreamer, Bertel's thoughts scattered. He struggled to order them in a way that made sense to Edela. Though, eventually, she heard his mostly clear opinion.

'You have no reason to think it wasn't Furia, and if she showed you symbols to keep you safe, it leads me to believe that she was helping you. If she hadn't been Furia, well, she could have killed you. Isn't that so? Right then and there?'

'Yes, she could have.'

'There are many who appear to want you dead, Edela Saeveld. Though I don't believe Furia is one. And I do think it was the goddess. It makes sense. She asked for your help, so it makes sense that something is happening with your family. And that's why you feel the discomfort.'

'Then I should be there, Bertel. Home. I should be home. They need me.' Edela felt tears coming. She wanted to weep. Everything had been so frightening, so terribly frightening, and despite Bertel's and Siggy's company and Korri's help, she felt the absence of those she loved. She imagined Axl's arm around her shoulder, giving her a squeeze, or Jael standing before her, poking fun with a wink. She saw a glimpse of Gisila holding onto Branwyn, both her daughters bereft, tears in their eyes.

Her own eyes sprang open, then quickly closed. 'We must never speak of this, Bertel. Please. Perhaps we can try this again? It seems to work quite effectively, and I do hope it is safe, though do not speak of what I have told you tonight. Not to anyone. Not even to me.'

'I won't, no. And if you need to talk about it again, we will do it this way. Our secret way.' He heard nothing further and soon felt Edela release his hand.

Somewhere, a man started singing. He had a mournful voice.

Opening his eyes, Bertel saw Edela staring at him with tears in her own.

He smiled at her, nodding, and taking her hand in his, he patted it.

***

Lying on her belly, back exposed and bleeding, an uncomfortable Jael had many questions.

So did Ratish, who had taken off her shoes only to find the stone. 'And what, pray tell, is this?'

'A... Tuuran symbol, an ancient one. It's supposed to... stop dreamers hearing or seeing,' she confessed with a whisper, struggling to command herself. The pain was intense, as though flames writhed beneath her skin, burning her from the inside out. Gasping, she gritted her teeth.

Ratish kept hold of the stone, turning it over. 'But why do you have it? What are you planning now?' He stepped closer to Jael's head, turned on its side, facing his many shelves, and now he bent down, whispering. 'You are planning another escape?'

She smiled at him. 'Of course. Why? You think I should let Arras get the better of me again?'

'But how?'

Jael shook her head. 'I won't tell you that, but I promise that soon you'll be free.'

'But I am no slave,' Ratish insisted, placing the stone on the table and smoothing Jael's hair away from her back. It was a tangled, filthy mess, and he didn't want even a strand touching her open wounds.

She flinched, shivering.

'The tincture I gave you will take effect soon,' the physician promised. 'I will wait a while longer before cleaning the wounds, though. It will hurt.' He picked up a clean cloth, gently soaking up the blood.

'You are... happy here?' she asked, trying to distract herself. 'You never wished to leave?'

'Those who come here do not leave,' Ratish said starkly, and now he stood, returning to his desk, where he proceeded to lay out the salves, needle and thread he needed.

'So you chose this path? To come to the isle?'

'I did, yes. It seemed a way out of a life I had grown weary of. The offer of a sanctuary? For that was what was promised... a sanctuary. It was an offer I did not think to refuse.'

'And you have, aarrghh, enjoyed this life?' Jael panted, closing her eyes.

'There were many reasons to enjoy it at first,' Ratish admitted, sitting in his chair, his back to Jael as he threaded the needle with squinting eyes. 'I left only bad memories behind. Though soon I could not ignore the reality of what this place truly meant to be.'

'And what was that?'

'A prison. For those who are free are few, and the enslaved so numerous, so cruelly treated, that I quickly began to realise that I was living in a prison.'

'Well, if that's the case,' Jael smiled, 'I can help you escape.'

The physician shook his head, chuckling as he turned around. 'Oh, I can just see you as a child, Jael Furyck. What trouble you must have gotten up to.'

***

'Jael's not back,' Alek noted, easing himself down onto his bed.

He'd spoken to his crew about plans for the morning. It would be an early start, hours before dawn, and he had reminded them about that too.

Opposite him, Rigg slipped off his shoes.

'Perhaps they'll keep her there?' Alek mused fretfully, keeping his on.

Rigg leaned towards him. 'Do you want the woman?'

'Want her?' Alek shook his head. 'For what?'

'Well, it's been lonely in here. A lot of lonely years. When did you last even lay eyes on a woman? I'm sure she'd look better with a wash. Brush all that hair out of her face, and you might see a real woman emerge.'

Alek scowled at him. 'I want my freedom, don't you? I lie here every night thinking about my freedom, my home, my sons, and Jael Furyck's my best chance of making that happen.' Seeing the doubt in Rigg's dark eyes, he turned away, determined to force himself to sleep. His body was frail, and no matter how much he ate, he never grew any stronger. Only weaker. 'Go to sleep,' he huffed. 'You've made your feelings about Jael clear enough. No need to say any more.' Lying down, Alek gasped, back aching. He eased himself onto his side, away from Rigg. 'Perhaps you'll get your wish? Maybe she won't be able to help us now? And if that's the case, we'll likely be stuck here forever, and there'll be no women then. Not ever.'

Rigg stared at Alek's back, fearing for the man; he appeared to be wasting away.

Rigg was thirty-six. He'd been captured as a slave eight years ago, eventually ending up on S'ala Nis. He never spoke about his own family, for no one was waiting for him. He wanted his freedom as much as Alek, as much as anyone on the isle, though there was no one to go home to.

Turning to lie down on his own mattress, he heard hushed conversations in corners of the sleeping hall, the odd grunt and rustle, though most men had stumbled down onto their beds, desperate for whatever comfort they offered until they were kicked awake and dragged back out into the sun for another day of endless torture.

The Furycks had killed his family.

Their men.

In the battles that they had started.

Rigg couldn't get past it.

He hadn't wanted Jael Furyck whipped. He hadn't imagined that's what Kosta would do. She was protected, he'd thought. Not to be harmed.

And now?

For Alek's sake, he hoped she'd return.

***

After supper, Dessalene found Kalina sitting alone on her bedchamber balcony, eyes closed. She laughed. 'Is this where you sleep now? Out here? It's hot enough, certainly, though surely not comfortable?' Coming around to face the queen, she peered at her. 'You're worried? About your father coming?'

'What happened to Jael Furyck?'

Dessalene wafted a hand. 'She can stand, speak, walk. No harm was done. Well, she's scarred for life, though as far as your father is concerned, she is here, waiting for him. Still in one piece!'

'Thanks to you,' Kalina said grudgingly, well aware that her stepmother had likely saved Jael's life twice now.

'Yes, of course thanks to me. Now come, dearest, it is time for bed. You must show your father a better face than that sack of wrinkles. Faith! I doubt he'll even recognise you!'

A frowning Kalina stood, taking Dessalene's hand. 'And what will he do? To me?'

Dessalene didn't want to admit that she didn't actually know. She shepherded Kalina into her bedchamber, where the soothing scents of myrrh and cypress burned in dishes on various tables in the immense chamber. She aimed her at the bed, where Mali was folding back a sheet. 'He will discuss his plans, I imagine. He has so many! For you know as well as I how ambitious he is.' She mumbled other such platitudes as she handed the queen into her capable slave's hands. 'Though think of other things, like your upcoming marriage and the children you will have. Think of names! And then sleep. That is what you must do most of all, Kalina. You must sleep.'

Dessalene slipped away before the queen could utter a word, not wanting to be drawn into a conversation, for she had her own plans for the night...

***

'What are you doing?' Fyn hissed at Mattie, who he'd found wandering around Hest's unoccupied hall.

Lost in her thoughts, she jumped, not having heard him coming. And feeling annoyed that, as a dreamer, she'd been caught unawares, she snapped back at him. 'Well, I could ask you the same!'

'I'm looking for something to drink,' Fyn told her. 'Kolarov won't stop complaining about his dry throat. Apparently, the herring was too salty, and he says he won't be able to sleep without something to drink, which sounds like a nightmare to me.'

'You didn't have anything in your chamber?'

'He drained everything we had, which put Thorgils in a foul mood. He's thirsty too.'

Mattie peered at him, seeing tired eyes above the flickering candle he held in his hand. 'And they sent you?'

Fyn grinned. 'I sent me, to get some peace. Those two can

moan at each other for a while.'

Mattie smiled. 'I can imagine. And as for me? I just feel odd. This place is odd.'

'It is. I've a lot of memories of Hest. Not good ones.'

'Mmmm, there's a darkness about it. It lingers. I feel it.'

'Not anymore,' Fyn assured her. 'Those who caused the Darkness, who killed everyone, they're gone now. The only dreamer in the city is Meena, according to Karsten, and you can see that she wouldn't hurt a fly.'

Mattie led him towards a long table in the main hall, where refreshments had thankfully been left out. Fyn immediately poured himself a cup of ale, drinking with gusto.

'The herring was too salty,' he admitted with a laugh. 'Kolarov's not wrong there.' Mattie didn't answer, and he turned to her, seeing that her eyes had drifted away from the table towards Karsten Dragos' throne: a great monstrosity standing astride a circular dais. It was a gruesome sight, for the stone dragon curling around the chair rested its feet on a stack of human skulls. He thought of Eadmund's and Jael's simple wooden thrones in Oss' hall and smiled. 'What darkness?' he asked. 'What do you feel?'

Mattie shrugged. 'Nothing I can put into words, just something I've felt since I arrived, and here, in this room, I feel it most strongly of all.'

'I've heard some of the things that happened in here,' Fyn told her, eyeing the table. 'If you don't want to go back to bed, I'm sure I could entertain you?'

Mattie turned back to him, still frowning. 'No, I'll just have a drink and be on my way. Entering the darkness won't help me now.'

Fyn was inclined to agree.

It felt strange to be in Hest as welcome guests rather than escaping fugitives. Though he couldn't wait to leave, to get back on *Bone Hammer* and return to TOWER OF BLOOD AND FLAME, hoping that Jael would still be there, waiting for them.

***

Ratish returned to his patient with a weary sigh. 'They will not let you stay the night,' he told her. 'I'm afraid I must send you on your way.'

Jael was disappointed to hear it, for she couldn't imagine moving. The tincture had dulled the pain, though she still felt the hot agony spreading in waves across her back, taking her breath away.

Ratish helped her to sit, then realising that her tunic was torn, just hanging off her, he left the room, returning with a familiar grey dress. 'I had a patient die recently...'

An unsteady Jael eyed it with trepidation.

'The pain,' Ratish warned. 'I would advise you to wear nothing, though that wouldn't be practical.'

'No, not especially.'

He pulled the torn tunic away from her back. 'Here, I will help you.' And dragging a stool towards the Queen of Oss, Ratish mounted it, dropping the dress over her head.

Jael let out an almighty groan as it fell past her shoulders, the rough fabric rubbing her stitches. 'I... appreciate your... help.'

A bothered Ratish shook his head, returning to the bed for Jael's stone, and as he slipped on her shoes, he pushed the stone down into the toe of one. 'Be careful,' he warned. 'And if you feel any strange heat, do come back. I don't want those wounds turning.'

'Strange heat?' Jael chuckled. 'I don't think I'd recognise a strange heat.'

A smiling Ratish ushered her to the door. 'No, perhaps not, though I will be here when you need me. Take care, my lady.' He smiled kindly at the grimacing slave and opened the door.

***

Dessalene heard footsteps outside her door, and pausing her ritual, she turned towards it. Though the footsteps soon padded away, and clearing her throat, seeking to refocus, she drew her attention back to her small altar. It was portable and entirely intimate – a collection of relics she had acquired over the years that both enhanced her power and protected her from malevolent forces. Her eyes were particularly drawn to a tiny amber figurine of the Siluran Goddess of Magic, Atikar. Eyshar's wife. Her body was that of a woman, though she had the head of a phoenix. It glowed as though ablaze, for Dessalene had lit many candles.

Pye had lit many candles, too, before she had shooed him away.

He had an obsession with fire bordering on madness, and she'd sent him from the chamber before he set the curtains alight.

He was a terrible nuisance.

A little froggy man.

Though useful in his own way.

As was Ronin Sardis, her husband. A handsome rogue in his prime. A man of few words but intense actions. She shivered at the memory of him. He never smiled, rarely spoke to her with kindness or affection, though he was thoroughly in love with her. She tried to tell herself that it was a one-sided arrangement, that she had no such desires for him, though her throbbing body soon told her otherwise. Blinking naked, candlelit visions away, she focused on her wedding band: a finely worked ring of gold embedded with nine tiny sapphires that Ronin had insisted were the perfect match for her eyes.

Dessalene couldn't help but agree.

The rogue. Always disarming her with his gruff charm.

Body heating again, she sought to return to her path. Her purpose.

For she had not come to her altar to pine for her husband.

She had come to see what games he was playing without her. And who he was playing them with.

***

After a slow, painful walk back through the city, once again under an armed escort, Jael returned to a mostly silent hall. She glimpsed a few bodies moving in a shadowy rhythm, and looking away, she quickly sought her bed, trying not to trip over a shoe or an arm.

If one of these men, long deprived of women's company, wanted to try something with her, this would certainly be the night to do so. She could barely lift an arm, and every movement caused the dress' rough homespun to brush her stitched wounds, slathered in Ratish's paste.

Stepping carefully, guided by tiny pools of moonlight, she soon found her bed. Glancing around, she saw movement from where Alek and Rigg slept, and soon the hulking shape of Rigg sat up. Kneeling on her bed, Jael sucked in every groan and gasp, just trying to keep that dress from touching her back.

Eventually, she lay down on her side, breathless.

She felt tired, though her mind was still busy with thoughts about what she'd seen on her journey to the harbour. And then she was imagining how she was even going to move in the morning.

Someone approached, and clenching her fists, she held her breath.

'Alek was worried about you.'

Jael didn't answer, still deciding whether she was going to pretend to be asleep. Though she soon opened her eyes, peering up at Rigg. 'And?' He shrugged, muttering something she couldn't hear. 'I need sleep,' she grumbled. 'So do you.'

Though Rigg remained, almost suspended before her. 'He

seems to think you're the only one who can lead us. Well, maybe before...'

Jael wanted him to go away, and staying silent wouldn't achieve that goal. 'I'll be fine, though I'm not sure about you. I'm not sure you'll ever be fine with me taking charge.'

Rigg was silent for some time. 'Your family are scum. Scum. But... in this instance, it makes sense for someone who has... led to... lead.'

Jael was too tired to feel surprised. 'Fine. That's fine.'

Neither could give the other what they wanted, for neither truly knew what they wanted.

Except sleep.

And soon a nodding Rigg left Jael's side, padding back to his mattress, leaving her to immediately sink into a disturbed sleep.

**

Dessalene saw her home in Zagora – one of many.

Thanks to Ronin's bounteous luck over the years, he now had a home in every kingdom in the Fire Lands. They barely visited most of them, though it was always worth keeping an ear to the ground, listening to the vibrations of what was happening around them.

She found him in their bed, a naked girl sitting astride him, two more lying nearby – all four having a wonderful time.

Ablaze with jealousy, Dessalene nearly jerked out of her trance. Despite nearing sixty, the man had an insatiable appetite for pleasures of the flesh, but to carry on like this in their bed? She twisted her lips, clenching her jaw before finally calming down and refocusing once more.

Pushing herself into the bedchamber, she stood beside Ronin, ignoring the moaning girl straddling him like a horse. She lifted her eyes to her husband's black and white beard, up to his bronzed face, to those strange pale green eyes – one slighter smaller than the other. Both cruel and kind, she thought. Well, perhaps not kind, but handsome. Desirable. Interesting.

He was all hers.

And yet, she could clearly see, not hers at all.

She bent to his ear, laying a hand on his temple. 'What are you thinking, my love?' she breathed. 'Dearest of all things to me. What are your plans?'

And finding the answer, unexpected but clear, she staggered back in horror.

PART THREE

Second Chances

CHAPTER TWENTY-FOUR

'You are not going!' Bayla exclaimed as Ulf entered her chamber dressed for sea. He was wearing his favourite old cloak, which he was only allowed to wear aboard a ship; she wouldn't allow such a garment inside the castle. 'It is bad enough that Karsten is handing them our fleet, but you, Ulf Rutgar? What are you thinking?'

Coming forward, Ulf took his difficult but exquisite woman in his arms. 'I am thinking that I'm the Master of the Fleet. It's my responsibility, Bayla. I'm in charge of our helmsmen. You think it makes sense for me to remain behind and wave them off?' He shook his head, grey hair escaping from behind his ears, earning another scowl.

Bayla tucked it back behind his ears, and though she was in no mood to be placated, she didn't wriggle out of his arms. They were solid, reliable arms, always comforting, and they held her tightly. 'But what if something happens?'

'Well, something can happen staying here, can't it? Look at the poor children, Eron and Kai. They died in their beds. In fact, it's the only place people have died in Hest for years now. We've had no trouble, and I'm not looking for any, but these are our men, and Karsten is my –'

'Your what? Hmmm?'

'My king,' Ulf went on.

'So you've become Hestian now, have you? No longer a

Brekkan? Yet you're running off to rescue a Brekkan queen.'

'She's an Islander now, but yes, Jael is still a Furyck, and I'll always feel a duty to help Ranuf Furyck's children. He was a friend to me, a fine man and a fierce king. I will not turn my back on his daughter. Or Karsten. I'm going to help the only way I know how. I'm going to steer my ship and command my men. And you're going to be here when I return, Bayla. For I will return to these arms, and this bed, and these lips.' And with a smile, Ulf bent his head and kissed them.

***

Gant tried to shake a clump of wet hair out of his mouth, though it wouldn't budge, and he was forced to take a hand off Gus' reins and scoop the sodden strands out himself. He rocked in the saddle, trying to unstick his trousers. The rain had been heavy for hours, and though not cold, it made even thinking an effort. The noise was intense, a driving roar that bored deep into his mind, disrupting the plans he was trying to make.

He glanced at a miserable-looking Rexon, who hunched over beside him, barely holding his mare's reins. Turning, he saw his man, Saki, looking just as depressed. And seeing a stretch of trees promising shelter, Gant aimed for it. 'Come on!' he urged. 'We'll take a break!'

Rexon's eyes flared.

They were heading for Borsund and Lord Edd Arnsten, who had always proven a reliable friend.

'We can carry on!' Rexon insisted, though he could barely see through the great wall of rain teeming down, and with an angry growl of acceptance, he turned his horse towards the trees.

Gant watched him, feeling hopelessly sad. Family was everything. He had no children, but he'd always cared for Jael and Axl like they were his own.

And as for Gisila...

He wasn't sure he would have left Saala's burning fort behind. Likely he would've shaken off his clear-thinking friends and charged for those gates.

Stopping his horse, Rexon ducked his head, refusing to meet anyone's eyes.

They were less exposed under the trees, though the noise of the rain soon increased, turning to hail.

Gant closed his eyes, wishing he was a dreamer who could see beyond the trees and the hail and the road to Borsund. He wanted to know where Edela and Jael had disappeared to; to see if Gisila was safe in Andala with Axl; to reassure them that he was.

Safe for now.

Though here, escaping enemies, Gant wasn't sure how long that would stay true.

***

The wind was picking up, their preparations for departing Hest were complete, and now it was simply a matter of getting everyone on board.

Thorgils was eager to get going and had headed to *Bone Hammer* early, helping Bolder organise the crew. 'What happened to you?' he laughed, seeing Eadmund approaching. He ran a hand over his curly mop. 'Where'd your hair go?'

A newly-shorn Eadmund, walking with Karsten and Ulf, peered up at his friend with a frown. Those on board turned their attention to the kings, and Eadmund squirmed, not wanting to reveal why he'd taken the drastic measure.

'Oh, that would be the lice!' Kolarov announced loudly,

popping up beside Thorgils. Though seeing Eadmund's scowling face, he quickly swung around as though called away.

Karsten peered at Eadmund. 'You have lice?'

'Lice? No. Just felt like a change. It's... so hot here.'

'Is it? Well, compared to your little block of ice, I imagine it is,' Karsten said, running a hand through his long blonde locks, rarely bothered by the heat himself.

Ulf wasn't thinking about hair. His eyes were fixed higher up, on the clouds blowing across the dirty grey sky. 'Wind's fair,' he decided.

Karsten laughed. 'That may be so, but you're still not going.'

Ulf looked confused. 'Why do you say that? I *am* going.'

'You think you're really going to go? Leave Bayla? That's not like you. You won't come. My mother's bound you to her like some dark dreamer. Tied you up with imaginary rope. You're hers. She won't let you go.'

Ulf grabbed his arm. 'I'm here, aren't I? My chest's already on board *Beloved*. What makes you think I'll change my mind now?'

'Because she's coming. See? Bayla's right behind us. All it will take is one little tear, one squeeze of your hand, held to her breast and –'

'Bah! You don't know what you're talking about, man.'

'Ulf!' Bayla called, lengthening her stride. 'Ulf Rutgar!'

Eadmund left them to it, deciding to run his eyes over the departing fleet before he joined his friends on *Bone Hammer*. Bolder seemed to have things under control, and Thorgils was loudly trying to sort out Kolarov and Mattie. But he wanted a moment to clear his head of all the noise. He was desperate to leave, to head back to sea and return to S'ala Nis, but they couldn't fail again.

He wouldn't leave Jael there a second time.

Five of the Hestian ships had been built with catapults, thanks to Karsten's unexpected foresight – a gift he couldn't help but marvel at. They had boulders and supplies of pitch, fire arrows, spears, bows and shields. Arras thought they certainly stood a chance of breaking into the harbour, though he feared the enormity of the task ahead.

Eadmund just hoped they'd be in time.

He knew what Arras had said about Jael not being killed, though he also knew his wife's inability to control her temper or her tongue. Smiling now, he shook his head; Jael was going to make it hard for her enemies to stick to that pledge. Still smiling, he nodded at a handful of Hestians who passed him carrying chests. He was pleased to see that the piers were clearing out as they got closer to their departure.

Including *Bone Hammer*, there were seventeen of them.

Though would it be enough?

Turning around, inhaling the sea, he remembered swimming into the dark tunnel.

Dripping and out of breath, he had run for his wife only to see that door close.

But not this time.

This time, he wouldn't let anything stand in his way.

***

It was time to say goodbye.

Having quickly sold the remainder of their furs, honey, and beeswax in Castala, Korri and his men planned to travel further inland, hoping to purchase turquoise and lapis lazuli with their profits, for those were the sort of luxuries that sold for hefty prices back in Alekka.

'You're sure you don't want to see the desert?' he asked Edela. 'They have camels!'

'What are camels?' Siggy wondered with big eyes.

'One of those creatures we saw with the humps,' Zen told her. 'Yesterday, remember? The man with the monkeys? They were riding on a camel.' He spoke without enthusiasm, his eyes dull, mostly turned towards his boots.

'Well, I don't think we're missing out on much not seeing a... camel?' Bertel muttered. 'How do you even ride something like that? With those humps?'

Korri laughed. 'We'll manage. Perhaps you'll find out for yourself sometime?'

Edela glanced at a clearly uninterested Bertel. 'Perhaps,' she chuckled. 'I wish you luck with your adventure. Hopefully, it's a much calmer experience for you. Without us, it's sure to be!'

Korri kissed her cheek. 'Well, what's life without some excitement? I'd rather have a few surprises than none at all. I'll ask about you when we return. See if you're still here.'

'Though hopefully, no one will know anything about our whereabouts,' Bertel told him. 'That's certainly our intention. This time, we move like shadows. Isn't that right, Edela?'

Edela held her tongue, lifting her eyes to the sky, which had lost its hazy blue of earlier, now appearing a dirty orange. The warm breeze had strengthened, and she heard snapping awnings, seeing dust swirling. 'Well, if the wind gets any stronger we'll be blown around like shadows!' she laughed, taking Siggy's arm. 'Farewell, Korri Torluffson, and thank you again. It was a most pleasant change to make friends rather than enemies!'

Korri and his men took their leave, heading away from the market to where they'd hired the camels to take them on an entirely new adventure.

'Are you sure you want to go with them?' Siggy asked Zen.

Zen lifted his eyes before glancing over his shoulder at Korri, feeling torn. 'I... I think so. Korri will look after me, and you've enough mouths to feed already.'

Bertel glanced at the boy, who appeared to have grown taller in the short time he'd known him. 'Well, you're right about that.'

Siggy frowned at him. 'But you can still stay with us if you want, can't he, Edela?'

'Of course,' Edela promised. 'If you change your mind, I'm sure you'll be able to find us.'

'Oh yes, just follow the next band of Silurans hunting us down!' Bertel chuckled, earning another frown from Siggy, who was now joined by Edela. Inhaling a mouthful of the swirling dust, he ignored them both, erupting into a noisy coughing fit.

And with a crooked grin, Zen shrugged and turned away.

Staring after him, Siggy felt certain she would see the boy again.

'Storm's coming,' Edela warned, touching her arm, hearing the wind start to whine. 'We should find whatever we need quickly and then hunker down.'

'Well, worst comes to worst, we can always stay on *Sea Queen*,' Bertel reminded her between coughs. 'Though I'd much rather have a bed and a roof! Come on!' And ducking his head as the wind stirred up more trouble, he led Edela and Siggy further into Castala's seething market.

***

Mattie held onto Otter, watching the golden city of Hest disappear in the distance. Kolarov stood to one side of her, Fyn on the other. *Bone Hammer's* sail was up, and everyone was making themselves comfortable.

Mattie felt like vomiting, though she wasn't convinced it was because of the ship. Otter was oddly still in her arms, and she felt tension in his body, which put her on edge. 'The dreamer will see us coming,' she fretted.

'Not now you've carved that symbol on every ship,' Fyn promised, turning to her with a reassuring smile. 'It will work. It will.'

'If you have it right. How do we even know you have it right?'

'Well, I expect we'll soon find out,' Kolarov chuckled. 'When we see a great wall of fire or serpents lunging out of the sea, trying to devour us!'

'Best not say that around Ulf,' Fyn warned. 'He actually saw a serpent lunge out of the sea, chomping his ship in two. And not just his ship...'

Kolarov's eyes bulged.

He saw Eadmund and Thorgils deep in conversation, almost not recognising the king with his new short haircut, which did indeed suit him. And then Mattie beside him, long hair whirling around a tense face, no doubt worried about her part in things.

'I think you should sit down with that cat and put your dreamer mind to work,' Kolarov suggested. 'We've got a fleet, weapons, and men, but the most important tool we brought along is you, Mattie Bilso. You are our greatest weapon and Jael Furyck's best hope, so why not see what you can find?'

Mattie hated being told what to do and almost told Kolarov what he could do with his suggestion, though he was right – she needed to be useful. So, with an almost agreeable nod, she lifted Otter up to her shoulder and stumbled away from the men, looking for a quiet place to sit.

***

As the dust storm descended upon Castala, the market emptied out with speed, its customers urgently seeking shelter.

Bertel led the way, cloak wrapped around his face, hoping not to swallow another mouthful of dust. He couldn't see, and then he couldn't stand. Someone had run across his path, elbowing him, and as he'd sought to rebalance himself, a gust of wind had blown him over, onto his knees.

'Bertel!' Siggy cried, bending down to help him up. 'We have to find shelter!'

Bertel agreed, and brushing off her helping hands, he

readjusted his cloak, trying to see.

'Let's aim for one of those buildings!' Siggy suggested, pointing towards a dusty silhouette of what might have been houses or perhaps shops. It was impossible to see as the dust swept around them. 'Hurry!' She turned back, now seeing only Bertel. 'Where's Edela?' she called. 'I can't see her!'

Bertel spun in a circle, squinting through the orange dust, cloak and tunic flapping, seeing no sign of the dreamer.

***

Edela had lost her companions so suddenly that she couldn't quite believe it. She had been telling Bertel to hurry, urging him to the left where she was sure they would find shelter.

Now she was alone in a whirlwind of orange dust, with no idea where she was.

No idea of where Bertel and Siggy were either.

Right hand out, left hand covering her mouth, Edela focused her attention on her feet. She could barely see her boots or the ground, though it was her only hope of not ending up walking into a great hole. Though it wasn't long before something hit her, blown by the wind, and she was knocked over, falling onto her side with a cry and a thump.

A hand grabbed her arm, pulling her back to her feet.

She didn't understand the man, but there was urgency in his voice as he bent to see if she was alright. She couldn't tell anything about him, or if he was even real.

'You understand the common tongue?' he said at last.

'Yes!'

'Come then! I will take you somewhere safe!'

And feeling the strength in that hand gripping hers, Edela didn't think she had any choice in the matter.

***

Bertel couldn't scream Edela's name.

Every time he opened his mouth, dust blew into it, and then he couldn't speak from coughing.

Siggy grabbed his arm. 'Come on! That way! That... way!' Soon she was coughing too.

She was pointing at something, though Bertel couldn't see a thing, merely allowing the girl to drag him along. Tunic flapping, wind roaring, he stumbled after her.

***

Suddenly, the noise was gone.

Almost, Edela thought, for her ears still rang with the sound of the vicious wind. Though now, she was inside a tunnel, and the only air she could feel was a flowing warmth around her face.

Her rescuer was leading her, turning occasionally to hurry her along.

Though as the urgency of escaping the dust storm diminished, she wasn't sure she wanted to follow him, fearing where he might be leading her.

Copper lanterns glowed in small alcoves set into the tunnel walls, lighting the way.

To where?

'I... where are you taking me?' Edela called. Nothing came to her – no hints of danger or safety or where her companions might be. She needed to go back and find them. They could come down into the tunnel, out of the wind too.

She needed to –

'You are Edela,' the man said, coming back to her. And

removing the wrappings from his face, his smile revealed a set of bright white teeth. 'Please, come. The Armless One is expecting you.'

CHAPTER TWENTY-FIVE

Atop the Tower of Eyshar, Jael was struggling. It was impossible not to move her arms, though every time she made the slightest motion, the wounds on her back burned.

Clenching her jaw and curling her toes in her shoes, she could feel the symbol stone, which calmed her. Releasing a long breath, she sought to focus.

Since she'd returned from the physician's and had been put back to work, Alek had fussed over her, repeatedly asking how she was. Rigg had nothing to say, though she often caught him watching her. There had been no sign of Argo Kosta, which was a relief, and Quint, who wouldn't meet her eye, had ensured that she was assigned lighter tasks. So that meant she was now permanently stationed at the top of the tower, overseen by Gardi, and by Alek, who, when he wasn't fussing over her, was breathless with frustration.

One of the pulleys had snapped, dropping a decorative frieze to the ground. Thankfully, it had remained intact, for it had taken weeks to craft. Though to get it back up the tower, the pulley needed to be repaired, and there was suddenly an absence of rope.

When Gardi finished his shift, Jael would take over, though instead of focusing on his very precise instructions, she was busy putting together everything she'd learned in her time on the isle.

According to Alek's calculations, the slaves amounted to ninety in every hundred S'ala Nis residents. That number was so staggering that Jael didn't quite believe it, though she hoped it was true. But having greater numbers wouldn't guarantee success. It certainly gave them a good chance of overthrowing the army and their masters, but it wasn't a given.

Alek called her away and they headed around the tower, the scaffolding planks bouncing beneath their feet. It was disconcerting and made Jael tense, for every jerk and bounce felt like it was rippling up her legs to those gashes on her back, rubbing against her tunic. Alek had quickly replaced her dress when she'd returned to the temple grounds, though she almost missed it, thinking how pleasant it would've felt to have no trousers sticking to her legs.

'What do you think?' he whispered when they were alone. 'Is it still possible? With your back?'

Jael peered at him. 'Is what still possible?'

'You? Leading us? I don't want to press you, but with the funeral coming, I fear you can't even raise an arm, let alone lead a battle. And it will be a battle.'

Jael glanced over her shoulder, wincing. 'I'll be fine. It's seven days till the funeral, though I could do it now if I had to. So could you.'

'To escape here, I could.'

'The greatest problem is that my army's invisible to me, and I'm invisible to them. I can't see them, talk to them, lead them. And how do we get everyone going in the same direction when no one knows the plan.'

'I have carefully cultivated my allies,' Alek insisted. 'They're intelligent and cautious. We've always had a basic understanding of what's required, but now, with the funeral as the focal point, everything's become much clearer. More possible. I will tell them what you need them to do. We can work together.'

'Though you tell the wrong person? Those getting paid to spy for the queen or for Kosta? What happens then?'

Alek swallowed, frantic eyes sweeping the cloudless sky, suddenly feeling small and vulnerable. 'Then we're tortured, killed. All of it. And it's over.'

'You've told them the signal? It's Quint's conch shell.'

Alek nodded. 'Rigg will steal it, and when it's time, he'll blow the signal. It's loud enough that our allies in the city will hear it. They'll blow their own signals, and we'll attack the soldiers in numbers throughout the isle. Though our greatest effort will have to be here.'

Jael agreed. 'The only way to disarm the soldiers effectively is with surprise and speed. I doubt they'll be watching the sacrifice with weapons in their hands. They'll be sheathed at first, so we'll need to knock them to the ground and steal their weapons. Kill them. There's no time for feelings. The slaves have to kill. One less man to overcome is one more chance of freedom.'

'Yes, of course.'

'And you? Can you use any sort of weapon?'

Alek squinted at her, mouth dropping open. 'Well, I...'

'None? Nothing?'

'Nothing,' he admitted sheepishly. 'Nothing at all.'

Jael's worry for the man increased.

'Except desire. I'll be armed with that.'

Sweat ran down Jael's back, seeping into her wounds, and she clenched her jaw. 'I should go back to Gardi.'

Alek smiled at her. 'It must hurt, your back.'

'I have children, dogs, horses, a husband, good friends, a missing grandmother and eight islands, and I'm stuck here, far away from them all. My back doesn't hurt nearly as much as that. So no, it may make things uncomfortable, but I've got more to concern me than whatever Kosta's whip did. Though when I find the bastard, I'll make him sorry he ever thought to touch me.'

***

Bertel's cloak flew away, lost in the storm, and though he cried out, there was nothing for it; they simply had to get inside before he was swept away after it.

Siggy had found a door, and pushing it open, she dragged Bertel through it, slamming it shut after them.

They were in some kind of workshop, Bertel realised, seeing that they weren't alone. He couldn't move, pressed in on every side as anxious people shuffled into groups, sheltering from the dust storm. It swirled angrily outside, rattling the window and banging the door, sweeping dust through cracks and under the door itself. Though inside the shop, they were safe from its worst.

He wondered how Korri and his men were faring, and then, most of all, he worried about Edela.

'Do you think someone took her?' Siggy hissed.

Looking down at the girl, Bertel wiped dust from his eyes. 'Well, knowing Edela as we do, it's entirely possible. What do you think? Do you see anything?'

Siggy shook her head, rubbing her own eyes. 'No, nothing at all.'

***

An unsettled Edela followed the man in the golden tunic down the tunnel into a cave, which glowed brightly, revealing a strange figure sitting behind a table.

Or was she imagining things?

Irritated by dust, Edela's eyes were little use, but as she approached the table, she eventually saw a person draped in shimmering red fabric. It fell over their face, covering their body, though recalling what the man had told her about this person's name, Edela soon became aware that the body did indeed appear armless.

'Sit,' came a voice inside her head.

Glancing over her shoulder, Edela saw a flash of gold as the man disappeared down the tunnel.

She saw a stool, and on the table, a little beaker filled with a reddish liquid, and despite a great sense of foreboding, she soon sat down. 'You knew I would come? You know who I am?' she asked, not daring to try and speak directly into The Armless One's mind.

Though The Armless One soon replied into hers. 'Yes, I am a seeress, and you are a dreamer. We are similar, I think, in many ways. I speak of the future.'

'For a price?' Edela wondered, already moving a hand towards her purse.

'No, you need not pay me, for I willed you to come. I have seen some of your journey, and though I do not entirely understand its ramifications, I believe I have information that will aid you.'

'Why?' Edela blurted out, once again checking over her shoulder. 'Most people I've encountered on my journey have only sought to hurt me.'

'Though in battle, there is more than one side, and perhaps I am on yours?'

Edela edged forward. 'Whatever you can share with me, I would be grateful to receive it. Though I... fear what it will cost me,' she admitted.

'Only a little time. While the wind rages and the dust blows, only a little of your time. Now, please, if you wish, take a drink and we shall begin.'

***

Quint blew his conch shell to signal the change in shift, which sent everyone rushing towards the nearest well or bucket of water.

With the changing rosters it had become a complex muddle now and there was a noisy confusion about who was supposed to stop and who had to do a double shift. Those foremen and their crews working at the base of the tower headed Quint's way, and soon he was surrounded by tired men waving hands in the air.

Jael knew she was on a double shift, though she was barely present as she climbed down the wobbling ladder fixed to the scaffolding, working hard to reduce every shudder and movement. Pain throbbed in her limbs, burning across her back, and she was trembling by the time she reached the ground.

She saw Quint talking to a stout woman with a mean-looking face. The woman kept peering around with squinting eyes, muttering to Quint.

His wife, Jael assumed, for she had the same squarish physique as Kosta, the same wide face; the scowl was familiar too. Seeing them both looking her way, she turned around, nearly banging into Rigg, who handed her a cup of muddy water. 'Do you think they add dirt to this?' she croaked at him.

He shrugged. 'Either way, better than just eating dirt.'

Rigg had been strange around her since her whipping. She wasn't sure what he thought or whether he felt somewhat responsible, though he'd snarled less and hadn't called her a loser once, which was something.

'I was talking to Alek –' she began, stepping closer.

'Why? Thinking you won't be able to go through with things? What with your back?'

Jael's smile was wry. 'No. Just that, what are we going to do with him?'

Rigg looked confused, and taking her elbow, he moved her away from the crowd. 'Meaning?'

'He can't use a weapon. He's defenseless and weak, so you'll need to protect him.'

Rigg stepped back. 'Me?'

'I'll be busy. I have to organise everyone. I can't be responsible for Alek's safety.' She thought of Sunni, remembering how it had turned out when she last tried helping someone escape the isle. 'You need to take him with you. Keep him close.'

An uptight Quint blew his shell again. 'Back to work! We must get back to work!' he called in the common tongue and then in Siluran. 'The king is returning! We must work quickly, for the king will be here for the funeral! He will return soon!'

Jael's eyes bulged.

She scratched her chin, frowning. Ideas sparked in her mind, and fears.

She remembered her vision of the king discussing the tunnel. He appeared to be a man who sought to prepare for everything, in which case their challenge had just become even tougher.

Rigg turned around, and their eyes met, both of them sensing problems.

***

Despite a mouthful of dust, Edela didn't dare sip the wine or whatever it was. She peered at The Armless One, desperate for answers but alert to danger.

There had been so much danger.

The Armless One appeared oblivious to her discomfort, her steady voice humming in Edela's ears. 'Many years ago, I gave a man a warning. I don't believe he heeded it, or perhaps there was nothing he could do? Though it appears that he did not speak of it to you. And yet now...'

'Man?'

'Ranuf Furyck. He visited Castala as a young man, when I was younger myself and not this...' The Armless One's voice trailed away.

It was a sad voice, Edela realised now. Deep but feminine. 'What was the warning?' Now she focused, fearing what the seeress would reveal next.

'He came to me seeking his destiny, though I had little to say that pleased him, for when I touched his hand, what I saw was the end of a dynasty. I saw that the Furyck line would die with his children. That he would father dead babies, feckless rulers and cowards. That they would preside over the downfall of that famous name. His children's weakness would be their undoing. His progeny, a failure.'

Edela spluttered in confusion. 'I do not recognise who you are speaking of. My grandchildren? They are neither feckless nor cowards. That is simply not true!'

'Your granddaughter is no longer a Furyck, Edela. She is a Skalleson. Gone from Brekka. Your grandson... do not lie to yourself. You doubt he has the strength of character to muster a long reign, and he certainly has no heirs.'

'Yet! And I promise you that my granddaughter still sees herself as a Furyck. She will always be one.'

'And Ranuf's secret son? Raymon?'

'He is dead.'

'No, he is not dead. Quite the contrary,' that sad voice hummed in her ears. 'He is here, in Castala. A runaway.'

***

After they exited the workshop they'd sheltered in, Bertel had to stop himself running off in a panic, though the fear of what might have happened to Edela lit a great fire within him.

Where could she be?

Siggy shared his sense of panic, though she thought it would be futile to search for Edela, at least for a while. Like them, she may simply have sought shelter once they'd been separated. She suggested heading for the great stone pillar in the middle of the square. It was the most obvious landmark, and even if she couldn't see where they were, perhaps Edela would simply head there anyway?

Bertel knew it made perfect sense, though as they waited, trying to distract themselves by studying the scenes of gods and battles wrapping around the tall pillar, seeing the great mounds of dust and dirt the storm had gathered around it, there was no sign of her.

'Perhaps I should go?' Bertel suggested eventually. 'I'll ask if anyone's seen her and return shortly. Just stay here and don't talk to anyone.'

Siggy shook her head. 'No! Bertel, that makes no sense. If we lose each other, what will I do?'

Bertel was about to argue, though seeing fear in the girl's blinking eyes, he nodded. 'Yes, yes, we'll stick together then. It makes sense. With the luck Edela's having, we've got to expect that something's gone wrong, so we must find her. And quickly!'

***

Edela felt the pull of her companions, hoping they were safe from the storm. She could almost hear Bertel calling her name. He would be fussing and fretting in that thoroughly irritating manner of his, and though she didn't wish to cause him further worry, there was much more she needed to know.

'Do not speak,' The Armless One warned. 'Not with your voice, Edela. This cave is protected. I have made it so, though ones such as us can never be certain what our enemies are truly capable of.'

Now Edela spoke into the seeress' mind. 'Is that why I'm here? In Castala? To find Raymon Vandaal?' She had a sudden memory of Esby and the ship she'd watched departing, shivers raising goosebumps on her dusty flesh. 'But how can I trust you to tell me the truth?'

'You cannot. You cannot trust anyone, though I reached out to you, for your enemies are my enemies. Those who seek to harm you have also harmed me, Edela. I wish to do what I can to even the scales.'

'Then what else can you tell me? Please. I must understand my path.'

'Your path is not something I am privy to, unfortunately. I can only tell you what I have seen myself. What I know. And now I have. There is nothing else I can offer.'

Edela felt heartily disappointed, beginning to realise that there were no easy answers to find in this mysterious quest of hers. Only pieces of a puzzle she was yet to understand.

***

In the comfortable silence on board *Bone Hammer*, Nico had approached his father.

Arras had wanted him to stay in Hest with Anika, though Nico had refused, and being a man, there was little his father could do about that. Like Arras, he had an interest in helping Jael Furyck escape. 'And,' he'd suggested, 'not just Jael, but all the slaves. Don't you think, Father? With the Hestian fleet Karsten Dragos has given us, don't you think there's a chance of taking the entire isle?'

It was an idea that, planted in Arras' mind, had blossomed until he had thought to take it to Eadmund Skalleson.

The King of Oss had no reason to care for anything he wanted. Arras had his freedom, as did his son. Eadmund didn't owe him anything. Well, perhaps a knife in the throat after what he'd done, stealing Jael as he had. It was all well and good to insist he'd had no choice, but was that entirely true? Wasn't there always a choice?

Seeing that Eadmund had left Thorgils behind, heading to the stern alone, Arras pursued him, noting a hint of annoyance in the king's eyes when he turned around.

'I've been thinking about what happens after we take the harbour,' Arras began. 'If Mattie can find out where Jael is, I can try and find her. I know my way around, so I can get us there quickly.' He saw Eadmund nod. 'But the rest of the slaves? We need to free them too. They deserve to go back to their homes or to try and find new ones. We can't just take Jael and leave them behind.'

Eadmund stared at him in disbelief. 'You thought we would just leave them behind?'

'Well, I...'

Eadmund shook his head. 'My father died a king, yet he was born a slave. He freed all the slaves on the islands, gave everyone the gift of a life to call their own, and you think I would just sail away, leaving those men and women as prisoners? No, we are going there to destroy the entire place.' He eyed Arras. 'Your queen made a mistake when she sent you after my wife. One I vow to make her regret till her dying day.'

***

Bertel had no idea where they were.

The storm had passed, though the cloying, warm air was still so murky that he could barely see where they'd been when they'd lost Edela. Though even if it were clear, he doubted he would've been any wiser.

'I...' he squinted, seeing the workshop they'd sheltered in again.

Now, he stepped out four paces and walked in a circle, head lowered. And on his next pass, he lifted it to waist height, narrowing his eyes further, desperate to sharpen his vision. On the third pass, he lifted it higher still, catching a glimpse of a man jumping onto a plinth, golden tunic shimmering in the sunlight. Looking up, Bertel was surprised to see the return of the sun, though mainly he saw an enormous blur of orange light seeking to blind him.

Looking back down, he noticed the man was smiling at him.

'Sir! Can I help you find what is lost?'

Frowning in surprise, Bertel tapped Siggy, and they hurried forward. 'Why do you ask?'

'Because I am a man of many talents, but mostly I watch people. And you, sir, are looking for something. Or perhaps someone...' Placing a finger to his temple, he smiled. 'Have you ever witnessed magic?' he asked with gleaming eyes.

Bertel was beginning to doubt the man's motives and he made to drag Siggy away, but the man lunged at him.

'Close your eyes, sir! Do close your eyes! And then turn around!'

Bertel snorted, though overcome with desperation, he closed his eyes and slowly turned around.

Waiting for the man to speak.

'Are you alright, Bertel?' came a familiar voice, and Bertel's eyes sprang open to Edela, standing before him with that familiar twinkle in her eyes.

'But I?' Bertel swung around to the man, though he was gone. And now he turned back to Edela, grabbing her forcefully. 'Oh, Edela!' He hesitated, caught for a moment, as though in his relief at finding her, he didn't know what to do with himself. Eventually, he released her arms and patted her head.

She looked at him in surprise, wrinkling her nose. 'Are you sure you're alright?'

'Yes, I... but where have you been, woman?' he snapped. 'Disappearing like that? You shouldn't make a habit of it, Edela.

We might not always be here to rescue you. It can be quite inconvenient!'

Ignoring him, Edela embraced Siggy. She held up a hand to silence Bertel, wanting instead to hear from the girl.

'I thought we'd never see you again,' Siggy said quietly, squeezing the dreamer. 'That the storm might have swept you away. Or those men. Perhaps they followed us?' She stepped back with tears in her eyes.

Edela wiped them away with a weary smile. 'Well, that would be a mistake on their part, don't you think? The danger we pose? They'd be wise to think twice before considering such a foolish idea.' She winked at Siggy and turned to Bertel, who had bent down to shake a pebble from his boot.

The words of The Armless One rang in her ears, and she remembered Raymon Vandaal. 'Put on your boot, Bertel Knutson!' she barracked, taking Siggy's hand. 'We haven't a moment to lose!'

CHAPTER TWENTY-SIX

Kalina swept through the palace like a rush of wind. Dressed in her newest gown, which felt far too loose in the bodice, her mind darted about. She fretted over the ill-fitting dress, knowing she'd barely eaten since Arras' departure, certain she looked like a skeleton. Turning around, she fed Mali a list of instructions, seeking to have everything ready for her father's imminent arrival.

She had never been entirely sure why he'd left S'ala Nis all those years ago with Dessalene. Ronin Sardis had always planned with the future in mind, for as his sole heir, they had both known that Kalina would eventually rule in his place. Though his departure had left her with questions that still remained unanswered. Perhaps he'd thought her ready? Or maybe he'd thought the opposite?

Kalina had occasionally sailed to visit him in exotic locations, though the last time she had seen her father had been nearly five years ago.

Taking Dessalene's advice, she had invited Argo Kosta and his daughter to supper, seeking to advance negotiations for the marriage. The thought of marrying such an ugly brute repulsed her, though she hoped it would put her father's mind at ease, knowing she was actively pursuing an heir.

And then there was Noor's funeral to think about.

Kalina had tried to put it all out of her mind, but now, with her father coming, she was consumed with urgency to have everything ready in time.

Swinging around, she stopped near a display of lilies. They perfumed the air with a pleasant sweetness, and for the first time since she'd woken, Kalina inhaled deeply. 'Send Marros to the temple and have him bring Inesh Seppo to me. I must hear his wishes for the funeral. Do that now, Mali, then find me in the Garden of the Gods. I will take tea there.' Dismissing her favourite slave without a glance, oblivious to the four slaves following at a discreet distance, Kalina swept around, silver earrings chiming together as she strode outside.

Five days.

Her father would arrive in five days' time.

***

Edela, Bertel, and Siggy pushed their way through the market, jostled by a sea of people moving as impatiently as ever, seemingly oblivious to the piles of dust or the recent storm. Castala was quickly coming back to life, the noise, once drowned out by the howling wind, now building again.

'What happened to you?' Bertel wanted to know, nudging Edela. 'You appeared swept away. One moment you were there, and then... gone!'

Edela laughed, feeling a sense of urgency but also exhaustion. 'I was! I turned around to find a way out of the storm, and when I looked back, I could only see the storm. I do hope Korri and his men are safe on those camels. And poor Zen.'

Siggy lifted her eyes to the sky, which was clearing. Those heavy clouds had peeled away, leaving an orange glow in their place. 'We need to find somewhere to stay.'

Bertel nodded. 'We certainly do. I don't want to be sleeping on that ship when another storm comes blowing through!'

'I was told about a place,' Edela revealed. 'A baker has rooms above his shop. We can rent one of them.'

Bertel frowned, inhaling a fresh dump of manure newly deposited nearby. 'Well, anything to get out of this. We need something to drink and somewhere to sit down for a moment. We need to make a plan.'

'Oh yes, we do, and now that we're together again, I'm sure we can come up with one.' And turning left, then right, Edela squinted, trying to see. 'It's that way!' she decided, pointing east. 'We'll find the baker's that way!'

The thought of what food the baker might be selling distracted them all. That and the idea of a roof over their heads. So much so that they didn't notice the small, dark-haired woman following them.

***

Sitting by herself in *Bone Hammer's* stern and aided by some of Kolarov's usha root, Mattie had slipped into a trance.

Kolarov was busy explaining all about the root to Arras Sikari, who watched the dreamer cradling her cat, eyes closed. Arras wondered how she could keep her balance on the constantly tilting ship. He doubted he could.

'Do you think that dreamer is waiting for us? On S'ala Nis?' Fyn asked. 'And the wolf ships? Maybe there are more?'

His questions had all three men frowning as they leaned over the shield rack, sipping ale.

Arras scratched the stitches on his forehead, thinking of Jael. They itched, though scratching was painful, and he dropped his hand as he turned to Fyn. 'When the king and his new wife left the isle, they didn't return. The queen travelled to visit them a few times, and I went along. I dined with the woman. More than once.'

Kolarov's bulging eyes widened further. 'Do tell, commander!'

'She was charming and playful but calculating,' Arras recalled. 'An attractive woman with a whip of a tongue. Quite... unique. I got the sense that she was dangerous. She certainly implied as much.'

'Where is she from?' Fyn wondered. 'Silura?'

Arras shook his head. 'I'm not sure where she comes from. Further north? She was very protective of her husband, supportive of him, so perhaps she saw what was happening and came to the isle by herself or with him? Hopefully, she was on one of those wolf ships, for if Dessalene is on S'ala Nis it's going to make our job nigh on impossible.'

Fyn was thoughtful. 'Though we have Mattie. And on the isle, we have Jael.'

But Arras wasn't convinced. 'I doubt Jael will be able to do much. Whatever has happened to her now, I doubt she'll be able to help at all.'

***

Jael was struggling, her back hurting so much that thinking became impossible. Sweat dripped from her hair, and she became distracted, just staring at those glistening drops forming bigger and bigger shapes until finally, they fell, dripping onto her tunic, joining the many others that had soaked it through. Head bowed, she didn't move, ears buzzing with the sound of a thousand bees.

Gardi shuffled back to her, barking orders with such a heavy accent that she could barely understand him. But lifting her head, she wiped sweat out of her eyes and got back to work, feeling his scowl but ignoring it anyway.

Alek soon made his way to her side of the tower to see what was happening.

And spying fresh streaks of blood across the back of Jael's tunic and the glazed look in her eyes, he told her to head down to the temple and find Inesh Seppo. The seer had mentioned wanting to check the placement of the crowning arch before it was mortared into place, so Alek decided that now was as good a time as any. Jael thought to argue, sensing that he'd taken pity on her, though she didn't have the energy. So, cleaning her trowels and leaving them in a bucket of water, she headed around the scaffolding, aiming for the ladder.

She saw herself riding Tig through the snow on Oss, the ice-cold wind chilling her face, numbing her body, the feel of him beneath her. Then, hearing a disturbance, she looked down at the courtyard, seeing the familiar bulky shape of Argo Kosta, whip out, striking a slave, who curled on his knees, covering his head.

Hands clenched into fists, she kept walking, deciding to head around the other side of the tower until he had gone. Then, hearing the plaintive cry of a horse, she swung around, wincing, just in time to see Kosta turn his whip on his own horse.

Jael's eyes widened in horror, heart thumping in her chest.

The horse was a fine bay stallion, at least sixteen hands, and she could see that he feared his owner. And as he reared up, pawing the air, trying to escape the lash of the whip, a furious Kosta struck him again.

Jael's eyes were drawn to Rigg, who stood watching with a look of horror on his face – one mirrored by all those nearby. Dropping his whip, Kosta lunged for his horse's bridle, and with a bellow of fury, he drew out his knife and slit the beast's throat.

Jael's breath caught in her own throat, hands trembling, gripping the scaffolding. She watched as the stallion threw back his head, as though trying to escape the God of Death coming to claim him. His body, no longer in his control, flopped down onto the dusty earth with a shuddering thump.

Silent slaves stared.

Red-faced with rage, Kosta hung over his horse, body heaving, knife dripping blood in his right hand. He stared for a moment, as though caught between wanting to stab the horse and not quite believing what he'd done. Head snapping around, he laid eyes on Rigg, calling him forward. 'Get rid of this creature!' he demanded. 'Have it thrown into the pits! And Quint! Quint! Find me another fucking horse!' He turned from the gory sight now, eyes up on the tower, and seeing Jael watching him, he staggered to a stop.

She thought about moving, about edging back, out of his line of sight, though it was too late. He was staring at her, seeing her.

Jael held his gaze, wanting to hurt the cruel, callous man.

That he would kill a horse? For what? She had no clue.

Eventually, Kosta swung around, heading for the tree-lined path to the temple entrance, shouting orders as he went.

The planks started bouncing, and soon Alek appeared, wanting to know what she was doing.

'That prick, Kosta, killed his horse.'

'What?' Alek peered down to where he could see the dead horse, and Rigg, calling for ropes, but knowing they were experiencing a real shortage, he doubted he'd find any. 'What did it do?'

Jael shrugged. 'I didn't see.'

'It's not the first time.'

'He's killed other horses?'

Alek nodded. 'More than horses. Animals tend to run from him, which tells you all you ever needed to know about Argo Kosta.'

Jael felt sick, and leaving Alek behind, she headed for the ladder, thinking of Tig, hoping he was safe on Oss.

She was vulnerable without her weapons, imprisoned far from home, far from her family. Remembering her dream of the pyres, she thought of Axl in Andala, wishing she'd left on better terms.

***

Axl clapped his arms around Hal Harbak, relieved to have both his friends back again. 'You took your time!'

'Did I?' Hal offered his king a crooked grin. 'Though there was much diplomacy to partake in, so I could hardly hurry home.'

Erling laughed, thinking of his journey to Hest. 'Yes, all that diplomacy tends to take a toll.'

'I'm not sure I've drunk so much in my life,' Hal sighed. 'None of it better than what we've got here, though I did have some nice mead.'

Erling groaned. 'Don't ever speak that word again.'

Hal's curiosity about that vanished as he noticed his friend's strange appearance. 'What happened to your hair? You look... different.'

Which Erling didn't take as a compliment and he shrugged as they followed Axl away from the stables towards The King's Axe. It had been too long since they'd all been together, holed up in the tavern, shutting out the world and the endless problems of the kingdom. 'Just a little change for summer.'

Hal wasn't sure it suited a narrow-faced Erling, though for once, he kept his opinions to himself. 'We need a meeting,' he said instead. 'I want to hear what happened in Hest, and you need to hear about my travels.'

Axl nodded. 'I sent Gerald to round up the women, though Getta went for a ride this morning. I'm not sure she's returned.'

'And what about your dreamer?' Erling wondered, eyes on Hal. 'Will you invite her?'

Hal's eyes bulged as Erling had intended, though he attempted to lessen his horror as he turned them on Axl. 'Dreamer? What's this?'

Axl was already tired of everyone's complaints about Helga. He had them himself, though he also felt grateful that the woman had come. Thinking about the amulet she had given him, feeling the cold metal against his chest, he hoped she would provide a bulwark against whatever sort to destroy him. 'Her name's Helga. She came down from Tuura with her grandson to help. So that's good. Now we've more insight, a window into whatever our enemies are planning.'

Hal had to stop himself from staring at Erling, who he sensed felt as troubled by this new development as he was. 'And what insight has she provided? Anything?'

Thinking about that, Axl shook his head. 'Nothing specific, though she certainly senses trouble on the horizon. It's why she came. We appear to be in desperate trouble.' And as those words sank in, he realised that it would do no good to keep the dreamer out. Helga had an unpleasant, abrupt manner, though he needed to see past that and work with her. 'I'll find Gerald, and he can bring Helga to the meeting. She may have seen something new, and it's best if she's there to hear your news too.' And seeing the tavern in the distance, Axl pulled up, deciding that he didn't feel like going in after all. 'I'll see you at the meeting,' he told his friends.

Erling looked surprised. 'You won't come in?'

'No, there's too much to do. I'll see Gerald, then go and find Ragnar. He can join us too. I think the more people we bring in, the better. We need to be fully informed about what's happening. About our strengths, our weaknesses and what we need to do.' Axl patted a frowning Hal on the shoulder. 'Have a cup for me, and I'll see you soon.' And with that, he was gone.

Hal stared after him before spinning towards Erling. 'Dreamer? What dreamer?'

Erling looked disturbed, though relieved to have him back. 'Exactly. This old duck just waddled down from Tuura, and now? Now she's busy wrapping our king around her filthy little finger. Come on, we need to make a plan. Decide what we're going to do about her before it's too late.'

***

Walking to the temple, eagerly looking forward to its offered shade, Jael glanced over her shoulder, gritting her teeth. She had visions of S'ala Nis' harbour, remembering her journey with Rigg. She imagined jumping on a ship, willing it to take her to Oss. Though she knew her departure from S'ala Nis would never be as simple as that.

Unfortunately.

Turning back around, she banged into Inesh Seppo.

Unlike the old, murdered Noor, Inesh was heavily bearded, with a thick mop of dark-brown hair brushed back from a dark face. He had thoughtful brown eyes shaded by bushy eyebrows.

Stumbling, he sought to grab hold of Jael, fearing he would knock her over. Though lurching backwards, she hurried out of his reach with a groan.

'Did I hurt you?'

She shook her head. 'I... my wounds. Sorry.'

Inesh nodded. 'I am the one who is sorry. To have been treated so viciously by that man?'

Jael blinked.

Inesh Seppo smiled. 'We are not all cruel here on S'ala Nis.'

They stood beneath an arch threaded with green leaves and white flowers. Jasmine, Jael saw, inhaling deeply, relieved not to feel the sun on her back for a moment.

'Did you need something?' Inesh prodded. 'I have been called to the palace to meet with the queen. About the funeral,' he added, seeing Jael's confusion. 'It will be greater than anything undertaken in my time, so there is much to organise. Much more than just finishing Eyshar's tower. Though that is important, too, for the god will have a say in proceedings. That is our hope, at least.'

'The stone masons are preparing to fit the arch. Alek said you wanted to see it in place first, to...' Jael sighed heavily, 'approve it?'

Inesh laughed. 'You are struggling to be a slave, perhaps?'

'Struggling?' Jael peered at him, unable to detect anything about the man's intentions; his thoughts were entirely walled off from her. She saw his smile but sensed that he was not all he appeared to be. 'No, I just want to go home.'

Inesh stared at her. 'You, perhaps more than any other, will struggle because you were not a farmer or a servant but a queen, daughter of a king. That struggle will take some time, though eventually, you will come to see that to fight against what is will only hurt you and deprive you of peace of mind. You are here now, so you must release all that has been, all that you may wish for. This isle is what you have now. It is your home.'

Jael was stunned. The seer's eyes were kind, but his words were cruel. She stiffened. 'Can I tell Alek when you'll come? He cannot bring the arch to you.'

'No, I imagine he can't,' Inesh chuckled, ignoring or perhaps oblivious to Jael's coldness. 'You may tell him I will come after my visit to the palace.' Glancing past her, he saw two slaves waiting with the shaded sedan chair they would carry him to the palace in. He took a breath, smoothing down his robe. 'I mustn't keep the queen waiting.'

***

Helga didn't appear happy to have been dragged away from Edela's cottage and into Axl's council meeting, though he tried not to become distracted by her surly scowls and his councillors' gawking glances. They had to work together now, for the sake of the kingdom.

'Hal, why don't you begin,' Axl invited, looking first at his friend before scanning the table, seeing Gisila sitting between Amma and Getta and an awkward Ragnar wedged in between

Hal and Erling. Helga sat to Axl's right, muttering darkly.

Hal tried not to stare at the intimidating dreamer as he began. 'We have little to worry about,' he declared brightly. 'Any losses experienced through the sicknesses have more than been made up for by time. Boys have become men in the intervening years, and despite struggling during the bad harvests, we haven't lost weapons. Quite the contrary, the weapons' stores from Sorn to Ording are in good order. It was a worthwhile journey, which certainly put my mind at ease. We have no problems.'

Helga's snort was explosive.

Everyone turned to her.

Picking up her cup, she sniffed.

'You disagree?' Hal posed with a frown. 'You see something else? Perhaps you'd like to share it with the rest of us, for we can hardly defend Brekka alone. From some invisible enemy, only apparent to a stranger like you?'

Helga slammed down her cup, eyes snapping to the round-shouldered Hal. 'You think the new King of Iskavall is invisible, do you? To whose eyes? Those of his people? His neighbours? Did you meet with him, speak to him, enquire as to why he was so desperate for the throne or what he intends to do with that power? With his army? His allies?' She sat back with a grunt, lips pressed together.

Silence.

All eyes now shifted to Axl, who turned to Hal. 'The King of Iskavall is a problem, as Getta has already informed us, and Helga has confirmed to me privately. He does not just seek to conquer Brekka, but all of Osterland. He wishes to rule every kingdom, to make them as one. An empire under his command.'

Surprise swept the chamber, accompanied by murmurs of discomfort.

Axl went on. 'So, although the news you bring is encouraging, Hal, it is only one piece of a much larger puzzle. Oren Storgard's ambitions are a threat to our very survival and, according to Gant, a man called Mutt Storman is busy accumulating power in the South.'

'Though I had a positive meeting with Karsten Dragos,' Erling put in. 'He reaffirmed Hest's commitment to Brekka and implied that his marriage to Freya Valens would only solidify the support of the Southern kingdoms. You cannot think that Oren Storgard or this Mutt Storman is any match against such might?'

Helga couldn't help herself – she snorted again.

Gisila looked furious with the woman, though ignoring them both, Axl spoke instead to Erling. 'The problem is that we're seeing what we want to see. What we know. That is how we assess a problem, by stacking it up against what has come before. We think because it was always one way, that that way will continue. That our enemies will arrive on a battlefield of our choosing. Though that will not be the case this time.'

A surprised Helga turned to the king. 'Yes.' She nodded now, twisting around until she was eyeing Gisila. 'I don't wish to be here any more than you want me here. Edela belongs here. This is her home, and it is where she should be. I am made for the forest, for I mostly despise the company of those on two feet. I do not hide who I am, who I have been, and I do not hide when called upon.'

'Called upon?' Gisila wondered.

'Your son is in danger,' Helga said bluntly. 'And more than anyone at this table, you know it, Gisila. You know it in your heart.'

Feeling that intense gaze fixed on her alone, Gisila's stomach twisted in knots, shivers rushing up her arms. She couldn't look away; it was as though the dreamer was holding her still.

'Swords and men to wield them is a useful place to begin,' Helga went on, shifting her attention to Erling and then Hal. 'Until it's not. A man like that? He is no fool. He does not sit upon Iskavall's throne as a lucky fool but as a calculating schemer with big ideas. I see him, and he is a snake.'

Amma clasped Getta's hand, feeling afraid.

'He knows his kingdom is smaller, weaker, yet he confidently pursues dreams of conquering Brekka. Which means what? Hmmm?' Now Helga turned to Axl, inviting the boy king to impress her once more.

'That he has other weapons. Magical ones.'

Helga smiled.

'Magical?' Getta looked doubtful, though she couldn't deny that it made sense, for how else did Oren Storgard anticipate conquering a much larger foe? 'Are you saying that Lina knows how to make magic? But I remember the silly girl. She was still a student in Tuura when I left Ollsvik. A child.'

Helga grunted, reaching for her cup, eyes lowered. 'Not the child,' she grunted. 'No, it is not the child dreamer we must concern ourselves with.'

'Then who?' Gisila wanted to know.

Though Helga didn't say.

***

Mattie's trance was interrupted by an urgent need to vomit, which surprised her. She had thought that after so many days at sea, she had gained control over that nauseating feeling. Though with her eyes closed, *Bone Hammer's* rocking motions had intensified the unpleasant sensations, and after she'd emptied her breakfast into the Adrano Sea, she turned around with a shudder, surprised to see Fyn watching her. 'What?'

'Just wondering if you'd seen anything?'

Mattie wiped her mouth, beckoning him closer. 'A little. I flew over the isle towards an enormous tower near the building with the strange tree sprouting from its centre.'

Fyn remembered what Kolarov had said. 'The temple.'

'I saw an old man in a white robe. He stood at the very top of the tower with his arms outstretched, covered in blood.'

Mattie shuddered, remembering what she'd seen next. 'He threw himself off the tower, and then... before he could hit the ground, he transformed into an eagle and flew away.'

Fyn became aware of Otter rubbing against his leg, no doubt hoping for another fish. 'What does that mean? Could it be the seer Kolarov mentioned?'

Mattie swallowed, needing some ale. 'I plan to ask him, though I fear it isn't good.'

'No.'

And seeing that Fyn had frozen before her, worried eyes fixed on some imaginary place in the distance, she patted his arm. 'I'll keep looking. I will keep looking, Fyn. Not all dreams are that confusing. There will be clues, and I will find them.'

Fyn nodded, encouraged by her confidence. 'You found a way in last time, a way to Jael,' he reminded her. 'I'm sure you can again.'

Ducking her head, Mattie stepped past him, not wanting to tell him that she'd already seen a glimpse of Jael Furyck.

And she had been covered in blood too.

CHAPTER TWENTY-SEVEN

Kalina had arranged to hold her meeting with Inesh Seppo in a private chamber. She did not wish the seer to even step foot inside the throne room for fear that he would see the truth of what had happened there.

Though could he have any doubt?

Sitting by an open door, she sought a cool breeze, though the air remained heavy, the sound of bees buzzing loudly, drilling into her mind.

'The king will arrive in five days!' Dessalene announced, wanting to move things along. After the formalities had ended and refreshments had been offered, Kalina had gone into some sort of trance and now appeared mute, so she tried moving things along herself. 'The isle is ready to rejoice in his long overdue and much-desired return. And it will! How fortunate I am here to guide us all in this little endeavour,' she purred, smiling at Inesh before turning her attention to Pye, who sat at a distance, shovelling cakes into his tiny mouth. Though one look from his mistress had him swallowing down the last doughy lump before sitting on his hands, head bowed in submission.

'It is a time of rejoicing,' Kalina agreed dully with a nod to her stepmother, who raised an eyebrow. She sat up straighter. 'Though also a time of reflection, for the passing of our beloved Noor must be treated with utmost respect and dignity.' She felt nervous sitting before the seer. He was little more than forty, an unsettlingly handsome man, but like Noor, she feared he could hear everything she was thinking.

Squirming in her chair, she once again lost the ability to speak, leaving Dessalene to carry on in her place.

'You are so right, dear queen,' the dreamer murmured. 'And so very wise. We must balance these two opposing forces with grace and dexterity. The gods are watching, especially now. Eyshar awaits your appointment with bated breath, lord seer. I am certain you feel that yourself?'

Dessalene was from Alekka; she had trained in Tuura.

Her gods were not Inesh's or even Kalina's.

They were not her husband's gods.

And that gave her an advantage over them all.

'I shall defer to you both,' Inesh said with a charming smile, the skin around his eyes wrinkling deeply. 'I have outlined the ritual sacrifice as it was retold to me by Noor. Here.' And opening a leather pouch, he took out a sheet of vellum.

'I intend to make many sacrifices,' Kalina piped up as Dessalene took the vellum, running her eyes over it. 'Many.'

Inesh bowed his head. 'Of course, my queen, for words without sacrifice hold no meaning to the gods. They are mute offerings.'

'I think Arras Sikari's horse can be one,' Kalina added. 'He is a fine beast. A gift from my father.'

Dessalene nodded. 'Though we must seek more than just four-legged beasts. Eyshar will also require those on two legs. Perhaps you, Pye?' she suggested, turning to her horrified man-servant. 'For what use have you been lately? I must say, you'll not find a more deserving candidate. I would do it myself if I had the time!' She smiled at the seer, drawn to his gentle brown eyes. Few men had a look of such attentiveness; it was quite unsettling. Blinking, she attempted to focus. 'Though I would hardly insult a noble god by offering up such an unpalatable tidbit. No, I will ensure we provide much worthier gifts.'

'I'm sure you'll be pleased to hear it,' Inesh chuckled, turning to smile at Pye, whose bulbous eyes remained on his mistress, not daring to look at the seer, who now turned back to the dreamer. 'I would gratefully request your help, my lady. For you to take a prominent role. If you notice, where Noor has outlined the sacrifice, he had one of the senior logi wielding Atikar's dagger, though he did not anticipate your presence here. I can think of no one better to take it on than you. You are a gifted weaver of magic, as I understand it, and Atikar is the Goddess of Magic herself. The timing is too perfect to ignore.'

Dessalene was further charmed. The seer's manner was so refreshingly genial. She was used to snarling men with angry eyes, grunting insults, curses and orders. But Inesh was like a tasty beverage, sweet on the lips, going down very smoothly.

She was quite taken.

Kalina turned to her slightly dazed stepmother. 'Dessalene?'

Dessalene blinked. 'Of course. I would be delighted to! Yes, I think that sounds like a very good idea indeed.'

***

Dusk took forever to arrive.

Though as the sky turned ever more vibrant shades of red and gold, slowly darkening into inky blues and greys, Gant sent a scout into Borsund's fort. He guessed they would shut the gates after night fell, knowing that left them a small window. Though he hadn't wanted to act earlier, much to Rexon's annoyance.

They had hidden in the trees, concealed from those coming and going from Lord Edd Arnsten's modest fort.

Rexon was mostly silent, though occasionally he would clench his fists, jaw pulsing and turn towards Gant with hissing complaints.

Gant was sympathetic, but if they made a mistake now,

there was no hope of returning to Saala. He had sent two men to Andala to alert Axl to what was happening, though the rest of his men remained with him and Rexon. Apart from the one he'd sent into the fort to determine whether Edd Arnsten remained loyal to the king.

Holding his breath, empty belly growling, he hoped they'd have an answer before long.

***

After a busy afternoon, Axl joined Amma for supper in the hall, pleased to see her looking plumper than she had in a long time. It was a good sign, he told himself. Perhaps this child would live? And Amma too. He placed a hand on her knee, smiling at her. 'Gisila tells me everything's organised for the journey. I suppose that's something. There's little for you to worry about now except yourself.'

Amma nodded. 'I'll miss you.'

'And I, you. As tedious as the wedding is likely to be, I'd rather be coming to Angard. I want to meet our allies face to face, to look in their eyes. Especially Oren Storgard.'

'Though will he even come?' Amma wondered, remembering Helga's words. 'If his intention is to claim Brekka and to kill you, he may remain behind.'

Axl wanted him to. He had tallied up Hal's numbers with Ragnar's and now possessed the clearest picture yet of where things stood.

Brekka was in a strong position.

Though in the back of his mind, he was desperate to know more about Gant's journey. He saw now that he'd been too slow to act on the trouble in Valso, and with news of this Mutt Storman emerging, he felt certain that the trouble was spreading.

Amma tapped his arm. 'Did you hear me?'

'No, I must have drifted off,' Axl smiled. 'I think this is the first time I've truly stopped today. Sorry.'

Amma kissed his cheek. 'Will you go to the tavern tonight?' She had enjoyed seeing more of her husband while his friends were gone, though with Hal returning, she feared Axl would slip away from her again.

Axl shook his head. 'I'd rather spend my time with you. Besides, Hal wasn't feeling well, so it would just be Erling, and he appears otherwise engaged.' He inclined his head to where Erling was engrossed in a conversation with Ragnar's blonde-haired daughter, Lise.

Amma yawned. 'Well, I don't imagine I'll be much company. I'll likely fall asleep as soon as we crawl into bed.'

'I hope you do,' Axl said, catching her yawn. His eyes drifted away from Amma to where he could see Gisila whispering to her sister, Branwyn. He guessed they were discussing Helga and her warnings from the meeting. Axl's chest tightened as though someone had wrapped a rope around him and was pulling it into a knot. He felt nauseous, wondering if he should let Amma and Gisila go to Angard. Wondering if he could trust Helga...

Without his father, Gant, Edela, and Jael, he had no one to talk to.

No one who didn't have a negative opinion of the dreamer.

There was no one to lean on at all, he realised, becoming overheated, fearing he might need to dash out of the hall, away from the fires burning in great pits. Fires that surely weren't needed on such a warm evening.

Jiggling a leg, he felt his heartbeat quickening.

Then a voice in his ear.

'Though you have yourself, Axl. My Axl. You have always been far wiser than you realised. Instinctive too. You don't grow up around a dreamer without learning a thing or two about instincts. So trust yourself. Trust that you will find your path, for I certainly do. I believe in you...'

Closing his eyes, Axl sought to find his grandmother in the darkness, though only the echo of her voice remained. She was gone. To where he didn't know, but he felt the loss of her like a great hole inside him, fearing he would never see her again.

***

Edela ate her supper beside a fidgeting Siggy, opposite a scowling Bertel, who wasn't enamoured with the meal they'd put together. Siggy had purchased a plate of fried squid, which was tough and flavourless, Edela had found some salted peas and flatbreads, and Bertel had bought a small cask of what he'd thought was ale but had turned out to be something so fiery and strong that nobody could drink it.

He sighed, peering around the little room above the baker's. Now that nothing moreish was cooking in the baker's ovens and over his fires, it smelled strongly of urine.

Bertel regretted that he hadn't sampled whatever he'd been lured into purchasing. In truth, he hadn't understood anything the taverner had said, and obviously, the man hadn't understood him. And now he was many coins lighter and desperately thirsty.

'We will find our way around this maze,' Edela promised her silent companions. 'And we'll certainly discover something more palatable than this!' She heard the noise from the street and the market and the buzzing hum of her own thoughts, though she tried to focus on those seated at the table.

'Will we stay here?' Siggy wondered, eyes darting to Bertel, who had returned to his cup of fire water, determined not to waste it. 'In Castala?'

'I think for now,' Edela murmured, and running a hand over her chin, she became quiet.

'You don't seem especially convinced,' Bertel noted, pushing away his cup.

'Oh no, I am convinced,' Edela assured him with a smile. 'Just a little tired. And hot. I wish there was a real window in here!' There was a long gap between the outer wall and the ceiling, though not big enough to put more than a hand through, and their faces were slick with sweat, hair stuck to their foreheads.

Bertel studied her. 'Well, if you'd like a walk, I'll return this cask and exchange it for something we can actually drink. I don't trust the look of the water from the well, and we'll die of thirst soon enough.'

'Well, perhaps not die,' Edela smiled. 'Though we can't drink that.'

And agreeing wholeheartedly, Bertel stood, pushing back his chair and eyeing Edela. He certainly wanted to try exchanging the cask, but he also wanted a private word with the dreamer. She'd been evasive and quiet since he'd found her in the market, and he wanted to know what had really happened to her in the dust storm.

'We won't be long,' Edela told Siggy. 'But lock the door, though, just in case.'

Siggy nodded. 'Maybe find some fruit? Something sweet would be nice.'

'I'll try,' Edela promised, and with a wink, she turned to follow Bertel through the door.

***

Gant's man slipped out of Borsund's gates as they were closing for the night, and mounting his horse, he headed down the main road until he was out of sight of those men on the ramparts. Turning his horse into the trees, he soon found Gant and Rexon waiting for him.

'What happened?' Rexon demanded, almost pouncing on the young man, who smelled of ale.

The man shook his head. 'Lord Arnsten's still there, though he's got a friend with him.'

Gant's stomach clenched. He thought of Gisila in Andala and felt an urgent need to go home. 'What friend?'

'From what I could pick up, he's an ally of Mutt Storman.'

Rexon swung around to Gant. 'How is that possible? This far north?'

Gant didn't know. He turned back to the young man. 'Anything else? Anything I need to know?'

'There were a lot of weapons, lord. Men were piling them up, counting them. It looked like they were preparing for battle.'

A stunned Gant ran a filthy hand over his mouth. He felt nauseous.

He'd called into various settlements and forts on his way to Saala, not thinking to stop at Borsund. Edd Arnsten had been loyal to Ranuf and had always shown great respect to Axl, so how had this come to pass? Had it all been an act, lulling them into a false sense of security? 'Then we ride for Rosby, aim to find a ship there and head to Andala.' He'd already known how Rexon would react to that, though there was little choice that he could see.

'We can get men from Folstad, from Tornas!' Rexon insisted, too loudly for Gant's liking, and he motioned for him to quieten down.

Though Rexon was exhausted, spent, inclined to shout all the louder. Grief made him reckless, though he lowered his voice, still clearheaded enough to know that alerting enemies to their position put them in danger. 'We've still got allies in the South.'

Gant hoped that was true, though he was beginning to doubt everything he'd seen and heard. 'But we have to get to Andala, Rexon. As much as I want to go back to Saala now, we risk everyone if we don't return with an army behind us. You're only of use to Demaeya and the children if you get to safety. We have to come back here in force and quickly, but only if we get out of here now. We have to find a ship, otherwise it's days riding back to Andala, and I fear Axl will have left for Angard before we arrive. We need to head for Rosby tonight.'

Gant had been one of Rexon's mentors when he'd lived in Andala as a young man. He'd learned everything at his and Ranuf Furyck's side, and though he wanted to rail against his words, he knew Gant was right. He heard the concern in his voice but also felt his steadiness. And now, despite his own frantic energy, he leaned towards him, seeking that calm direction. His heart was torn, bleeding in his chest, though Gant was right.

They had to get to Andala.

***

After her enjoyable time with Inesh Seppo, Dessalene was forced to attend a tedious evening with Kalina's greedy old lords, who had arrived at the palace with their hideous wives, all of them preening and fretting, wanting reassurance that the isle wasn't about to be devoured by Eyshar and his vengeful brother Herash, God of Death.

And after gliding about with a charming smile, offering comforting words and promises, Dessalene retreated to a corner of the dining hall, where she sought a moment's peace before the first course was served. She remembered the welcome calm of her meeting with the seer and how attentive he had been – so interested in her thoughts. Nothing like her husband, who only sought to take, like a pig at a trough, feeding until he was unconscious.

Sipping from a silver goblet, bejewelled with flaming garnets, Dessalene watched the queen, seeing how effectively she was charming her guests – among them a bellicose Argo Kosta and his humourless daughter. The hulking commander wasn't as ugly as she remembered, though she saw that his face had been scarred by fire, which had melted his right ear into a fleshy lump. Dessalene wondered why the man persisted with such a cropped hairstyle. Surely it made sense to grow it longer to mask the hideous sight?

Turning away, she headed for Pye, who lingered near a billowing curtain on the opposite side of the dining hall, as though thinking about slipping outside and heading for the harem.

She wouldn't have put it past him.

'What have you heard, my little toad? Anything worth bringing to my attention?' Then, immediately holding up a hand, Dessalene cut him off. 'Though do not bore me, Pye. You know how I detest being bored.'

Pye's moist lips quivered, bulbous eyes zipping left and right. Lips parting, he leaned forward. 'Argo Kosta killed his horse today.'

Turning around, Dessalene saw the commander eyeing Kalina with a look of hunger, though busy talking to Krissia, the queen didn't appear to notice. She arched an eyebrow. 'And? Have you ever known me to care about an animal? Except you, of course. My favourite one of all.' And now she scratched Pye under his hairless chin, seeing him shudder with joy. 'Tell me why I should care. About him?'

'Because he is reckless! Not to be trusted. It was his own horse, Mistress. What man does that?'

Dessalene dismissed his worries about Kosta for now, wanting answers to other questions. 'And what have you heard about Inesh Seppo, the Noor-Elect? What do you know of him?' She flicked a hand at an annoying slave, who kept pestering her with a tray of honey-glazed door mice – a thought too hideous to imagine.

'He is well-favoured, Mistress. Apprenticed to the old Noor. The logi speak highly of him. They follow him without question.' Pye shrugged. 'There's nothing of interest there.'

Dessalene narrowed her eyes. 'Though I cannot read the

man's thoughts.'

'He is a seer, Mistress. I doubt he could read yours.'

Dessalene cuffed him around the ears. 'Impertinent! Of course he couldn't read mine. What? Do you think I just crawled out of a latrine as fresh as a new turd? No, toad, of course he couldn't read mine, but I should have been able to read his. He is all charm, but what else? You will find out and tell me. From what you say about that brute Kosta causing trouble, the temple is the place for you to be. And, of course, the she-man Jael Furyck is there, isn't she?'

Pye smiled.

'What? What do you know of her?' Now Dessalene grabbed him by his red ear, pinching it.

'I... ow, I... Mistress!' Pye yelped.

But ignoring his complaints and the sudden interest of Kalina and her guests, Dessalene dragged her little spy outside, only releasing him when they were alone.

'If you think to keep secrets from me, Eppypyrus...'

The wincing man backed away from her, fearing what the use of his real name portended. 'But there are no secrets, Mistress. None! She is just pretty. A pretty woman!'

Dessalene's blue eyes flared in horror. '*Pretty*? You are deluded. A deluded little man! I shall have your eyes tested. I'm sure the physicians can tell if you are going blind!' And curling her lips in disgust, she headed back inside. Though stopping by the curtains, she swung around to Pye, who had followed her. 'No.No, thank you. You return to the temple and find some patch of earth to curl up on like the dirty rodent you are. And do not return without a useful tidbit. Otherwise...' She drew a hand across her throat, and with a sneering grin, slipped through the curtains.

CHAPTER TWENTY-EIGHT

'What do you see?' Fyn asked, watching his cousin, who sat beside him with his eyes closed.

'Ketil's. I'm at a table. Two of the children are on my knees, the rest sitting beside me. Isaura's opposite me, and it's snowing. They're laughing. Even Mads.'

Fyn smiled, closing his own eyes, trying to picture the sight of Oss' long-seen square, covered in snow. Ketil would have his braziers flaming, meat on long metal skewers turning slowly over the fires.

He licked cracked lips.

'Isaura's pouring a cup of Munder Sandvik's ale. He makes the best ale in all the islands.'

Fyn nodded in agreement.

'She hands me a cup, and I put down my meat stick just long enough to take a sip. Then Mads steals it away, jumping down into the snow, running into Jael. Ha! She sends him back to the table with one of those looks, and I have my meat stick again.'

Fyn laughed, opening his eyes. 'I can see the look on Jael's face.'

'I can see the look on Mads'!' Thorgils opened his own eyes and sighed, seeing nothing but shadows moving around *Bone Hammer* in the dark. Most of the crew was sleeping or getting ready to. A few were sharing cups of ale and talking amongst themselves. Kolarov belched repeatedly as he fussed around his cabinet, creaking doors and squeaking drawers. Mattie was sound asleep on her side with Otter, and Eadmund was chatting to Bolder at the steering oar.

'We just have to save Jael and go home,' Fyn told him. 'That's all. And then we'll see Oss again.'

'I like how optimistic the young are,' Thorgils grinned. 'So optimistic! You really think it's going to be that simple for us?'

'I choose to believe it will. I want to go home and see Bram and...'

Leaning his head back against the gunwale, Thorgils yawned. 'We all deserve a summer, a little reprieve before the next shit storm comes for us.'

Fyn joined Thorgils in his yawning. 'You forget that it's Jael. She sacrificed herself to save that slave girl, but she won't be sitting on her hands. She'll be working on a plan. You know her.'

'Course she'll be working on a plan, and hopefully, it won't get us all killed! Or her...'

Eadmund's attention was drawn to Thorgils and Fyn, talking loudly in the distance. Or, at least, Thorgils was.

Beside him, Bolder had gone quiet.

'You've done more to help us than I could have imagined,' Eadmund told the helmsman. 'More than anyone could've asked.'

Bolder turned with a shrug. 'Jael should have been my queen in Brekka. Everyone thought it. Axl's a fair enough king, but Jael was destined for the throne.'

Eadmund smiled. 'Well, luckily for me, Ranuf Furyck made other plans.'

'You'll be glad to go home.'

'I will. We will. I don't imagine we'll leave again for a year. We can visit the islands and then... ' Eadmund patted Bolder, feeling weary. 'You'll be rewarded. Enough to buy yourself another two ships. I'll see to that.' He yawned. 'Think I'll take to my bed, or whatever you call a wet fur on a wooden deck.'

Bolder's mouth had fallen open, and he was too shocked to reply as the King of Oss bid him goodnight and headed for his friends.

***

Edela's mind was on Raymon Vandaal as she took a seat outside a tavern opposite Bertel. He had negotiated to exchange his cask and now poured them each a measure of what looked and smelled a little more promising into two tiny cups.

Edela sniffed hers, sipping and smiling. 'Ale,' she sighed. 'That's better.'

Bertel, though, wrinkled his nose. 'Bitter,' he decided.

'Though perfectly drinkable. And after those salty peas, I'm glad of it.'

Bertel quickly finished his cup, and placing it on the table, he took Edela's hand.

She was so surprised that she almost snatched it away.

'We can talk. As before. If you think it's wiser?'

And understanding his meaning, she closed her eyes, placing her left hand on top of his.

'My disappearance wasn't an accident. I didn't get lost,' she explained into Bertel's mind. His hand jerked, but she held on, feeling him become still again. 'The man in the golden tunic took me to a cave where I met a woman called The Armless One.' She felt Bertel shudder. 'And yes, she certainly appeared to have no arms. I could barely see in the cave, and she was hidden beneath a cloth, but I...'

Bertel squeezed Edela's hand, trying to focus her.

'The woman is a seeress who met with Ranuf Furyck here many years ago. She warned him then that his line would die out, that the Furyck dynasty would end with his children.' Edela felt tears coming, but she hurried on, knowing they needed to get back to Siggy. 'And there's more. According to The Armless One, Raymon Vandaal isn't dead. He's here, in Castala.'

Now Bertel jerked away from Edela entirely and she opened her eyes, staring at him. Mouth gaping, he peered at her. 'What?'

Taking his hand, Edela encouraged him back into the silence.

'When I was in Esby, I had the strongest sense that I was missing something. As though it was staring me in the face, though I remained entirely blind. I remember watching a ship departing the harbour. What if he was on that ship?'

Bertel immediately made to speak, but keeping his lips closed, he sought to merely think instead, hoping Edela would understand him. 'But if Raymon Vandaal is here, who died in Ollsvik and why?'

'The Armless One said he ran away, so I fear he planned it himself. That it was all a ruse to escape.'

'From who?'

'I don't know, but we need to find him.'

'And what? Force him to return to Iskavall? Though with Oren Storgard in charge, how would that even be possible?'

'I'm not sure.'

'The man ran away, Edela, so why should we intervene?'

Again, Edela had no answers.

'Besides, if this armless woman saw the end of the Furycks, shouldn't you return to Osterland to see your grandson? Ranuf Furyck had two sons, so what if you've been sent after the wrong one?'

***

Mattie lurched out of her dream like a dragur breaking through the earth, and rising to her feet, she gulped in big mouthfuls of cold air. Turning, she saw Kolarov swaying towards her, feeling the warm comfort of Otter rubbing against her legs.

'My king!' Kolarov called, turning to where he'd last seen Eadmund sharpening his sword. 'My king! The dreamer is awake!' He swung back to Mattie, who stood before him, shaking with cold. 'Tell me, my dear, what did you see? Something to aid us? Something of the isle?'

Mattie nodded, not entirely sure what she had seen. It had been so loud, a chaotic scene, though an organised one, she thought now.

Everything had been bright white and blue skies.

An explosion of voices, drums, horses.

A curdling scream.

Shaking her head, she tried to focus on Kolarov. 'It was a... parade. Perhaps? Like nothing I've seen before. All these people in white. There were flowers, white flowers, and there was... blood.'

***

Linas was asleep, the black dog sent on his way with a full belly, and Helga welcomed the silence of the cottage into her mind, steadying her thoughts.

She wasn't used to so many people or so much conversation.

Her only daughter had died birthing Linas, and for months after, grief had rendered her mute. Even now, she had little to say to the boy, though they communicated well enough in their own way, she knew, checking to see that he was covered and sleeping.

Turning back to the fire, she saw not flames but blood. She saw walls and bodies, great cries of anguish and pain. And edging closer, Helga held out her hands, chanting in a low voice, not wanting to wake Linas. And soon she saw those flames changing from red and gold to blue and green.

Moving her hands, she parted them, revealing the sight of what she feared most of all: Oren Storgard sitting on his throne, his dreamer wife by his side.

A new king in a small kingdom with fewer resources, married to an inexperienced girl who likely didn't even know how to conjure a spell. Not as a student of Tuura...

So why did she keep coming back to this scene?

To this man. That woman.

Why did she tremble and fear for her boy and for the King of Brekka, who was little more than a boy himself.

Oren Storgard vanished, and now she saw an old lady walking with Axl Furyck. White-haired and tiny, she had an energy about her, squeezing the king's arm, keeping him close. Her eyes twinkled, and she looked up at Axl with affection and love. Bending down, he laughed, kissing her cheek as they went on their way.

Helga dropped her hands, and the flames merged once more, returning to their warm burnished glow. Linas called out in his sleep, nothing she could understand, though pushing herself out of the chair, she padded towards him. Bending down, she lifted the fur up to his chin, smoothing down his dark hair. It would grow back, she thought with a rare smile, feeling the unevenness of her efforts.

He was a good boy. Her boy.

So she would do what was best for him. It was what her daughter would have wanted: protecting Linas, giving him a future. And if Oren Storgard was allowed to fulfill his ambitions, there would be no future for boys like Linas at all.

***

Mattie's dream piqued Eadmund's curiosity, and he quickly woke Arras, wanting him to make sense of it.

The commander approached with a now-familiar frown, and shaking his head to wake himself up, he squatted down, joining the small huddle of Eadmund, Mattie, and Kolarov. 'A parade?' His frown deepened, remembering the many parades he'd been forced to take part in during his time on the isle. 'Did you recognise anything about it? Anything strange?'

Mattie looked up as Thorgils and Fyn approached, and curious about what was going on, they bent down to join the circle.

'What's happening?' Thorgils wondered, gnawing a sliver of salted pork.

'Mattie had a dream,' Eadmund explained. 'About the isle. There was a parade.'

Thorgils frowned. 'Parade? What were they celebrating?'

'I'm not sure they were celebrating. I can't tell. They were dressed all in white.'

Arras blinked. '*Everyone* was in white?'

'Some were in grey, I think,' Mattie clarified.

'The slaves, they always wear grey. But those in the parade?'

'They were in white.'

'White is worn for a funeral,' Arras explained.

'Even the flowers were white,' Mattie added.

'Then definitely a funeral.'

'It can't be Jael,' a worried Fyn decided. 'They wouldn't celebrate that, would they?'

Arras agreed. 'No, it's not Jael. They wouldn't celebrate her at all. Not the lords and ladies. Not the free. She's a slave. She is nothing to them.'

'Then who died?' Eadmund asked. 'Who was the funeral for?'

Mattie had no clues. *Bone Hammer* dipped, and she lost her balance, falling onto Arras, who grabbed her arm. And blinking, she saw a flash of something. 'A horse. A black horse covered in blood.'

Arras tensed. 'Did it have a star? A white star on its forehead?' Mattie nodded, and pushing her away, he stood, struggling to catch his breath.

Eadmund soon joined him. 'What is it? *Your* horse?'

Arras was almost too upset to speak. 'There are more horses than mine who are black with white stars,' he said, working to convince himself that it was merely a coincidence. 'Many more, I'm sure.'

'But why would they kill your horse?' Thorgils wondered, rising to his own feet.

'A sacrifice to the gods?' Kolarov suggested.

Arras turned to him with a shiver. 'Yes, I expect so. It would be like Kalina to sacrifice my horse, though I cannot blame her. She knew what he meant to me, I knew what he meant to me, and yet, I left him behind. I imagine she will take her revenge.' His heart ached for Tito, his beloved horse of twelve years. He turned back to Mattie. 'And his throat was slit?'

Mattie struggled to her feet. 'Not that I saw. I just saw the blood, heard a terrible noise.'

'Someone died, there was a funeral procession and a sacrifice,' Kolarov recounted. 'They would have made such a sacrifice where?' he asked Arras. 'At the temple?'

A still-stunned Arras nodded. 'If it was a funeral, the procession would finish there, and then the sacrifices would begin.'

'Sacrifices?' Eadmund wondered.

Arras frowned, trying to focus. 'Someone important has died.'

'The queen?' Thorgils suggested.

Mattie shook her head, drawing everyone's attention her way. 'I saw a dark-haired woman wearing a crown. She rode in a gilded carriage, flanked by many slaves.'

'That sounds like the queen,' Arras said.

'So if it's not her and it's not Jael, who is it?' Eadmund asked, fearing in his heart that it was Jael. He had no sense of her, and Mattie hadn't seen a glimpse of her since they'd left the isle behind, so despite everyone's assurances, his heart throbbed with dread.

'I saw that man throwing himself off the temple, remember?' Mattie exclaimed, clutching Arras. 'He transformed into an eagle and flew away. He wore a white robe, and it was covered in blood!'

Arras blinked at her. 'This man, what did he look like?'

Mattie sucked in a breath, trying to remember. She wrinkled her nose, dropping her arm back to her side. 'He had the look of leather. Old and hairless. I remember that he looked oddly hairless.'

Arras' mouth dropped open. 'That is Noor of the Dragon Blood Tree.'

'Which would explain such an occasion,' Kolarov decided, taking Fyn's offer of a hand to pull him back to his feet. 'But why are you seeing such a thing?' he wondered, eyeing Mattie.

Who shrugged. 'I don't know, but I'll keep searching for answers,' she promised. 'Hopefully, there'll be more to see and an understanding of why it all matters.'

***

Gisila couldn't sleep. Whether it was Helga's snarling words or Gant's messages, she felt disturbed. Not the sort of disturbance a slovenly servant or a lost necklace would evoke, but a gnawing fear that grew with each passing day. She had longed for a dreamer to provide insight and assurance, though Helga's arrival had peeled open the doors to a nightmare she had been fearing for some time.

She had been excited to go to Angard, looking forward to such an occasion, but now? Nibbling a hanging fingernail, she headed away from her bedchamber, deciding to find a little mulled wine, hoping it would soothe her back to sleep. But in the hall, she found Axl sitting at the table, staring at his hands as though seeking some invisible answers.

He looked up in surprise, motioning for her to join him. 'Can't sleep?'

'Without Gant, it's never easy,' Gisila admitted. 'I always feel more at ease when he's around. As though I can relax and let him worry about everything.' She chuckled, certain that wasn't true, though his presence had always given her comfort. 'I just wish he was here. That I could see him before we leave.'

'He won't be far away,' Axl promised. 'And he won't know what to do without you. It will be so quiet here.'

Gisila stared at him blankly before shaking her head. 'Your father used to say that to me before I went away. He'd tell me how much he intended to eat while I was gone. How much he would drink without me sitting beside him, tapping his hand and whispering in his ear.' Now she laughed. 'And when I returned, he would say how terrible it had been without me. How he'd lost his appetite entirely, waiting for my return.'

Axl smiled. 'He did love you. I know he did.'

'Well, yes, he did, for a time. And for a time, I loved him. Though fate intervened and tore us apart. Fate and grief. There was so much grief and loss. And Tuura. Not to mention Ravenna Vandaal, of course.' Gisila shook her head, turning to her son. 'Marriage is like a seed. You must plant it in fertile soil, water it, nurture it, care for it. Though if the gods see fit to send too much rain or sun or snow, it will not thrive, and in some instances, it will stop blooming and simply die. So you must care for your marriage, for your wife, through these hardships, Axl. Your father and I grew apart as I struggled. I certainly pushed him away, which didn't help. Losing my babies made me feel less of a woman and less of a wife. Certainly less of a queen. And once pushed away, your father did not return to me. We stayed at a distance, watching it fall apart without ever truly being aware of it until it was too late, and we had simply become strangers.' Taking Axl's hand, Gisila squeezed it. 'Cherish what you have, my son. Never take your life or your wife for granted.'

'I won't, Mother, I promise. And I hope you can enjoy yourself in Angard. Please leave your worries here. They'll be waiting for you when you return. As will I.'

Gisila nodded. 'You must take care and listen to that dreamer.'

Axl sat up in surprise.

'Well, I am choosing to trust her. I don't see another option, do you?'

'No.'

'So listen to her, though never stop thinking for yourself. You have many enemies, Axl, and you can be sure they all want you dead.' Bolts of fear shot through Gisila's body, though her face revealed nothing. 'Never forget you're a Furyck, and Andala is where you belong. Do not let anyone tell you otherwise.'

***

That evening, Jael sat down with a smile.

She had rarely noticed whether she was sitting or standing before. Tending to always be in a hurry, mind overflowing with things to do, the discomfort of the present had rarely affected her. Until she'd been forced to stand or squat in the full glare of the sun for twenty hours a day. Until her joints burned and her legs trembled with the need to rest. Until her back throbbed and her wounds pulsed like flames.

Her shoulders, twisted into painful knots, started unwinding as she swallowed a few spoonfuls of the evening broth, which tasted fishy and foul but was so welcome after a day spent in the burning sun. The liquid soothed her parched throat and almost made her want to speak again.

Opposite her, a quiet and still Alek coughed.

Looking up, Jael blinked at him.

He chuckled. 'Just clearing my throat. You carry on. You look hungry.'

'I think this might be the best meal I've ever eaten,' she lied with a wink, shifting her attention to Rigg, who sat opposite her, finishing his bowl of broth, and back to Alek again. 'Not hungry?'

Rigg looked up and around to Alek, then down at his friend's bowl, which was indeed still full. 'You need to eat.'

Alek nodded, brushing off their worries. 'Sometimes I get so tired I lose my appetite and the thought of eating? You're welcome to it,' he said, nudging the bowl towards Rigg, who pushed it right back.

'It tastes like shit, but I'd happily eat shit to stay alive in this place. You know what happens to those who stop eating, Alek.'

'I haven't stopped eating. It's one bowl. I just want to get to bed. These longer days are trying. I... need some sleep more than I need that broth.'

Jael peered at Alek, thinking that his big eyes looked sunken, his cheekbones more pronounced. 'Though you need both to keep going. If you skimp on either, you'll end up paying a price. A few spoonfuls would be useful for tomorrow.' Leaning forward, she lowered her voice. 'We need you.'

And finding himself penned in by his fussing companions, Alek picked up his spoon and dipped it into the now-congealed bowl of broth, hoping to shut them both up.

Watching him, Jael's shoulders dropped, all humour gone from her eyes. Tension throbbed in her chest and at her temples like a heartbeat.

She barely knew these men, who slumped over tables, desperate to head to bed. They were broken men, unhappy men, exhausted and abused men.

But were they fighting men?

Would they fight for her, for their freedom?

In seven days, Jael knew she'd find out.

CHAPTER TWENTY-NINE

Before leaving Hest's capital, Eadmund had agreed to meet up with the Hestians in the small town of Solt to go over their plans one last time.

The Hestians arrived slowly, led by Ulf in a magnificent ship called *Beloved*. It was a strange name for a ship, Eadmund thought. Most warships were named to intimidate, but this ship was named as if in honour of someone. And it wasn't hard to guess who.

He clapped a cheerful-looking Ulf on the back. 'Good trip?'

Ulf nodded. 'She sails like a seal, slipping over the waves. It was a delightful way to spend a few days.'

A yawning Thorgils lifted his arms up, out of his cloak, as though trying to touch the clouds. They hung above the beach in an almost straight row, light grey and feathery, blocking the sun. 'I don't imagine you get set free much these days, what with Bayla keeping you close.'

Ulf laughed. 'Bayla's the last woman to want me close, I assure you. I keep my own counsel about that.' And saying nothing more, he turned his attention to the small town bordered by wicker fences on a lean, as though permanently buffeted by a strong wind. He'd often thought that Solt needed better defenses but had never pushed Karsten hard enough to do something about it. With the King of Silura being such a close ally, their coastal defenses hadn't been front of mind. Though now, with trouble brewing in the Fire Lands and beyond, it was time to push harder to make some sensible changes.

'What's on offer here?' Thorgils wondered, striding across the beach with purpose. His belly rumbled loudly, for breakfast had been a meagre affair of cheese and nuts, and he was ready for something more substantial.

'What you'd expect,' Ulf grinned. 'Just on a smaller scale. Though we're not here for the food,' he warned, promptly ignored by Thorgils Svanter, who quickly moved past him.

Eadmund shook his head, realising that everyone was of the same mind, as crews from every ship soon flooded the beach, heading after Thorgils. 'We're not staying long!' he warned, seeing Thorgils waving a hand and otherwise ignoring him. Soon he was joined by Fyn and Kolarov, both men eager to experience whatever Solt had to offer.

Arras walked further back with Mattie, who carried Otter in her arms, wanting to learn more about what the dreamer had seen. 'I wish you could see something of Jael,' he said, keeping his voice low. Eadmund was walking ahead with Ulf, and he didn't want the king hearing him. 'I know she'll likely have those fetters back on again, but still...'

Mattie stopped him, dropping Otter to the ground. 'Perhaps I have, though maybe it's not something I want to talk about?'

'Why? What did you see?'

Mattie couldn't tell Eadmund or Fyn. She certainly didn't want to tell Kolarov, who tended to blabber whatever he heard. And realising that she needed to tell someone, she drew closer to Arras. 'I did see a glimpse of Jael. She was covered in blood, and these men, they... threw her into a hole.'

Arras stiffened. 'A *hole*?'

'There were many holes, I think,' Mattie murmured. 'Pits and troughs and mounds. It was a vast area. A field of dirt and dust. I... perhaps it was a burial ground?'

Arras sighed heavily. 'Of sorts,' he said. 'Yes, if you get thrown into the pits, you are left to die. There are tiny holes dug into the earth, with lids on top, and once the lid is locked, there's little air, and in the heat... it doesn't take long.'

A horrified Mattie clamped a hand over her mouth. She glanced up the beach at Eadmund, who had turned to encourage everyone to hurry.

'And that was your only sight of her?'

The dreamer nodded. 'So we might be going back to S'ala Nis for nothing. Jael might be... dead.' She peered at Arras, then back at Eadmund. 'What are we going to do? How am I going to tell the king?'

***

Axl held Amma close, feeling the swell of her belly against his own. He smiled, imagining their child growing inside his wife – a strong, healthy child. Closing his eyes, he inhaled the summery smell of her hair. She had bathed the day before and now smelled like a flowering meadow.

Pulling back, he kissed her. 'You look perfect,' he breathed. 'A perfect queen. My queen.'

Amma gulped, feeling a nervous wreck. Remembering the dreamer's stark words, she feared she would never see Axl again.

The dreamer had joined the well-wishers lining the piers as those leaving for Angard hurried to ready themselves, under orders from impatient helmsmen and barracked by Gisila, who was ready to depart.

She had said her goodbyes to her son and now stood on board *Death Weaver*, hands on hips, wishing Amma would hurry along. Spinning around, she realised that Getta had disappeared. And with an annoyed sigh, she headed towards her sister, hoping she knew where she was.

'Stay safe,' Amma pleaded. 'Axl, you must stay safe here.'

He smiled, stroking her hair. 'Brekka has always been the strongest kingdom in Osterland. That hasn't changed, and it won't. Besides, I have Helga looking for problems. And I'll have Erling and Ragnar here, helping me. We'll all be here, waiting for your return.' He took her hand, leading her towards *Death Weaver*.

Amma glanced over her shoulder, seeing Getta hurrying towards her, followed by a loping Hal Harbak. She cringed, hoping he would choose to sail on the other ship, where he could keep the upset horses company. She knew Axl wanted Hal to go along to keep them safe, though she would have preferred anyone else. Even Erling. Though his sister was still unwell, so his parents had tasked him with staying behind to care for her. Which was strange, she thought, wondering why Kamilla Venberg hadn't wanted to stay herself. Though seeing her fussing with her hair in *Death Weaver's* stern, she knew the ambitious woman wouldn't want to miss out on such an important event, no doubt hoping to return with a bride for her bachelor son.

'There you are!' Gisila called, relieved to see Getta. 'We must leave. We really must, Axl!' And glaring imploringly at her son, she watched as he planted a final kiss on his wife's lips before hoisting her into the ship. 'I have a chest organised for you, my dear. Over here, yes, move please... come along, Amma. Over here!'

Axl held up a hand as his wife turned away, then feeling a clap on his back, he turned around to Hal. 'Look after Amma,' he said. 'My mother too. I don't like that I won't be there, keeping them safe.'

'In Angard?' Hal was half-asleep, hungover, and not looking forward to a long journey to Angard with Gisila bossing him about, though he sought to reassure his fretting king. 'We'll be safe, Axl, surrounded by allies. It's Andala you need to worry about, for you're sending your best warrior away.'

'What? Who?'

'Me!' Hal grinned. 'Though I suppose you'll have Erling for

company and, of course, your old friend Helga. She's sure to keep you warm at night!'

Axl laughed, pushing Hal towards *Death Weaver*. 'If you don't hurry, Gisila will have you in the sea!' he warned, turning to an out-of-breath Getta, who stopped beside him. 'Do you have everything?'

Getta had dashed back to the hall for Amma's sick bowl, doubting her sister, the queen, would want to hang over the gunwales like everyone else.

She frowned. 'Hopefully, though I'm not armed with any confidence.'

Peering at her miserable face, Axl was concerned. 'Confidence?'

'About any of it,' Getta hissed. 'Going there, leaving you here. Eren Venberg.'

Axl blinked, bending down to her. 'What?'

'Well, she's staying behind, isn't she? And without Amma here to distract you –'

'It is over. It is. I had no part in her staying.'

Getta eyed him doubtfully, deciding it was pointless to pursue the matter any further. Axl was a grown man, a king, and she couldn't make him bend to her will or choose right over wrong. Though hurting her sister was very wrong indeed. 'I will keep Amma safe,' she said instead.

Axl nodded. 'Your sister means everything to me, Getta. I know you don't believe me, but she does. I've made mistakes, I just hope...'

Though not wanting to hear any more, Getta turned away, knowing that she'd made her own but fearing that her brother-in-law was about to make some more.

In fact, she was certain of it.

***

The rain hadn't stopped for two long days, and a tired and sodden Gant began to fear it never would. Their journey from Borsund to Rosby, along Brekka's eastern cliffs, had gone slowly because that rain had caused flooding and slips, and the path, far too close to the sheer cliffs for Gant's liking, had kept them cautious. Even Rexon, who had been mute for much of the journey north, had tempered his horse's desire to move faster, eager to get out of the rain. Though there had been no escaping it until those first hints of smoke reached their dripping noses.

Smoke and the smell of fish.

Soon they saw a glimpse of Rosby's ramparts, newly constructed and rising out of the steaming gloom. The sun had risen somewhere, though it was impossible to tell, for the sky remained a heavy grey blanket, slashed with rain.

Gant held Rexon back. 'I'll send Saki in.'

A morose Rexon didn't argue, hoping upon hope that Mutt Storman hadn't infiltrated their allies this far north. Turning around, he ran his eyes over Gant's bedraggled men and miserable horses. They all needed food, water, ale, and, most of all, somewhere dry. He nodded. 'I'll move everyone back into the trees.'

Gant was pleased to see a hint of the leader return, and he smiled, then with a sigh, he called to Saki, ordering him to approach the fort like a man, not a warrior. They stripped him of his shield, leaving him with a plain cloak and a swordbelt carrying only knives. His grey gelding was a fine horse, though he was a Brekkan, so there was nothing unusual about that. And content with how he looked, Gant sent Saki on his way before turning back to wait with Rexon and his men. As impatient as they were, it wouldn't do for Saki to head in and out with speed.

He wished they could make a fire, but that risked drawing attention.

At least he could stand, so slipping out of the wet saddle, he patted Gus, giving his head an affectionate rub, smiling as his loyal horse bumped his head against his chest, wanting more.

'We wait,' he told his men. 'Give the horses a break. Stretch!'

They were getting closer to Andala, and if they could help themselves to one of Rosby's ships, they'd be in Brekka's capital in a day.

He missed Gisila. The feel of her body as she stroked his face, tidying up his beard. And his eyebrows. He smiled, turning to see Rexon standing by himself, staring into the trees like a man who'd lost every reason to live.

Blowing out a tense breath, Gant didn't want to think it was truly possible. That Rexon's wife and their three children were all dead? Burned in that fire?

And if they weren't?

Whatever the case, it was time to deal with the trouble in the South once and for all.

Saki eventually returned, giving everyone a lift.

'It's safe!' he called, spurring his horse forward. 'There's no trouble! We can go –' An arrow took him in the head and knocked out of the saddle, he hung from his horse, one boot wedged into a stirrup.

The spooked horse took off as though shot himself, plunging into the forest, leaving everyone scrambling to mount their own horses.

***

Helga, Linas, and Gully joined Axl as the two ships left the harbour.

'You have much to do,' the dreamer bluntly told the king as Gully charged off after a cat, Linas following close behind.

Axl barely heard her, his attention still focused on the disappearing ships, suddenly regretting sending Amma away. Perhaps it was safer to stay here? To stay together?

Getting no response, Helga grunted. 'You must turn to what is happening here. Your fortress is not safe!'

Now Axl blinked, finally drawing his eyes towards the dreamer. 'How so?'

'You have enemies within. Just as you have spies in Ollsvik, Oren Storgard has spies here, so you must weed them out if you are to shield yourself from that man. As well as symbols. They will help.'

'We have symbols,' Axl told her, glancing over his shoulder for one more look at the ships before turning to follow Helga towards the harbour gates. 'They've kept us safe.'

She laughed out loud. 'But what real danger have you faced these past few years? No, you need to use my symbols. I've kept myself hidden in the forest for years, and not by chance, I –' She froze, feeling a pain in her chest, lungs burning as though she'd been running.

'Is something wrong? Helga?'

She stared at him, breathless, unable to put her thoughts into words. 'Show me what you have, and I will... make a plan.' Images flooded her mind, surging towards her like rain on the wind, but she couldn't make sense of them. Something was happening, something important, though until she knew what, she couldn't say anything.

She wouldn't.

Feeling the king's concerned eyes on her, Helga bent her head and bustled away.

***

Saki was gone, his dead body likely still dragged behind his horse, though there was no chance of helping him now.

Gant, Rexon, and their men were under attack.

Arrows took out two more men in quick succession as Gant ordered everyone into the trees. He knew the area around Rosby well and immediately took the lead on Gus, urging his men to follow.

Shouts of pain and surprise rose over the hammering rain, disorienting them all.

It was hard to sense where the attack was coming from, as first, men on Gant's left flank were struck, and then those on his right. The rain came down heavily, streaming through gaps in the forest canopy, and he turned Gus in a circle, trying to see a way out. He saw Rexon's horse stabbed with an arrow, and then Rexon himself, struck in the arm. 'Move!' Gant bellowed. 'We have to move!' And finally choosing his path, he ducked his head, spurring Gus deep into the trees.

He had to protect his men, Rexon, and his horse, too, but more than anything, Gant knew he had to get back to Andala and warn Axl of the danger heading his way.

***

'We'll arrive at S'ala Nis in four to five days. Likely five,' Arras told the helmsmen gathered around the long trestle table set up in Solt's underwhelming square. Crowds of curious onlookers gathered around the strangers, wanting to know what they were discussing. Fyn and Nico had been tasked with keeping them far enough away so that no information reached their ears. Both men clasped cups of ale, and in the warm sunshine, they seemed content with the task.

Arras moved a finger to where he'd marked S'ala Nis on the map. He'd drawn the map on a hide before they left Hest, where the general outline of their plan had been formulated, but now he needed to focus Bolder, Ulf, and Eadmund on the intricate nature of what would be required. 'Last time you headed for The Maiden's Reach...' Mattie was included in the huddle as well, and Arras immediately became distracted, remembering what she'd seen of Jael and her fears that the queen was dead.

He was acting as though she was alive, talking to her husband about how he should rescue his wife – the woman who had saved him.

Though shouldn't he say something?

Shouldn't he give Eadmund some warning?

'This time, we'll be aiming here, at the harbour, where we'll be met by a strong response. Ulf, you'll need to lead the way with your catapult ships.' Turning his body so he could no longer see Mattie, Arras tried to focus, wanting to see S'ala Nis' harbour in his mind. Not the pits. Not the pits the dreamer had seen Jael thrown into, doomed to die an agonising death.

Blinking, he sought to focus.

'So there's only one harbour? One place to moor ships?' Thorgils mumbled between bites of a moreish almond cake. He chewed with his mouth open, eyes on Arras.

'Only one, to ensure we know who comes in and out. We could drop anchor and swim, though that makes little sense. Wet men wielding slippery weapons puts us at a disadvantage. Once Ulf's ships take out the ballistas, we can move into the harbour at speed.'

'Sails?' Bolder wondered.

'Yes. All the way in,' Arras advised. 'There are five piers and three entrances into the isle from the harbour. Straight down the main road, the tunnels to the south or the tunnels to the north.'

'And where will Jael be?' Eadmund asked, growing tense, seeing how many pieces crowded the gaming board now. He looked from Arras to Mattie, both of whom appeared to freeze. 'Any clues? Any idea where we'll find her? That's where I want to head. Aim me at my wife.' He looked back to the map before fixing his attention on a tight-lipped Mattie. 'Have you seen any sign of her?'

Mattie looked past Eadmund to Arras, who dropped his eyes to the map.

Seeing the look on the dreamer's face, Eadmund shivered. 'You've seen something, haven't you? Something bad?'

Thorgils gulped down the last of his cake. 'Tell us, Mattie. What have you seen?'

And backed into a corner, Mattie couldn't lie. 'I saw Jael, yes. A glimpse of her. She was covered in blood, as though she'd been attacked.'

Eadmund lunged at her, eyes flaming. 'But you didn't say?' He furiously scratched his newly shorn hair. 'Why not?' And now he swung around to Arras, who didn't appear to be blinking. 'But you know? You told him, didn't you? Why?' He turned back to Mattie. 'What did you really see?'

'She saw Jael being thrown into a pit,' Arras said, not wanting everything to fall on Mattie. 'She didn't want to worry you. She didn't quite understand what it meant. We spoke only now, on the beach.'

'A pit?' Eadmund's throat had immediately dried up; he could barely swallow. 'What pit?'

'I can't say,' Arras tried to explain.

'I think you can!' Eadmund bellowed. 'Tell me!'

'The pits are prison holes.'

Thorgils frowned. 'But I thought they wanted to keep Jael alive? That she wasn't allowed to die?'

Arras nodded. 'Which is why I was hesitant to say anything. It doesn't make sense unless –'

'Unless?' Eadmund snapped. 'What?'

'Unless the queen lost her mind.'

Silence swept over the table like a heavy snow cloud as they all let that sink in.

The oinking sounds of an escaping piglet echoed around the square, though no one looked away.

'And you think she might have?' Eadmund asked in a small voice. 'Lost her mind?'

Arras shrugged. 'It's always possible. Kalina is prone to fits of anger. Tantrums. She likes getting her own way. She was thrown from a horse as a young woman and immediately had it killed. I... I wouldn't put it past her.' It hadn't been what he'd intended to say, planning to veer closer to a path of hope. Though it was the truth, and in the end, he felt he owed Eadmund his honesty.

Eadmund felt as though he was being swept away from all he'd clung to, as though the current was too strong and he would soon lose his grip.

On hope.

On the prospect of ever seeing his wife again.

'We don't know that it's real,' Mattie put in. 'What I saw. I may have seen it wrong, or it was another time, or –'

'Whether Jael's alive or not, we carry on,' Thorgils said, speaking on behalf of Eadmund, who he could tell was struggling to speak at all. 'To the isle. It's what Jael would want us to do. To liberate those slaves. Though knowing her, she's already busy doing it herself.' He felt odd, struggling to keep his spirits up, though he needed to. For all of them. 'We carry on!'

Eadmund didn't even nod in reply.

Since Jael had been taken, since they'd left S'ala Nis without her and escaped the wolf ships and the fire walls, he'd wondered if the gods were with them. Did they want to help Jael or hurt her? Furia was her protector, but had she turned against her? Or were other gods now seeking to bring her down?

It wasn't a helpful line of thinking, though Eadmund feared that no matter what he thought or did, he was doomed never to see her again.

CHAPTER THIRTY

Having told the king where she intended to apply new symbols to the gates and around Andala's walls, and leaving him with a flea in his ear about the spies in his fort, Helga went looking for Linas.

The boy was used to Tuura's forest, which he'd known since he could crawl, though he didn't know a busy fort or its self-interested people. He was curious and quick but with the mind of a dog hankering after a treat; he would not stop and ask questions. She almost smiled, thinking about the dog, who was now Linas' dog. She could see that well enough.

A pale-faced woman rushed around the corner before her, hand over her mouth, eyes sweeping the alley, and seeing no alternative, she turned to a small midden pit and threw up.

Helga stopped, and frowning, she waited for the woman to finish.

Wiping her mouth as she turned around, Eren Venberg gasped, seeing the stout woman staring at her. 'Who are you?'

The rear of a row of workshops cast long shadows over the alley, a strong smell of urine fouling the air. Helga guessed they were near the tanner's, which might have explained why the woman had become nauseous.

But not quite.

'It is unfortunate, I think, or perhaps desirable. To you, at least.'

Eren shivered, holding her ground, fearing that this was the dreamer Erling had told her about, and then quickly sure of it. 'What are you talking about?'

'Your child. It is one way to keep a man, of course, but just as easily a reason to push him far away. Unless you plan to use it as leverage? To bring him back to you, to keep your silence in return for his love?'

Eren turned to vomit again, though she wasn't sure if it was from nausea or fear.

Now Helga approached, not wishing to spread gossip. 'The king doesn't love you. A child will not change that. No matter what you say or do, you cannot steal a heart. It is given.' And with that, she turned to leave, though frowning, she turned back to Eren Venberg. 'There is something about you that concerns me. Not just the child in your belly but your intentions. I am old, and my vision is failing, though I will never be blind while there is breath in my lungs. Wherever you go, whatever you do, know that I will be watching.' And with a grunt, Helga stomped off, feeling the woman's eyes following her every step.

***

They had talked awhile longer, refreshed their stores of ale and water, filled chests and baskets with food, then headed back to sea.

The wind had dropped considerably, making Bolder tense, though seeing Eadmund traipsing up and down *Bone Hammer's* deck with hunched shoulders, worries etched into his face, he held back his own.

Having heard what Arras and Mattie had revealed to the king, Kolarov joined him, hoping to put his mind at ease. 'I have seen these pits,' he said. 'My lord was shown them. The Lord of

Bhat. From Agerra, south of Zagora. I was employed by the man for nearly a year. He was educated. A wealthy, ambitious lord. He sought to create the same sort of private kingdom the King of S'ala Nis had built. He wanted to understand everything, so he found his way to an invitation to the isle, and I was taken along.'

Eadmund stopped, wondering where this was leading. Suppressing a sigh, he looked down at the man, tension pulsing in his jaw.

'We were shown to the pits. A horrible place, teeming with flies. Oh, the filth!' Kolarov worked to hold himself back, trying to refocus. 'Our guide explained that those doomed to die were dropped into the holes and locked in. It was a feeding ground for Venusta, Goddess of Souls, though I imagine the God of Death also made use of the place.' Though seeing that only made Eadmund more concerned, Kolarov hurried on, eyes averted. 'The guide also said that the pits were used as a deterrent and that, sometimes, all that was needed was a few hours. It would give a troublesome slave a good scare, and then they'd be hauled out and cause no further problems.'

Eadmund's face suddenly relaxed. 'So the queen may just have sought to threaten Jael? To punish her?'

'Yes. Exactly! She would wish to please her father, surely? To be his heir and then go against his wishes? For surely they are his wishes?'

'So there's a chance...'

'I think there's more than a chance. I cannot believe that woman would die in a hole. She is far too special for that. Jael Furyck?' Tears welled in Kolarov's eyes. 'I have not seen her in many a year. Not since her father's untimely death. Though my memories of her are still vivid and full of life, like she is. I saw her fighting often, and never once was she defeated. No, I tell you, dear king, your wife lives still. I feel it.'

Eadmund stared at him, tears in his own eyes, and placing his hands on Kolarov's shoulders, he nodded. 'So do I, my friend. So do I.'

***

That night, there was a disturbance in the slaves' sleeping quarters.

Someone had been found dead.

But as everyone scurried around, trying to find out what had happened, Jael lay on her side, listening, confident that the man had simply died of natural causes.

Well, not natural, she realised.

The pressure the slaves' bodies were being put under, the strain of such long working hours and brutal conditions wasn't natural at all.

She imagined Kalina Sardis sleeping in her bed. Closing her eyes, she saw a high bed requiring steps to climb into it. It was draped in silk sheets and finely woven blankets, crowned by a ring of enormous feather-stuffed pillows, encased in fine muslin curtains. And...

Jael blinked, wondering if she was imagining things or was she really seeing the queen's bedchamber? A tingle at the back of her neck had her wondering. Since Sunni's death, she'd struggled to see much. She certainly wanted to, though something was holding her back.

Rigg squatted down before her. 'Looks like Esten just died. No sign of any wounds or weapons. Poor sod. We arrived here together, I remember. Thought he'd been looking a bit off-colour.'

A frowning Jael didn't know why he was suddenly talking to her.

'This place will kill us all.'

Jael didn't answer, sensing something else was coming.

'Alek says the only way to succeed...' Now Rigg dropped lower, leaning his head until it was shadowing Jael's face. 'Is to have one leader, which should be me, of course, though he wants it to be you. He thinks your coming here is some sort of sign from the gods, and he doesn't want to displease them.' He saw glimpses of Jael's face. She looked in pain, he thought, seeing her lying on her side with her face scrunched up.

He wondered how she was even going to lift an arm to help them rise up.

But shaking his head, he carried on. 'So, it's you. I... it's you.'

Jael was almost too tired to answer, though she cleared her throat. 'Good. So we can't go in different directions anymore. Only mine.'

'Because you're a dreamer?'

Jael made a noise that sounded almost like a laugh. 'No, because I'm a leader. It's what I do. I will lead us out of here.'

***

The eagle soared above S'ala Nis.

From this height, the isle was tiny, the sea encircling its rocky cliffs like shimmering blue glass.

Silence.

The bird's brown wings extended like great sails on either side of its body. Feathers fluttering ever so gently, it angled its head, diving now, aiming for S'ala Nis' temple.

Dessalene watched.

Lying in her bed, lost in a dream, she watched that magnificent bird with an open mouth.

Eagles were heroic creatures, sacred to Artis, God of War.

She refocused on the bird, seeing it swooping towards the Dragon Blood Tree. And skimming its furry green top, it rose again, wings flapping, lifting higher.

Dessalene felt cold air on her cheeks, fingers twitching.

The eagle's wings now spread out in perfectly straight lines as it raced over the city. She recognised the harbour, the palace, and the main road leading to the temple grounds. She saw crowds of people fixed in place, and she realised it was the funeral procession.

Kalina was there. Argo Kosta and his ugly daughter.

She saw herself.

And a body wrapped in a white funeral shroud, resting on a bier, carried by eight red-robed logi.

She suddenly noticed that the eagle had something in one of its talons.

A rat.

And as Dessalene looked on, the bird released its sharp claws, dropping the rat down onto the procession before lifting its head and flying away.

***

The men who'd attacked them at Rosby had followed them into the forest, taking down three more riders before Gant and his men had finally managed to leave them behind.

It was dark, still wet, and the horses were tired.

No one could see through the rain.

No one knew where they were.

But finding a clearing near a stream, Gant ordered everyone off the horses, wanting to sleep but knowing they had to stay alert.

'We've gone back on ourselves,' one of his men muttered. 'I feel like we've turned around.'

Gant barely heard him over the thundering rain, though he feared it himself.

He'd lost six men. Six horses.

And he was no closer to getting back to Andala.

Walking Gus to the stream, he dropped his head to the side, trying to relieve a spasm in his neck.

'You think we lost them?' Rexon wondered, conscious of the arrow in his arm. He'd snapped the end off, though he needed someone to cut it out. 'I don't feel we have.'

'No, I don't think we lost them. To follow us for hours in this weather? They're not looking for coins.'

'They want to stop us reaching Andala,' Rexon decided, leaving his injured mare beside Gus and turning with a sigh. He brought his wet hands up to his wet face, sweeping away the rain. Though it soon returned in force, and he blinked at his friend with dripping eyelashes, trying to find some hope in the darkness.

'It's hard to know what to do because we didn't see much of them. I'd be tempted to split us in two, send half to lead them on a wild goose chase and the rest to Andala. Though what if there's an army?'

Rexon thought about that, and stepping closer to Gant, he lowered his voice. 'If we don't tell Axl what's happening, there's no chance. There's no guarantee those messengers got through, and if there is an army...' His meaning conveyed, Rexon stepped back, running a hand over his horse's rump. He'd cut out the first arrow that had hit her in Saala, but she'd been struck again at Rosby, and now he snapped that in half, knowing there was nothing he could do till morning. She whinnied in discomfort and stepped away, dropping her head to the stream.

Gant made his decision. 'We'll rest for a while and give the horses a break. I'll take first watch, then we'll separate. You lead the men to Andala. I'll take the rest deeper into the woods and hopefully distract anyone still following us.'

Rexon was surprised. 'Hallow Wood?'

A weary Gant grinned. 'There's nothing to fear in there now except more rain and whoever's got a mind to stop us. Hopefully, they won't feel so inclined to enter the woods.'

'You're sure you don't want to go to Andala?'

Gant shook his head, peeling away his cloak from his tunic, hoping to find something to eat in his pouch. 'If it all goes wrong, you need to get back to Saala and those children. I may love my wife, but your children need their father.'

Rexon held his gaze for a moment before looking away.

'I'll tell the men.'

***

In Jael's dream, she was in Andala.

Everything looked so achingly familiar.

She saw the King's Hall, wishing she was a girl, running inside to see her father, though she walked alone in an eerie silence. There was no one in the square, no one coming and going through the open hall doors. The workshops were quiet. She heard no hammering sounds. No clanging. No chatter.

Just an oddly heavy silence.

Moving slowly, Jael sensed everything becoming darker. She peered over her shoulder, feeling a presence, though seeing nothing; nothing but moonlight now, streaked across the ground.

Turning back, she heard a creak.

A crack.

Lengthening her stride, she was soon heading past the hall.

And then she was running, heart pounding.

It wasn't a crack or a creak but a great shattering of wood, as Andala's main gates broke open and a flurry of men swept inside, weapons glinting in moonlight, teeth bared. They were screaming, charging at her.

She had no weapon, nothing to hand, and she was knocked to the ground, trampled underfoot, bones snapping, chest crushed.

Waking with a shout, Jael saw that Quint was already in the sleeping hall, rousing the slaves with a kick and a shove, urging everyone to hurry. Soon he put his shell to his lips and blew loudly.

She didn't even look his way.

In the heat of the stuffy hall, she felt chilled to the bone.

'Jael?' Alek had crept over to see if she was alright. He moved to put a hand on her shoulder, though quickly thought better of it.

She turned to him, hearing his familiar voice, seeing his kind face. Her heart was still racing, body trembling. 'I...' She nodded slowly. 'Fine. I'm fine.'

He turned away to answer a question, though Jael didn't move.

She was still there, watching those warriors charging through Andala's gates.

***

A tired Dessalene sat like a statue at breakfast.

Pye hovered nearby, slipping in and out of the dining hall curtains as he was wont to do. Beside her, Kalina picked at a plate of figs and olives. She heard the delicate patter of slippers across marble as slaves moved around the table in silence. From the open doors came a steady hum of industry, the squawking, chirping, singing sounds of birds in the courtyard and the plentiful gardens beyond.

Yet Dessalene's mind remained in her dream. She had returned to it many times over the past two days. The eagle had dropped a rat; it seemed clear enough. Though what did the rat signify? Or who?

She hadn't had a dream since, nothing to further inform her thinking, and it left her disturbed and unsettled.

Who was the rat?

Glancing at Kalina, she wished the woman would lift herself out of her puddle of self-pity. She was an embarrassment, carrying on like a broken-hearted girl when her indulgent father had made her a powerful queen. How could she rule her people when she appeared incapable of commanding herself?

Blinking, Dessalene moved her head, watching the silent

slaves, noting their subtle glances at the queen and their shared looks of concern.

Foundations didn't crumble overnight.

The weakening of great dynasties happened out of sight for months, even years before the first wall fell. A great catastrophe was the result of many small instances, each one adding to create a destructive sum of its parts.

Leaning forward, Dessalene raised her goblet. 'A toast!' she announced loudly. 'To your upcoming nuptials! I had a dream last night of you and your husband.' Keeping her eyes fixed on a curious Kalina, she sensed that the nearby slaves had pricked up their ears.

'You did?' Kalina turned towards her stepmother, raising her own goblet.

'Yes, you and he were on a ship. A fine wolf ship, surrounded by your children. Three little boys and a daughter. You held the girl in your arms, her dark hair shimmering like perfect obsidian, just like yours. It was quite the scene. I woke with tears on my cheeks, dearest. Tears of happiness for you and Kosta.'

Kalina stared blankly at Dessalene, unable to imagine such a future.

Unless she replaced Argo Kosta with Arras Sikari and then it became entirely possible. Despite her anger at her traitorous former husband-to-be, the memory of his face teased a smile out of her at last.

Dessalene felt relieved. 'Those other men were ill-suited to you, but Kosta is cut from a different cloth entirely. He will be both a loyal consort and a mighty ruler of our army. He will keep you and your children and S'ala Nis safe.' A tired Dessalene doubted every word, and soon her smile faltered, though not before she offered a toast to Olera.

This time, Kalina didn't raise her goblet, watching as Dessalene drank from hers. Her stepmother kept talking in that loud, attention-seeking voice of hers, though Kalina was no longer listening.

Would Arras return?

Would he come back to S'ala Nis and save her from having to marry Argo Kosta?

***

Kosta stopped his new horse by the temple well, swinging down to the ground with a grunt. Quint came running towards him, seeing that his wife had accompanied her father.

Carefully placing Krissia on the ground, Kosta turned to glare at a sweating Quint. 'That scaffolding is still up. Why is it still up? We discussed it yesterday, man. I want it down! We have more work to do than just the tower. These grounds are a mess! A fucking mess! There is planting to be done, and I must ensure the platform is prepared for the sacrifice, so why is that tower still not finished?'

A fretful Quint bowed his head. 'The men are working as fast as they can, though we have lost time with the...' Lifting his head, he eyed his pouting wife. 'Deaths.'

'What? Speak up!' Kosta snapped. 'I cannot hear the mutterings of mice!'

'There have been a great number of deaths, lord. Since the pace was accelerated, it has become a struggle.'

Kosta snarled, snapping his fingers at a slave to see to the horses. And taking his daughter's hand, he slipped it into the crook of his arm. 'You think we are lacking slaves, Quint? Is that what you're saying? That on an isle brimming with slaves, we cannot find any to finish the job?'

Quint was a bowing, bending, nervous wreck around his father-in-law. 'I've enough who can lift and mix. It's the cutting and the point work that takes skill, and I've just lost two of my best men. The arch is fiddly, lord. It must be done right.'

It was a reasonable answer and certainly a quandary, but for Argo Kosta, future consort of S'ala Nis, betrothed to a very particular queen, it was not good enough. He aimed his daughter at the temple, seeking to deposit her in the shade while he made his way up the tower to find out what to do about this nagging problem.

The funeral was in four days, and he felt confident that with a final push, they could finish the tower and ready the grounds, but he wanted everything looking presentable for the king's return. For he knew Ronin Sardis would hurry to the temple to make an offering to Eyshar upon his arrival.

The grounds simply could not remain in this chaotic state any longer.

Handing Krissia off to her husband, he called three slaves to him. He knew no names; they were just bodies. 'You there! And you! You too! Come!' And when the three surprised and anxious-looking slaves approached, Kosta gave them their orders. 'You will clear this courtyard. I want every bucket, every rock, every speck of dust gone. The tower mightn't be finished, but the courtyard will no longer look like a building site, understood?' Squinting in the harsh glare of the morning sun, he narrowed sharp eyes at the three men, whose heads were bowed and bobbing. 'Good, see that it's done.' And turning on his heels, Kosta headed after Quint and Krissia, who had been stopped by the Noor-Elect, dressed in a dark blue robe trimmed in silver thread.

'A good morning to you, commander. And to your lovely daughter,' Inesh Seppo smiled, inclining his head.

Despite all his bluster, Kosta had a great reverence for the gods and their emissaries, and he bobbed his own head. 'You must be eager for the mess and noise to be gone, lord seer?'

Inesh laughed. 'It is like the sound of birds and bees to me now. I am certain I would not recognise the silence!' He motioned his guests towards the open doors of the temple, where shade beckoned. Here was another world entirely, and peace descended as they crossed the impressive mosaic floor, weaving between pools swimming with lilies and lotuses. Suddenly, the sounds of shouting and hammering lessened, a sweet chorus of birdsong filling the air.

'Still, we must have it completed in time for the funeral. And for the king, who arrives within days.'

'I have great faith that it will be. I know Quint has his men working night and day, so do not fear, commander. I have seen that all will come together as we intend. Have faith.'

The seer's words soothed Kosta's tension, and he smiled at his daughter, whose eyes were immediately drawn to the matching statues of Eyshar and his wife, Atikar. 'Would you be kind enough to show my Krissia around? Quint is going to take me to the top of the tower so I can assess our progress from above.'

'Of course,' Inesh said. 'I would be delighted.' He fixed his attention on the sour face of Krissia, who barely offered a smile as her father turned away, heading back into the sun.

And to the scaffolding.

Where he would climb the tower.

CHAPTER THIRTY-ONE

The rain had finally stopped in the night, though Gant was still soaked through and shivering as he led his men deep into Hallow Wood.

They rode silently behind him, unhappy about the mission they'd been set.

Warriors disappeared in Hallow Wood. Everyone knew that.

They had all heard tales of what lurked amongst the strange trees. It was like a different world in here. Everything had a tinge of blue, as though the light filtering down through the tree canopy came from an entirely different sun. Or perhaps it was abandoned by the gods altogether?

Except those with dark intentions...

Gant wasn't a dreamer, though he could almost hear the unspoken fears swirling around him.

Leaning forward, he patted an oddly still Gus. Gus remembered this place, and not fondly, he guessed, judging by his lack of interest in his surroundings. It was as though he was just trying to get through the woods in one piece.

One of Gant's men, Osgar, rode up beside him, eyes darting left and right. 'Would they have followed us, lord? In here?'

Gant shrugged. 'Not if they're smart.' Now he grinned, patting the young man on the back, seeing fear in his tired eyes. 'Though we've nothing to fear from the woods. Whatever lingered in here is long gone.'

***

Kneeling at the top of the tower, trowel in hand, Jael's mind wandered like a river. She couldn't fix it in one place. It returned to her dream of Andala before flowing past thoughts of the battle to come, stopping briefly at Alek, who she was growing increasingly worried about, her children and Milla Ulfsson, and finally lingering on Eadmund for a time.

She wondered what he had done after leaving S'ala Nis.

Where he had gone...

Despite her best efforts, she hadn't been able to bring anything to her. She had seen him being chased by ships, so had he made an escape?

Was he safe?

Body tensing, she stopped what she was doing.

'Is something wrong?' Alek asked, seeing Jael's hand shaking mid-air. He'd come to check her progress, and pleased with what he saw, he'd started to smile, but seeing her expression, he frowned instead.

Jael shook her head, hearing a scream in the distance, feeling silly for worrying about her own wounds. Likely someone had just broken a bone or lost a limb or perhaps their life. 'No, nothing.' Turning her head, she peered up at him. 'And you?'

Their attention was immediately diverted by the sight of an eagle soaring past the tower.

Jael laughed. 'He's following me.'

'The eagle?'

She nodded. 'I've been seeing him for days now.'

'Well, I'm glad you've got some company up here.'

'The best sort,' Jael assured him. 'Anything but people.'

They heard a disturbance, soon feeling vibrations as the planks started rippling like waves.

Alek looked past Jael, immediately stiffening. 'Kosta,' he warned, inclining his head for her to stand.

Which she eventually did, with some effort, just in time to see the big brute staring at her as he stopped, shadowed by a muttering Quint.

Rigg had happily informed Jael that Kosta had thrown a number of slaves off the tower already, displeased with their work. He'd warned her of what might happen if she were ever paid a visit by the commander.

Jael quickly woke herself up, assessing the situation. She backed up to the tower wall, not wanting to get anywhere near the edge of the scaffolding. She held a trowel in her right hand, and she had her fetters, which were weapons in themselves, though it wasn't just herself to worry about. Alek was as thin as vellum. If Kosta decided to have a problem with him, he could simply blow him over the side.

Seeing the slave queen, Kosta glowered at her. 'You have been given this task? Why? What did you promise to earn this place? What did you have to do?'

Alek was quick to intervene. 'She has skill with the finer work, commander. Gardi chose her to help him. She works fast too. Faster than anyone we've had up here, even with...' He trailed off, realising he had chosen the wrong path.

'Even with?' Kosta demanded, almost bumping his chest into a clearly intimidated Alek.

'Even with her weakness as a woman,' Alek hurried to explain. 'Weakness of mind and body. She is... effective here. And we need speed if we're to finish on time.' He glanced at Quint, who looked as nervous as Alek felt.

Kosta grunted, moving away from Alek towards Jael, forcing her to step back until her wounds were touching the stone tower. He knew he'd hurt her, and now he would remind her of that. Though watching her eyes, he saw no indication of pain. The sunlight was bright on her face, and her eyes sparkled like gems. Bending close, he poked a finger at her nose. 'Soon the king will be here, and I imagine he'll want to see his prize. And what will he do to you? What does he want you for? I'd say you're about to find out.' Jael's face remained impassive, and incensed by that, Kosta had to resist the urge to grab her by the tunic and fling her off the tower.

Hands pulsing by his sides, he clenched them into fists, hearing another scream in the distance, soon followed by a loud thud. And motioning with his head, he indicated for Quint to go and find out what had happened. Lunging at Jael, he grabbed her by the throat. 'You'd better be on your best behaviour, bitch, for if I hear even one whisper that you're falling behind, taking it easy, I'll have you down in that quarry, hefting stones as big as Alek here. Hear me now, for if this tower isn't finished on time, I'll make you wish you were dead.'

***

Edela walked past the plinth where the man in the golden tunic was trying to tempt customers for The Armless One. Their eyes met for a moment before she carried on, though her attention was drawn back to the seeress' words and then Bertel's.

Raymon Vandaal had run away.

But was she really here to try and convince him to return home?

And to what?

A ruined hall, a new king, and little hope of reclaiming his throne?

A throne he didn't appear to even want?

Jostled by an impatient woman, who elbowed her sharply, Edela toppled towards Bertel, who righted her with a grunt.

'You must look around, Edela! These people are like galloping horses, with little care for us. Do stay alert!' And taking Edela's arm, he proceeded to walk briskly.

Siggy, who had been ranging ahead, came running back to

them with bright eyes. 'There's a statue on top of that mountain!' she called, pointing into the distance. 'To Sibela. She's the Siluran Goddess of Wisdom. A woman told me you can go up there and make a wish. The goddess will tell you what you want to know if you pay her a silver coin!'

Bertel laughed. 'And who takes all those coins, I wonder?'

Though an earnest Siggy shook her head. 'No, there's a great pool and an altar. You throw them in for the goddess, and she keeps them!'

Though Bertel wasn't enthusiastic. 'It sounds like too much walking to me. Up a mountain?'

Edela felt torn. She was desperate for more insight, but like Bertel, the thought of all that walking wasn't appealing in such energy-sapping heat. 'It's been a while since we walked up a mountain, though I haven't forgotten how horrific it was!'

'And you only had to walk up it once,' Bertel grumbled. 'Hmmm, and how reliable is this goddess?'

Edela laughed. 'I'm not sure you should be questioning the integrity of a goddess, Bertel Knutson. Besides, a little walk might do us some good.'

'A little walk?' Bertel scratched his head. 'Where is this mountain?' Now he spun around, trying to see through the frothing sea of people and the orange haze burning across the sky. 'I see no mountain!' Though stopping abruptly, he thought he did spy a dark lump rising in the distance.

'It's not far,' Siggy promised. 'And we could always take a wagon?'

'Now that's thinking!' Bertel declared, glancing around with squinting eyes. 'Let's ask that man up there!' And pointing at an old man standing in a wagon, an enthusiastic Bertel bounded away.

***

Anticipating the arrival of her husband, Dessalene strode around the palace with the urgency of a warrior preparing for battle, demanding that every piece of furniture and every ornament was free of dust, that the rugs were taken outside and beaten, and then, still unhappy with the state of them, beaten again. That every vase was emptied of its flowers, its foul-smelling water refreshed. And more of them, for the king was coming.

'The king is coming!' she bellowed at Pye, who followed closely behind, trying not to step on her swishing blue dress.

He blinked, offering no soothing words or offers of comfort.

She glared at him.

'And the king will be so pleased to see you, Mistress. He will not care for flowers or be disturbed by dust. He is coming to see you!'

Dessalene swung back around, snorting loudly. 'What an impudent little toad you are. He isn't coming to see me. He wants to inspect his prize, and he wishes to see what his daughter has been up to. And if he sees the truth? The mess Kalina has made of everything?'

'Though you have the power to paint the picture you desire him to see,' Pye purred. 'Any picture you wish.'

It was true, and taking a breath, Dessalene marched on into the foyer, where she mounted the stairs, aiming for her bedchamber. Hearing Pye clopping behind her, she turned around, shaking her head. 'Not you, creature. Hop away and find me a tasty tidbit! Something useful to make me smile. I shall reward you.' And bending down, she tickled him under the chin. 'Hurry along now.'

Pye looked excited by the prospect of a reward and soon scuttled away, leaving a tense Dessalene staring after him.

Something was wrong.

In all that was right, something felt off. And not dirty rugs or drooping flowers, but something she could not see.

Her dream filtered back to her, and she remembered the rat.

And if there was a rat on S'ala Nis, she needed to be a cat.

***

Jael heard Alek coming long before he arrived.

'Your cough is getting worse,' she told him when he stopped to offer her a cup of water. Jael was certain the water was upsetting her stomach, but her throat was so dry that she quickly threw the muddy water down it.

Alek frowned, working to suppress the cough tickling the back of his throat. 'I fear you're trying to convince me that we shouldn't follow through with our plan.'

Handing him back the empty cup, Jael dropped her shoulders, longing for an ice-cold bath. 'You're not a child, Alek, and I'm not your mother.'

He leaned towards her. 'I may be two steps from the outstretched hand of the God of Death, but I am still two steps, Jael. I will not give in to whatever ails me. I've come through worse. The heat and the dust?' Now he coughed freely, drawing up a great rattling noise from deep in his lungs. He stumbled, nearly dropping the cup.

Taking his arm, she sought to steady him. 'I need your help with this pattern.' Inclining her head to the bricks she'd laid out according to Gardi's instructions, she bid Alek to sit down. 'If you could just stay here awhile, make sure I have it right. Just for a while. The sun's moved away, and it's almost shaded here.'

Alek was too busy trying to catch his breath to answer. But looking up at Jael as she forced him onto the ground, he smiled. 'You are –'

'I need more mortar. If you can just wait here, I'll find Abez. He'll have some more. Just wait here for me.'

Alek nodded.

'I won't be long.' And slowly moving away from the foreman, not wanting to bounce the planks, Jael blew out a long breath. Her worry for Alek was growing. She hadn't been here long, but he appeared to be fading away before her eyes.

Leaving him sitting, she decided to go and see Quint.

***

With Siggy's help, Bertel had commandeered a wagon to take them up the mountain and they all felt happy about that.

Edela turned to them with a smile. Her companions sat together on one side of the wagon, squeezed between barrels of what smelled like fish, while she perched on the bench next to the driver: a sullen, silent old man who refused to make eye contact with her.

Bertel had quickly offended the man, who had threatened to drive away, though Siggy had convinced him to take their coins. She was certainly growing in confidence away from Tuura's temple and those girls who had made her feel unworthy of her place amongst them. Here, on this strange adventure, she had a freedom never experienced before – a true journey of discovery – and though it had been frightening, dangerous, and most of all, confusing, Edela saw that it was exactly what Siggy had needed.

It was as though she had been freed from every doubt, forced to live in the moment. Forced to rely on instincts and gifts that had always been present, though buried under a mountain of doubt.

Smiling wryly, Edela shook her head, feeling buried beneath her own doubts.

Lifting a hand, she shielded her eyes from the sun, which appeared to be burning a great hole through the haze. She felt stuck to the bench, feeling sweat cascading down her back. They had purchased skins, filling them with small ale, though after the long ride up the mountain, Edela doubted they had a drop left between them. She hoped there would be somewhere to refill them, though turning to the scowling driver, she didn't dare ask him.

As the haze burned off, the view from the mountain sharpened, and Edela could see the great city of Castala disappearing from view. It was a relief to be away from the crushing noise and the impatient crowds. She longed for the open spaces offered by Andala, the trees and the rain, her garden, her cottage.

Peace.

She had certainly taken it for granted over the years, but since leaving Tuura behind with Bertel and Siggy, she had known none, just a continual churning of fear and confusion.

'A far better way to climb a mountain!' Bertel called to her as the wagon jolted over a rock. He grabbed the siding, not wanting those to be his last words, for up here, it was steep, and the driver had moved his wagon far to the edge of the mountain path to avoid oncoming traffic.

'You'd better hold on, Bertel,' Siggy warned, eyes bulging as the wagon tilted sharply, creaking as though it was about to come apart.

Edela turned back to them again. 'See the statue up there! Have you ever seen something so tall? It's enormous!'

The impressive statue of Sibela rose from the mountain like a bird, the arms on either side of her long body appearing to flutter like wings in the sunlight. Her body had a rosy hue, which was quite striking after the gold and brown tones of the city.

Staring up at Sibela's face, Edela saw a haughty-looking woman. The goddess appeared to be snarling, as though willing away those who came to make offerings, which didn't bode well.

Turning back around, she heard Siggy's excitement and Bertel's efforts to rein in the girl's enthusiasm, feeling her own trepidation about what lay ahead.

The old driver snapped the reins, urging his oxen up the last of the rapidly steepening incline, and then they were at the top of the mount, approaching a great square with the appearance of a market. Much like Castala itself, there were food sellers and stalls and peddlers hawking their wares – a great humming buzz of industry. In front of the statue, people formed lines on the steps leading to the stone altar fronting the great pool, eager to toss their offerings into the water, hoping Sibela would grant them an answer or a wish.

Siggy had jumped down before the wagon had completely stopped, earning another grumble from Bertel, who urged her to stay where she was.

To no avail.

'I won't go far!' she promised. 'Only over there!'

Amongst the various peddlers were those selling food, and the appetising aromas had quickly attracted a hungry Siggy.

'Oh, let her go, Bertel,' Edela laughed. 'She has a few coins, so let her spend them. Besides, you need to pay this man for his trouble and then help me down. I'm eager to see what all the fuss is about!'

Bertel turned away from Siggy, hopping down from the wagon in a tangle of limbs and twisted clothes. He hurried to rearrange himself before grabbing Edela by the waist and lifting her down. She turned to smile at the driver, who ignored her, keeping his eyes on Bertel, who was busy digging into his pouch, where he pulled out the agreed-upon sum of coins.

The driver quickly pocketed the coins and picked up the reins, clicking his tongue.

'No! Wait! You must wait here to take us back down! I have more coins for the return journey!' Bertel called. 'To the city! You must wait!'

But ignoring him, the driver turned his oxen in a slow circle, aiming them back down the mountain.

A laughing Edela grabbed Bertel's flailing arm. 'We'll find someone else. Look! There are so many coming and going. It appears that the goddess is good for business. We'll find another wagon. For now, let's just enjoy this magnificent view!'

Siggy came running back to them with two slices of a dark-coloured cake. 'I bought us something to eat!' she said, handing one to Edela and the other to Bertel.

'Though where is yours?' Edela wondered, sniffing the cake,

intrigued by hints of fruit and spice.

'I ate it already! I want to go and see the woman selling jewellery. She has necklaces and amulets. Could I, maybe, spend a few more coins?'

Already shaking his head, Bertel opened his mouth, though it was Edela who spoke. 'You most certainly can. It will be lovely to have a little keepsake, not just a faint memory of all the different foods we tried!' And thinking of food, she took a bite of the cake, closing her eyes to savour the complex medley of flavours.

Bertel followed her lead, both of them watching as Siggy scampered away towards the dark-haired woman selling jewellery.

***

Quint had nothing helpful to say about Alek. 'He's knowledgeable, useful at managing his crew, and a hard worker. It'll be a shame to lose him, but what can I do?'

'Send for the physician,' Jael insisted. 'You need to send for the physician or take Alek there. He needs something for his cough. A tonic.'

Quint laughed, looking past Jael to the slaves bringing in the wagon-loads of dirt needed for the new gardens around the tower. 'I don't have time to be down a man. I can't be!' He felt rising panic, for Krissia had warned him that if the tower wasn't finished on time, her father intended to place all the blame on him. 'He just needs to stop complaining! Stop complaining about ill health and get on with his work!'

His spittle hit Jael's face, and she stepped back with a scowl. 'You'll have no one left soon if that's your attitude. These men don't want to die, yet they're dying in droves out here in the sun, doing this impossible task –'

'Do you want to be whipped again? Or thrown in the pits?' Quint snarled uncharacteristically. 'Because if you don't shut your mouth and get back to work, I can assure you that will happen. The commander doesn't tolerate failure. He...' Shoulders sagging, he ran out of anger. He went to bed every night beside his far-from-affectionate wife, though he rarely slept anymore. He lay on his comfortable mattress, resting his head on his feather-stuffed pillow, fretting and worrying about the tower.

It was the centrepiece of the sacrifice to come.

As though Eyshar himself would be looking down on them; a part of the ritual.

And if it were to remain unfinished?

Quint felt a stabbing pain, as though his father-in-law had reached into his chest and squeezed his heart. He could almost smell the commander's breath, always so strong and sour. He drank the notoriously potent black wine, morning till night, and even his skin reeked of the stuff.

'You needn't fear the commander,' Jael said.

Quint blinked at her. 'What?'

'I... to help the men finish the tower on time, you need to bring a physician here. It would help speed things along. He could see the men with ailments and wounds and help to remedy them. It would mean healthier men, happier men, faster men.'

Quint peered at the woman. She frowned intently at him, as though in pain. He saw her eyes imploring him, and they were quite mesmerising eyes. And her words... it was as though they were in his head.

Blinking, he called over a man he often used as a messenger. 'Go to the physician's. Request their presence down at the tower. We have men needing attention. And quickly. Return as quickly as you can.' Quint glanced at Jael, seeing her eyes brighten and intensify. He moved a hand to dismiss her, feeling as though it wasn't even attached to his body.

And with a smile, she was gone.

Though Quint remained, watching her, the slave queen's

words echoing in his ears.

***

Helga toured Andala's fort in the company of Linas and Gully, though the boy and the dog mainly ignored her, and when she stopped to inspect the main gates, they left her behind, heading down the well-worn path to the forest. 'Do not go far!' she warned, though only Gully turned his head in acknowledgement.

Helga's eyes, though, were on a man watching from the trees.

He held the bridle of his horse, which was mostly hidden by the thick trunk of an oak, his eyes roaming the ramparts and then the open gates, watching those coming and going.

She narrowed her eyes, murmuring a quick chant, searching for that which remained hidden.

Closing her eyes, she saw a lord – a man with dark brown hair.

'Look like one of them. Blend in and head down. Find Emmet. He's working at the docks, staying with a woman from the tavern. You'll find him easily enough.'

Opening her eyes, Helga called Linas to her. Hands on hips, she waited, seeing no sign of the boy, though within a few heartbeats, Gully came bounding out of the trees and back onto the path, Linas charging after him.

She felt the man moving out of the trees now, though she didn't return her gaze to him. She kept it on the dog and the boy, though she sensed the man making his way towards her, his heartbeat quickening as he approached the gates. His smell was in her nostrils, and now Helga turned around.

'We weren't going far!' Linas promised with a freckly grin.

His grandmother ignored him and the dog, who looked up at her joyously, hoping to be rewarded for his obedience. Grunting, she turned around. 'That may be so, though you don't know this forest, boy. It's not our forest. We're not in Tuura now.'

The man was close, passing Linas, though she would not look his way.

Or the boy's.

Instead, she pushed an idea into her grandson's mind.

Linas peered up at her, frowning.

And then he nodded.

'Come on, Gully!' he called. 'Let's go see the ships! They might have brought back some treasure!'

Helga sensed the man staring after the boy. She slowed to a stop, putting a hand to her back, seeing that man pass her by, eyes trained on the boy, who he was now following.

***

The dark-haired woman held a silk-covered tray, showing a selection of necklaces and amulets to Siggy. There were other customers wishing to inspect her wares, though her eyes remained on the girl.

The necklaces first caught Siggy's eye – made with glass beads and stones. She fingered them, lifting them up, seeing the way the sun lit up the tiny balls of blue and green glass as though they were made of liquid. There was another necklace of red carnelian stones that captured her interest and then something else entirely: a round silver disc on a silver chain. It wasn't beautiful, but somehow, it quickly became the most mesmerising of all.

'What does it mean?' Siggy wondered, picking up the amulet and fingering the interlocking symbol carved into the silver disc.

'It is Memtek's symbol. He is the God of Protection. You wear this under your dress, next to your heart. It is not as pretty or eye-catching as the rest, but it is the most powerful.'

'Powerful?' Siggy squinted at the woman, whom she noticed for the first time. She was middle-aged and small, with curly black hair. Her cheeks were deeply pitted as though she had lived through a serious illness. Her eyes were kind, perhaps weary, Siggy thought.

She wondered if the woman had to walk up the mountain to sell her wares each day. It would be exhausting, especially in the heat.

'You wear it to protect those you love. To keep them safe.'

'Those you love?'

Placing the tray on the ground, the woman slipped a hand into her bodice and pulled out her own amulet, which had the same symbol carved into a similar silver disc. 'I pray to Memtek each morning and every night to keep my children safe. I wear this in honour of him. My children are grown now, with their own families, so it has certainly worked for me.'

Siggy stared past her to the great statue of Sibela, then over her shoulder at Bertel and Edela, who weren't looking her way. 'I will take it,' she decided quickly. 'Please.'

The woman smiled. 'You will wear it now?'

Siggy nodded, looping it over her head.

'Remember to keep it safe, next to your heart, and to offer up a prayer to Memtek each night before you close your eyes. It is your special amulet, so make sure to keep it just for you.'

A happy Siggy tucked the necklace beneath her dress and paid the woman the three coins. 'Thank you.'

'No,' the woman smiled. 'Thank you.'

CHAPTER THIRTY-TWO

Ratish was happy to leave his rooms behind, eager to do what he could to help those slaves under the most intense pressure on the isle.

Having tended to horrific injuries and deformities over the years, he had tried to counsel Argo Kosta about his treatment of the slaves. He knew that Arras Sikari had petitioned the queen about it, to no avail, for the commander's cruelty had persisted. And those men forced to work demanding hours, lifting heavy stones into dangerous positions, had suffered, died, or been maimed forever.

Now was a chance to help at least a few of them.

'This man needs to rest for the day,' he told a muttering Quint, who hovered over the physician's shoulder, shuffling impatiently.

Ratish had been invited to set up a temporary clinic in the temple foyer by Inesh Seppo, who had ordered his logi to bring in mattresses and cups of wine.

Ratish was grateful, though Quint was starting to fear that Kosta would arrive and shut the whole thing down. He half wished he would. At this rate, the number of men waiting to see the physician would outnumber those working on the tower.

'No one can afford a rest!' he sighed. 'No one! I'm losing too many! Just patch them up, give them something to drink, and send them on their way. You're here to help them carry on, not to stop them from working altogether!'

The physician peered up at him from where he squatted on the mosaic tiles, touching the slave's head. 'Then assign this man somewhere out of the sun. He clearly has heat stroke. If he goes back into the sun, he will die. So please, put him somewhere else.'

Quint rolled his eyes, turning to find Alek staring at him. 'What now?'

Alek blinked at him in surprise. 'I... I'm next in line.'

And grunting with annoyance about that, Quint strode away, wanting to see exactly how long the line now was.

Ratish smiled at Alek. 'Please, lie down on that mattress over there, and I'll be with you shortly.'

***

Edela and Siggy made a small offering of coins to the scowling Goddess of Wisdom while Bertel shuffled impatiently behind them, muttering his opinions about that. Eventually, he headed off to the latrines, leaving them in peace.

'Here's hoping he'll be some time,' Edela laughed. 'He may even get lost!' Though thinking it, she glanced around, wanting to remember in which direction he had headed.

Siggy was thoughtful. She tipped back her head, trying to see the face of the statue. The goddess appeared angry, as though she hated her job. She remembered the necklace she'd bought and was going to show it to Edela, though recalling what the woman had told her, she decided to keep it to herself. The idea that she could help keep Edela and Bertel safe mattered to her. If she told them about it, perhaps they wouldn't understand?

'Why don't you go after Bertel?' Edela suggested. 'I'll stay here for a moment. I need to think.'

People crowded the altar, tossing their offerings into the pool.

Most threw coins or stones, some jewellery or knives. Siggy saw a sword and a child's toy in the water. There were even scattered bones.

A few of the gathered crowd looked upset, clinging to each other with tears in their eyes. She felt their concerns for their loved ones, their fears for themselves, and she offered a sympathetic smile as she headed after Bertel.

Edela shut her out. She shut the noise of the crowd out too.

And closing her eyes, she took herself into the calming darkness, looking for answers.

She immediately saw the burned hall in Ollsvik and its new king with his gleaming, gloating face. She saw a terrified Lina in tears, sitting beside her husband. He held her hand tightly, as though hurting her.

Edela thought of Raymon, and soon his face was before her and he was in Esby, boarding a ship. He turned, and she saw herself in the little rowboat with Siggy, the rain pouring down on them both.

He turned away, dropping his hood lower, and then he was gone.

'To Castala,' someone said. 'We are heading for Castala.'

The vision vanished, darkness returned, and Edela burst out of it, staring up at the statue of the goddess, certain now that she had been sent here to find Raymon Vandaal.

***

Dessalene usually enjoyed entertaining, though she had quickly grown tired of Kosta and his frumpy daughter, who dressed like a woman with a great fortune but no taste whatsoever. She was a diminutive dumpling whose lavender dress was so extravagantly busy that it appeared to be drowning her. Her little head poked out of a collar of ruffles, her earrings so heavy they dragged her ears towards her shoulders.

And as for her hair...

Thin, mousy strands had been wound into curls that had now gone limp and merely hung about her like wind chimes seeking a breeze.

It was quite the sight.

Though it was Krissia's father who claimed most of Dessalene's attention. The man drank like a commoner, gulping down goblet after goblet of the queen's black wine – her strongest. He was a man of high standing on the isle, so she'd been surprised to discover that he reeked like a drunk. And though she kept a pleasing smile fixed on her face, it was making her cheeks hurt.

Kalina felt much the same, willing time to move faster. She thought of her bedchamber, imagining the feel of her legs rubbing against the cool sheets. Here, she felt on display, like a treasure Kosta sought to claim. She was no dreamer, but she could certainly see the intentions in the man's eyes.

They ate on the patio, under an awning, surrounded by flaming torches and an army of statue-like slaves holding platters and jugs. The air was sweetened with honey and jasmine, the gentle calls of night jars like music in the distance.

'Your father's return has captured the attention of the isle,' Kosta told Kalina. 'There has always been much speculation about why he left or whether he was even alive, so now to return so suddenly...'

Kalina and Dessalene exchanged a glance.

'Well, the motives and movements of a king have never been the concern of slaves or even lords,' Dessalene said with a hint of irritation, smile faltering now. 'My husband values privacy above all things, as I'm sure he'll remind you when he arrives.'

Kosta heard the rebuke in the dreamer's words, and his jaw clenched. Sitting opposite him, Krissia stared at her father with a warning in her eyes, knowing that he possessed a volcanic temper that she'd always feared would ruin them both.

Ignoring her, Kosta now turned to the dreamer with a grimacing sort of smile. 'I respect any man who knows his own mind, who keeps his own counsel. And certainly a king. It's the type of consort I intend to be.' Now his attention shifted from the king's thin-lipped wife to the luscious lips of the attractive queen, who quickly averted her eyes. 'A man who knows his own mind and his desires.'

Swallowing down a lump of distaste, Kalina reached for her goblet, taking a big gulp of wine. She understood Dessalene's rationale for this match, though if she had been in her right mind, she would have fought harder against it.

She would talk to her father. He would –

Then, remembering the mess she'd made by choosing Arras Sikari and the six dead husbands before him, not to mention murdering Noor of the Dragon Blood Tree, she sighed, sipping her wine.

Wishing it was stronger.

'And the tower?' Dessalene enquired, seeking to draw everyone's attention away from Kalina. 'I hear there is trouble.'

Kosta looked surprised. 'You do? Well...' He violently scratched his salt and pepper beard, scattering a flurry of dandruff onto his plate. 'Perhaps there was a hiccup or two initially, though we will be ready to host the sacrifice. In fact, Krissia's husband excused himself from our supper because he is so keen to deliver the tower on time, my lady. It will be done, I assure you.' Fixing his eyes on the dreamer, he remained unblinking until she looked away, motioning for a slave to bring her guests more wine.

And when his goblet was once again filled to the brim, a tense Kosta drained it dry.

***

It had taken some time to find a wagon to drive them down the mountain, so it was late when Edela, Bertel, and Siggy returned to the city, though thankfully, there was still time to buy fried fish from one of the vendors near the docks. The fish was warm and tasty, a little spicy but otherwise pleasant, and while Bertel and Siggy walked ahead of her, aiming for the baker's and their room, Edela lingered further back, feeling weary.

She held her wrapped fish in one hand, no longer eating. Her mouth hummed with spice, and she thought of offering it to Siggy, though in the next moment, it had been snatched from her hand by someone running past, knocking her to the ground.

Crying out in surprise, Edela bit her tongue, feeling a sharp pain in her knees and then a hand on her arm, pulling her up. In the darkness, she felt afraid, though the man's voice was reassuring and oddly familiar. He righted her onto her feet, then seeing her, his eyes bulged in horror, and dropping his hood over his face, he spun away, immediately sucked into the crowd.

Bertel hurried back to Edela. 'What happened? Are you alright?'

Siggy was soon beside him, looking a dishevelled Edela over.

Though the dreamer could only gape at them in horror, unable to offer any words, certain that the man who had helped her had been Raymon Vandaal.

***

Erling joined Axl in the hall after supper.

'How's Eren?' Axl wondered, not having seen her around the fort. He imagined Getta's face but blinked away her angry scowl, telling himself that he was simply interested in his friend's sister's health.

Erling took the goblet of wine Gerald handed him without

acknowledging the steward and turned to Axl. 'She's well enough. Women's troubles, I suspect. The less I know, the better.'

'Oh?' Axl took a seat by a brazier, indicating for Erling to join him. They were alone in the hall, apart from those servants tidying the high table and finishing up in the kitchen. It was so oddly quiet that he felt grateful for Erling's company.

'Well, as I said, she's not been herself, though I'm none the wiser. As long as she's alive when my mother returns, then I'm in the clear!'

'You'll make such a responsible father one day with those high standards.'

Erling grinned. 'I can't imagine it, being a father. And a husband? It needs to happen, and my mother certainly wants it to, though I like my freedom too much to think about being tied to one woman. One woman?'

'Then you've never been in love, my friend, for if you had, you'd know how desirable such a proposition can be.' Though remembering his dalliance with Erling's sister, Axl stopped smiling. He felt embarrassed and ashamed, a disappointment to himself and his family.

And not for the first time.

'Though, according to Helga, the harbinger of doom, I should be fearing the end of the kingdom. It's hardly the time to make plans for marriage and children.'

Axl smiled. 'I'm not sure why everyone hates Helga.'

'You're not sure? Why? Don't your eyes work? Or your ears? Or your nose, come to think of it. You can smell the wild beast coming. Her and her rabid boy.'

The hall doors opened, and Gully rushed inside, followed by Linas and Helga. The boy and the dog headed for the high table, where Gully immediately slid onto his belly, searching for anything the servants may have missed.

Though Helga had her squinting eyes fixed on Erling Venberg in the dark hall, and she glowered at the man as she stomped forward.

A horrified Erling abruptly sat up, peering at Axl, who looked just as surprised by the dreamer's sudden arrival. Unsettled too. It was late, and he hadn't been expecting any other visitors.

Now Erling stood. 'I must get back to my sister. I... don't want to leave her alone.'

Helga raised an eyebrow, lips clamped together, watching as a flustered Erling nearly knocked over Linas in his attempt to hurry out of the hall.

'Is something wrong?' Axl asked, leaving his goblet on a table as he approached the dreamer. 'Have you seen something?'

Helga glanced at Linas, who disappeared under the high table with Gully. She saw that the servants had left the hall, and hearing no one nearby, she indicated for Axl to return to his chair. And when he had, she took a seat next to him. 'Your friend's sister is not unwell. She is pregnant with your child.'

Axl felt as though he'd been hit in the face or smacked in the stomach. He felt deprived of air and thoughts, just feelings that immediately started bubbling inside him: fear, anger, annoyance, anxiety.

Panic.

Heat rushed up his body until he tugged at his tunic, feeling breathless.

'There is nothing to do about that,' Helga said plainly. 'Except keep your mouth closed and ensure that she does the same. The gods will decide the fate of that child and the woman, as they will decide yours, Axl Furyck.'

Axl sagged in the chair, eyes drifting to his goblet.

'I did not come to discuss her, though. There is a man. I found him today. His name is Hardar, and he came here to join up with someone called Emmet, who is working on your new pier. A lord sent him. Not a lord friendly to you.'

All thoughts of Eren Venberg flew out of Axl's mind. 'What lord?'

A shrugging Helga didn't know. 'You must have the men watched and followed by someone you trust. Not me,' she added quickly. 'There will be men you can ask. Those who can blend in.'

Axl nodded. 'I'll find someone.'

Helga stood, waiting as Linas returned to her side.

'I'm hungry,' the boy said, peering up at her.

His grandmother ignored him. 'Come to me when you have anything to report. And I will find you if I learn more. I suggest that speed is your best friend now... my lord.' And shooing the boy towards the doors, Helga headed out of the hall, leaving the open-mouthed king staring after her.

***

Alek looked better that evening, sipping from the tiny glass phial Ratish had given him.

The slaves had been gifted the surprise of an early meal, too, which Jael knew had also come thanks to the physician.

She smiled, pleased to see a hint of colour on Alek's sunken cheeks.

Even Rigg looked cheerful, gobbling down what appeared to be mutton and pea soup, though the meat was so overcooked that it had lost all colour and could have been anything. Jael swallowed without chewing, trying not to imagine what it was.

Alek looked at his bowl with less enthusiasm as he picked up his wooden spoon and scooped some stringy meat into his mouth. 'I hear you're to thank for the physician coming today.'

Lifting his head, Rigg looked surprised.

'Who said that?' Jael wondered.

Alek grinned. 'Quint got himself worked up when so many lined up to be seen. Said he regretted ever listening to that stupid woman. Wished he never had. I can only think he meant you. That wife of his would hardly offer charity to anyone.'

Rigg chuckled, surprising them both. 'What? You don't

think I'm happy to have an early supper? I've been starving since breakfast. A man like me, living off scraps? I'll look like Alek soon enough!'

'Thanks.'

Leaning across the table, Rigg eyed Jael. 'How did you convince Quint then? Did you promise to fuck him?'

'Rigg!' Alek wasn't impressed. 'You think a queen would propose that? Are you drunk?'

Jael wasn't offended in the slightest, though she changed the subject, lowering her voice. 'Have you been passing on messages to your allies? About our plans?'

Alek nodded, still frowning at Rigg. 'I've confirmed the timing and the signal. Word has gone out, though news of the king's arrival has worried a few.'

It worried Jael, too, but the funeral procession and the sacrifice at the tower was their best chance to make something happen. Everything was easier in numbers; there was confidence and support amongst a crowd. In such a setting, you could lose your identity entirely and become not an individual but a weapon.

At least, Jael hoped that would be the case.

'Where will you go when you leave here?' she wondered, eyeing Rigg. 'Back to Hest?'

He looked annoyed, instantly reminded of why he hated her and her family so much. 'I've already said. I've no home any longer. No place I belong.'

'Then come with me,' Alek offered. 'To Brekka. Stora isn't much, though it's paradise compared to here. It rains!' He laughed, never having thought he would miss those gloomy Brekkan days as winter signalled its approach. 'There are trees, forests, grass. Come with me, Rigg, and we can start again together.'

'What will you do?' Jael asked Alek.

'Set up a workshop. Though for that, I'll need coins.'

'Which you'll have,' she assured him. 'You will. These lords and ladies have plenty to spare. And spare them they will,' she added darkly.

Rigg peered at her. 'Why do you want to help the likes of us? What's in it for you?'

'I like to think we're helping each other,' Jael began, watching as one of Alek's men approached the table, wanting a word.

'From the goodness of your heart?' Rigg scoffed when the man had departed.

Jael eyed him. 'You think a Furyck has a heart? How big of you, Rigg. No, I want to get out of here as much as you. I have things to do, people to hunt down and kill, and if we work together, soon we'll all get what we want.'

**

'Siggy's asleep,' Bertel sighed. 'So now you must tell me, Edela. You've had your lips sewn together all evening, though now I'll hear no more excuses. What is wrong, for surely something is? I've never seen you so quiet. You're a shadow of your usually boisterous self.'

Edela suppressed a laugh. '*Boisterous*? I'm not sure I've ever been described as boisterous before. Not even as a child.'

Bertel pulled his chair around the table, stopping it beside her. 'And?' He glanced at Siggy, who lay perfectly still on the floor. 'What has happened? Something?'

'I... I think I saw Raymon Vandaal.'

Bertel plopped down onto the chair in surprise, and shaking his head, he frowned. 'In a dream, you mean? A vision?'

'No, I actually saw his face, tonight, when I was robbed of my supper. The man who helped me up, I think it was the king. He... must have recognised me, for he immediately ran away.'

Bertel was doubtful. 'And you've met him before?'

'Oh yes, before he decided to shun Axl and Jael. I know he only did it to survive in that snake pit, though before then, he came to Andala a number of times. I remember that face. It grows more and more like his father's, and of course, there's a resemblance to Axl and Jael. I... I'm sure it was him.'

'Though it was dark.'

'It was, but I'm not entirely blind, Bertel Knutson. He was very close. I saw him clearly. It was him.'

Siggy flopped over, and they held their breaths, willing her to remain asleep. She didn't need to know all their troubles.

'Well, if that's the case, what can we do? He's gone to an awful lot of trouble not to be the King of Iskavall, so I doubt a few words from us will change his mind.'

'Mmmm, and he's obviously not looking to be found. Not by anyone. He recognised me, though he looked like he'd seen a ghost. He couldn't run away fast enough.'

Bertel raked his beard, and finding knots, he dug into his pouch and pulled out a fine ivory comb, working it through his grey beard as he worked on his thoughts. 'So what are we supposed to do?'

'Well, something,' Edela decided. 'If I could just speak to him, find a way to speak to him, maybe I could understand what it was all about?' Her eyes drifted towards Siggy again and up to the little gap in the wall, wishing it would usher in a breeze. The room was stifling, and the thought of sleeping was unappealing, though they would need sleep, for tomorrow they had to scour the city for a runaway king.

***

In her dream, it was so hot that Siggy felt as though the flames were licking her legs.

And her back.

She spun around, fearing they were, but the wall of flames

remained at a distance.

A woman was talking to her in a quiet voice. It was gentle and familiar. And now she came closer, with a smile on her face, hands out.

It was the woman who had sold her the amulet, Siggy realised. The woman with the curly dark hair.

She reminded Siggy of her mother, and though she felt afraid, she smiled.

'I am so pleased you came, my dear,' the woman said. 'To me, for I can help you. You knew that, didn't you, when we met? Come closer, and I will show you how we can help each other...'

CHAPTER THIRTY-THREE

Jael hadn't slept much since Kosta had taken his whip to her, so she was wide awake as the first hints of dawn lit up the sleeping quarters. She heard the odd groan and fart, someone crying out in their sleep, but it was a mostly peaceful time.

Her eyes hurt more than her back, which she took as a good sign.

It was healing. And by the day of the funeral, she would be ready to wield a sword again.

She couldn't wait.

Alek was the brains behind the revolt, but he had tasked her with being the sword, and she knew she needed to be able to use one. There was simply no choice.

Pushing herself up into a sitting position, she winced, feeling the rough threads of her tunic move across her back. Though breathing deeply, she worked the pain into a place where it was manageable, rubbing her eyes. Glancing around, she saw she was the only one sitting. Those sleeping men would not rouse themselves until Quint blew his shell. Until then, they would claim every last moment of rest.

The pain came again, blaring loudly, but she kept breathing, pushing it back, moving through it. Lifting her left arm, she brought it across her body, bracing it with her right, stretching her injured back.

It hurt, though not as much as it had done yesterday and

even less than the day before.

She sat there for some time before repeating the process with her right arm.

'What are you doing?' Rigg wondered behind her, sitting up with a loud yawn.

'Preparing.'

'You think you'll be ready to fight?'

Jael heard the doubt and even scorn in his voice, and for a moment, she was back in Harstad, smelling the dragur. Barely alive, she'd pulled herself out of that bed and fought off those revolting creatures intent on killing her. 'I don't mind the pain.'

'What sort of woman are you?' he scoffed.

Irritable and tired, she wriggled around to face him. 'Perhaps the truth is, Rigg, you just like it here? You'd prefer to stay here where you're treated so kindly by your masters. By their rich lords and friends. Perhaps the truth is that you simply like being someone's bitch?'

Rigg lunged for her, but Jael held out an arm, keeping him back, eyes flaming. 'You don't know me. You have no idea about me at all.'

'I know you're a Furyck.'

She shook her head, turning away. It was like talking to a tree.

Nothing would change the man's mind about her.

'Choose a side,' she hissed, glancing over her shoulder. 'You can't be on this one if you're against me. And if you don't want to be on my side, then get out of my way.'

And with that, she stood, suppressing a groan, deciding to go outside and take a piss.

***

Siggy seemed different when she woke that morning, and Edela hesitated to tell her about Raymon Vandaal. 'Did you have a dream?'

A frowning Siggy tried pulling a comb through her knotted curls. 'I don't remember. I was... tired.'

'Oh, so was I,' Edela sighed. 'All that walking. I can't feel my feet. Imagine if we hadn't found those wagons!'

Bertel had come back inside after a long visit to the latrine. He seemed in a good mood and had brought back something for breakfast. 'Well, sit a while longer and try one of these,' he suggested, offering a round fruit to Edela. 'No idea what it tastes like, but it was recommended by the baker. He makes pies with them, apparently.'

Taking the oddly textured fruit in her hand, Edela peered at it. It was furry, like a short-haired cat. 'And I'm supposed to... eat it?'

Bertel bit into his, blinking. 'It's called a peach. Quite tart, but juicy.' He took another bite. 'Mmmm, I don't mind that.'

Edela merely held onto her peach, eyeing Siggy, who still seemed too sleepy to be aware of anything.

'So are we off to find the king then?' Bertel wondered cheerfully, quickly demolishing his peach.

'King?' Siggy looked confused and then nervous. 'Are we going to visit the King of Silura?' Now she was wide awake.

Bertel laughed. 'Didn't Edela tell you? No, we're off to find Raymon Vandaal. He's here. Edela saw him last night.'

Siggy's mouth fell open. 'What? *Alive*?' She blinked some more.

'Yes, I believe he's the man who helped me when I was knocked over. I think he's escaped to here.' Edela absentmindedly bit into the soft peach, surprised when juice spurted down her chin.

'But he was dead, in Ollsvik's hall,' Siggy remembered, feeling confused. 'How did he get out of the burning hall?'

'Well, perhaps he wasn't even there?' Bertel suggested,

handing Edela the scrap of cloth they used to dust the room. She dabbed her chin, then her dress, fearing the stains wouldn't come out.

Siggy was quiet, her thoughts moving slowly, then she shuddered as though struck by lightning. 'You mean he pretended to die? That he ran away?'

Bertel shrugged. 'Well, seems to me that if he hadn't run away, he'd still be in Osterland with his wife, trying to get back his kingdom. No other reason he'd be here unless it's to hide.'

'From who?' Siggy asked.

No one knew.

'And we're going to search for him?'

'We may as well try to,' Edela said. 'If only to offer our help. Someone to talk to.'

Bertel laughed. 'I doubt he's come all this way because he's looking for someone to talk to, Edela. You are funny! Someone to talk to?' And he laughed some more.

Edela stared at him, stony-faced. 'Says the man who's never had a child or a grandchild. Young men often lose their way. Young women too. And Raymon is very young, younger than my Axl. I can certainly offer him guidance and, as a dreamer, the insight he may be needing. It's worth reaching out. If we can find him, that is.'

'Do you have any idea where to look?' Siggy wondered.

'No,' Edela realised, handing a hungry-looking Bertel the rest of her peach. 'Though don't you worry, I'm sure something will come to me as we walk around.'

***

Dessalene remained in bed later than usual, clinging to the remnants of a dream.

There was no eagle, no rat, but there was a horse.

He was quite magnificent as horses went, she thought, seeing the sheen of his rich black coat glistening in the sun. She felt that sun herself, burning her cheek. And holding up a hand, Dessalene was forced to shield her eyes, trying to see through the intense glare. Though everything immediately became even brighter until all she could see was a white light.

And then something coming.

A flash of lightning striking her cheek.

Screaming, she fell, seeing the black horse rising above her, hooves in the air.

Crashing down on her.

Lurching upright with a gurgling gasp, she shook all over.

Shivering and shuddering, she didn't move.

Those hooves had crushed her bones. The pain...

Closing her eyes, Dessalene quickly drew a symbol for healing and one for calm, weaving them together as she returned to her breath, finding the room inside her mind where reality existed.

The now.

She had to return to the now.

Legs on silk, hands on legs.

Chest moving up and down.

And now Dessalene opened her eyes, wondering what her dream had meant.

***

After a nauseating breakfast, Alek led his crew outside into the blistering heat.

'Is it ever cool?' Jael wondered. 'Does it ever rain?'

Alek laughed in response. 'Apparently Kosta plans to spend the day here, making sure we finish the tower.'

Rigg grunted as he stretched behind them, lifting his arms and rolling his shoulders. 'And what's he going to do if we don't? Throw us all off the tower? And then what? The man's a fool.'

Alek saw Quint coming towards them with his second-in-command – an old grouch named Berros – and he turned around to Rigg with a frown. 'Though there's nothing we can do to change that. We're this close,' he reminded his friend, pinching his fingers together. 'This close. So head down and work fast.' He turned back around, smiling at Quint. 'Are you ready?'

A swollen-eyed Quint looked confused. 'Ready for what?'

Reading his thoughts, Jael could hear him fretting about the terrible arguments he'd been having with his wife. She had nothing against the man. He wasn't a slave, though wedged between the dominant figures of Argo and Krissia Kosta, he was as good as one.

'Ready to finish the tower,' Alek told him. 'We're so close.'

'Haven't you heard? Abez died during the night.'

Jael was shocked, having worked with the man. 'How?'

'Slipped and fell in the dark, or at least that's what I imagine happened. Gardi went to check his progress and found him missing. It took some time to locate the body. And without him? We lost hours last night.'

Jael felt sad. These men had to hold on now. It was only three days till the funeral, three days till the slaves would rise up and reclaim their lives.

They just had to hold on.

'You need to rally everyone, Quint,' Alek suggested. 'Bring everyone together. We need a final push now. Any men who are too tired should be rested, replaced by those able to work. We need our best on board, and those men can do more. Just for this final push.'

Quint peered at him as though he was speaking Siluran. He didn't answer.

Frozen to the spot, he just stared.

Alek nudged him towards the centre of the courtyard. 'Grab

your shell. Give it a blow and call the meeting.'

'We can't afford the time,' Quint insisted.

'A few minutes at most,' Alek promised. 'That's all. Just a few minutes.'

Jael glanced at Rigg, who quickly looked away.

She felt the earth vibrating beneath her feet, and turning around, she saw the approach of Argo Kosta on his new horse.

***

'I have ordered my carriage to take us to the temple. It will be here directly,' Kalina told Dessalene when she finally came down for breakfast. Though the queen had long since finished hers and was sitting with her hands in her lap while Mali brushed her hair.

Dessalene stared at her blankly.

'Inesh Seppo invited us,' Kalina reminded her stepmother. 'You are to help with the sacrifice, remember? He asked us to come so he could explain your role. To show you the platform where it will all take place, and the tower. You haven't seen it yet, I imagine?'

Dessalene shivered as the ripples of her odd dream returned to unsettle her anew. The feeling of those giant hooves breaking her bones into tiny little shards, crushing her chest... it was visceral and disturbing. 'Yes, yes. And where is Pye this morning?'

'I haven't seen him.'

Dessalene was puzzled, too nauseous to eat, mind darting about, tired eyes slow to follow. 'Your father will arrive tomorrow.'

'Tomorrow?' Kalina had known that, though her stepmother's words made her nauseous.

Turning to the breakfast table, Dessalene poured wine into an empty goblet, drinking greedily. Blinking at the queen, she shook her head. 'We will visit the temple then return to ready everything for his arrival. I must give the cooks their orders. Your father will be ravenous.' Now she smiled, imagining her surly husband with his big, rough hands. She had missed him.

Kalina felt nervous, shooing Mali away. She smoothed down her shining dark hair and turned to the dreamer. 'And what will you tell him?'

Dessalene stroked her stepdaughter's cheek. 'What a good question you pose, dearest.' Hearing clopping hooves, she dropped her hand. 'Let us see how the day proceeds. I shall think on it, for I am your father's wife but also his dreamer. I owe him honesty in all matters.'

Kalina's eyes shone with fear.

'Though we shall talk, and I shall see. Do not fear, precious one, whatever the outcome, we both know Ronin Sardis. I am certain he will be most understanding!' And tittering with laughter, Dessalene swept into the entrance hall, where the footmen were now waiting.

Kalina watched her go, as confused as ever. Dessalene kept her spinning like a child's toy, leaving her unsure if she could trust the woman. Just as she was starting to feel close to her, the dreamer would twist the knife, choosing cruelty over kindness. And always, always playing games.

It was as though she was two different people.

And when it came to her father and what the dreamer was going to tell him, that provided no comfort at all.

***

Amongst the panicked slaves, their stressed foremen, and the frazzled Quint, the logi were finalising their preparations for Noor's funeral under the watchful eye of Inesh Seppo.

Which was giving Kosta a headache.

'We can transport the smaller animals in wagons,' he told the seer.

Much like his predecessor, Inesh Seppo had a slow, deliberate manner, and he let the commander's clipped words roll over him like a wave cresting a beach. Then smiling, he eventually replied. 'Though it is important that the animals come of their own volition. They must agree to their part in the sacrifice. They must assent. Packing them into wagons and driving them here deprives them of such a choice in the very first instance.'

Kosta stared at the man, not understanding.

Someone shouted down a warning from the tower, and everyone scattered. Soon a block of stone crashed to the earth, breaking in two.

Stomping away from the seer, a furious Kosta lifted a hand to shield his eyes, tipping back his head. 'I hope that wasn't fucking important!' he bellowed. 'It's broken now!' Spinning around, he spied Alek. 'Where's Quint? What's going on up there?'

Alek came closer. 'I'm not sure, my lord. He may have gone to check on supplies. We're running out of ash to make the mortar.'

'Running out? Is that why the stone fell? There's not enough mortar?'

Alek didn't know, and he shrugged apologetically.

Kosta wanted to hit him, though he stormed away instead. Stopping, he glanced over his shoulder at the seer. 'I will return momentarily. I must ensure nothing else falls off that tower. And you,' he growled at Alek. 'You will help the Noor-Elect with whatever he needs.'

Alek turned to the seer in surprise.

Inesh grinned at him as Kosta strode away. 'Do not worry, I need nothing from you or your men. I have my own attendants, my logi, and their arms and legs have more life in them than yours. Of that I am certain.'

Knowing that Inesh Seppo was a seer, soon to be the new Noor, Alek had many questions. He feared that he would die before he ever left the isle. He feared his sons were dead or that his wife had remarried a cruel man who abused them. He –

Inesh placed a hand on his arm. 'You have a tired body but a very active mind, my friend. What you need is some shade and a little faith. Come. The commander wishes you to help me, so come into the cool of the temple and you can advise me on the more... practical matters of the sacrifice.'

Alek's lips parted, ready to protest, though before he could speak, both men heard the clattering of a carriage, and turning around, they saw the queen arriving with her stepmother.

Leaving Alek behind, Inesh hurried forward, watching as a stool was produced by the footmen, who silently offered their hands to each lady, helping them dismount in turn.

Kalina gagged, trying not to inhale. A breeze blew across the courtyard, carrying a terrible stink all the way from the pits and she was soon flapping at a dark cloud of flies. 'My father will arrive tomorrow, so we must see how everything is coming along.' Tilting back her head and shielding her eyes, Kalina saw how much the tower had changed since her last visit. 'It is nearly finished!' she exclaimed in delight.

'Yes, my queen, the men have worked hard, ably led by Quint and his loyal foremen,' Inesh told her. He smiled at the dreamer, who appeared to be studying everything with sharp eyes.

'And Argo Kosta?' Dessalene wondered. 'For surely the success of the tower is his? Not some mere offsider I have never heard of.'

Inesh nodded. 'Indeed. The commander has gone up the tower to inspect it himself, though he will return soon and give us his assessment, which I feel will be favourable.'

Dessalene felt relieved, as did Kalina, who jumped as a rat scurried past, chased by a mangy-looking cat. She looked up at the seer with distaste. 'Well, I hope he can do something about the vermin. How disgusting!'

Inesh smiled apologetically, urging the queen towards the temple.

Though Dessalene didn't follow.

Her attention was on that cat, bounding after the rat.

'I will join you inside,' she murmured. 'I won't be long.' And lifting her hem out of the dirt, she stalked away.

***

Axl stood in a daze, watching Helga's grandson, Linas, fishing off a pier with two boys he appeared to have befriended. It was such a surprise not to see him alone or in the company of Gully that he stared, remembering his own childhood and how inseparable he'd been with Hal and Erling.

How quickly time had passed.

Now he was hoping for a child of his own.

He started, remembering Helga's words, and turning away, he wondered what he should do. He'd barely slept, going over the ramifications of Eren's pregnancy and the possible courses of action.

He should have been thinking about the man Helga had told him about and the one he was going to meet, though if he started snooping about, it would likely spook both men. He'd sent his trusted messenger, Torun, to work on the new pier, wanting him to appear disgruntled, unhappy with the king. He hoped the ruse would work, and in the meantime, he had to focus on tracking down every other spy in the fort.

Turning away from the fishing boys, Axl decided to head for the main gates. The toll master and his assistants kept a strict watch on the harbour, inspecting those who came and went, and Axl wanted to ensure that the men on the main gates were enforcing a similar level of security.

He saw Erling coming towards him with Eren and sought to spin away and somehow make himself invisible, but it was too late, for Erling had a hand in the air, calling his name.

'You look lost!' Erling laughed, ducking his head as a squawking gull swooped low.

Axl peered at him. 'Lost?'

'Not in the hall.'

Axl's cheeks were warm, his mouth suddenly dry as he nodded at Eren, hurriedly shifting his gaze to Erling. 'There's so much to do. I just need to ensure we're as prepared as possible.'

Eren looked confused. 'For what?'

'There will likely be an attack soon.'

Now Erling was confused. 'By who? Iskavall? But surely that's a guess? There's no information that suggests it will happen. Is there? I know about the problems in the South, but Iskavall?'

'Helga sees that Oren Storgard will come. That he seeks to defeat Brekka. And me.'

Eren shivered. 'The dreamer?'

Axl wished she'd stop speaking. He didn't want to look at her, though he could hardly ignore her. 'Yes.'

Erling rolled his eyes. 'You're putting an awful lot of trust in this dreamer, Axl. A woman you'd never met before a few days ago. A woman who bustled in here like a snarling old crone and found herself a new home and a benevolent king, wheedling her way into his confidence.'

'Matters regarding my dreamer are not your concern, Erling,' Axl snapped. 'As king, I must do everything to ensure the safety of my people. And employing the advice of a skilled dreamer makes sense. I have no reason not to trust the woman, and nor do you.' He glared at Erling, bobbed his head at Eren, and turned to go. 'We'll be meeting this afternoon. You, me, Helga and Ragnar, so I hope you can put your feelings about the dreamer to one side.' And with that, he was gone.

Eren grabbed her brother's arm, watching Axl stride away. 'The dreamer is a problem,' she hissed. 'She is going to be a problem.'

And turning to watch the quickly disappearing king, Erling Venberg feared his sister was right.

CHAPTER THIRTY-FOUR

The cat chased the rat around the back of the tower, forcing Dessalene to move faster than she was used to, and restrained by her dress, she was breathing heavily by the time she stopped, seeing a woman filling a bucket from the well.

The rat scuttled away, though the cat remained, and now it sat down.

Watching the woman.

A panting Dessalene looked from the cat to the woman.

Who, she could clearly see, was Jael Furyck.

Looking up, Jael saw the dreamer watching her and she froze.

'Taking a break, are we? Hiding away?' Dessalene purred, coming forward with a smile. She worked quickly to calm her breathing, smoothing her flowing auburn hair away from her shining face.

'I need water to mix the mortar,' Jael explained, covered in a dusting of ash and lime. 'The slave who did it was taken away. Likely he'll die.'

'Ahhh, and they say the Goddess of the Sun is a benevolent force. Well, perhaps not where I come from! You have a friend, I see,' she added, forcing Jael to stop.

Jael stared at the cat before lifting her eyes to the dreamer. 'I've never seen it before.'

'No? Though it seems to like you well enough. Or perhaps not? Perhaps it is watching you?'

Jael laughed. 'I'd be glad for the company, though I have to climb back up the tower soon, so I doubt it'll keep following me for long.'

Dessalene stepped closer. 'You have been busy, from what I hear, working like a man. You must be happy, not having to clean floors and wash clothes like women do?'

'Well, happiness isn't what it was. I take what I get, nothing more. And you? I hear your husband is arriving tomorrow. You must be happy to see him? I imagine it's painful being apart?' Jael stared at the dreamer, wanting to dig deep into her mind, though she found only walls keeping her out.

Walls she hoped that she too possessed.

Lunging at her, Dessalene grabbed one of Jael's fetters, checking it was still clamped tightly around her wrist. She checked the other fetter, then bending down, she checked the ones around her ankles too.

Jael held her breath, fearing the woman would see the scratched symbols or force her to take off her shoes, revealing her stone.

Though standing up, Dessalene smiled, blue eyes flashing with menace. 'My husband pines for me, you know. A brutish man with the heart of a needy child. I couldn't be happier with my choices. Though soon you'll see for yourself, for he will want to meet you. After all he went through to claim you? And why? Perhaps he'll tell you? I imagine you are *burning* to know.' Dessalene glanced at the cat, who continued to stare at the slave queen. 'I'm not like your frail old grandmother, Jael Furyck. Tuuran dreamers tend to be so unambitious, squandering their real power. No, where I come from, the Goddess of Magic herself teaches us. She claims us and gifts us *extraordinary* powers. You simply cannot imagine how much pain I could cause to those you love and how quickly I could do so.' And with a triumphant smile, Dessalene spun on her heels and strode away.

***

'How are we feeling?' Thorgils wondered, stopping before Eadmund with an enormous shiver. Rugged up in a thick woollen cloak, he didn't feel especially cold. His face was frozen, his nose and ears numb, though his body was warm enough, he supposed, being at sea again.

It was more a nervous kind of energy.

Perhaps even a sense of excitement building now?

Eadmund stared at him with dead eyes. He didn't know how he felt. Perhaps petrified? Petrified that his wife was a corpse in a hole.

It was all he'd thought about since they had sailed away from Solt, aiming for S'ala Nis. In the silence, he feared he could actually hear the truth. That he had some magical insight into what had happened.

He feared the worst.

Fyn approached. 'Bolder says to hunker down. Storm's coming.'

Thorgils sighed. 'And here's me thinking we'd get through the journey without some disaster befalling us.'

'Go speak to Mattie,' Eadmund told Fyn. 'See what she can see.'

A nodding Fyn headed past the men, who swayed before each other in silence.

Thorgils clapped his friend on the shoulder. 'I've never had faith in anyone like I have in Jael,' he said without even a hint of humour in his eyes. 'Not even your father, and that's saying something. That woman...' He shook his head. 'She's wrangled more beasts and bastards than anyone I know of. And you want to doubt her now? I think she'd have something to say about that.' He stared into Eadmund's eyes, trying to see a flicker of life.

Eadmund swallowed, turning away. Picking his nails, he heard the mournful cry of the wind. If he let his mind wander, that sound merged into one deafening howl, as though all the gods were weeping.

For Jael.

Furia's daughter.

The mighty Jael Furyck.

And remembering his wife's dream of those pyres and her own body lying amongst them, he felt sick, swirling in a whirlpool of worries.

'What I think or feel doesn't matter,' he muttered. 'It doesn't matter now.'

'Exactly. We'll see soon enough. And in the meantime, let Jael handle whatever's being thrown at her. She can. We both know she can handle warriors and dreamers alike. Don't worry, Eadmund, we'll be there soon. And so will she. Waiting for us.'

**

Edela led Bertel and Siggy on a long, meandering journey, searching for any sign of Raymon Vandaal, convinced that her path away from Osterland, across the Valgeir Sea, had led her here for a reason.

A Furyck reason.

And stopping, at last, to the great relief of her companions, panting loudly behind her, she turned around.

'Finally!' Bertel exclaimed. 'We have to find a well, Edela. I'm parched, and as for poor Siggy –'

'I'm fine. Though I've got a hole in my boot.' And taking advantage of the break, Siggy took off her boot and shook out some gravel.

Edela turned to her. 'That's not good to hear. We need that lovely shoemaker from Bakkar, don't we? What was her name?'

'Anna,' Siggy said. 'But where are we, Edela?'

'Good question,' Bertel huffed. 'Nowhere near a well, that's for sure.'

'We are at a crossroads,' Edela told them. 'See.' And motioning past her companions, she showed them what was entirely obvious: a narrow tower with a symbol on top, marking a bustling crossroads, with nine narrow paths leading off it.

'Deary me,' Bertel sighed, taking it all in. 'And you know which path to take?'

'I will,' Edela assured him, suddenly not feeling confident about that. 'After I catch my breath. Over there,' she suggested, pointing to a bench, empty bar a few birds making a mess. 'We'll give our poor feet a break, and I'll close my eyes.'

Bertel shook his head. 'You'll only draw attention to yourself, woman.'

'I'll pretend to be asleep!' she laughed. 'That won't look out of place at all. I certainly feel like taking a nap.'

Siggy limped after Edela with a grimace. 'I've got a terrible blister.' And shooing three squawking birds away, she sat down, showing Edela her foot.

'Oh dear, that does look painful,' Edela said, glancing around. 'You stay here, and I'll try that shop over there. I've been meaning to find a healer. I'm completely useless with no supplies.'

Bertel, who had bent to sit, now straightened up. 'I'll come with you.'

Edela laughed. 'For what reason? Company? In truth, I'd enjoy a moment alone.'

Bertel looked offended as Edela continued to chuckle. 'I have my coins, so you take a seat, and I'll return presently. Perhaps I'll find something tasty to eat while I'm gone?'

'Well, don't go far,' Bertel warned. 'You mustn't go far!' Though he was calling into the noise of the crossroads, and a bustling Edela didn't even turn around.

***

'Where have you been?' Alek asked when he found Jael, still mixing her bucket of mortar on a plank of wood balanced on two boulders.

'Gardi was taken away and there's no one else free. I've had to come down and do it myself.'

'And you know how?' Alek wondered.

Jael nodded. 'Gardi taught me.'

'What happened to him?'

'He just started slurring his words, then he slumped over. Quint and Berros had to come and carry him down.'

Alek sighed. 'They're dropping like flies.' And batting a cloud of actual flies away, he edged closer to Jael. 'The queen and her stepmother went into the temple with Inesh Seppo.'

Jael peered at him, sensing there was more. The flies moved towards her now, though with one hand stirring and another pouring the water, she couldn't swat them away. 'And?'

'Apparently, he's invited the dreamer to be part of the sacrifice. To lead it.'

Jael was confused, unsure what she thought of Inesh Seppo and his motives. Was he like the old Noor, who had sacrificed himself and given her hope? Or was he an enemy masking his true intentions with a pleasing manner and an earnest smile? 'The dreamer is a worry. She made a lot of pointed threats to me just now.'

Alek looked worried himself. 'Do you think she can see past your symbol?' he whispered, though with a hoarse, dry throat, he was soon coughing.

Wanting to give him confidence, Jael shook her head. 'No. No, I don't believe so. Though you must take care not to speak to anyone who doesn't have a stone. You have your leaders and your messengers, so only rely on them. Encourage them to hold their tongues too.'

He nodded. 'They know to do that.'

'There will always be spies. Dreamers or not, there will always be spies. We just have to get to the funeral. Here. With all those slaves here, we'll outnumber them.'

'Though will it be enough?' Alek was suddenly doubtful of his long thought-through, much-discussed plan. Jael was right about the numbers. He'd spent years on the numbers, and in his head or scratched in dirt, it had all seemed possible. Hopeful. Now he saw how broken and exhausted these men were. How would they have the strength for such an important fight against armed, energised warriors? Men skilled with weapons, who went home every night. Who slept in beds and ate real food and didn't live with the fear of death hanging over their heads?

And then there was Jael herself.

She could barely lift her arms.

His doubts created a churning noise that Jael heard loudly. 'Fear breeds fear,' she told him as two men approached. 'In a battle, fear quickly becomes like a sickness. If you can frighten your enemy, that fear can do more harm than any blade. If you can command their minds, tell them what to think and feel, you will weaken them. But if the opposite happens?' Standing back, she shrugged. 'We have to stay strong in our minds. You've managed it this far, Alek, and I'll need you. So will those men you've chosen to lead. Don't wobble now.'

Alek felt very wobbly as the two men stopped before him, one with a question, one with a command from Kosta to meet him atop the tower. He nodded at one, answered the other, and with a determined smile, left Jael to it.

Watching him go, she was reminded of the dreamer's threats, fearing that everything she'd just told Alek was a bunch of lies and that Dessalene Sardis had heard them all.

***

The healer's shop was fragranced with a mishmash of intriguing aromas, and as Edela closed the door behind her, she picked out hints of lavender and ginger, though many scents were entirely foreign to her nose.

The middle-aged man behind the thick wooden counter eyed her with interest.

He spoke the common tongue in the first instance, recognising that this old woman was not from the Fire Lands. 'And from whence have you come?' he enquired, twirling his moustache with a flourish. 'I have visitors from all over Varmyr. North, South, East and West, I've had them all through my door!'

Edela peered at the diminutive man, deciding that he seemed trustworthy enough, though she wouldn't reveal anything about herself. 'I am from Alekka. Visiting. My granddaughter has a terrible blister, so I wanted some marigold for it, and mallow if you have it. Also some witch hazel. Yes, and garlic. Oh, how I long for garlic!'

The man arched an unruly eyebrow. 'You are a healer?'

Edela laughed. 'I have healed as a mother, a grandmother, and now as an old woman. I'm not sure that makes me a healer, though I do know my way around a blister.'

The man smiled. 'I am Tarkel. A physician. Please, I have just what you need as it happens. I've been making pots of my favourite healing balm, for burns, bruises, and cuts. It should work perfectly for a blister.'

'What is in it?' Edela wondered.

Tarkel hesitated, for his concoctions were his own. 'You are just visiting?'

Edela nodded. 'I will return home before the end of the month.'

'Well, there is no harm in sharing a little knowledge between friends,' Tarkel decided with a wink. 'Please, go through the archway and take a seat in my waiting room. I shall just step upstairs and grab one of my pots.' He ushered Edela through the archway, where a young woman was tying an apron over a plain black dress. 'Lilia, please look after the shop.' And with that, the physician disappeared up the stairs.

Edela smiled at the woman in passing, intrigued by the many shelves and intense smells in the physician's waiting room. She barely heard the shop door open and close but soon became aware of a man's voice and then the young woman replying.

Shivers tingled Edela's arms as she crept back towards the archway, and lifting her hood over her head, she saw that the man who'd entered the shop was none other than Raymon Vandaal.

***

Jael had discovered that there was something hypnotic about her work, and despite her discomfort, the repetitive movements were oddly soothing. She perched on the scaffolding, trowels in hand, working to a steady rhythm, pleased to be mostly alone.

Her thoughts wandered, the sun beating on her head like a drummer. It was so hot that she became sleepy.

She saw Eadmund's face, feeling his beard beneath her fingers. She watched herself kissing a sleeping Bo, riding a glistening Tig.

Killing.

She saw the rhythmic dance of blades, the sharpened edges cutting flesh, drawing blood. It flew through the air like little red baubles. Baubles in the sun.

That sun, it burned, and she saw her back, striped and stitched.

Argo Kosta's face.

Sunni lying dead.

And she saw herself standing on the sacrifice platform before the tower, the sun striking her face, lighting her up like flames.

Igniting her.

The plank she crouched on wobbled violently, and jerked out

of her vision, she saw a man approach. 'Didn't you hear? Break time! Take too long and there'll be no water for you.'

Jael peered at the man. Berros. That creep.

She nodded. 'Coming.' And after cleaning her trowels on a cloth and leaving them in the bucket of water, she stood, turning to stare at the hazy blue sky and the great golden sun.

Eyshar was the God of Fire, Alek had told her.

And also the God of Providence.

A powerful god indeed.

So whose side was he on?

***

Upon seeing the familiar face of Edela Saeveld, Raymon's feet started shuffling, eyes snapping to the door. Though he didn't move as the dreamer came through the archway towards him.

The physician's assistant turned away to find something on the shelves, and Raymon dropped his head, swallowing a mouthful of bile.

'Hello,' Edela said softly. 'I had hoped to see you again.'

Raymon frowned, eyes darting to the assistant and then the dreamer before returning to his boots. 'You are following me? You have followed me here?' he whispered.

The woman turned back with a small linen pouch. 'You must crush the leaves and mix with the salt. Hold them in your mouth, on the tooth, for at least an hour. More if necessary. If it doesn't help, please return, and I will find you something stronger.'

A nodding Raymon paid the woman with fumbling fingers, eventually turning back to Edela, clasping the linen pouch, unsure of what to say.

'May we use your rear door?' Edela asked sweetly, forgetting all about the balm the physician had left to find. 'A more private exit would be preferable for my young friend and me.'

The woman looked surprised on both counts, though she silently ushered Edela and Raymon through the archway, into the waiting room, a full store room, and finally, through the back door.

Edela flashed her a grateful smile. 'Please tell the physician I will return presently. I just have a... matter to attend to.'

The woman nodded, closing the door, leaving Edela and Raymon alone in a dank alley, penned in by tall buildings cloaking them in shadow.

Edela saw a litter of miaowing kittens, thinking of Siggy, who she needed to return to. But not yet.

'Why are you here?' Raymon wanted to know. 'Who sent you after me? Axl? Who knew I was here?'

'No one at all,' Edela promised, seeking to calm him, fearing he would simply run away again. 'At least not that I'm aware of. I am here by chance. I saw you by pure chance, but once I did, I had to see you again. I was in Ollsvik the day after the fire, you see. It was quite upsetting. And then to see you here? I wondered if I was imagining things. But no, here you are, Raymon. Very much alive.'

Raymon turned away, trying to make sense of things. 'You were in Ollsvik? Why?' He turned back to Edela, too surprised to be wary now.

'There was an attack in Tuura. I was staying there, helping at the temple and... well, I saw the danger just in time and managed to escape with my companions. One of them was Lina Storgard. We took her home to Ollsvik, to her family.'

Raymon's frown deepened, his confusion intensifying. 'Lina?' Now he nodded. 'She was a dreamer.'

'And soon to be the Queen of Iskavall.'

That was a shock that quickly had Raymon shivering. 'So Oren Storgard was victorious?'

'You didn't think he would be? When you ran away, you didn't imagine he would claim your throne?'

Raymon shook his head. 'I hadn't meant that to happen when

I...' He turned to the physician's door, fearing someone would come out. Staring back down the alley, he saw the kittens now playing with a dead mouse. 'I did what I did, Edela. I can't undo it, and I... I don't want to. I don't want to return.'

'But what about your wife? Your people?'

Raymon's laugh was bitter. 'Many of my people sought to kill me. My wife certainly would've, given a better offer. I have nothing in Ollsvik, nothing I want. That place, it killed everyone I loved, and I knew before long that it would kill me too.'

'So you killed yourself first?'

'You don't understand what it was like, what it felt like to live in that prison, watched by my enemies. I was afraid of every mouthful of food, every cup of wine, every pair of eyes. A man would slip his hand inside his cloak and I'd fear he'd have a knife.' Shaking his head, he trembled at the memories. 'I... I will not return. I cannot.'

Edela felt his pain, and nodding, she offered a smile. 'I am not here to make any demands, Raymon. I merely wanted to understand, to see if I could help.'

He peered at her. 'But why are you in Castala, Edela? So far from home? You went from Ollsvik to Silura?'

'Yes, eventually,' she chuckled. 'I'm not entirely sure how I've ended up here or why, though it appears that people are trying to kill me. They've certainly tried very hard, though I'm still standing.'

'Kill you? Why?'

'Unfortunately, I have no answers for that, though I am hunted, and I fear returning to Osterland until I understand why.'

Raymon's worry for himself vanished as he looked down on the kind old woman – Jael and Axl's grandmother. She had always been so nice to him, and now she was in danger. 'You're not alone, though, are you? You have help?'

Edela smiled. 'I do. I have two companions keeping me on my feet, so you needn't worry about me. And being a dreamer, I have a few tricks up my sleeve too.'

'And coins? You have enough?'

'Yes, I do. Oh, yes, plenty.' Digging into her purse, Edela ferreted around, eventually pulling out a small shard of green tourmaline. 'Here, take this. Keep it on you, and if you ever find yourself in trouble, in need of help, you can hold it and think of me, and I will try and find you.'

Raymon peered at the stone before lifting his eyes to the dreamer. 'Well, I...'

'I would take you with me now if I could,' she grinned. 'Though I'm well aware that you want to leave all vestiges of your old life behind. But we all need help sometimes, so don't be afraid to reach out for it. If I am close, I will come. And even if I'm far away, I will make my way to you, Raymon. If you find yourself in danger, I will do all I can to help you.'

'Why?' he wondered, tears in his eyes as he finally took the stone, rubbing a finger over its surface, feeling indentations. 'Why care about me?'

'Because you are a Furyck, of course. We share a family, whether you want to believe so or not. I know you thought it helped you to forget about being a Furyck, though you will always be one. I see it so clearly. You are Ranuf's boy, and he loved you so very much. I've often seen images of him with you as a child. The love he bore for you was all over his face. That and his love for your mother.'

A tear spilled from Raymon's eye, trailing down his cheek.

'You will always be a Furyck, always have a home in Brekka, if you decide you want it. Or with Jael, on Oss. Axl and Jael would both welcome you. We all would. Wherever you go, however lost you become, always know that you have a home with your family.' Taking his hand, Edela gave it a comforting squeeze. 'Be careful, Raymon. You may think you have escaped your enemies, though your actions will not have gone unnoticed by those who mean the Furycks harm.' Bobbing her head, she stepped past a stunned Raymon towards the physician's back door. 'Take care now.'

He turned, watching her go. 'And you, Edela. And you.'

PART FOUR

Return of the King

CHAPTER THIRTY-FIVE

Axl had decided to keep Helga's discovery to himself, so he hadn't mentioned it at the previous day's meeting. The fewer people who knew about the spies, the better. It wasn't that he didn't trust Erling or even Ragnar. There was just more risk of having word spread, and he needed to keep the men talking so he could uncover their plans.

He sent word to his messenger, Torun, now acting as his spy, arranging to meet the young man in the forest.

Torun was late, and Axl was growing concerned, scuffing pine needles with his boots, constantly glancing over his shoulder, at last hearing a horse coming.

An apologetic Torun dismounted with red cheeks, hurrying to his king. 'I couldn't get away, my lord. I am sorry.'

Axl shook his head, wanting to be quick. 'And what have you found? These men? Have you... befriended them?'

'Hardar and Emmet? Yes, it was easy enough. We're all working for Elred on the new pier.'

'And these men, what have they told you?'

Torun sucked in a breath, seeing a golden beam of sunlight shining through the trees. 'Emmet's quiet.'

'I don't know him,' Axl admitted. 'I can't put a face to the name.'

'He's not Andalan,' Torun explained. 'He's come up from Rosby. He's disgruntled, alright. Says he doesn't like the state of things. Not since your father died, my lord.'

Axl frowned. 'And the other man? Hardar?'

'He's from Rosby too. They know each other.'

'*Rosby*?' Axl was confused. 'So they're not Iskavallan?'

'No, lord.'

Axl thought of the Lord of Rosby, Henk Layborg. He was new to that position, having taken over from his brother during the recent sickness. Much of his family had perished, from memory. He didn't know the man well, though he had sworn an oath to his king.

An oath that was now...

Axl didn't know.

Perhaps it was nothing? It was common for people to move about, seeking better opportunities. Life was rarely stagnant, and when circumstances changed, people often left what was familiar for a new beginning. Perhaps Hardar had simply come to Andala because his friend had, and now they were working together?

Though he remembered Helga's words.

A lord sent him. Not a lord friendly to you.

There could be no doubt, and realising it, he eyed Torun. 'Keep in with them. The pier's barely started, so there's plenty to keep you all busy. See if you can draw them out. Share your own unhappiness with your king.' Torun looked uncomfortable about that, though Axl smiled encouragingly. 'It's no different than carrying messages. It's what your king is asking you to do, and it could save all our lives. Find out what those men want. My dreamer thinks they're enemies, so I need to find out the truth before it's too late.'

***

Dessalene pinched Pye, who squeaked as she'd intended. 'I need more from you than tittle-tattle about Kalina's lords and their revolting proclivities, you pointless toad. What I want are things I can actually use! Do you understand me? I am searching for a rat, not breadcrumbs!'

Pye sat opposite her in the carriage they were taking to the harbour, where the king was soon to arrive. Kalina had gone on ahead, wanting to ensure that everything was perfect.

Having seen what her husband had been up to since she'd left his side, Dessalene felt less inclined to rush, though it wouldn't do to create problems. There would be time to take him to task for his *indulgences*.

'I did hear something...' Pye teased.

'Something you've been sitting on?'

He shook his head. 'I thought to gather more information before I brought it to you, Mistress, but as you are so very impatient –'

'I abhor games, Pye, unless I'm the one playing them. Ronin will be here any moment, which, as always, is both a curse and a blessing, so I need to know everything. And I need to know it now!'

'There is talk of a revolt, Mistress.'

'Revolt?' The carriage dipped into a rut, and Dessalene jerked forward, almost onto Pye's lap. 'What? By the slaves?'

He nodded. 'There is talk that they'll rise up and overthrow the lords. Even the queen herself!'

Dessalene laughed. 'Silly Pye, that isn't new. Such talk is always present, for what prisoner doesn't speak of freedom? It is nothing to concern ourselves with, unless there is something more?'

Pye wasn't sure.

'And where did you hear this?'

'One of the kitchen slaves. She heard rumours about how it was coming. They would rise up soon, she said, and she was worried. She feared what they would do to those who worked for the queen, in the palace. She worried they wouldn't be spared and that the women would all be raped!' Pye's bulging eyes became more pronounced.

Though Dessalene eyed him with scorn. 'The word of one gossiping slave is hardly proof of a conspiracy, Pye. Surely you know that?'

He slunk back with a grunt, slumped in defeat. 'It is something. I tell you it is something,' he muttered.

The dreamer ignored him, turning to look at the great forest of masts marking the harbour in the distance. She had no love of ships or the men who sailed them. They were generally a smelly, uncouth bunch. Apart from Arras Sikari, she thought with a scowl. And though that charming man had slipped away from her prowling wolves, she wouldn't forget him.

She would ensure the traitor was brought to justice one day.

One day soon.

The carriage started rocking from side to side as they approached the harbour entrance, where Dessalene could see Kalina flanked by a small army of slaves, issuing orders to her temporary Commander of the Waves.

Their attention appeared fixed on one ship in particular, and as the carriage rumbled closer, Dessalene could see her husband gripping its wolf head prow.

***

Bone Hammer was abuzz with activity as everyone scrambled to find something for breakfast. Strict rationing was in place, though it hadn't stopped a greedy few helping themselves when no one was looking.

Including Thorgils Svanter, who did his best impression of an innocent man as Bolder grumbled about where all the cheese had gone.

Shaking his head, Fyn turned to Mattie. 'Well, I hope you didn't feel like cheese.'

She grinned. 'I prefer soft cheese. I like to mix it with fresh dewberries and a little cream and serve it with crispbreads.' She shrugged. 'It's not to everyone's taste.'

Though Fyn looked intrigued. 'I wouldn't mind trying that.'

'Well, I imagine you'd have to come to Sonderberg. I doubt you have dewberries on Oss.'

Fyn shrugged. 'Traders are always stopping by, so likely we've got more than you might expect. But no, I've never heard of them.'

'And do you like living there? Your cold little island?'

Fyn laughed. 'It's certainly cold, though it's not so little, and I do. It's home. Everyone knows each other, so it's like a big family really. And with Jael and Eadmund on the throne, it just feels... right.' Turning his head, he saw the horizon like a great road in the distance, wondering how far he was from home now. How far from Bram and his horse, Yara. From the children and Biddy. Isaura and Ayla.

Home.

He wondered if Milla was there, and thinking of her, he smiled.

'We've been away for too long,' he decided, eyes back on Thorgils, who was fighting Kolarov for a half-frozen sausage. 'Especially Thorgils. His wife was pregnant when we left. He worries about her. Her last birth was a bit frightening for them both.'

'And you want that, do you? A wife and children on your little island?'

Fyn shrugged. 'I'm still young, so I'm happy as I am. I'll wait and see what the gods have in store for me. For now, it's all about getting our queen and going home.' He peered at a silent Mattie, surprised by how calm she was. The dreamer had become increasingly tense as their journey progressed, so it was unusual to find her so relaxed. 'And you? You will go back to Tuura? To your village?'

Mattie bent down, picking up her miaowing cat. 'Of course. It's just the two of us, so yes, we'll go home and pick up where we left off.'

'And will you marry again?'

'Me?' Mattie laughed. 'Why would I ever want to? I already found my true love. I won't search for another. I'm content now to live with Otter and my memories.'

Fyn thought to encourage her to think differently, to hope for a family and another man she could love, though she was a stubborn woman. A woman who certainly knew her own mind. Her happiness was her own.

Not his business.

He spun around as Thorgils lobbed a stale roll at him.

'You'll lose a tooth on that,' Mattie warned with a wink.

'Not hungry?'

She shook her head. 'I want to close my eyes and see where the day takes me. I'll eat when all the fuss dies down. Besides, I don't think anyone should get between Thorgils and his empty belly.'

Fyn laughed, watching as she stumbled away from him, one hand hugging Otter to her chest, one held out for balance.

He hoped she would find something.

Something to give them hope that Jael was still alive.

***

A breathless slave arrived at the temple grounds with news that the king's ships had been sighted in the harbour.

Sipping from a cup of water, shielding her eyes from the already blazing sun, Jael became tense.

Ronin Sardis sounded like a formidable man. To have created

his own private kingdom? To have built it up with such speed that it resembled an ancient city? And to do it all under a shield of privacy? From the scant information she'd managed to gather, he was an ambitious man, protected and supported by powerful friends.

Her enemy.

Beside her, Alek bent over, coughing. 'We must be... careful,' he warned, trying to clear his throat. Jael offered him her water, though he shook his head. 'Kosta might be a brute, a hammer, but from what I've heard, Ronin Sardis is a wolf. He's careful in what he does, careful in who he trusts and always primed to attack.'

'Well, we just have to hope that any loose lips are sewn shut until the funeral.'

'Is that possible, though? In a place this size?' Alek fretted. 'If one conversation is overhead, one person changes their mind and talks...'

Jael yawned, taking in those men sucking the last drips of moisture from their small cups. They looked ready to fall down where they stood and sleep until winter. She doubted any would want to sabotage their chance of freedom. Though it wasn't unthinkable for someone to be overheard or that sharp-eyed dreamer to uncover what they were planning. 'Either way, remember what you know, what you believe to be true. Your mind will start tricking you now, especially in the heat and after all these hours of working. But you can't forget what you know, Alek.' He was still coughing, trying to suppress it, though she could see that he was struggling. 'You know numbers. Your work has all been up here,' Jael said, tapping her aching head. 'Let them try to stop us. We'll crush them anyway.' And with a smile, she headed to where Quint stood near the men who had drawn up four buckets of water from the well, though she doubted it would last long.

Alek turned to watch her go, struggling to catch his breath.

He saw the streaks of blood leaking from her wounds, the patches of sweat staining her tunic. She was as exhausted as the rest of them, but Jael Furyck walked like a queen.

A queen who would soon set them free.

***

'You have been missed, Wife,' Ronin Sardis grunted, pulling Dessalene towards him, kissing her with a need that soon had them both breathing heavily.

Dessalene pulled away, inclining her head to where Pye sat opposite them, looking on with bulging eyes.

'What's that fuck doing here?' Standing up, Ronin demanded the driver's attention, and sitting back down as the carriage pulled to an abrupt halt, he swung open the door. 'Out you go! Crawl back to the palace, you little prick! Or better yet, go find a kennel to sleep in!'

A horrified Pye glanced at Dessalene, who shrugged at him, and with a reluctant sigh, he crept towards the open door, almost falling through it as Ronin threatened him with a boot.

'You are cruel,' Dessalene chided with a smile, paying no attention to a plaintive-looking Pye, who watched as the carriage clattered away, leaving him in a cloud of dust. She had missed the smell of this man, though remembering what she'd seen in her dreams, her smile soured. 'To *me*. So cruel, Ronin. I came to comfort and help your poor barren daughter while you remained behind, entertaining young girls in *our* bed.'

Ronin grabbed Dessalene's arm, tugging her towards him. 'Young girls? Well, younger than you, my old wife. But never as desirable, never as powerful, never as important as you are to me. Though I am a man. What else am I to do when you abandon me? I am a *king*. My needs must be met, Dessalene, and if not by you, then whoever's to hand.'

'Must they, though?' She smiled as he kissed her, rushing a

hand up her dress. 'It is only a... brief journey to the palace,' she warned with a gasp.

'Take me on a tour!' Ronin barked at the driver, his pale green eyes never leaving Dessalene's. 'And you, Wife, will remind me of what I've been missing.'

***

After his surprising encounter with Edela Saeveld, Raymon felt all at sea. Any peace he may have claimed since leaving Osterland had been swept away in a wave of confusion.

Had the dreamer truly just stumbled upon him?

He couldn't quite believe it.

Despite a night's sleep, her words still rang in his ears, warning him of enemies he hadn't anticipated. Once he'd left Ollsvik, he had hoped no one would think of him again. His kingdom would have yet another king, his wife, who hated him, would find another husband, and he would...

Raymon hadn't exactly known.

His travels had so far been almost surreal, as though he'd not been able to experience all that was new and strange. He had changed his name three times already, unable to decide who he wanted to be. But hearing his own name spoken again and being looked upon by someone who had known him as a king made him feel ashamed.

A coward.

Raymon turned right with no idea of where he was going. He'd hoped to wake up knowing what he wanted to do and where he wanted to go, though the new day had brought no clarity. He thought about finding some breakfast, remembering that he hadn't eaten supper. Maybe food was what he needed to start thinking clearly again?

Eyes sweeping the flock of people surging towards him, occasionally turning around to check who was behind him, he was determined not to bump into Edela again.

He remembered the baker who sold delicious date cakes, immediately turning right, hoping he could find his way there.

His thoughts tangled.

Perhaps he needed to leave Castala today? He could find a camel or a horse and disappear into the desert.

He could...

Now Raymon turned left. The alleys were so narrow there was barely any space between opposing rows of houses. There was a pervasive smell of shit, though, a reeking stench that had his nostrils flaring, once again focusing his mind.

He would buy some food and return to his room, pack his things and decide what to do.

He couldn't be anywhere someone might find him – someone from his past.

If he was a coward, then so be it, but he wouldn't return to that life.

He wouldn't return to Iskavall.

He turned a sharp corner, tunic snapping as he hurried away.

Not noticing the man in the hooded cloak following some distance behind.

***

After greeting her father and realising it was Dessalene he most wanted to be with, Kalina had made a quick escape in her carriage, heading back to the palace. Her father was notoriously quick-tempered and detested when things weren't exactly to his liking, so she felt an urge to ensure the palace was in order one last time.

The carriage pulled up outside the palace steps, footmen and doormen scurrying to and fro.

She saw Argo Kosta waiting near the open doors, and taking a footman's hand, she descended the carriage steps, frowning. 'Is something wrong, commander? My father is on his way, I... if something is wrong, perhaps it is best to tell me first. I do not wish to ruin his homecoming with problems.'

Kosta looked confused and incredibly clean, Kalina realised as she approached, sensing Mali behind her, untangling her train.

'Your stepmother invited me,' he explained in a halting voice. He was more comfortable with weapons and warriors, and dressed in a new linen tunic and trousers, absent any armour, he felt almost naked. 'She wanted me here. I thought you knew, my queen. Kalina.'

Kalina blinked at him, swallowing a sigh. 'Of course. Well, do come inside. We mustn't loiter out here with the slaves.'

She was a queen, Kalina knew. What she thought mattered little now.

A queen needed a husband and heirs, and because of her poor choices, she had lost the opportunity to take matters into her own hands. It was S'ala Nis that mattered now; there was nothing else to be said.

So, sweeping past her betrothed into the palace, she left all thoughts of Arras Sikari behind.

***

Ronin and Dessalene's carriage entered the temple grounds, its impressive new tower reaching into the clear morning sky. The sun had set it alight, enhancing every feature, and Ronin took a moment to study it, feeling pleased with its overall impact on the site. Though his attention quickly skipped ahead. 'Is she here then? My prize?' he breathed in a dishevelled Dessalene's ear, feeling her warm and limp beside him.

'Oh yes,' his wife promised. 'She has been working on that tower herself, like the good little slave she is.'

'Not stirring up trouble?' Ronin wondered, turning to stroke her cheek. 'Not trying to start a war? You left in such a fluster. I had imagined coming here to find the place on fire and Jael Furyck sitting on the throne.'

Dessalene laughed. 'You give the woman too much credit. She is mortal, Ronin, not a goddess.'

He kissed her. 'Though from what you just told me, she nearly escaped, no thanks to Kalina.'

'Kalina is the reason she didn't escape. Her spies alerted her to the danger, and they stopped her.'

'Though not Arras Sikari,' Ronin scowled. It was hard not to feel betrayed by that. The man had been like a son to him. He had raised him up so high, now regretting every misjudgment he had made, reliving his poor choices.

'The girl fell in love! I'm sure you remember what that feels like?' Dessalene murmured, watching her husband's jaw pulsing.

'Perhaps I remember,' he growled, fingering her lips.

She nibbled his finger. 'Well, let us forgive Kalina her little sins and forget about Arras Sikari entirely. As I said, I've already arranged for her to marry Argo Kosta. It is an eminently suitable match, and he has a bastard on the way with a slave. Before long, Kalina will have a child in her arms and a consort by her side, and we can return to our own plans.'

And thinking of their plans, Ronin's eyes were drawn back to that impressive tower. He saw the empty stadium before the sacrifice platform and the temple, mostly unchanged since he had left the isle, but it was the tower that held his attention. Sunlight surged through holes in the walls like orange and gold flames.

He thought of Eyshar, and edging away from his wife, he tidied up his trousers and tunic. 'I will make an offering,' he murmured. 'Alone. It has been too long.'

'Then I shall carry on and send the carriage back for you,'

Dessalene decided.

Kissing her, Ronin frowned. 'But first, tell me what happened to Noor. How did he die?'

***

Hallow Wood was a strange place, and after riding through it for nearly three days, Gant was beginning to feel strange himself.

He was tired, he knew that, though he was sure he kept passing the same tree. It was an old oak with a knot in its trunk, curled into the shape of a heart.

He was convinced he'd seen it four times now, starting to wonder if he was seeing things. Turning around, he called Osgar to him. 'We need to stop for a drink. You ride ahead and find a stream.' The young man nodded, spurring his mare ahead.

Gus' white ears had started swivelling for the first time since they'd ridden into the woods, inviting Gant to worry some more. Then blinking and attempting to wake himself up, he thought of Gisila and Andala and Axl.

He couldn't let his mind wander down meandering paths. He had to stay on this path, leading any pursuers far away from Andala.

Turning around, he winked at the nearest man. 'Osgar might find us somewhere we can –' Hearing a scream and certain it was Osgar, Gant swung back around, spurring Gus down the road.

CHAPTER THIRTY-SIX

Edela, Bertel, and Siggy ate in silence, perched outside a busy tavern, enjoying an early supper of seafood broth and bread. The broth was salty, and the bread was a little charred, though overall, it was a hearty meal that filled them up.

Bertel kept trying to ply Edela for information while they ate, wanting to know what they were going to do about finding Raymon Vandaal. After only one day of searching, she no longer seemed interested in pursuing him any further.

'I told you, I've no clues about where he might be,' she insisted. 'It feels like a dead end. Perhaps not a path to follow at all? Besides, we can hardly keep wandering around in circles. If I was meant to find him, I'm sure I would have been shown something by now.' Edela wasn't exactly sure why she wanted to keep her meeting with Raymon a secret, except that she'd felt something when she was standing before him – a dark foreboding, as though he was in grave danger. She had felt such an urgency to find him, though now she felt foolish, fearing she may have led her enemies to a new target.

Were they linked?

She didn't know, but Furia herself had feared for those Edela loved.

And The Armless One had said as much in her prophecy to Ranuf Furyck.

The Furyck line would soon end.

Gulping, she placed her spoon back in the bowl and her hands in her lap. 'You can have mine,' she offered, first to Siggy, who shook her head, then to Bertel, who nodded his.

The bowls were barely big enough to feed a child, he thought, happy to have two. They were trying to conserve the coins Edela had earned in Bakkar, so he'd worked to suppress his appetite, keeping his thoughts to himself.

Except those about Raymon Vandaal.

Though no longer wishing to even talk about the poor young man, Edela changed the subject. 'We need to find a way to earn more coins while we're here. What do you think we could do? Anything but fortune telling!' she laughed, winking at a quiet Siggy, who looked up in that dazed manner again. Edela frowned. 'I'm starting to think you're ill. You have a look about you. Does your head hurt, or perhaps your throat?'

Siggy nodded. 'My head has been hurting since yesterday. I thought it would go away, but it hasn't.'

A disturbed Bertel edged away from her, earning a stern look from Edela. 'Well, I have something for that in my purse!' she announced happily. 'Though I must return to that physician for a few more supplies. I need to keep us all in good working order, don't I?' She squeezed Siggy's hand. 'Why don't we leave Bertel to gobble that down, and we'll head back to the baker's room. I can make you up a drink that will soon send that headache on its way.'

Siggy stood with a grateful smile. 'I'm sorry. I don't mean to be unhelpful.'

Edela wrapped an arm around her. 'Oh, you're never unhelpful, Siggy Larsen. Quite the opposite.'

'But you can't go on your own!' Bertel spluttered, splashing his spoon down into the bowl. 'I...!' He took another quick mouthful before rushing up from the table and hurrying after them. 'It's not safe!' he called, receiving a few filthy looks.

Edela was laughing when he caught them. 'You still don't think I can keep myself safe? *Still*?'

Bertel swept a hand over his forehead, wiping away a layer of sweat. 'I think you think you can keep yourself safe, though I doubt Iker Rayas is going to give up so easily. If he was promised a reward, he will hunt you down like the prize you are, no matter how many injuries he has.' Moving ahead of his companions, Bertel sought to clear a space, without much luck. Everyone moved with urgency, demonstrating no tolerance for those standing in their way.

Edela let him do what he needed to, keeping Siggy close. 'It won't be long. We're nearly there.'

Beneath all her curls, Siggy tried to smile, though she still felt odd.

Something was wrong. Something she couldn't put her finger on.

Something inside her.

***

Gant's heart was throbbing as he turned Gus into the trees, fearing he'd led his men into danger once again.

He heard more screaming as he charged deeper into the woods, leaving the path behind.

Branches snapping, horses blowing, Gant and his men ploughed on, following those agonising noises.

It sounded as though Osgar was in terrible pain.

The forest darkened around them, first a greenish blue light, then an inky black. Gant was struggling to even breathe, let alone see now, though just as he was about to stop and turn his men around, he came to a clearing.

He could smell smoke.

And squinting, he could see a cottage...

***

Quint had lost his voice after days of yelling at his men, so his offsider, Berros, had to make his speech after supper to those slaves who had been allowed to stop for a meal. 'We'll be working through the night! All of us! One hour's rest only!'

There were surprised looks and disappointed groans at that news.

Jael eyed Alek, who looked ready for a long sleep, though he nodded at her, attempting enthusiasm. Rigg, on the other hand, appeared ready to jump up from the bench and rip Berros' head off.

'One hour,' he grumbled, ignoring the rest of whatever nonsense the man was spouting. 'They want men climbing up that tower in the dark on one hour's sleep? Men who've been pushed day after day, night after night? And they think that will get their tower finished?' He leaned forward, dropping his head to his hands, and bristling with annoyance, he scratched his head. 'Tired men are clumsy men and clumsy men –'

'One more night, though,' Alek reminded him. 'We're supposed to be finished by tomorrow.'

'And if we're finished tomorrow, they'll put us on something else,' Rigg's neighbour muttered, head bowed as though he couldn't even lift it. 'The king or the queen or some rich lord will put us on something else. Some pretty tower or building or temple they can look at, not caring how many of us are buried to make it for them.'

Jael eyed the man, who was given to grumbling, though he wasn't wrong. 'Where do you come from?' she asked.

Lifting his head, the black-eyed man named Hepa peered at her. 'Silura. A place called Opat, far in the desert. I made the mistake of venturing to Castala one summer. It was like stepping into the mouth of a serpent, and before I knew it, he'd clamped his teeth together and I was trapped. Taken here.'

Jael had first-hand knowledge of a serpent's mouth, though she didn't say. 'I went there many years ago,' she said instead. 'To visit the King of Silura.'

The three men turned towards her, wanting to know more.

'And how did you find him?' Hepa asked. 'Last I heard, he'd gone mad. Locked away in his compound. His own prisoner now.'

Jael had heard something similar. 'It must have been ten years since I saw him. He seemed content then, with his family around him. His palace with its gardens was enormous. I remember seeing wild beasts.' She shook her head, feeling odd. Her father had taken her and Aleksander, leaving Axl behind with Gisila. It had opened her mind to how big Varmyr was, to how much there was to see.

'All his family slowly died,' Hepa added. 'Some taken by illness. Many murdered. It doesn't always pay to be a ruler of men, as those in power here will soon find out.'

Rigg nudged the man. 'Keep your mouth shut about that, Hepa.'

Hepa eyed him angrily. 'You think I'd risk Quint finding out? Risk an opportunity to see my home again?' He lowered his voice. 'No. I'll slit the man's throat myself and piss on his dying body.'

Jael stared at him, seeing anger seething from his pores like sweat.

She felt her own, though she had nothing against Quint.

He appeared caught in a trap of his own making. Every way he turned, he was bound to encounter an enemy – even in his own house.

Berros had finally finished speaking, and soon everyone in the hall dragged themselves back to their feet, accompanied by a chorus of groans, creaks, and clicks. Bodies that couldn't take any more would only be offered one hour to recover, and they needed to use every second of it.

Jael closed her eyes, willing herself on.

Two days.

In two days, she would find her way home.

***

'It is so good to have you home, Father,' Kalina said nervously.

Ronin had excused them both, leaving Dessalene to entertain Kosta while he ushered Kalina into the throne room, quietly closing the doors.

No slaves were present, though every lamp and candle was burning – a sweet, musky aroma infusing the air.

'I'm not sure you mean that, Kalina. Truly? You do know Dessalene told me about Arras and about Noor. That you murdered him?' Ronin's voice was a hiss and a snarl. '*Here*? In this very chamber?'

Kalina didn't blink, though she felt a familiar tightness in her chest. 'He betrayed me,' she insisted, holding her ground.

'How? *How*?' Ronin demanded, and grabbing her wrist, he pulled her to him.

'He told me that Arras and I would be together. He lied! He was playing games. To make such things up? To *lie*?' She shook her head. 'I knew he wasn't loyal. Not to me or S'ala Nis. He let Arras escape! It was his fault. He should have seen!' She was trembling with terror, feeling her father squeezing her wrist.

'But to murder a seer? Chosen by Eyshar himself? But that great god raised me up, turned me from a lowly slave into a powerful king. And to betray him so cruelly in my name? Without thought to the consequences, Kalina?' Dropping her arm, Ronin spun away. 'I'm disgusted that you could commit such a crime. Against me! Against the trust I have placed in you! And why? Because your *heart* was broken?' Ronin laughed, swinging back around. 'Do you think a queen should have a heart, Daughter? A heart of what? Blood? No!' He shook his head. 'To rule with power and strength, a queen must possess no heart at all.'

Kalina blinked at him.

'Your people do not care if you are happy. They care little for who lies beside you at night, who holds your hand and whispers in your ear. *No!* They care that they are safe and prosperous. And you have made us less safe, Kalina. Arras is gone from here, and what will he reveal of our secrets? What aid will he give to our enemies?'

Kalina still didn't understand why Arras had left.

He'd shown no signs of unhappiness – not until he'd returned from Osterland with that woman.

A dreamer, who had certainly bewitched him.

'Perhaps Jael Furyck is to blame?' she offered. 'Perhaps she convinced Arras to escape? To take her away? Noor denied it, though I didn't believe him.'

'Why? Because *you* are a dreamer, Kalina? Is that it? You are a seeress, a dreamer? That is a great revelation, if true!'

Kalina's temper stirred, though under the steely gaze of her dominating father, it soon retreated. 'I didn't believe him,' she repeated, sounding defeated now. 'I cannot explain why.'

Ronin's anger wasn't tempered, and he pounded a fist against his leg. 'I *trusted* you! Your mother, that silly, addled woman, tried to turn you into her little doll, but I saw intelligence and a quick mind. I saw strength and a leader in you. My heir! I *chose* you! And you? You have disrespected that choice, ruling not as a queen but as a petulant child, making impulsive, reckless decisions!'

Kalina recalled a childhood spent hiding from her father's violent outbursts. 'I am... sorry, Father. I am. Though S'ala Nis has not suffered. The isle thrives.'

Ronin swung around, remembering his guest. 'You may think so,' he seethed. 'Yes, you may think so, Daughter, but power is so finely balanced on the isle. You rule as one woman. You sit in this chamber on that throne and make everyone on the isle believe that you are more powerful than all of them combined.

That Eyshar chose you to rule in my steed, just as he chose Noor. The Noor you *murdered.*' He turned to look back at his daughter, pinching his fingers together. 'This is the margin between success and failure, between the powerful and the powerless. If you give these people a reason to doubt you, to doubt your ability to command Eyshar's favour...' And now he clamped his fingers together, eventually dropping his shoulders. 'Come, we must rejoin your betrothed. I'm sure he has missed you already.' And without lifting an eyebrow in humour, King Ronin Sardis strode out of the throne room, leaving his trembling daughter behind.

***

Knowing they were only allowed one hour's rest, Jael hadn't imagined that sleep would come. She'd eased herself down onto the mattress, lying on her side, mind whirring, though within a few heartbeats, she had plunged into a dream.

She walked in the snow, and it was cold.

Jael had forgotten cold, and this was freezing in a way that kept her blinking. Her lower legs were buried in it, her arms and legs shivering, nose numb.

It made her smile.

It was Oss. Home.

She saw Sigmund throwing snowballs at Mads, both boys swathed in layers of wool and fur, red cheeks bright against the white snow. The sky was a dull grey behind them, merging with the pillars of smoke writhing into the air.

Jael turned to see Thorgils helping his stepdaughters make their own snowballs. He was crouched down between two of the girls, who urged him to hurry.

She wanted to join them, though her eyes were soon on Oss' old hall, seeing its familiar roof like an upturned ship, its doors shut against the cold.

Beaming with pleasure and impatient to get inside, she hurried up the steps as Isaura walked out, carrying Elina. Turning around to smile after them, Jael was momentarily distracted, seeing another familiar face.

Everything looked so familiar.

She turned back and frowned.

Not everything.

The interior of the hall wasn't as she remembered it.

She saw the two simple wooden thrones on the hide-covered dais.

Eadmund's was on the left, and on the right... a woman sat on Jael's throne.

Ayla?

She looked different, a confused Jael thought, coming closer, seeing Eadmund emerge from behind a curtain. It wasn't green. The green curtain had gone.

He came towards the dais, and stepping up to Ayla, he bent down and kissed her – on the lips.

Jael felt as though she had lost her balance, her hold on the dream.

She started vibrating.

Eadmund kissed Ayla, then touched her belly.

Her very pregnant belly.

Staring in horror, Jael watched as he left the dais behind, heading out of the hall straight past her. She could smell him; every scent that was so achingly familiar; every memory of his hands, his lips and...

Turning to follow him, desperate to understand what was happening, she headed out of the hall to where Eadmund had stopped by Thorgils.

'How's Ayla?'

'Better, I think. She slept more last night.'

Thorgils peered at his friend. 'And you? How are you?' Stepping away from the children, he kept his voice low. 'Thinking about Jael?'

Eadmund ran a hand through his sandy curls. He stared at his friend with sad eyes. 'I know she's gone, but I... I still wake up every morning not believing it's real. That she's not here?' He shook his head, dropping it, arms hanging by his sides. 'How is it even real? That I have to live my life without her?'

Thorgils patted his back. 'Though you do have to live, Eadmund. And you know Jael would want you to.'

'And Bo?' Eadmund raised his head. 'I miss her. So does Sigmund.'

Thorgils turned to look at the children and at the little blonde head of Sigmund Skalleson, now curly like his father.

Hands shaking by her sides, Jael stared at that little boy with a deep longing. He wasn't her blood, but he was her heart.

'Though we have to think about what we have here. We both do. Sigmund and Ayla and the baby? There's still a lot to be grateful for. There is.' Thorgils looked ready to cry, though he attempted a smile. 'Come on. Let's show these children of ours how to have a real fight.'

Eadmund didn't smile, though he was soon following him towards the children, trying to drum up some enthusiasm.

Shivering in Oss' snowy square, Jael stared after them.

Tears freezing on her cheeks.

***

When it was dark, and the street outside the baker's was mostly quiet, Siggy sat up, heart thumping.

She'd heard a voice.

Glancing around, seeing moonglow creeping across the walls, falling over the beds, she saw that both Bertel and Edela were sound asleep.

They hadn't spoken.

She glanced at the door, squinting, noting that the bolt was firmly in place.

Feeling confused, she soon felt the pull of her mattress. It was warm and sticky in the room, though she was simply too tired to care.

Then the voice again.

Looking down, Siggy saw that she had something clasped in her hand: the silver disc from her necklace. She must have been clutching it when she went to sleep.

And now she crawled away from her mattress towards the table where Edela had left a plate of figs for breakfast. Her eyes shifted from the table to the cloaks draped over the chairs. Siggy saw her own and then Edela's. The dreamer's belt hung over it, and attached to that belt was a leather purse in which Edela kept stones and nuts and all sorts of useful supplies.

Glancing over her shoulder, checking that the dreamer was still asleep, Siggy froze. Then, shaking her head, curls trembling, she turned back to that purse, silently lifting its flap and sliding her silver disc inside.

And with one more look over her shoulder, she touched the purse and padded back to her mattress, lying down, immediately drifting back into a deep sleep.

***

The man who kicked Jael received a surprised shout in return. She lurched off her mattress, crying out in pain, shaking with tiredness. Her bed was wet through where she'd been lying, her hair damp and stuck to her face. She felt stiff and strange, as though she hadn't slept at all.

The men around her were complaining loudly, used to

little sleep, but not this little. It was torture. They moved slowly, barracked by Quint's offsider, Berros, for Quint was still sleeping in his bed with his wife and would be for some hours yet.

'Come on!' Rigg growled, raising his hoarse voice. 'We've two days till the funeral! Two days till we...' He sneezed loudly and then a second time. 'Till we rest!'

Jael's disturbing dream returned like a splash of cold water. She shivered, remembering the snow and the playing children and her husband, who appeared to have married Ayla.

Because she was dead.

And Bo?

'You too!' Rig grunted, flapping a hand at her. 'Our queen. Aren't you supposed to set a good example for your subjects?'

Jael glared at him. 'Fuck off.' And dropping her head to her hands, she rubbed her eyes, trying to make the dream disappear. Though it lingered, taunting her.

Her dream of the pyres hadn't disturbed her as much as this.

Eadmund had another wife. A pregnant wife.

And there was no Bo.

Lifting her head, she saw Rigg trying to rouse Alek, who remained lying down, and shaking off her own worries, she stood. 'Is he alright?'

'I'm fine,' came Alek's weak voice, mingled with a yawn. 'Just... tired.'

Jael smiled. 'Two days till the funeral,' she reminded him. 'It's just two more days.' Berros' helpers were moving around the hall with glowing lanterns, urging speed. She looked back to Alek, seeing how gaunt he was. He coughed, and it rattled his bones. 'You can just sit somewhere for a while. Let Berros run after everyone. You just sit.'

Between Jael and Rigg, they managed to help Alek up into a sitting position and then onto his feet. He wobbled unsteadily, coughing some more, though he offered his friends a smile.

'Two days,' he echoed. 'And then –'

'Get moving!' came the urgent cry. 'Kosta's on his way!'

That was a worse thought than anything that might happen on the building site, and whether true or not, it shot a spark of fear at the tired slaves, who now hurried to drag their shattered bodies and broken spirits towards the doors.

'Hope they give us something to drink,' Rigg croaked.

Jael hoped so too. 'You take Alek outside. I'll go and ask. He needs water.' Alek couldn't clear his throat and kept coughing, now bent over. She felt increasingly worried about him, about her dream, about their chances.

If she was dead, when had it happened?

Ayla looked heavily pregnant, Sigmund maybe a year older. So when had she died?

Here?

Still trying to shake off the dream, she headed for the shouting Berros, looking for something to drink.

***

'I did miss you,' Ronin sighed, stroking his wife's flaming hair. Her head lay on his naked chest, her fingers in his chest hair, their bodies still vibrating.

'I find that hard to believe, Ronin Sardis. You looked so busy when I saw you.'

He laughed. 'I told you, those women are never a replacement for you. They're merely a distraction. A way to pass the time, to relax. I have so much on my mind. I do need to relax, Dessalene.'

'Oh, I'm sure you do. Perhaps you'll need to pay a visit to your old harem while you're here for some more... relaxing? From what Pye tells me, it's stocked to the brim with nubile young *distractions*.'

Ronin laughed. 'And what would he know about such things? I didn't think he even liked women.'

'Pye? Oh, he has quite the appetite, hungry little beast that he is. Man or woman, he's never been fussy. Though looking like that, he has to take what he can get.'

Ronin bent down, and lifting her chin, he kissed her. 'And you? How is your appetite, Dessalene?'

She stared at him. 'I'm quite full, to be honest. Perfectly sated.'

He looked disappointed.

'But surely you must sleep, darling one? After your journey? And with all there is to attend to? Let your body and mind rest now, and perhaps my appetite will return before dawn?'

He grunted, still hungry for his wife, though she wasn't wrong – he was exhausted. 'And you?'

'Well, I have one or two matters to attend to.'

Ronin lifted an eyebrow, preparing to sit up, but his naked wife pushed him back down, reaching for her silk robe. 'My matters,' she assured him. 'I shall return shortly.'

'How shortly?'

'Very shortly,' she promised, and bending down to kiss him, she patted his head. 'Be a good boy now, and I may even wake you when I return.' She didn't mean it, for Ronin Sardis had always slept like the dead. Once she left the chamber, he would barely take a breath before falling into a deep sleep.

A yawning Ronin stretched out his legs, cracking his toes. 'Don't be long,' he warned, and pulling more pillows towards him, he dropped his head, promptly closing his eyes.

Watching him, Dessalene smiled, and turning around, she inhaled a deep breath, ready to get to work.

***

After Jael had propped Alek on a bench and given him a cup, which, to his surprise, contained ale, she turned away, ready to start work.

'Jael, wait,' Alek implored, touching her elbow. 'I want to talk about what will happen.'

Turning back, she frowned. 'Happen?'

'At the sacrifice. After the signal, how it will all unfold.'

Jael bent down to him, eyes darting around the dark courtyard. Braziers had been set up around its square perimeter, though their flames did little to brighten the dense night. 'We've already discussed it. I know what to do, and so do you.'

Alek was struggling to breathe. He lowered his cup to his lap, holding it in an unsteady hand. 'I'm just... I don't know what I can do now. I'm... worried.'

She patted his hand. 'Rigg will take care of you. We've decided. Between the two of us, we'll keep you safe.' Jael's dream lurched out of the darkness, and she feared that wasn't true. Squeezing his hand, she tried to reclaim a sense of certainty. 'I know where to go. I can see the path, Alek. When Rigg blows the signal, I'll find a sword, grab a horse and rally everyone. Once I'm on horseback, it'll be easier. You don't have to worry. Just rest and let us finish the tower.'

She stood to go, but taking another sip of the delicious ale, Alek cleared his throat. 'I don't want to kill Quint.'

'No, nor do I, though he's not on our side. If he had to make a choice, he'd sacrifice us. He may not want to be where he is, but he can't escape it now. I won't kill him unless I have to, though likely someone else will.'

Alek nodded, motioning for her to leave. 'You'll see the sun rise,' he told her. 'Up there. It will be beautiful.'

She smiled. 'Yes, I imagine it will.'

**

A vibrating Dessalene took a seat at her table.

Into its smooth obsidian surface were carved four circles filled with intricate symbols. They opened whichever door she wished to unlock. It was simply a matter of deciding exactly where she wanted to go.

She sensed problems.

Running the pads of her fingers around the circles, she certainly sensed problems.

Kalina appeared to have come back into line, Ronin was here, which meant she could keep a closer eye on him. Jael Furyck was alive, lucky not to have been murdered twice, and Inesh Seppo had preparations for the funeral under control – a competent man indeed.

There was still the matter of her dream about the eagle and the rat.

Though that wasn't why she had left her husband sleeping. She had far more important matters to attend to now.

Important matters that were long past needing to be resolved...

Touching a symbol with her right index finger, Dessalene watched it glow, bright white like a tiny moon. Behind her, the crackling fire was a comforting sound. The doors to the balcony were open, and though it was a warm night, a fire always helped her slip into a trance.

The symbol extinguished, and now Dessalene tried another, this time with her left index finger, holding it on a symbol that resembled a hook. Its glow intensified, quickly lighting up the table, and feeling the relief of finding her path, Dessalene Sardis now closed her eyes.

CHAPTER THIRTY-SEVEN

That night, Axl paid a visit to Helga.

It was late, Linas was sound asleep, though she had been expecting him, for she opened the door before he could knock, silently ushering him into the cottage, inclining her head to the boy.

Axl wasn't surprised to see Gully greet him with a big slobbering tongue, though Helga shooed him back to the bone he'd been enjoying by the fire.

'You have word? About those men?' she wondered in a quiet voice, motioning to the stool in front of the fur-lined chair.

Axl took a seat without thinking about his grandmother. Helga was here now, and he needed her insight. 'They're not from Iskavall. They're Brekkan. Likely not sent by Oren Storgard or any of his lords, but by one of mine.'

She grunted, surprised by that. 'You have more enemies than I can count, which is nothing new for a king. I don't imagine any king sleeps with both eyes closed.'

Axl stared at her, desperate to unburden himself.

But not to Helga.

He stiffened. 'Torun is working with them on the new pier. He will try to find out more, but in the meantime, you need to help me. Gant's gone to find answers, and he's been gone a long time now.'

Helga looked confused.

'My stepfather, my... he's... Gant. My father's best friend. He taught me everything I know. He's...' Becoming worried, Axl's words trailed off.

'He's a reliable, experienced man,' Helga murmured, seeing an image of a grey-haired man sitting astride a big white horse. Something pricked at her. That strange feeling again, and she realised that perhaps she'd found a clue.

'What is it?' Axl asked, seeing her deepening frown.

She shook her head. 'I will hunt for answers, of course, though they do not always come when bidden. Not like that dog, who is an obedient creature.' She looked down at a happy Gully, gnawing away on his bone. 'I can search for him, but do not expect the truth to be revealed. Sometimes...' She blinked.

'Sometimes?'

'Sometimes bad things are simply meant to happen.'

Now Axl blinked, seeing sadness in Helga's eyes. He thought of Aleksander and his father. No dreamer had been able to see or stop what had happened to them. Not in time, at least.

'Though I will keep looking. It makes sense to. For now.'

Axl nodded, seeing Linas wriggling in the little bed Ayla used to sleep in, and Biddy before her.

'Know that you are at war, Axl Furyck. Your enemies may not be knocking on your gates, but they are circling you. I feel it. Be ready for it, for it is coming.'

***

Arras couldn't sleep.

He had tried, though memories of S'ala Nis kept him disturbed in both body and mind. He remembered what it had felt like to be taken to that place, removed from all he knew. Relieved of his freedom.

He had it back now, though was he about to throw it away? And his life? Not to mention Nico's?

His son lay sleeping next to him, beside Fyn Gallas, who seemed like a nice young man. They all seemed nice, but were they good enough to overcome whatever Kalina and her army would throw at them?

If Ronin Sardis and his wife were there, perhaps not.

He noticed Otter's fluffy brown tail flicking in a pool of moonlight, and looking up, he saw the dreamer approaching.

She stopped before him. 'Can't sleep?'

Arras nodded, and deciding that he needed to clear his head, he stood. 'We're getting closer, I just...'

'Wonder if you're doing the right thing? Going back?' Mattie inclined her head for him to follow her away from the sleeping bodies. They walked to the stern, where Otter had returned to Mattie's pile of furs, scratching them into a lumpy heap.

'It's the right thing to try and rescue Jael, to free the slaves, though I do fear I'm simply taking my son back to be a prisoner. Or worse.' Peering at the dreamer, Arras hoped the moon would reveal what she thought about that, though her face remained in shadow. 'As a parent, I...'

Leaning on the stern, Mattie's eyes were drawn to the churning sea in *Bone Hammer*'s wake. 'Though the gods have already decided your fate. Yours and your son's.'

Dragging a hand through his beard, Arras nodded. 'What do you see? Anything about the isle?'

'Nothing new,' Mattie admitted. 'It's as though a shroud has dropped over it. I just see clouds now.'

'Perhaps that's the dreamer?'

Mattie feared he was right. 'Do you know her? You must, for how else did you find Jael? How else did you know where she was?' She turned to Arras, seeing nothing in the man's eyes that told her he was lying, though she needed to be certain which side he was on.

Arras stared at her. 'I didn't know her well. We barely spoke.'

'Though she led you to Jael?'

'Dessalene?' He shook his head. 'No, it was the queen who asked me to find the men for the mission to Osterland. She gave us our instructions and sent us away.'

Having heard about Jael's journey from Alekka to Tuura, Mattie was confused by that. 'Though Jael didn't have plans to go to Tuura. She went to Andala. Going to Tuura came out of the blue, a spur-of-the-moment decision, so how did you end up there?'

Arras began to wonder if he was under attack. 'Well, I –'

'Someone helped you?'

'There was someone...'

Mattie almost pounced on him.

'A voice in my ears. It was like a dream, as though I was imagining things. I don't know who it was, but I'm sure it wasn't Dessalene. It wasn't a voice I'd heard before.'

'What did it tell you?'

'Where to go and when. Where Jael would be.' Arras remembered that night so clearly, full of regret but also gratitude now, for without Jael, he would never have found a way to escape S'ala Nis.

Mattie felt strange, fearing how many dreamers were helping their enemies. She frowned, becoming nauseous.

'You have a gift,' Arras assured her, guessing the reason behind the dreamer's silence. 'So whoever you have to face, you should feel confident. We all saw what you did to stop those arrows. You made that magic.'

Mattie screwed up her face. 'If that's what it was. I don't know –'

'Of course it was, you know it was. *You* did it. And if called upon, you'll do it again. I remember walking into the Arena, matched up against the king's champion. I wasn't a warrior. I'd learned some things here and there to survive, though I'd never killed a man. Yet I held my own. I defeated that champion. He was too cocky, too sure that he'd crush me just because he'd crushed every man he'd faced before. Confidence can help you, but it can also trick you into thinking you're unstoppable. And that's where people like us can come into our own.'

Mattie held her breath, hanging on every word, feeling her fears writhing inside her.

'If Dessalene is there, if she's watching, she will try to stop us. And you. Prepare for that, but don't let it defeat you, for I'm certain that she's the one who should be fearing you.'

***

The path was paved with stars, leading to a door.

Dessalene's heart pounded like footsteps as she approached, suddenly hot in the darkness.

The door was short; she would have to bend her head to enter. Grabbing the handle, she turned, though it didn't open. She felt the resistance of the bolt on the other side, though with a deep breath, that bolt soon slid back. Silently. And with a twist of the handle, she was inside.

A smelly little room.

A box with no windows, she thought, seeing a sliver of moonlight revealing two beds and three sleeping bodies.

She saw the girl curled up on a mattress wedged between the two beds.

The two old people lying stretched out, mouths open.

Smiling now, she stepped further inside, seeing the silver disc glowing brightly in the old dreamer's purse.

Dessalene moved around the little table, only just stopping herself falling over a basket. She inhaled shoes and lavender mingled with fish, and wrinkled her nose. Then, stopping her wandering thoughts, she focused on the old woman.

Edela Saeveld.

And silently approaching her bed, Dessalene held out a hand.

***

In the dark, working at the top of the tower, Jael was struggling to function. Sleep deprivation had always been her least favourite form of torture. And knowing how much she hated giving up sleep, her father and Gant had thought it amusing to wake her in the middle of the night, taking her outside to train. Aleksander too. He'd blamed her for that, and quite rightly, as he'd never had a problem with being hauled out of bed before.

She smiled, mind wandering again, seeing Edela approaching the training ring with her familiar shuffle. Her grandmother had often spent hours perched on her moon-watching bench, returning to her cottage past the training ring, offering words of encouragement.

Jael wanted to reach out and stop her, but she was moving too quickly.

Hand in the air, Edela chuckled, smiling at her granddaughter. 'Keep going! You can do it! I believe in you, Jael!'

Jael stared at her, desperate to say something.

'Where are you?' she wanted to ask. 'Are you still alive?'

'Come and find me when you're done! I shall have a hot tea waiting!'

'No, Grandmother. No,' Jael pleaded silently. 'Wait for me.'

And then darkness, and she was staring at the stone wall and Berros was bounding along the plank towards her, barking with unhappiness.

'It won't be finished by wishing it!' he snapped. 'Lift your trowel and get going, woman!'

Ignoring him, Jael could still see those sparkling blue eyes peering at her in the darkness. 'Wait for me, Grandmother,' she urged. 'And when I'm free, I will come and find you.'

***

Edela sat up, hearing a strange humming in her ears.

Glancing around, she slipped her eating knife out from under her pillow. Bertel was snoring opposite her, Siggy was sleeping silently on the floor, the room illuminated by a ghostly moonbeam.

Lifting her head, she saw that the door was open.

Hurrying out of bed, Edela stepped over Siggy, reaching for her belt and cloak. She wrapped the belt around her waist, threw her cloak around her shoulders and slipped on her boots. She thought about waking her companions, though she didn't want to worry them.

Not till she knew there was something to worry about.

Perhaps they had simply not bolted the door?

Either way, she would quickly find out.

Stepping around the table, she tiptoed towards the open door.

Glancing around, she saw nothing unusual. She heard no footsteps or anything to cause her concern. It was late. No noises were coming from either of their neighbours.

Feeling confused, Edela turned around, sniffing.

And though she swung back with speed, she was too late.

Something was thrown over her head, and after that, there was nothing.

***

The coming dawn woke a tired Fyn, who wasn't sure he'd slept much.

He felt stiff all over, stretching his arms, legs, even his toes in an effort to get moving. He longed for warmth: a fire, a hot drink – something to thaw his frozen nose and fingers. Squeezing his hands together, he tried waking them up, and finally, with a yawn, he stood, seeing Kolarov already busy preparing a cup of his favourite concoction. It had such an unappetising smell that Fyn wondered why he chose to drink it, and smiling now, he approached the explorer. 'Breakfast?'

Kolarov looked up. 'Well, a form of it, yes. This tonic is my elixir. It keeps me young!' He glanced up at the tall, supple figure of Fyn Gallas, feeling anything but. 'Not something you need to worry about for many a year, though men my age start to lose their spark after a time. So this is how I try to reignite myself!'

Fyn sat down on a chest. 'You seem full of energy to me.'

'Yes, all thanks to my elixir! I developed it myself, you know. My own little recipe formulated from my discoveries. Perhaps I should set up a shop and sell it? I would certainly make a fortune. It is quite the wonder.'

'Back in Castala?'

'Well...' And now Kolarov's enthusiasm retreated somewhat. 'I am beginning to wonder if I'll ever see Castala again.'

'Do you love it?'

Kolarov was so surprised by the question that he struggled for an answer. 'It is... where I was born, where I always returned to, but love?' He looked sad then. 'I do not think of love. Love has never been a part of my life.'

'You never wanted a family?'

Kolarov immediately looked away, fussing with his cabinet drawers. 'Men like me, we are... not made for that sort of life. No, I seek other pleasures. Other worlds! A simple family life? Ha, I am certain I would shrivel up and cease to exist!' His bluster and bravado were back, though sadness lingered in his eyes. 'Though men like you? I imagine you cannot wait to return to Oss and find a mate. Unless, of course, you've already found her?' he wondered with a wink.

Fyn looked confused. 'What?'

'Mattie,' Kolarov murmured. 'I've seen the two of you together. You make quite the pair. Yes, and she's a lonely widow, looking for a husband, desperately wanting a family.'

'Mattie?' Fyn looked horrified. '*Mattie*?'

'Yes?'

Both men turned to the dreamer, who stared at Fyn in confusion. 'You wanted me?'

Kolarov suppressed a laugh.

A slightly dazed Fyn shook his head. 'No, no, I don't.'

'Oh.' Mattie looked from Fyn to Kolarov with no idea of what was going on.

'We were just... talking about tomorrow,' Fyn muttered. 'It will be tomorrow, won't it? That's what I've heard. About what you might have seen in your dreams. Hopefully, something.'

Mattie sighed. 'I've seen nothing, so unless this mist in my head blows away, we'll be sailing into the harbour blind.'

That soon swept away all thoughts of wives and home. 'Blind?' Fyn repeated, staring at the dreamer.

'Yes, blind.'

***

Bertel couldn't see.

His eyes were almost glued together, the room a muggy cave. He felt so weary that he wasn't sure it was morning, though the cheerful chatter of birds filtering through the gap at the top of the wall told him otherwise.

He heard a familiar bustling sound coming from the market and could smell that the baker was cooking his first loaves of bread, which immediately had his empty stomach growling. Though inside the room, he heard no hints of movement at all. And used to waking after Edela, Bertel was surprised by that. He finally peeled open his eyes, squinting at the dreamer's bed, where he realised that she was already awake.

And gone.

Glancing around the small room, he saw Siggy sprawled on the floor, sound asleep. Turning to look at the table, he noticed that Edela's cloak and belt were missing, her boots too. And hoping she'd slipped out to find some breakfast, he considered going back to sleep, though that was hardly setting a good example for Siggy. So, instead, he sat up, feeling stiffer than ever. Old age was no fun, and nor was sleeping on a door, which was what lay beneath his very thin, straw-stuffed mattress. Yawning loudly, he adjusted his tunic and trousers and stood. Immediately unbalanced, he stumbled towards Siggy, accidentally kicking her awake.

She sat up with a splutter, peering up at him through a fringe of damp curls. Brushing them away, she blinked. 'What... happened?'

'Happened? Just morning. Time to wake up! Edela will hopefully be back soon with something to eat. I certainly don't think a few figs will fill us up.'

Siggy looked around, feeling so exhausted that she almost didn't know where she was, though seeing Edela's empty bed, something jumped out at her, glowing in the dim light. Arms tingling, she peered down at her right hand, clenched in a fist. Though opening it, she saw nothing but a memory.

Standing in a hurry, she stumbled towards the table, to the chair where Edela's cloak and belt had been. Lifting her right hand, she remembered slipping the silver disc into the dreamer's purse. And frowning, she turned back to look at the bed.

She swung around, seeing nothing disturbed in the cottage.

Though the door was open.

Which was odd.

Though not as odd as her dream.

Slipping a hand into the pocket of her grey dress, she pulled out the silver chain, seeing no disc attached.

And now she turned to Bertel with horror in her eyes.

***

Dessalene was in such a joyous mood at breakfast that she was even nice to Pye, who remained in a corner of the dining hall, awaiting instructions.

'I will see Jael Furyck today,' Ronin decided, surprising his wife.

Dessalene peered at him. '*See* her? What? For a little chat?'

Ronin laughed as he watched a slave topping up his goblet. 'A chat? Do you think I wish to get to know her? To see how much we have in common and discuss our shared interests?' Picking up the goblet, he sampled the black wine he'd been so fond of during his time on the isle. He blinked, having forgotten how potent the stuff was. Sensing his wife stiffen opposite him, he turned instead to his open-mouthed daughter. 'Unless you have actually managed to kill her, Kalina? Pushed her too hard, broken her body, deprived her of everything needed to keep her alive?' His smile darkened, and his pale eyes hardened. 'Though my orders were to keep her very much alive, weren't they? To keep her alive for me.'

Kalina looked from her father to Dessalene, whose lips rose into a cat-like grin. 'Yes... they were, and I... she is alive, Father. Of course.'

'I hope so. For your sake, I do hope so.'

Kalina suddenly remembered something Kosta had said at supper about happily sacrificing a number of slaves to get the tower finished in time. He was an arrogant man, given to hyperbole, though she didn't doubt he meant it, and he appeared to have a particular dislike of Jael Furyck...

She dropped her eyes to her plate.

'If she is dead, I shall happily find another heir, Kalina. The woman's life is mine, and only I choose when to end it.'

A flustered Kalina swallowed a fishbone. It stuck in her throat, and feeling herself panic, she grabbed her goblet, guzzling down a mouthful of wine – almost spitting it out.

Dessalene laughed. 'What a brute you are, Ronin! Your poor daughter only wishes to please her beloved father, and there you are, threatening to throw her into the sea. And not for the first time!'

Ronin gazed at his wife with a knowing look. 'I dislike betrayal, I despise failure, and I detest incompetence most of all. Though...' And now he turned back to his daughter, patting her hand. 'Kalina would never let me down, would you?' Leaning towards her, he kissed her flushed cheek. 'Come, finish up, and we will head to the temple. I wish to meet this Noor-Elect too. He may be the chosen heir, though I still have to approve the man. As does Eyshar himself.'

Dessalene lifted an eyebrow at Kalina, who hurried to dab her lips with a napkin. 'Well, do enjoy yourselves!'

'You are not coming, Wife?'

'To that building site again?' Dessalene shook her head. 'No. I have too many things to prepare that do not involve leaving the palace. I shall see you both upon your return.'

Ronin wasn't happy about that, though Dessalene had always been a secretive creature, plotting away in the shadows, so her having other plans didn't come as a surprise. He nodded, finishing his breakfast in silence, and when he was ready, he stood, helping a nervous Kalina to her feet. 'Well, come along, Daughter. Let us go and greet my long-awaited prize!'

***

Edela didn't know where she was.

Or who had taken her from the room above the baker's.

She had been awake for only moments, yet her senses were quickly alert and vibrating with urgency.

Something was draped over her head, preventing her from seeing where she was or who was with her. She heard boots scuffing floorboards, inhaling the sweat of male bodies. Her throat was painfully dry, though she felt too afraid to ask for a drink.

Her hands were bound, too heavy to lift; something hard and cold was wrapped around them.

And then the mask was yanked off her head and a gasping Edela saw that she was sitting across a table from a one-eyed Iker Rayas.

CHAPTER THIRTY-EIGHT

'What do you mean? *Amulet*?' Bertel didn't understand as Siggy panicked before him, tugging his tunic in terror. 'You lost an amulet?'

A frustrated Siggy took a breath and started again. 'When we went up the mountain to visit the goddess, this woman... she had jewellery for sale. Necklaces and amulets.'

'Yes, yes,' an impatient Bertel grumbled. 'You've already said. Move to the part where she tricked you. What does that mean?'

'I don't know. The woman... I bought an amulet from her. She told me it would protect those I cared about but that I needed to keep it to myself.'

Bertel frowned. 'Sounds a bit strange. What was this amulet?'

'I don't have it,' Siggy admitted, showing him the chain. 'Well, I have the chain, but the disc with the symbol on it –'

'*Symbol*?' An increasingly concerned Bertel almost lunged at the girl. 'What symbol?'

'Protection, the woman said. It was the God of Protection's symbol, and then... I think I felt strange.'

Bertel peered at her. 'You were strange. Quiet. You had a sore head.'

'I did, but it's gone now, and so is Edela!'

A now frantic Bertel grabbed both of Siggy's arms, shaking her. 'What does that mean?'

'I think I led someone to Edela. I think the amulet was a trap.

And now, what if I've gotten her killed?'

***

Iker Rayas looked different from when she'd last seen him, Edela thought, trying not to reveal any disgust she might feel about his gruesome appearance. In trying to be helpful, Zen had flung a knife at his eye, and now a bloody bandage was wrapped around his face, hiding it. He had new wounds, too, roughly stitched, though she could smell that they were festering.

Slamming his hands on the table, Iker grinned at her. 'I have hunted you for weeks, and now, you're finally mine.'

Glancing down, Edela saw the heavy iron fetters clamped around her wrists.

Iker laughed. 'They will stop your magical powers, old woman. Stop everything you seek to do. Stop anyone finding you too.'

Edela's mind raced back to Bertel and Siggy. She tried to remember what had happened.

She had crept out of their room to check on the open door, and if only she had thought to say something, to not be so stubborn, so reckless... perhaps...

Tears pricked her eyes, lips quivering, as she realised that she had finally run out of luck. This man had sworn to kill her, and now, with her imprisoned and helpless, he finally could. She balled her hands into fists, trying to stop her tears from falling. 'You wish to take my life? To end it?' Forcing a smile, she tried a look of nonchalance, which she doubted was effective, for she trembled like a leaf. Now she shook her head. 'I confess to feeling flattered. An old woman clinging to the last years of her life? I had not expected to find myself fleeing a band of warriors intent on murdering me.'

'Then what sort of dreamer does that make you?' Iker wondered, indicating for one of his men to fill his cup with ale.

A desperately parched Edela looked longingly at that ale jug, though there was no cup for her. 'Well, a failed one,' she confessed. 'The Tuuran gods guide me, so I assume their silence is a statement in itself.' She wasn't sure she believed what she was saying. The words coming from her dry lips evoked no feelings of fear or regret. She felt displaced, disconnected from her body.

Iker smiled, though now he didn't look happy. 'Perhaps, though my orders have changed. It appears you have a reprieve, but only a small one.' Edela blinked, though he revealed nothing further, and standing with a grunt, he headed out of the room.

***

Argo Kosta was standing beside a fidgeting Quint when the queen's carriage pulled up outside the temple. Though before either man could speak, a flock of slave children hurried down the temple steps, followed by a smiling Inesh Seppo and six yellow-robed logi.

Pulling up before the king, first the slave children and then the seer and his attendants bowed deeply.

'Father, this is Inesh Seppo,' Kalina mumbled with a tense smile.

Ronin stepped forward. 'I do not remember you,' he said bluntly, ignoring the children, who were soon shooed away, curious about this man who had risen so high without his knowledge or approval. 'When did you arrive on S'ala Nis?' Ignoring Kosta and Quint, and not even glancing at the tower, the king kept his attention on the seer.

'Nine years ago now, my king. I had a vision that brought me to Noor, and after we met, he asked me to stay. He saw that I should succeed him.'

A deeply uncomfortable Kalina nodded. 'Yes, Noor sought my approval, and Inesh has been here ever since, learning what is expected of him. He has many gifts.'

Ronin studied the man. 'You are young.'

'I do not always feel it, my king,' Inesh joked. 'Though I understand your concern. I had it myself when Noor approached me, though he insisted that age was no guarantee of wisdom, and nor should it be used to prohibit those qualified from serving. Eyshar spoke to him and, according to Noor, chose me, and I have answered that call. I had expected many more years to pass before I assumed his place, though Noor saw that his time was ending. We both did.' He glanced at Kalina before averting his eyes.

Ronin wasn't sure what he thought of this confident, youthful man. His memories of Noor were of a silent, still sage who spoke in riddles that were always maddening, though often revelatory. He half-doubted Inesh Seppo was a seer at all, though he knew Eyshar would have the final say on that.

Now Ronin's attention returned to why he had come, and he shifted his eyes away from the seer towards Kosta. 'Tell me, where can I find my very special slave?'

***

Pye scuttled along behind Dessalene, who had decided on bathing. 'I do not require your company,' she informed him with a flapping hand. 'Go be with your own kind, toad.'

Though a determined Pye caught up with her instead. 'I have more!'

Dessalene turned around with a scowl. 'More? More what? I am going to bathe, Pye. Do not pester me with nonsense. Do not!'

'More about the slaves, Mistress. They truly are making plans to revolt.'

'Is this your little kitchen friend again?' Dessalene wondered with narrowed eyes. 'And what are you paying her for all these tasty morsels?'

'She wishes to be helpful,' Pye insisted.

'To me? A *slave*?' Dessalene laughed. 'But no slave wishes to aid their mistress from the goodness of their miserable little hearts! No, Pye, this woman, whoever she is, seeks to gain something for herself through a gullible fool like you!'

'She has a son!'

Dessalene shrugged.

'She fears he will be killed, Mistress! She wishes to stop the revolt. To save his life.'

Dessalene remained unconvinced, though remembering her dream of the eagle and the rat, she knew it would not do to overlook such a threat at this delicate time. 'Bring the woman to my chamber, though be discreet,' she warned. 'I'll have no word of this meeting spread about like shit in a stable. Now go! I will need at least an hour.'

Problems amongst the slaves was the last thing she wanted to worry about, so she fixed her mind on more pleasing matters.

Like Edela Saeveld.

Things were looking up.

And with a spring in her step, Dessalene Sardis turned around and swept down the hall.

***

Jael was brought down from the top of the tower by an uptight Quint, who told her that the king was in the temple, waiting on her.

The king and his daughter, the queen.

Jael's tired thoughts refused to order themselves as she carefully climbed down the scaffolding. She clung to the sides of the ladder, well aware that one exhausted man had fallen today. He hadn't died, but word was that he'd broken nearly every bone in his body. She swallowed, moving with even more care, until she was down on the ground, out of breath and covered in dust.

Following behind an impatient Quint, she enjoyed a brief respite from the sun as she entered a shaded colonnade before heading out into the temple courtyard, where she first saw Kosta, then Inesh Seppo, the queen, and finally a big man, who turned to her with a look that chilled her to the core.

'My king,' Quint mumbled, bowing to Ronin, then the queen, and mumbling some more, he shuffled backwards, leaving Jael standing by herself, stared at by her enemies.

'I met your father once,' Ronin said by way of introduction, his words clipped, his tone sharp. He spoke the common tongue with a heavy accent. There was no smile in his eyes, no welcome in his voice. 'Such an arrogant prick of a man. He talked about you, I remember. About how you would be his heir. The Furyck line, he told me, would carry on through you. How odd, I later thought, when I heard that he had chosen your brother instead. How odd that he had lost faith in you.' Ronin smiled now, staring at his own daughter, whose face was a mask beside him. 'But now I see you, broken and filthy, a defeated prisoner, and I realise how right he was to discard you. You are celebrated in many parts of Osterland, from what I hear, as a hero, a saver of the light, yet how easily you were trapped! Like a novice. Like that boy you keep beside you. What was his name?' Ronin tapped his chin. 'Fyn, that's right. Fyn Gallas.'

A horrified Jael felt like a tiny piece on a giant's gaming board.

She saw her home, her friends, her family, everyone she loved, and Ronin Sardis looming over the board, moving those pieces around with enormous, powerful hands.

Pushing back her shoulders, she projected something else entirely. 'Well, I was never much of a dreamer.'

'So I've heard,' Ronin grinned. 'And what a shame for you.' He stared at the slave queen, seeing defiance in her eyes. They were compelling eyes, drawing his attention to her face. She was tall, and though she appeared weary, she still carried herself as though she thought she was important.

Which she wasn't.

As she would soon find out.

***

Fearing that Siggy was right about the amulet and Edela, Bertel sought to formulate a plan.

'Edela can take care of herself,' he kept reminding them both as they sat outside the baker's, hunched over a plate of cakes. It wasn't the most appropriate breakfast, though Bertel had needed to feed the girl, and having given her some coins, he'd left her to pick what she wanted to eat.

She'd chosen two slices of the delicious date cake, though sitting at the table without Edela, worrying about Edela, neither of them had an appetite.

'But this feels different,' Siggy insisted. 'If Edela had known there was danger, she would still be here with us. She's seen it every time before, but this?' Dropping her head to her hands, she burst into tears. 'It's all my fault!'

Bertel glanced around, conscious of those sitting nearby, turning to stare. 'Now, now,' he soothed awkwardly. 'I... we just need help, don't we?' And thinking of help, he remembered the man in the golden tunic who had taken Edela to the seeress' cave. 'There might be someone who can find her,' he murmured, leaning closer until he was whispering in Siggy's ear, explaining everything.

When he'd finished, Siggy blinked at him, wiping her eyes.

'I know where he is!' And jumping to her feet, she grabbed the cakes off the table, stuffed them into her purse and with a quick look at Bertel, bounded away.

***

After a long and luxurious bath, Dessalene remembered Pye and his gossiping slave. She sighed, having her own matters to attend to, though if there was an actual revolt being planned, she would do well to uncover it quickly.

Entering her private chamber, which she did not share with her husband, she saw that her loyal toad was already there, offering his guest some wine. A horrified Dessalene was at a loss to understand why he'd even given the woman a seat, let alone refreshments, which Pye appeared to realise as the dreamer entered, nearly knocking over his goblet as he rushed to his feet. The slave looked as disturbed by Dessalene's arrival as her companion, and the pair of them were silent and twitching as she approached the table.

'It appears you have started our little meeting without me,' Dessalene seethed.

Pye hurried to pull out a chair for his mistress. 'Nanna was thirsty. I thought it would be easier for her to speak if her throat was... moist.'

Nanna was a small buxom woman of perhaps forty, with the sort of motherly look Dessalene knew Pye was drawn to. He liked being fussed over and petted, like a cat, rather than the slimy little toad he actually was.

She forced a smile and took a seat.

When Nanna moved as though to sit back down, Dessalene's head snapped around, quickly removing such a notion from the slave's misguided mind. 'You will tell me why I am giving you my time. It is a valuable prize, my time, and I do not gift it to mere chattels. Not without cause. So make this sacrifice on my part worthwhile, or I shall have Pye club you to death.' She smiled brightly, showing off perfectly straight teeth.

The dreamer's words tied a shocked Nanna's tongue in knots, and she couldn't even begin until a helpful Pye nudged her along.

'You told me about what you'd heard, about there being a revolt? Soon?'

Nanna nodded. 'The leaders are trying to recruit everyone.'

'Which leaders?' Dessalene demanded. 'Give me names!' She grabbed the slave's hand, squeezing it hard. 'What are the names of these rebel leaders?'

Nanna's mouth dropped open, a look of confusion crossing her face. 'I have no names, lady.' She bobbed her head apologetically.

'No names? Then what do you expect me to do? Who do you expect me to kill if you cannot point them out?'

'*Kill*?' Nanna sought a hasty retreat, regretting that she'd spoken up, though Dessalene had a firm hold of her hand, and she couldn't move. 'But I –'

'Anyone attempting to revolt against the queen will be thrown into the pits! I will see to that myself! Now, tell me, where did you hear talk of this revolt?'

'F-f-from, f-f-from,' Nanna stuttered, the pain of the dreamer's grip making her eyes water. 'Ingrid! She works in the kitchen garden. I... aarrghh, she overheard men talking in the street.'

Dropping the woman's hand, Dessalene stood. 'You are useless to me. Get rid of her!' And swinging around, green dress swirling around her thin body, she headed to the door. 'Get rid of her, Pye, and find the woman who actually has the information I need. And do not waste my time again!' Flinging open the door, she turned to hiss at the slave. 'If we should ever have the misfortune of meeting again, that will be a very bad day for you.' And turning to glare at Pye, she watched as he hurried Nanna through the door. Slamming it after them, she spun around, bristling with anger.

Furious at her little toad for wasting her time.

***

Edela was taken to a small, windowless room.

Where she was locked in.

The fetters made any sort of movement cumbersome. They were incredibly heavy, and she moved slowly.

The dark room was sparsely furnished with a single short bed, a bucket, a dirty cup and a jug of water.

There was no food, though she assumed that would come in due course as Iker Rayas now apparently wanted her to live. Or, at least, whoever had sent him after her did.

She tried to recall the woman's face. Her words.

'Bring me the dreamer, she will be my prize.'

A prize?

A puzzled Edela collapsed onto the bed with a sigh.

Hearing footsteps, she glanced at the door, though they soon moved away. She wondered where she was. The noise from the market had found her everywhere she went in Castala, though here, she heard little but the blaring sound of her rising fears.

She thought of Bertel and Siggy, who were hopefully back at their room unharmed. They would try to find her, come after her, though that would only put them in terrible danger.

She remembered creeping out of their room into the dark hallway with only her knife, wondering what madness had bewitched her. Now her knife was gone, and so was she, locked away in this room. Glancing down, she saw that she was wearing her belt, and seeing her purse, she opened the flap, feeling even more confused. She had been carrying her symbol stone, which surely shielded her from the view of whoever was seeking her?

Unless Iker Rayas had simply spotted her in a street and

followed her?

Feeling around in the purse, she found the familiar smooth surface of her stone. She saw a few nuts, which might come in handy, and something shiny that caught her eye. And then, digging deeper, she found a silver disc with a strange symbol on it.

***

When Siggy led Bertel towards the plinth she'd often seen the golden man standing on, she was devastated to discover that he wasn't there.

'Perhaps he's taking a break?' Bertel muttered, glancing around. Though he saw no sign of a golden tunic amongst the bustling crowd. 'We can go and find a seat over there. On that bench. He'll come back eventually.'

Siggy hoped that was true, and pushing through the crowd, she approached the bench, whose availability was likely explained by the splatters of bird shit fouling its surface.

A sighing Bertel looked around, and seeing no alternative, he spat on his sleeve and started wiping.

Eventually, they sat down, eyes on the plinth.

A man in a brown tunic arrived, and mounting the plinth, he started his presentation to the crowd. He spoke many dialects, eventually repeating his message in the common tongue, trying to tempt both Siggy and Bertel to venture the short journey to his stall down at the harbour, where they could purchase fried fish.

Thinking of food, Siggy pulled the squashed cakes out of her purse.

Bertel pointed at them. 'They'll be like rocks before long. You should have them. Edela wouldn't want you to starve.'

Siggy stared at him as though he was mad. 'But it's my fault!

It's all my fault, Bertel! She's missing because of me!' She was very loud, scaring away the birds who had thought to approach, wanting the cakes for themselves.

'You must stop this. Edela wouldn't blame you. She's been fooled enough herself not to blame you for any of this. If it's those men again, they would've found her one way or another. What we need to do is find some help. Someone who might have seen her. I can ask around. We passed that tavern a few roads back. I'll return there and ask if anyone's seen Edela. You stay here and wait for the golden man.' Standing now, Bertel peered at Siggy, wondering if that was a sound plan. 'You have your knife?'

She nodded.

'Well, maybe some time alone will do you good? You might have a vision.' Siggy looked ready to cry, so Bertel patted her shoulder. 'What would Edela say? You have proven yourself a dreamer, Siggy Larsen. All you need now is a little confidence. I'm not saying you have to find Edela, that it's all on you, but just that you try opening your mind. Who knows where it will lead you?' And with a squeeze of her shoulder, he turned away. 'Wait here for me!' he called. 'I won't be long!'

CHAPTER THIRTY-NINE

When Quint finally blew his conch shell for a break, Jael hurried down the ladder, eager to find out how Alek was, though she couldn't see him anywhere. So, after helping herself to a cup of water, she made her way to Quint. 'Have you seen Alek?'

'I put him in the temple. He's assisting Inesh Seppo with preparations for tomorrow.'

Lifting a hand to shield her eyes, Jael peered at the overseer. 'He's worse then?'

Quint looked away. 'The seer needed help, and Alek's good at organising. He knows this place better than most.'

Reading his thoughts, Jael suppressed a grin, pleased to know she'd been right about Quint. He did, in fact, appear to be a half-decent man, unlike Ronin Sardis, who, Jael was convinced, was evil to the core.

They stood side by side, turning to look up at the tower.

'I didn't think we'd finish it in time,' Quint sighed. 'Though soon it will be ready, and then we'll all move on to something else. Some other monument or building. Some great monstrosity...'

He looked defeated, Jael thought, and tired. The bags under his eyes had grown more pronounced since she'd arrived. His wife tormented him, and his father-in-law was a vicious bully, though as much as she thought to offer him advice, she had enough problems of her own.

And he certainly wouldn't welcome her interference.

'What did you want Alek for?' Quint wondered, waking himself up.

'To take him some water, to see how he was.'

'Hmmm, well, if he makes it to tomorrow, I'll ensure he has a seat at the sacrifice.'

'An actual seat? How generous.' And with a grin, Jael dropped her head and aimed for the temple. Though after a few steps, Quint blew his shell again, ordering everyone back to work.

Glancing over her shoulder, she glowered at him, and with a sigh, turned and headed back to the tower.

***

Gripping the silver disc between trembling fingers, Edela hoped to feel something, wanting to discover what the symbol meant. Though knowing that the bonds around her wrists and ankles were put there to prevent her seeing anything, she eventually dropped it back into her purse.

She saw the nuts again, though she had more of an urge to vomit than eat. Her head hurt, absent any clarity. It felt as though her fears had imprisoned her as much as the fetters.

Wanting to understand more about them, Edela held her right arm out, moving the fetter around, trying to see. There was no window in the room, though light came streaming under the door and through countless holes in the walls and ceiling. She moved the fetter around until a beam of sunlight revealed symbols. A squinting Edela thought she could make out one. Perhaps? She moved the fetter again, now seeing nothing. The fetter itself was locked tight, and she imagined Iker Rayas guarded the key.

She would have no luck there.

She remembered her knife, though apart from her purse, her belt was empty.

And feeling more desperate by the moment, she closed her eyes, seeking answers in the darkness of her mind.

***

After Jael Furyck had been sent back up the tower, Ronin had taken leave of his companions to spend some time alone at the Dragon Blood Tree.

The old tree was sacred, a gift from Eyshar himself. Drops of his dragon's blood had fallen from the sky, from which the tree had grown, now towering above the temple itself, infusing the isle with good fortune.

To Eyshar, Ronin owed a mighty debt, the weight of which he carried with him. The God of Providence and Fire had paved his path in gold, taking him from a slave, born of a slave, to a king. And soon, with Eyshar's blessing, he would seek to claim more.

Though he knew that such success could not be taken for granted, and in the silence of the temple courtyard, he could feel the god's displeasure chilling him. Looking up now, Ronin saw a cloud, dark and small, hovering above his head. It blocked the sun, and he stood in shadow, shivering with worry.

If Eyshar removed his favour, what would become of his ambitions?

What would become of all that he and Dessalene had planned?

***

The sun had reached its zenith when Dessalene emerged from her private chamber, hunting for Pye, who had not returned to her.

She found him out on the balcony, stuffing his face with grapes.

'What is this?' she exclaimed in horror, spying the grapes and feeling like some herself. Leaning down, she snatched his plate away. 'Have you forgotten who you serve, Eppypyrus?'

Pye recoiled. 'No, Mistress. Never!'

'Then why are you sitting here, feasting like a king instead of bringing me that slave you promised? The garden slave? The one with all the information?'

'She's dead, Mistress. I was coming to tell you, but then I was faint from hunger. I thought to eat. It makes sense to eat.'

Dessalene took a seat. 'Dead how?'

Pye leaned forward, though he didn't speak. Looking around surreptitiously, he edged even closer before finally opening his tiny mouth. 'A... plague.'

'A what?' Dessalene recoiled in horror, hand to her throat. 'A *what*?'

'The woman collapsed, carried away to the physician's. She was there for a few days but never recovered. They whisper of a plague.'

'Who whispers?'

Pye shrugged unhelpfully, earning a pinch. 'I don't know!' he yelped, cradling his cheek. 'I'm only telling you what I heard. They say the woman's face swelled with boils of pus. Hideous things! She was coughing up blood. Blood in her eyes too!' Pye shuddered. 'We shouldn't stay!'

Dessalene agreed, though tomorrow was Noor's funeral, and for the good of the isle and to ensure Ronin's prosperity, they could hardly decamp now. 'I need you to find someone,' she whispered. 'Someone... disposable.'

Pye didn't understand.

'I do not want you returning to that garden, you fool. Back to where that woman died?' She pushed back her chair and stood, moving far away from him. 'You do not come into the palace again. Understood? And you certainly do not breathe a word of this, Pye. Not to anyone.' Glancing back at the open doors, she saw no slaves lurking about, though surely there would be one?

'Can't you do something?' Pye pleaded, not wanting to be cast out.

'Against a plague?' Dessalene mouthed. 'You have the mind of an ass. No, no, a plague is sent by the gods themselves. A punishment!' And remembering what Kalina had done, murdering Noor as she had, she wondered if this was just the beginning? Their luck upended, like a bounteous harvest ruined by a deluge of rain? 'Find someone, a slave of no consequence. Have them go to the kitchen and shut them all in. This cannot spread. Not the sickness and not the gossip. Make sure it is contained there, Pye. I am relying on you. And whatever you do, do not come back inside the palace. Send word that you have completed this task.'

Pye looked concerned. 'And where am I to sleep, Mistress?'

Dessalene didn't care. 'In a doorway? Under a wagon? I shall be sleeping in my bed, so why should I concern myself about where you'll be? For all I know, you're already full of disease. This may very well be our last moment together.' Holding a hand to her nose, Dessalene turned away.

'Mistress!' Pye called to her, bulbous eyes shining with fear, though he had no response as the dreamer disappeared into the palace without looking back.

***

Bolder handed Raal the steering oar, and massaging his cold, stiff hands, he brought Eadmund and his friends close to discuss how things stood. 'Do you think they'll keep everything the same?' he asked, fearing that whatever knowledge Arras had was out of date.

Arras frowned, the crease between his bushy eyebrows deepening. 'Likely they replaced me with Victor Omani.' He looked at Nico, who nodded. 'My deputy. He's a useful man with a sound mind. And unless he was told otherwise, he wouldn't have suddenly changed every system we had in place. Things ran smoothly, and my departure shouldn't have altered that.'

Eadmund hoped he was right. 'So they'll change shifts at sundown? Those guarding the harbour?'

Arras nodded. 'It's always been the same. When the bell is rung to change shifts, there's a rhythm to it, a slower pace. I never minded that. The men take a little time to ease their way in and out. They're more relaxed in those moments, so if we make our move then, we'll catch them off guard.' Arras knew his soldiers. Most were good men, and the thought of storming the harbour and trying to kill them didn't sit right with him. Though Kalina would never relinquish her prisoner, and she wouldn't free the slaves unless forced to.

There was no other choice that Arras could see.

Nico looked just as uncomfortable opposite him.

'The timing of our approach will be crucial,' Arras added. 'And around The Corridor, it's never easy to anticipate the wind. It can blow about unpredictably.'

'That's comforting,' Bolder groaned, eyeing Mattie. 'Perhaps you can find a clue?'

Mattie stared at him. 'About the *wind*?'

'There are wind spells, you know,' Kolarov put in helpfully. 'Old women in The Murk speak of binding the wind.'

Mattie felt a great rush of heat surge up her frozen body. She shook her head. 'I can't simply know how to do everything, Kolarov! About the wind?'

'I can tell you what I know,' he said quietly. 'It may help.'

'Do it,' Eadmund ordered. 'You two go over there and sort that out.' And ignoring Mattie's gaping mouth, he turned back to Arras. 'When we arrive in the harbour, you'll need to lead us. You'll need to lead me to Jael.' He experienced a shudder of uncertainty as he spoke, though it made sense. Arras had escaped the isle and would not be welcomed back. He needed to do everything he could to survive, so Eadmund chose to trust him.

And though it made sense, the gathered men were silently surprised.

Especially Arras, who blinked at an equally shocked Nico before turning to look at the king. Scratching his cheek and dragging dirty nails through his scraggy beard, he thought quickly. 'It makes sense. Nico can lead the assault with Ulf. He knows the harbour.' He looked at Fyn and Thorgils. 'Fyn, you should come with us. We'll need to move with speed through the tunnels. When Ulf's catapults announce themselves, Victor will send everyone to counter the attack. I can only hope he doesn't send too many to guard the tunnels. If Mattie can't tell me where Jael is, once I'm inside the city, I'll find someone who can. Everyone will be talking about her after the fight in the Arena. Someone will know where she is.'

Eadmund hoped that was true. 'Thorgils, you go with Nico. We'll stop Ulf before we reach the isle, and you can hop on board *Beloved*.'

Thorgils would have preferred to join the hunt for Jael, though he didn't argue, ready to do his part.

Eadmund clapped him on the back. 'So it's agreed? Nico and Thorgils will join Ulf and attack the harbour. Arras, Fyn, and I will lead *Bone Hammer's* crew through the tunnel into the city.'

Arras nodded. 'The tunnel will take us into a bathhouse, a garden, and then we'll be out on the street. I'll find my way to Jael then.'

'Take a sword for her,' Thorgils suggested.

A smiling Arras remembered how much trouble Jael had caused Otho Dimas. 'Not sure she'll need one. Not if she's got those fetters back on. She seemed able to handle herself without any blade at all.'

A sense of anticipation was building now, a nervous energy buzzing around the ship.

Eadmund glanced over his shoulder at Mattie and Kolarov arguing in the distance. The explorer was waving a small section of rope in her face, and she was batting it away. He shook his head, uncertain how that would go, but whatever the case, in little more than a day, they would arrive at the isle.

***

Ronin Sardis approached his wife with an unfamiliar sense of trepidation.

They had planned everything so carefully, and yet he had an overwhelming desire to go against one of the centrepieces of their plan.

Dessalene was in the Pleasure Garden, gliding around a fountain in a trance. Looking up at the sound of his footsteps, she cocked her head to one side. 'You have come.'

'I needed to speak to you.'

'And I you.'

'We have to kill Jael Furyck,' they blurted out together.

Ronin blinked. '*You* think we should kill her?'

'I do,' Dessalene said in surprise. 'And you? Why?'

Reaching his wife, Ronin took her hands. 'I spent much time in contemplation in the temple, before the tree. I left my offerings, I gave Eyshar my apologies and my promises, though I sensed a great unease, a darkness descending upon the isle, upon Kalina and upon me. The god has been unhappy for some time, Dessalene. I feel it. I know it. He will not be satisfied with the blood of oxen and goats, no matter if we send him a hundred. After what Kalina did, murdering Noor? Eyshar's voice on the isle? His eyes?' A tense groan escaped his lips. 'It was such a lapse in judgement on her part, to lose her temper so recklessly. A betrayal! If we wish to solidify Kalina's place on the throne and secure Eyshar's continued support, I believe we must offer him that which I most desire. A true sacrifice, something I do not wish to lose. We must offer him Jael Furyck.'

'Though our plans?'

'There are other ways, we both know this. Other ways to make it happen.'

Dessalene sighed. 'I fear you are right, for there is another problem.' Ronin's grip on her hands intensified, though yanking them away, the dreamer stepped back with a disgusted shiver. 'Pye has uncovered what appears to be a plague.'

'What? On the isle?'

Dessalene nodded. 'A woman working in the kitchen garden died in a particularly revolting manner.'

'In the kitchen?' Ronin looked concerned. 'Where our meals have been prepared?'

'In the garden, dearest,' Dessalene repeated. 'I have enquired further, and the woman had no access to the kitchen itself. She was more of a gardener.'

'Still...'

Dessalene lifted her head. 'The sacrifice of a Furyck, a queen, will certainly please Eyshar. Her blood will appease him, and S'ala Nis' destiny will be assured. It will be as we intend once more, and our plans will simply be remade.' Now Dessalene slipped her arms around his waist. 'Eyshar has granted you the most glorious destiny, my love, though you must demonstrate your gratitude. And you will. Tomorrow.'

CHAPTER FORTY

Kolarov Radic enjoyed studying people.

He was an observant man, drawn to the unseen. He had visited exotic places, climbed mountains and trekked through jungles, sailed oceans and feasted in palaces, though studying people remained his favourite adventure of all.

Conversations involved listening and speaking, and though Kolarov enjoyed using his voice, he mostly used his eyes. And as he tried to get through to a very resistant Mattie, what he saw was a fearful girl. She stood before him as a determined woman, full of bluster, though her eyes revealed the girl who'd never felt good enough to be a dreamer. The girl that, when pushed, had run away from the Temple of Tuura, never to return. And now that girl stood before him, speaking with the voice of an angry twenty-six-year-old woman.

'You're talking gibberish!' Mattie insisted, fiddling with her belt. 'And what can I do with that? I don't know this god. Isvarr? I don't know anything about Alekka or The Murk. I know Tuura. And as far as I'm aware, there is no God of the Wind in Tuura!'

Kolarov weathered her storm of doubt, and when she fell silent, he took her hand, patting it gently. 'Though there's no harm in trying, is there? These men are fortunate having a dreamer on board. You've already saved their lives! They would have died without you, Mattie. And Arras and his son wouldn't be here if you hadn't uncovered that tunnel. You have exceeded any expectations already. Far exceeded. Now is just something you can try.' He shrugged nonchalantly, seeking to relax her. 'There is no certainty that binding the wind is even possible. Of course not! Though you have already proven your worth many times over. All you need to do now is have a little... try.'

Mattie's shoulders remained tense, up near her ears. 'Try?'

'To bind the wind.'

'And then?'

'Release it at exactly the right moment to spur us along. Like kicking a horse from a trot to a gallop. We will fly through that corridor of stone and into the harbour!'

Mattie stared at him, feeling that gentle pressure on her hand. It was oddly comforting, and she didn't try to draw it away. 'Show me again,' she said. 'But this time, go slowly, Kolarov. I need to understand you.'

Watching with Eadmund and Fyn, Thorgils chuckled. 'If Mattie was a bit stronger, I've a feeling she'd tip Kolarov overboard.'

Fyn smiled, though Eadmund remained tense, scratching his head. His belly was mostly empty and noisy with it, but he was becoming nauseous, continually running through what would happen and what could go wrong.

Thorgils nudged him. 'Jael might see us coming. She might be watching us now.'

Blinking at him, Eadmund hoped it was true.

'So we should try and look more confident about this plan of ours, don't you think?'

Now Eadmund grinned, blowing out a long breath. 'I'd say so. She's probably rolling her eyes, imagining she's going to have to do it all herself.'

'And not for the first time!' Thorgils added. 'Come on, let's find some more ale. We've talked enough for one day. Best thing we can do now is let it all go. In the morning, we'll wake up ready to do our part. You know, to help Jael with whatever plan she's magicked up!' He was laughing as he headed off in search of ale, remembering his queen and her hair-brained schemes.

Hoping she was busy making more.

***

Jael wiped her nose. A breeze had swept dust up it, and she couldn't stop sneezing. She felt like falling on her face. Just the thought of lying down was so enticing that nothing else entered her mind.

She had come down from the scaffolding, having been sent on her way by Berros.

Looking up, she could see that only the last touches to the crowning arch remained to complete.

The tower was almost done.

Rigg approached, sneezing himself. 'Where'd the breeze come from? I didn't think Eneko knew where to find S'ala Nis!'

A sniffing Jael turned around in confusion.

'Eneko. The Siluran God of the Wind.'

'Oh, well, it's not cool, but it's better than nothing, I suppose.'

'Are you done up there?' Rigg asked, picking a scab on his wrist.

'I am. Finally.'

'So you're off to bed then?' The sun was setting, still hot, like a fire on his face, which glowed.

'Oh yes, off for a nice long sleep,' Jael joked, knowing how many more tasks she'd been assigned. 'This time tomorrow it will start,' she realised, watching the sun's slow descent. She turned to see its golden rays hitting the tower arch, and though not yet pushing through it, they were already blazing like fire.

Turning further, she saw the circular platform with the high-backed stone chairs and the enormous altar where the sacrifices would take place. It stood alone, cut off from what looked like an empty moat, with a little bridge leading up to it. According to Alek, the animals would be led across that bridge to where Dessalene Sardis and Inesh Seppo's logi would sacrifice them to Eyshar, filling the moat with blood.

The thought was sickening. All that blood spilled to honour a god?

Remembering what Rigg had said, she turned back to him. 'They're bringing more plants and dirt, apparently. Quint's gone to hurry up the gardeners. Now we have to start digging.'

'I thought there'd be ale,' Rigg grumbled. 'To celebrate.'

'Well, when we crush our enemies, you can go to the palace and drink the queen's wine.'

Rigg's beady eyes popped open at the thought of it. 'And what are we going to do with the queen?' he wondered.

'Not that,' Jael said, reading his thoughts.

He blinked at her, all innocent surprise. 'What?'

'She's a woman, so it's not hard to imagine what you want to do with her,' she muttered, finally seeing the return of Quint, followed by a procession of slaves pushing hand carts. 'Though she's not the woman we need to worry about.'

Rigg was confused. 'Who then?'

'The dreamer. She'll be leading the sacrifice, and when we start the attack I've no idea what she might do.' Lowering her voice, Jael swung around in a circle, checking no one had snuck up on them. 'I've seen dreamers so powerful they can –' Stopping abruptly, she tried to prevent the memory of the Vale returning, though it was quickly before her as though she was living it again.

'Can what?'

'Kill with symbols and spells. I've seen them kill.'

Rigg thought about scoffing, though he saw how troubled the usually cocky queen looked. 'Though you're a dreamer, too, aren't you? You can stop her.'

Jael laughed, though she was soon whispering again. 'I see things, hear things. I've gone into trances and spoken to gods, but magic? No, give me a sword or a bow and I'll be useful, but spells?

I know nothing about them.' She scratched her head, fearing that might soon become a problem. Looking at Rigg, she saw his tension and tried to reassure him. 'I'll deal with the dreamer one way or another. Don't worry, I won't let her get in our way.'

***

It had been a fruitless, exhausting day for Bertel and Siggy, who had eventually given up on the man in the golden tunic and walked around Castala, searching for Edela. And as dusk painted the sky deepening shades of amber, they stopped outside a tavern to decide their next move.

Bertel had purchased two pots of what appeared to be some sort of bean stew with his last coins, regretting that he'd left Edela holding most of them. Still, that wasn't a worry Siggy needed, and he kept his fears about how he would feed them to himself.

Siggy felt like crying. 'Do you think they've already killed her?'

Looking down at his beaker of wine, Bertel thought about throwing it back in one big gulp, though he knew he'd quickly regret that. He took a sip instead. 'I'm not sure.' Just saying that made him shiver. 'Edela was adept at alluding them, so to have disappeared like that? I don't know.'

'That branded man from Bakkar... he said he wanted to kill her. That there was a price on her head.'

Bertel took another sip, resting his elbows on the table. 'They took her away,' he mused. 'If they'd intended to simply kill her, they would have burst in and killed us all, wouldn't they?'

Siggy shrugged. 'I want to try and sleep,' she decided, having had enough of the bean stew. It had been tasty, though she felt too distracted to eat any more. 'I need to dream. I've been trying to see something all day, but there are so many people and too much noise. We've looked everywhere, but I want to look inside my dreams.' She had become quieter as she spoke and now looked completely uncertain.

Unable to resist the temptation of his wine any longer, Bertel tipped the remainder of it down his throat, and wiping a hand over his mouth, he stood. 'We'll head back to our room then, but let's check the docks on the way. We haven't been there today. You never know, whoever took her might have made a hasty escape.'

Siggy looked horrified to think such a thing, but she nodded. 'Hopefully, we'll find something there.'

***

Edela hadn't seen Iker Rayas again.

She hadn't seen anyone. Not even with food.

She had carefully rationed her jug of water and still had a little left. The windowless room was becoming stuffier as the day turned to night. She tried imagining where she was. Somewhere in view of the setting sun, she thought. So, west?

Back aching, she attempted to get her bearings, though in the end, her thoughts tangled like a ball of yarn, and she couldn't unpick them. She was starving and tired, and the lack of both food and sleep had left her drained.

The symbols inside the fetters were stopping her seeing beyond her prison walls or using any magic to escape. She couldn't reach out to Siggy or Bertel, and she knew that Siggy wouldn't be able to find her.

Heart galloping, Edela started panicking.

Footsteps approached, and though she feared what that meant, she was also desperate for food and information.

Iker Rayas unlocked the door, stepping inside with a wooden

trencher. He placed it on the floor, eyeing the old woman sitting on the bed. 'You've been quiet in here. Thought I'd best come check whether you still lived.'

'I hardly think you'd worry either way. You did want me dead.' Edela didn't move from the bed, though the fishy aromas coming from the trencher had her belly growling.

'Still do. Though I'm not the one who gets to decide such matters. Not now. My mistress... well. We all answer to another, don't we? There's always someone above us.'

'I wouldn't know. I don't tend to go around kidnapping people for coins.'

Iker laughed, readjusting his filthy bandage. 'You think I need coins? That I'm scraping about to make my fortune?' He shook his head. 'No, old woman, I'm the son of a lord, a wealthy man of influence. Where I come from, I'm friends with a queen.'

Edela's surprise was impossible to mask. 'Is she your mistress, this queen?'

Realising that he'd said too much, Iker backed up to the door. 'Enjoy your meal, for who knows? It might be your last.'

'Wait!' Edela launched herself off the bed, desperate for more clues. 'You could earn a far greater fortune by releasing me. Perhaps your father is a wealthy man, but not you? In Osterland, you could be rich in your own right.'

Iker burst out laughing. 'But I thought you were a dreamer? Now I'm not sure why I have those fetters on you at all. You're obviously just a useless fucking crone!'

Edela didn't understand what he meant, though she feared it.

'We'll be leaving tomorrow, so best get some rest.' And with that, Iker turned back to the door. 'Your family can't help you now. No one can.'

Edela watched him leave with unblinking eyes, feeling like a fool.

A frightened old fool.

Why had she ever left Osterland?

Looking down at her hands, she saw the truth in Iker

Rayas' words: her skin, so mottled with age; her crooked fingers trembling.

The fetters trapping her.

Why had she ever left her family behind?

Head sinking, eyes closing, Edela feared she would never see them again.

***

Ronin and Dessalene enjoyed a private supper with Kalina that evening, eager to share their plans.

Though having heard them, Kalina was confused. 'But I thought you wanted Jael Furyck to remain here? Alive? I thought she was to live out her life as a slave?'

Slaves came and went from the table, removing bowls and spoons, refilling goblets, replacing carafes and napkins. More slaves hovered in the distance, dealing with flies and bugs, securing flapping curtains and relighting candles.

It was unusual for the city to experience a notable breeze, let alone a strong wind, though as the day ended, that wind was sweeping through the city all the way to the palace.

Hearing a door slam, Dessalene spun around, eyeing the slaves before answering her stepdaughter. 'We must adapt to circumstances as they change. Like the weather! It appears we may have challenges to confront tomorrow, though we will, Kalina. And sacrificing Jael Furyck will balance the scales you so abruptly tipped against us all. After Noor's murder and Arras Sikari's escape, I fear there is a shift. A dangerous one.'

'Dangerous?'

'Dessalene has discovered a plague,' Ronin explained.

Kalina rose in her chair before sitting back down in horror. '*Plague?*'

'I have Pye inquiring further, though the kitchen has been shut down.'

'What? *My* kitchen?' Kalina clutched her throat, staring at Dessalene, wondering if that's why her stepmother hadn't eaten her meal.

Dessalene looked nonplussed. 'There is nothing to fear! It is only one woman so far... that I know of.' She turned to Ronin, seeking his support.

'The sacrifice tomorrow is how we reset everything,' Ronin told his daughter. 'We will offer contrition and demonstrate our gratitude. Remember, Kalina, actions always have consequences. You killed Noor. You took a knife to Eyshar's seer.' Ronin did not lower his voice, for he cared little about the slaves; he didn't notice them at all. Reaching for his wine, he inhaled the fruity bouquet, swilling it in the goblet, imagining blood. He wondered if they were doing the right thing, killing the Furyck woman, though looking up, he smiled confidently at his wife.

Eyshar needed his thirst quenched.

And Jael Furyck's death was sure to please him.

***

Fires burned in braziers, lighting up the harbour, though Bertel remained wary. He'd already been jostled once, sensing that the man hadn't merely fallen against him but had been seeking to steal his pouch. He'd slipped his arm through Siggy's after that, keeping her close as they walked down the docks together. 'Those men appear to be working,' Bertel told her, seeing three men in similar dark tunics, two holding scrolls. 'We can ask if they've seen anything.' Moving with purpose and not seeing a man turn into his path, he immediately stumbled into him.

The burly man reeked of ale, unsteady on his feet. He spun

back to Bertel and swung for his head. Siggy screamed and Bertel ducked, thumping his fist into the man's belly. He'd reacted on instinct, quickly regretting it as his knuckles smashed into what felt like a wall of rock. The man appeared to be wearing many layers, masking his true physique, and it was only now that Bertel realised what a mistake he'd made.

Hand throbbing, he shook it by his side, stepping back as the big man sought to come for him again.

'No! Bertel!' Siggy cried in warning. '*Bertel!*' She glanced past him to those men with their scrolls. 'Please help!' Though the men remained where they were, showing no interest in intervening.

Bertel ducked and dodged the swinging fist, realising that with Siggy behind him, there was little to do but try and hold his own. They wouldn't be able to outrun this man, who soon had two friends flanking him. One made to move around the fighting pair, trying to grab Siggy. 'No!' Bertel yelled. 'Siggy! *Move!*'

He felt a sharp pain, then an explosion of heat as he fell to the pier.

***

At supper, Jael was pleased to see Alek return.

He looked pale as he sat down before her and Rigg with a small helping of stew that had been slopped into his bowl. Fish of some sort.

It smelled off.

Rigg eyed him with a crooked grin. 'Thought you'd be moving in with the logi now? Tucked up in bed, wearing one of their pretty robes?'

Alek laughed throatily. 'Well, it was one way to spend the day. They're certainly determined to get everything right tomorrow. It's the first funeral of a Noor on the isle, so they want to ensure everything goes to plan.'

Rigg yawned, not caring. 'Did you get anything to eat?'

'I wasn't especially hungry, though a few things here and there.'

'Fresh fruit, I bet,' Rigg sighed, looking down at the greyish dregs in his bowl. 'Dripping with sweet juice.' Closing his eyes, he saw himself biting into a black-red plum.

'Perhaps.' Alek didn't want to say any more. The logi had offered him many delicacies and treated him kindly, though he'd felt nauseous and tired, working hard just to breathe. Still, he smiled for his friends. 'I hear you've turned into a gardener now,' he said to Jael.

She showed him her black fingernails. 'And not a good one. Ask my grandmother. I was never made for digging in the dirt. I couldn't think of a worse way to pass the time.' Both men blinked at her. 'Well, perhaps I can,' she laughed wearily. 'I can't think straight. I need to go to bed.'

'What for?' Rigg wondered bitterly. 'You put your head down and someone will be kicking you awake one minute later. We may as well just stay here.'

Alek looked from one to the other, wondering if they were starting to get along.

'You do what you want,' Jael grumbled, eyes closing. 'But I'll take any sleep I can get. I have to find some way to stop that dreamer tomorrow.'

Alek nodded. 'She has an important role, presiding over the sacrifices. The seer mainly watches until his part. It's Dessalene Sardis who will lead his logi.'

Jael shivered, seeing a slave approaching their table. It was late, and she yawned, sensing him trying to meet her eye. She couldn't remember the man's name, though he'd always acted respectfully towards her, and even now he bobbed his head as he slid onto the bench beside Alek.

Everyone stared at him.

'Skarpi,' Rigg said. 'You've something to say?'

The black-haired Skarpi sat perfectly still, fearing he would get in trouble, wondering if he should take such a risk, but knowing what they were planning tomorrow, he feared he had no choice. 'I've had a message from our friend at the palace.'

Turning to him, Alek became tense. 'What message?'

Though Skarpi's eyes remained on Jael. 'They say you're going to be sacrificed tomorrow, my lady. Along with the animals. The queen intends to offer you to Eyshar.'

CHAPTER FORTY-ONE

Bertel couldn't hear anything.

He saw only shadows. Someone held his tunic, moving his head around.

He thought he heard a familiar voice.

Siggy?

No, no...

Head falling forward, he slid back into the darkness.

Siggy was panicking. 'We need to get him somewhere safe! To lie down. He needs...' She didn't know. Edela knew about that. And realising that both Bertel and Edela might die, she burst into tears.

Korri Torluffson put his arm around her. 'Don't worry, we'll carry him back to the ships. It's going to be alright, Siggy. Bertel's tougher than you think, he's just taken a knock to the head. That man was a mountain, though no match for my beauty,' he said with a nod to his bloody sword, with which he'd gutted the man who had sought to kill Bertel.

A sobbing Siggy nodded through her tears, surprised to see Zen arrive with more of Korri's men.

Upon seeing her, he pulled up. 'Siggy?'

She burst into tears again, happy to see him, though not quite understanding why they were all back in Castala.

'Let's head for the ships!' Korri called to his men. 'Zen, help Anders with Bertel.' He glanced around. 'And where's Edela?'

'Gone,' Siggy sniffed, immediately feeling even worse. 'We were trying to find her. All day. But... it's my... fault. She's been taken!'

Korri and his men turned towards the girl in horror. 'By who?'

'I think the same man from Bakkar. Iker Rayas. I... think it was him.' She blinked at Zen, who didn't look happy to hear that.

'Well, let's get Bertel on board and we'll think on what to do. Don't worry, we won't let anything happen to Edela.' He said it with a smile, though having lost men to those Siluran warriors in Bakkar, Korri felt worried by the thought of confronting them again. And after a disaster in the desert, he was down even more men than before. Still, he kept smiling as he ushered Siggy towards the nearest pier, following behind those men who had picked up an unconscious Bertel, carrying him between them.

He thought of Edela, remembering her mischievous blue eyes and generous smile, knowing he would do everything in his power to find her.

***

Jael finally closed her mouth.

It had dropped open at Skarpi's words, and she'd been unable to say anything in response.

Though a frantic Alek and Rigg were busy pressing Skarpi for more information.

'How did Kito hear this?' Alek wanted to know. 'Everything we've been told is that Jael is to be kept alive. A slave for life.'

Rigg nodded with sharp eyes, looking from Skarpi to a clearly shocked Jael. 'Who told Kito?'

'He has a woman in the palace. She heard it tonight at supper. The queen and her father were talking. He announced it.'

Jael blew out a breath. 'Well, that changes things.'

'For you, maybe,' Rigg told her. 'We still have to mount an attack. I can lead, as before.'

Alek turned to him in horror. 'What? You'll just move on past that, will you? Just forget about Jael?'

Rigg didn't understand. 'If the king himself wants to sacrifice her, what can we do to stop it?'

For a time, Jael couldn't think of anything to say.

To be sacrificed? It seemed too strange to be real.

Her unsettling dream about Eadmund and Ayla returned, though she quickly blinked it away. Leaning forward, she interrupted the arguing men. 'We stick to the plan. I'll still lead us.'

Rigg snorted. 'I thought you'd have some understanding of sacrifices and how they work.'

'We don't offer human sacrifices where I come from,' Jael snarled. 'Perhaps that's only a Hestian thing?'

Rigg bared his teeth, carrying on with pleasure now. 'Well, let me tell you then. You'll have to be bathed, prepared, dressed in special robes. They'll give you things to addle your mind. You won't even know where you are. I've seen it. When they bring a human to sacrifice, they're usually no longer present. Not in their minds, at least.'

Jael remained defiant. She remembered the tunnel and Eadmund calling her name. She would not fail this time.

This time, she would go home.

Her dream of Oss taunted her, but she shut it out with a slamming door.

Standing up, jaw clenched, she moved past Rigg. 'I'm going to bed. We can talk more in the morning.'

The three men stared after her in silence.

'She can't die,' Alek said, feeling his hopes leaving with her. 'I don't believe she can die. I was promised that she would get us out of here.'

'By who?' Rigg wondered, though Alek didn't say as he

stood, following Jael to the sleeping hall.

***

Waking from a nightmare, a disturbed Thorgils turned to Eadmund, who was sharpening a sword in no need of sharpening beside him. At sea, there was no real sense of time. No birds, no people. Once darkness fell, it was simply night. 'You ever planning on getting some sleep?' he yawned, rubbing aching eyes. 'You'll need it.'

'I expect I will, though I want to be ready. There's a lot to work through in my mind. How it will go. What will happen.'

'Well, I can already tell you that,' his friend grinned. 'We'll free your wife, free those slaves, become heroes. She'll grumble her thanks but secretly be pleased. That sort of thing.'

Eadmund smiled. 'I like how simple you make everything. Sounds entirely possible.'

'It does, and why not? Nothing more than we've done before. We've done the impossible, Eadmund. You know that. We've been up against creatures and dreamers and gods, so we can certainly do this.'

'We can,' Eadmund agreed without confidence, then seeing Thorgils still staring at him, unconvinced, he straightened up, laying his sword across his lap and his whetstone on the deck. 'I've never understood how I ended up with a friend like you.'

Thinking it was an insult, Thorgils readied his own, though Eadmund's hand was soon on his shoulder.

'You've always stood beside me. All my life, Thorgils Svanter. I wouldn't be here without you. Wouldn't have a chance to save my wife.'

Thorgils was too surprised to speak.

'And when we get home, I'm going to build you a new house.

The finest on Oss.'

'What? But what about the timber? You were saving it for more ships.'

'We can import more from Brekka. We'll need it to build you something big enough for all your children. Though perhaps we'll have to build Isaura her own house so she can lock you out!'

Thorgils couldn't imagine such a thing. 'We've decided to stop at ten.'

'Ten children?' Eadmund was incredulous. 'Your poor wife.'

Thinking of his wife, Thorgils sat back with a contented sigh. 'She likes children, so who am I to stop the woman? I can't blame her, of course, wanting to be surrounded by little Svanters.'

Eadmund sat back himself, resting his head on the gunwale, eyes on the stars. And for a moment, he was back on Oss, walking around the fort in moonlight.

'What's your favourite star?' Jael asked him, looking up at the sky, trying to spot her own.

'Atoya,' Eadmund told her. 'It was my mother's favourite.' He pointed. 'Past the anchor, left a little.'

Jael nodded, moving closer to him, shoulders touching. 'That's mine,' she said, pointing east. 'Not one, but five. In Brekka, we call it Furia's Axe. My father always told me that's where Furia watches over us.'

'You Furycks even have your own stars?' Eadmund laughed. 'Well, us poor Islanders just have to adopt the stars we like. The gods don't care about us. They don't see us at all.'

'Though Furia is watching over you,' Jael promised, coming around to face her husband, placing her cold hands on his face. 'So now you know. Whenever we're apart, I'll be watching you from the stars too.'

'Mmmm, now I know,' Eadmund breathed, kissing her.

Blinking open his eyes and hearing Thorgils snoring beside him, Eadmund searched the night sky for any sign of Furia's Axe. Would he see it here, this far from home?

Nothing looked familiar as he searched and searched.

Eventually, heart sinking, he gave up, eyes too heavy to keep open. And slipping his sword into its scabbard and his whetstone back into his pouch, he rested his head against the gunwale and closed his eyes.

***

An uptight Jael had gone to sleep with Dessalene in mind. Lying on her stomach, right hand balled into a fist, she had held onto her memory of the dreamer, seeking to understand what the woman was planning.

To sacrifice her?

She had thought she was part of a game she couldn't understand.

So now to just kill her?

It made no sense.

'The Furycks are not who they claim to be,' hissed a voice. 'Furia's famed line is all a lie! A trick!'

Jael didn't know the voice.

She felt the heat of flames, inhaling ashy smoke, and squinting into the distance, she saw a great trail of hot lava flowing down a mountain.

A volcano?

She sought to draw more information from the blurry shapes, though the silhouettes and shadows teased her, revealing nothing further.

She started walking, bare feet on warm sand, quickly sinking into it.

'And they will pay!' the voice called as it returned, now loud enough to drown out every other thought. 'I will make them pay!'

And soon that sand was crumbling away, and Jael lost her footing, sinking into the darkness.

***

Dessalene slid out of bed, hurrying on her robe. Turning to look at her sleeping husband, she frowned. Her dreams had been fraught, disturbed by hideous visions of plague-ridden bodies lining the streets.

Shivering in disgust, she swept out of their shared bedchamber into her private room down the hall, where she was surprised to find Pye sprawled in the middle of the bed, sound asleep. 'What are you doing!' she shouted, not caring who she disturbed. 'Sleeping in my bed? In here? Get up! Get out!'

Pye screamed in fright, crawling up to the headboard, then seeing that he wasn't being assaulted by a ghoulish demon but a screeching dreamer in a silk robe, he sighed. 'I came looking for you, Mistress. To tell you more.'

'Though I forbade you to come near me again, Eppypyrus! And certainly that included not rolling around in my sheets like a disobedient puppy!' Stepping back to the door, Dessalene was seething.

'There have been more deaths!' Pye called. 'I thought you should know. We must leave this place at once!'

'*We*? You and your friends the slaves? But when I leave, you will have to remain with them.'

'No! I am not sick!'

'You are not sick *yet*, and perhaps you will not be touched by it, but I won't have you on a ship, Pye. I won't bring that plague with us. The king and I will leave together, and you will remain here.'

'To die?'

Dessalene laughed. 'How dramatic! I'm sure you have nothing to fear, and besides, you are due a break. A rest. So take your time here, helping Kalina, and I will allow you back when the plague has passed.'

Pye dropped to his knees now, staring at his mistress in

horror. 'I have helped you.'

'We have helped each other, toad, and we will again in the future. Though for now, you must go.' Pulling open the door, Dessalene motioned with a hand. 'Do not fret, little Pye. If you live, I am sure we will meet again.'

A still-stunned Pye shuffled off the bed, moving like a reluctant child, dragging his feet towards an impatient Dessalene, who left the door wide open and hurried to the other side of the chamber, far away from him.

'You are wrong,' he told her. 'This is wrong. I am not a slave. I never was.'

'Perhaps, but without me you are no more than a lump of misshapen parts for someone to abuse and use. I found you and made you into something more useful. And you have been, though now I want you out of my sight. As far away as possible.' She turned her back on him, heading for her altar, though her ears were open in case Pye decided to become hysterical.

Though hearing nothing, she soon turned around.

Seeing that he had gone.

**

Bertel woke up feeling strange, having no idea where he was. Not on land, he soon realised, quickly panicking. And standing up, he almost toppled over. The pain in his head was excruciating, and he stumbled, reaching for the gunwale.

He tried recalling what had happened.

Those men... and Siggy!

He turned, blinking open aching eyes. He had to find Siggy, he had to get off the ship, he had to –

A hand on his arm had him jumping.

'Bertel?'

Bertel bit his tongue, swinging around to the familiar face of Korri Torluffson. 'What are you doing here? How did I...?' Pain crashed in on every side of Bertel's head, and he fell against Korri. 'Oh, I...'

'Let's sit you down,' Korri said kindly. 'After what you've been through, I'm not sure you should be walking around.'

'I don't understand,' Bertel kept repeating. 'You were... in the desert.' He relaxed his limbs, letting Korri ease him back down onto a fur. They were on *Sea Queen*, moored in the harbour, Bertel soon realised, smelling the goat and hearing the chickens. 'But what happened?'

Korri shook his head. 'We were attacked, robbed, not long after passing through a village. I suspect we were part of a plot. The villagers had welcomed us in, shared a meal with us, then after we left, they sent warriors to track us down.' He sighed heavily, joining Bertel on the deck. 'They came upon us at night, took everything we had, killed Amos and Selvi. It was some battle, rolling around in the sand, trying to fight them off. Eventually, they took off on horses, moving with speed. I had injured men, I...' Korri dropped his head to his hands. 'I lost everything I earned in Bakkar. All those coins I was going to buy the stones with.'

Bertel was horrified. 'But you... have more to sell? Here?'

'I had some ivory, a bit of tin. Not much, but the men I left behind to guard the ships stole everything. I've been shat on left and right. Any gods who may have seen fit to favour me have gone elsewhere. I'm entirely ruined.'

'I'm so sorry. That's terrible to hear. But I... how did I end up on your ship? And where's Siggy?'

'She's sleeping over there. See?' Korri pointed to where Siggy had fallen asleep beside Zen.

Bertel nodded. 'And me?'

'Well, you seemed to have gotten yourself into a bit of bother. We were returning from a tavern and heard Siggy calling your name. And just in time. That man had taken his full share of drink. He was aiming to kill you.'

Bertel winced. The pain in his head was sharp, painting slashes of darkness over every memory he sought to reclaim. 'I'm very grateful, Korri. It seems that we've found each other again at just the right time.'

'You mean Edela?'

Bertel nodded. 'Did Siggy tell you what happened? About the amulet?'

'She tried to, though the poor girl was so upset that she didn't make a lot of sense. She blames herself for Edela going missing.'

'Well, she was lured into a trap by some malevolent creature, though I would hardly expect a child to see through that sort of game. She's lucky to be alive.'

'And Edela? You think it's the same man from Bakkar?'

Bertel became distracted, hoping for something to drink. 'His name is Iker Rayas, and he... wants to kill her. I don't know why everyone wants to kill Edela, but they seem to and I...'

'Soon as the sun's up, I'll send my men out. We'll scour this place until we find her,' Korri promised, smiling at the old man. 'Now, do you want to try sleeping again, or would you like some ale?'

Bertel peered at him, feeling oddly emotional. 'I think you must have been sent by the gods. You're a surprisingly good man.'

'Surprisingly?'

'Well, we haven't encountered many allies on our travels,' Bertel sighed, thinking of Elmer Falson. And once again his mind returned to Edela.

Standing up, Korri turned to where he'd last seen an ale jug. 'Rest now. I'll get you something to drink, and in the morning, we'll go and find your dreamer.'

***

In her dream, Jael stood on the sacrifice platform in bare feet, wearing her familiar grey dress.

She turned, seeing Dessalene Sardis flinging drops of blood from a switch she'd dipped in a golden bowl.

The dreamer moved around Jael, eyes blinking slowly.

Everything was moving slowly, Jael saw.

Those drops, flung through the air, the sound of her heartbeat in her ears.

Like hooves clopping, slow and steady.

Though not calm, she thought, tension rising.

As the dreamer moved past her, she saw the men sitting on tall stone chairs. Eight dressed in red, and the man in the centre in white.

Inesh Seppo.

He stared at her, a great wooden staff in one hand, its gnarled pommel like a claw that he rolled his fingers over and stood. Stepping towards Jael, his face oddly stern, no hint of those smiling eyes now, he stopped and lifted his staff, pointing it at her.

Jael cried out, kicked in the back.

Eyes bursting open, she jerked forward, away from that boot.

'Up! Up! We have a funeral to prepare for!' Kosta bellowed, striding away from Jael, kicking more of the sleeping slaves awake. 'What do you think this is? A day off?'

In fact, the slaves had been promised this special day off, though Kosta had seen that, despite their valiant efforts, the area around the tower and the walkway to the temple were in urgent need of attention.

Dawn hadn't broken, but Kosta feared that his future hinged on this day, and so did Krissia, who had sent Quint from their house with a flaming lantern, urging him to ensure that everything was perfect. Quint had woken his father-in-law, who had joined him in his wagon without complaint. As soon as the sacrifice was over and the new Noor had been anointed, Kosta would press forward with his marriage to the queen.

And then everything would change.

'Up! Now!' he barked, kicking Rigg, who'd been slow to move, catching his knee. A yelping Rigg rolled away, soon up on his feet, one eye open. He glanced around the sleeping hall, seeing Jael but no Alek.

His bed was empty.

Forcing open his reluctant left eye, Rigg approached the slave queen. 'Where's Alek?'

Jael swung around. 'I don't know.' She saw Quint's offsider, Berros. 'Have you seen Alek?'

'Outside.'

Rigg felt relieved.

'Surprised he's still standing. You didn't hear? He couldn't breathe in the night. Kept coughing. Thought we'd have to carry him away.'

Rigg turned to Jael, who looked shocked; she hadn't heard a thing.

'There'll be no food until I'm happy with how the courtyard looks!' Kosta bellowed from the doorway. 'So if you want to eat you'll have to –' A slave interrupted him, much to his annoyance. 'What?' He bent down to the small man, who spoke with purpose but softly, conscious of the early hour despite the rising noise in the sleeping hall.

Kosta frowned, making the man repeat himself before turning around to find Jael. 'Our favourite slave is going to the palace!'

'The sacrifice,' Rigg mouthed, seeing the messenger coming Jael's way. 'They'll prepare you.'

Ignoring him, Jael didn't move. 'You need to talk to Alek.'

Rigg nodded.

'Nothing changes,' she insisted quickly. 'I've a knife in my mattress. Take it and hide it on yourself. Use it if you need to. We keep to the plan. If Alek or I...' Jael was almost drunk with tiredness, though she worked to order her thoughts. 'Steal Quint's shell and wait for my signal.'

Rigg stared at her. 'Alek believes in you. No idea why he

trusts a Furyck, but he does, so you can't let him down, slave queen.'

Jael heard his thoughts. He was nervous, worried it would all go wrong now.

'I won't,' she promised, remembering Sunni. She had been so tired, so busy that she hadn't thought about the girl in days. Lifting her head, she pushed back her shoulders, feeling blood trickling down her back where Kosta had kicked her. 'Enjoy your day off!' she called loudly. 'I look forward to seeing you all soon!'

Reaching the glowering commander, Jael sensed that he was ready to kick her again, but knowing she was going to the palace, he held himself back.

'You think you'll return in a pretty dress, with the queen as your new friend? That they'll have changed their minds about you, and now everything will be flowers and cakes?'

'No,' Jael assured him. 'No, I don't think so at all.' She turned to Quint. 'Good luck today.'

He looked surprised to receive her good wishes, as did Kosta, who scowled after her as she took one last look at Rigg and those slaves standing in the sleeping hall, peering at her with tension in their swollen eyes.

And swallowing down her doubts, Jael smiled broadly and strode outside into the blazing sun.

PART FIVE

Homecoming

CHAPTER FORTY-TWO

Fyn had been awake for hours, and finally seeing the first hints of dawn, he poured himself something to drink. Realising that the dreamer was awake, he brought her a cup too.

She wasn't thirsty but took it anyway.

Otter rubbed against Fyn's leg, and smiling at the cat, he bent down to pat him. He'd discovered that he didn't hate cats as much as he'd thought, which had surprised him after a lifetime of avoiding them. Though Otter was a different kind of cat, he realised. There was something about him that Fyn enjoyed. He was almost human in the way he knew when to comfort and when to sound the alarm. Like a dog, Fyn decided, thinking of Ido and Vella.

'Have you finished?' Mattie wondered, eyeing him.

'Finished?' Fyn straightened up.

'With Otter. I need your help here.'

A surprised Fyn blinked at her. 'With what?'

'My trance. If I'm to bind the wind...' She tried not to roll her eyes, knowing that achieving anything was impossible if you kept telling yourself you couldn't. 'Kolarov's misplaced his usha root, so I have to fall into a trance on my own. I've got these herbs from Hest, and Meena Dragos showed me some things, but I need your help feeding them into the brazier. And lighting the brazier. And watching Otter. I need -'

'I'll help,' Fyn promised. 'You can sit down and prepare, and

I'll get everything ready.'

Mattie nodded, twisting the rope around her hand. 'It may not work.'

'No, though it's not essential. Useful, I imagine, though the wind does what the wind does. We'll be fine either way.'

Mattie stared at him before looking down at the rope, trying to pull some useful tidbit from her memory. She thought of those sneering elders and secretive dreamers, none of whom had warmed to her; her mother, who had never listened to her or cared that she was a dreamer.

And her husband, Theo.

He had believed in her, she remembered with a smile.

He had held her in his arms and promised that she could do anything.

***

Going to the palace was the last thing Jael wanted to do, though as the sun rose, promising another scorching day, absent last night's wind, she was pulled out of a wagon and pushed up the steps into the royal palace. Four doormen greeted her with suspicious scowls, ushering her through the open doors, where the slaves were already hard at work, washing the floor and dusting every surface in preparation for their mistress' arrival.

Nothing Jael had dreamed had been helpful, she realised as her thoughts rushed to the forefront of her mind. She had hoped to find something useful about the dreamer, something she could use, but apart from becoming certain she was going to be sacrificed, nothing more had been illuminated.

'There you are!' an elegantly dressed Dessalene called, having been up early, preparing for her departure to the temple. 'Our little slave queen, ready for her big day!' Coming closer, the dreamer's smile faltered. 'Though I'm not sure we have enough time to prepare you. The state of that hair and your skin. It's hideous!'

'Prepare me?' Jael attempted a look of confusion.

'You have a very important role to play,' Dessalene explained. 'In the ritual. You will be our guest of honour!'

Jael stared at her, trying to read the dreamer's thoughts but finding only resistance. 'Guest of honour?'

Ronin Sardis strode in from the dining hall, devouring a slice of sesame cake. His eyes flicked to Jael Furyck, then back to his wife. 'I am having my doubts, Dessalene. Are we sure about this?'

The dreamer nodded, brushing sesame seeds out of his beard. 'Yes. A Furyck? Of course. There could be nothing more appetising to a hungry god.'

'I don't understand,' Jael tried. 'Why am I here?'

'Because we are going to sacrifice you, which makes today the last day of your life!' Dessalene announced. 'It is an honour, such an honour to be chosen as a sacrifice to noble Eyshar.'

Jael stared at her. 'And you think, what? That your god will forgive the murder of your seer if you kill me? That he'll simply forget what the queen did, stabbing the old man like that?' Both Ronin and Dessalene stiffened, smiles vanishing, and pleased about that, Jael carried on. 'I doubt your god is a fool. Have you met him?'

Dessalene looked confused. 'Met a god? What are you talking about? Are you suggesting *you* have met a god?'

'I have spoken to Daala, Mother of All. And Furia. Darroc too. I've met a number of gods.'

Shock pried open Dessalene's pursed lips, sharpening her cheekbones. 'Daala? Why? Why did she come to you?'

'To help me. To protect me.'

Ronin narrowed his pale green eyes. 'Why should we believe you?'

'I don't care if you do. Do with it what you will. If you wish to kill me, then I welcome it. I give you thanks for it. Do you truly think I'd rather live here, under the thumb of your spoiled daughter, watching good men and women die around me? And all for your vanity? No, kill me and bleed me, let your god drink my blood and eat my flesh, but know that you will never appease him. You killed his seer. There will be no forgiveness. Your god will destroy this isle and everything you've worked so hard for. Today.'

Ranuf Furyck had always encouraged his daughter to hold her tongue, though Ranuf Furyck wasn't about to be sacrificed, so Jael had to use her only weapon to hand.

She couldn't read Ronin's or Dessalene's thoughts.

Though she could see their faces.

A furious Ronin grabbed her by the tunic, tugging her close enough that she could smell honey on his breath. 'You think yourself better than me? Than us? That somehow your death will be avenged? You smug bitch. But you're just the beginning. My vow is to kill every Furyck. Every living one. And when you burn, and your bones are crushed up and dropped into a hole, buried and forgotten, I will take my ships to sea and tear your brother's head from his body. One brother, then two. And then I will find your daughter.' Twisting her tunic around his hand, Ronin spat at her. 'I gift you that, Jael Furyck. The knowledge that those you love will die, and so will your name. I will wipe the Furycks out.' Releasing his hand, Ronin pushed Jael back until she stumbled against one of the guards.

Heart thumping, she watched as he smiled at her, nodded at his wife and strode away.

***

Arras stood near Bolder, helping the helmsman navigate the treacherous Arc of Herash and its dangerous waters, while

Kolarov recounted the many disasters it had caused to an annoyed Thorgils.

'You need to go and sit down!' Thorgils snapped at him, and not taking no for an answer, and with one eye on the sea swirling like ale in a cup, he shepherded the explorer back to the stern.

Mattie heard his complaining as she tried to push herself deep into a trance.

She was worried about the sea, too, feeling the ship almost falling away beneath her. She thought about Fyn breathing next to her and her cat, fearing he wasn't safe. If only she'd thought to leave him in Hest with the very distracting Kolarov.

There was her need to find a way to bind the wind, her constant fear that Jael Furyck was already dead.

And the isle.

She couldn't stop thinking about what awaited her on S'ala Nis.

Death.

The rasping voice in her ears promised death.

'You know magic is for the depraved, don't you, girl? The desperate and depraved who have lost sight of the gods! They cling to the darkness, seeking to mask their weakness! They cower in shadows, afraid to live in the light like those who embrace the true gods. You understand that, don't you, girl?'

Mattie trembled at the memory of Mirna – a vicious elder who had whipped her and a friend when she'd found them trying to make magic. Just that once. Mattie's friend had found an old spell and thought to try it. And though Mattie had been doubtful that such things were even possible, she'd eagerly gone along. Now Inga had been sent home from the temple in disgrace, and she was about to join her.

The old woman had a stain on her robe, Mattie noticed, a dark moustache framing her scowling lips. She was not like the other elders, most of whom tried to offer guidance and help. Mirna had cruel intentions; she liked to cause pain.

Mattie's eyes were drawn to that stain as Mirna snapped at

her, spittle flying from moist lips. Berries, she thought. The old woman had eaten berries for breakfast, yet as the elder overseeing the kitchen, she ensured that the dreamer novices received only watery porridge.

A red berry. Dark, deep red.

Like blood, Mattie thought, transfixed by the stain, watching it spread over Mirna's sagging breasts, dying her robe red.

Blood.

The woman grabbed her chest as though in pain, face contorting before her, and looking down, Mattie saw that her hand was in a fist and she was squeezing the words from Mirna's throat. And then her heart. She would crush it, squeeze and squeeze until there was no life left. No heartbeat. No blood. All of it gone.

She hated the old woman, who had made every day a nightmare since she'd arrived.

Blood and death.

White robe.

Old woman.

Mirna sank to the flagstones like a bird falling from the sky. A slow twirling dance to the end. To earth.

And where would she go?

A cruel old woman like that?

Mattie's fingers released their hold on the spell, her arm falling back to her side, now staring at the body of an old man, blood seeping through his white robe, eyes fixed open. He called to her, his lips never moving, though he said her name.

Mattie bent down to him, closer and closer, until she could hear his final whispers as he breathed them into her ear.

***

Jael was hurried through the palace towards the baths.

Dessalene accompanied her, soon stopped by the queen, who had just emerged from the baths herself, hair unbound, loose and damp on her shoulders.

'What is this?' Kalina wondered, looking from Jael to her stepmother. 'Why is she here?'

'Well, we can hardly offer up this piece of filthy rubbish to Eyshar. No, dearest, we must purify her first. Cleanse all the grime from her body, dress her in something more... appropriate.'

'And then?' Kalina asked, temper sparking.

'She will join the procession. We will make her walk to her death!'

Kalina had presided over more than one human sacrifice in her time, and she narrowed her eyes. 'And will you give her anything?'

'Give her what? Something to take away the terror and the pain? To make it easier? To take her somewhere else?' Dessalene sneered. 'Oh no, but your father has insisted that she feel everything. This mighty warrior here? She is more than used to pain and fear. I'm sure there's no one better equipped to deal with what awaits!' And needing to prepare herself for the sacrifice, Dessalene left Jael Furyck in the hands of Kalina's most useful slave, Mali, and four capable looking guards. 'I must leave for the temple,' she told her stepdaughter as Jael was led away.

'Now?' Kalina stared after the disappearing slave queen, reminded of Arras and her broken heart. 'Why now?'

'Inesh Seppo and I have much to do. We will be preparing together.'

'Though you have all day.'

'Which just may be long enough!' Dessalene laughed, spirits rising. She thought of Pye and the plague cases, which had already exploded since he'd first alerted her. It would get so much worse, she saw, deciding to speak to Ronin before she left for the temple.

To ensure their safety, they could not linger when it was all done.

***

Mattie emerged from her trance with an open mouth, turning to stare at Fyn, who was stroking Otter beside her.

He saw that she was no longer clutching the rope in her hand. 'What happened? Did you bind the wind?'

Mattie just stared at him, visions rushing back to her in gruesome colour.

Mirna's death.

Then the old seer; the man who had flown off the temple.

Noor of the Dragon Blood Tree.

Scrambling to her feet, mouth still open, she swayed towards Kolarov. Her mind felt stuffed with cloth, and instead of hearing the familiar creaking of the ship and a bellowing Bolder, she heard her own thoughts and her racing heart.

Kolarov saw the look in her eyes, and rising to his feet, he grabbed her hands as she started tipping to one side. 'What did you see? Mattie, my dear, do sit and tell me.' Edging the dreamer towards his chest, Kolarov kept a firm hold of her hands, tottering before her.

'I... there was a... Noor of the Dragon Blood Tree. I saw him!'

'The old seer?'

Mattie nodded. 'He was murdered!'

Kolarov spun around in horror. 'Commander!' he called. 'Come! You must come!'

Arras left Bolder behind, moving to the stern, soon joined by a curious Fyn. 'What's happened?'

'The dreamer says Noor of the Dragon Blood Tree was murdered!'

Arras stared at him in horror before turning to Mattie.

'By the queen. He told me. The queen killed him.'

Arras' mouth gaped open. 'She will be cursed. The isle will be cursed.'

'Why did you see this?' Fyn wondered. 'How does it help us?'

Mattie stared at him, shaking her head. 'I... because I know where Jael is going to be. The seer told me that to appease their god, they will... sacrifice her.'

***

As the slaves cleared the roads around the temple and hastily planted the last garden beds, Rigg received word from the palace that Jael was being prepared for the sacrifice.

The messenger brought more than tidings about Jael, though. He had come armed with a list of concerns from those allies around the isle. For as news about Jael spread, there was panic, no one knowing whether the revolt would proceed as planned. There had been rumours about Alek taking ill too.

'He'll be fine,' Rigg told the messenger. 'That man's been hanging on by his fingernails for years. You think he'll just slip away now? Today of all days? That's not Alek Orlan. He'll see this day through like the rest of us.'

'But Kito wants to know if it's still happening. Word's spreading fast that it's over.'

A furious Rigg grabbed the man by the shoulders. 'That's a lie. Jael and Alek and I... we're not giving in or giving up. That woman has a plan.'

'To start a revolt while being sacrificed?'

Rigg thought of all the things he wanted to say about Jael Furyck, biting them down. 'You think she wants to die like a goat? Throat slit and tossed away? That she'd let that be her legacy? A Furyck?' Rigg shook his head. 'You go back and tell the truth. Nothing changes. I'll blow the signal, and when you hear it, you will attack, and we'll all be with you as planned.'

'We have this one chance.'

Rigg agreed. 'So go back and tell everyone. We proceed as planned.'

***

Dessalene watched her husband being dressed by two male slaves. At nearly sixty, Ronin had the body of a man some twenty years younger. He was still muscular, his arms and torso defined and hard. She smiled. 'There is a ship moored in the cove.'

Looking around, Ronin was puzzled. 'Of course. There's always a ship moored in the cove.'

'Though you need to send a crew to ready it. I wish to depart in haste after the sacrifice,' Dessalene purred. 'We cannot linger here. Your fleet will leave quickly, but we must leave soonest of all, my love.'

'Because of the...' Ronin turned, becoming aware of the slaves. '*Issue* Pye uncovered?'

'Exactly.'

'But Kalina?'

'She is the queen.' Dessalene hardened her expression and her voice. 'It would not do for her to leave her people. Not in a time of... crisis. I see no problem there. Nothing to concern you.'

Ronin narrowed his eyes, feeling concerned, though in all their years together, Dessalene had never let him down. She saw danger, opportunities, and she'd always kept him moving forward, towards his destiny. 'I shall have the ship readied.'

'Good, now I must hurry away to the temple. Inesh Seppo appears diligent enough, though I have concerns about any man being able to organise such an event. I doubt he's even out of bed!' She kissed her husband with a sigh. 'Until we meet again, sweet love, enjoy the day. You have waited a lifetime for this. To see a Furyck die?' Dessalene smiled, looking forward to that herself. 'Now the wait is finally over, and soon you will watch that woman bleed for your god. You will see, Ronin. I will show you.'

***

Jael needed a plan.

Head back, eyes closed as she enjoyed the cool water of the deep pool she'd been forced into, she saw Aleksander. Her Aleksander.

He had come to her in that tiny hole, urging her to live. To fight.

She saw his dark eyes now, peering at her. She felt pressure on her hand, a soothing voice in her ear, and then a different pair of eyes. Hazel and mischievous. Sometimes sad. Always full of love.

For her.

'Are you ready to fight?' Eadmund asked.

'Fight?' Jael smiled. 'I was born to fight.'

'I'm not leaving you behind,' he told her. 'Not this time. This time I will take you home.'

She thought of her dream of Eadmund with Ayla, and his face faded, plunging her into darkness again.

'I was born to fight,' came her echoing voice.

Though she heard someone laughing now.

***

Arras didn't know what to make of Mattie's vision, though piecing it together with everything else she'd told him, he made a guess. 'I can't say why Kalina may have killed Noor, except that he promised her things that didn't happen. She has a history of killing those who displease her. A lack of hesitation about it too. It's why I sought to escape with Nico.'

Eadmund and Thorgils had joined their huddle now, both

men keeping quiet, eager to hear more.

'I had meetings with Noor about his funeral,' Arras went on. 'We discussed what would happen, the ceremonies, and what would be required. He wanted the transition to be seamless. He had his successor picked out. I met him –'

'So the funeral you saw is actually happening?' Thorgils interrupted.

Mattie nodded. 'And Jael will be sacrificed.'

Thorgils turned to Arras. 'Was that part of the seer's plan? A sacrifice?'

'Yes, of course, and in return, the god would bless his successor.'

'And now the sacrifice is to be Jael?' Thorgils' brow furrowed with worry.

'Which means she's alive,' Eadmund told them, working to find a place where he could set aside his fears and simply cope with leading these men into battle. 'She's alive, which means she has a chance.'

'More than a chance,' Arras told him. 'She has us. We just need to get there in time. I walked through every step of that sacrifice with Noor.'

'Why?' Kolarov wondered. 'Why you? I thought you were the Commander of the Waves? Though surely the temple belongs to the Commander of the Rocks?'

Arras offered a wry smile. 'Well, Argo Kosta's not a man for details or delicacy. Noor didn't like or trust him.'

'And who will kill Jael?' Kolarov asked, blinking at Eadmund. 'At least, who will... try to?'

Arras thought about that. 'There were to be many sacrifices. There is a stone ditch, a moat. The blood would run into it, offered to the god. The carcasses would be roasted on spits and boiled in great vats, and everyone would share in the meal.'

Fyn grimaced.

'Arras!' Bolder called from the steering oar.

'If I think of anything else, I'll find you,' Arras promised. 'But don't worry, we have a clearer picture now, and it helps us.'

'How?' Eadmund wanted to know.

'Because everyone will gather at the temple grounds. The procession will lead there. It helps us.'

Eadmund stared after him, doubts squawking like angry birds, pecking away at his confidence until it hung around him in tatters. Though he turned back to his men with a nod. 'Nothing changes. We proceed as planned.'

CHAPTER FORTY-THREE

Argo Kosta brought his daughter to the palace.

'I thought Krissia could attend to you,' he told the confused queen with a smile.

Smiling didn't suit him, Kalina noticed, wishing he would stop. 'Of course. I would be delighted for your company, Krissia. We will be family after the wedding, so it makes sense to become more... acquainted.'

Krissia beamed, as ill-suited to joy as her father.

'You will accompany my father in the procession?' Kalina asked the commander, motioning to the balcony where her slaves had prepared a selection of delicacies to break her fast.

'Yes, I am to see him next.'

'He intends to depart the isle after the sacrifice,' Kalina told him. Kosta was boorish and grotesque, though with both Noor and Arras gone, she felt the need to lean on someone. 'He will not stay for our wedding.'

Kosta was surprised and slightly offended. 'No?'

'My father is a very busy man.'

Busy doing what, Kosta wondered, though he didn't ask. 'I imagine he is,' he said instead, holding out a chair for the queen and then his daughter before taking a seat himself.

Kalina watched him closely.

Everything he did appeared clumsy and unnatural, and he sat down looking uncomfortable. He was used to fine things but not bred for it.

And it showed.

'Though after he leaves, we will have matters of urgency to attend to before our marriage ever takes place,' Kalina warned discreetly, waiting for the slaves to leave.

Krissia looked concerned but left her father to enquire.

Kosta's eyes were on the queen's slender hand, raising a small beaker of wine. 'Urgent matters?'

'There is a... plague.'

Krissia gasped, sitting back in horror, eyes immediately seeking her father.

Who responded with calm assurance. 'Bad news, of course, though nothing we haven't faced before. I am sure the sacrifices to Eyshar will reestablish goodwill with the god and that he'll once again bless us with his favour.'

Remembering how she had murdered the seer, Kalina was doubtful. She wanted to confess everything, to ask for forgiveness.

There had been so many missteps...

Kosta placed his hand over the queen's. 'Do not worry, Kalina. After today, Eyshar will return only good fortune to you and me, and our family to come.'

***

Dessalene's carriage was waiting. She had been reminded of that twice now, though she'd made a return to her chamber, feeling the call of her altar.

And her mistress.

Throwing out the slaves making the bed and remembering how that vile toad had thought to soil them, she hurried to pull the curtains closed, needing darkness.

It was not offered.

The sun was a beacon of light, forcing its way through the almost sheer curtains. Though refusing to be unsettled by that, Dessalene removed a candle from a flaming candelabra, lighting the tiny lamps on her altar. And when she was done, she left the candle burning in a dish of frankincense, soon sending whirls of smoke into the air.

Now she sat on the floor, resting on her heels.

Closing her eyes, her breaths, at first trapped and tense, lengthened and as she steadied her breathing and calmed her mind, she heard a voice.

'Vainglorious Dessalene! So concerned with her own needs, so certain in her power and magnificence that she doesn't think to look around. To look away from that prize she is so desperate to claim for herself.'

'Mistress, I –'

'You will not speak! You will only listen. To *me*.'

Though then there was only silence, and Dessalene lingered in the darkness like a fish dangling from a hook, until it tugged, and she heard the return of the voice she knew so well.

'Look around you, dreamer. The gods are not on our side. They help our enemies! And you? Who will you help today, Dessalene? Yourself? Well, know that I shall be watching. I shall be watching you...'

***

The sun was still rising in the east as Korri and his men searched for Edela. Bertel and Siggy were joined by Zen, who offered to help.

Despite lingering grief, he seemed eager to be useful, and Bertel wasn't about to say no. Besides, he was good company for Siggy, who talked to him about the places they could go.

Bertel trailed behind them with his sword hilt exposed. He wanted to be ready for anything. It was time, he thought, lifting his aching head. Long past time to remember what he could do. He was old, but he had been born with talent. Over the years, he had turned that talent into skill, which was surely still there. His confidence may have retreated over the years, though not his memories.

Siggy turned around to him. 'There are two options,' she said with sudden clarity, causing both Zen and Bertel to stop with her. 'They will either kill Edela here or take her away. And I think... if they were going to kill her here, they would have done so.' The thought brought tears to her eyes, knowing that she had certainly led Edela to her death. 'But if they are to take her away, then it must be either by sea or through the desert.'

Bertel nodded patiently, for they had already discussed this.

'And they didn't kill her in our room, so I think... no, I feel that they will take her away from here. To someone. The one who wants her dead. The one killing the dreamers.'

'By sea or land?' Zen asked.

Put on the spot, Siggy couldn't answer, though feeling a sensation, like someone tapping her shoulder, she spun around, seeing the man in the golden tunic standing on the plinth, watching her.

***

Bone Hammer led the way through The Corridor – a passage of sheer volcanic rock that rose like walls on either side of them.

Eadmund headed to the stern to see Ulf following behind in *Beloved*.

They had agreed on the use of signal flags before departing Hest, though Eadmund's mind was suddenly blank, trying to remember which colour signified each action.

Turning back, he lifted his head to the mast, sensing that since they'd entered The Corridor, the wind had left them. He saw the sail sagging, no longer a taut round belly but a dimpled flapping napkin. Nibbling cracked lips and running a hand over his shorn head, he aimed for Mattie. 'Did you find out how to command the wind?'

Mattie shook her head. 'I didn't, I'm sorry. It was all about the seer. I can try again.' She could see the sail herself. 'I'll try again.'

Eadmund nodded. 'If your vision comes to pass, we can't be late, Mattie. My wife tends to forge her own path, though I'm certain she'd appreciate our help. And yours.'

A blinking Mattie headed to the stern, determined to find Kolarov's missing usha root.

Eadmund let her go, his gaze once again drifting up to the sail, then beyond it to the walls leading them towards S'ala Nis' harbour and its deadly ballistas.

Closing his eyes, he gripped the shield rack, wanting to reach his wife.

***

Jael sat on a chair, once again dressed in a grey dress.

It was clean, as she was clean.

Her wet hair hung down her back, soaking the dress, and despite the cool bath, she was hot and tense.

One of the guards had gone for a physician, for her wounds had started bleeding and wouldn't stop.

Looking down, Jael saw the pool of watery blood beneath the chair.

The slave, Mali, looked up as the guard returned with Ratish.

He frowned as he approached, and shooing away the slave

and the guards, he sought to speak privately to Jael. 'I don't understand. What is happening?'

Jael smiled. 'I'm about to be sacrificed to Eyshar, so things aren't going to plan.'

Ratish stared at her in confusion, though sensing the guards approaching, he looked Jael over, quickly seeing the blood seeping through the back of her dress. 'I must examine you.' Turning back to the guards, he frowned. 'If this woman is to be sacrificed, why does she still have her bonds on? I fail to understand the point. Do you fear she could defeat four of you? That she is some sort of magical creature?' He laughed mockingly. 'Come now, remove them so I may treat these wounds. I have to re-stitch some, by the look of things. Hurry now. I am sure your mistress doesn't want to be kept waiting.'

'We have no key,' one of the guards told him.

An annoyed Ratish turned back in disgust, lowering his voice. 'I have to remove your dress. I will find somewhere to lay you down.' Straightening up, he headed back to the huddle of guards. 'I need a table or a bed. Where can I take her?'

Mali spoke up. 'The chamber next door is a dressing room. There is a long couch.'

'Good. Let us take her there. Hurry now,' Ratish urged. 'Though you men will wait outside. The woman must retain some semblance of dignity. She is a queen, after all.' He was grumbling and complaining, concerned about what Jael had said.

A sacrifice?

He didn't know how he could help her now.

Mali led them to the next chamber, where Ratish shooed the guards away and closed the door. 'You will help her undress, but gently now,' he said, seeing Mali heading for the slave. 'Gently.' He heard Jael's mostly silent gasps as she lifted her arms in the air, allowing the slave to pull the dress over her head before helping her to lie down, face first on the couch.

It was softer than anything she'd experienced in some time, and Jael wished she could simply fall asleep.

Ratish spoke to Mali in the common tongue, though the slave shook her head, and he reverted to Siluran, which she understood perfectly. He bid her to sit by the door, ensuring no one entered while he tended to the slave's wounds. And then he turned to Jael, unpacking his kit of supplies, whispering in her ear. 'What can I do? How can I help you?'

'Just stitch me up the best you can. Wrap me in bandages if you have to. And ask that slave to braid my hair.'

***

Siggy hurried towards the man in the golden tunic, closely followed by Bertel and Zen. 'Hello!' she called. 'Hello?'

The man turned with a beaming smile, and bending down, he lowered his voice. 'Ahhh, the little dreamer. You seek answers, I see... though can you pay for them? For help does not always come for free.' He turned over a hand, revealing a deeply lined palm.

Zen dug into his pouch, pulling out five silver coins of good size and quality, dropping them into that palm. 'Is that enough?'

The man looked unimpressed, though the coins soon disappeared.

He motioned with his head for Siggy to follow him, shaking it when her two companions sought to join them. 'You will wait here. We shall return presently.'

Bertel looked uncertain, though Siggy wasn't waiting. 'I won't be long, Bertel. Stay here!'

And then she was gone, vanishing into the crowd with the golden man.

***

Raymon Vandaal had been up early, having spent a restless night choosing his next path.

He'd thought hard about what he wanted and where he wanted to be.

Though Edela's words kept returning him to Ollsvik and Oren Storgard. He had abandoned his throne and his people, leaving them in the hands of a man who would rule as a tyrant. Those who had lived under his father and then him would suddenly be at the mercy of that ambitious man, who would think little of their lives in his march to power.

Still, dismissing any lingering guilt, Raymon packed up his few possessions, paid his landlord and headed to the harbour, still mulling over his options.

***

The Armless One had not wished to draw further attention to herself, though she had wanted to help the young girl, who had been cruelly tricked.

And the old dreamer.

She had seen that.

Siggy sat before the table, trembling with fear. She knew of Edela's visit to the seeress, but the sight of the armless woman draped in cloth was unnerving, and she struggled to locate her tongue.

The Armless One spoke into her ears.

'Edela is hidden from me,' she told her. 'And you. Yet we have the power to see, so what does that tell you, I wonder?'

Siggy blinked. 'That a dreamer has captured her? A dreamer

is hiding her from us?'

It was a good answer but not one The Armless One wanted to hear out loud. 'Share your thoughts with me, child. Silently. You can do that.'

Siggy wasn't sure she could, though she clamped her lips together and tried. 'They must be using symbols.'

'Indeed. To hide Edela, though not themselves... which means that you can find the men who took her. So there is my advice, the only advice I am able to offer. Look for the man with the branded cheeks. He makes little effort to hide himself, so find him, child, and you will find your dreamer.'

CHAPTER FORTY-FOUR

A freshly stitched Jael was led through the palace by the four guards. Mali had spent some time combing and braiding her hair, and with it off her face and out of her eyes, she almost felt like herself.

The guards ushered her outside onto the palace steps, where chaos was unfolding. The panicked voices all spoke Siluran, and trying to understand what was happening, she glimpsed a man being carried away.

Ronin Sardis was stomping around with flailing hands, barking orders, slaves scattering before him. He caught a glimpse of Jael and froze. This woman looked nothing like the dirty wreck he'd threatened earlier. With her braided dark hair pulled back from a clean face, he saw strong cheekbones and vibrant green eyes.

This woman looked like a queen.

Kalina arrived, followed by six slaves holding up the long train of her gown. She was dressed entirely in white, as was the custom for such solemn occasions, though she was still fretting, not wanting to draw too much attention to herself.

Not at the funeral of the man she had murdered.

Dessalene had picked out the extravagant gown with its enormous train, though Kalina wasn't sure it was appropriate. 'What is happening?' she asked, glancing at Jael in surprise before returning her attention to her father. 'Is something wrong?'

'Nothing,' her father insisted. 'There is nothing wrong. It was the heat! Only the heat! The man fainted from the heat!'

And sensing that wasn't true, Kalina flicked a hand at the slaves and approached her father alone. 'What really happened?'

'It doesn't matter!' he snapped, becoming tense. 'A slave fainted. It doesn't matter! We simply must begin the procession. We are to be at the temple as the sun sets, and at this rate, we'll be arriving beneath the fucking stars!' He looked past his daughter to where Jael Furyck appeared to be trying to understand what was going on.

Doubt flared.

He had sought to keep her. After years of planning how to capture her, he finally had, and now to just toss her away like something that didn't matter?

Though, he reminded himself, Eyshar certainly wouldn't think so.

'Bring the slave queen to me. She will walk before me. And that horse. I want that horse!'

Jael turned to see Arras' horse, Tito, being tugged forward. He was a reluctant guest, hooves seeking purchase in the gravel, tail flicking, eyes rolling. She saw an image of Arras riding his horse, and then he was standing on a ship, tension in his eyes, sword in his hand. He stared at her, saying nothing, turning his head, revealing the man by his side.

A short-haired Eadmund.

She clung to that image, seeking to go deeper as the voices around her became louder.

'We must be on our way!' Ronin called, eyeing Tito, who looked ready to nip him. 'Once I give this beast a talking to.' He turned to wink at his daughter, seeking to steady the rocking ship. 'Where's Kosta?' He saw Krissia emerge onto the steps and trained his eyes on her.

She froze, not wanting to reveal that her father had gone to the latrines some time ago. 'He is... attending to matters.'

'Matters?' Ronin looked confused, then annoyed as Tito

butted him in the back. Swinging around with a snarl, he yanked the beast towards him. Though before he could push for more information, Kosta emerged from the palace, red-faced and flustered as he resettled his armour. 'Finally! It appears we are finally ready to get this procession underway.'

'Apart from one important guest, my lord,' Kosta said, turning to the red-robed logi bringing out the bier with Noor of the Dragon Blood Tree's body. Intense aromas of beeswax and pine masked the rank smell of his decaying flesh, though Kalina still shuddered when she turned around, seeing the wrapped corpse of the man she had killed. His face was uncovered, though not wanting even a glimpse of it, she turned away, meeting her father's eyes. His displeasure remained unspoken, though it cowed her nonetheless, and she was silent as she urged her slaves to once again pick up her train and help her into the carriage.

Jael was shoved forward into the procession, ordered to stand between two wagons draped in silk and flowers, carrying golden statues of what she could only guess were gods.

'I want everyone to see you!' Ronin Sardis called to her as he mounted a skittish Tito. 'To see the queen who will die!'

Jael didn't turn to him, she didn't reply, though for once, she was in total agreement.

She wanted everyone lining the streets to see her too.

***

The man in the golden tunic returned a breathless Siggy to Bertel and Zen before disappearing back to his plinth.

'What happened?' Bertel asked, looking her over. 'Are you alright?'

Siggy nodded. 'She said that we can't find Edela because she can't find Edela, which means a dreamer is doing something to hide her. That's why I haven't been able to see where she is.'

Bertel's shoulders sagged.

'Though we can find that man, Iker Rayas. We can try and find him!'

'Yes, of course!' Lifting his head, Bertel scratched it. 'The three things a man like that will want are food, ale, and women.'

Siggy peered at him.

'I'm only guessing,' Bertel said, almost leaping ahead of her. 'There's the place we passed last night, where that half-naked woman accosted me.'

Zen turned to Siggy with questions in his eyes, though Siggy could only shrug.

'We'll start there!' Bertel called, hurrying away.

Siggy grabbed Zen's hand. 'Come on! We have to hurry!'

***

As the afternoon wore on, everyone grew tense on board *Bone Hammer*.

Bolder was under orders from Arras, who had instructed him to drop anchor before the end of The Corridor, knowing that the moment they passed beyond its protective walls, their presence would no longer be a secret, and likely nor would their intentions.

Ulf instructed the Hestian fleet to fall in line, slowing to a crawl before dropping their own anchors, while he brought *Beloved* alongside *Bone Hammer* and came on board.

'We've got new information,' Eadmund told him as they crouched in the stern, eyes on the top of the chest Arras had scratched a map onto, wanting to outline his intentions. 'About Jael.'

Ulf glanced at him, reaching for the cup of ale Fyn offered.

'We anticipate that she's going to be here,' Arras told him, using the point of his eating knife to mark the temple grounds.

'Apparently, she's going to be sacrificed,' Thorgils said, much to Ulf's horror.

A blinking Ulf now focused on Arras. 'And we...'

'Thorgils and Nico will switch ships and come with you. Nico will guide you into the harbour towards the ballistas. He knows their range and what's possible. Let him run the catapults.'

Ulf peered at the young man, who he'd never even spoken to before; he looked little more than a teenager. 'And you?'

'Once we're in the harbour, Bolder will aim us west, near this tunnel, which will take us into the city. The various doors and gates are guarded, but we'll have enough men to overcome them. It shouldn't be a problem.'

Ulf nodded. 'So you'll look for Jael?'

'Yes,' Eadmund said. 'And you and your Hestians will need to push through the harbour as fast as you can. Take out their defenses and move through the city.'

'What sort of resistance are we looking at?' Ulf wondered.

'We talked about the change in shift at sunset,' Arras reminded him. 'Though now we have new information from the dreamer. According to her, the sacrifice will take place after the procession, which, if that holds true, means that most of the isle will be at the temple grounds or on their way there. They tend to hold such events in the afternoon, going late into the night.'

Ulf looked hopeful. 'So we might have an easier time?'

'Unless the dreamer sees us coming,' Mattie piped up. 'I feel her sometimes, or someone. As though they're watching. That we're not alone.'

No one liked the sound of that.

'Either way, we're not turning around and going home,' Eadmund insisted. 'We move forward regardless. Ulf, Thorgils, Nico, you need to go. Do we all remember the signals?'

Ulf nodded, tapping his head. 'Like it's tattooed in here,' he promised with a wink. Nerves fluttered in his belly, rising to his heart. He felt displaced, rocking in a strange ship in a strange sea, surrounded by mostly strangers. Though seeing the look of fear in Eadmund Skalleson's eyes, his purpose clarified. Jael had been taken by these people, who were preparing to sacrifice her. And as a Brekkan, once loyal to Jael's father, Ulf Rutgar knew exactly what he had to do.

Gulping down his ale, he handed the empty cup back to Fyn. 'Anything else, or shall we just get going?'

Arras lifted his eyes to Eadmund, who turned to meet them.

'No,' Eadmund said, heart thumping like a drum, urging him on. 'Nothing else. Let's go and get my wife.'

**

The slaves who'd worked to build the Tower of Eyshar – those who had lived to see it finished – had been brought together by Quint, who, in honour of the occasion, had organised for each man to receive one cup of ale.

He hadn't told Kosta, having secured the barrel himself, ensuring it was mixed with water so it would last.

'Drink up!' he urged. 'You've certainly earned it!' Turning around, eyes on the completed tower, relief washed over him. His shoulders, which had throbbed painfully night and day for months, finally started to loosen, and shaking his head, he almost smiled. Seeing one of the logi heading his way, he left his cup behind and headed towards the man.

And deciding that was his chance, Rigg winked at Hepa, who turned and whispered to the slaves nearby. Moving ahead of the big man, they came together like a shield wall, blocking him from sight.

Rigg slipped away, hurrying to Quint's empty wagon. He'd spent days being ferried around in that wagon. He'd delivered the cask of ale on it, leaving the driver to serve the men, ensuring no one would get more than their fair share.

And seeing that the wagon was empty and that Quint's attention was elsewhere, Rigg dropped a hand over the siding, searching for the conch shell.

***

Jael walked near the back of the slow-moving funeral procession as it clattered towards the temple grounds, feeling strange. The sight of the smiling, waving slave children disturbed her.

Though it motivated her too.

Having little care for the solemnity of the occasion, they ran alongside the wagons and horses and marching soldiers, eager to catch one of the flowers being thrown into the crowd. Some were brave enough to try touching Noor's body, for it was good luck to touch a seer, dead or alive. Jael knew that if Sunni had been running with them she would certainly have tried to.

She walked with her head held high, back straight, conscious of the stone in her shoe and the fetters around her ankles. They were almost part of her now. She had spent so much time compensating for their weight that she half-wondered if she could walk without them.

At first, few appeared to know who she was. Some pointed and stared, but initially, most of the crowd's attention was on the king, the queen, and Noor's body. Though soon whispers swept around like wind, eyes turning from the front of the procession, where units of soldiers marched, and from the king, riding before his daughter, whose open carriage moved her forward as though she sat atop a gilded throne.

And now they turned to Jael, becoming reverential in their silence.

Riding further behind, Ronin sensed the hush moving

through the crowd as Noor's body approached. The seer had been like a pillar holding up the isle, the eyes and ears of Eyshar and the gods, and here, witnessing his dead body carried to the temple, he saw uncertainty in the eyes of many.

Anger at his daughter was quickly extinguished by the memory of his quick-thinking wife, who had rushed to the isle to limit the damage Kalina's rash actions had wrought. Though with news of the plague spreading, he feared she'd been too late.

That this was all too late.

Blowing out a breath, he lifted his chin, pleased that Arras Sikari's temperamental horse had submitted to him and now walked calmly under his hold. He was a fine beast, as Arras had been a fine man, until he'd turned against him, betrayed his daughter and abandoned his post. And now, like the rest of his enemies, he was a traitor doomed to die.

Twitching with tension, Ronin had to stop himself from snapping Tito's reins and driving them all to the temple in haste. Lifting his eyes, he saw the setting sun, its glaring rays dazzling him, feeling his heartbeat outstripping the plodding rhythm of the drummers, who followed at the back of the procession.

Impatient to get to the temple.

***

As the late afternoon sun streamed through holes in the walls of her prison room, Edela started to panic. Another day was passing, and she sensed that she wouldn't remain in the room for long. And as she thought it, footsteps echoed outside the door, and soon it was flung open, revealing Iker Rayas dressed in a cloak.

Blinking at him as the room filled with more light, Edela swallowed; he hadn't been wearing a cloak before.

'On your feet, old woman!' he barked, and stepping towards

the bed, he yanked Edela up by the arm. She stumbled against him, unbalanced by the fetters. 'Ship's leaving.'

'Ship?' she croaked, long since having finished her water. 'Ship to where?'

He laughed. 'But aren't you the dreamer?' Now he snarled, tugging her forward as another man entered the room.

'Sure you want to move her while it's still light? What if she squawks?'

'Then she'll sound like every other fucking bird in this place,' Iker grinned, unsheathing a knife, which he brandished at Edela's face. 'You even open your mouth and I'll stick you with this.'

Edela trembled before that lethal-looking blade, knowing that with the fetters blocking her power, she was entirely helpless against it. And him. 'You're not supposed to kill me now.'

He laughed. 'I know what will kill a man or an annoying old woman. I know how to keep you alive too. You won't lose much blood where I intend to stab you, but it will hurt, so quiet now.'

Edela nodded, eyeing that knife, which Iker soon dropped to his side.

'We're going to walk to the harbour. It's not so far. We'll make you nice and comfortable for our journey.'

To where, Edela wondered.

To where was he taking her?

And to whom?

***

Korri and three of his men came across Bertel, Siggy, and Zen as they emerged from a brothel. He raised an eyebrow at a blushing Bertel. 'Any luck?'

Bertel shook his head, glancing over his shoulder. 'No, no,' he answered, still flustered by the very hands-on women he'd encountered inside, wishing he'd thought to leave Siggy and Zen outside. 'You?'

'Not a peep. We may as well return to the ships and plot our next move.'

Though Bertel wasn't ready to stop yet. 'We haven't checked the crossroads. That physician is there, and surely he sees many people coming and going. He might have heard something? Or seen something?'

Korri looked intrigued. 'Crossroads?'

Turning around, Bertel stared into the sun. 'Back past the textile merchants. It's not too far.'

'Then let's take a look,' Korri decided. 'It sounds like a useful place to start.'

***

'You want to scream?' Iker growled, yanking Edela closer; close enough that she could smell his sweat as though it was her own. She turned her head, though immediately feeling the press of his blade against her waist, she spun back to look at him, almost blinded by the sinking sun.

'No,' she insisted. 'No.'

'No, you don't,' Iker smiled. 'That's right. One little word and I'll bleed you.' He turned back around, eager to move with speed.

Edela was too afraid to breathe. All her attention had to be on keeping that knife away from her side. They were being jostled as they walked. In front of them, Iker's men attempted to beat back the crowd, though it throbbed around them, impatient people hurrying into every available space, barely conscious of others. She tripped, nudging a man, who looked sympathetically at her before disappearing.

She thought of Bertel and Siggy, knowing they would be

looking for her, hoping to see their faces amongst the crowd, though she moved in a sea of strangers with no idea of where she was or of where she was going.

Perhaps it was for the best, for what could they possibly do against Iker Rayas and his five armed men?

And thinking of Jael, knowing her granddaughter would certainly be able to do something, Edela felt tears coming. She blinked them away, though, hearing Jael's voice in her ears, urging her to focus on what would come next.

She had to stay safe.

She had to stay alive.

CHAPTER FORTY-FIVE

Dessalene had arrived at the temple with fluttering nerves, almost regretting that she'd agreed to take such a prominent role in the sacrifice. It would have been much easier to have ridden with Ronin, sitting beside him, his hand on her leg. Her thoughts were a swirling mass of concerns: her mistress' warning, fear of whatever plague was spreading on the isle, and the lingering memory of her dream about the eagle and the rat.

From his chair in the temple courtyard, where he had gathered his logi, Inesh Seppo could see that the dreamer was troubled. 'My lady!' he called, motioning with a hand. 'Is something wrong?'

Dessalene shook her head. 'I am... no. I am eager to begin, I...' She stopped, moving her hands rather than her lips, distracting thoughts competing for her attention, merging to form a great hive of noise in her head.

Inesh stood, leading Dessalene to a table laden with ceremonial goblets. Picking up one, he offered it to the dreamer. The logi soon moved forward, taking their own.

Dessalene sniffed the dark liquid, sighing as its pleasant aromas immediately worked to soothe her.

'Moonflower, henbane, and a little apple,' Inesh told her. 'Amongst other things. Noor was precise in his instructions, right down to this very drink. He was a meticulous man, a man of deep conviction. The isle was beloved to him, and he wished to preserve it, to nurture its people. He was a healer of souls, a bringer of hope. That is how he saw himself at the end. A bringer of hope.'

Sipping the sweet-smelling liquid, Dessalene felt her frazzled spirit being smoothed. Licking her lips, she smiled. 'And he did not see his own death coming?'

'I believe he did, my lady. Yes. We had spoken the night before, and I sensed a shift in him. He was a quiet man, careful with his words. That night, though, he had much to say to me. He took me for a walk in the gardens, and we discussed the tower and his desire to see it finished. I sensed he had knowledge of what would come, for there was a peace about him, an acceptance of his fate.' Finishing his drink, the seer placed his goblet back on the table.

'And yet he did not fight against it? Did not try to prevent such an end...' Dessalene couldn't quite believe anyone would be so foolish. To offer himself up to such a death? Surely it was no noble sacrifice to surrender to the queen's temper tantrum?

'Prevent what the gods had chosen?' Inesh shook his head. 'But that would go against everything he believed in. The destiny that befell our beloved Noor was one he walked towards with his head held high.' He stared at Dessalene intently, noting that she was no longer blinking. Her pupils had dilated, fixed on his. 'Come, and let us make an offering before we head to the tower. The procession will be here soon. There is not much time.'

The dreamer turned to him, lips parted, though the thought that had rushed into her mind evaporated, and she could only nod.

***

Having finally made his decision, Raymon bought passage on a trading ship heading east. Few of the men spoke the common tongue, though the helmsman did, and he'd offered Raymon a place on board if he was prepared to work for it. He had to pay with coins but also with labour. The man was down three hands since his arrival from Zagora, and he liked the look of the young man's strapping shoulders, certain he could put him to good use.

Raymon wasn't sure how he felt about his decision. The lanky helmsman had many questions and inquisitive eyes, though he needed to get out of Castala quickly.

He needed to –

Turning around, he heard the crew calling out in greeting, watching in horror as a gruesome-looking man brought Edela Saeveld towards the ship. And eyes dropping from her terrified face, he soon saw that her hands were bound and that the man beside her was holding a knife to her side.

He made to turn away, though the helmsman patted him on the shoulder, introducing him.

'Iker! I've found us another pair of hands!'

A scowling Iker looked Raymon over. 'Where are you from?'

Raymon turned from the helmsman to the branded man, avoiding Edela's eyes. He had no choice but to repeat his lie; he'd used it often since leaving Iskavall behind. 'Alekka.'

Iker grunted, moving past him with barely a glance. 'We need more than one, though, Vito. I thought I told you to find more?'

Raymon was confused, soon realising that the helmsman wasn't the lord of this ship, though he had certainly made himself out to be.

The ship had a crew of some twenty-five men, though seeing the new arrivals, Raymon put the count nearer thirty. And with that many men, he didn't know how he could help Edela. She'd said she was travelling with companions, but surely she didn't mean these men? 'When will we leave?' he asked one of the crew, who didn't understand him. The helmsman had turned away with the man called Iker, and Edela, and he couldn't ask him.

'Here!' Vito barked. 'What was your name again?'

Raymon turned around. 'Markus.'

'Well, Markus, hop on board! Earning your way starts now! You'll pick up things as you go.'

Iker turned as Raymon jumped on board. 'You can start by looking after my little old grandmother here.'

Raymon blinked at him, eyes dropping to the knife. 'Your grandmother?'

A laughing Iker sheathed his knife, pushing Edela towards Raymon. 'Someone's grandmother. Who gives a fuck? Just take her to the stern, sit her down and keep her quiet. If she makes a noise, stuff something in her mouth.'

Edela looked up at Raymon with tears in her eyes, more certain than she had been in weeks that Furia was watching over her.

***

The crowds slowly escorted the funeral procession to the temple grounds, where Jael's attention was drawn to the Tower of Eyshar, gilded by the setting sun.

She thought of the hours she'd spent perched atop that tower like a nesting bird, imagining this day. Though she had never seen herself as part of it.

Not like this.

She heard bursts of singing, a mingling of joy and sorrow, as white flowers were thrown over Noor's body.

He had been beloved, Jael could see, wondering about the man who had died protecting her, shielding the truth of her escape from the queen, saving his last words for her.

She shivered. He had wanted her to escape.

To help Alek free the slaves.

She imagined the old man now, standing before her, hand out, urging her forward. He stood in a flare of sunlight, as white as the light behind him. 'You are the sword,' he told her. 'You are the sword to set these people free.'

Jael looked down at those now familiar fetters. She thought of *Toothpick* for the first time in days, missing her beloved sword, which had felt a part of her for so long. As her horse, Tig, had. And Oss. Her family.

'Don't you dare die, Jael Furyck,' she heard Eadmund say. 'Don't you dare.'

She curled her hands into fists, clenching so tightly she could feel her nails digging into her palms.

'I am the sword,' she repeated. 'I am the sword.'

***

Arriving at the crossroads, Korri and his men headed west, leaving Bertel, Siggy, and Zen to go east, though no one had seen any sign of a man resembling Iker Rayas' description. Or Edela's.

They met back at the signpost and then separated again, this time heading north and south.

The sun was setting as Siggy walked beside Bertel. Zen roamed ahead of them, all of them moving as though in a trance, trying to find the unmistakable face of Iker Rayas amongst knots of ordinary-looking strangers.

Siggy saw herself rowing that tiny boat from Ollsvik to Esby, drenched in rain, encouraged by Edela's endlessly cheerful chatter. The dreamer had told her to hurry. A ship was making room for them, so they had to hurry.

Edela had been drawn to Esby's harbour, Siggy remembered, as though the river itself was her path, a road she needed to follow.

Out to sea.

A dazed Siggy turned away from Bertel, feeling a breeze.

Smelling the ocean.

They would take the dreamer away.

They would take her to sea!

Wheeling back around, Siggy lunged at Bertel, tugging his sleeve. 'I know where Edela is! But we must hurry!'

***

As the seer, the dreamer, and the logi made their preparations on the sacrifice platform, the sun continued its languid descent, the air heavy and warm.

The slaves who weren't packed into standing rows, eyes on the lords and ladies comfortably seated in the stadium surrounding the platform, were helping to bring in the animals to be sacrificed.

It was taking forever, and the waiting was driving an uptight Rigg mad.

He had secured Quint's shell on the ground between his feet, and surrounded by his fellow slaves, who stood shoulder to shoulder, he remained shielded from view. Though, waiting nervously beside him, aware of that shell's presence and the occasional inspection by an armed soldier, Alek feared it would be discovered. Having the shell itself wasn't necessarily enough to get them whipped, though he tried to think of an excuse, a reason it might be there, just in case.

Inhaling a shaky breath, he could finally hear the funeral procession edging closer, the sinking sun now flaming in the sky. He hoped they would hurry. Where he stood in a group of some hundred-odd slaves, he was near the front, and as the soldiers lined up in ceremonial dress before them, facing the platform, Alek had already chosen who he would go for: a cocky prick who had kicked him more than once. He wasn't a big man, though he was a bully, arrogant enough to think that his gods would always protect him on his precious isle with his wealthy friends and his boundless freedom.

Rigg nodded at him, feeling Jael's knife tucked down his waistband.

After he blew the shell, he'd surge forward and stab the soldier closest to him in the back, get him down, slit his throat and steal his sword. He kept walking through it in his mind, remembering Jael's words. She'd sneered that he didn't know how to lead, though he was determined to show her otherwise. He had to lead these men to rise up while Jael worked to extract herself from whatever the dreamer and the logi intended to do to her.

Timing was everything.

Hearing wheels clattering over cobblestones, the beat of drums and the rising hum of the crowd surging closer, Rigg glanced around, inhaling a tense breath as he met Alek's eyes.

Soon.

***

Beloved led them forward under the command of Ulf Rutgar, accompanied by Thorgils and Nico Sikari, and flanked by four more catapult ships.

On board *Bone Hammer* with Arras and Fyn, Eadmund's mouth dried up. He tried to swallow, though it was becoming increasingly difficult. 'Fyn! Bring me some ale!' he croaked from the bow, where he'd stopped to assess how things were going.

The Hestian ships had left the protection of The Corridor behind, emerging into the exposed stretch of sea before the isle.

Arras stood beside him. 'They'll spot us soon enough, though remember what I said. The change in shift is coming.' He glanced up, seeing the sun sinking, almost bleeding into the sky. 'Those men ready to leave their posts will have their minds on going home, on meeting up at the tavern. They'll be distracted, talking, thinking about what comes next, not focused on what's before them. They won't be looking out to sea.'

Eadmund ran a hand over his head as Fyn arrived, hoping he was right. He took the offered cup of ale with gratitude in his eyes, gulping it down. 'Are the buckets full?' he asked, wiping his beard and leaving the cup on the deck. 'Full of water?'

Fyn nodded.

'Has Mattie seen anything?' Arras wondered, adjusting his swordbelt, shoving his sword in tight, then his knives, thinking of Nico.

Fyn shook his head. 'Nothing else. She's with Kolarov, keeping out of the way. If she sees anything, she'll let us know.'

Eadmund turned back to Arras. 'Can I trust you? It's not some trap?'

'No, it's not a trap. I'm risking my life, my son's life to go back to that place. I'd rather go anywhere but back there, for if it all goes wrong?'

If it all goes wrong, Eadmund thought.

But it couldn't. It wouldn't.

Not this time.

***

Edela couldn't talk to Raymon or even make eye contact with him. Revealing that they knew each other would likely get him killed, though she desperately needed his help.

The crew had readied the ship, preparing to get underway.

Apparently, some of Iker's men were still missing – those who had been sent for ale – and no one wanted to leave without that on board.

Edela could hear Iker Rayas becoming angry, arguing with

the helmsman, who happily argued back, and seeing that they were distracted, she whispered to Raymon. 'Give me your knife.'

He spun around, blinking at her before quickly looking away, muttering under his breath. 'I can't.'

'The symbols inside these fetters are magical, stopping me saving us both. You don't want to go with these men, Raymon. They're dangerous killers, taking us to who knows where. Please, if you shield me, I can scratch through the symbols, and then I can... save us.'

They had been left in the stern, where the space was taken up with barrels and chests. Edela sat on a chest, mostly hidden from view, and making his decision, Raymon turned, handing her his knife, spinning back as one of the crew walked over. 'You must hurry, Edela,' he whispered.

'Yes, yes. Even if I scratch one, I'll be able to do something.'

'Ssshhh,' Raymon hissed. And turning around with a frown, he made as if to check on her.

'Everything alright?' the helmsman called.

Raymon held up a hand, nodding, praying that Edela would hurry.

***

Dessalene felt fluid as she surveyed the temple grounds, as though made of ribbons undulating in a gentle breeze.

Inesh Seppo's delicious tonic had relieved her of that which was irrelevant, focusing her mind on what was vitally important. She stood in the embrace of the sun, red clouds raging across the sky like a hungry fire, body vibrating in the presence of the god.

Could they please Eyshar with their offerings? Secure his forgiveness for Kalina's recklessness? In that perfect moment, a confident Dessalene thought of Jael Furyck and knew they could.

Behind her, the red-robed logi moved with calm purpose, for each man had undertaken training for his role in the ritual and now carried out his duties with the skill of one performing a dance.

The seer sat silently in the middle of the row of nine stone chairs, draped in his white ceremonial robes.

He would not officially begin his role until he had been anointed. Until then, he would remain a neutral observer, watching the sacrifices.

Dessalene now saw the first horses arrive at the temple grounds, moving through the slaves, who had been pushed back to create a road fenced by rows of heavily armed soldiers. Wearing black and gold tunics, they shone in the sun.

The slaves appeared in a festive mood, cheering loudly at the first sight of the procession.

She turned to the stadium where the lords and ladies and their families sat, feeling the heat of the sun on her back, all thoughts of plagues gone from her mind now. Her eyes sparkled, eager to see her husband sitting amongst them.

Dessalene's thoughts continued to flow as she turned back to the procession, watching it merge into the crowd now, searching for the gift she would offer the god.

It was time for that vile woman to die.

And stepping forward to a stone plinth draped in red velvet, she lifted a pure obsidian dagger from its rest, and carefully cutting the tip of her left index finger with its vicious blade, she painted a symbol on her forehead.

The symbol of Alari.

The Alekkan Goddess of Magic.

***

Edela worked furiously to scratch through the symbols inside her wrist fetters – cutting herself countless times. The blood made everything harder, and with the sun blinding her, she struggled to even see. She raked that blade down each fetter, hoping to feel some spark, some sense that she was freed from its magical bonds.

Raymon spun around, bending down, and yanking the knife from her hand, he stood up as Iker Rayas approached.

Iker eyed the young man, then Edela. 'She's dangerous, my prisoner, so whatever you do, don't turn your back on her again. Understood? I told you to watch her, and unless you've got eyes in the back of your head, you're looking in the wrong direction, boy.'

Raymon tried not to stare at the man's gruesome wounds. He sought to focus on his eyes, though only one was uncovered, glowering at him, so eventually, he stared past his head, nodding.

Iker leaned forward, looking past Raymon to Edela, who blinked at him, then back at Raymon. 'I don't know you.'

'I've paid for passage,' Raymon explained. 'I'm heading for Kadak.'

'Why? What's there? You're not from around here.'

'No, I left home for an adventure.'

'Alone?' Iker was becoming suspicious.

Raymon nodded, feeling it. 'I... had a falling out. I'm just looking to start again. Somewhere no one knows me.'

'Where in Alekka are you from? North or South?'

Raymon felt a wave of heat rush up his body to his neck, soon burning his cheeks. 'South. A small village.'

'Called?'

'B-B-Bola. It's very small, a tiny place. You wouldn't know it.'

Iker's eye lit up. 'I do know it! Near Sondermay. On the Oglund River. It's a nice place.'

A horrified Raymon started babbling. 'Yes... it is. I... was... sad to leave, but I –'

Iker clamped a hand around Raymon's wrist, and lifting it up, he snatched the knife from his hand, turning to aim it at his throat. 'I know Sondermay, and though it's in Southern Alekka, that river's in the North.'

Raymon froze, his heart beating a warning in his ears. 'Well, no, you're wrong. There's... more than one,' he tried, though Iker wasn't convinced.

'Vito!' he called. 'Where'd you get this prick?'

The gangly helmsman came down the deck towards them. 'Why? What are you doing, Iker? He's paid me to sail to Kadak. We need the help.'

'From this boy? This liar?'

'I, I...' Raymon spluttered, struggling to think.

The helmsman laughed. 'What? You think we're a band of innocent men with nothing to hide? No secrets? Come on, give him a chance. He's young. Look at those arms. He'll be of use, Iker.'

Though Iker wasn't convinced. 'You've got his coins?'

Vito nodded.

'Good, then I'll take his life. Stick to Silurans from now on. Men I can trust.'

'What? *No!*' Raymon cried, stepping back, and drawing his sword, he aimed its newly sharpened tip at Iker Rayas' furious eye.

CHAPTER FORTY-SIX

An exhausted Bertel realised that he hadn't stopped running since he'd come across Edela Saeveld in Tuura's forest, and he was panting as he trailed Korri and his men down the steps to the docks. There were countless piers to check – perhaps as many as twenty – and Bertel feared they would be too late.

That they would simply run out of time.

A sharp pain in his side slowed him down, and stopping to take a breath, he bent over, sucking in warm air.

'Do you need help?' a woman asked.

There was a kind look in her eyes as she approached him, head cocked to one side, hand out.

'I... I'm looking for someone,' Bertel rasped. 'A man with... ruined cheeks. Brands and an eye –' Seeing a flicker of recognition in the young woman's eyes, he cut himself off. 'You've seen him?'

She nodded with a shudder. 'Him and his crew. They passed here not long ago. That way,' she said, pointing in the opposite direction to where Korri had led his men. 'See that big ship with the yellow sail? They went there!'

Bertel looked around, seeing no sign of Korri now. Or Siggy. 'I... if my friends return, a girl with curls, a man with a long beard, and a tall boy... tell them where I went. Please!' And with a grateful smile, he wheeled around, his side immediately aching again. But squeezing his right hand around his sword grip, Bertel Knutson started running.

***

On board *Beloved*, Nico stood close to Thorgils Svanter. He pointed west. 'That tower first. It has the only signal bell. The other one was being replaced when I left.'

Thorgils nodded, nerves humming, mind sharpening as he ran through each stage of their plan. No thoughts of his wife and children or his home entered his head now. He didn't even think of Eadmund and what *Bone Hammer* might be doing behind them. It was all *Beloved* now.

And *Beloved* was leading them towards the harbour.

It was on Nico Sikari to know when they were within range. To predict the moment just before those crews watching from the cliffs, running the ballistas, would spring into action.

***

Raymon swung his sword at Iker Rayas, who threw his knife at his face, just missing his cheek before unsheathing his own sword, scattering the crew standing nearby.

'Fuck! *Iker!*' Vito exclaimed. 'We need to leave!' Though he was soon stepping back, urging his men to keep their distance. He knew Iker, as they knew Iker.

This young man didn't stand a chance.

Edela closed her eyes, shutting away her fears for Raymon. She became still, focused, cloaking herself in darkness while she worked to help them both.

Raymon screamed as Iker's blade sliced across his wrist. He wore a plain tunic and cloak, a swordbelt, and little else. His only defense was to be better than this man, who was stocky and muscular but moved with real speed, feet never still. Raymon was soon breathless, sweeping from side to side, parrying each strike, searching for a way through the man's defenses. Slashes of sunlight dazzled him, and he stumbled, Iker Rayas' blade dragging across his chest. Eyes bursting open, Raymon cried out. The intense sting distracted him at first, then quickly focused him. Pushing onto the front foot, blood dripped from his wrist, oozing between his fingers. He tightened his grip, and turning his hand, he pointed his sword like a spear. Feinting right, he left Iker Rayas chasing shadows as he veered back, stabbing the man in the waist.

Iker jerked back, growling, and remembering something Jael had taught him, Raymon dropped low, spearing the man's knee. Iker's growl became a roar as he stumbled back, hopping, though Raymon quickly realised that his problems had only doubled as Vito now unhooked an axe from his belt and stepped forward, flanked by half the crew, who appeared to have lost patience with the whole mess.

'Time for you to leave,' the tall helmsman warned darkly, eyeing Raymon as Iker shook off his injuries and lurched back into action.

'Edela! *Edela!*'

Hearing Bertel calling for her, Edela's eyes bulged in surprise, but quickly closing them again, she moved with speed, realising that she had to do something to help before Iker Rayas and his men killed them all.

***

The funeral procession finally came to a halt at the temple grounds, now packed with slaves, soldiers, and animals, looked down upon by a stadium full of the isle's elite, and watched over by Inesh Seppo and his logi.

Ronin was pleased with what he saw, and dismounting Arras Sikari's horse, he made his way to the royal carriage, where he removed his golden helmet, offering his daughter a hand. 'You are fortunate, Kalina,' he murmured as he helped her dismount. 'That Dessalene saved you and my isle. To think what might have befallen it without her timely intervention.'

Kalina weathered his displeasure in silence, holding his hand as they walked ahead of the logi transporting Noor's body to the platform, where he would rest during the ceremony before later being buried in the temple – after they had feasted on the meat of the sacrificed animals.

Kalina's stomach turned at the thought of it.

She saw Krissia Kosta heading into the stadium on the arm of her father and felt even worse, though quickly remembering that the entire mess was of her own making, she bit down on her revulsion and put on a smile.

Up ahead, Jael had found Rigg in the crowd. He nodded at her, his face a slab of tension. His wasn't the only face turned her way, and she soon became aware of how many slaves were watching her. All those men she had suffered alongside to finish that tower. Men desperate for their freedom, though full of doubt that they possessed the strength to claim it.

Scared men.

She saw Alek and sought to reach him. 'Stay safe. Let Rigg protect you and stay safe. I will get you home.'

And now she was dragged away by two soldiers, almost off her feet.

Jael heard goats bleating and a horse whinnying, and turning, she saw the procession of animals being shepherded towards a bridge leading up to the platform, where the dreamer waited, dressed in a long black gown, wielding a long black dagger. Spotting Tito, Jael once again saw a vision of Arras and Eadmund side by side. They were talking, pointing at something. She was shoved, ordered to move, though she tried to hold onto that vision.

The two men were staring at something.

The vision faded, though not before Jael had seen a glimpse of what they were pointing at: tall, jagged cliffs, upon which stood two giant ballistas.

***

Edela had to do something.

Raymon was surrounded by Iker Rayas and his men, and a bellowing Bertel had just announced his presence to everyone. She couldn't say anything to put him in danger or alert him at all, so chanting in furious whispers, she quickly brought symbols into her mind.

'*Bertel!*'

Now Edela recognised Siggy's voice, and panic exploding, she sought to hurry.

'Edela!' Bertel called. 'We are coming for you! Hold on!'

The shouting came at just the right time for Raymon, who swung at a distracted Vito, taking him in the throat. 'Stay there, Edela!' he warned, seeing that they had help. 'Stay down!'

The bleeding helmsman dropped to the deck with a gurgle, and Raymon moved forward, taking the next man on the wrist, chopping off his hand. He spun, stabbing another man in the thigh. He had to be fast now, to move like the wind. Nerves leaving him, he sought to kill.

Edela's fetters sprang open, and so did her eyes. She shook off her bonds as Bertel jumped down into the ship, brandishing his sword. 'No!' she cried. 'Bertel! *No!*'

'Stay back, Siggy! Zen, take her!'

Edela blinked, and in the next moment, Korri Torluffson and a handful of men jumped down after Bertel, and quickly taking the lead, swords in the air, they charged.

***

As Ronin Sardis took his seat on the royal dais beside his silent daughter, his eyes were drawn to his wife's glistening auburn hair. The setting sun was sinking quickly now, and soon it would reach the tower arch.

Ronin's eyes drifted past Dessalene to the woman in the plain grey dress, waiting with the rest of the animals.

His left hand twitched, regretting that he wasn't the one to take Jael Furyck's life. But though she wouldn't die by his blade, she would die on his isle, her life ended by his powerful wife. And seeing Dessalene turning to him as though hearing his thoughts, he smiled.

***

An angry Korri led the attack against the ship's crew, having lost good men to these Silurans in Bakkar. He could see that they'd taken Edela prisoner. She hunched in the stern, cowering and afraid.

Or was she?

Shouting orders at his men, he urged speed. '*Bertel!*' he warned as one of the Silurans aimed for the old man's back.

A focused Bertel swung around, shearing his sword across the man's nose. He was much taller, his stance higher, and he cut that nose in two. Shifting his feet and twisting his grip, he attacked the man again, and slitting his throat, he ended his life.

Flashes of the past ignited inside him, and he moved up to flank Korri, desperate to make his way to Edela.

Iker Rayas was back on his feet now, and pushing down on his injured leg, he lunged for a distracted Raymon, knocking his sword from his hand.

'Raymon!' Edela shouted in warning, causing more than one head to turn her way, though there was nothing Korri or his men could do, blocked by the crew as they were. Raymon had taken back his knife, so she had to move with speed to find one for herself. Everyone was here because of her. They couldn't sacrifice themselves.

She wouldn't let them.

So, hopping off the chest, Edela crawled across the deck, searching for a weapon.

***

Two soldiers in black and gold tunics flanked Jael, who stood in a sea of animals, penned in by fences and panicking. They butted against each other, seeking an escape.

Though there was nowhere to go.

Jael waited near the front beside Tito, Arras' fretting horse, lifting a hand to comfort him. He sensed, as all the animals did, that something was terribly wrong, and he shifted around anxiously beside her, bumping her with his head. She thought of Tig, soothing Tito with quiet words, speaking slowly and softly, working to keep them both calm. His coat was smooth, and stroking it made her feel better too.

There was little she could do to help the other animals; there were simply too many.

The drummers from the funeral procession had made their way onto the platform, still drumming as they took their places behind the seated logi and Inesh Seppo.

Dessalene Sardis prowled the platform in a headdress of red feathers and gold antlers, her tall, angular body moving like a predator at times, at other times like a graceful bird. Fragrant smoke blew towards Jael, and inhaling, she recognised the familiar scent of mugwort, though her attention quickly shifted to the dreamer speaking in what sounded like Siluran.

The drummers' rhythm steadily increased, Dessalene following with a chant, so that soon the beating drum and the dreamer's words became a thumping heartbeat, not happening around Jael but inside of her. The powerful smoke blew towards her, and she blinked as it stung her eyes.

She saw Arras again.

No, she realised, shaking her head. Nico. She saw Nico Sikari with Thorgils, standing beside...?

Jael frowned intensely, not understanding.

Whatever was lurking in that smoke was already undoing her mind, for she was certain she saw Ulf. Ulf Rutgar? Closing her eyes, she pursued the vision, that drumbeat rolling her forward as though she stood atop a wave. And now she saw that it was indeed Ulf, standing beside Thorgils at the helm of a Hestian ship.

Shifting her eyes, holding the vision, she turned to see more ships.

Quickly counting at least twelve.

A Hestian fleet coming to S'ala Nis.

***

A breathless Raymon was jabbing and swaying, working to keep Iker Rayas back, though now weaponless, he knew he wouldn't hold out the skilled warrior for long. Dropping low, he released a leg, seeking to knock over the already unbalanced man, who hopped about, slashing his sword. But Iker quickly brought down his blade, chopping into Raymon's shoulder before losing his balance, both men collapsing to the ground.

'*Aarrghh!*' Raymon bellowed, falling with a crash.

Bertel's right arm was becoming heavy, as though he was wielding an anchor. The man facing him looked Korri's age, sprightly and snarling, light on his feet. He'd cut Bertel's cheek and his arm, and a panting Bertel was starting to flag. Breathing burned his lungs, though he kept trying to draw in breaths, hoping to spur himself on.

Knocked in the back, he lost his balance, tipping towards his enemy's knife. He was shunted out of the way by Korri, who fell with Bertel, both men losing their swords, now towered over by two Silurans, who drew back their axes, ready to strike.

Watching from the pier, held back by an anxious Zen, Siggy screamed. 'No! Edela! *Do* something!'

Edela was trying to. Having scooped up Iker Rayas' knife, she'd sliced it across her hand, and now, face and hands dripping with bloody symbols, she rose to her feet, swaying like a tree in a gale.

Her chanting was thunder, and she was a storm.

These men had tormented them for too long; hunted and tracked them, terrorised and hurt them, and now it would end.

She would end it.

Here.

***

'Wait for me,' Jael murmured. 'We have to wait.' She thought of Rigg, then Alek, not certain she'd gotten through to either man. 'Please, wait for me.'

The sun now burnished the top of the stadium, flaring off the golden helmet the king cradled in his lap. She saw Ronin Sardis, who had threatened to wipe out her entire family.

Why?

She needed to kill him, to stop him, though she wanted

answers from him first.

She kept Thorgils' face in her mind. He was on that lead ship with Ulf. Their connection had always been strong, she knew, almost smiling as Dessalene pointed to her, motioning her forward.

The slaves became still, anxious, fearing that their hopes rested on the future of this one woman. Once a queen, now a slave like they were.

She had promised to lead them, but would she get the chance?

They stood shoulder to shoulder in orderly rows under the ever-watchful eye of Argo Kosta, who sat beside the queen in the stands. Jael feared that his presence was intimidating the slaves. Though if they stumbled now they would never be free.

Their fears and doubts swirled around her as she sought to keep her composure.

There was no guarantee the slaves would rise as one.

No guarantee they would keep going in the face of soldiers skilled with their lethal weapons.

She heard Tito whinny, the beating drums rolling like thunder.

Her heart thumped, keeping in time with Thorgils'.

She saw the catapults on Ulf's ship, blinking in surprise, thinking of Karsten.

She would know.

When they struck the first ballista, she would know.

***

Edela could feel the ship shuddering beneath her. A darkness vibrated in the sea, and she lifted it higher with her left hand, using her right to bring a cloud down over the sun. She drew them closed like curtains, encasing the ship in a sheath of darkness.

The dark frightened many, but not Edela, who worked quickly now, twisting her hands, weaving glowing red symbols through that darkness like sparkling threads of yarn.

She saw the trails of the symbols as she wound and bound them together, hearing the clash of blades only faintly now and Siggy crying out so far away.

Jerking forward, Edela's back arched, arms lifting as the two symbols ignited in an explosion of sparks that blinded her. She cried out in surprise, rising off the deck, all the breath rushing from her lungs as she hung in the air, suspended, hands lost amongst a shower of red sparks.

The Silurans froze before her, turning their eyes to the levitating old woman.

They couldn't look away.

The red light blinded them, though they couldn't turn their heads. They couldn't even blink or lift a hand to shield their eyes.

Edela had claimed them, wound her symbol around them like rope, and now they were her prisoners.

They were hers.

Iker Rayas felt his sword arm burning, blazing from his shoulder to his fingers until he had no choice but to release his weapon.

It clattered to the deck, joined by those of his men.

Swords fell from hands, knives and axes, even hammers. Every weapon gone.

And now those men?

In that moment, Edela felt Furia standing with her.

The goddess was wild with anger.

Furia had sent her away to safety, and she had had enough of these men pursuing the dreamer. So had Bertel, Siggy, even Korri and Zen. They had all had enough of living in fear.

Turning her palms up to the dark sky, hearing the screams of Iker Rayas and his Silurans, loud in her ears, Edela lifted her arms into the darkness, reaching into those roiling clouds, and now she claimed them, pulling them to her chest until every red spark vanished and she was the darkness itself.

This was no magic learned in Tuura's temple.

For Edela was no longer in Tuura, and with a roar, she flung out her arms, sending the clouds of darkness sweeping over Iker Rayas and his helpless men.

Killing them all.

***

Standing beside Rigg, Alek was holding his breath, eyes fixed on the platform and the terrifying dreamer. He heard Jael's voice in his ears and turned to peer at Rigg, who looked at him strangely, as though he had heard it too. Tugging his friend's sleeve, Alek pulled him close. 'We wait.'

A nervous Rigg wasn't sure he agreed.

He shuffled his feet, now gripping the conch shell in his hands, holding it low. His eyes met Alek's before sweeping over the rows of slaves. He was vibrating with tension, doubts working to undo the certainty he'd felt only moments earlier.

If they waited too long, if he waited too long to blow the shell, would the slaves lose their appetite for the fight? Before them was a great show of pomp and power. A reminder that those who proclaimed themselves their owners were in complete control. According to everything he'd heard, the dreamer was dangerous and powerful, and if she...

Alek tugged his sleeve again. 'We wait for Jael, Rigg. We trust in Jael.'

CHAPTER FORTY-SEVEN

Jael saw the bloody symbol painted on Dessalene's forehead. In the heat, it had run into her eyes, bleeding over her cheeks and down her black dress.

She smiled, and her teeth were bloody too.

There was much a dark dreamer could do, Jael remembered, ripples of trauma returning to unsettle her. Shaking them away, she focused on ways to protect herself from whatever magic the woman was weaving.

'I am the sword,' she reminded herself silently. 'I am the sword.'

The first rays of sunlight flared through the tower's arch, burnishing the top of Inesh Seppo's dark head. Glancing at the man, she was surprised to see him watching her. His eyes were suddenly guarded, and once again, she wondered whose side he was on.

Dessalene brandished the long obsidian dagger as she chanted words Jael couldn't understand, though she guessed the dreamer was blessing the altar where the sacrifices would be offered.

It was made of a dark granite, glistening in the sun, a narrow channel attached to feed blood into the deep moat encircling the platform.

Not wanting to think about that, Jael turned away from the dreamer, eyes on the red-robed logi flanking the seer. Each man took his seat, hands clasped in his lap. One held the wooden staff they would present to Inesh Seppo as he was being anointed.

The setting sun had gilded half the stadium now, those lords and ladies sparkling like golden stars.

And Jael suddenly felt Thorgils' heart racing.

***

The catapults were loaded, Ulf's men waiting for the signal to strike.

No one spoke, *Beloved's* crew holding their breaths and their shields as they waited, all eyes up on the cliffs and on those enormous ballistas aimed their way.

'Now!' Nico urged, turning to look at Thorgils as *Beloved* crossed the invisible line that only he could see. 'Fire!' The ship's well-trained catapult crew moved with speed, releasing the hammer, already preparing to reload as it swung back, launching its boulder, just before the ballista crew discharged their giant missile.

***

The dark clouds that had rolled over Iker Rayas' ship like a dust storm quickly evaporated, the sky lightening above their heads, and soon everyone could see that the Silurans were dead.

They lay sprawled around the deck as though felled in battle. There was no blood, though their eyes were red, wide open and unblinking, weapons lost from their hands.

Edela lay on the deck too.

A bleeding Bertel had rushed to her side, rolling her onto

her back, though she hadn't moved. He couldn't hear her heart beating, couldn't feel her breathing.

His own breath stuck in his throat, horror and sadness freezing him as he stared at the dreamer in disbelief.

Siggy jumped down into the ship with Zen, crying out as she ran forward. 'No! *Edela*!'

Raymon swayed on his feet, and Korri was there, clutching an arm to his chest, all of them crowding around the fallen dreamer.

Bertel took Edela's hand, once again listening to her chest, desperate to hear her heart beating.

'Edela!' Siggy sobbed, kneeling beside him. The darkness was lifting now, the setting sun returning, and she saw the ghostly pallor of Edela's face beneath all that blood. '*Please*! You must come back to us! Please, Edela! We need you! *I* need you!'

Tears fell from her eyes onto the dreamer's face.

Which twitched, eyelashes gently fluttering.

'She moved!' Korri exclaimed. 'Did you see?'

Siggy did, and wiping her tears away from Edela's face, she kissed her forehead.

'Edela?' Bertel prodded, seeing those eyelashes moving with real purpose now.

And then a cough.

Pushing a crying Siggy out of the way and certain he wasn't crying himself, Bertel scooped an arm under Edela's back, and with Korri's help, they raised her to a sitting position.

She opened her eyes, blinking. 'I...'

'Don't speak,' Bertel told her.

'But what happened?' Siggy asked.

Bertel glared at the girl. 'She shouldn't speak. She needs rest.'

'What I need is for you to... move out of my face, Bertel Knutson,' Edela grumbled. 'How can I take a breath with you so close?'

Watching the dreamer batting away her companions, relief washed over Raymon. Relief that the Silurans were dead and the dreamer was alive. Edela Saeveld was beloved by Brekkans and

Tuurans alike and by her family most of all. Then, remembering how much he wanted to forget who he was and where he came from, he turned to go. The buzzing in his ears reminded him that he was wounded, that he couldn't lift his arm. He would have to find someone to help him. He would go to the physician's and –

The buzzing came for him like a swarm of angry bees, and Raymon Vandaal, former King of Iskavall, fell to the deck with a thud.

***

'Red flag!' Ulf bellowed to his men positioned in the stern and on both gunwales. 'Red flag!' His hands loosened on the steering oar, almost forgetting he was responsible for driving them into the harbour. 'Keep her steady,' he told himself, imagining what Karsten would say if he sunk his prize ship.

Beloved's boulder struck the ballista's spear, shattering it. But with that threat gone, they had to quickly fire again and take out the ballista itself.

'Reload!' Ulf cried.

'They're signalling!' Nico warned, turning to see another boulder launched from the ship, and flying free, it struck the eastern ballista. 'Again!' he urged. 'Fire!'

***

Trailing *Beloved* and the four Hestian catapult ships, Bolder's hands tightened around the steering oar. He saw another enormous spear-like missile coming for the fleet. It only just missed the ship trailing *Beloved* before diving into the sea.

Pulling the steering oar, Bolder aimed for the western side of the harbour, where they would drop anchor nearest the tunnel, into which Arras, Eadmund, and their men would disappear, looking for Jael.

Hoping the queen could hold on.

***

Dessalene finished her chant, eyes glazed like fine blue glass as she stared at the glowing tower, imagining Eyshar watching her. Sweeping around, she ran her eyes over the logi and the seer, raising them to find Ronin in the stadium before dropping them to her first victim.

The raven-haired queen. Furia's daughter.

Though not for long.

And now the dreamer glided towards the little bridge Jael had been dragged onto by two soldiers, who Dessalene didn't see at all. Her attention remained on the woman. She could feel Ronin as though he was looking over her shoulder, breathing in anticipation. He wanted this moment to be theirs together, though it was Dessalene who would cut the woman's throat.

Dessalene, who would gift her blood to Eyshar.

Jael watched the dreamer coming towards her, unable to prevent herself moving forward. In fact, she needed to get closer. To have any chance of stopping the dreamer, she was going to have to get as close as possible.

The two soldiers shunted her onto the platform towards Dessalene and her obsidian dagger. The drumming felt as though it was reaching a crescendo; the logi and the seer as still as statues, staring at her.

Keeping her lips pressed together, Jael sought to reach Alek, her eyes never leaving the dreamer's face. 'Hold,' she urged silently. 'Hold.'

'You will hold her arms,' Dessalene told the soldiers. 'Keep her still.'

In her mind, Jael heard the shatter of wood, boulders crashing onto the ballistas, and heart thumping, mouth open, she shouted at the top of her lungs, calling the slaves to action. 'Rigg! *Now!*'

Her shouting caught an entranced Dessalene by surprise, the men holding Jael, too, and feeling their grip on her arms loosen, she pushed forward, viciously headbutting the dreamer, who dropped the dagger as she fell to the ground, knocked unconscious.

Tugging her left arm out of the grip of one soldier, a dazed Jael heard Rigg blowing the conch shell.

Once.

Twice.

Three times.

A furious roar swept around the temple grounds. A roar of joy and anger.

And purpose.

Jael swung her fetter at the soldier, breaking his jaw, and turning to the other man, who'd dropped her arm, aiming to unsheathe his sword, she smashed him in the nose. Elbowing him in the throat, she helped herself to his sword. There was a flurry of movement in the stadium as the lords and leaders hurried to react to what was happening. From high up in the stands, she heard a bellowing Kosta ordering his men into the fight, seeing a flash of gold, knowing that the king was on his feet. Though Jael couldn't worry about those men – she had to organise the slaves.

Spinning around, she ran across the bridge, jumping down to Tito, and seizing the reins, she threw herself into the saddle. Raising her sword, she clung on as Tito reared up, nearly unseating her, goats and oxen panicking around him, desperately trying to get out of his path. 'Kill them!' Jael cried in Siluran. 'Kill them!' she yelled in the common tongue, and now Tito dropped his front hooves back to the ground, and she urged him on, past the frightened animals and out into the courtyard as the clanging sound of signal bells rose into the air.

***

One of the Hestian ships had been speared by a missile, though Ulf's attention was on trying to destroy the remaining ballista before it could do any further damage.

He could hear the clanging in the distance as the bells alerted the isle to danger.

Thorgils turned, calling to Ulf. 'Nudge it! We have to hit it square on!'

Ulf didn't even nod, trying to line *Beloved* up directly before that ballista, still just a lump on the cliff to him, wishing his eyes were twenty years younger.

'Turn!' he heard someone shout from a nearby ship, sensing another missile had been fired; they looked like spears a giant would wield. Two more boulders were quickly launched into the air, one knocking the missile off course, and soon it splashed into the sea, almost clipping *Bone Hammer*.

Biting his tongue, Bolder swore loudly, tugging the steering oar. 'I don't intend to swim to this fucking island! Why can't they crush it?' Though in the next moment, he heard an explosion as *Beloved's* newly-launched boulder struck the ballista down the middle.

A cheer went up on board more than one ship, though neither Arras nor Eadmund were celebrating.

'I planned for this sort of attack. As commander,' Arras told the king, eyes never leaving the harbour they were now aiming at. 'It won't be easy.'

Thinking she might vomit, Mattie turned away from the

men, remembering her rope. She had left it with Kolarov, who had a firm hold on Otter. And now, pushing up the deck, past the strained faces of concentrating men, she aimed for the explorer. 'I need to try the rope!'

He peered up at her in confusion, ears ringing with noise.

'The rope!' Mattie cried, and bending down, she felt around, finding it under her fur. 'We're not going fast enough! We need speed now!'

Straightening up, she immediately lost her balance, falling onto an unimpressed Otter, who bounded away. Scrambling back to her feet, Mattie gripped the stern in her left hand and the rope in her right.

And turning around, she braced herself, closing her eyes.

***

Jael drove Tito at the soldiers, who had turned back to fight off the attacking slaves.

It was all about momentum now, and she had to drive it.

She caught a glimpse of Alek, immediately knocked off his feet, fearing for him. Though he was Rigg's responsibility now, because if she didn't spur these men on, there'd be death for them all.

She thought of Eadmund and Arras, Thorgils and Fyn.

They were coming.

But not yet.

Alek and Rigg had taught her a few useful phrases in Siluran, and now she screamed them at the top of her lungs. 'Grab their weapons! Take their swords! Attack! Attack!'

***

Taking to the stadium's steps, a furious Ronin watched Kosta charging towards the courtyard, calling his men to arms. Turning to Kalina, he seized her elbow. 'You must get to the palace! You'll be safe there!' He motioned to two guards as a terrified Krissia approached. 'Take the women to the palace, and keep your queen safe! Use the back road and go now!' And unsheathing his sword, he ran after Kosta, eyes fixed, not on Jael Furyck or the slaves, but on the fallen figure of his wife, who lay sprawled on the platform. 'Dessalene!' he bellowed, seeing the sun beaming through every hole in the tower's arch now, flaming on the faces of Inesh Seppo and his logi as they rose to their feet.

'Fan out!' Inesh ordered, using a firm voice to command his red-robed men. And taking Noor's staff, he banged it down on the platform, calling for Eyshar to guide and protect them.

Reaching the platform, Ronin barrelled past him, aiming for Dessalene. Falling to his knees, he brushed hair away from her bleeding face. Her nose appeared broken, blood gushing over her cheeks, pooling in her ears. Her eyes were closed, and scooping an arm under her back, he kissed her, desperate to bring her back to life. Back to him.

She stirred, spluttering, and releasing her, Ronin felt relief, oblivious to the chaos swirling around him.

'Help me... up!' Dessalene urged, and unable to breathe through her nose, she started to panic. 'She... broke my nose! Ronin! You must kill that woman! My... nose!' And flinging out a hand, she now swayed up to her feet. 'Leave me!' she raged. 'And go! *Kill* her!' Sending her husband on his way, she turned from the horrified look in his eyes. She didn't dare touch her face, not wanting the extent of her injuries becoming more real.

It was enough to feel them.

'Stay safe!' Ronin called with a final look at his wobbling wife before running for the bridge.

Watching him leave and seeing the chaos Jael Furyck appeared in charge of, Dessalene knew she needed to do something quickly. So, lifting a trembling hand to her broken nose, she scooped up a finger of blood. And drawing symbols on each palm, she started chanting.

***

Mattie's thoughts screamed at her that it wasn't possible to control the wind, though she pushed ahead anyway, wanting to help.

In her cold hands, the rope felt coarse as she untied the first of the three knots she'd made earlier. She felt them like strands of hair blowing in a breeze. The breeze was gentle.

It moved them along.

Kolarov had told her about Isvarr – a god of both moderate and extreme temperaments. He would rise when the moment required it, and even though she was far from home, she felt as though she was back in Tuura, running through a field, hands spread like wings, hat blowing off her head.

Kolarov had said that Isvarr was just. A just god who wasn't afraid to come for his enemies.

She wondered if he would venture this far from home?

Now she untied the second knot. She wouldn't reach for the third.

They just needed a moderate wind.

Enough to blow them into the harbour at pace.

***

'Blue flag!' Ulf ordered as *Beloved* started picking up speed, grateful that the wind was strengthening in their favour.

The archers came forward, readying their fire arrows.

Braziers had been burning steadily since they'd emerged from The Corridor, but now those flames became erratic and the archers had to take care, holding their arrows in the fire, waiting for them to catch alight.

Nico Sikari stalked the deck as the men holding the blue signal flags waved them wildly.

'Arrows!' Thorgils yelled behind him, hearing a whistle and throwing up his shield.

Nico ducked behind his own. Ulf had no spare hands, though his second-in-command was holding a shield and worked to protect them both.

Beloved remained the lead ship, reaching for the harbour now, well within range of those archers who had flooded the piers.

The arrows sprayed over the Hestian fleet, two striking *Beloved's* mast, one piercing her sail. Another struck the prow, the remainder shooting into the sea.

'Hestians!' Thorgils cried. 'Nock!' Dropping his shield, he turned, carrying his booming voice to the two rows of archers, all seeking their balance, who emerged from behind the shield-bearers. 'Aim!' *Beloved* was heading into the harbour at speed now, Thorgils could see, as he turned back. '*Fire!*'

***

Jael spun Tito around, raking her sword down a soldier's back. He fell forward, howling in agony as she drove the horse on, calling to the slaves. '*Move!*' she roared, throat burning. 'Take their weapons! Knock them down! Faster!'

Turning the horse back to the platform, she saw the bloody-faced dreamer on her feet, arms extended, hands aimed in her direction. Quickly sliding off Tito, Jael slapped him away, needing a shield, though fearing it wouldn't be enough against the powerful witch.

She quickly found a dead soldier, relieving him of his useless shield, and feeling more like herself than she had in weeks, she pushed past the penned-in animals, seeking the bridge to the platform where the dreamer waited.

Watching her, body trembling, a frustrated Dessalene couldn't make any magic. Try as she might, she couldn't bring a symbol to her mind. Every word she thought to speak wouldn't leave her tongue.

She felt no spark, no energy. Nothing at all.

Seeing Jael Furyck coming for her, armed with weapons, she panicked. Spinning around, she saw the sun blazing through the arch, lighting up Inesh Seppo. He shone like a golden coin in that perfect moment, and blinking, she finally found her voice. 'Help me! You must... help!'

Though instead, the seer closed his eyes, hands wrapped around his staff.

He was doing something, Dessalene realised, terror exploding now as she felt a strange force, like a wall between them.

He was working against her. Blocking her power.

Jael roared, seeking to claim the dreamer's attention, though she was hit on the head by a flying rock and knocked to the ground.

***

Rigg saw a helmeted Argo Kosta barging through his men, hacking at every weaponless slave in his path, urging his soldiers to crush the revolt, demanding they snuff it out before it spread.

He had quickly found Alek a shield and a knife, and keeping his friend close, he started pushing towards where he'd last seen Jael. She'd dismounted the black horse, aiming for the sacrifice platform.

He hadn't seen her since.

The men around him were looking for direction, losing momentum. He had to lead.

Some had already been injured and were clutching bleeding wounds, trying to escape the melee rather than fight on. Others appeared to be hanging back, waiting to see what would happen before they committed themselves, eyes on a furious Kosta.

And knowing that momentum was everything, Rigg sought to spur them on.

Lifting his voice, he gripped his new sword like a long-lost friend, urging the terrified men in grey tunics to fight for their lives. 'For freedom! Fight for your freedom or die at their hands!'

'Fight! Fight!' came the cry around him, strengthening now as slaves fought off blades with fists and heads and feet. They fought their own fear that they wouldn't be strong enough to overcome armed warriors of skill and experience.

But fight they did.

Behind Rigg, Alek swung up his shield, nearly knocking himself over, but finding a strength he'd feared he didn't possess, he gritted his teeth, smashing a soldier in the mouth. Blood spurted from broken teeth and cut lips, spraying his face, and gulping in horror, he stumbled after Rigg.

'Take their weapons!' Rigg demanded in Siluran, quickly repeating it in the common tongue. 'Take every fucking weapon and make them yours! Eyshar is with us! Every god is on our side!'

On the ground, struggling to get back to her feet amongst walls of legs, many kicking her, Jael heard him, and screaming, she rolled over, pushing herself up. Quickly getting her bearings, she saw that she'd been driven away from the platform and the dreamer, back into the throng of wrestling men.

'Arras Sikari is here!' she shouted, seeking to give the slaves hope. 'He's brought a fleet of warriors to free us!' Swinging around, she parried an axe, teeth gritted. A few ears pricked up, and she carried on, seeking to drive that stake through the heart of the soldiers' defenses. 'Arras Sikari is here! In the harbour! He has returned to free you!'

She stabbed a soldier in the thigh, immediately bringing her blade up under his chin, dragging it across his throat. And working her elbows, she spun away, needing to find Tito.

She caught a glimpse of the king's helmet.

Gleaming gold and studded with colourful jewels, it was a beacon, drawing her to him. Unleashing a long, broad sword, he swung it in two hands, chopping at every bare head, seeking to stamp out every pocket of resistance.

***

Eadmund and Arras moved into *Bone Hammer's* bow in front of their men as a handful of archers, protected by shield-bearers, remained, giving them cover.

Waiting just behind Eadmund, Fyn vibrated with tension, trying to shut out his fears of what might go wrong. Mattie and Kolarov would stay behind with Bolder in case they needed to make a hasty escape, and he could only hope they'd be safe on board.

Ulf's Hestians were burning the harbour to their right, setting fire to the ballistas, crushing them with boulders that flamed and smoked, sending dark clouds and stinking pitch into the air.

'Stay here!' he called to Mattie. 'Don't leave the ship!'

The dreamer clung to her rope, though she no longer needed it. Kolarov hugged Otter beside her. They both nodded at him.

'I'll return,' Fyn promised with a crooked smile. 'This time with Jael!'

'Hurry!' Mattie urged, feeling a sharp pain in her heart, seeing glimpses of battle now. 'Jael needs you! You must hurry!'

Hearing that, Eadmund almost jumped out of the ship, though they were still a few lengths from the pier. 'Get us close!' he demanded, not wanting to swim. It would slow them down, and as Mattie said, they needed speed. 'Come on!'

'I'm trying!' Bolder snapped, swaying from side to side, attempting to see through the billowing smoke and the choking pitch. 'Take the oar!' he yelled at Raal. 'Hold her steady! I need to see!' And running to the starboard gunwale, he was struck by an arrow. It took him in the side, knocking him over.

'Bolder!' Mattie screamed, scrambling towards him.

Plonking Otter down, Kolarov crawled after her.

Eadmund spun around, mouth open, and though he feared for his friend, he couldn't help him now. 'Get us there fast!' he yelled at Raal. 'Hurry!'

CHAPTER FORTY-EIGHT

Ronin Sardis sensed that his men were faltering under the slaves' onslaught. His soldiers had experience. They were armed and skilled, though they were being crushed by the sheer number of slaves in the temple grounds. It had been a mistake, he saw in hindsight, to cram so many into one tight space.

They were overwhelmed.

Those on horseback had been brought down, weapons had been ripped away, and his soldiers were being beaten by fists, kicked and stoned, armour torn from bodies, heads caved in.

More and more rocks were being used as weapons, and Ronin ducked and weaved, keeping his head on a swivel. He was experienced enough to expect the ebb and flow of battle, knowing that an inexperienced enemy would often claim early success, though it was important not to let that momentum solidify into something substantial. Once the slaves ran out of breath, he was sure his trained men would assert themselves again, instilling fear into those who dared overthrow them.

Glancing at Kosta, bludgeoning a slave with his sword, Ronin thought about what he'd heard Jael Furyck shouting. That Arras Sikari was in the harbour? That he was here to liberate the slaves?

Having heard the signal bells, he feared she was right.

Though surely he hadn't returned alone...

'Kosta!' he shouted, slashing a path towards the commander. 'You need to head for the harbour!'

Kosta swung around with confusion in his eyes.

'You heard the bells! Something's wrong! Get down there! If Arras Sikari's back?' Ronin knew he couldn't afford to spare any men, but if they were under attack from an outside force, that force would be fully armed, and coming in from the harbour, it would crush his soldiers. He had to risk it all now or expose himself to an attack from behind. 'Take half your men and go! Gather more on the way! You will hold them back! Hold them back and defeat them at the harbour!'

Kosta looked so unsure that Ronin was forced to shove him. 'You will *go*! I'll command here! And my wife, she will help! Now leave!'

***

Bone Hammer hit the pier with a thump, knocking a handful of the crew off their feet, weapons clattering.

Eadmund wondered fleetingly if his loyal helmsman was alive, and then he was vaulting off the ship onto the pier. Sword swinging from a clenched fist, he took the first man across his padded chest. Arras landed behind him with a thud, sweeping down the pier with precision, elbowing one surprised man into the sea, spearing another with his blade. He yelled at those men rushing down the pier, warning them that he had come to free the slaves and that they would either help him or die by his hand.

Eadmund saw hesitation in the eyes of those men, though their new commander barked orders for them to charge, and instinct taking over, they moved down the pier in unison, shields at their chests, swords and axes gripped in claw-like hands.

Fyn glanced over his shoulder, seeing the familiar figure of Thorgils on *Beloved* as the Hestian ship approached the piers, red hair flowing in the sun. Bright and intense, it streamed into Fyn's eyes as he turned back around, hearing more boulders smashing the harbour, flames crackling as they rose up from shattered wagons, barrels, and bodies.

'Move! Move! Move!'

Arras' shout focused his attention, and Fyn extended his stride until he was level with him. Shifting his body slightly to the right, he saw a flash of the day Jael had taught him how to hold his sword, remembering it like it was yesterday. And squeezing his hand around his hilt, he roared. 'For Jael!'

Eadmund didn't speak as he released his own sword, sliding it across the neck of a warrior, but he thought it.

For Jael.

**

Jael saw Kosta gathering his men together, heading away from the temple grounds, and now she had a decision to make: stay at the temple or move to stop him gaining control over the rest of the island?

He turned to look over his shoulder at her, smiling.

And back burning, sword arm twitching, her decision was made.

She swung back around, parrying a shot to the head, then veering sharply, she elbowed her way towards Tito, who had sought refuge amongst the herd of frightened animals offered a reprieve by the attack.

He didn't look pleased to see her, but having made her decision, Jael once again threw herself into the saddle, and hitching up her dress, she slipped her shoes into the stirrups. Tito made to rear up again, though a few strong words kept him grounded, and soon she was driving him towards Rigg. 'Out of my way!' she warned, not wanting to knock down any slaves.

She saw Quint, who, having lost his sword, was working to fend off three slaves with a shield alone. Though she couldn't help the man. He was simply on the wrong side.

Finding Rigg, she shouted at him. 'Kosta's going for the harbour! I have to go after him! You're in charge! Push them forward! Secure things here, then move up to meet me!'

Rigg nodded, spinning away, headbutting a soldier trying to attack him from behind.

'Where's Alek?'

Rigg stepped to the side, almost tripping over a body, revealing that Alek and his shield were still there, wobbling beside him.

'Forward!' she cried. 'There's more of you now! Kosta's taking men with him!' Tito skittered beneath her, nostrils flaring, the pungent stench of blood unsettling him further.

Rigg lifted his eyes, meeting Jael's and with a nod, he swung away.

'Alek! Stay safe!' Jael called, eyes on the frail man, fearing for them both, though there was no time for it.

She had to get after Kosta.

***

Arras took them into the tunnel, having dispatched those men guarding it with relative ease. Their hesitation about attacking their former commander had rendered their defense ineffective, and Arras had quickly left their bodies behind, plunging into the darkness. 'Run!' he urged. 'It's long, but we have to run!' He heard rumbles like thunder as the Hestian boulders destroyed the harbour in the distance now, fixing his mind on what lay ahead.

He would aim for the female slave's bathhouse, where he'd first taken Jael. Through there was a quick route into a garden and then out onto the main street.

And what would be waiting for them?

Or who?

***

A groggy and bleeding Dessalene was horrified to see Kosta departing with half those men previously holding back the slaves surging across the temple grounds.

She didn't understand what Ronin was thinking... sending the man away?

She could see nothing herself.

She could bring nothing to her, and becoming enraged, she spun around to Inesh Seppo and his circle of logi, fearing they were enemies but too desperate to care. 'You will do something! I... need you to do something!'

Inesh looked at her blankly.

'What is wrong with you?' Dessalene shrieked, ready to throttle the man. 'Why aren't you *doing* anything?' The noise crashed in from every side, her aching face pounding. Wiping blood from her eyes, she strode towards the seer and his men.

Inesh looked confused. 'You wish us to fight, my lady? But we know no magic, no spells. And you? I had heard that you did...'

A furious Dessalene peered into those deep brown eyes, seeing defiance.

She couldn't read the man's thoughts, couldn't read any of their thoughts, and turning away with a howl of rage, she left him behind.

She was disarmed of her weapons – every one of them, apart from her instincts.

And they told her that Ronin was in desperate trouble.

***

With Jael gone, Rigg took the battle at the temple grounds by the reins. He urged the slaves on, sensing that with the bellowing king rallying his soldiers, the slaves' momentum had faltered.

'They will kill us all!' he warned. 'We have to kill –'

A knife took him in the head, right between the eyes.

Beside him, Alek's mouth dropped open. 'Rigg! Rigg!' He stumbled down beside him, seeing that his friend was dead, eyes fixed open in surprise. Terror flooded Alek's veins. Terror and sadness.

Grabbing Rigg's sword, he stood, heart in mouth, knowing that Jael had gone.

Jael had gone, the king was leading his men, seeking to overcome their stuttering assault.

And Rigg was dead.

'I will not die here!' he shouted, voice breaking. Beside him, men glanced his way. 'They killed Rigg, but I will not die here! I miss my sons! I want to go home! Don't you?' He turned, screaming at the men around him, seeking to blast any doubt out of their hearts, wanting to replace it with fire and belief. 'Don't you?'

He was immediately knocked to the ground, kicked by soldiers working to push back the slaves. Crying out, he felt a sharp pain in his ribs. And then a hand on his shoulder and another lifting him to his feet, and soon he was flanked by two of his crew. They weren't as big as Rigg, not warriors, but men who had slaved over that tower beside him and under him. Men who had given their all and who now stood on the precipice of death or freedom beside him.

And those men chose to fight.

'Push forward!' Alek rasped. '*Push!*'

***

Jael spurred Tito after Kosta and his men, wishing she had a bow and a quiver of arrows, though they seemed in short supply on S'ala Nis. She saw skirmishes breaking out along the main road as groups of slaves banded together, throwing rocks and anything else they had to hand. Some even threw their shoes.

Kosta's men ran beside and rode after their commander, moving with trained precision. Swaying from side to side in Tito's saddle, Jael watched as he ordered some of those men to peel off, urging them to crush those slaves rebelling in the main street.

She rode after him alone, calling those slaves to her, seeking to infuse them with hope. 'Arras Sikari is coming!' she bellowed. 'Arras Sikari is coming to save you!' She doubted they knew her or cared for anything she might say, but she knew how much they admired their favourite commander.

Her bellowing finally caught Kosta's attention, and brutally jerking his horse around, he aimed him at the big-mouthed slave queen.

***

Jumping down onto a pier packed with enemies, Thorgils took a man in the cheek, chopping hard. Yanking back his blade, he drove it into the man's belly. Blood showering over him, he moved away from Nico Sikari towards where Ulf was rallying his Hestians to pick up their pace.

'Faster!' Ulf snapped, momentarily blinded by the last of the sun. 'You want some gold? To please your king? Then move yourselves! *Move!*' He threw his axe, striking a head, and unsheathing his sword, he swept towards the man, wanting it back.

Thorgils skidded on a trail of blood, chomping down on his tongue, and grimacing, he remembered Jael's advice that a clear head was a better weapon than any sword. Shrugging, he lashed out with his sword anyway, shattering a shield, sending its holder scrambling backwards. 'Move on!' he shouted, spitting out a gob of blood. 'Through the harbour! *Move!*' A rush of energy pumped through his vibrating body, heating it like boiling water.

Blades were flying, the odd arrow picking off their men, but Thorgils Svanter felt a lift. These bastards had kept his queen a prisoner. His queen, his friend.

Jael.

And he was here to get her back.

***

Kosta drove his horse back through his men, urging them to follow his second-in-command to the harbour, where they would make their stand against whoever sought to join the unrest. 'Protect the city!' he urged. 'Protect the queen!' He feared for Kalina as he drew back his sword, hoping his daughter had made it to safety with her.

Reaching Jael, he released his blade, though he didn't swing for the woman.

He swung for the horse.

Jael jerked the reins, pulling Tito back, hooves in the air. She clung to him, legs gripping his belly, left hand wrapped around the reins, and bringing him back to the ground, she saw Kosta's game. Her back was numb or burning – she couldn't tell. The last of the sun streamed into her eyes, and in the middle of the street where she had walked with Sunni, she slid off Tito's back, slapping him away, deciding to make her stand.

***

Arras turned left, leading them down the tunnel, sword dripping with blood, gripped in a vibrating hand. He thought of Nico, hoping his son was safe, regretting he'd brought him back, exposing him to more danger than ever. 'The courtyard's coming up!' he warned. 'Through there another tunnel and then the bathhouse. We're getting closer!'

He didn't look over his shoulder to see whether Eadmund had heard him.

Though Eadmund had, and turning around to Fyn, he nodded.

***

Jael's stolen sword had nothing on Kosta's beautiful weapon. He was an arrogant, proud, bullish brute, though he knew how to handle it with skill. Dismounting with a thump, he sent his own horse away and now confronted Jael with a sneer and a slash of his blade, skipping towards her with surprising gracefulness.

'I'll shatter that stick in two!' he taunted. 'You could run? Well...' He glanced down at her fetters. 'Perhaps not!' Sweeping forward, he swung again.

Jael's movements were hampered by both sets of fetters and by the dratted grey dress. She couldn't move her feet with speed, her arms were slower than she wanted them to be, and she only just managed to parry his strike. The power behind Kosta's blow nearly bounced the sword out of her hand. She clung on, though, thoughts scattering.

Eadmund was coming with Arras Sikari. She saw glimpses of the harbour and Thorgils' face. Ulf was there with his Hestians, but they were not having an easy time of it.

Slaves swarmed the street behind Jael, chased by soldiers, a great screaming cacophony rising into the darkening sky. Women hung out of windows, tipping buckets of water over the fighting masses. The two horses charged away, seeking an escape as a snarling Kosta lunged forward, aiming to stab Jael in the chest.

Lurching back, she tripped over a cobblestone, lifting her sword, which Kosta easily broke in two.

Hubris was a cruel mistress, a stumbling Jael thought, staring at the broken blade, regretting everything that had made her think that, imprisoned by her fetters and hampered by her back, with a stranger's sword in her hand, she would be any match for this man.

The cobblestones were unforgiving. There was nowhere to slide to. No knife down her boot, no belt at her waist. No Fyn by her side.

Though hearing Fyn's voice in her ears, she knew he was coming.

And if she could just hang on...

***

Arras, Eadmund, and their twenty-odd men were held up in a courtyard. Having heard the signal bell, soldiers had been sent into the tunnels, taking a shortcut to the harbour, so there weren't just four men guarding the doors to the next tunnel but fifteen.

'Spread out!' Eadmund called, motioning for Fyn to take the right flank. 'We can't slow down! Finish them!'

But recognising Arras, a soldier held up his hand, keeping them back. 'Commander! Why are you here?'

Arras knew the young man well; he was a good friend of Nico's. 'I've come to free the slaves, Ravil! To free Jael Furyck.

This is her husband. We are here to liberate the isle!'

The blue-eyed man blinked at him. 'And Nico?'

'He's with us! Coming through the harbour. Join us! Join us or die! We outnumber you. We will kill you! You must join us or die!'

And not feeling inclined to die, Ravil urged his men to stand down and fall in line.

***

Still holding her broken sword, Jael slipped out of the sheering arc of Kosta's blade, which struck the road with a crash.

'Bitch!' he seethed, swinging back that mighty blade again, ready to fell her like a tree. 'You plotting bitch! This was your plan all along? With Sikari? To come here and free the slaves?'

Ignoring him, a grunting Jael swung her right leg, tearing her dress as she sought to knock Kosta's sword from his hand. But moving with ease, he switched the sword to his left hand and once again unleashed it at her. Jael dropped her leg, unbalanced, trying to move more quickly than her fetters would allow, and legs tangling, they tripped her.

She fell on her side. Pain blinding her, she swung out her broken blade, aiming for Kosta's leg.

He brought down his sword with a grunt, eyes gleaming hungrily, but Jael swerved to the side, stabbing the jagged blade into his ankle. He howled, furious, kicking her in the back with his good leg.

'*Aarrghh*!' Jael screamed, the intense pain stealing her vision. She entered the darkness, seeing her father's face as he sat before that pyre. She heard Ronin Sardis' voice as he threatened her family.

Kosta kicked her again and again. She tried to move, to

wriggle away, to crawl to her feet, unable to hear anything now but her heartbeat thumping in her ears.

It stuttered. She couldn't breathe, couldn't see.

The broken sword fell from her hand.

And Argo Kosta laughed, bringing down his blade.

***

Arras charged out of the garden, eyes up, ears open, hearing a thundering roar from the harbour, blades clashing in the street. 'Move!' he urged as Eadmund fell in behind him, keeping pace with Fyn.

Nico's friend Ravil moved up to Arras' right. 'What's the objective, commander?'

He spoke in Siluran, and neither Eadmund nor Fyn understood him. They followed close, running down a cobblestoned alley at pace, turning abruptly after the commander.

'We were at the temple,' Ravil explained. 'Sent to the harbour by Kosta. He was being chased by that woman, Jael Furyck. He sent us on. He went back for her.'

A shiver rippled through Arras' body.

Argo Kosta.

That bastard.

CHAPTER FORTY-NINE

'Roll!' Aleksander's voice blared in Jael's ears.

Eyes bursting open, she reacted on instinct, rolling as though she was back in Andala, training with him, bellowed at by her father and Gant.

'*Roll!*' he screamed again. 'Up on your feet!'

Jael's back had frozen; she couldn't breathe. She thought of her other Aleksander – Alek – seeing glimpses that Rigg was dead and that Alek was leading those men on his own. And rolling again, she heard someone calling her name.

'*Jael!*'

Now it was Eadmund's voice in her ears.

Dragging herself onto her knees with a pained roar, blood pouring from her mouth, she swayed away from Kosta's blade, and clamping her forearms together, fetters touching, she swung for his waist. He was moving to the left, and she took him on the hip, knocking him off balance.

Keeping her forearms pressed together, Jael swung low, striking his knee. Now up on her feet, she ducked his blade as he stumbled, seeking to come for her again. Dropping her hands, she pushed off her thighs, drawing in every bit of strength she possessed, and leaning on her left leg, she flung her right at Kosta's head. Clipping his ear with her fetter, she hurt him. Though made of stone, he merely grunted, soon swinging back at her, blade glinting.

***

The main road was choked with fighting.

Soldiers were being pulled from horses, uniforms stripped from dying bodies. The soldiers' helmets were being used as weapons against them, and even children had joined the battle, some armed with slingshots and stones, others trying their luck with knives. Arras saw more than one child lying injured, perhaps dead.

'Which way?' Eadmund demanded, knocked against Fyn as Kosta's soldiers backed towards them, seeking to escape a showering of rocks. Most didn't have shields, and they joined with Ravil's men, who did. There were curious glances as some of the men recognised Arras, and those loyal to Kosta weren't happy to see him. One man turned on Arras with a fist. Another brandished his blade.

Eadmund swung away, grabbing Ravil. 'Where's my wife? Jael Furyck? Which way?'

Ravil pointed to his left, ducking a flying rock.

'Take the men!' Arras told him, realising he was going to be penned in. 'I'll keep Ravil's. Push south. I'll head north and work my way back to Nico!'

A nodding Eadmund was immediately spinning away. '*Jael!*'

'Jael!' Fyn echoed beside him, elbowing someone out of the way. The young man didn't appear armed, he realised, feeling bad about that. 'Jael Furyck?' he asked hopefully as the man righted himself.

'Fighting Kosta! That way! He's killing her!'

And with one look at Eadmund, Fyn Gallas put down his head and barrelled forward.

***

Sucking air down a throat that burned, Jael tried reminding herself that she had many options. Twenty years of fighting had taught her a lot.

If only she could remember any of them.

She swayed out of Kosta's reach, though not far enough. Feet heavy and fetters cumbersome, she was too slow, and his sword cut her upper arm.

Wincing, she dropped down, and with an agonised grunt, she bent her head, slamming it into his belly. He wore a padded vest, and it was a soft enough landing, she supposed, working quickly to grab the sides of the vest. Hanging from it, she almost tore it off him as she brought him crashing down to the ground.

Eadmund was near. She heard him shouting for people to move.

Fyn too.

Kosta hit the ground with a thud, helmet rolling off his head. Swinging back onto her knees, Jael kicked his sword out of his hand, hearing it skitter across the cobblestones.

Stopped by a boot.

Mouth full of blood, back dripping blood, braids undone, stuck to her face, she swung her left fetter at Kosta's nose, shattering it, and then her right at his mouth, breaking his teeth. Roaring now, she staggered to her feet, blowing like a horse, swaying backwards, and as Kosta tried to move, gurgling blood, seeking to get back to his feet, she turned to her right.

Taking the sword her husband handed her.

Tears welled in her eyes as she turned back around.

Her husband.

And with a mighty bellow, Jael swung that heavy sword down on Argo Kosta, missing his neck entirely and shattering his ribs. She swayed, tears streaming down her bloody face, sobbing now. And pulling back the sword until it rose past her shoulder, she brought it down across his neck, killing him.

Dropping the sword, she wobbled, and turning, she fell into Eadmund's arms.

***

Shocked to see his horse galloping up the street, Arras called to him. Tito's ears pricked up, then swivelled around and spying his long-seen owner, he soon headed his way.

After a brief reunion, Arras mounted his loyal stallion, spurring him towards the harbour. He could see scores of soldiers ahead of him, knowing they sought to stop the Hestians' assault.

He needed help.

'I have returned to free you!' he called to the slaves. 'Come with me and be free! You can go home to your loved ones! Set yourselves free!' He repeated it in the common tongue and even in Kalmeran, quickly drawing more slaves into the street. Windows were flung open, women and children peering out, seeing the beloved commander who had once been one of them.

He had not forgotten them.

He had returned.

'Join me!' he cried. 'And you will be free!'

***

Eadmund made to wrap his arms around his sobbing wife's back, though she jerked out of his reach, waking herself up.

'No!' Wiping a bloody hand over her eyes, trying to see, Jael turned around, revealing a torn dress slashed with blood. 'I... we have to go. Arras?' Jael could hear the commander calling the slaves to him.

'Heading for the harbour. Thorgils is coming through with Nico.'

Jael saw Fyn and didn't want to cry again, but the relief, the joy was like nothing she'd experienced in her life.

They had come to take her home.

'We have to go back to the temple! The king!' she remembered, blinking tears from her eyes. 'And Alek!' Thinking quickly, she picked up Kosta's sword, handing it to Eadmund. 'Swap?'

Nodding, he unsheathed his own sword, taking the fine blade she now offered, staring at the mess of her in horror. 'Can you even walk?'

Turning around with a grimace, Jael looked for a horse. 'I can ride. But we have to hurry!'

**

Pushing forward with Nico, Ulf, and the Hestians, Thorgils' confidence rose.

They'd made it out of the harbour, suffering few losses. Ulf's men were vicious, Thorgils was pleased to see, which, given that they were Hestians, wasn't surprising. He'd been struck by a rock and could only hear a ringing in his left ear, so he kept turning, needing to see what was coming for him from every side.

'Push on!' Nico shouted, picking up his pace. He could see how few soldiers were out in the streets. He'd expected to have encountered more resistance, though maybe his father was helping with that?

Soon they heard a thundering of boots, and turning the corner, they saw a wall of black and gold tunics coming for them, shields at the ready.

'To me!' Thorgils urged, spinning to Ulf. 'Form up on me! Shield wall! Do not let them past!'

**

Kosta's men had abandoned their horses in the street, some of them dragged off them by brave slaves, so Jael, Eadmund, Fyn, and their men grabbed what they could, and following after Jael, they headed to the temple.

Jael rode a black stallion, which seemed entirely appropriate, Eadmund thought, watching her. His eyes were drawn to the bloody streaks across her dress, wondering what had happened, though Jael wasn't even looking his way as she rode, one-handed, driving the horse back through surging rows of slaves, who appeared to have gotten the better of Kosta's soldiers.

Turning around, she motioned to the tower in the distance. 'There! Follow me!' And darting down an alley that she hoped was a shortcut, she saw glimpses of a struggling Alek, fearing she'd be too late.

***

Alek had been knocked out, left on the ground some time ago.

When he'd come to, he'd tried pulling himself back to his feet, though his legs were trapped. He couldn't even see them, couldn't move them. Bodies were tumbling around him, screams cut off, blood flung around like buckets of water. Gasping, his voice just a thin croak, he tried calling for help. The man lying over his legs, he soon realised, was two men. Both dead. Both heavy as stone.

He was bleeding from his head wound, which had run into his mouth, and lying down, he turned to the ground to vomit. The pungent smell of death polluted the warm evening air. 'Help,' he could only mouth in despair.

Screaming men couldn't hear him, though. They didn't see him.

Then another body fell on his chest.

***

Jael leaned left, hoping her horse had quicker reactions than she did, for here the alleys were narrow, lined with barrels, handcarts pushed against houses, rubbish piled high. She almost ran over a pregnant dog, who waddled slowly across her path, teats nearly touching the ground.

Veering right, she heard hooves thumping behind her, loud on the cobblestones. Holding her breath, she emerged back onto the main road, having avoided the throng of slaves just before the entrance to the temple grounds.

She thought of the king, certain she saw a glimpse of his golden helmet.

But only fleetingly.

She had to save Alek.

***

Kosta's men were not backing down.

They were not going to be pushed back either. These men had come to take their island, and they were determined to hold it until their commander arrived with reinforcements.

Nico saw men he knew, many he despised, and feeling motivated for the fight, he shunted his shield forward, stabbing low with his sword, aiming at thighs and knees. He would hobble anyone to stop them getting past.

They needed to be a wall now. To keep the soldiers back.

Beside Thorgils, Ulf went down, speared in the leg.

Dropping his shield, Thorgils reached down and yanked him back. Turning with a thump and a roar, he speared a man in the chest.

There was no time to think, to care, to feel.

He would survive. He would survive and save his queen.

The sudden surge of black and gold soldiers seemed to part like waves, and soon they heard a familiar voice and a whinnying horse. Looking up, Nico saw his father on Tito, coming behind those warriors, sword crashing down like a hammer. And then a cheer loud enough to drown out all other thoughts.

The slaves, Nico realised, seeing flashes of grey.

The slaves were rising.

***

Jael steered her horse into the temple grounds, tightening her grip on the reins, bloody hands shaking now. To her surprise, she saw that Inesh Seppo and his logi remained on the platform like colourful statues.

There was no sign of Dessalene.

She saw the king's soldiers grouped in a huddle, trying to hold off a swarming mass of slaves. They were vastly outnumbered, surrounded, and, by the look of things, out of weapons. Rocks were being lobbed in the air, supported by fists and knives. The screaming, desperate slaves appeared to have gone over the edge, past the point of backing down.

Scanning the darkening temple grounds, Jael turned in the saddle, though there was no sign of the king either. She pushed her stallion to the edge of the melee, raising Eadmund's sword in the air, desperate to find Alek. She knew he was in trouble, though where, she had no idea.

Behind her, Eadmund ordered his men to fan out, circling the fight.

'You have won!' Jael called over the noise, her horse blowing in protest, not wanting to go any further. She kneed him, though, forcing him into the crowd, seeing Hepa. 'Tell them you've won! We can take prisoners! Don't let another man die!' He nodded, repeating her words in Siluran as Jael echoed them in the common tongue, her black stallion shuffling left, then right. There was no sign of Alek, but spotting Quint's conch shell, abandoned and blood-splattered, she jumped down from her horse with a grunt, spinning around to Eadmund. 'You need to keep your men back. Let Hepa talk them down. Hold the line!' And gripping Eadmund's sword, she moved into the crush of bodies, aiming for that shell.

'Jael!' Fyn cried, seeing a flying shield aiming for her head. '*Jael!*'

***

Calling down to his son from atop Tito, Arras started organising for peace, wanting to stop the bloodletting, though he sensed he was going to have problems. He didn't blame the slaves, many of whom had been stolen from their homes and families and brought to this strange island. They had been beaten and raped, had their hope and freedom stripped from them, so he didn't begrudge them their frustration or their desire for revenge.

But now, he needed them to listen. To get behind him and follow him to the temple to complete their victory, to vanquish their enemies and free themselves once and for all.

'With me!' he shouted, encouraging Nico and the Hestians to follow his lead. 'To the temple! We need to find the king!'

Those words pierced the red mist, Arras saw, and heads popping up, more and more pairs of eyes fixed on him.

***

Wriggling on the ground, Jael saw a familiar pair of eyes.

She'd turned just in time to avoid the flying shield, though her ankle fetter had caught on something, and legs tangled, she'd crashed down onto a pile of bodies with a soft thump. And there she caught a glimpse of a groggy Alek, trying to escape a heap of blood-soaked bodies. 'Alek!' Untangling her legs, Jael crawled towards him, seeing no sign of recognition in his eyes as they closed. She could only see his face, and soon that was buried as well. Forcing herself back to her feet, she saw Fyn and Eadmund barrelling towards her, pulling and pushing bodies out of the way. 'Help me! Help me get him out!' And handing Eadmund's sword back to him, Jael lunged for Alek's hand as the stack of bodies started shifting away from her.

Dropping the giant sword and sheathing his own, Eadmund plunged in after her.

'Alek! Hold on!' Jael urged, hearing Hepa calling for a cease to the fighting. She grabbed Alek's hand.

Freeing his own hands, Fyn joined Eadmund in pushing the dead bodies off the man, whose eyes fluttered open.

'Jael?' Alek's eyes closed again and he didn't speak.

Fyn shoved the last man away, and Eadmund pulled Alek out of the crush, throwing him over his shoulder and moving away as Jael hurried to grab Quint's shell. Knocked into left and right, she lifted the shell to her lips and took a breath, blowing loudly.

She felt the battle almost shudder to a stop around her. 'You have... won!' she cried, hearing Hepa echo her in Siluran. 'You are free!' And seeing glimpses of the devastated harbour and the slaves united behind Arras, she knew that was finally true.

Again, Alek opened his eyes, trying to peer at her from over Eadmund's shoulder. And turning to look at him, Jael was sure she saw him smile.

'What now?' Fyn asked. He couldn't stop staring at his queen.

She looked different, her tanned face drawn. Older. Though perhaps it was all the blood?

'The king. We need to find where he's gone. Leave Alek on the platform,' she told Eadmund, seeing that the logi were already coming forward, eyes on the fallen foreman. 'And come with me!' Then, waking herself up, she ran back to Eadmund, kissing him as she unsheathed his sword. And flashing a bloody smile at her surprised husband, she ran for her horse.

CHAPTER FIFTY

'What is wrong with you, woman?' Ronin snapped at his wife as they ran down an alley. 'Are you truly powerless?'

Dessalene was a bloody mess beside him, her thoughts in knots, her magic gone, though she knew that they had lost. The cheers rising into the dusky sky weren't coming from victorious soldiers. Sweat trickled down her back, but she shivered, fearing they wouldn't escape the wrath of those liberated slaves.

'Answer me!' Ronin snarled, pushing Dessalene closer to the wall. And stopping, he shrugged off his golden armour, not wanting to attract any attention. Bending down, he dropped it on the ground. It had taken a year to make and cost a fortune, though now he would abandon it like an unwanted child.

Thinking of children, he felt the pain of regret, knowing he was leaving Kalina, though she had been taken to the palace on the opposite side of the city, and he couldn't reach her now. 'You cannot help us?'

'I can always help!' Dessalene spat, anger masking her fear that she was lying to them both. 'And you? What help have you been? Just get us to the cove, Ronin! We will not die here, you and I. Our plans will not be destroyed by that woman!'

Snatching his wife's bloody hand, Ronin yanked her down the alley, looking for the symbol etched into the wall. It had been years since his friend Pero had built the tunnels leading towards the sea and the cove, and he hoped he could still find the way in.

Running a hand along the stone panels, hearing horses coming, he desperately sought to find the symbol.

***

With Jael it was usually best not to ask questions, Fyn knew as he urged his unfamiliar horse over the scattered remains of a wagon. He smelled smoke and saw a soldier being dragged into a house, its door slamming.

Before him, Jael didn't even turn her head. He saw those big red slashes across her torn dress, his mind full of more questions, though head down, he simply focused on following her.

Jael saw a flash of flames, hearing her horse whinnying beneath her, sensing that he was unhappy about that, and then she saw a vision of golden armour in an alley.

Ronin Sardis had created the tunnel to the sea.

Glancing around, seeing little to recognise in the fading light, she could only follow her instincts, and swinging right, she aimed her horse down an alley barely big enough to fit through. It wasn't long, and soon, after a sharp left turn, inhaling a terrible smell, she saw two figures running far ahead. Though, as she stared at them, sharpening her vision, they disappeared from view. 'Go! Go!' she bellowed at her confused horse, driving him harder, Fyn on her heels, Eadmund and seven of Bolder's men tucked up behind them.

All light was draining from the sky, and by the time Jael arrived at where she thought she'd seen the two figures, it was almost dark. Sliding off the horse, she hurried to the wall, needing to find the symbol. 'I have to see!'

'What?' Fyn dropped down beside her, soon joined by Eadmund and his men.

'A symbol. I need to find a symbol.' And though there was

no light, Jael placed her hands on the wall, heart thumping, back burning. Panic and pain melded together in an explosion of urgency inside her. 'I...' Opening her eyes, she shuffled to the left, hand trailing along the stone wall, suddenly stopping as though she'd touched a spark. 'Here!' And reaching up, she found indentations. And now, placing both hands on the wall, she pushed, feeling it release, opening like a door. 'Hurry!'

As he plunged into the darkness after his wife, Eadmund realised, to his surprise, that this was the tunnel – the other side of the tunnel he'd swum into.

'We have to stop... the king!' Jael panted. 'Run!'

***

'Someone's coming!' Dessalene hissed, stumbling beside her husband, whose grip on her arm was becoming painful.

'And what? You want me to stop and fight them on my own? Or you?' Ronin growled. 'You can use magic again? We are in no position to fight, Dessalene. I don't know how many men are coming, do you?'

Dessalene heard footsteps. 'Too many,' she decided quickly. 'Hurry!'

***

Running with the fetters made an exhausted Jael incredibly slow, and panting, she urged everyone ahead of her. 'Go... please...'

Eadmund charged past her into the darkness, and Jael felt a memory stab her, seeing Sunni. The girl had run away from her.

The girl had died.

She tried to pick up her feet, to move more quickly.

'I see them!' Eadmund cried from somewhere up ahead.

Jael thought to tell him to stop, but her husband wasn't Sunni. 'Go!' she bellowed instead. 'Stop them!'

He tried, she could see, drawing on every reserve to move faster, though as Jael rounded the corner, she saw a shadowy movement as a door opened. It welcomed in hints of light, revealing a glimpse of Ronin Sardis. He looked almost regretful, as though he wanted to stay and fight. Then the door was slammed shut, plunging the tunnel back into darkness.

Eadmund ran up to the door on the right.

'They went that way!' he called to Jael, who stopped, then turning around, she ran back up the tunnel, remembering where Sunni had died, reliving every moment of what had happened.

And dropping to her knees, she dug around where she'd hidden the key.

Though it was gone.

She searched every crevice, hands raking through gravel, scraping bloody knuckles across stone, though there was no sign of that key. And with a defeated sigh, she slumped forward in a heap, head bowed, knowing that the king and his dreamer wife had gone.

***

Arriving at the temple grounds on Tito, Arras saw familiar faces everywhere he turned. The slaves had overcome the soldiers, and those soldiers still standing were being corralled like cattle.

He saw actual cattle penned in by the platform and Bolder's men on horses and on the ground, trying to halt the ongoing skirmishes.

It was dark, though braziers burned brightly around the platform, lighting up the Tower of Eyshar and the logi, who were following behind Inesh Seppo.

Nudging his horse forward, Arras ordered Thorgils and Nico to help Bolder's men quell the fighting. From his position, he could see that, like elsewhere, the soldiers had simply been outnumbered.

'Take prisoners!' he told his son before turning his horse towards the seer. Approaching the bridge, he stopped and dismounted.

'You have come!' Inesh greeted the commander. 'To liberate your people!'

In the darkness, Arras couldn't see Inesh's eyes, though as the seer came closer, he soon saw a flash of white teeth.

The man was smiling. 'You have come, Arras Sikari. Home.' And bending forward, he placed his hands on the commander's arms, blessing him.

***

A panting Jael returned to Eadmund, Fyn, and their men. 'There was a key, but I –'

Eadmund touched her arm, wanting to see her eyes, though her face was only darkness. He'd tried both doors again, urging his men to help, though there was no way through. 'We can't worry about him, Jael. We have to get out of here, back to the men. We need to finish this.'

Jael couldn't smile, though she'd said those words herself. Many times. Instead, she simply nodded, allowing Eadmund to lead her back through the tunnel to their horses, which they rode back to the temple grounds, where she eventually found Arras.

He stared at her with a gaping mouth. 'You.'

Jael finally found a smile, aching shoulders sagging. 'Hello, again.'

Arras narrowed his eyes, emotions bubbling inside him. Nico stood nearby watching, safe. The slaves had been talked down, tasked with taking prisoners under the watchful guidance of Inesh Seppo and his logi. Arras had sent the Hestians into the city to keep order, remaining on the platform where Alek was lying.

Turning away, Jael hurried towards him. 'Alek!' Dropping to her knees, she took his hand. 'Are you alive?' She didn't need his answer; she could feel it. And squeezing his hand, she bent to his ear. 'I promised I'd get you home.'

He nodded, tears in his eyes. 'I always knew you would.'

Jael rocked back on her heels, the pain in her body, dulled since she'd killed Kosta, returning like slashes of lightning. Her eyes started watering. 'I'm not sure I did.'

Alek tried to laugh, but he coughed instead. 'I'm no dreamer, Jael Furyck, but I don't believe that for a moment.'

Hearing a familiar holler, she released Alek's hand, pushing herself to her feet, desperate to get the dratted fetters off. Turning quickly, she wasn't in time to avoid being swept into a bear hug by a grinning Thorgils Svanter.

'My queen! Jael!'

'*No!*' she yelped in agony. 'Get... off me!' The tears in her eyes watered with ever greater ferocity as his strong arms squeezed her tightly. 'Thorgils... Svanter... get the fuck off me!' And ready to headbutt him, she finally pushed out of his embrace, seeing his look of surprise, even hurt. Though having missed him and his bear hugs, she turned around, showing him what she could feel was the bloody mess of her back. It was dark, though she heard his gasp, and turning back around, she kissed his cheek instead.

'You're hurt?'

Jael shook her head, then nodded it. 'But it doesn't matter now because you're here.' Eadmund came to one side of her and Fyn the other as Arras turned to Nico. 'You're here,' she said, tears blurring her eyes. Leaning on Eadmund's arm, she reached for his hand. Entwining her fingers with his, tears trailing down her cheeks, she felt him squeeze her gently.

She closed her eyes, ready to sleep.

And then her eyes burst open as she remembered that Edela was missing.

That Ronin Sardis had threatened to kill her brothers.

To kill her daughter.

She remembered Milla Ulfsson's smile and her dream of Oss.

And looking up at Eadmund, Jael knew there wasn't a moment to lose.

It was time to go home.

THE END

EPILOGUE

A red-faced Gerald almost ran into his king as he rounded the corner.

It was late, but Axl couldn't sleep, thoughts of Eren prodding him like nails. He'd headed to the kitchen, knowing that the cook always left out a plate of leftovers. And returning to his chamber, lost in his thoughts, he hadn't heard the old man coming and only just pulled up in time. 'Gerald! Why are you running around at this time of night?'

'Men, lord. Men are here!'

Axl's mind immediately went to Oren Storgard.

Heart racing, he turned and ran for his chamber.

Behind him, Gerald inhaled a breath and hurried out a word. 'Rexon!'

Stopping as though striking a wall, Axl swung around. 'Rexon is here? Rexon Boas?'

Gerald nodded. 'In the, the... hall, my lord.'

Axl left him behind, not bothering to dress, still wearing a tunic and trousers, his feet bare. When he arrived in the hall, he saw Rexon and a handful of men standing beside a fire pit. Its flames revealed tired faces and filthy clothes. He saw men he knew. Andalans.

The men who had left with Gant.

'What's happened? Why are you here?'

Rexon bobbed his head, then shook it in surprise. 'Gant's not here?'

'Gant? I... thought he was with you.' Once again, Axl stared at those Andalan men, who he could see, looked deeply troubled. Though not as troubled as a gaunt-looking Rexon. 'What's happened?' he asked again.

'We... Saala,' Rexon sighed. 'It's been taken. I've no idea what that means for my family, but I... they were burning the hall.'

Axl swallowed, thoughts immediately with Amma, regretting that she wasn't here with him.

'We sought help from Borsund, from Rosby, but they are no longer loyal. Mutt Storman, he is coming for you, my lord. He is coming here.'

Axl heard Gerald gasp, looking up as the hall doors opened and Helga stepped inside. Crumpled face pinched into a frown, she approached the men.

Axl ignored her, focusing on one thing in particular.

One very important piece of information.

'But where's Gant?' he asked, already knowing that he didn't want an answer. 'Where is he?'

Rexon shrugged. 'I... I don't know. We were set upon and followed out of Rosby, and Gant thought we should separate. He led half the men into Hallow Wood, hoping to draw our enemies away from Andala.'

'Hallow Wood?' Axl's eyes bulged, and before him, Helga's mouth fell open.

'Hallow Wood?' the dreamer echoed.

'Yes, though he should've been back by now. I... something must have happened.'

Mouth open, Axl sought to find out more, though his words stuck in his throat as Andala's signal bells started ringing in the harbour.

WHAT TO READ NEXT

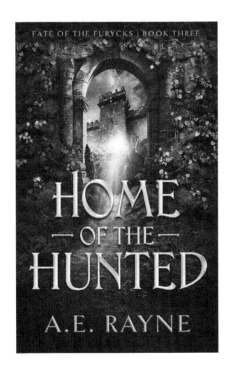

KINGS OF FATE FOR FREE!

Sign up to my newsletter and get *Kings of Fate,*
my Furyck Saga prequel novella,
for FREE!

www.aerayne.com/sign-up

THE FURYCK SAGA

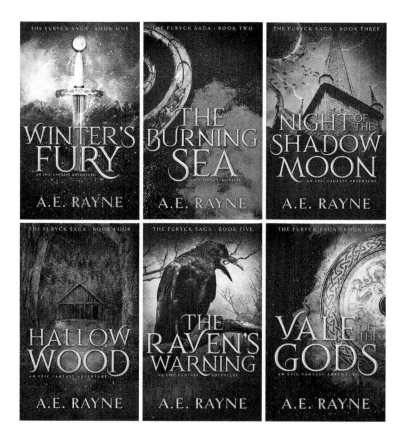

THE FURYCK SAGA

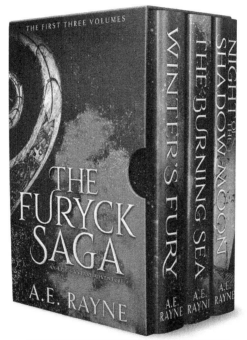

The Furyck Saga: Books 1-3

AUDIOBOOKS

THE FURYCK SAGA

THE LORDS OF ALEKKA

THE LORDS OF ALEKKA

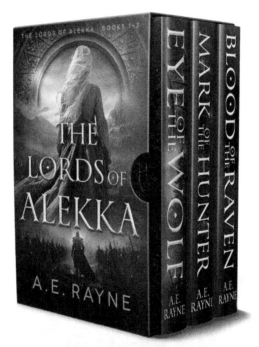

The Lords of Alekka: Books 1-3

AUDIOBOOKS

LORDS OF ALEKKA

FATE OF THE FURYCKS

AUDIOBOOKS

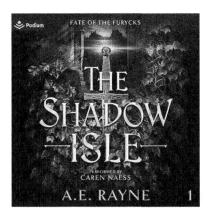

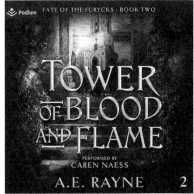

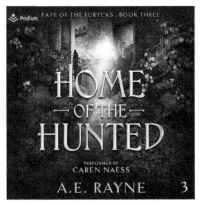

COMING SOON

ABOUT A.E. RAYNE

I survive on a happy diet of historical and fantasy fiction and I particularly love a good Viking tale. My favourite authors are Bernard Cornwell, Giles Kristian, Robert Low, C.J. Sansom, and Patrick O'Brian. I live in Auckland, New Zealand, with my husband, three children and three dogs.

I promise you characters that will quickly feel like friends and villains that will make you wild, with plots that twist and turn to leave you wondering what's coming around the corner. And, like me, hopefully, you'll always end up a little surprised by how I weave everything together in the end!

***

Sign up to my newsletter for pre-sale and new release updates
www.aerayne.com/sign-up

Contact me:
a.e.rayne@aerayne.com
www.aerayne.com/contact